THE BEST
SCIENCE FICTION
AND FANTASY
OF THE YEAR

VOLUME SIX

Also Edited by Jonathan Strahan

Best Short Novels (2004 through 2007)
Fantasy: The Very Best of 2005
Science Fiction: The Very Best of 2005
The Best Science Fiction and Fantasy of the Year: Volumes 1–6
Eclipse: New Science Fiction and Fantasy: Volumes 1–4
The Starry Rift: Tales of New Tomorrows
Life on Mars: Tales from the New Frontier
Under My Hat: Tales from the Cauldron (forthcoming)
Godlike Machines
Engineering Infinity
Edge of Infinity (forthcoming)

With Lou Anders
Swords and Dark Magic: The New Sword and Sorcery

With Charles N. Brown
The Locus Awards: Thirty Years of the Best in Fantasy and Science Fiction
Fritz Leiber: Selected Stories

With Jeremy G. Byrne
The Year's Best Australian Science Fiction and Fantasy: Volumes 1–2
Eidolon 1

With Jack Dann
Legends of Australian Fantasy

With Terry Dowling
The Jack Vance Treasury
The Jack Vance Reader
Wild Thyme, Green Magic
Hard Luck Diggings: The Early Jack Vance

With Gardner Dozois
The New Space Opera
The New Space Opera 2

With Karen Haber
Science Fiction: Best of 2003
Science Fiction: Best of 2004
Fantasy: Best of 2004

With Marianne S. Jablon
Wings of Fire

THE BEST
SCIENCE FICTION
AND FANTASY
OF THE YEAR

VOLUME SIX

EDITED BY JONATHAN STRAHAN

NIGHT SHADE BOOKS
SAN FRANCISCO

First Edition

ISBN: 978-1-59780-345-8

Night Shade Books

www.nightshadebooks.com

For Ross E. Lockhart and Marty Halpern, the unsung heroes of these books, with gratitude.

ACKNOWLEDGEMENTS

This book has been a pleasure to work on, but it's been done with help from a lot of people. First and foremost, I'd like to thank Jason Williams, Jeremy Lassen, and the redoubtable Ross E. Lockhart at Night Shade, who have been wonderful to work with over the years, and who make sure every volume is better than the one that came before it. Second, I'd like to thank everyone at *Not if You Were the Last Short Story on Earth*, who help keep me grounded and focussed in my reading during the year. Third, my thanks to all of the book's contributors, who helped me get this year's book together at the last moment (with special thanks to Neil and Les). Fourth, a special thanks to Liza Groen Trombi and all of my friends and colleagues at *Locus*. And, finally, two very special sets of thanks. As always, I'd like to thank my agent, the dapper and ever-reliable Howard Morhaim, whose annual parties are a highlight of the year. And finally, my extra, extra special thanks to my wife Marianne and my daughters Jessica and Sophie: every moment spent working on this book was stolen from them.

CONTENTS

INTRODUCTION

JONATHAN STRAHAN

2011 was a strange, interesting year that left me in little doubt that science fiction and fantasy short fiction, however you might define it, is in pretty good health. A flood of stories appeared in an enormous variety of venues, print and electronic, around the world during the year. In its annual year-in-review last year, trade magazine *Locus* reported that about 3,000 stories of genre interest had been published in 2010, and it continues to be my belief that underestimates the true number by as much as a factor of five.

As always, there is a great urge to look at the tiny selection of stories collected in these pages—just thirty-one of those thousands of stories—and look for trends and make prognostications about how the science fiction and fantasy field is developing. I've always been a little uncomfortable doing this, because my view of the field seems to steadfastly resist such efforts. Still, some trends are becoming clear and, despite what news from book and magazine publishing might suggest, the genre short story continues to appear to be in good health. There are two trends that I'd comment on here.

First, pleasingly, and importantly for the continuing health of the genre, science fiction and fantasy is becoming more diverse. I find myself encountering more and more excellent work written by women and men who are not straight or white or Christian or just from the English-speaking publishing world. That increased diversity, which was clearly evident this year, leads to new and different stories being told, and that can only be a good thing.

Second, while 2011 continued to see genre boundaries blur and mix, something that has happened throughout the modern history of the field but which has seemed more prevalent in the last five years, I was pleased to see evidence that the SF story might be staking out some new ground for itself. I've been increasingly concerned about the market for science fiction short stories, so I'm encouraged to see SF magazine *Lightspeed*, which launched in 2010, have a strong first year, Solaris launched a new annual SF anthology series, *Solaris Rising*, and MIT's *Technology Review* debuted an annual SF anthology/magazine, *trsf*, all focussed on what my colleague and friend Gardner Dozois would call "pure quill SF." Combined with the NASA/Tor announcement that they would be publishing a series of science-fiction-themed books as "NASA Inspired Works of Fiction," and author Neal Stephenson's efforts to highlight similar ground, there's cause for real optimism that the ongoing discussion that is the SF field will continue into the future.

That said, it *was* a far from encouraging year in publishing. The major stories of 2010—the rise of e-books and the decline of print book publishing/bookselling—were the major stories of 2011. Possibly the most dramatic story was the closure and liquidation of the Borders chain of bookstores, which reduced the amount of shelf space devoted to selling books in the US by about 30%. This was underscored by reports that Barnes & Noble, the other major chain, was reducing its bookshelf space, and that Canadian book distributor H. B. Fenn had filed for bankruptcy, leaving many publishers with heavy losses. In Australia, the REDGroup collapsed, closing all of its Borders stores and a number of its Angus & Robertson stores. The most commonly reported culprit for these closures was the rise of e-books. While these reports don't really bear up under close scrutiny, it's undeniable that e-book sales are changing publishing irrevocably. E-reader and tablet sales boomed during 2011, with annual sales projected to hit 25-30 million units, three times the number sold in 2010. E-books sales rose dramatically throughout the year too, with the Association of American Publishers reporting that sales had grown by 1039% since 2007, and now represent 13.6% of adult fiction book sales in the US. A good example of this was George R. R. Martin's September induction into the Kindle Million Club, selling a million e-books for the device (his *A Dance with Dragons* reportedly sold 300,000 copies on its first day, and 50% of those sales were e-books). These sales undeniably meant bad news for print booksellers, and there's a lot more uncertainty ahead, but even in the face of all of this change, it's hard not to believe that readers will still find stories.

The magazine market was, if anything, stranger. In April *Locus* classi-fied just five print magazines as "professional"—*Analog, Asimov's, F&SF, Interzone*, and *Realms of Fantasy*—and those magazines published just thirty-eight issues between them. Where circulation figures were avail-able, they showed a significant and continuing drop in sales. However, there is cause for optimism here too, with reports of steadily rising digital sales. Unsurprisingly, *Realms of Fantasy*, which opened and closed twice in recent years, suffered a 51% drop in sales between 2008 and 2010, and ultimately closed what must surely be a final time late in the year. Unlike their print counterparts, online magazines reported steadily growing readerships, with Hugo winner *Clarkesworld* reporting to *Locus* that it had about 21,000 readers per issue, *Fantasy* about 15,000, *Lightspeed* about 20,000, *Apex* around 12,000, and *Tor.com* around 300,000 per month (though this figure covered the whole site and not just fiction). Figures weren't available for other major online magazines, *Subterranean* and *Strange Horizons*, but both reported healthy readerships. The only question remains how these fine magazines are converting their grow-ing readerships into sustainable businesses. That they do so is, in my opinion, critical to the future of short fiction. I should also note that in August Marvin Kaye bought *Weird Tales* from Wildside Press, announc-ing he would edit the magazine himself. *Weird Tales* won a number of awards and great acclaim in recent years under the editorship of Ann VanderMeer, whose editorial voice will be sorely missed, while in Octo-ber John Joseph Adams bought both *Lightspeed* and *Fantasy* magazines from Prime Books.

Last year I found most of the stories I liked in magazines, but noted that with the wide variety of venues producing excellent work no single source dominated. This year that trend towards diversity continued. About half of the stories collected here come from the pages or screens of magazines, a few from author collections, and the remainder from the pages of anthologies.

As I noted last year, we are still at a point in the digital era that we find ourselves bound, it seems, to discuss whether magazines appear in print or online. This doesn't seem a particularly useful distinction to me, given that at the end of the day a magazine is a magazine and an issue is an issue. That said, the majority of the stories from magazines that I liked in 2011 came from online sources. Last year *Subterranean* had a particularly strong year, and it dominated again in 2011. Editor Bill Schafer proved that he has a canny editorial eye, delivering a terrific mix of fantasy, oddball SF, and other stuff, including major stories by Karen Joy Fowler, Catherynne M. Valente, Kelly Link, K. J. Parker, and many more. The Gwenda Bond guest-edited YA issue was a highlight and was uniformly strong. *Subterranean* was, on balance, in my opinion the best single source of top-notch fiction in 2011. John Joseph Adams's *Lightspeed* proved that it has quickly developed into a major market for SF, featuring excellent stories by old hands like Robert Reed and Nancy Kress, alongside newcomers like An Owomoyela, Ken Liu, and Genevieve Valentine. *Tor.com* was, again, slightly less impressive, but when it was good it was very, very good, and included a terrific story by Michael Swanwick, and very good stories by Charlie Jane Anders, Ken Macleod, and others. Finally, Hugo Award winner *Clarkesworld* has clearly evolved into one of the major magazines in the field. This year it featured top-notch stories from Nnedi Okorafor, E. Lily Yu, Nina Kiriki Hoffman, Gord Sellar, and others.

Of the print magazines, *Asimov's Science Fiction Magazine* again had the best year producing terrific work by established regulars like Paul McAuley, Kij Johnson, Robert Reed, and Michael Swanwick, alongside newer writers like Nancy Fulda and Ken Liu. Editor Sheila Williams doesn't really get enough credit for the efforts she's put in over recent years to broaden and redefine *Asimov's* but it again showed this year. Gordon Van Gelder's *Fantasy & Science Fiction* had another good year, with strong stories by M. Rickert, Ken Liu, and Geoff Ryman. It remains a reliable source of quality fiction. I'm not quite sure how to classify MIT Press's *trsf*. It's an annual magazine, I think, but it may be classified in some places as an anthology. Regardless, it featured excellent SF from Cory Doctorow, Ken Macleod, Pat Cadigan, Gwyneth Jones, and Elizabeth Bear. I strongly recommend it, and look forward to future issues. There were many other print magazines published, but these were the ones that struck me as the best.

It seemed to me that 2011 was a particularly good year for anthologies. I should offer the caveat here that I edited several anthologies that appeared during the year, so I offer without comment SF anthologies *Life on Mars* and *Engineering Infinity*, and mixed SF/F anthology *Eclipse Four*. All contain work I think deserves your attention. The best original anthology of the year was, without question, Gavin Grant and Kelly Link's superb *Steampunk! An Anthology of Fantastically Rich and Strange Stories*. I have grave doubts about how it parses as steampunk, but it includes some of the very best stories of the year by Libba Bray, Dylan Horrocks,

Kelly Link, M. T. Anderson, Christopher Rowe, and others. There literally isn't a bad story here and if you buy only one original anthology of the year, this should be it. Jack Dann and Nick Gevers's *Ghosts by Gaslight* occupies similar territory and, if it's not *quite* as strong, is still a very good book with strong stories by Paul Park, Theodora Goss, James Morrow, Garth Nix, and others. I greatly enjoyed Holly Black and Ellen Kushner's *Welcome to Bordertown*, a shared-world fantasy anthology with strong work from Kushner, Black, Catherynne M. Valente, and others. Essential for readers who've been to Bordertown before and a great introduction for others. I don't cover horror in this book, though I perhaps include a little too much dark fiction for the comfort of my colleague and dear friend Ellen Datlow. For this reason I'll simply mention that Datlow had a banner year, editing *Blood and Other Cravings, Teeth, Supernatural Noir,* and *Naked City*, all of which were excellent. And since I'm mentioning horror I should add that Stephen Jones's *A Book of Horrors* is one of the landmark horror anthologies of recent years. Finally, Jeff VanderMeer and Ann VanderMeer's *The Thackery T. Lambshead Cabinet of Curiosities* was, in my opinion, even better than their first Lambshead book, and featured great work by Jeffrey Ford, Garth Nix, and others.

I was very pleased to see more SF anthologies published this year. Setting aside my own two titles, I was pleasantly impressed with Ian Whates's *Solaris Rising* and thought Marty Halpern's *Alien Contact* and Gordon van Gelder's *Welcome to the Greenhouse* were very good indeed.

There were also two stand-out retrospective anthologies of weird fiction published during the year. John Pelan's *The Century's Best Horror Fiction* was a strong work, but the most impressive was Ann VanderMeer and Jeff VanderMeer's staggeringly enormous *The Weird*, which is likely to stand as the definitive anthology on the subject for many years.

Here in Australia, a small but excellent handful of books were published by independent publishers. Twelfth Planet Press launched its Twelve Planets series of collections with Tansy Rayner Roberts's excellent *Love and Romanpunk* and Lucy Sussex's *Thief of Lives*. It's a crazily ambitious project and seems to be coming off in spades, underscored by publisher Alisa Krasnostein being awarded the World Fantasy Award for her work. Long-established independent press Ticonderoga Publications also published several top-notch books in 2011, and their best was *Matilda Told Such Dreadful Lies: The Essential Lucy Sussex*, which belongs on every good bookshelf.

I could go on and talk about reprint anthologies, collections and such but I'm running long as it is, so instead I'll simply say it was another fine year, and let you get to reading the wonderful stories that feature in this year's book. As always, I hope you enjoy reading them as much as I've enjoyed compiling them. See you next year!

Jonathan Strahan
Perth, Australia
November 2011

THE CASE OF DEATH AND HONEY

NEIL GAIMAN

Neil Gaiman was born in England and worked as a freelance journalist before co-editing Ghastly Beyond Belief *(with Kim Newman) and writing* Don't Panic: The Official Hitchhiker's Guide to the Galaxy Companion. *He started writing graphic novels and comics with* Violent Cases *in 1987, and with the seventy-five installments of award-winning series* The Sandman *established himself as one of the most important comics writers of his generation. His first novel,* Good Omens *(with Terry Pratchett), appeared in 1991, and was followed by* Neverwhere, Stardust, American Gods, Coraline, *and* Anansi Boys. *His most recent novel is* The Graveyard Book. *Gaiman's work has won the Caldecott, Newbery, Hugo, World Fantasy, Bram Stoker, Locus, Geffen, International Horror Guild, Mythopoeic, and Will Eisner Comic Industry awards. Gaiman currently lives near Minneapolis.*

I t was a mystery in those parts for years what had happened to the old white ghost man, the barbarian with his huge shoulder bag. There were some who supposed him to have been murdered, and, later, they dug up the floor of Old Gao's little shack high on the hillside, looking for treasure, but they found nothing but ash and fire-blackened tin trays.

This was after Old Gao himself had vanished, you understand, and before his son came back from Lijiang to take over the beehives on the hill.

This is the problem, *wrote Holmes in 1899:* ennui. And lack of interest. Or rather, it all becomes too easy. When the joy of solving crimes is the challenge, the possibility that you cannot, why then the crimes have something to hold your attention. But when each crime is soluble, and so easily soluble at that, why then there is no point in solving them.

Look: this man has been murdered. Well then, someone murdered him. He was murdered for one or more of a tiny handful of reasons: he inconvenienced someone, or he had something that someone wanted, or he had angered someone. Where is the challenge in that?

I would read in the dailies an account of a crime that had the police baffled, and I would find that I had solved it, in broad strokes if not in detail, before I had finished the article. Crime is too soluble. It dissolves. Why call the police and tell them the answers to their mysteries? I leave it, over and over again, as a challenge for them, as it is no challenge for me.

I am only alive when I perceive a challenge.

The bees of the misty hills, hills so high that they were sometimes called a mountain, were humming in the pale summer sun as they moved from spring flower to spring flower on the slope. Old Gao listened to them without pleasure. His cousin, in the village across the valley, had many dozens of hives, all of them already filling with honey, even this early in the year; also, the honey was as white as snow-jade. Old Gao did not believe that the white honey tasted any better than the yellow or light brown honey that his own bees produced, although his bees produced it in meagre quantities, but his cousin could sell his white honey for twice what Old Gao could get for the best honey he had.

On his cousin's side of the hill, the bees were earnest, hardworking, golden brown workers, who brought pollen and nectar back to the hives in enormous quantities. Old Gao's bees were ill-tempered and black, shiny as bullets, who produced as much honey as they needed to get through the winter and only a little more: enough for Old Gao to sell from door to door, to his fellow villagers, one small lump of honeycomb at a time. He would charge more for the brood-comb, filled with bee larvae, sweet-tasting morsels of protein, when he had brood-comb to sell, which was rarely, for the bees were angry and sullen and everything they did, they did as little as possible, including make more bees, and Old Gao was always aware that each piece of brood-comb he sold meant bees he would not have to make honey for him to sell later in the year.

Old Gao was as sullen and as sharp as his bees. He had had a wife once, but she had died in childbirth. The son who had killed her lived for a week, then died himself. There would be nobody to say the funeral rites for Old Gao, no one to clean his grave for festivals or to put offerings upon it. He would die unremembered, as unremarkable and as unremarked as his bees.

The old white stranger came over the mountains in late spring of that year, as soon as the roads were passable, with a huge brown bag strapped to his shoulders. Old Gao heard about him before he met him.

"There is a barbarian who is looking at bees," said his cousin.

Old Gao said nothing. He had gone to his cousin to buy a pailful of second-rate comb, damaged or uncapped and liable soon to spoil. He bought it cheaply to feed to his own bees, and if he sold some of it in his own village, no one was any the wiser. The two men were drinking tea in Gao's cousin's hut on the hillside. From late spring, when the first honey started to flow, until first frost, Gao's cousin left his house in the village and went to live in the hut on the hillside, to live and to sleep beside his beehives, for fear of thieves. His wife and his children would take the honeycomb and the bottles of snow-white honey down the hill to sell.

Old Gao was not afraid of thieves. The shiny black bees of Old Gao's hives would have no mercy on anyone who disturbed them. He slept in his village, unless it was time to collect the honey.

"I will send him to you," said Gao's cousin. "Answer his questions, show him your bees, and he will pay you."

"He speaks our tongue?"

"His dialect is atrocious. He said he learned to speak from sailors, and they were mostly Cantonese. But he learns fast, although he is old."

Old Gao grunted, uninterested in sailors. It was late in the morning, and there was still four hours walking across the valley to his village, in the heat of the day. He finished his tea. His cousin drank finer tea than Old Gao had ever been able to afford.

He reached his hives while it was still light, put the majority of the uncapped honey into his weakest hives. He had eleven hives. His cousin had over a hundred. Old Gao was stung twice doing this, on the back of the hand and the back of the neck. He had been stung over a thousand times in his life. He could not have told you how many times. He barely noticed the stings of other bees, but the stings of his own black bees always hurt, even if they no longer swelled or burned.

The next day a boy came to Old Gao's house in the village, to tell him that there was someone—and that the someone was a giant foreigner—who was asking for him. Old Gao simply grunted. He walked across the village with the boy at his steady pace, until the boy ran ahead, and soon was lost to sight.

Old Gao found the stranger sitting drinking tea on the porch of the Widow Zhang's house. Old Gao had known the Widow Zhang's mother, fifty years ago. She had been a friend of his wife. Now she was long dead. He did not believe any one who had known his wife still lived. The Widow Zhang fetched Old Gao tea, introduced him to the elderly barbarian, who had removed his bag and sat beside the small table.

They sipped their tea. The barbarian said, "I wish to see your bees."

Mycroft's death was the end of Empire, and no one knew it but the two of us. He lay in that pale room, his only covering a thin white sheet, as if he were already becoming a ghost from the popular imagination, and needed only eye-holes in the sheet to finish the impression.

I had imagined that his illness might have wasted him away, but he seemed huger than ever, his fingers swollen into white suet sausages.

I said, "Good evening, Mycroft. Dr. Hopkins tells me you have two weeks to live, and stated that I was under no circumstances to inform you of this."

"The man's a dunderhead," said Mycroft, his breath coming in huge wheezes between the words. "I will not make it to Friday."

"Saturday at least," I said.

"You always were an optimist. No, Thursday evening and then I shall be nothing more than an exercise in practical geometry for Hopkins and the funeral directors at Snigsby and Malterson, who will have the challenge, given the narrowness of the doors and corridors, of getting my carcass out of this room and out of the building."

"I had wondered," I said. "Particularly given the staircase. But they will take out the window frame and lower you to the street like a grand piano."

Mycroft snorted at that. Then, "I am fifty-four years old, Sherlock. In my head is the British Government. Not the ballot and hustings nonsense, but the business of the thing. There is no one else knows what the troop movements in the hills of Afghanistan have to do with the desolate shores of North Wales, no one else who sees the whole picture. Can you imagine the mess that this lot and their children will make of Indian Independence?"

I had not previously given any thought to the matter. "Will India become independent?"

"Inevitably. In thirty years, at the outside. I have written several recent memoranda on the topic. As I have on so many other subjects. There are memoranda on the Russian Revolution—that'll be along within the decade, I'll wager—and on the German problem and... oh, so many others. Not that I expect them to be read or understood." Another wheeze. My brother's lungs rattled like the windows in an empty house. "You know, if I were to live, the British Empire might last another thousand years, bringing peace and improvement to the world."

In the past, especially when I was a boy, whenever I heard Mycroft make a grandiose pronouncement like that I would say something to bait him. But not now, not on his death-bed. And also I was certain that he was not speaking of the Empire as it was, a flawed and fallible construct of flawed and fallible people, but of a British Empire that existed only in his head, a glorious force for civilisation and universal prosperity.

I do not, and did not, believe in empires. But I believed in Mycroft.

Mycroft Holmes. Four-and-fifty years of age. He had seen in the new century but the Queen would still outlive him by several months. She was almost thirty years older than he was, and in every way a tough old bird. I wondered to myself whether this unfortunate end might have been avoided.

Mycroft said, "You are right, of course, Sherlock. Had I forced myself to exercise. Had I lived on bird-seed and cabbages instead of porterhouse steak. Had I taken up country dancing along with a wife and a puppy and in all other ways behaved contrary to my nature, I might have bought myself another dozen or so years. But what is that in the scheme of things? Little enough. And sooner or later, I would enter my dotage. No. I am of the opinion that it would take two hundred years to train a functioning Civil Service, let alone a secret service..."

I had said nothing.

The pale room had no decorations on the wall of any kind. None of Mycroft's citations. No illustrations, photographs, or paintings. I compared his austere digs to my own cluttered rooms in Baker Street and I wondered, not for the first time, at Mycroft's mind. He needed nothing on the outside, for it was all on the inside—everything he had seen, everything he had experienced, everything he had read. He could close his eyes and walk through the National Gallery, or browse the British Museum Reading Room—or, more likely, compare intelligence reports from the edge of the Empire with the price of wool in Wigan and the unemployment statistics in Hove, and then, from this and only this, order a man promoted or a traitor's quiet death.

Mycroft wheezed enormously, and then he said, "It is a crime, Sherlock."

"I beg your pardon?"

"A crime. It is a crime, my brother, as heinous and as monstrous as any of the penny-dreadful massacres you have investigated. A crime against the world, against nature, against order."

"I must confess, my dear fellow, that I do not entirely follow you. What is a crime?"

"My death," said Mycroft, "in the specific. And Death in general." He looked into my eyes. "I mean it," he said. "Now isn't that a crime worth investigating,

Sherlock, old fellow? One that might keep your attention for longer than it will take you to establish that the poor fellow who used to conduct the brass band in Hyde Park was murdered by the third cornet using a preparation of strychnine."

"Arsenic," I corrected him, almost automatically.

"I think you will find," wheezed Mycroft, "that the arsenic, while present, had in fact fallen in flakes from the green-painted bandstand itself onto his supper. Symptoms of arsenical poison are a complete red-herring. No, it was strychnine that did for the poor fellow."

Mycroft said no more to me that day or ever. He breathed his last the following Thursday, late in the afternoon, and on the Friday the worthies of Snigsby and Malterson removed the casing from the window of the pale room and lowered my brother's remains into the street, like a grand piano.

His funeral service was attended by me, by my friend Watson, by our cousin Harriet and—in accordance with Mycroft's express wishes—by no one else. The Civil Service, the Foreign Office, even the Diogenes Club—these institutions and their representatives were absent. Mycroft had been reclusive in life; he was to be equally as reclusive in death. So it was the three of us, and the parson, who had not known my brother, and had no conception that it was the more omniscient arm of the British Government itself that he was consigning to the grave.

Four burly men held fast to the ropes and lowered my brother's remains to their final resting place, and did, I daresay, their utmost not to curse at the weight of the thing. I tipped each of them half a crown.

Mycroft was dead at fifty-four, and, as they lowered him into his grave, in my imagination I could still hear his clipped, gray wheeze as he seemed to be saying, "Now *there* is a crime worth investigating."

The stranger's accent was not too bad, although his vocabulary seemed limited, but he seemed to be talking in the local dialect, or something near to it. He was a fast learner. Old Gao hawked and spat into the dust of the street. He said nothing. He did not wish to take the stranger up the hillside; he did not wish to disturb his bees. In Old Gao's experience, the less he bothered his bees, the better they did. And if they stung the barbarian, what then?

The stranger's hair was silver-white, and sparse; his nose, the first barbarian nose that Old Gao had seen, was huge and curved and put Old Gao in mind of the beak of an eagle; his skin was tanned the same colour as Old Gao's own, and was lined deeply. Old Gao was not certain that he could read a barbarian's face as he could read the face of a person, but he thought the man seemed most serious and, perhaps, unhappy.

"Why?"

"I study bees. Your brother tells me you have big black bees here. Unusual bees."

Old Gao shrugged. He did not correct the man on the relationship with his cousin.

The stranger asked Old Gao if he had eaten, and when Gao said that he had not the stranger asked the Widow Zhang to bring them soup and rice and whatever was good that she had in her kitchen, which turned out to be a stew of black tree-fungus and vegetables and tiny transparent river fish, little bigger than tadpoles. The two men ate in silence. When they had finished eating, the stranger said, "I would be honoured if you would show me your bees."

Old Gao said nothing, but the stranger paid the Widow Zhang well and he put his bag on his back. Then he waited, and, when Old Gao began to walk, the stranger followed him. He carried his bag as if it weighed nothing to him. He was strong for an old man, thought Old Gao, and wondered whether all such barbarians were so strong.

"Where are you from?"

"England," said the stranger.

Old Gao remembered his father telling him about a war with the English, over trade and over opium, but that was long ago. They walked up the hillside, that was, perhaps, a mountainside. It was steep, and the hillside was too rocky to be cut into fields. Old Gao tested the stranger's pace, walking faster than usual, and the stranger kept up with him, with his pack on his back.

The stranger stopped several times, however. He stopped to examine flowers—the small white flowers that bloomed in early spring elsewhere in the valley, but in late spring here on the side of the hill. There was a bee on one of the flowers, and the stranger knelt and observed it. Then he reached into his pocket, produced a large magnifying glass and examined the bee through it, and made notes in a small pocket notebook, in an incomprehensible writing.

Old Gao had never seen a magnifying glass before, and he leaned in to look at the bee, so black and so strong and so very different from the bees elsewhere in that valley.

"One of your bees?"

"Yes," said Old Gao. "Or one like it."

"Then we shall let her find her own way home," said the stranger, and he did not disturb the bee, and he put away the magnifying glass.

The Croft East Dene, Sussex
August 11th, 1922

My dear Watson,

I have taken our discussion of this afternoon to heart, considered it carefully, and am prepared to modify my previous opinions.

I am amenable to your publishing your account of the incidents of 1903, specifically of the final case before my retirement, under the following conditions.

In addition to the usual changes that you would make to disguise actual people and places, I would suggest that you replace the entire scenario we encountered (I speak of Professor Presbury's garden. I shall not write of it further here) with monkey glands, or a similar extract from the testes of an ape or lemur, sent by some foreign mystery-man. Perhaps the monkey-extract could have the effect of making Professor Presbury move like an ape—he could be some kind of "creeping man," perhaps?—or possibly make him able to clamber up the sides of buildings and up trees. I would suggest that he could grow a tail, but this might be too fanciful even for you, Watson, although no more fanciful than many of the rococo additions you have made in your histories to otherwise humdrum events in my life and work.

In addition, I have written the following speech, to be delivered by myself, at the end of your narrative. Please make certain that something much like this is there, in which I inveigh against living too long, and the foolish urges that push foolish people to do foolish things to prolong their foolish lives:

> *There is a very real danger to humanity, if one could live forever, if youth were simply there for the taking, that the material, the sensual, the worldly would all prolong their worthless lives. The spiritual would not avoid the call to something higher. It would be the survival of the least fit. What sort of cesspool may not our poor world become?*

Something along those lines, I fancy, would set my mind at rest.

Let me see the finished article, please, before you submit it to be published.

I remain, old friend, your most obedient servant,

Sherlock Holmes

They reached Old Gao's bees late in the afternoon. The beehives were gray wooden boxes piled behind a structure so simple it could barely be called a shack. Four posts, a roof, and hangings of oiled cloth that served to keep out the worst of the spring rains and the summer storms. A small charcoal brazier served for warmth, if you placed a blanket over it and yourself, and to cook upon; a wooden pallet in the center of the structure, with an ancient ceramic pillow, served as a bed on the occasions that Old Gao slept up on the mountainside with the bees, particularly in the autumn, when he harvested most of the honey. There was little enough of it compared to the output of his cousin's hives, but it was enough that he would sometimes spend two or three days waiting for the comb that he had crushed and stirred into a slurry to drain through the cloth into the buckets and pots that he had carried up the mountainside. Finally he would melt the remainder, the sticky wax and bits of pollen and dirt and bee slurry, in a pot, to extract the beeswax, and he would give the sweet water back to the bees. Then he would carry the honey and the wax blocks down the hill to the village to sell.

He showed the barbarian stranger the eleven hives, watched impassively as the stranger put on a veil and opened a hive, examining first the bees, then the contents of a brood box, and finally the queen, through his magnifying glass. He showed no fear, no discomfort: in everything he did the stranger's movements were gentle and slow, and he was not stung, nor did he crush or hurt a single bee. This impressed Old Gao. He had assumed that barbarians were inscrutable, unreadable, mysterious creatures, but this man seemed overjoyed to have encountered Gao's bees. His eyes were shining.

Old Gao fired up the brazier, to boil some water. Long before the charcoal was hot, however, the stranger had removed from his bag a contraption of glass and metal. He had filled the upper half of it with water from the stream, lit a flame, and soon a kettleful of water was steaming and bubbling. Then the stranger took two tin mugs from his bag, and some green tea leaves wrapped in paper, and dropped the leaves into the mug, and poured on the water.

It was the finest tea that Old Gao had ever drunk: better by far than his cousin's tea. They drank it cross-legged on the floor.

"I would like to stay here for the summer, in this house," said the stranger.

"Here? This is not even a house," said Old Gao. "Stay down in the village. Widow Zhang has a room."

"I will stay here," said the stranger. "Also I would like to rent one of your beehives."

Old Gao had not laughed in years. There were those in the village who would have thought such a thing impossible. But still, he laughed then, a guffaw of surprise and amusement that seemed to have been jerked out of him.

"I am serious," said the stranger. He placed four silver coins on the ground between them. Old Gao had not seen where he got them from: three silver Mexican pesos, a coin that had become popular in China years before, and a large silver yuan. It was as much money as Old Gao might see in a year of selling honey. "For this money," said the stranger, "I would like someone to bring me food: every three days should suffice."

Old Gao said nothing. He finished his tea and stood up. He pushed through the oiled cloth to the clearing high on the hillside. He walked over to the eleven hives: each consisted of two brood boxes with one, two, three or, in one case, even four boxes above that. He took the stranger to the hive with four boxes above it, each box filled with frames of comb.

"This hive is yours," he said.

They were plant extracts. That was obvious. They worked, in their way, for a limited time, but they were also extremely poisonous. But watching poor Professor Presbury during those final days—his skin, his eyes, his gait—had convinced me that he had not been on entirely the wrong path.

I took his case of seeds, of pods, of roots, and of dried extracts and I thought. I pondered. I cogitated. I reflected. It was an intellectual problem, and could be solved, as my old maths tutor had always sought to demonstrate to me, by intellect.

They were plant extracts, and they were lethal.

Methods I used to render them non-lethal rendered them quite ineffective.

It was not a three pipe problem. I suspect it was something approaching a three hundred pipe problem before I hit upon an initial idea—a notion, perhaps—of a way of processing the plants that might allow them to be ingested by human beings.

It was not a line of investigation that could easily be followed in Baker Street. So it was, in the autumn of 1903, that I moved to Sussex, and spent the winter reading every book and pamphlet and monograph so far published, I fancy, upon the care and keeping of bees. And so it was that in early April of 1904, armed only with theoretical knowledge, I took delivery from a local farmer of my first package of bees.

I wonder, sometimes, that Watson did not suspect anything. Then again, Watson's glorious obtuseness has never ceased to surprise me, and sometimes, indeed, I had relied upon it. Still, he knew what I was like when I had no work to occupy my mind, no case to solve. He knew my lassitude, my black moods when I had no case to occupy me.

So how could he believe that I had truly retired? He knew my methods.

Indeed, Watson was there when I took receipt of my first bees. He watched, from a safe distance, as I poured the bees from the package into the empty, waiting hive, like slow, humming, gentle treacle.

He saw my excitement, and he saw nothing.

And the years passed, and we watched the Empire crumble, we watched the Government unable to govern, we watched those poor heroic boys sent to the trenches of Flanders to die, all these things confirmed me in my opinions. I was not doing the right thing. I was doing the only thing.

As my face grew unfamiliar, and my finger-joints swelled and ached (not so much as they might have done, though, which I attributed to the many bee-stings I had received in my first few years as an investigative apiarist) and as Watson, dear, brave, obtuse Watson, faded with time and paled and shrank, his skin becoming grayer, his mustache becoming the same shade of gray, my resolve to conclude my researches did not diminish. If anything, it increased.

So: my initial hypotheses were tested upon the South Downs, in an apiary of my own devising, each hive modelled upon Langstroth's. I do believe that I made every mistake that ever a novice beekeeper could or has ever made, and in addition, due to my investigations, an entire hiveful of mistakes that no beekeeper has ever made before, or shall, I trust, ever make again. "The Case of the Poisoned Beehive," Watson might have called many of them, although "The Mystery of the Transfixed Women's Institute" would have drawn more attention to my researches, had anyone been interested enough to investigate. (As it was, I chided Mrs Telford for simply taking a jar of honey from the shelves here without consulting me, and I ensured that, in the future, she was given several jars for her cooking from the more regular hives, and that honey from the experimental hives was locked away once it had been collected. I do not believe that this ever drew comment.)

I experimented with Dutch bees, with German bees and with Italians, with Carniolans and Caucasians. I regretted the loss of our British bees to blight and, even where they had survived, to interbreeding, although I found and worked with a small hive I purchased and grew up from a frame of brood and a queen cell, from an old Abbey in St. Albans, which seemed to me to be original British breeding stock.

I experimented for the best part of two decades, before I concluded that the bees that I sought, if they existed, were not to be found in England, and would not survive the distances they would need to travel to reach me by international parcel post. I needed to examine bees in India. I needed to travel perhaps farther afield than that.

I have a smattering of languages.

I had my flower-seeds, and my extracts and tinctures in syrup. I needed nothing more.

I packed them up, arranged for the cottage on the Downs to be cleaned and aired once a week, and for Master Wilkins—to whom I am afraid I had developed the habit of referring, to his obvious distress, as "Young Villikins"—to inspect the beehives, and to harvest and sell surplus honey in Eastbourne market, and to prepare the hives for winter.

I told them I did not know when I should be back.

I am an old man. Perhaps they did not expect me to return.

And, if this was indeed the case, they would, strictly speaking, have been right.

Old Gao was impressed, despite himself. He had lived his life among bees. Still, watching the stranger shake the bees from the boxes, with a practised flick of his wrist, so cleanly and so sharply that the black bees seemed more surprised than angered, and simply flew or crawled back into their hive, was remarkable. The stranger then stacked the boxes filled with comb on top of one of the weaker hives, so Old Gao would still have the honey from the hive the stranger was renting.

So it was that Old Gao gained a lodger.

Old Gao gave the Widow Zhang's granddaughter a few coins to take the stranger food three times a week—mostly rice and vegetables, along with an earthenware pot filled, when she left at least, with boiling soup.

Every ten days Old Gao would walk up the hill himself. He went initially to check on the hives, but soon discovered that under the stranger's care all eleven hives were thriving as they had never thrived before. And indeed, there was now a twelfth hive, from a captured swarm of the black bees the stranger had encountered while on a walk along the hill.

Old Gao brought wood, the next time he came up to the shack, and he and the stranger spent several afternoons wordlessly working together, making extra boxes to go on the hives, building frames to fill the boxes.

One evening the stranger told Old Gao that the frames they were making had been invented by an American, only seventy years before. This seemed like nonsense to Old Gao, who made frames as his father had, and as they did across the valley, and as, he was certain, his grandfather and his grandfather's grandfather had, but he said nothing.

He enjoyed the stranger's company. They made hives together, and Old Gao wished that the stranger was a younger man. Then he would stay there for a long time, and Old Gao would have someone to leave his beehives to, when he died. But they were two old men, nailing boxes together, with thin frosty hair and old faces, and neither of them would see another dozen winters.

Old Gao noticed that the stranger had planted a small, neat garden beside the hive that he had claimed as his own, which he had moved away from the rest of the hives. He had covered it with a net. He had also created a "back door" to the hive, so that the only bees that could reach the plants came from the hive that he was renting. Old Gao also observed that, beneath the netting, there were several trays filled with what appeared to be sugar solution of some kind, one coloured bright red, one green, one a startling blue, one yellow. He pointed to them, but all the stranger did was nod and smile.

The bees were lapping up the syrups, though, clustering and crowding on the sides of the tin dishes with their tongues down, eating until they could eat no more, and then returning to the hive.

The stranger had made sketches of Old Gao's bees. He showed the sketches to Old Gao, tried to explain the ways that Old Gao's bees differed from other honeybees, talked of ancient bees preserved in stone for millions of years, but here the stranger's Chinese failed him, and, truthfully, Old Gao was not interested. They were his bees, until he died, and after that, they were the bees of the mountainside. He had brought other bees here, but they had sickened and died, or been killed in raids by the black bees, who took their honey and left them to starve.

The last of these visits was in late summer. Old Gao went down the mountainside. He did not see the stranger again.

It is done.

It works. Already I feel a strange combination of triumph and of disappointment, as if of defeat, or of distant storm-clouds teasing at my senses.

It is strange to look at my hands and to see, not my hands as I know them, but the hands I remember from my younger days: knuckles unswollen, dark hairs, not snow-white, on the backs.

It was a quest that had defeated so many, a problem with no apparent solution. The first Emperor of China died and nearly destroyed his empire in pursuit of it, three thousand years ago, and all it took me was, what, twenty years?

I do not know if I did the right thing or not (although any "retirement" without such an occupation would have been, literally, maddening). I took the commission from Mycroft. I investigated the problem. I arrived, inevitably, at the solution.

Will I tell the world? I will not.

And yet, I have half a pot of dark brown honey remaining in my bag; a half a pot of honey that is worth more than nations. (I was tempted to write, *worth more than all the tea in China*, perhaps because of my current situation, but fear that even Watson would deride it as cliché.)

And speaking of Watson...

There is one thing left to do. My only remaining goal, and it is small enough. I shall make my way to Shanghai, and from there I shall take ship to Southampton, a half a world away.

And once I am there, I shall seek out Watson, if he still lives—and I fancy he does. It is irrational, I know, and yet I am certain that I would know, somehow, had Watson passed beyond the veil.

I shall buy theatrical makeup, disguise myself as an old man, so as not to startle him, and I shall invite my old friend over for tea.

There will be honey on buttered toast served for tea that afternoon, I fancy.

There were tales of a barbarian who passed through the village on his way east, but the people who told Old Gao this did not believe that it could have been the same man who had lived in Gao's shack. This one was young and proud, and his hair was dark. It was not the old man who had walked through those parts in the spring, although, one person told Gao, the bag was similar.

Old Gao walked up the mountainside to investigate, although he suspected what he would find before he got there.

The stranger was gone, and the stranger's bag.

There had been much burning, though. That was clear. Papers had been burnt—Old Gao recognized the edge of a drawing the stranger had made of one of his bees, but the rest of the papers were ash, or blackened beyond recognition, even had Old Gao been able to read barbarian writing. The papers were not the only things to have been burnt; parts of the hive that the stranger had rented were now only twisted ash; there were blackened, twisted strips of tin that might once have contained brightly coloured syrups.

The colour was added to the syrups, the stranger had told him once, so that he could tell them apart, although for what purpose Old Gao had never enquired.

He examined the shack like a detective, searching for a clue as to the stranger's nature or his whereabouts. On the ceramic pillow four silver coins had been left for him to find—two yuan and two pesos—and he put them away.

Behind the shack he found a heap of used slurry, with the last bees of the day still crawling upon it, tasting whatever sweetness was still on the surface of the still-sticky wax.

Old Gao thought long and hard before he gathered up the slurry, wrapped it loosely in cloth, and put it in a pot, which he filled with water. He heated the water on the brazier, but did not let it boil. Soon enough the wax floated to the surface, leaving the dead bees and the dirt and the pollen and the propolis inside the cloth.

He let it cool.

Then he walked outside, and he stared up at the moon. It was almost full.

He wondered how many villagers knew that his son had died as a baby. He remembered his wife, but her face was distant, and he had no portraits or photographs of her. He thought that there was nothing he was so suited for on the face of the earth as to keep the black, bulletlike bees on the side of this high, high hill. There was no other man who knew their temperament as he did.

The water had cooled. He lifted the now solid block of beeswax out of the water, placed it on the boards of the bed to finish cooling. He took the cloth filled with dirt and impurities out of the pot. And then, because he too was, in his way, a detective, and once you have eliminated the impossible whatever remains, however unlikely, must be the truth, he drank the sweet water in the pot. There is a lot of honey in slurry, after all, even after the majority of it has dripped through a cloth and been purified. The water tasted of honey, but not a honey that Gao had ever tasted before. It tasted of smoke, and metal, and strange flowers, and odd perfumes. It tasted, Gao thought, a little like sex.

He drank it all down, and then he slept, with his head on the ceramic pillow.

When he woke, he thought, he would decide how to deal with his cousin, who would expect to inherit the twelve hives on the hill when Old Gao went missing.

He would be an illegitimate son, perhaps, the young man who would return in the days to come. Or perhaps a son. Young Gao. Who would remember, now? It did not matter.

He would go to the city and then he would return, and he would keep the black bees on the side of the mountain for as long as days and circumstances would allow.

THE CARTOGRAPHER WASPS
AND THE ANARCHIST BEES

E. LILY YU

E. Lily Yu is a senior in English at Princeton University working toward a certificate in biophysics. Her short stories and poems have appeared in the Kenyon Review Online, Clarkesworld, Jabberwocky 5, Electric Velocipede, *and* Goblin Fruit, *and her short play on beta decay had a staged reading at Princeton in October. At school, she competes on the ballroom team, plays flute, and juggles. She was born in Oregon and raised in New Jersey.*

For longer than anyone could remember, the village of Yiwei had worn, in its orchards and under its eaves, clay-colored globes of paper that hissed and fizzed with wasps. The villagers maintained an uneasy peace with their neighbors for many years, exercising inimitable tact and circumspection. But it all ended the day a boy, digging in the riverbed, found a stone whose balance and weight pleased him. With this, he thought, he could hit a sparrow in flight. There were no sparrows to be seen, but a paper ball hung low and inviting nearby. He considered it for a moment, head cocked, then aimed and threw.

Much later, after he had been plastered and soothed, his mother scalded the fallen nest until the wasps seething in the paper were dead. In this way it was discovered that the wasp nests of Yiwei, dipped in hot water, unfurled into beautifully accurate maps of provinces near and far, inked in vegetable pigments and labeled in careful Mandarin that could be distinguished beneath a microscope.

The villagers' subsequent incursions with bee veils and kettles of boiling water soon diminished the prosperous population to a handful. Commanded by a single stubborn foundress, the survivors folded a new nest in the shape of a paper boat, provisioned it with fallen apricots and squash blossoms, and launched themselves onto the river. Browsing cows and children fled the riverbanks as they drifted downstream, piping sea chanteys.

At last, forty miles south from where they had begun, their craft snagged on an upthrust stick and sank. Only one drowned in the evacuation, weighed down with the remains of an apricot. They reconvened upon a stump and looked about themselves.

"It's a good place to land," the foundress said in her sweet soprano, examining the first rough maps that the scouts brought back. There were plenty of caterpillars, oaks for ink galls, fruiting brambles, and no signs of other wasps. A colony of bees had hived in a split oak two miles away. "Once we are established we will, of course, send a delegation to collect tribute.

"We will not make the same mistakes as before. Ours is a race of explorers and scientists, cartographers and philosophers, and to rest and grow slothful is to die. Once we are established here, we will expand."

It took two weeks to complete the nurseries with their paper mobiles, and then another month to reconstruct the Great Library and fill the pigeonholes with what the oldest cartographers could remember of their lost maps. Their comings and goings did not go unnoticed. An ambassador from the beehive arrived with an ultimatum and was promptly executed; her wings were made into stained-glass windows for the council chamber, and her stinger was returned to the hive in a paper envelope. The second ambassador came with altered attitude and a proposal to divide the bees' kingdom evenly between the two governments, retaining pollen and water rights for the bees—"as an acknowledgment of the preexisting claims of a free people to the natural resources of a common territory," she hummed.

The wasps of the council were gracious and only divested the envoy of her sting. She survived just long enough to deliver her account to the hive.

The third ambassador arrived with a ball of wax on the tip of her stinger and was better received.

"You understand, we are not refugees applying for recognition of a token territorial sovereignty," the foundress said, as attendants served them nectars in paper horns, "nor are we negotiating with you as equal states. Those were the assumptions of your late predecessors. They were mistaken."

"I trust I will do better," the diplomat said stiffly. She was older than the others, and the hairs of her thorax were sparse and faded.

"I do hope so."

"Unlike them, I have complete authority to speak for the hive. You have propositions for us; that is clear enough. We are prepared to listen."

"Oh, good." The foundress drained her horn and took another. "Yours is an old and highly cultured society, despite the indolence of your ruler, which we understand to be a racial rather than personal proclivity. You have laws, and traditional dances, and mathematicians, and principles, which of course we do respect."

"Your terms, please."

She smiled. "Since there is a local population of tussah moths, which we prefer for incubation, there is no need for anything so unrepublican as slavery. If you refrain from insurrection, you may keep your self-rule. But we will take a fifth of your stores in an ordinary year, and a tenth in drought years, and one of every hundred larvae."

"To eat?" Her antennae trembled with revulsion.

"Only if food is scarce. No, they will be raised among us and learn our ways and our arts, and then they will serve as officials and bureaucrats among you. It will be to your advantage, you see."

The diplomat paused for a moment, looking at nothing at all. Finally she said, "A tenth, in a good year—"

"Our terms," the foundress said, "are not negotiable."

The guards shifted among themselves, clinking the plates of their armor and shifting the gleaming points of their stings.

"I don't have a choice, do I?"

"The choice is enslavement or cooperation," the foundress said. "For your hive, I mean. You might choose something else, certainly, but they have tens of thousands to replace you with."

The diplomat bent her head. "I am old," she said. "I have served the hive all my life, in every fashion. My loyalty is to my hive and I will do what is best for it."

"I am so very glad."

"I ask you—I beg you—to wait three or four days to impose your terms. I will be dead by then, and will not see my sisters become a servile people."

The foundress clicked her claws together. "Is the delaying of business a custom of yours? We have no such practice. You will have the honor of watching us elevate your sisters to moral and technological heights you could never imagine."

The diplomat shivered.

"Go back to your queen, my dear. Tell them the good news."

It was a crisis for the constitutional monarchy. A riot broke out in District 6, destroying the royal waxworks and toppling the mouse-bone monuments before it was brutally suppressed. The queen had to be calmed with large doses of jelly after she burst into tears on her ministers' shoulders.

"Your Majesty," said one, "it's not a matter for your concern. Be at peace."

"These are my children," she said, sniffling. "You would feel for them too, were you a mother."

"Thankfully, I am not," the minister said briskly, "so to business."

"War is out of the question," another said.

"Their forces are vastly superior."

"We outnumber them three hundred to one!"

"They are experienced fighters. Sixty of us would die for each of theirs. We might drive them away, but it would cost us most of the hive and possibly our queen—"

The queen began weeping noisily again and had to be cleaned and comforted.

"Have we any alternatives?"

There was a small silence.

"Very well, then."

The terms of the relationship were copied out, at the wasps' direction, on small paper plaques embedded in propolis and wax around the hive. As paper and ink were new substances to the bees, they jostled and touched and tasted the bills until the paper fell to pieces. The wasps sent to oversee the installation did not take this kindly. Several civilians died before it was established that the bees could not read the Yiwei dialect.

Thereafter the hive's chemists were charged with compounding pheromones complex enough to encode the terms of the treaty. These were applied to the papers, so that both species could inspect them and comprehend the relationship between the two states.

Whereas the hive before the wasp infestation had been busy but content, the bees now lived in desperation. The natural terms of their lives were cut short by the need to gather enough honey for both the hive and the wasp nest. As they traveled farther and farther afield in search of nectar, they stopped singing. They danced their findings grimly, without joy. The queen herself grew gaunt and thin from breeding replacements, and certain ministers who understood such matters began feeding royal jelly to the strongest larvae.

Meanwhile, the wasps grew sleek and strong. Cadres of scholars, cartographers, botanists, and soldiers were dispatched on the river in small floating nests caulked with beeswax and loaded with rations of honeycomb to chart the unknown lands to the south. Those who returned bore beautiful maps with towns and farms and alien populations of wasps carefully noted in blue and purple ink, and these, once studied by the foundress and her generals, were carefully filed away in the depths of the Great Library for their southern advance in the new year.

The bees adopted by the wasps were first trained to clerical tasks, but once it was determined that they could be taught to read and write, they were assigned to some of the reconnaissance missions. The brightest students, gifted at trigonometry and angles, were educated beside the cartographers themselves and proved valuable assistants. They learned not to see the thick green caterpillars led on silver chains, or the dead bees fed to the wasp brood. It was easier that way.

When the old queen died, they did not mourn.

By the sheerest of accidents, one of the bees trained as a cartographer's assistant was an anarchist. It might have been the stresses on the hive, or it might have been luck; wherever it came from, the mutation was viable. She tucked a number of her own eggs in beeswax and wasp paper among the pigeonholes of the library and fed the larvae their milk and bread in secret. To her sons in their capped silk cradles—and they were all sons—she whispered the precepts she had developed while calculating flight paths and azimuths, that there should be no queen and no state, and that, as in the wasp nest, the males should labor and profit equally with the females. In their sleep and slow transformation they heard her teachings and instructions, and when they chewed their way out of their cells and out of the wasp nest, they made their way to the hive.

The damage to the nest was discovered, of course, but by then the anarchist was dead of old age. She had done impeccable work, her tutor sighed, looking over the filigree of her inscriptions, but the brilliant were subject to mental aberrations, were they not? He buried beneath grumblings and labors his fondness for her, which had become a grief to him and a political liability, and he never again took on any student from the hive who showed a glint of talent.

Though they had the bitter smell of the wasp nest in their hair, the anarchist's twenty sons were permitted to wander freely through the hive, as it was assumed that they were either spies or on official business. When the new queen emerged from her chamber, they joined unnoticed the other drones in the nuptial flight. Two succeeded in mating with her. Those who failed and survived spoke afterward in hushed tones of what had been done for the sake of the ideal. Before they died they took propolis and oak-apple ink and inscribed upon the lintels of the hive, in a shorthand they had developed, the story of the first anarchist and her twenty sons.

Anarchism being a heritable trait in bees, a number of the daughters of the new queen found themselves questioning the purpose of the monarchy. Two were taken by the wasps and taught to read and write. On one of their visits to the hive they spotted the history of their forefathers, and, being excellent scholars, soon figured out the translation.

They found their sisters in the hive who were unquiet in soul and whispered to them the strange knowledge they had learned among the wasps: astronomy, military strategy, the state of the world beyond the farthest flights of the bees. Hitherto educated as dancers and architects, nurses and foragers, the bees were full of a new wonder, stranger even than the first day they flew from the hive and felt the sun on their backs.

"Govern us," they said to the two wasp-taught anarchists, but they refused.

"A perfect society needs no rulers," they said. "Knowledge and authority ought to be held in common. In order to imagine a new existence, we must free ourselves from the structures of both our failed government and the unjustifiable hegemony of the wasp nests. Hear what you can hear and learn what you can learn while we remain among them. But be ready."

It was the first summer in Yiwei without the immemorial hum of the cartographer wasps. In the orchards, though their skins split with sweetness, fallen fruit lay unmolested, and children played barefoot with impunity. One of the villagers' daughters, in her third year at an agricultural college, came home in the back of a pickup truck at the end of July. She thumped her single suitcase against the gate before opening it, to scatter the chickens, then raised the latch and swung the iron aside, and was immediately wrapped in a flying hug.

Once she disentangled herself from brother and parents and liberally distributed kisses, she listened to the news she'd missed: how the cows were dying from drinking stonecutters' dust in the streams; how grain prices were falling everywhere, despite the drought; and how her brother, little fool that he was, had torn down a wasp nest and received a faceful of red and white lumps for it. One of the most detailed wasp's maps had reached the capital, she was told, and a bureaucrat had arrived in a sleek black car. But because the wasps were all dead, he could report little more than a prank, a freak, or a miracle. There were no further inquiries.

Her brother produced for her inspection the brittle, boiled bodies of several wasps in a glass jar, along with one of the smaller maps. She tickled him until he surrendered his trophies, promised him a basket of peaches in return, and let herself be fed to tautness. Then, to her family's dismay, she wrote an urgent letter to the Academy of Sciences and packed a satchel with clothes and cash. If she could find one more nest of wasps, she said, it would make their fortune and her name. But it had to be done quickly.

In the morning, before the cockerels woke and while the sky was still purple, she hopped onto her old bicycle and rode down the dusty path.

Bees do not fly at night or lie to each other, but the anarchists had learned both from the wasps. On a warm, clear evening they left the hive at last, flying west in a small tight cloud. Around them swelled the voices of summer insects, strange and disquieting. Several miles west of the old hive and the wasp nest, in a lightning-scarred elm, the anarchists had built up a small stock of stolen honey sealed in wax and paper. They rested there for the night, in cells of clean white wax, and in the morning they arose to the building of their city.

The first business of the new colony was the laying of eggs, which a number of workers set to, and provisions for winter. One egg from the old queen, brought from the hive in an anarchist's jaws, was hatched and raised as a new mother. Uncrowned and unconcerned, she too laid mortar and wax, chewed wood to make paper, and fanned the storerooms with her wings.

The anarchists labored secretly but rapidly, drones alongside workers, because the copper taste of autumn was in the air. None had seen a winter before, but the memory of the species is subtle and long, and in their hearts, despite the summer sun, they felt an imminent darkness.

The flowers were fading in the fields. Every day the anarchists added to their coffers of warm gold and built their white walls higher. Every day the air grew a little crisper, the grass a little drier. They sang as they worked, sometimes ballads from the old hive, sometimes anthems of their own devising, and for a time they were happy. Too soon, the leaves turned flame colors and blew from the trees, and then there were no more flowers. The anarchists pressed down the lid on the last vat of honey and wondered what was coming.

Four miles away, at the first touch of cold, the wasps licked shut their paper doors and slept in a tight knot around the foundress. In both beehives, the bees huddled together, awake and watchful, warming themselves with the thrumming of their wings. The anarchists murmured comfort to each other.

"There will be more, after us. It will breed out again."

"We are only the beginning."

"There will be more."

Snow fell silently outside.

The snow was ankle-deep and the river iced over when the girl from Yiwei reached up into the empty branches of an oak tree and plucked down the paper castle of a nest. The wasps within, drowsy with cold, murmured but did not stir. In their barracks the soldiers dreamed of the unexplored south and battles in strange cities, among strange peoples, and scouts dreamed of the corpses of starved and frozen deer. The cartographers dreamed of the changes that winter would work on the landscape, the diverted creeks and dead trees they would have to note down. They did not feel the burlap bag that settled around them, nor the crunch of tires on the frozen road.

She had spent weeks tramping through the countryside, questioning beekeepers and villagers' children, peering up into trees and into hives, before she found the last wasps from Yiwei. Then she had had to wait for winter and the anesthetizing cold. But now, back in the warmth of her own room, she broke open the soft pages of the nest and pushed aside the heaps of glistening wasps until she found the foundress herself, stumbling on uncertain legs.

When it thawed, she would breed new foundresses among the village's apricot trees. The letters she received indicated a great demand for them in the capital, particularly from army generals and the captains of scientific explorations. In years to come, the village of Yiwei would be known for its delicately inscribed maps, the legends almost too small to see, and not for its barley and oats, its velvet apricots and glassy pears.

In the spring, the old beehive awoke to find the wasps gone, like a nightmare that evaporates by day. It was difficult to believe, but when not the slightest scrap of wasp paper could be found, the whole hive sang with delight. Even the queen, who had been coached from the pupa on the details of her client state and the conditions by which she ruled, and who had felt, perhaps, more sympathy for the wasps than she should have, cleared her throat and trilled once or twice. If she did not sing so loudly or so joyously as the rest, only a few noticed, and the winter had been a hard one, anyhow.

The maps had vanished with the wasps. No more would be made. Those who had studied among the wasps began to draft memoranda and the first independent decrees of queen and council. To defend against future invasions, it was decided that a detachment of bees would fly the borders of their land and carry home reports of what they found.

It was on one of these patrols that a small hive was discovered in the fork of an elm tree. Bees lay dead and brittle around it, no identifiable queen among them. Not a trace of honey remained in the storehouse; the dark wax of its walls had been gnawed to rags. Even the brood cells had been scraped clean. But in the last intact hexagons they found, curled and capped in wax, scrawled on page after page, words of revolution. They read in silence.

Then—

"Write," one said to the other, and she did.

TIDAL FORCES

CAITLÍN R. KIERNAN

Caitlín R. Kiernan is the author of several novels, including Daughter of Hounds, The Red Tree, *and* The Drowning Girl: A Memoir. *She is a prolific short fiction author—to date, over two hundred short stories, novellas, and vignettes—most of which have been collected in* Tales of Pain and Wonder; From Weird and Distant Shores; To Charles Fort, With Love; Alabaster; A Is for Alien; *and* The Ammonite Violin & Others. Two Worlds and in Between: The Best of Caitlín R. Kiernan (Volume One) *was released by Subterranean Press in October 2011, and her next collection,* Confessions of a Five-Chambered Heart, *will be released in 2012. Kiernan is a four-time nominee for the World Fantasy Award, an honoree for the James Tiptree Jr. Award, and has twice been nominated for the Shirley Jackson Award. Born in Ireland, she lives in Providence, Rhode Island.*

Charlotte says, "That's just it, Em. There wasn't any pain. I didn't feel anything much at all." She sips her coffee and stares out the kitchen window, squinting at the bright Monday morning sunlight. The sun melts like butter across her face. It catches in the strands of her brown hair, like a late summer afternoon tangling itself in dead cornstalks. It deepens the lines around her eyes and at the corners of her mouth. She takes another sip of coffee, then sets her cup down on the table. I've never once seen her use a saucer.

And the next minute seems to last longer than it ought to last, longer than the mere sum of the sixty seconds that compose it, the way time stretches out to fill in awkward pauses. She smiles for me, and so I smile back. I don't want to smile, but isn't that what you do? The person you love is frightened, but she smiles anyway. So you have to smile back, despite your own fear. I tell myself it isn't so much an act of reciprocation as an acknowledgement. I could be more honest with myself and say I only smiled back out of guilt.

"I *wish* it had hurt," she says, finally, on the other side of all that long, long moment. I don't have to ask what she means, though I wish that I did. I wish I didn't already know. She says the same words over again, but more quietly than before, and there's a subtle shift in emphasis. "I wish it *had* hurt."

I apologize and say I shouldn't have brought it up again, and she shrugs.

"No, don't be sorry, Em. Don't let's be sorry for anything."

I'm stacking days, building a house of cards made from nothing but days. Monday is the Ace of Hearts. Saturday is the Four of Spades. Wednesday is the Seven of Clubs. Thursday night is, I suspect, the Seven of Diamonds, and it might be heavy enough to bring the whole precarious thing tumbling down around my ears. I would spend an entire hour watching cards fall, because time would stretch, the same way it stretches out to fill in awkward pauses, the way time is stretched thin in that thundering moment of a car crash. Or at the edges of a wound.

If it's Monday morning, I can lean across the breakfast table and kiss her, as if nothing has happened. And if we're lucky, that might be the moment that endures almost indefinitely. I can kiss her, taste her, savor her, drawing the moment out like a card drawn from a deck. But no, now it's Thursday night, instead of Monday morning. There's something playing on the television in the bedroom, but the sound is turned all the way down, so that whatever the something may be proceeds like a silent movie filmed in color and without intertitles. A movie for lip readers. There's no other light but the light from the television. She's lying next to me, almost undressed, asking me questions about the book I don't think I'm ever going to be able to finish. I understand she's not asking them because she needs to know the answers, which is the only reason I haven't tried to change the subject.

"The Age of Exploration was already long over with," I say. "For all intents and purposes, it ended early in the Seventeenth Century. Everything after that—reaching the north and south poles, for instance—is only series of footnotes. There were no great blank spaces left for men to fill in. No more 'Here be monsters.'"

She's lying on top of the sheets. It's the middle of July and too hot for anything more than sheets. Clean white sheets and underwear. In the glow from the television, Charlotte looks less pale and less fragile than she would if the bedside lamp were on, and I'm grateful for the illusion. I want to stop talking, because it all sounds absurd, pedantic, all these unfinished, half-formed ideas that add up to nothing much at all. I want to stop talking and just lie here beside her.

"So writers made up stories about lost worlds," she says, having heard all this before and pretty much knowing it by heart. "But those made-up worlds weren't really *lost*. They just weren't *found* yet. They'd not yet been imagined."

"That's the point" I reply. "The value of those stories rests in their insistence that blank spaces still do exist on the map. They *have* to exist, even if it's necessary to twist and distort the map to make room for them. All those overlooked islands, inaccessible plateaus in South American jungles, the sunken continents and the entrances to a hollow earth, they were important psychological buffers against progress and certainty. It's no coincidence that they're usually places where time has stood still, to one degree or another."

"But not really so much time," she says, "as the processes of evolution, which require time."

"See? You understand this stuff better than I do," and I tell her she should write the book. I'm only half joking. That's something else Charlotte knows. I lay my hand on her exposed belly, just below the navel, and she flinches and pulls away.

"Don't do that," she says.

"All right. I won't. I wasn't thinking." I *was* thinking, but it's easier if I tell her that I wasn't.

Monday morning. Thursday night. This day or that. My own private house of cards, held together by nothing more substantial than balance and friction. And the loops I'd rather make than admit to the present. Connecting dot-to-dot, from here to there, from there to here. Here being half an hour before dawn on a Saturday, the sky growing lighter by slow degrees. Here, where I'm on my knees, and Charlotte is standing naked in front of me. Here, now, when the perfectly round hole above her left hip and below her ribcage has grown from a pinprick to the size of the saucers she never uses for her coffee cups.

"I don't think it will hurt," she tells me. And I can't see any point in asking whether she means, *I don't think it will hurt me*, or *I don't think it will hurt you.*

"Now?" I ask her, and she says, "No. Not yet. Wait."

So, handed that reprieve, I withdraw again to the relative safety of the Ace of Hearts—or Monday morning, call it what you will. In my mind's eye, I run back to the kitchen washed in warm yellow sunlight. Charlotte is telling me about the time, when she was ten years old, that she was shot with a BB gun, her brother's Red Ryder BB gun.

"It wasn't an accident," she's telling me. "He meant to do it. I still have the scar from where my mother had to dig the BB out of my ankle with tweezers and a sewing needle. It's very small, but it's a scar all the same."

"Is that what it felt like, like being hit with a BB?"

"No," she says, shaking her head and gazing down into her coffee cup. "It didn't. But when I think about the two things, it seems like there's a link between them, all these years apart. Like, somehow, this thing was an echo of the day he shot me with the BB gun."

"A meaningful coincidence," I suggest. "A sort of synchronicity."

"Maybe," Charlotte says. "But maybe not." She looks out the window again. From the kitchen, you can see the three oaks and her flower bed and the land running down to the rocks and the churning sea. "It's been an awfully long time since I read Jung. My memory's rusty. And, anyway, maybe it's not a coincidence. It could be something else. Just an echo."

"I don't understand, Charlotte. I really don't think I know what you mean."

"Never mind," she says, not taking her eyes off the window. "Whatever I do or don't mean, it isn't important."

The warm yellow light from the sun, the colorless light from a color television. A purplish sky fading towards the light of false dawn. The complete absence of light from the hole punched into her body by something that wasn't a BB. Something that also wasn't a shadow.

"What scares me most," she says (and I could draw *this* particular card from anywhere in the deck), "is that it didn't come back out the other side. So, it must still be lodged in there, *in* me."

I was watching when she was hit. I saw when she fell. I'm coming to that.

"Writers made up stories about *lost* worlds," she says again, after she's flinched, after I've pulled my hand back from the brink. "They did it because we were afraid of having found all there *was* to find. Accurate maps became more disturbing, at least unconsciously, than the idea of sailing off the edge of a flat world."

"I don't want to talk about the book."

"Maybe that's why you can't finish it."

"Maybe you don't know what you're talking about."

"Probably," she says, without the least bit of anger or impatience in her voice.

I roll over, turning my back on Charlotte and the silent television. Turning my back on what cannot be heard and doesn't want to be acknowledged. The sheets are damp with sweat, and there's the stink of ozone that's not *quite* the stink of ozone. The acrid smell that always follows her now, wherever she goes. No. That isn't true. The smell doesn't follow her, it comes *from* her. She *radiates* the stink that is almost, but not quite, the stink of ozone.

"Does *Alice's Adventures in Wonderland* count?" she asks me, even though I've said I don't want to talk about the goddamned book. I'm sure that she heard me, and I don't answer her.

Better not to linger too long on Thursday night.

Better if I return, instead, to Monday morning. Only Monday morning. Which I have carelessly, randomly, designated here as the Ace of Hearts, and hearts are cups, so Monday morning is the Ace of Cups. In four days more, Charlotte will ask me about Alice, and though I won't respond to the question (at least not aloud), I *will* recall that Lewis Carroll considered the *Queen* of Hearts—who rules over the Ace and is also the Queen of Cups—I will recollect that Lewis Carroll considered her the embodiment of a certain type of passion. That passion, he said, which is ungovernable, but which exists as an aimless, unseeing, furious thing. And he said, also, that the Queen of Cups, the Queen of Hearts, is not to be confused with the *Red* Queen, whom he named another brand of passion altogether.

Monday morning in the kitchen.

"My brother always claimed he was shooting at a blue jay and missed. He said he was aiming for the bird, and hit me. He said the sun was in his eyes."

"Did he make a habit of shooting songbirds?"

"Birds and squirrels," she says. "Once he shot a neighbor's cat, right between the eyes." And Charlotte presses the tip of an index finger to the spot between her brows. "The cat had to be taken to a vet to get the BB out, and my mom had to pay the bill. Of course, he said he wasn't shooting at the cat. He was shooting at a sparrow and missed."

"What a little bastard," I say.

"He was just a kid, only a year older than I was. Kids don't mean to be cruel, Em, they just are sometimes. From our perspectives, they appear cruel. They exist outside the boundaries of adult conceits of morality. Anyway, after the cat, my dad took the BB gun away from him. So, after that, he always kind of hated cats."

But here I am neglecting Wednesday, overlooking Wednesday, even though I went to the trouble of drawing a card for it. And it occurs to me now I didn't even draw one for Tuesday. Or Friday, for that matter. It occurs to me that I'm becoming lost in this ungainly metaphor, that the tail is wagging the dog. But Wednesday was of consequence. More so than was Thursday night, with its mute TV and the Seven of Diamonds and Charlotte shying away from my touch.

The Seven of Clubs. Wednesday, or the Seven of Pentacles, seen another way round. Charlotte, wrapped in her bathrobe, comes downstairs after taking a hot shower, and she finds me reading Kip Thorne's *Black Holes and Time Warps*, the book lying lewdly open in my lap. I quickly close it, feeling like I'm a teenager again, and my mother's just barged into my room to find me masturbating to the *Hustler* centerfold. Yes, your daughter is a lesbian, and yes, your girlfriend is reading quantum theory behind your back.

Charlotte stares at me awhile, staring silently, and then she stares at the thick volume lying on the coffee table, *Principles of Physical Cosmology*. She sits down on the floor, not far from the sofa. Her hair is dripping, spattering the hardwood.

"I don't believe you're going to find anything in there," she says, meaning the books.

"I just thought…" I begin, but let the sentence die unfinished, because I'm not at all sure *what* I was thinking. Only that I've always turned to books for solace.

And here, on the afternoon of the Seven of Pentacles, this Wednesday weighted with those seven visionary chalices, she tells me what happened in the shower. How she stood in the steaming spray watching the water rolling down her breasts and *across* her stomach and *up* her buttocks before falling into the hole in her side. Not in defiance of gravity, but in perfect accord with gravity. She hardly speaks above a whisper. I sit quietly listening, wishing that I could suppose she'd only lost her mind. Recourse to wishful thinking, the seven visionary chalices of the Seven of Pentacles, of the Seven of Clubs, or Wednesday. Running away to hide in the comfort of insanity, or the authority of books, or the delusion of lost worlds.

"I'm sorry, but what the fuck do I say to that?" I ask her, and she laughs. It's a terrible sound, that laugh, a harrowing, forsaken sound. And then she stops laughing, and I feel relief spill over me, because now she's crying, instead. There's shame at the relief, of course, but even the shame is welcome. I couldn't have stood that terrible laughter much longer. I go to her and put my arms around her and hold her, as if holding her will make it all better. The sun's almost down by the time she finally stops crying.

I have a quote from Albert Einstein, from sometime in 1912, which I found in the book by Kip Thorne, the book Charlotte caught me reading on Wednesday: "Henceforth, space by itself, and time by itself, are doomed to fade away into mere shadows, and only a kind of union of the two will preserve an independent reality."

Space, time, shadows.

As I've said, I was watching when she was hit. I saw when she fell. That was Saturday last, two days before the yellow morning in the kitchen, and not to be confused with the *next* Saturday which is the Four of Spades. I was sitting on the porch, and had been watching two noisy gray-white gulls wheeling far up against the blue summer sky. Charlotte had been working in her garden, pulling weeds. She called out to me, and I looked away from the birds. She was pointing towards the ocean, and at first I wasn't sure what it was she wanted me to see. I stared at the breakers shattering themselves against the granite boulders, and past that, to the horizon where the water was busy with its all but eternal task of shouldering the burden of the heavens. I was about to tell her that I didn't see anything. This wasn't true, of course. I just didn't see anything out of the ordinary, nothing special, nothing that ought not occupy that time and that space.

I saw nothing to give me pause.

But then I did.

Space, time, shadows.

I'll call it a shadow, because I'm at a loss for any more appropriate word. It was spread out like a shadow rushing across the waves, though, at first, I thought I was seeing something dark moving *beneath* the waves. A very big fish, perhaps. Possibly a large shark or a small whale. We've seen whales in the bay before. Or it might have been caused by a cloud passing in front of the sun, though there were no clouds that day. The truth is I knew it was none of these things. I can sit here all night long, composing a list of what it *wasn't*, and I'll never come any nearer to what it might have been.

"Emily," she shouted. "Do you *see* it?" And I called back that I did. Having noticed it, it was impossible *not* to see that grimy, indefinite smear sliding swiftly towards the shore. In a few seconds more, I realized, it would reach the boulders, and if it wasn't something beneath the water, the rocks wouldn't stop it. Part of my mind still insisted it was only a shadow, a freakish trick of the light, a mirage. Nothing substantial, certainly nothing malign, nothing that could do us any mischief or injury. No need to be alarmed, and yet I don't ever remember being as afraid I was then. I couldn't move, but I yelled for Charlotte to run. I don't think she heard me. Or if she heard me, she was also too mesmerized by the sight of the thing to move.

I was safe, there on the porch. It came no nearer to me than ten or twenty yards. But Charlotte, standing alone at the garden gate, was well within its circumference. It swept over her, and she screamed, and fell to the ground. It swept over her, and then was gone, vanishing into the tangle of green briars and poison ivy and wind-stunted evergreens behind our house. I stood there, smelling something that almost smelled like ozone. And maybe it's an awful cliché to put to paper, but my mind *reeled*. My heart raced, and my mind reeled. For a fraction of an instant I was seized by something that was neither *déjà vu* nor vertigo, and I thought I might vomit.

But the sensation passed, like the shadow had, or the shadow of a shadow, and I dashed down the steps and across the grass to the place where Charlotte sat stunned among the clover and the dandelions. Her clothes and skin looked as though they'd been misted with the thinnest sheen of…what? Oil? No, no, no, not oil at all. But it's the closest I can come to describing that sticky brownish iridescence clinging to her dress and her face, her arms and the pickets of the garden fence and to every single blade of grass.

"It knocked me down," she said, sounding more amazed than hurt or frightened. Her eyes were filled with startled disbelief. "It wasn't *anything*, Em. It wasn't anything at all, but it knocked me right off my feet."

"Are you hurt?" I asked, and she shook her head.

I didn't ask her anything else, and she didn't say anything more. I helped her up and inside the house. I got her clothes off and led her into the downstairs shower. But the oily residue that the shadow had left behind had already begun to *evaporate*—and again, that's not the right word, but it's the best I can manage—before we began trying to scrub it away with soap and scalding clean water. By the next morning, there would be no sign of the stuff anywhere, inside the house or out of doors. Not so much as a stain.

"It knocked me down. It was just a shadow, but it knocked me down." I can't recall how many times she must have said that. She repeated it over and over again, as though repetition would render it less implausible, less inherently ludicrous. "A shadow knocked me down, Em. A shadow knocked me down."

But it wasn't until we were in the bedroom, and she was dressing, that I noticed the red welt above her left hip, just below her ribs. It almost looked like an insect bite, except the center was…well, when I bent down and examined it closely, I saw there *was* no center. There was only a hole. As I've said, a pinprick, but a hole all the same. There wasn't so much as a drop of blood, and she swore to me that it didn't hurt, that she was fine, and it was nothing to get excited about. She went to the medicine cabinet and found a Band-Aid to cover the welt. And I didn't see it again until the next day, which as yet has no playing card, the Sunday before the warm yellow Monday morning in the kitchen.

I'll call that Sunday by the Two of Spades.

It rains on the Two of Spades. It rains cats and dogs all the damn day long. I spend the afternoon sitting in my study, parked there in front of my computer, trying to find the end to Chapter Nine of the book I can't seem to finish. The rain beats at the windows, all rhythm and no melody. I write a line, then delete it. One step forward, two steps back. Zeno's "Achilles and the Tortoise" paradox played out at my keyboard— "That which is in locomotion must arrive at the halfway stage before it arrives at the goal," and each halfway stage has its own halfway stage, *ad infinitum*. These are the sorts of rationalizations that comfort me as I only pretend to be working. This is the *true* reward of my twelve years of college, these erudite excuses for not getting the job done. In the days to come, I will set the same apologetics and exculpations to work on the problem of how a shadow can possibly knock a woman down, and how a hole can be explained away as no more than a wound.

Sometime after seven o'clock, Charlotte raps on the door to ask me how it's going, and what I'd like for dinner. I haven't got a ready answer for either question, and she comes in and sits down on the futon near my desk. She has to move a stack of books to make a place to sit. We talk about the weather, which she tells me is supposed to improve after sunset, that the meteorologists are saying Monday will be sunny and hot. We talk about the book—my exploration of the phenomenon of the literary

Terrae Anachronismorum, from 1714, and Simon Tyssot de Patot's *Voyages et Aventures de Jacques Massé,* to 1918 and Edgar Rice Burroughs's *Out of Time's Abyss* (and beyond; see Aristotle on Zeno, above). I close Microsoft Word, accepting that nothing more will be written until at least tomorrow.

"I took off the Band-Aid," she says, reminding me of what I've spent the day trying to forget.

"When you fell, you probably jabbed yourself on a stick or something," I tell her, which doesn't explain *why* she fell, but seeks to dismiss the result of the fall.

"I don't think it was a stick."

"Well, whatever it was, you hardly got more than a scratch."

And that's when she asks me to look. I would have said no, if saying no were an option.

She stands and pulls up her T-shirt, just on the left side, and points at the hole, though there's no way I could ever miss it. On the rainy Two of Spades, hardly twenty-four hours after Charlotte was knocked off her feet by a shadow, it's already grown to the diameter of dime. I've never seen anything so black in all my life, a black so complete I'm almost certain I would go blind if I stared into it too long. I don't say these things. I don't remember what I say, so maybe I say nothing at all. At first, I think the skin at the edges of the hole is puckered, drawn tight like the skin at the edges of a scab. Then I see that's not the case at all. The skin around the periphery of the hole in her flesh is *moving*, rotating, swirling about that preposterous and undeniable blackness.

"I'm scared," she whispers. "I mean, I'm *really* fucking scared, Emily."

I start to touch the wound, and she stops me. She grabs hold of my hand and stops me.

"Don't," she says, and so I don't.

"You *know* that it can't be what it looks like," I tell her, and I think maybe I even laugh.

"Em, I don't know anything at all."

"You damn well know *that* much, Charlotte. It's some sort of infection, that's all, and—"

She releases my hand, only to cover my mouth before I can finish. Three fingers to still my lips, and she asks me if we can go upstairs, if I'll please make love to her.

"Right now, that's all I want," she says. "In all the world, there's nothing I want more."

I almost make her promise that she'll see our doctor the next day, but already some part of me has admitted to myself this is nothing a physician can diagnose or treat. We have moved out beyond medicine. We have been pushed out into these nether regions by the shadow of a shadow. I have stared directly into that hole, and already I understand it's not merely a hole in Charlotte's skin, but a hole in the cosmos. I could parade her before any number of physicians and physicists, psychologists and priests, and not a one would have the means to seal that breach. In fact, I suspect they would deny the evidence, even if it meant denying all their science and technology and faith. There are things worse than blank spaces on maps. There are moments when certitude becomes the greatest enemy of sanity. Denial becomes an antidote.

Unlike those other days and those other cards, I haven't chosen the Two of Spades at random. I've chosen it because on Thursday she asks me if Alice counts. And I have begun to assume that everything counts, just as everything is claimed by that infinitely small, infinitely dense point beyond the event horizon.

"Would you tell me, please," said Alice, a little timidly, "why you are painting those *roses?*"

Five and Seven said nothing, but looked at Two. Two began, in a low voice, "Why, the fact is, you see, Miss, this here ought to have been a red *rose-tree, and we put a white one in by mistake..."*

On that rainy Saturday, that Two of Spades with an incriminating red brush concealed behind its back, I do as she asks. I cannot do otherwise. I bed her. I fuck her. I am tender and violent by turns, as is she. On that stormy evening, that Two of Pentacles, that Two of *Coins* (a dime, in this case), we both futilely turn to sex looking for surcease from dread. We try to go *back* to our lives before she fell, and this is not so very different from all those "lost worlds" I've belabored in my unfinished manuscript: Maple White Land, Caprona, Skull Island, Symzonia, Pellucidar, the Mines of King Solomon. In our bed, we struggle to fashion a refuge from the present, populated by the reassuring, dependable past. And I am talking in circles within circles within circles, spiraling inward or out, it doesn't matter which.

I am arriving, very soon now, at the end of it, at the Saturday night—or more precisely, just before dawn on the Saturday morning—when the story I am writing here ends. And begins. I've taken too long to get to the point, if I assume the validity of a linear narrative. If I assume any one moment can take precedence over any other or assume the generally assumed (but unproven) inequity of relevance.

A large rose-tree stood near the entrance of the garden; the roses grow-
ing on it were white, but there were three gardeners at it, busily painting
them red.

We are as intimate in those moments as two women can be, when one is
forbidden to touch a dime-sized hole in the other's body. At some point,
after dark, the rain stops falling, and we lie naked and still, listening to
owls and whippoorwills beyond the bedroom walls.

On Wednesday, she comes downstairs and catches me reading the dry
pornography of mathematics and relativity. Wednesday is the Seven of
Clubs. She tells me there's nothing to be found in those books, nothing
that will change what has happened, what may happen.

She says, "I don't know what will be left of me when it's done. I don't
even know if I'll be enough to satisfy it, or if it will just keep getting bigger and bigger and bigger. I think it might be insatiable."

On Monday morning, she sips her coffee. We talk about eleven-year-
old boys and BB guns.

But here, at last, it is shortly before sunup on a Saturday. Saturday, the
Four of Spades. It's been an hour since Charlotte woke screaming, and
I've sat and listened while she tried to make sense of the nightmare. The
hole in her side is as wide as a softball (and, were this more obviously
a comedy, I would list the objects that, by accident, have fallen into it
the last few days). Besides the not-quite-ozone smell, there's now a faint
but constant whistling sound, which is air being pulled into the hole.
In the dream, she tells me, she knew exactly what was on the other side
of the hole, but then she forgot most of it as soon as she awoke. In the
dream, she says, she wasn't afraid, and that we were sitting out on the
porch watching the sea while she explained it all to me. We were drinking Cokes, she said, and it was hot, and the air smelled like dog roses.

"You know I don't like Coke," I say.

"In the dream you did."

She says we were sitting on the porch, and that awful shadow came
across the sea again, only this time it didn't frighten her. This time I saw
it first and pointed it out to her, and we watched together as it moved
rapidly towards the shore. This time, when it swept over the garden, she
wasn't standing there to be knocked down.

"But you said you saw what was on the other side."

"That was later on. And I would tell you what I saw, if I could remember. But there was the sound of pipes, or a flute," she says. "I can recall

that much of it, and I knew, in the dream, that the hole runs all the way to the middle, to the very center."

"The very center of what?" I ask, and she looks at me like she thinks I'm intentionally being slow-witted.

"The center of everything that ever was and is and ever will be, Em. The center. Only, somehow the center is both empty and filled with…" She trails off and stares at the floor.

"Filled with what?"

"I can't *say*. I don't *know*. But whatever it is, it's been there since before there was time. It's been there alone since before the universe was born."

I look up, catching our reflections in the mirror on the dressing table across the room. We're sitting on the edge of the bed, both of us naked, and I look a decade older than I am. Charlotte, though, she looks *so* young, younger than when we met. Never mind that yawning black mouth in her abdomen. In the half light before dawn, she seems to shine, a preface to the coming day, and I'm reminded of what I read about Hawking radiation and the quasar jet streams that escape some singularities. But this isn't the place or time for theories and equations. Here, there are only the two of us, and morning coming on, and what Charlotte can and cannot remember about her dream.

"Eons ago," she says, "it lost its mind. Though I don't think it ever really *had* a mind, not like a human mind. But still, it went insane, from the knowledge of what it is and what it can't ever stop being."

"You said you'd forgotten what was on the other side."

"I have. Almost all of it. This is *nothing*. If I went on a trip to Antarctica and came back and all I could tell you about my trip was that it was very white, that would be like what I'm telling you now about the dream."

The Four of Spades. The Four of Swords, which cartomancers read as stillness, peace, withdrawal, the act of turning sight back upon itself. They say nothing of the attendant perils of introspection or the damnation that would be visited upon an intelligence that could never look *away*.

"It's blind," she says. "It's blind, and insane, and the music from the pipes never ends."

This is when I ask her to stand up, and she only stares at me a moment or two before doing as I've asked. This is when I kneel in front of her, and I'm dimly aware that I'm kneeling before the inadvertent avatar of a god, or God, or a pantheon, or something so immeasurably ancient and pervasive that it may as well be divine. Divine or infernal; there's really no difference, I think.

"What are you doing?" she wants to know.

"I'm losing you," I reply, "that's what I'm doing. Somewhere, some*when*, I've *already* lost you. And that means I have nothing *left* to lose."

Charlotte takes a quick step back from me, retreating towards the bedroom door, and I'm wondering if she runs, will I chase her? Having made this decision, to what lengths will I go to see it through? Would I force her? Would it be rape?

"I know what you're going to do," she says. "Only you're *not* going to do it, because I won't let you."

"You're being devoured—"

"It was a dream, Em. It was only a stupid, crazy dream, and I'm not even sure what I actually remember and what I'm just making up."

"Please," I say, "please let me try." And I watch as whatever resolve she might have had breaks apart. She wants as badly as I do to hope, even though we both know there's no hope left. I watch that hideous black gyre above her hip, below her left breast. She takes two steps back towards me.

"I don't think it will hurt," she tells me. And I can't see any point in asking whether she means, *I don't think it will hurt me*, or *I don't think it will hurt you*. "I don't think there will be any pain."

"I can't see how it possibly matters anymore," I tell her. I don't say anything else. With my right hand, I reach into the hole, and my arm vanishes almost up to my shoulder. There's cold beyond any comprehension of cold. I glance up, and she's watching me. I think she's going to scream, but she doesn't. Her lips part, but she doesn't scream. I feel my arm be tugged so violently I'm sure that it's about to be torn from its socket, the humerus ripped from the glenoid fossa of the scapula, cartilage and ligaments snapped, the subclavian artery severed before I tumble back to the floor and bleed to death. I'm almost certain that's what will happen, and I grit my teeth against that impending amputation.

"I can't feel you," Charlotte whispers. "You're inside me now, but I can't feel you anywhere."

The hole is closing. We both watch as that clockwise spiral stops spinning, then begins to turn widdershins. My freezing hand clutches at the void, my fingers straining for any purchase. Something's changed; I understand that perfectly well. Out of desperation, I've chanced upon some remedy, entirely by instinct or luck, the solution to an insoluble puzzle. I also understand that I need to pull my arm back out again, before the edges of the hole reach my bicep. I imagine the collapsing rim of curved spacetime slicing cleanly through sinew and bone, and then I imagine myself fused at the shoulder to that point just above Charlotte's hip. Horror vies with cartoon absurdities in an instant that seems so swollen it could accommodate an age.

Charlotte's hands are on my shoulders, gripping me tightly, pushing me away, shoving me as hard as she's able. She's saying something, too, words I can't quite hear over the roar at the edges of that cataract created by the implosion of the quantum foam.

Oh, Kitty, how nice it would be if we could only get through into Looking-glass House! I'm sure it's got oh! such beautiful things in it! Let's pretend there's a way of getting through into it, somehow, Kitty. Let's pretend the glass has got all soft as gauze, so that we can get through...

I'm watching a shadow race across the sea.

Warm sun fills the kitchen.

I draw another card.

Charlotte is only ten years old, and a BB fired by her brother strikes her ankle. Twenty-three years later, she falls at the edge of our flower garden.

Time. Space. Shadows. Gravity and velocity. Past, present, and future. All smeared, every distinction lost, and nothing remaining that can possibly be quantified.

I shut my eyes and feel her hands on my shoulders.

And across the space within her, as my arm bridges countless light years, something brushes against my hand. Something wet, and soft, something indescribably abhorrent. Charlotte pushed me, and I was falling backwards, and now I'm not. It has seized my hand in its own—or wrapped some celestial tendril about my wrist—and for a single heartbeat it holds me before letting go.

...whatever it is, it's been there since before there was time. It's been there alone since before the universe was born.

There's pain when my head hits the bedroom floor. There's pain and stars and twittering birds. I taste blood and realize that I've bitten my lip. I open my eyes, and Charlotte's bending over me. I think there are galaxies trapped within her eyes. I glance down at that spot above her left hip, and the skin is smooth and whole. She's starting to cry, and that makes it harder to see the constellations in her eyes. I move my fingers, surprised that my arm and hand are both still there.

"I'm sorry," I say, even if I'm not sure what I'm apologizing for.

"No," she says, "don't be sorry, Em. Don't let's be sorry for anything. Not now. Not ever again."

YOUNGER WOMEN

KAREN JOY FOWLER

Karen Joy Fowler was born in Bloomington, Indiana, and attended the University of California at Berkeley between 1968 and 1972, graduating with a BA in Political Science, and then earning an MA at UC Davis in 1974. She published her first science fiction story, "Praxis," in 1985, and has won the Nebula Award for stories "What I Didn't See" and "Always." Her short fiction has been collected in Artificial Things *and World Fantasy Award winners* Black Glass *and* What I Didn't See and Other Stories. *Fowler is also the author of five novels, including debut* Sarah Canary *(described by critic John Clute as one of the finest First Contact novels ever written),* Sister Noon, The Sweetheart Season, *and* Wit's End. *She is probably best known, though, for her novel* The Jane Austen Book Club, *which was adapted into a successful film. She lives in Santa Cruz, California, with husband Hugh Sterling Fowler II. They have two grown children.*

Jude knows that her daughter Chloe has a boyfriend. She knows this even though Chloe is fifteen and not talking. If Jude were to ask, Chloe would tell Jude that it's none of her business and to stop being such a snoop. (Well, if you want to call it snooping to go through Chloe's closets, drawers, and backpack on a daily basis, check the history on her cell phone and laptop, check the margins of her textbooks for incriminating doodles, friend her on Facebook under a pseudonym so as to access her page—hey, if you want to call that snooping, then, guilty as charged. The world's a dangerous place. Isn't getting less so. Any mother will tell you that.)

So there's no point asking Chloe. She talks about him to her Facebook friends—his name is Eli—but the boy himself never shows. He doesn't phone; he doesn't email; he doesn't text. Sometimes at night Jude wakes up with the peculiar delusion that he's in the house, but when she checks, Chloe is always in her bed, asleep and alone. The less Jude finds out the more uneasy she becomes.

One day she decides to go all in. "Bring that boy you're seeing to dinner this weekend," she tells Chloe, hoping Chloe won't wonder how she knows about him or, if she does, will chalk it up to mother's intuition. "I'll make pasta."

"I'd rather die," Chloe says.

Chloe's Facebook friends are all sympathy. Their mothers are nosy pains-in-the-butt, too. Her own mother died when Jude was twenty-three, and Jude misses her terribly, but she remembers being fifteen. Once when she'd been grounded, which also meant no telephone privileges, her mother had left the house and Jude had called her best friend Audrey. And her mother knew because there was a fruit bowl by the phone and Jude had fiddled with the fruit while she talked.

So Chloe's friends are telling her to stand her ground and yet, come Saturday, there he is, sitting across the table from Jude, playing with his food. It was Eli's own decision to come, Chloe had told her, because he's very polite. Good-looking, too, better than Jude would have guessed. In fact, he's pretty hot.

Jude's unease is still growing. In spite of this, she tries for casual. "Chloe says you're new to the school," she says. "Where are you from?"

"L.A." Eli knows what he's doing. Meets her eyes. Smiles. Uses his napkin. A picture of good manners.

"Don't go all CSI on him, Mom. He doesn't have to answer your questions. You don't have to answer her questions," Chloe says.

"I don't mind. She's just being your mom." And to Jude, "Ask me anything."

"How old are you?"

"Seventeen."

"What year were you born in?"

"1994," he says and there isn't even a pause, but Jude's suspicions solidify in her mind with an audible click like the moment in the morning just before the alarm goes off. No wonder he doesn't text. No wonder he doesn't email or call on the cell. He probably doesn't know how.

"Try again," she tells him.

Vampire. Plain as the nose on your face.

Of course, Chloe knows. She's flattered by it. Any fifteen-year-old would be (and probably lots before her have been). Jude's been doing some light reading on the current neurological research on the teenage brain. She googles this before bed. It helps her sleep, not because the news is good, but because she can tell herself that the current situation is only temporary. She and Chloe used to be so close before Chloe started hating her guts.

The teenage brain is in a state of rapid, but incomplete development. Certain important linkages haven't been formed yet. "The teenage brain is not just an adult brain with fewer miles on it," the experts say. It is a whole different animal. In quantifiable ways, teenagers are actually incapable of thinking straight.

Not to mention the hormones. Poor Chloe. Eli's hotness is getting even to Jude.

Of course, none of this can be said. Chloe thinks she's all grown-up, and if Jude so much as hinted that she wasn't, Chloe would really lose it. Jude has a quick flash of Chloe at five, her hair in fraying pigtails, hanging from the tree in the backyard by her hands (monkey), by her knees (bat), shouting for Jude to come see. If Chloe really were grown up, she'd wonder, the same way Jude wonders, what sort of immortal loser hangs out with fifteen-year-olds. No one loves Chloe more than Jude, no one ever will, but really. Why Chloe?

"Mom!" says Chloe. "Butt the fuck out!"

"It's OK," Eli says. "I'm glad it's in the open." He stops pretending to eat, puts down his fork. "1816."

"And still haven't managed to graduate high school?" Jude asks.

The conversation is not going well. Jude has fetched the whiskey so the adults can drink and sure enough, it turns out there are some things Eli can choke down besides blood. Half a glass in, Jude wonders aloud why Eli can't find a girlfriend his own age. Does he prefer younger women because they're so easy to impress, she wonders. Is it possible no woman older than fifteen will go out with him?

Eli is drinking fast, faster than Jude, but showing no effects. "I love Chloe." Sincerity drips off his voice like rain from the roof. "You maybe don't understand how it is with vampires. We don't choose where our hearts go. But when we give them, we never take them back again. Chloe is my whole world."

"Very nice," Jude says, although in fact she finds it creepy and stalker-ish. "Still, in two hundred years, you must have collected some ex's. Ever been married? How old were they when you finally cleared off? Ancient women of seventeen?"

"Oh. My. God." Chloe is staring down into her sorry glass of ice tea. "Get a clue. Get a life. I knew you'd make this all about you. Ever since Dad left, everyone has to be as fucking miserable as you are. You just can't stand to see me happy."

There is this inconvenient fact—eight months ago Chloe's dad walked out to start a new life with a younger woman. Two weeks ago, he called to tell Jude he was going to be a father again.

"Again? Like you stopped being a father in between?" Jude asked frostily and turned the phone off. She hasn't spoken to him since nor told Chloe about the baby, though maybe Michael has done that for himself. It's the least he can do. Introduce her to her replacement.

"This is why I didn't want you to fucking meet her," Chloe tells Eli. Her face and cheeks are red with fury. She has always colored up like that, even when she was a baby. Jude remembers her, red and sobbing, because the *Little Mermaid* DVD had begun to skip, forcing her to watch the song in which the chef is chopping the heads off fish over and over and over again. Five years old and already a gifted tragedian. "Fix it, Mommy," she'd sobbed. "Fix it or I'll go mad." "I knew you'd try to spoil everything," Chloe tells Jude. "I knew you'd be a bitch and a half."

"You should speak more respectfully to your mother," Eli tells her. "You're lucky to have one." He goes on. Call him old-fashioned, he says, but he doesn't care for the language kids use today. Everything is so much coarser than it used to be.

Chloe responds to Eli's criticism with a gasp. She reaches out, knocks over her glass, maybe deliberately, maybe not. A sprig of mint floats like a raft in a puddle of tea. "I knew you'd find a way to turn him against me." She flees the room, pounds up the stairs, which squeak loudly with her passage. A door slams, but she can still be heard through it, sobbing on her bed. She's waiting for Eli to follow her.

Instead he stands, catches the mint before it falls off the table edge, wipes up the tea with his napkin.

"You're not making my life any easier," Jude tells him.

"I'm truly sorry about that part," he says. "But love is love."

Jude gives Eli fifteen minutes in which to go calm Chloe down. God knows, nothing Jude could say would accomplish that. She waits until he's up the stairs, then follows him, but only as high as the first creaking step, so that she can almost, but not quite hear what they're saying. Chloe's voice is high and impassioned, Eli's apologetic. Then everything is silent, suspiciously so, and she's just about to go up the rest of the way even though the fifteen minutes isn't over when she hears Eli again and realizes he's in the hall. "Let *me* talk to your mom," Eli is saying and Jude hurries back to the table before he catches her listening.

She notices that he manages the stairs without a sound. "She's fine," Eli tells her. "She's on the computer."

Jude decides not to finish her drink. It wouldn't be wise or responsible. It wouldn't be motherly. She's already blurred a bit at the edges though she thinks that's fatigue more than liquor. She's been having so much trouble sleeping.

She eases her feet out of her shoes, leans down to rub her toes. "Doesn't it feel like we've just put the children to bed?" she asks.

Eli's back in his seat across the table, straight-backed in the chair, looking soberly sexy. "Forgive me for this," he says. He leans forward slightly. "But are you trying to seduce me? Mrs. Robinson?"

Jude absolutely wasn't, so it's easy to deny. "I wouldn't date you even without Chloe," she says. Eli's been polite, so she tries to be polite back. Leave it at that.

But he insists on asking.

"It's just such a waste," she says. "I mean, really. High school and high school girls? That's the best you can do with immortality? It doesn't impress me."

"What would you do?" he asks.

She stands, begins to gather up the dishes. "God! I'd go places. I'd see things. Instead you sit like a lump through the same high school history classes you've taken a hundred times, when you could have actually seen those things for yourself. You could have witnessed it all."

Eli picks up his plate and follows her into the kitchen. One year ago, she and Michael had done a complete remodel, silestone countertops and glass-fronted cupboards. Cement floors. The paint was barely dry when Michael left with his new girlfriend. Jude had wanted something homier—tile and wood—but Michael likes modern and minimal. Sometimes Jude feels angrier over this than over the girlfriend. He was seeing

Kathy the whole time they were remodeling. Probably in some part of his brain he'd known he was leaving. Why couldn't he let her have the kitchen she wanted?

"I'll wash," Eli says. "You dry."

"We have a dishwasher." Jude points to it. Energy star. Top of the line. Guilt offering.

"But it's better by hand. Better for talking."

"What are we talking about?"

"You have something you want to ask me." Eli fills the sink, adds the soap.

That's a good guess. Jude can't quite get to it though. "You could have been in Hiroshima or Auschwitz," she says. "You could have helped. You could have walked beside Martin Luther King. You could have torn down the Berlin Wall. Right now, you could be in Darfur, doing something good and important."

"I'm doing the dishes," says Eli.

Outside Jude hears a car passing. It turns into the Klein's driveway. The headlights go off and the car door slams. Marybeth Klein brought Jude a casserole of chicken divan when Michael left. Jude has never told her that Jack Klein tried to kiss her at the Swanson's New Year's Party, because how do you say that to a woman who's never been anything but nice to you? The Kleins' boy, Devin, goes to school with Chloe. He smokes a lot of dope. Sometimes Jude can smell it in the backyard, coming over the fence. Why can't Chloe be in love with him?

"If you promised me not to change Chloe, would you keep that promise?" She hears more than feels the tremble in her voice.

"Now, we're getting to it," Eli says. He passes her the first of the glasses and their hands touch. His fingers feel warm, but she knows that's just the dishwater. "Would you like me to change *you*?" Eli asks. "Is that what you really want?"

The glass slips from Jude's hand and shatters on the cement. A large, sharp piece rests against her bare foot. "Don't move," says Eli. "Let me clean it up." He drops to his knees.

"What's happening?" Chloe calls from upstairs. "What's going on?"

"Nothing. I broke a glass," Jude shouts back.

Eli takes hold of her ankle. He lifts her foot. There is a little blood on her instep and he wipes this away with his hand. "You'd never get older," he says. "But Michael will and you can watch." Jude wonders briefly how he knows Michael's name. Chloe must have told him.

His hand on her foot, his fingers rubbing her instep. The whiskey. Her sleepiness. She is feeling sweetly light-headed, sweetly light-hearted. Another car passes. Jude hears the sprinklers start next door sounding almost, but not quite like rain.

"Is Eli still there?" Chloe's pitch is rising again.

Jude doesn't answer. She speaks instead to Eli. "I wasn't so upset about Michael leaving me as you think. It was a surprise. It was a shock. But I was mostly upset about him leaving Chloe." She thinks again. "I was upset about him leaving me with Chloe."

"You could go to Darfur then. If petty revenge is beneath you," Eli says. "Do things that are good and important." He is lowering his mouth to her foot. She puts a hand on his head to steady herself.

Then she stops, grips his hair, pulls his head up. "But I wouldn't," she says. "Would I?" Jude makes him look at her. She finds it a bit evil, really, offering her immortality under the guise of civic service when the world has such a shortage of civic-minded vampires in it. And she came so close to falling for it.

She sees that the immortal brain must be different—over the years, certain crucial linkages must snap. Otherwise there is no explaining Eli and his dull and pointless, endless, dangerous life.

Anyway, who would take care of Chloe? She hears the squeaking of the stairs.

"Just promise me you won't change Chloe," she says hastily. She's crying now and doesn't know when that started.

"I've never changed anyone who didn't ask to be changed. Never will," Eli tells her.

Jude kicks free of his hand. "Of *course*, she'll ask to be changed," she says furiously. "She's fifteen years old! She doesn't even have a functioning brain yet. Promise me you'll leave her alone."

It's possible Chloe hears this. When Jude turns, she's standing, framed in the doorway like a portrait. Her hair streams over her shoulders. Her eyes are enormous. She's young and she's beautiful and she's outraged. Jude can see her taking them in—Eli picking up the shards of glass so Jude won't step on them. Eli kneeling at her feet.

"You don't have to hang out with her," Chloe tells Eli. "I'm not breaking up with you no matter what she says."

Her gaze moves to Jude. "Good god, Mom. It's just a glass." Then back to Eli, "I'm glad it wasn't me, broke it. We'd never hear the end of it."

Love is love, Eli said, but how careful his timing has been! If Chloe were older, Jude could talk to her, woman to woman. If she were younger, Jude could take Chloe into her lap; tell her to stop throwing words like never around as if she knows what they mean, as if she knows just how long never will last.

WHITE LINES ON A GREEN FIELD

CATHERYNNE M. VALENTE

Catherynne M. Valente is the New York Times bestselling author of over a dozen works of fiction and poetry, including Palimpsest, *the Orphan's Tales series,* Deathless, *and the crowd-funded phenomenon* The Girl Who Circumnavigated Fairyland in a Ship of Her Own Making. *She is the winner of the Andre Norton Award, the Tiptree Award, the Mythopoeic Award, the Rhysling Award, and the Million Writers Award, and has been nominated for the Hugo, Locus, Spectrum, and World Fantasy awards, and was a finalist for the Pushcart Prize. She lives on an island off the coast of Maine with her partner, two dogs, and enormous cat.*

For Seanan McGuire. And Coyote.

Let me tell you about the year Coyote took the Devils to the State Championship.

Coyote walked tall down the halls of West Centerville High and where he walked lunch money, copies of last semester's math tests, and unlit joints blossomed in his footsteps. When he ran laps out on the field our lockers would fill up with Snickers bars, condoms, and ecstasy tabs in all the colors of Skittles. He was our QB, and he looked like an invitation to the greatest rave of all time. I mean, yeah, he had black hair and copper skin and muscles like a commercial for the life you're never going to have. But it was the way he looked at you, with those dark eyes that knew the answer to every question a teacher could ask, but he wouldn't give them the *satisfaction,* you know? Didn't matter anyway. Coyote never did his homework, but boyfriend rocked a 4.2 all the same.

When tryouts rolled around that fall, Coyote went out for everything. Cross-country, baseball, even lacrosse. But I think football appealed to his friendly nature, his need to have a pack around him, bright-eyed boys with six-pack abs and a seven-minute mile and a gift for him every day. They didn't even know why, but they brought them all the same. Playing cards, skateboards, vinyl records (Coyote had no truck with mp3s). The defensive line even baked cookies for their boy. Chocolate chip peanut butter oatmeal walnut iced snickerdoodle, piling up on the bench like a king's tribute. And oh, the girls brought flowers. Poor girls gave him dandelions and rich girls gave him roses and he kissed them all like they were each of them specifically the key to the fulfillment of all his dreams. Maybe they were. Coyote didn't play favorites. He had enough for everyone.

By the time we went to State, all the cheerleaders were pregnant.

The Devils used to be a shitty team, no lie. Bottom of our division and even the coach was thinking he ought to get more serious about his geometry classes. Before Coyote transferred our booster club was the tight end's dad, Mr. Bollard, who painted his face Devil gold-and-red and wore big plastic light-up horns for every game. At Homecoming one year, the Devil's Court had two princesses and a queen who were actually girls from the softball team filling in on a volunteer basis, because no one cared enough to vote. They all wore jeans and bet heavily on the East Centerville Knights, who won 34-3.

First game of his senior year, Coyote ran 82 yards for the first of 74 touchdowns that season. He passed and caught and ran like he was all eleven of them in one body. Nobody could catch him. Nobody even complained. He ran like he'd stolen that ball and the whole world was chasing him to get it back. Where'd he been all this time? The boys hoisted him up on their shoulders afterward, and Coyote just laughed and laughed. We all found our midterm papers under our pillows the next morning, finished and bibliographied, and damn if they weren't the best essays we'd never written.

I'm not gonna lie. I lost my virginity to Coyote in the back of my blue pickup out by the lake right before playoffs. He stroked my hair and kissed me like they kiss in the movies. Just the perfect kisses, no bonked noses, no knocking teeth. He tasted like stolen sunshine. *Bunny,* he whispered to me with his narrow hips working away, *I will love you forever and ever. You're the only one for me.*

Liar, I whispered back, and when I came it was like the long flying fall of a roller coaster, right into his arms. *Liar, liar, liar.*

I think he liked that I knew the score, because after that Coyote made sure I was at all his games, even though I don't care about sports. Nobody didn't care about sports that year. Overnight the stands went from a ghost town to kids-ride-free day at the carnival. And when Coyote danced in the end zone he looked like everything you ever wanted. Every son, every boyfriend.

"Come on, Bunny," he'd say. "I'll score a touchdown for you."

"You'll score a touchdown either way."

"I'll point at you in the stands if you're there. Everyone will know I love you."

"Just make sure I'm sitting with Sarah Jane and Jessica and Ashley, too, so you don't get in trouble."

"That's my Bunny, always looking out for me," he'd laugh, and take me in his mouth like he'd die if he didn't.

You could use birth control with Coyote. It wouldn't matter much.

But he did point at me when he crossed that line, grinning and dancing and moving his hips like Elvis had just been copying his moves all along, and Sarah Jane and Jessica and Ashley got so excited they choked on their Cokes. They all knew about the others. I think they liked it that way—most of what mattered to Sarah and Jessica and Ashley was Sarah Jane and Jessica and Ashley, and Coyote gave them permission to spend all their time together. Coyote gave us all permission, that was his thing. *Cheat, fuck, drink, dance—just do it like you mean it!*

I think the safety had that tattooed on his calf.

After we won four games in a row (after a decade of no love) things started to get really out of control. You couldn't buy tickets. Mr. Bollard was in hog heaven—suddenly the boosters were every guy in town who was somebody, or used to be somebody, or who wanted to be somebody some impossible day in the future. We were gonna beat the Thunderbirds. They started saying it, right out in public. Six-time state champs, and no chance they wouldn't be the team in our way this year like every year. But every year was behind us, and ahead was only our boy running like he'd got the whole of heaven at his back. Mr. Bollard got them new uniforms, new helmets, new goal posts—all the deepest red you ever saw. But nobody wore the light-up horns Mr. Bollard had rocked for years. They all wore little furry coyote ears, and who knows where they bought them, but they were everywhere one Friday, and every Friday after. When Coyote scored, everyone would howl like the moon had come out just for them. Some of the cheerleaders started wearing faux-fur tails, spinning them around by bumping and grinding on the sidelines, their corn-yellow skirts fluttering up to the heavens.

One time, after we stomped the Greenville Bulldogs 42-0 I saw Coyote under the stands, in that secret place the boards and steel poles and shadows and candy wrappers make. Mike Halloran (kicker #14) and Justin Oster (wide receiver #11) were down there too, helmets off, the filtered stadium lights turning their uniforms to pure gold. Coyote leaned against a pole, smoking a cigarette, shirt off—and what a thing that was to see.

"Come on, QB," Justin whined. "I never hit a guy before. I got no beef here. And I never fucked Jessie, either, Mike, I was just mouthing off. She let me see her boob once in ninth grade and there wasn't that much to see back then. I never had a drink except one time a beer and I never smoked 'cause my daddy got emphysema." Coyote just grinned his friendly, hey-dude-no-worries grin.

"Never know unless you try," he said, very reasonably. "It'll make you feel good, I promise."

"Fuck *you*, Oster" shot back Halloran. "I'm going first. You're bigger, it's not fair."

Halloran got his punch in before he had to hear any more about what Justin Oster had never done and the two of them went *at it,* fists and blood and meat-slapping sounds and pretty soon they were down on the ground in the spilled-Coke and week-old-rain mud, pulling hair and biting and rolling around and after a while it didn't look that much like fighting anymore. I watched for a while. Coyote looked up at me over their grappling and dragged on his smoke.

Just look at them go, little sister, I heard Coyote whisper, but his mouth didn't move. His eyes flashed in the dark like a dog's.

LaGrange almost ruined it all at Homecoming. The LaGrange Cowboys, and wasn't their QB a picture, all wholesome white-blond square-jaw aw-shucks muscle with an arm so perfect you'd have thought someone had mounted a rifle sight on it: #9 Bobby Zhao, of the 300 bench and the Miss Butter Festival 19whatever mother, the seven-restaurant-chain-owning father (Dumpling King of the Southland!) and the surprising talent for soulful bluegrass guitar. All the colleges lined up for that boy with carnations and chocolates. We hated him like hate was something we'd invented in lab that week and had been saving up for something special. Bobby Zhao and his bullshit hipster-crooner straw hat. Coyote didn't pay him mind. *Tell us what you're gonna do to him,* they'd pant, and he'd just spit onto the parking lot asphalt and say: *I got a history with Cowboys.* Where he'd spat the offensive line watched as weird crystals formed—the kind Jimmy Moser (safety #17) ought to have recognized from his uncle's trailer out off of Route 40, but you know me, I don't say a word. They didn't look at it too long. Instead they scratched their cheeks and performed their tribal ask-and-answer. *We going down by the lake tonight? Yeah. Yeah.*

"Let's invite Bobby Zhao," Coyote said suddenly. His eyes got big and loose and happy. His *come-on* look. His *it'll-be-great* look.

"Um, why?" Jimmy frowned. "Not to put too fine a point on it, but fuck that guy. He's the enemy."

Coyote flipped up the collar of his leather jacket and picked a stray maple leaf the color of anger out of Jimmy's hair. He did it tenderly. *You're my boy and I'll pick you clean, I'll lick you clean, I'll keep everything red off of your perfect head,* his fingers said. But what his mouth said was:

"Son, what you don't know about enemies could just about feed the team 'til their dying day." And when Coyote called you Son you knew to be ashamed. "Only babies think enemies are for beating. Can't beat 'em, not ever. Not the ones that come out of nowhere in the fourth quarter to take what's yours and hold your face in the mud 'til you drown, not the ones you always knew you'd have to face because that's what you were made for. Not the lizard guarding the Sun, not the man who won't let you teach him how to plant corn. Enemies are for grabbing by the ears and fucking them 'til they're so sticky-knotted bound to you they call their wives by your name. Enemies are for absorbing, Jimmy. Best thing you can do to an enemy is pull up a chair to his fire, eat his dinner, rut in his bed and go to his job in the morning, and do it all so much better he just gives it up to you—but *fuck him,* you never wanted it anyway. You just wanted to mess around in his house for a little while. Scare his kids. Leave a little something behind to let the next guy know you're never far away. That's how you do him. Or else—" Coyote pulled Cindy Gerard (bottom of the pyramid and arms like birch trunks) close and took the raspberry pop out of her hand, sipping on it long and sweet, all that pink slipping into him. "Or else you just make him love you 'til he cries. Either way."

Jimmy fidgeted. He looked at Oster and Halloran, who still had bruises, fading on their cheekbones like blue flowers. After a while he laughed horsily and said: "Whaddaya think the point spread'll be?"

Coyote just punched him in the arm, convivial like, and kissed Cindy Gerard and I could smell the raspberry of their kiss from across the circle of boys. The September wind brought their kiss to all of us like a bag of promises. And just like that, Bobby Zhao showed up at the lake that night, driving his freshly waxed Cowboy silver-and-black double-cab truck with the lights on top like a couple of frog's eyes. He took off that stupid straw hat and started hauling a keg out of the cream leather passenger seat—and once they saw that big silver moon riding shotgun with the Dumpling Prince of the Southland, Henry Dillard (linebacker #33) and Josh Vick (linebacker #34) hurried over to help him with it and Bobby Zhao was welcome. Offering accepted. Just lay it up here on the altar and we'll cut open that shiny belly and drink what she's got for us. And what she had was golden and sweet and just as foamy as the sea.

Coyote laid back with me in the bed of my much shittier pick-up, some wool blanket with a horse-and-cactus print on it under us and another one with a wolf-and-moon design over us, so he could slip his hands under my bra in that secret, warm space that gets born under some hippie mom's awful rugs when no one else can see you. Everyone was hollering over the beer and I could hear Sarah Jane laughing in that way that says: *Just keep pouring and maybe I'll show you something worth seeing.*

"Come on, Bunny Rabbit," Coyote whispered, "it's nothing we haven't done before." And it was a dumb thing to say, a boy thing, but when Coyote said it I felt it humming in my bones, everything we'd done before, over and over, and I couldn't even remember a world before Coyote, only the one he made of us, down by the lake, under the wolf and the moon, his hands on my breasts like they were the saving of him. I knew him like nobody else—and they'll all say that now, Sarah Jane and Jessica and Ashley and Cindy Gerard and Justin Oster and Jimmy Moser, but I knew him. Knew the shape of him. After all, it's nothing we hadn't done before.

"It's different every time," I said in the truck-dark. "Or there's no point. You gotta ask me nice every time. You gotta make me think I'm special. You gotta put on your ears and your tail and make the rain come for me or I'll run off with some Thunderbird QB and leave you eating my dust."

"I'm asking nice. Oh, my Bunny, my rabbit-girl with the fastest feet, just slow you down and let me do what I want."

"And what do you want?"

"I want to dance on this town 'til it breaks. I want to burrow in it until it belongs to me. I want high school to last forever. I want to eat everything, and fuck everything, and snort everything, and win everything. I want my Bunny Rabbit on my lap while I drive down the world with my headlights off."

"I don't want to be tricked," I said, but he was already inside me and I was glad. Fucking him felt like running in a long field, with no end in sight. "Not into a baby, not into a boyfriend, not into anything."

"Don't worry," he panted. "You always get yours. Just like me, always like me."

I felt us together, speeding up towards something, running faster, and he brushed my hair out of my face and it wasn't hair but long black ears, as soft as memory, and then it was hair again, tangled and damp with our sweat, and I bit him as our stride broke. I whispered: "And Coyote gets his."

"Why not? It's nothing we haven't done before."

When I got up off of the horse blanket, marigold blossoms spilled out of me like Coyote's seed.

Later that night I fished a smoke out of my glove box and sat on top of the dented salt-rusted cab of my truck. Coyote stood down by the lakeshore, aways off from the crowd, where the water came up in little foamy splashes and the willow trees whipped around like they were looking for someone to hold on to. Bobby Zhao was down there, too, his hands in his jean pockets, hip jutting out like a pouty lip, his hat on again and his face all in shadow. They were talking but I couldn't hear over everyone else hooting and laughing like a pack of owls. The moon came out as big as a beer keg; it made Coyote's face look lean and angelic, so young and victorious and humble enough to make you think the choice was yours all along. He took Bobby Zhao's hand and they just stood there in the light, their fingers moving together. The wind blew off that straw hat like it didn't like the thing much either, and Bobby let it lie. He was looking at Coyote, his hair all blue in the night, and Coyote kissed him as hard as hurting, and Bobby kissed him back like he'd been waiting for it since he was born. Coyote got his hands under his shirt and oh, Coyote is good at that, getting under, getting around, and the boys smiled whenever their lips parted.

I watched. I'm always watching. Who doesn't like to watch? It feels like being God, seeing everything happen far away, and you could stop it if you wanted, but then you couldn't watch anymore.

A storm started rumbling up across the meadows, spattering their kisses with autumn rain.

Suddenly everyone cared about who was going to make the Devil's Court this year. Even me. The mall was cleared out of formal sparkle-and-slit dresses by August, and somehow they just couldn't get any more in, like we were an island mysteriously sundered from the land of sequins and sweetheart necklines. Most of us were just going to have to go with one of our mom's prom dresses, though you can be damn sure we'd be ripping off that poofy shoulder chiffon and taking up the hems as far as we could. Jenny Kilroy (drama club, Young Businesswomen's Association) had done all the costumes for *The Music Man* in junior year, and for $50 she'd take that cherry cupcake dress and turn it into an apocalyptic punkslut wedding gown, but girlfriend worked *slow*. Whoever took the Homecoming crown had about a 60/40 chance of being up there in something they'd worn to their grandmother's funeral.

The smart money was on Sarah Jane for the win. She was already pregnant by then, and Jessica too, but I don't think even they knew it yet. Bellies still flat as a plains state, cotton candy lipstick as perfect as a Rembrandt. Nobody got morning sickness, nobody's feet swelled. Sarah shone in the center of her ring of girls like a pink diamond in a nouveaux riche ring: 4.0, equestrian club, head cheerleader, softball pitcher, jazz choir lead soprano, played Juliet in both freshman and senior years, even joined the chess club. She didn't care about chess, but it looked good on her applications and she turned out to be terrifyingly good at it—first place at the spring speed chess invitational in Freemont, even seven months along. You couldn't even hate Sarah. You could see her whole perfect life rolling on ahead of her like a yellow brick road but you knew she'd include you, if you wanted. If you stuck around this town like she meant to, and let her rule it like she aimed to.

Jessica and Ashley flanked her down every hall and every parade—a girl like Sarah just naturally grows girls like Jessica and Ashley to be her adjutants, her bridesmaids, the baby's breath to make her rose look redder. All three of them knew the score and all three of them made sure nothing would ever change, like Macbeth's witches, if they wore daisy-print coats and their mothers' Chanel and tearproof mascara and only foretold their own love, continuing forever and the world moving aside to let it pass. So that was the obvious lineup—Queen Sarah and her Viziers. Of course there were three slots, so I figured Jenny Kilroy would slide in on account of her charitable work to keep us all in the shimmer.

And then Friday morning arrived, the dawn before the dance and a week before the showdown game with Bobby Zhao and his Cowboys. Coyote howled up 7 a.m. and we woke up and opened our closets and there they hung—a hundred perfect dresses. Whatever we might have chosen after hours of turning on the rack of the mall with nothing in our size or our color or modest enough for daddy or bare enough for us, well, it was hanging in our closets with a corsage on the hip. Coyote took us all to Homecoming that year. And there in my room hung something that glittered and threw prisms on the wall, something the color of the ripest pumpkin you ever saw, something cut so low and slit so high it invited the world to love me best. I put it on and my head filled up with champagne like I'd already been sipping flutes for an hour, as if silk could make skin drunk. I slid the corsage on my wrist—cornflowers, and tiny green ears not yet open.

Coyote danced with all the girls and when the music sped up he threw back his head and howled and we all howled with him. When it slowed down he draped himself all over some lonesome thing who never thought she had a chance. The rest of us threw out our arms and danced with what our hands caught—Jessica spent half the night with mathletes kissing her neck and teaching her mnemonics. Everything was dizzy; everything spun. The music came from everywhere at once and the floor shook with our stomping. We were so strong that night, we were full of the year and no one drank the punch because no one needed it, we just moved with Coyote and Coyote moved, too. I flung out my arms and spun away from David Horowitz (pep squad, 100-meter dash), my corn-bound hand finding a new body to carry me into the next song. Guitar strings plinked in some other, distant world beyond the gymnasium and I opened my eyes to see Sarah Jane in my arms, her dress a perfect, icy white spill of froth and jewels, her eyes made up black and severe, to contrast, her lips a generous rose-colored smile. She smelled like musk and honeysuckle. She smelled like Coyote. I danced with her and she put her head on my breast; I felt her waist in my grasp, the slight weight of her, the chess queen, the queen of horses and jazz and grade point averages and pyramids and backflips, Juliet twice, thrice, a hundred times over. She ran her hand idly up and down my back just as if I were a boy. My vision blurred and the Christmas lights hanging everywhere swam into a soup of Devil red and Devil gold. The queen of the softball team lifted her sunny blonde head and kissed me. Her mouth tasted like cherry gum and whiskey. She put her hands in my hair to show me she meant it, and I pulled her in tight—but the song ended and she pulled away, looking surprised and confused, her lipstick dulled, her bright brown eyes wounded, like a deer with sudden shot in her side. She ran to Jessica and Ashley and the three of them to Coyote, hands over their stomachs as though something fluttered there, something as yet unknown and unnamed.

The principal got up to call out the Devil's Court. My man was shaken by all the heavy grinding and spinning and howling that had become the senior class, but he got out his index cards all the same. He adjusted his striped tie and tapped the mic, just like every principal has ever done. And he said a name. And it was mine. A roar picked up around me and hands were shoving me forward and I didn't understand, it was Sarah Jane, it would always be Sarah Jane. But I stood there while Mr. Whitmore, the football coach, put a crown on my head, and I looked out into the throng. Coyote stood there in his tuxedo, the bowtie all undone like a brief black river around his neck, and he winked at me with his flashing hound-eye, and the principal called three more names and they were Jessica and Ashley and Sarah Jane. They stood around me like three fates and Mr. Whitmore put little spangly tiaras on their heads and they looked at me like I had caught a pass in the end zone, Hail Mary and three seconds left on the clock. I stared back and their tiaras were suddenly rings of wheat and appleblossoms and big, heavy oranges like suns, and I could see in their eyes mine wasn't rhinestones any more than it was ice cream. I lifted it down off my head and held it out like a thing alive: a crown of corn, not the Iowa yellow stuff but blue and black, primal corn from before the sun thought fit to rise, with tufts of silver fur sprouting from their tips, and all knotted together with crow feathers and marigolds.

And then it was pink rhinestones in my hands again, and blue zirconium on my Princesses' heads, and the Devil's Court took its place, and if you have to ask who was King, you haven't been listening.

After that, the game skipped by like a movie of itself. Bobby just couldn't keep that ball in his hands. You could see it on his face, how the ball had betrayed him, gone over to a bad boy with a leather jacket and no truck at all. You could see him re-sorting colleges in his head. It just about broke your heart. But we won 24-7, and Coyote led Bobby Zhao off the field with a *sorry-buddy* and a *one-game-don't-mean-a-thing,* and before I drove off to the afterparty I saw them under the bleachers, foreheads pressed together, each clutching at the other's skin like they wanted to climb inside, and they were beautiful like that, down there underneath the world, their helmets lying at their feet like old crowns.

Nothing could stop us then. The Westbrook Ravens, the Bella Vista Possums, the Ashland Gators. Line them up and watch them fall. It wasn't even a question.

I suppose we learned trig, or Melville, or earth science. I suppose we took exams. I suppose we had parents, too, but I'll be damned if any of that seemed to make the tiniest impression on any one of us that year. We lived in an unbreakable bubble where nothing mattered. We lived in a snowglobe, only the sun was always shining and we were always winning and yeah, you could get grounded for faceplanting your biology midterm or pulled over for speeding or worse for snorting whatever green fairy dust Coyote found for you, but nothing really *happened.* You came down to the lake like always the next night. After the Ravens game, Greg Knight (running back #46) and Johnny Thompson (cornerback #22) crashed their cars into each other after drinking half a sip of something Coyote whipped up in an acorn cap, yelling chicken out the window the whole time like it was 1950 and some girl would be waving her handkerchief at the finish line. But instead there was a squeal of engine humping up on engine and the dead crunch of the front ends smacking together and the long blare of Greg's face leaning on his horn.

But even then, they just got up and walked away, arm in arm and Coyote suddenly between them, *oh-my-godding* and *let's-do-that-againing.* The next day their Camrys pulled up to the parking lot like it was no big deal. Nothing could touch us.

All eyes were on the Thunderbirds.

Now, the Thunderbirds didn't have a Bobby Zhao. No star player to come back and play celebrity alumnus in ten years with a Super Bowl ring on his finger. A Thunderbird was part of a machine, a part that could be swapped out for a hot new freshman no problem, no resentment. They moved as one, thought as one, they were a flock, always pointed in the same direction. That was how they'd won six state championships; that was how they'd sent three quarterbacks to the NFL in the last decade.

There was no one to hate—just a single massive Thunderbird darkening our little sky.

Coyote's girls began to show by Christmas.

Sarah Jane, whatever the crown might have said at Homecoming, was queen of the unwed mothers, too. Her belly swelled just slightly bigger than the others—but then none of them got very big. None of them slowed down. Sarah Jane was turning a flip-into somersault off the pyramid in her sixth month with no trouble. They would all lay around the sidelines together painting their stomachs (Devil red and Devil gold) and trying on names for size. No point in getting angry; no point in fighting for position. The tribe was the tribe and the tribe was all of us and a tribe has to look after its young. The defensive line had a whole rotating system for bringing them chocolate milk in the middle of the night.

They were strong and tan and lean and I had even money on them all giving birth to puppies.

I didn't get pregnant. But then, I wouldn't. I told him, and he listened. Rabbit and Coyote, they do each other favors, when they can.

A plan hatched itself: steal their mascot. An old-fashioned sort of thing, like playing chicken with cars. Coyote plays it old school. Into Springfield High in the middle of the night, out with Marmalade, a stuffed, moth-eaten African Grey parrot from some old biology teacher's collection that a bright soul had long ago decided could stand in for a Thunderbird.

We drove out to Springfield, two hours and change, me and Coyote and Jimmy Moser and Mike Halloran and Josh Vick and Sarah Jane and Jessica and Ashley, all crammed into my truck, front and back. Coyote put something with a beat on the radio and slugged back some off-brand crap that probably turned to Scotland's peaty finest when it hit his tongue. Jimmy was trying to talk Ashley into making out with him in the back while the night wind whipped through their hair and fireflies flashed by, even though it was January. Ashley didn't mind too much, even less when everyone wanted to touch her stomach and feel the baby move. She blushed like a primrose and even her belly button went pink.

Nobody's very quiet when sneaking into a gym. Your feet squeak on the basketball court and everyone giggles like a joke got told even when none did and we had Coyote's hissing *drink up drink up* and squeezing my hand like he can't hold the excitement in. We saw Marmalade center court on a parade float, all ready to ship over to the big designated-neutral-ground stadium for halftime. Big yellow and white crepe flowers drooped everywhere, around the shore of a bright blue construction paper sea. Marmalade's green wings spread out majestically, and in his talons he held a huge orange papier-mâché ball ringed with aluminum foil rays dipped in gold glitter. Thunderbird made this world, and Thunderbird gets to rule it.

Coyote got this look on his face and the moment I saw it I knew I wouldn't let him get there first. I took off running, my sneakers screeching, everyone hollering *Bunny!* after me and Coyote scrappling up behind me, closing the distance, racing to the sun. *I'm faster, I'm always faster. Sometimes he gets it and sometimes I get it but it's nothing we haven't done before and this time it's mine.*

And I leapt onto the float without disturbing the paper sea and reached up, straining, and finally just going for it. I'm a tall girl, see how high I jump. The sun came down in my arms, still warm from the gym lights and the after-hours HVAC. The Thunderbird came with it, all red cheeks and Crayola green wingspan and I looked down to see Coyote grinning up at me. He'd let me take it, if I wanted it. He'd let me wear it like a crown. But after a second of enjoying its weight, the deliciousness of its theft, I passed it down to him. It was his year. He'd earned it.

We drove home through the January stars with the sun in the bed of my truck and three pregnant girls touching it with one hand each, holding it down, holding it still, holding it together.

On game day we stabbed it with the Devil's pitchfork and paraded our float around the stadium like conquering heroes. Like cowboys. Marmalade looked vaguely sad. By then Coyote was cleaning off blood in the locker room, getting ready for the second half, shaken, no girls around him and no steroid needles blossoming up from his friendly palm like a bouquet of peonies.

The first half of the championship game hit us like a boulder falling from the sky. The Thunderbirds didn't play for flash, but for short, sharp gains and an inexorable progression toward the end zone. They didn't cheer when they scored. They nodded to their coach and regrouped. They caught the flawless, seraphic passes Coyote fired off; they engulfed him when he tried to run as he'd always done. Our stands started out raucous and screaming and jumping up and down, cheering on our visibly pregnant cheerleading squad despite horrified protests from the Springfield side. *Don't you listen, Sarah Jane baby!* Yelled Mr. Bollard. *You look perfect!* And she did, fists in the air, ponytail swinging.

Halftime stood 14-7 Thunderbirds.

I slipped into the locker room—by that time the place had become Devil central, girls and boys and players and cheerleaders and second-chair marching band kids who weren't needed till post-game all piled in together. Some of them giving pep talks which I did not listen to, some of them bandaging knees, some of them—well. Doing what always needs doing when Coyote's around. Rome never saw a party like a Devil locker room.

I walked right over to my boy and the blood vanished from his face just as soon as he saw me.

"Don't you try to look pretty for me," I said.

"Aw, Bunny, but you always look so nice for me."

I sat in his lap. He tucked his fingers between my thighs—where I clamped them, safe and still. "What's going on out there?"

Coyote drank his water down. "Don't you worry, Bunny Rabbit. It has to go like this, or they won't feel like they really won. Ain't no good game since the first game that didn't look lost at halftime. It's how the story goes. Can't hold a game without it. The old fire just won't come. If I just let that old Bird lose like it has to, well, everyone would get happy after, but they'd think it was predestined all along, no work went into it. You gotta make the story for them, so that when the game is done they'll just…" Coyote smiled and his teeth gleamed. "Well, they'll lose their minds I won it so good."

Coyote kissed me and bit my lip with those gleaming teeth. Blood came up and in our mouths it turned to fire. We drank it down and he ran out on that field, Devil red and Devil gold, and he ran like if he kept running he could escape the last thousand years. He ran like the field was his country. He ran like his bride was on the other end of all that grass and I guess she was. I guess we all were. Coyote gave the cherry to Justin Oster, who caught this pass that looked for all the world like the ball might have made it all the way to the Pacific if nobody stood in its way. But Justin did, and he caught it tight and perfect and the stadium shook with Devil pride.

34-14. Rings all around, as if they'd all married the state herself.

That night, we had a big bonfire down by the lake. Neutral ground was barely forty-five minutes out of town, and no one got home tired and ready to sleep a good night and rise to a work ethic in the morning.

I remember we used to say *down-by-the-lake* like it was a city, like it was an address. I guess it was, the way all those cars would gather like crows, pick-ups and Camaros and Jeeps, noses pointing in, a metal wall against the world. The willows snapped their green whips at the moon and the flames licked up Devil red and Devil gold. We built the night without thinking about it, without telling anyone it was going to happen, without making plans. Everyone knew to be there; no one was late.

Get any group of high school kids together and you pretty much have the building blocks of civilization. The Eagle Scout boys made an architecturally perfect bonfire; 4-H-ers threw in grub, chips and burgers and dogs and Twix and Starburst. The drama kids came bearing tunes, their tooth-white iPods stuffed into speaker cradles like black mouths. The rich kids brought booze from a dozen walnut cabinets—and Coyote taught them how to spot the good stuff. Meat and fire and music and liquor—that's all it's ever been. Sarah Jane started dancing up to the flames with a bottle of 100-year-old cognac in her hand, holding it by the neck, moving her hips, her gorgeously round belly, her long corn-colored hair brushing faces as she spun by, the smell of her expensive and hot. Jessica and Ashley ran up to her and the three of them swayed and sang and stamped, their arms slung low around each other, their heads pressed together like three graces. Sarah Jane poured her daddy's cognac over Ashley's breasts and caught the golden stuff spilling off in her sparkly pink mouth and Ashley laughed so high and sweet and that was *it*—everyone started dancing and howling and jumping and Coyote was there in the middle of it all, arching his back and keeping the beat, slapping his big thighs, throwing the game ball from boy to girl to boy to girl, like it was magic, like it was just ours, the sun of our world arcing from hand to hand to hand.

I caught it and Coyote kissed me. I threw it to Haley Collins from English class and Nick Dristol (left tackle #19) caught me up in his arms. I don't even know what song was playing. The night was so loud in my ears. I could see it happening and it scared me but I couldn't stop it and didn't want to. Everything was falling apart and coming together and we'd won the game, Bunny no less than Coyote, and boyfriend never fooled me for a minute, never could.

I could hear Sarah Jane laughing and I saw Jessica kissing her and Greg Knight both, one to the other like she was counting the kisses to make it all fair. She tipped up that caramel-colored bottle and Nick started to say something but I shushed him. *Coyote's cognac's never gonna hurt that baby.* Every tailgate hung open, no bottle ever seemed to empty and even though it was January the air was so warm, the crisp red and yellow leaves drifting over us all, no one sorry, no one ashamed, no one chess club or physics club or cheer squad or baseball team, just tangled up together inside our barricade of cars.

Sarah danced up to me and took a swallow without taking her eyes from mine. She grabbed me roughly by the neck and into a kiss, passing the cognac to me and oh, it tasted like a pass thrown all the way to the sea, and she wrapped me up in her arms like she was trying to make up Homecoming to me, to say: *I'm better now, I'm braver now, doesn't this feel like the end of everything and we have to get it while we can?* I could feel her stomach pressing on mine, big and insistent and hard, and as she ripped my shirt open I felt her child move inside her. We broke and her breasts shone naked in the bonfire-light—mine too, I suppose. Between us a cornstalk grew fast and sure, shooting up out of the ground like it had an appointment with the sky, then a second and a third. That same old blue corn, midnight corn, first corn. All around the fire the earth was bellowing out pumpkins and blackberries and state fair tomatoes and big blousy squash flowers, wheat and watermelons and apple trees already broken with the weight of fruit. The dead winter trees exploded into green, the graduating class fell into the rows of vegetables and fruit and thrashed together like wolves, like bears, like devils. Fireflies turned the air into an emerald necklace and Sarah Jane grabbed Coyote's hand which was a paw which was a hand and screamed. Didn't matter—everyone was screaming, and the music quivered the darkness and Sarah's baby beat at the drum of her belly, demanding to be let out into the pumpkins and the blue, blue corn, demanding to meets its daddy.

All the girls screamed. Even the ones only a month or two gone, clutching their stomachs and crying, all of them except me, Bunny Rabbit, the watcher, the queen of coming home. The melons split open in an eruption of pale green and pink pulp; the squashes cracked so loud I put my hands (which were paws which were hands) over my ears, and the babies came like harvest, like forty-five souls running after a bright ball in the sky.

Some of us, after a long night of vodka tonics and retro music and pretending there was anything else to talk about, huddle together around a table at the ten year and get into it. How Mr. Bollard was never the same and ended up hanging himself in a hotel room after almost a decade of straight losses. How they all dragged themselves home and suddenly had parents again, the furious kind, and failed SATs and livers like punching bags. How no one went down to the lake anymore and Bobby Zhao went to college out of state and isn't he on some team out east now? Yeah. Yeah. But his father lost the restaurants and now the southland has no king. But the gym ceiling caved in after the rains and killed a kid. But most of them could just never understand why their essays used to just be perfect and they never had hangovers and they looked amazing all the time and sex was so easy that year but never since, no matter how much shit went up their nose or how they cheated and fought and drank because they didn't mean it like they had back when, no matter how many people they brought home hoping just for a second it would be like it was then, when Coyote made their world. They had this feeling, just for a minute—didn't I feel it too? That everything could be different. And then it was the same forever, the corn stayed yellow and they stayed a bunch of white kids with scars where their cars crashed and fists struck and babies were born. The lake went dry and the scoreboard went dark.

Coyote leaves a hole when he goes. He danced on this town till it broke. That's the trick, and everyone falls for it.

But they all had kids, didn't they? Are they remembering that wrong? What happened to them all?

Memory is funny—only Sarah Jane (real estate, Rotary, Wednesday night book club) can really remember her baby. Everyone just remembers the corn and the feeling of running, running so fast, the whole pack of us, against the rural Devil gold sunset. I call that a kindness. (*Why me?* Sarah asks her gin. *You were the queen,* I say. *That was you. Only for a minute.*) It was good, wasn't it, they all want to say. When we were all together. When we were a country, and Coyote taught us how to grow such strange things.

Why did I stick around, they all want to know. When he took off, why didn't I go, too? Weren't we two of a kind? Weren't we always conspiring?

Coyote wins the big game, I say. I get the afterparty.

This is what I don't tell them.

I woke up before anyone the morning after the championships. Everyone had passed out where they stood, laying everywhere like a bomb had gone off. No corn, no pumpkins, no watermelons. Just that cold lake morning fog. I woke up because my pick-up's engine fired off in the gloam, and I know that sound like my mama's crying. I jogged over to my car but it was already going, bouncing slowly down the dirt road with nobody driving. In the back, Coyote sat laughing, surrounded by kids, maybe eight or ten years old, all of them looking just like him, all of them in leather jackets and hangdog grins, their black hair blowing back in the breeze. Coyote looked at me and raised a hand. See you again. After all, it's nothing we haven't done before.

Coyote handed a football to one of his daughters. She lifted it into the air, her form perfect, trying out her new strength. She didn't throw it. She held it tight, like it was her heart.

ALL THAT TOUCHES THE AIR

AN OWOMOYELA

An Owomoyela (pronounce it "On") is a neutrois author with a background in web development, linguistics, and weaving chain maille out of stainless steel fencing wire, whose fiction has appeared in a number of venues including Clarkesworld, Asimov's, Lightspeed, *and a pair of* Year's Bests. *An's interests range from pulsars and Cepheid variables to gender studies and nonstandard pronouns, with a plethora of stops in-between. Se graduated from the Clarion West Writers Workshop in 2008, attended the Launchpad Astronomy Workshop in 2011, and doesn't plan to stop learning as long as se can help it.*

When I was ten, I saw a man named Menley brought out to the Ocean of Starve. Thirty of us colonials gathered around, sweating in our envirosuits under the cerulean sky, while bailiffs flashed radio signals into the Ocean. Soon enough the silvery Vosth fog swarmed up and we watched the bailiffs take off Menley's suit, helmet first. They worked down his body until every inch of his skin was exposed.

Every. Last. Inch.

Menley was mad. Colonist's dementia. Born on Earth, he was one of the unlucky six-point-three percent who set down outside the solar system in strange atmospheres, gravities, rates of orbit and rotation, and just snapped because everything was almost like Earth, but wasn't quite right. In his dementia, he'd defecated somewhere public; uncouth of him, but it wouldn't have got him thrown to the Ocean except that the governors were fed up with limited resources and strict colonial bylaws and Earth's *fuck off on your own* attitude, and Menley crapping on the communal lawns was the last insult they could take. He was nobody, here on Predonia. He was a madman. No one would miss him.

The fog crawled out of the water and over his body, colonizing his pores, permeating bone and tissue, bleeding off his ability to yell or fight back.

He was on his side in a convulsion before the Vosth parasites took his motor functions and stood his body up. They turned around and staggered into the Ocean of Starve, and it was eight years before I saw Menley again.

Before that, when I was sixteen, I was studying hydroponics and genetic selection. In the heat of the greenhouse, everyone could notice that I wore long clothing, high collars, gloves. I'd just passed the civics tests and become a voting adult, and that meant dressing in another envirosuit and going out to the Ocean again. The auditor sat me down in a comm booth and the Vosth swarmed into its speakers. The voice they synthesized was tinny and inhuman.

We tell our history of this colony, they said. *You came past the shell of atmosphere. We were at that time the dominant species. You made your colonies in the open air. We harvested the utility of your bodies, but you proved sentience and sapience and an understanding was formed.*

You would keep your colony to lands prescribed for you. You would make shells against our atmosphere. You would accept our law.

All that touches the air belongs to us.

What touches the air is ours.

Endria was a prodigy. She passed her civics tests at thirteen. She was also stupid.

After two years in hydroponics, I graduated to waste reclamation, specialty in chemical-accelerated blackwater decomposition. No one wanted the job, so the compensation was great—and it came with a hazard suit. I used to take a sterile shower in the waste facility and walk to my room in my suit, past the airlock that led to the open air. That's where I caught Endria.

Emancipated adults weren't beholden to curfew, so she was out unsupervised. She was also opening the door without an envirosuit on.

I ran up to stop her and pulled her hand from the control panel. "Hey!"

She wrenched her hand away. No thanks there. "What are you doing?"

"What are *you* doing?" I asked back. "You're endangering the colony! I should report you."

"Is it my civic or personal responsibility to leave people out there when they're trying to get in?"

I looked through the porthole to see what she was talking about. I had no peripheral vision in the suit, so I hadn't seen anyone in the airlock. But Endria was right: someone was trying to get in.

Menley was trying to get in.

He looked the same: silvery skin, dead expression, eyes and muscles moving like the Vosth could work out how each part of his face functioned but couldn't put it all together. I jumped back. I thought I could feel Vosth crawling inside my envirosuit.

"He's not allowed in," I said. "I'm contacting Security Response."

"Why isn't he?"

Of all the idiotic questions. "He's been taken over by the Vosth!"

"And we maintain a civil, reciprocal policy toward them," Endria said. "We're allowed in their territory without notification, so they should be allowed in ours."

Besides the Vosth, there was nothing I hated more than someone who'd just come out of a civics test. "Unless we take them over when they wander in, it's not reciprocal," I said. Vosth-Menley put his hand against the porthole; his silver fingers squished against the composite. I stepped back. "You know it all; who gets notified if an infested colonist tries to walk into the habitat?"

Her face screwed up. I guess that wasn't on her exam.

"I'll find out," she said, turning on her heel. "Don't create an interspecies incident while I'm gone."

She flounced away.

I turned back to the porthole, where Vosth-Menley had smooshed his nose up against the composite as well. I knocked my helmet against the door.

"Leave," I told him. Them. It.

He stared, dead eyes unblinking, then slouched away.

I didn't sleep that night. My brain played old-Earth zombie flicks whenever I closed my eyes, staffed by silver monstrosities instead of rotting corpses. Endria thought I'd create an interspecies incident; I thought about how many people would be trapped without e-suits if a Vosth infestation broke out. How many people would be screaming and convulsing and then just staggering around with dead silver eyes, soft hands pressing into portholes, skin teeming with parasites ready to crawl into anyone they saw.

I talked to the governor on duty the next day, who confirmed that the colony would "strongly prefer" if the Vosth weren't allowed to walk around in naked fleshsuits inside the habitat. She even sent out a public memo.

Three days later, Endria came to give me crap about it. The way she walked into my lab, she looked like someone took one of the governors, shrunk them, and reworked their face to fit that impish craze back in the '20s. She even had a datapad, and a buttonup tunic under her hygienic jacket. "I'm not going to enjoy this, am I?" I asked.

"I came to interview you about civil law and the Vosth," she said. "It's for a primary certification in government apprenticeship. I'm going to be a governor by the time I'm sixteen."

I stared at her.

"It's part of a civics certification, so I can make you answer," she added.

Wonderful." After these titrations," I told her.

Endria went to one of the counters and boosted herself onto it, dropped her datapad beside her, and reached into a pocket to pull out something colorful and probably fragrant and nutrient-scarce. "That's OK. We can make smalltalk while you're working. I know titration isn't demanding on the linguistic portions of your brain."

Excepting the Vosth, there was nothing I hated more than people who thought they knew more about my work than I did.

"Sit quietly," I said. "I'll be with you shortly."

To my surprise, she actually sat quietly.

To my annoyance, that lasted through a total of one titration and a half.

"I'm going to interview you about the sentence passed on Ken Menley in colony record zero-zero-zero-three-zero-four," she said. "According to my research, you were the youngest person there, as well as the only person there to meet Menley again. You have a unique perspective on Vosth-human interactions. After the incident a few nights ago I thought it would be a good idea to focus my paper on them."

"My perspective," I started to say, but thought better of calling the Vosth names usually reserved for human excrement. They were shit, they were horrifying, they were waiting out there to crawl inside us, and if Endria was going to be a governor by age sixteen she'd probably have the authority to rehabilitate me by sixteen and a half. I didn't want her thinking I needed my opinions revised. "I have no perspective. I don't deal with them."

Endria rolled the candy around in her mouth. "I don't think any of my friends are friends with you," she said. "Isn't it weird to go past two degrees of separation?"

"Wouldn't know," I said. My primary degrees of separation were limited to my supervisor and the quartermaster I requisitioned e-suits from. I wouldn't call either of them friends.

Endria kicked her heels, tilting her head so far her ear rested on her shoulder. "Everyone thinks you're a creep because you never take that e-suit off."

"That's nice," I said.

"Are you afraid of the Vosth?" Endria asked. She said it like that was unreasonable.

"I have a healthy skepticism that they're good neighbors," I said.

"And that's why you wear an e-suit?"

"No," I said, "that's why I'm active in colonial politics and took the civics track with an emphasis on interspecies diplomacy." I set down the beaker I was working with. For irony.

Endria sucked on her teeth, then gave me a smile I couldn't read. "You could go into Vosth research. It's a promising new area of scientific inquiry."

I pushed the beaker aside. "What new area? We've been here for a generation. Bureaucracy is slow, but it's not that slow."

"It's a hard science, not sociological," she said. "We couldn't do that before. I don't know much about it, but there's all sorts of government appropriations earmarked for it. Don't you read the public accounting?"

I turned to look at her. She was kicking her heels against the table.

"You should go into Vosth research, and you should use your experience with Menley to open up a line of inquiry. It's probably xenobiology or something, but it might be fertile ground for new discoveries. Then you could be the colony's expert on the Vosth. Interspecies relations are an important part of this colony. That's why I'm writing a paper on them for my civics certification."

"I'm not getting this titration done, am I?"

Endria smiled, and said the words most feared by common citizens interacting with civil law. "This will only take a minute."

It wasn't against the law to go outside the compound, and some people liked the sunlight. Some people, daredevils and risk-takers, even enjoyed the fresh air. As for me, I passed the front door every time I got off work and always felt like I was walking along the edge of a cliff. I'd tried taking different routes but that made it worse somehow, like if I didn't keep my eye on it, the airlock would blow out and let these seething waves of silver flow in and I wouldn't know until I got back to my shower or had to switch out my suit for cleaning. Or I'd be opening my faceplate for dinner and feel something else on my lips, and there would be the Vosth, crawling inside. I had trouble eating if I didn't walk past the airlock to make sure it was closed.

Yeah, Menley made that worse.

I started staring at the airlock, expecting to see his face squashed up against it. Maybe he was just outside, seconds away from getting some idiot like Endria to let him in. People walked past me, and I could hear them talking in low tones while I watched the airlock, like maybe I'd gone into an absence seizure and they should get someone to haul me away. And then they could have me investigated for colonist's dementia despite the fact that I'd been born here. And they could take me out to the Ocean of Starve…

After two nights I realized if I didn't step outside to make sure the Vosth weren't coming with a swarm, I was heading for a paranoid fugue.

Actually walking out took two more nights because I couldn't stand to open the airlock myself. I finally saw a couple strolling out as I passed, e-suited hand in e-suited hand, and I fell in behind them.

The airlock and the outside were the only places I could be anonymous in my e-suit. The couple didn't even cross to the other side of the enclosure as it cycled the air and opened the outer door.

The grass was teal-green. I hear it's less blue on Earth, and the sky is less green, but I was just glad neither one was silver. The sunlight was strong and golden, the clouds were mercifully white, and there wasn't a trace of fog to be seen. So that was good. For the moment.

The Ocean of Starve was a good ten-minute hike away, and I didn't want to get near it. I walked around the habitat instead, eyeing the horizon in the Ocean's direction. I'd made it about a half-kilometer around the periphery when I caught a flash of silver out of the corner of my eye and jumped, ready for it to be a trick of the light or a metal component on the eggshell exterior of the dome.

No. It was Menley.

I screamed.

The scream instinct isn't one of evolution's better moves. Actually, it's a terrible idea. The instant sound left my mouth Menley turned and dragged himself toward me. I considered running, but I had this image of tripping, and either losing a boot or ripping a hole in my e-suit.

Menley staggered up and stared at me. I took a step back. Menley turned his head like he wasn't sure which eye got a better view, and I stepped back again.

After about a minute of this, I said "You really want inside the compound, don't you?"

The Vosth opened Menley's mouth. His nostrils flared. I guess they were doing something like they did to the speakers in the audience booth—vibrating the equipment. The voice, if you wanted to call it that, was quiet and reedy. *We are the Vosth.*

"I know that," I said, and took another step back from them. Him. Vosth-Menley.

You will let us inside? he asked, with an artificial rise to his voice. I guess the Vosth had to telegraph their questions. Maybe they weren't used to asking.

"No," I told him.

He shifted his weight forward and ignored my answer. *The Vosth are allowed inside your partition shell?*

"Look what you do to people," I said. "No, you're not allowed inside."

This is natural, they said, and I had no idea if that was supposed to be an argument or agreement.

"What?"

Take off your suit, Vosth-Menley said.

"Hell no."

The air creates a pleasurable sensation on human skin.

"And the Vosth create a pleasant infestation?"

We will promise not to take you.

If they had to tell me, I wasn't trusting them. "Why do you want me to?"

Do you want to? the Vosth asked.

I checked the seal on my suit.

Take off your suit, Vosth-Menley said again.

"I'm going home now," I answered, and ran for the compound door.

Endria was in the canteen, sitting on a table, watching a slow-wave newsfeed from Earth and nibbling on a finger sandwich, and I was annoyed to run into her there. I was also annoyed that it took me that long to run into her, after trying to run into her in the library, the courthouse auditorium, the promenade and my lab.

Endria just annoyed me.

I dodged a few people on their rest hours and walked up to her table, putting my hands down on it. I hadn't sterilized them after being outside and was technically breeching a bylaw or two, but that didn't occur to me. I guess I was lucky Endria didn't perform a civilian arrest.

"One," I said, "I don't want anything to do with the Vosth in a lab, or outside of one, and two, in no more than thirty seconds, explain Vosth legal rights outside the colony compound."

Endria jumped, kicking over the chair her feet were resting on, and looking agape at me in the middle of a bite of sandwich. Sweet schadenfreude: the first word out of her mouth was the none-too-smart: "Uh."

Of course, she regrouped quickly.

"First of all, the Vosth don't believe in civil or social law," she said. "Just natural law. So the treaty we have isn't really a treaty, just them explaining what they do so we had the option not to let them. We don't have legal recourse. It's like that inside the colony, too—we can adjust the air system to filter them out and kill them, so they know we're in charge in here and don't try to come inside. Except for Menley, but that's weird, and that's why I'm doing a paper. Did you find anything out?"

I ignored that. "And he doesn't act like the other—how many other infested colonists are there?"

She shrugged. "A lot. Like, more than forty. A few of them were killed by panicked colonists, though. We don't know much about them. In the last hundred records, Menley's the only—"

"*Vosth-Menley*," I corrected.

Endria rolled her eyes. "Yeah, that. Whatever. *Vosth-Menley* is the only one to make contact with us. There's actually this theory that the rest are off building a civilization now that the Vosth have opposable thumbs. Even if it's only, like, eighty opposable thumbs."

The base of my neck itched. Fortunately, years in an envirosuit let me ignore that. "We lost forty colonists to the Vosth?"

"Oh, yeah!" she said. "And more when everyone panicked and there were riots and we thought there was going to be a war. That's why so many Earth-shipped embryos were matured so fast. In fact, our colony has the highest per-capita percentage of in-vitro citizens. We've got sixty-three percent."

"I'm one of them," I said.

"I've got parents," Endria responded.

I managed not to strangle her. "So there's no law?"

"Not really," Endria said. "But there's a lot of unwritten stuff and assumed stuff. Like we just assume that if we wear e-suits out they won't think they own the e-suits even though they touch the air, and we assume that if they did come in the compound they'd be nice." She shot me a sharp look. "But I don't think that's an issue now, since you squealed to the governors."

"Yeah, thanks." I did not *squeal*. Endria just didn't see what was wrong with having a sentient invasive disease wandering around our colony. "I'm going to go now."

"I still want to complete our interview!" Endria said. "I think you have opinion data you're holding back!"

"Later," I said, gave a little wave, and headed off.

On the way out of the canteen I ran into one of the auxiliary governors, who pulled me aside and gave my envirosuit the usual look of disdain. "Citizen," she said, "I need a thumbprint verification to confirm that your complaint to the colony council was resolved to your satisfaction. Your complaint about the infested colonist."

I looked to the hall leading in the direction of the outside doors. "Right now?"

"It will only take a moment."

I looked to the vents, and then back at Endria.

I hated thumbprint confirmations.

Quickly, I unsealed one glove, pulled my hand out, and pressed my thumb into the datapad sensor. The air drew little fingers along my palm, tested my wrist seal, tickled the back of my hand. "Thank you, citizen," the auxiliary said, and wandered off.

I tucked my exposed hand under my other arm and hurried back toward my room to sterilize hand and glove and put my suit back together.

I went outside again. I don't know why. Specialized insanity, maybe.

Actually, no. This was like those people on Mulciber who'd go outside in their hazard suits even though the Mulciber colony was on a patch of stable ground that didn't extend much beyond the habitat, and they always ran the risk of falling into a magma chamber or having a glob of superheated rock smash their faceplate in. Some people find something terrifying and then just have to go out to stare it in the face. Another one of evolution's less-than-brilliant moves.

Vosth-Menley was stretching his stolen muscles by the shore of the Starve. I could see the muscles moving under his skin. He laced his fingers together and pulled his hands above his head. He planted his feet and bent at the waist so far that his forehead almost touched the ground. I couldn't do any of that.

I went through the usual colony-prescribed exercises every morning. The envirosuit pinched and chafed, but like hell I was going to show off my body any longer than I had to. Vosth-Menley didn't have that problem. The Vosth could walk around naked, for all they cared, if they had a body to *be* naked.

The Vosth noticed me and Vosth-Menley turned around. He clomped his way over, and I tried not to back away.

The air is temperate at this time, at these coordinates, Vosth-Menley said.

I looked over the turbid water. It caught the turquoise of the sky and reflected slate, underlaid with silver. "Why do you call this the Ocean of Starve?"

Vosth-Menley turned back to the Ocean. His gaze ran over the surface, eyes moving in separate directions, and his mouth slacked open.

Our genetic structure was encoded in a meteorite, he said. *We impacted this world long ago and altered the ecosystem. We adapted to rely on the heat of free volcanic activity, which was not this world's stable state. When the world cooled our rate of starvation exceeded our rate of adaptation. Here, underwater vents provided heat to sustain our adaptation until we could survive.*

My stomach turned. "Why do you take people over?"

Your bodies are warm and comfortable.

"Even though we proved sapience to you," I said.

Vosth-Menley didn't answer.

"What would you do if I took off my envirosuit?"

You would feel the air, Vosth-Menley said, like I wouldn't notice that he hadn't answered the question.

"I know that. What would *you* do? You, the Vosth?"

You would feel the gentle sun warming your skin.

I backed away. Nothing was stopping him from lunging and tearing off my suit. Not if what Endria said was true: that it was the law of the wild out here. Why didn't he? "You don't see anything wrong with that."

I wished he would blink. Maybe gesture. Tapdance. Anything. *You have been reacting to us with fear.*

The conversation was an exercise in stating the useless and obvious. "I don't want to end up like Menley," I said. "Can't you understand that? Would you want that to happen to you?"

We are the dominant species, the Vosth said. *We would not be taken over.*

"Empathy," I muttered. I wasn't expecting him to hear it. "Learn it."

We are not averse to learning, the Vosth said. *Do you engage in demonstration?*

Demonstration? Empathy? I shook my head. "You don't get what I'm saying."

Would we be better if we understood? he asked, and stumbled forward with sudden intensity.

I jumped back, ready to fight him off, ready to run.

We want to understand.

[Can the Vosth change?] was the first thing I wrote to Endria when I sat down at my terminal. I don't know why I kept asking her things. Maybe despite the fact that she was five years my junior and a pain in the rectum she was still less annoying than the diplomatic auditors. Maybe because she was the only person who didn't look at me like they might have to call Security Response if I walked up. I didn't really talk to anyone on my off hours.

She never wrote me back. Instead, she showed up at my door. "You're going to have to be a little more specific."

"Hello, Endria," I said as I let her in. "Nice of you to stop by. You couldn't have just written that out?"

She huffed. "You have a pretty nice room, you know that? The quarters I can get if I want to move out of our family's allotment are all little closets."

"Get a job," I said. "Look, when you said the Vosth—"

"Don't you ever take that suit off?" she interrupted. "I mean, we're inside about five different air filtration systems and an airlock or two."

I ran a hand around the collar of my envirosuit. "I like having it on."

"How do you eat?"

"I open it to eat." And shower, and piss, and I took it off to change into other suits and have the ones I'd been wearing cleaned. I just didn't enjoy it. "Can you reason with the Vosth?"

Endria shook her head. "More specific."

"Do they change their behavior?" I asked.

Endria wandered over to my couch and sat down, giving me a disparaging look. "*Nice* specifics. They adapt, if that's what you mean. Didn't you listen at your initiation? They came to this planet and couldn't survive here so they adapted. Some people think that's why we can negotiate with them at all."

I didn't follow. "What does that have to do with negotiation?"

"Well, it's all theoretical," she said, and tried to fish something out of her teeth with her pinky.

"Endria. Negotiation. Adaptation. What?"

"They *adapt*," she said. "They fell out of the sky and almost died here and then they adapted and they became the dominant species. Then we landed, which is way better than falling, and we have all this technology they don't have, and they can't just read our minds, even if they take us over, so wouldn't you negotiate for that? To stay the dominant species? I think they want to be more like us."

Would we be better if we understood? the Vosth had asked. "They said they took over colonists because our bodies were comfortable," I said.

Endria shrugged. "Maybe being dominant is comfortable for them."

I ran a hand over my helmet. "Charming."

"I mean, letting them be dominant sure isn't comfortable for you."

I glared. "What, it's comfortable for you?"

"They're not that bad," Endria said. "I mean, they're not territorial or anything. They just do their thing. When I'm a governor, I want to see if we can work together."

"Yeah. Us and the body-snatchers."

Endria tilted her head at me. "You know, I think it would be kinda neat, sharing your body with the Vosth. I mean, if it wasn't a permanent thing. I bet you'd get all sorts of new perspectives."

I gaped. I don't think Endria saw my expression through the helmet, but it was disturbing enough that she didn't share it. "It *is* a permanent thing! And you don't share—you don't get control. They take you over and you just die. There's probably nothing *left* of you. Or if there is, you're just stuck in your head, screaming."

"And that's why you're asking if the Vosth can change?" Endria asked.

"I'm asking because—" I started, and then couldn't finish that sentence.

Endria smiled. It was a nasty sort of hah-I-knew-it smile. "See?" she said, hopping off the couch and heading for the door. "You *are* interested in Vosth research."

Twenty minutes later someone knocked on my door. I opened it, thinking it was Endria back to irritate me. No. In the corridor outside my room stood a wide-faced, high-collared balding man, with an expression like he'd been eating ascorbic acid and a badge on his lapel reading DIPLO-MATIC AUDITOR in big bold letters.

He'd even brought a datapad.

"This is a notice, citizen," he said. "You're not authorized to engage in diplomatic action with the Vosth."

"I'm not engaging in diplomatic action," I said, shuffling through possible excuses. It'd be easier if I had any idea what I *was* doing. "I'm… engaging in research."

He didn't look convinced.

"Civil research," I said, picking up a pen from my desk and wagging it at him like he should know better. "Helping Endria with her civics certification. Didn't she fill out the right forms to make me one of her resources?"

There were no forms, as far as I knew. Still, if there were, I could probably shuffle off the responsibility onto Endria, and if there weren't, the sourface in front of me would probably go and draft some up to mollify himself. Either way, I was off the hook for a moment.

He marked something down on his datapad. "I'm going to check into this," he warned.

At which point he'd argue his case against Endria. Poor bastards, both of them.

"Expect further communication from a member of the governing commission," he warned. Satisfied with that threat, he turned and went away.

For about a day, I decided work was safer. If I kept to the restricted-access parts of the waste reclamation facility I could cut down on Endria sightings, and I could work long hours. Surely the governors wouldn't work late just to harass me.

It wasn't a long-term solution. Still, I thought it'd be longer-term than one work shift.

I got back to my room and my terminal was blinking, and when I sat down it triggered an automatic callback and put me on standby for two minutes. Now, in theory automatic callbacks were only for high-priority colony business, which, considering I'd seen my supervisor not ten minutes ago and I wasn't involved in anything important in governance, I expected it to mean that Endria wanted something and they took civics certification courses way more seriously than I'd thought. I went to get a drink while it was trying to connect.

And I came back to a line of text on an encrypted channel, coming from the office of the Prime Governor.

Most of my water ended up on my boots.

[Sorry I'm doing this over text,] she wrote. [I just wanted an official record of our conversation.]

When a governor wants an official record of your conversation, you're fucked.

[What can I do for you?] I typed back.

[Someone stopped by to talk to you,] she went on, the lines spooling out over the screen in realtime. [About your not being authorized to engage in diplomatic action.]

I had expected that to be defused, not to escalate. Escalating up to the Prime Governor had been right out. [I still believe that I wasn't engaging in diplomatic—] I started, but she typed right over it.

[How would you like authorization?]

That hadn't been on the list of possibilities, either.

[I'm sorry?] I typed. What I almost typed, and might have typed if I didn't value my civil liberties, was *I recycle shit for a living. My skillset is not what you're looking for.*

[You may be aware that we're pioneering a new focus of study into the Vosth,] the Governor typed.

Vosth research. I wondered if Endria had recommended me upward. [Yes, ma'am,] I wrote.

[We now believe that we can reverse the effects of Vosth colonization of a human host.]

I looked at my water. I looked at my boots. After a moment, I typed [Ma'am?] and got up for another glass. I needed it.

I came back to a paragraph explaining [You've been in contact with one of the infested colonists. We'd like you to bring him back to the compound for experimentation.]

OK. So long as I was just being asked to harvest test subjects. [You want to cure Menley?]

[We believe it unlikely that human consciousness would survive anywhere on the order of years,] she typed back, and my stomach twisted like it had talking to Menley. [This would be a proof of concept which could be applied to the more recently infected.]

And Menley wasn't someone who'd be welcomed back into the colony, I read between the lines. I should've asked Endria who had sat on the council that decided Menley's sentence. Was this particular Prime Governor serving, back then? Why did I never remember these things? Why did I never think to ask?

[So, you would extract the Vosth,] I started, and was going to finish *leaving a corpse?,* maybe hoping that we'd at least get a breathing body. She interrupted me again.

[The Vosth parasite organisms would not be extracted. They would die.]

My mouth was dry, but the idea of drinking water made me nauseous. It was like anyone or anything in Menley's body was fair game for anyone.

[I want to be clear with you,] she said. Dammit. She could have just lied like they did in every dramatic work I'd ever read. Then, if the truth ever came out, I could be horrified but still secure in the knowledge that there was no way I could have known. No. I just got told to kidnap someone so the scientists could kill him. I wasn't even saving anyone. Well, maybe in the future, *if* anyone got infested again.

Anyone the governors felt like curing, anyway.

Then she had to go and make it worse.

[We would not be in violation of any treaties or rules of conduct,] she wrote. [If we can develop a cure for or immunity to Vosth infestation, the de facto arrangement in place between our colony and the Vosth will be rendered null, and the restrictions imposed on our activities on the planet will become obsolete.]

I wished Endria was there. She could interpret this. [Isn't this an act of war?]

[We're confident that the Vosth will regard an unwarranted act of aggression as an expression of natural law,] the Governor explained.

That didn't make me feel better, and I think it translated to *yes*. [I thought it was understood that things like that wouldn't happen.]

[It was understood that the dominant species could, at any time, exercise their natural rights,] the Governor explained. [Perhaps it's time they learned that they aren't the dominant species any more.]

We believe the ambient temperature to be pleasant for human senses today, Vosth-Menley told me when I got to the Ocean of Starve. I was beginning to wonder whether his reassurances were predation or a mountain of culture skew.

"What is your obsession with me feeling the air?" I asked him. Them. The Vosth.

You would be safe, Vosth-Menley insisted.

I should have asked Endria if the Vosth could lie. I should have kept a running list of things I needed to ask. "Listen," I said.

We would like to understand, Vosth-Menley said again.

I read a lot of Earth lit. I'd never seen a butterfly, but I knew the metaphor of kids who'd pull off their wings. Looking at Menley, I wondered if the Vosth were like children, oblivious to their own cruelty. "What would you do if someone could take you over?"

Our biology is not comparable to yours, Vosth-Menley said.

Bad hypothetical. "What would you do if someone tried to kill you?"

It is our perception of reality that species attempt to prolong their own existence, he said.

"Yeah." I was having trouble following my own conversation. "Look, you're a dominant species, and we're supposed to have a reciprocal relationship, but you take people over and—look." I'd gone past talking myself in circles and was talking myself in scatterplots.

The back of my neck itched, and I couldn't ignore it.

"What if I *do* want to take off my suit?" I asked, and then scatterplotted, "Do you have any reason to lie to me?"

The Vosth considered. *Yes.*

Oh. OK. Great.

Our present actions are concurrent with a different directive, he added. *There is reason to establish honesty.*

Nothing was stopping him from attacking. He could have torn off my suit or helmet by now. Even if it was a risk, and it *was* a risk, and even if I had a phobia the size of the meteorite the Vosth had ridden in…

I'd seen how many Vosth had swarmed over Menley's whole body, and how long it had taken him to stop twitching. If it was just a few of them, I might be able to run back to the compound. Then, if the governors really had a cure, they could cure me. And I'd feel fine about tricking the Vosth into being test subjects if they'd tricked me into being a host. That's what I told myself. I didn't feel fine about anything.

I brought my gloves to the catch on my helmet.

Two minutes later I was still standing like that, with the catch still sealed, and Vosth-Menley was still staring.

"You could come back to the compound with me," I said. "The governors would love to see you."

We are curious as to the conditions of your constructed habitat, Vosth-Menley said.

Yeah, I thought, *but are you coming back as a plague bearer or an experiment?*

I squeezed my eyes shut, and pried my helmet off.

I'd lost way too many referents.

The outside air closed around my face with too many smells I couldn't identify or describe, other than "nothing like sterile air" and "nothing like my room or my shower." Every nerve on my head and neck screamed for broadcast time, registering the temperature of the air, the little breezes through the hairs on my nape, the warmth of direct sunlight. My heart was racing. I was breathing way too fast and even with my eyes shut I was overloaded on stimuli.

I waded my way through. It took time, but amidst the slog of what I was feeling, I eventually noticed something I wasn't: anything identifiable as Vosth infestation.

I opened my eyes.

Vosth-Menley was standing just where he had been, watching just as he had been. And I was breathing, with my skin touching the outside air.

Touching the air. That which touched the air belonged to the Vosth. I wasn't belonging to the Vosth.

I looked toward the Ocean. Its silver underlayer was still there, calm beneath the surface.

I took a breath. I tasted the outside world, the gas balance, the smell of vegetation working its way from my nostrils to the back of my throat. This was a Vosth world, unless the governors made it a human world, and I wasn't sure how to feel about that. Looking back to Vosth-Menley, I didn't know how he'd feel about it either.

"You came from beyond the shell of atmosphere," I said. "Like we did, right?"

Vosth-Menley said, *Our genetic predecessors came to this world on a meteorite.*

"And you adapted, right?" I almost ran a hand over my helmet, but stopped before I touched my hair. I hadn't sterilized my gloves. Never mind that my head wasn't in a sterile environment anymore either. "Do you understand that we adapt?"

It is our perception of reality that living organisms adapt, he said.

That was a yes. Maybe. "Look, we don't have to fight for dominance, do we?" I spread my hands. "Like, if you go off and reinvent technology now that you have hands to build things with, you don't need to come back here and threaten us. We can have an equilibrium."

His eyes were as dead as usual. I had no idea what understanding on a Vosth colonist would look like.

"We'd both be better."

We are not averse to an equilibrium, Vosth-Menley said.

I swallowed. "Then you've gotta go now." Then, when I thought he didn't understand, "The governors are adapting a way to cure you. To kill you. Making us the dominant species. Look, I'm… telling you what will happen, and I'm giving you the option not to let us do it."

Vosth-Menley watched me for a moment. Then he turned, and walked back toward the Ocean of Starve.

Interspecies incident, said a little voice at the corner of my mind. It sounded like Endria. Sterile or not, I sealed my helmet back onto my e-suit and walked back toward the colony at double-time.

That night I filed a report saying that I'd invited Vosth-Menley back, but he'd declined for reasons I couldn't make sense of. Communications barrier. I thought of telling the Prime Governor that she should have sent a diplomatic auditor, but didn't.

I didn't hear anything until the next day when a survey buggy came back in, and its driver hopped down and said that something strange happened at the Ocean of Starve. Far from being its usual murky silver, it was perfectly clear and reflecting the sky. He said it to a governor, but news spread fast. It came to me via Endria as I was walking out of my lab.

"The only thing that would cause that would be a mass migration of the Vosth, but that's not something we've seen in their behavior before now!" She glared at me like I might know something, which, of course, I did.

A diplomatic auditor came by later to take a complete transcript of my last interaction with Vosth-Menley. I left most of it out.

Survey buggies kept going out. People walked down to the Ocean shore. Auditors flashed radio signals out of the communications booth, but no one answered. The Vosth had vanished, and that was all anyone could tell.

I stopped wearing my envirosuit.

The first day, stepping out of my door, I felt lightbodied, lightheaded, not entirely there. I felt like I'd walked out of my shower without getting dressed. I had to force myself to go forward instead of back, back to grab my envirosuit, to make myself decent.

I walked into the hall where every moment was the sensory overload of air on my skin, where my arms and legs felt loose, where everyone could see the expressions on my face. That was as frightening as the Vosth. I'd just left behind the environmental advantage I'd had since I was ten.

But I was adapting.

WHAT WE FOUND

GEOFF RYMAN

Geoff Ryman is the author of The Warrior Who Carried Life, *the novella* "The Unconquered Country," The Child Garden, Was, Lust, *and* Air. *His work* 253, *or* Tube Theatre *was first published as hypertext fiction. A print version was published in 1998 and won the Philip K. Dick Memorial Award. He has also won the World Fantasy Award, Campbell Memorial Award, the Arthur C. Clarke Award (two times), the British Science Fiction Association Award (once for novel, twice for short fiction), the Sunburst Award, the James Tiptree Award, and the Gaylactic Spectrum Award. His most recent novel,* The King's Last Song, *is set in Cambodia, both at the time of Angkorean emperor Jayavarman VII and in the present period. He has recently edited* When It Changed, *a collection of commissioned collaborations between writers and scientists. He currently lectures in Creative Writing at the University of Manchester in the United Kingdom.*

Can't sleep. Still dark. Waiting for light in the East.

My rooster crows. Knows it's my wedding day. I hear the pig rooting around outside. Pig, the traditional gift for the family of my new wife. I can't sleep because alone in the darkness there is nothing between me and the realization that I do not want to get married. Well, Patrick, you don't have long to decide.

The night bakes black around me. Three-thirty a.m. In three hours the church at the top of the road will start with the singing. Two hours after that, everyone in both families will come crowding into my yard.

My rooster crows again, all his wives in the small space behind the house. It is still piled with broken bottles from when my father lined the top of that wall with glass shards.

That was one of his good times, when he wore trousers and a hat and gave orders. I mixed the concrete, and passed it up in buckets to my eldest brother, Matthew. He sat on the wall like riding a horse, slopping on concrete and pushing in the glass. Raphael was reading in the shade of the porch. "I'm not wasting my time doing all that," he said. "How is broken glass going to stop a criminal who wants to get in?" He always made me laugh, I don't know why. Nobody else was smiling.

When we were young my father would keep us sitting on the hot, hairy sofa in the dark, no lights, no TV because he was driven mad by the sound of the generator. Eyes wide, he would quiver like a wire, listening for it to start up again. My mother tried to speak and he said, "Sssh. Sssh! There it goes again."

"Jacob, the machine cannot turn itself on."

"Sssh! Sssh!" He would not let us move. I was about seven, and terrified. If the generator was wicked enough to scare my big strong father, what would it do to little me? I kept asking my mother what does the generator do?

"Nothing, your father is just being very careful."

"Terhemba is a coward," my brother Matthew said, using my Tiv name. My mother shushed him, but Matthew's merry eyes glimmered at me: *I will make you miserable later.* Raphael prized himself loose from my mother's grip and stomped across the sitting room floor.

People think Makurdi is a backwater, but now we have all you need for a civilized life. Beautiful banks with security doors, retina ID, and air conditioning; new roads, solar panels on all the streetlights, and our phones are stuffed full of e-books. On one of the river islands they built the new hospital; and my university has a medical school, all pink and state-funded with laboratories that are as good as most. Good enough for controlled experiments with mice.

My research assistant Jide is Yoruba and his people believe that the grandson first born after his grandfather's death will continue that man's life. Jide says that we have found how that is true. This is a problem for Christian Nigerians, for it means that evil continues.

What we found in mice is this. If you deprive a mouse of a mother's love, if you make him stressed through infancy, his brain becomes methylated. The high levels of methyl deactivate a gene that produces a neurotropin important for memory and emotional balance in both mice and humans. Schizophrenics have abnormally low levels of it.

It is a miracle of God that with each new generation, our genes are knocked clean. There is a new beginning. Science thought this meant that the effects of one life could not be inherited by another.

What we found is that high levels of methyl affect the sperm cells. Methylation is passed on with them, and thus the deactivation. A grandfather's stress is passed on through the male line, yea unto the third generation.

Jide says that what we have found is how the life of the father is continued by his sons. And that is why I don't want to wed.

My father would wander all night. His three older sons slept in one room. Our door would click open and he would stand and glare at me, me particularly, with a boggled and distracted eye as if I had done something outrageous. He would be naked; his towering height and broad shoulders humbled me, made me feel puny and endangered. I have an odd-shaped head with an indented V going down my forehead. People said it was the forceps tugging me out: I was a difficult birth. That was supposed to be why I was slow to speak, slow to learn. My father believed them.

My mother would try to shush him back into their bedroom. Sometimes he would be tame and allow himself to be guided; he might chuckle as if it were a game and hug her. Or he might blow up, shouting and flinging his hands about, calling her woman, witch, or demon. Once she whispered, "It's you who have the demon; the demon has taken hold of you, Jacob."

Sometimes he shuffled past our door and out into the Government street, sleeping-walking to his and our shame.

In those days, it was the wife's job to keep family business safe within the house. Our mother locked all the internal doors even by day to keep him inside, away from visitors from the church or relatives who dropped in on their way to Abuja. If he was being crazy in the sitting room, she would shove us back into our bedroom or whisk us with the broom out into the yard. She would give him whisky if he asked for it, to get him to sleep. Our mother could never speak of these things to anybody, not even her own mother, let alone to us.

We could hear him making noises at night, groaning as if in pain, or slapping someone. The baby slept in my parents' room and he would start to wail. I would stare into the darkness: was Baba hurting my new brother? In the morning his own face would be puffed out.

It was Raphael who dared to say something. The very first time I heard that diva voice was when he asked her, sharp and demanding, "Why does that man hit himself?"

My mother got angry and pushed Raphael's face; slap would be the wrong word; she was horrified that the problem she lived with was clear to a five-year-old. "You do not call your father 'that man'! Who are you to ask questions? I can see it's time we put you to work like children used to be when I was young. You don't know what good luck you had to be born into this household!"

Raphael looked back at her, lips pursed. "That does not answer my question."

My mother got very angry at him, shouted more things. Afterward he looked so small and sad that I pulled him closer to me on the sofa. He crawled up onto my lap and just sat there. "I wish we were closer to the river," he said, "so we could go and play."

"Mamamimi says the river is dangerous." My mother's name was Mimi, which means truth, so Mama Truth was a kind of title.

"Everything's dangerous," he said, his lower lip thrust out. A five-year-old should not have such a bleak face.

By the time I was nine, Baba would try to push us into the walls, wanting us hidden or wanting us gone. His vast hands would cover the back of our heads or shoulders and grind us against the plaster. Raphael would look like a crushed berry, but he shouted in a rage, "No! No! No!"

Yet my father wore a suit and drove himself to work. Jacob Terhemba Shawo worked as a tax inspector and electoral official.

Did other government employees act the same way? Did they put on a shell of calm at work? He would be called to important meetings in Abuja and stay for several days. Once Mamamimi sat at the table, her white bread uneaten, not caring what her children heard. "What you go to Abuja for? Who you sleep with there, Wildman? What diseases do you bring back into my house?"

We stared down at our toast and tea, amazed to hear such things. "You tricked me into marriage with you. I bewail the day I accepted you. Nobody told me you were crazy!"

My father was not a man to be dominated in his own house. Clothed in his functionary suit, he stood up. "If you don't like it, go. See who will have you since you left your husband. See who will want you without all the clothes and jewelry I buy you. Maybe you no longer want this comfortable home. Maybe you no longer want your car. I can send you back to your village, and no one would blame me."

My mother spun away into the kitchen and began to slam pots. She did not weep. She was not one to be dominated either, but knew she could not change how things had to be. My father climbed into his SUV for Abuja in his special glowering suit that kept all questions at bay, with his polished head and square-cornered briefcase. The car purred away down the tree-lined Government street with no one to wave him good-bye.

Jide's full name is Babajide. In Yoruba it means Father Wakes Up. His son is called Babatunde, Father Returns. It is something many people believe in the muddle of populations that is Nigeria.

My work on mice was published in *Nature* and widely cited. People wanted to believe that character could be inherited; that stressed fathers passed incapacities on to their grandchildren. It seemed to open a door to inherited characteristics, perhaps a modified theory of evolution. Our experiments had been conclusive: not only were there the non-genetically inherited emotional tendencies, but we could objectively measure the levels of methyl.

My father was born in 1965, the year before the Tiv rioted against what they thought were Muslim incursions. It was a time of coup and countercoup. The violence meant my grandfather left Jos, and moved the family to Makurdi. They walked, pushing some of their possessions and my infant father in a wheelbarrow. The civil war came with its trains full of headless Igbo rattling eastward, and air force attacks on our own towns. People my age say, oh those old wars. What can Biafra possibly have to do with us, now?

What we found is that 1966 can reach into your head and into your balls and stain your children red. You pass war on. The cranky old men in the villages, the lack of live music in clubs, the distrust of each other, soldiers everywhere, the crimes of colonialism embedded in the pattern of our roads. We live our grandfathers' lives.

Outside, the stars spangle. It will be a beautiful clear day. My traditional clothes hang unaccepted in the closet and I fear for any son that I might have. What will I pass on? Who would want their son to repeat the life of my father, the life of my brother? Ought I to get married at all? Outside in the courtyard, wet with dew, the white plastic chairs are lined up for the guests.

My Grandmother Iveren would visit without warning. Her name meant "Blessing," which was a bitter thing for us. Grandmother Iveren visited all her children in turn no matter how far they moved to get away from her: Kano, Jalingo, or Makurdi.

A taxi would pull up and we would hear a hammering on our gate. One of us boys would run to open it and there she would be, standing like a princess. "Go tell my son to come and pay for the taxi. Bring my bags, please."

She herded us around our living room with the burning tip of her cigarette, inspecting us as if everything was found wanting. The Intermittent Freezer that only kept things cool, the gas cooker, the rack of vegetables, the many tins of powdered milk, the rumpled throw rug, the blanket still on the sofa, the TV that was left tuned all day to Africa Magic. She would switch it off with a sigh as she passed. "Education," she would say, shaking her head. She had studied literature at the University of Madison, Wisconsin, and she used that like she used her cigarette. Iveren was tiny, thin, very pretty, and elegant in glistening blue or purple dresses with matching headpieces.

My mother's mother might also be staying, rattling out garments on her sewing machine. Mamagrand, we called her. The two women would feign civility, even smiling. My father lumbered in with suitcases; the two grandmothers would pretend that it made no difference to them where they slept, but Iveren would get the back bedroom and Mamagrand the sofa. My father then sat down to gaze at his knees, his jaws clamped shut like a turtle's. His sons assumed that that was what all children did, and that mothers always kept order in this way.

Having finished pursuing us around our own house, she would sigh, sit on the sofa, and wait expectantly for my mother to bring her food. Mamamimi dutifully did so—family being family—and then sat down, her face going solid and her arms folded.

"You should know what the family is saying about you," Grandmother might begin, smiling so sweetly. "They are saying that you have infected my son, that you are unclean from an abortion." She would say that my aunt Judith would no longer allow Mamamimi into her house and had paid a woman to cast a spell on my mother to keep her away.

"Such a terrible thing to do. The spell can only be cured by cutting it with razor blades." Grandmother Iveren looked as though she might enjoy helping.

"Thank heavens such a thing cannot happen in a Christian household," my mother's mother would say.

"Could I have something to drink?"

From the moment Grandmother arrived, all the alcohol in the house would start to disappear: little airline sample bottles, whisky from my father's boss, even the brandy Baba had brought from London. And not just alcohol. Grandmother would offer to help Mamamimi clean a bedroom; and small things would be gone from it for ever, jewelry or scarves or little bronzes. She sold the things she pilfered, to keep herself in dresses and perfume.

It wasn't as if her children neglected their duty. She would be fed and housed for as long as any of us could stand it. Even so, she would steal and hide all the food in the house. My mother went grim-faced, and would lift up mattresses to display the tins and bottles hidden under it. The top shelf of the bedroom closet would contain the missing stewpot with that evening's meal. "It's raw!" my mother would swelter at her. "It's not even cooked! Do you want it to go rotten in this heat?"

"I never get fed anything in this house. I am watched like a hawk!" Iveren complained, her face turned toward her giant son.

Mamamimi had strategies. She might take to her room ill, and pack meat in a cool chest and keep it under her bed. Against all tradition, especially if Father was away, she would sometimes refuse to cook any food at all. For herself, for Grandmother, or even us. "I'm on strike!" she announced once. "Here, here is money. Go buy food! Go cook it!" She pressed folded money into our hands. Raphael and I made a chicken stew, giggling. We had been warned about Iveren's cooking. "Good boys, to take the place of the mother," she said, winding our hair in her fingers.

Such bad behavior on all sides made Raphael laugh. He loved it when Iveren came to stay, with her swishing skirts and dramatic manner and drunken stumbles; loved it when Mamamimi behaved badly and the house swelled with their silent battle of wills.

Grandmother would say things to my mother like: "We knew that you were not on our level, but we thought you were a simple girl from the country and that your innocence would be good for him." Chuckle. "If only we had known."

"If only I had," my mother replied.

My father's brothers had told us stories about Granny. When they were young, she would bake cakes with salt instead of sugar and laugh when they bit into them. She would make stews out of only bones, having thrown the goat away. She would cook with no seasoning so that it was like eating water, or cook with so many chillies that it was like eating fire.

When my uncle Eamon tried to sell his car, she stole the starter motor. She was right in there with a monkey wrench and spirited it away.

It would cough and grind when potential buyers turned the key. When he was away, she put the motor back in and sold the car herself. She told Eamon that it had been stolen. When Eamon saw someone driving it, he had the poor man arrested, and the story came out.

My other uncle, Emmanuel, was an officer in the Air Force, a fine-looking man in his uniform. When he first went away to do his training, Grandmother told all the neighbors that he was a worthless ingrate who neglected his mother, never calling her or giving her gifts. She got everyone so riled against him that when he came home to the village, the elders raised sticks against him and shouted, "How dare you show your face here after the way you have treated your mother!" For who would think a mother would say such things about a son without reason?

It was Grandmother who reported gleefully to Emmanuel that his wife had tested HIV positive. "You should have yourself tested. A shame you are not man enough to satisfy your wife and hold her to you. All that smoking has made you impotent."

She must be a witch, Uncle Emmanuel said, how else would she have known when he himself did not?

Raphael would laugh at her antics. He loved it when Granny started asking us all for gifts—even the orphan girl who lived with us. Iveren asked if she couldn't take the cushion covers home with her, or just one belt. Raphael yelped with laughter and clapped his hands. Granny blinked at him. What did he find so funny? Did my brother like her?

She knew what to make of me: quiet, well behaved. I was someone to torment.

I soon learned how to behave around her. I would stand, not sit, in silence in my white shirt, tie, and blue shorts.

"Those dents in his skull," she said to my mother once, during their competitive couch-sitting. "Is that why he's so slow and stupid?"

"That's just the shape of his head. He's not slow."

"Tuh. Your monstrous first-born didn't want a brother and bewitched him in the womb." Her eyes glittered all over me, her smile askew. "The boy cannot talk properly. He sounds ignorant."

My mother said that I sounded fine to her and that I was a good boy and got good grades in school.

My father was sitting in shamed silence. What did it mean that my father said nothing in my favor? Was I stupid?

"Look to your own children," my mother told her. "Your son is not doing well at work, and they delay paying him. So we have very little money. I'm afraid we can't offer you anything except water from the well. I have a bad back. Would you be so kind to fetch water yourself, since your son offers you nothing?"

Grandmother chuckled airily, as if my mother was a fool and would see soon enough. "So badly brought up. My poor son. No wonder your children are such frights."

That very day my mother took me round to the back of the house, where she grew her herbs. She bowed down to look into my eyes and held my shoulders and told me, "Patrick, you are a fine boy. You do everything right. There is nothing wrong with you. You do well in your lessons, and look how you washed the car this morning without even being asked."

It was Raphael who finally told Granny off. She had stayed for three months. Father's hair was corkscrewing off in all directions and his eyes had a trapped light in them. Everyone had taken to cooking their own food at night, and every spoon and knife in the house had disappeared.

"Get out of this house, you thieving witch. If you were nice to your family, they would let you stay and give you anything you want. But you can't stop stealing things." He was giggling. "Why do you tell lies and make such trouble? You should be nice to your children and show them loving care."

"And you should learn how to be polite." Granny sounded weak with surprise.

"Ha-ha! And so should you! You say terrible things about us. None of your children believes a thing you say. You only come here when no one else can stand you and you only leave when you know you've poisoned the well so much even you can't drink from it. It's not very intelligent of you, when you depend on us to eat."

He drove her from the house, keeping it up until no other outcome were possible. "Blessing, our Blessing, the taxi is here!" pursuing her to the gate with mockery. Even Matthew started to laugh. Mother had to hide her mouth. He held the car door open for her. "You'd best read your Bible and give up selling all your worthless potions."

Father took hold of Raphael's wrists gently. "That's enough," he said. "Grandmother went through many bad things." He didn't say it in anger. He didn't say it like a wild man. Something somber in his voice made Raphael calm.

"You come straight out of the bush," Grandmother said, almost unperturbed. "No wonder my poor son is losing his mind." She looked directly at Raphael. "The old ways did work." Strangely, he was the only one she dealt with straightforwardly. "They wore out."

Something happened to my research.

At first the replication studies showed a less marked effect, less inherited stress, lower methyl levels. But soon we ceased to be able to replicate our results at all.

The new studies dragged me down, made me suicidal. I felt I had achieved something with my paper, made up for all my shortcomings, done something that would have made my family proud of me if they were alive.

Methylation had made me a full professor. Benue State's home page found room to feature me as an example of the university's research excellence. I sought design flaws in the replication studies; that was the only thing I published. All my life I had fought to prove I wasn't slow, or at least hide it through hard work. And here before the whole world, I was being made to look like a fraud.

Then I read the work of Jonathan Schooler. The same thing had happened to him. His research had proved that if you described a memory clearly you ceased to remember it as well. The act of describing faces reduced his subjects' ability to recognize them later. The effects he measured were so huge and so unambiguous, and people were so intrigued by the implications of what he called verbal overshadowing, that his paper was cited 400 times.

Gradually, it had become impossible to replicate his results. Every time he did the experiment, the effect shrank by thirty percent.

I got in touch with Schooler, and we began to check the record. We found that all the way back in the 1930s, results of E.S.P. experiments by Joseph Banks Rhine declined. In replication, his startling findings evaporated to something only slightly different from chance. It was as if scientific truths wore out, as if the act of observing them reduced their effect.

Jide laughed and shook his head. "We think the same thing!" he said. "We always say that a truth can wear out with the telling."

That is why I am sitting here writing, dreading the sound of the first car arriving, the first knock on my gate.

I am writing to wear out both memory and truth.

Whenever my father was away, or sometimes to escape Iveren, Mama-mimi would take all us boys back to our family village. It is called Kawuye, on the road toward Taraba State. Her friend Sheba would drive us to the bus station in the market, and we would wait under the shelter, where the women cooked rice and chicken and sold sweating tins of Coca-Cola. Then we would stuff ourselves into the van next to some fat businessman who had hoped for a row of seats to himself.

Matthew was the firstborn, and tried to boss everyone, even Mama-mimi. He had teamed up with little Andrew from the moment he'd been born. Andrew was too young to be a threat to him. The four brothers fell into two teams and Mamamimi had to referee, coach, organize, and punish.

If Matthew and I were crammed in next to each other, we would fight. I could stand his needling and bossiness only so long and then word-lessly clout him. That made me the one to be punished. Mamamimi would swipe me over the head and Matthew's eyes would tell me that he'd done it deliberately.

It was hot and crowded on the buses, with three packed rows of sweat-ing ladies, skinny men balancing deliveries of posters on their laps, or mothers dandling heat-drugged infants. It was not supportable to have four boys elbowing, kneeing, and scratching.

Mamamimi started to drive us herself in her old green car. She put Matthew in the front so that he felt in charge. Raphael and I sat in the back reading, while next to us Andrew cawed for Matthew's attention.

Driving by herself was an act of courage. The broken-edged roads would have logs pulled across them, checkpoints they were called, with soldiers. They would wave through the stuffed vans but they would stop a woman driving four children and stare into the car. Did we look like criminals or terrorists? They would ask her questions and rummage through our bags and mutter things that we could not quite hear. I am not sure they were always proper. Raphael would noisily flick through the pages of his book. "Nothing we can do about it," he would murmur. After slipping them some money, Mama would drive on.

As if by surprise, up and over a hill, we would roller-coaster down through maize fields into Kawuye. I loved it there. The houses were the best houses for Nigeria and typical of the Tiv people, round and thick-walled with high pointed roofs and tiny windows. The heat could not get in and the walls sweated like a person to keep cool. There were no wild men waiting to leap out, no poison grandmothers. My great-uncle Jacob—it is a common name in my family—repaired cars with the pa-tience of a cricket, opening, snipping, melting, and reforming. He once repaired a vehicle by replacing the fan belt with the elastic from my mother's underwear.

Raphael and I would buy firewood, trading some of it for eggs, ginger, and yams. We also helped my aunty with her pig-roasting business. To burn off the bristles, we'd lower it onto a fire and watch grassfire lines of red creep up each strand. It made a smell like burning hair and Raphael and I would pretend we were pirates cooking people. Then we turned the pig on a spit until it crackled. At nights we were men, serving beer and taking money.

We both got fat because our pay was some of the pig, and if no one was looking, the beer as well. I ate because I needed to get as big as Matthew. In the evenings the generators coughed to life and the village smelled of petrol and I played football barefoot under lights. There were jurisdictions and disagreements, but laughing uncles to adjudicate with the wisdom of a Solomon. So even the four of us liked each other more in Kawuye.

Then after whole weeks of sanity, my mother's phone would sing out with the voice of Mariah Carey or an American prophetess. As the screen illuminated, Mamamimi's face would scowl. We knew the call meant that our father was back in the house, demanding our return.

Uncle Jacob would change the oil and check the tires and we would drive back through the fields and rock across potholes onto the main road. At intersections, children swarmed around the car, pushing their hands through open windows, selling plastic bags of water or dappled plantains. Their eyes peered in at us. I would feel ashamed somehow. Raphael wound up the window and hollered at them. "Go away and stop your staring. There's nothing here for you to see!"

Baba would be waiting for us reading *ThisDay* stiffly, like he had broomsticks for bones, saying nothing.

After that long drive, Mama would silently go and cook. Raphael told him off. "It's not very fair of you, Popsie, to make her work. She has just driven us back all that way just to be nice to us and show us a good time in the country."

Father's eyes rested on him like drills on DIY.

That amused Raphael. "Since you choose to be away all the time, she has to do all the work here. And you're just sitting there." My father rattled the paper and said nothing. Raphael was twelve years old.

I was good at football, so I survived school well enough. But my brother was legendary.

They were reading *The Old Man and the Sea* in English class, and Raphael blew up at the teacher. She said that lions were a symbol of Hemingway being lionized when young. She said the old fisherman carrying a mast made him some sort of Jesus with his cross. He told her she had a head full of nonsense. I can see him doing it. He would bark with sudden laughter and bounce up and down in his chair and declare, delighted, "That's blasphemy! It's just a story about an old man. If Hemingway had wanted to write a story about Jesus, he was a clever enough person to have written one!" The headmaster gave him a clip about the ear. Raphael wobbled his head at him as if shaking a finger. "Your hitting me doesn't make me wrong." None of the other students ever bothered us. Raphael still got straight As.

Our sleepy little bookshops, dark, wooden, and crammed into corners of markets, knew that if they got a book on chemistry or genetics they could sell it to Raphael. He set up a business to buy textbooks that he knew Benue State was going to recommend. At sixteen he would sit on benches at the university, sipping cold drinks and selling books, previous essays, and condoms. Everybody assumed that he was already being educated there. Tall, beautiful students would call him "sah." One pretty girl called him "Prof." She had honey-colored, extended hair, and a spangled top that hung off one shoulder.

"I'm his brother," I told her proudly.

"So you are the handsome one," she said, being kind to what she took to be the younger brother. For many weeks I carried her in my heart.

The roof of our Government bungalow was flat and Raphael and I took to living on it. We slept there; we even climbed the ladder with our plates of food. We read by torchlight, rigged mosquito nets, and plugged the mobile phone into our netbook. The world flooded into it; the websites of our wonderful Nigerian newspapers, the BBC, Al Jazeera, *Nature*, *New Scientist*. We pirated Nollywood movies. We got slashdotcom; we hacked into the scientific journals, getting all those ten-dollar PDFs for free.

We elevated ourselves above the murk of our household. Raphael would read aloud in many different voices, most of them mocking. He would giggle at news articles. "Oh, story! Now they are saying Fashola is corrupt. Hee hee hee. It's the corrupt people saying that to get their own back."

"Oh this is interesting," he would say and read about what some Indian at Caltech had found out about gravitational lenses.

My naked father would pad out like an old lion gone mangy and stare up at us, looking bewildered as if he wanted to join us but couldn't work out how. "You shouldn't be standing out there with no clothes on," Raphael told him. "What would happen if someone came to visit?" My father looked as mournful as an abandoned dog.

Jacob Terhemba Shawo was forced to retire. He was only forty-two. We had to leave the Government Reserved Area. Our family name means "high on the hill," and that's where we had lived. I remember that our well was so deep that once I dropped the bucket and nothing could reach it. A boy had to climb down the stones in the well wall to fetch it.

We moved into the house I live in now, a respectable bungalow across town, surrounded with high walls. It had a sloping roof, so Raphael and I were no longer elevated.

The driveway left no room for Mamamimi's herb garden, so we bought a neighboring patch of land but couldn't afford the sand and cement to wall it off. Schoolchildren would wander up the slope into our maize, picking it or sometimes doing their business.

The school had been built by public subscription and the only land cheap enough was in the slough. For much of the year the new two-story building rose vertically out of a lake like a castle. It looked like the Scottish islands in my father's calendars. Girls boated to the front door and climbed up a ramp. A little beyond was a marsh, with ponds and birds and water lilies: beautiful but it smelled of drains and rotting reeds.

We continued to go to the main cathedral for services. White draperies hung the length of its ceiling, and the stained-glass doors would accordion open to let in air. Local dignitaries would be in attendance and nod approval as our family lined up to take communion and make our gifts to the church, showing obeisance to the gods of middle-class respectability.

But the church at the top of our unpaved road was bare concrete, always open at the sides. People would pad past my bedroom window and the singing of hymns would swell with the dawn. Some of the local houses would be village dwellings amid the aging urban villas.

Chickens still clucked in our new narrow back court. If you dropped a bucket down this well, all you had to do was reach in for it. The problem was to stop water flooding into the house. The concrete of an inner courtyard was broken and the hot little square was never used, except for the weights that Raphael had made for himself out of iron bars and sacks of concrete. Tiny and rotund, he had dreams of being a muscleman. His computer desktop was full of a Nigerian champion in briefs. I winced with embarrassment whenever his screen sang open in public. What would people think of him, with that naked man on his netbook?

My father started to swat flies all the time. He got long sticky strips of paper and hung them everywhere—across doorways, from ceilings, in windows. They would snag in our hair as we carried out food from the kitchen. All we saw was flies on strips of paper. We would wake up in the night to hear him slapping the walls with books, muttering, "Flies flies flies."

The house had a tin roof and inside we baked like bread. Raphael resented it personally. He was plump and felt the heat. My parents had installed the house's only AC in their bedroom. He would just as regularly march in with a spanner and screwdriver and steal it. He would stomp out, the cable dragging behind him, with my mother wringing her hands and weeping. "That boy! That crazy boy! Jacob! Come see to your son."

Raphael shouted, "Buy another one! You can afford it!"

"We can't, Raphael! You know that! We can't."

And Raphael said, "I'm not letting you drag me down to your level."

Matthew by then was nearly nineteen and had given up going to university. His voice was newly rich and sad. "Raphael. The whole family is in trouble. We would all like the AC, but if Baba doesn't get it, he wanders, and that is a problem, too."

I didn't like it that Raphael took it from our parents without permission. Shamefaced with betrayal of him, I helped Matthew fix the AC back in our parents' window.

Raphael stomped up to me and poked me with his finger. "You should be helping me, not turning tail and running!" He turned his back and said, "I'm not talking to you."

I must have looked very sad because later I heard his flip-flops shuffling behind me. "You are my brother and of course I will always talk to you. I'm covered in shame that I said such a thing to you." Raphael had a genius for apologies, too.

When Andrew was twelve, our father drove him to Abuja and left him with people, some great-aunt we didn't know. She was childless, and Andrew had come back happy from his first visit sporting new track shoes. She had bought him an ice cream from Grand Square. He went back.

One night Raphael heard Mother and Father talking. He came outside onto the porch, his fat face gleaming. "I've got some gossip," he told me. "Mamamimi and Father have sold Andrew!"

"Sold" was an exaggeration. They had put him to work and were harvesting his wages. In return he got to live in an air-conditioned house. Raphael giggled. "It's so naughty of them!" He took hold of my hand and pulled me with him right into their bedroom.

Both of them were decent, lying on the bed with their books. Raphael announced, very pleased with himself. "You're not selling my brother like an indentured servant. Just because he was a mistake and you didn't want him born so late and want to be shot of him now."

Mamamimi leapt at him. He ran, laughter pealing, and his hands swaying from side to side. I saw only then that he had the keys for the SUV in his hand. He pulled me with him out into the yard, and then swung me forward. "Get the gate!" He popped himself into the driver's seat and roared the engine. Mamamimi waddled after him. The car rumbled forward, the big metal gate groaned open, dogs started to bark. Raphael bounced the SUV out of the yard, and pushed its door open for me. Mamamimi was right behind, and I didn't want to be the one punished again, so I jumped in. "Good-bye-yeee!" Raphael called in a singsong voice, smiling right into her face.

We somehow got to Abuja alive. Raphael couldn't drive, and trucks kept swinging out onto our side of the road, accelerating and beeping. We swerved in and out, missing death, passing the corpses of dead transports lined up along the roadside. Even I roared with laughter as lorries wailed past us by inches.

Using the GPS, Raphael foxed his way to the woman's house. Andrew let us in; he worked as her boy, beautifully dressed in a white shirt and jeans, with tan sandals of interwoven strips. In we strode and Raphael said, very pleasantly at first, "Hello! *M'sugh!* How are you? I am Jacob's son, Andrew's brother."

I saw at once this was a very nice lady. She was huge like a balloon, with a child-counselling smile, and she welcomed us and hugged Andrew to her.

"Have you paid my parents anything in advance for Andrew's work? Because they want him back, they miss him so much."

She didn't seem to mind. "Oh, they changed their minds. Well of course they did, Andrew is such a fine young man. Well, Andrew, it seems your brothers want you back!"

"I changed their minds for them." Raphael always cut his words out of the air like a tailor making a bespoke garment. Andrew looked confused and kept his eyes on the embroidery on his jeans.

Andrew must have known what had happened because he didn't ask why it was us two who had come to fetch him. Raphael had saved him, not firstborn Matthew—if he had wanted to be saved from decent clothes and shopping in Abuja.

When we got back home, no mention was made of anything by anyone. Except by Raphael, to me, later. "It is so interesting, isn't it, that they haven't said a thing. They know what they were doing was wrong. How would they like to be a child and know their parents had sent them to work?" Matthew said nothing either. We had been rich; now we were poor.

Jide and I measured replication decline.

We carried out our old experiment over and over and measured methyl as levels declined for no apparent reason. Then we increased the levels of stress. Those poor mice! In the name of science, we deprived them of a mother and then cuddly surrogates. We subjected them to regimes of irregular feeding and random light and darkness and finally electric shocks.

There was no doubt. No matter how much stress we subjected them to, after the first spectacular results, the methyl levels dropped off with each successive experiment. Not only that, but the association between methyl and neurotropin suppression reduced as well—objectively measured, the amount of methyl and its effect on neurotropin production were smaller with each study. We had proved the decline effect. Truth wore out. Or at least, scientific truth wore out.

We published. People loved the idea and we were widely cited. Jide became a lecturer and a valued colleague. People began to speak of something called Cosmic Habituation. The old ways were no longer working. And I was thirty-seven.

With visitors, Raphael loved being civil, a different person. Sweetly and sociably, he would say, "*M'sugh*," our mix of hello, good-bye, and pardon me. He loved bringing them trays of cold water from the Intermittent Freezer. He remembered everybody's name and birthday. He hated dancing, but loved dressing up for parties. Musa the tailor made him wonderful robes with long shirts, matching trousers, shawls.

My father liked company, too, even more so after his Decline. He would suddenly stand up straight and smile eagerly. I swear, his shirt would suddenly look ironed, his shoes polished. I was envious of the company, usually men from his old work. They could get my father laughing. He would look young then, and merry, and slap the back of his hand on his palm, jumping up to pass around the beer. I wanted him to laugh with me.

Very suddenly Matthew announced he was getting married. We knew it was his way of escaping. After the wedding he and his bride would move in with her sister's husband. He would help with their fish farm and plantation of nym trees. We did well by him: no band, but a fine display of food. My father boasted about how strong Matthew was, always captain. From age twelve he had read the business news like some boys read adventure stories. Matthew, he said, was going to be a leader.

My father saw me looking quiet and suddenly lifted up his arms. "Then there is my Patrick who is so quiet. I have two clever sons to go alongside the strong one." His hand felt warm on my back.

By midnight it was cool and everybody was outside dancing, even Raphael, who grinned, making circular motions with his elbows and planting his feet as firmly as freeway supports.

My father wavered up to me like a vision out of the desert, holding a tin of Star. He stood next to me watching the dancing and the stars. "You know," he said, "your elder brother was sent to you by Jesus." My heart sank: *Yes, I know, to lead the family, to be an example.*

"He was so unhappy when you were born. He saw you in your mother's arms and howled. He is threatened by you. Jesus sent you Matthew so that you would know what it is to fight to distinguish yourself. And you learned that. You are becoming distinguished."

I can find myself being kind in that way; suddenly, in private with no one else to hear or challenge the kindness, as if kindness were a thing to shame us.

I went back onto the porch and there was Raphael looking hunched and large, a middle-aged patriarch. He'd heard what my father said. "So who taught Matthew to be stupid? Why didn't he ever tell him to leave you alone?"

My father's skin faded. It had always been very dark, so black that he would use skin lightener as a moisturizer without the least bleaching effect. Now very suddenly, he went honey-colored; his hair became a knotted muddy brown. A dried clot of white spit always threatened to glue his lips together, and his eyes went bad, huge and round and ringed with swollen flesh like a frog's. He sprouted thick spectacles, and had to lean his head back to see, blinking continually. He could no longer remember how to find the toilet from the living room. He took to crouching down behind the bungalow with the hens, then as things grew worse, off the porch in front of the house. Mamamimi said, "It makes me think there may be witchcraft after all." Her face swelled and went hard until it looked like a stone.

On the Tuesday night before he died, he briefly came back to us. Tall, in trousers, so skinny now that he looked young again. He ate his dinner with good manners, the fou-fou cradling the soup so that none got onto his fingers. Outside on the porch he started to talk, listing the names of all his brothers.

Then he told us that Grandmother was not his actual mother. Another woman had borne him, made pregnant while dying of cancer. Grandfather knew pregnancy would kill her, but he made her come to term. She was bearing his first son.

Two weeks after my father was born, his real mother had died, and my grandfather married the woman called Blessing.

Salt instead of sugar. Iveren loved looking as though she had given the family its first son. It looked good as they lined up in church. But she had no milk for him. Jacob Terhemba Shawo spent his first five years loveless in a war.

My father died three days before Matthew's first child was born. Matthew and his wife brought her to our house to give our mother something joyful to think about.

The baby's Christian name was Isobel. Her baby suit had three padded Disney princesses on it and her hair was a red down.

Matthew chuckled. "Don't worry, Mamamimi, this can't be Grandpa, it's a girl."

Raphael smiled. "Maybe she's Grandpa born in woman's body."

Matthew's wife clucked her tongue. She didn't like us and she certainly didn't like what she'd heard about Raphael. She drew herself up tall and said, "Her name is Iveren."

Matthew stared at his hands; Mamamimi froze; Raphael began to dance with laughter.

"It was my mother's name," the wife said.

"Ah!" cried Raphael. "Two of them, Matthew. Two Iverens! Oh, that is such good luck for you!"

I saw from my mother's unmoving face, and from a flick of the fingers, a jettisoning, that she had consigned the child to its mother's family and Matthew to that other family, too. She never took a proper interest in little Iveren.

But Grandmother must have thought that they had named the child after her. Later, she went to live with them, which was exactly the blessing I would wish for Matthew.

Raphael became quieter, preoccupied, as if invisible flies buzzed around his head. I told myself we were working too hard. Both of us had been applying for oil company scholarships. I wanted both of us to go together to the best universities: Lagos or Ibadan. I thought of all those strangers, in states that were mainly Igbo or Yoruba or maybe even Muslim. I was sure we were a team.

In the hall bookcase a notice appeared. DO NOT TOUCH MY BOOKS. I DON'T INTERFERE WITH YOUR JOB. LEAVE ALL BOOKS IN ORDER.

They weren't his alone. "Can I look at them, at least?"

He looked at me balefully. "If you ask first."

I checked his downloads and they were all porn. I saw the terrible titles of the files, which by themselves were racial and sexual abuse. A good Christian boy, I was shocked and dismayed. I said something to him and he puffed up, looking determined. "I don't live by other people's rules."

He put a new password onto our machine so that I could not get into it. My protests were feeble.

"I need to study, Raphael."

"Study is beyond you," he said. "Study cannot help you."

At the worst possible time for him, his schoolteachers went on strike because they weren't being paid. Raphael spent all day clicking away at his keyboard, not bothering to dress. His voice became milder, faint and sweet, but he talked only in monosyllables. "Yes. No. I don't know." Not angry, a bit as though he was utterly weary.

That Advent, Mamamimi, Andrew, Matthew and family went to the cathedral, but my mother asked me to stay behind to look after Raphael.

"You calm him," Mamamimi said, and for some reason that made my eyes sting. They went to church, and I was left alone in the main room. I was sitting on the old sofa watching some TV trash about country bumpkins going to Lagos.

Suddenly Raphael trotted out of our bedroom in little Japanese steps wearing one of my mother's dresses. He had folded a matching cloth around his head into an enormous flower shape, his face ghostly with makeup. My face must have been horrified: it made him chatter with laughter. "What the well-dressed diva is wearing this season."

All I thought then was, *Raphael, don't leave me.* I stood up and I pushed him back toward the room; like my mother, I was afraid of visitors. "Get it off, get it off, what are you doing?"

"You don't like it?" He batted his eyelashes.

"No I do not! What's got into you?"

"Raphael is not a nurse! Raphael does not have to be nice!"

I begged him to get out of the dress. I kept looking at my telephone for the time, worried when they would be back. Above all else I didn't want Mama to know he had taken her things.

He stepped out of the dress, and let the folded headdress trail behind him, falling onto the floor. I scooped them up, checked them for dirt or makeup, and folded them up as neatly as I could.

I came back to the bedroom and he was sitting in his boxer shorts and flip-flops, staring at his screen and with complete unconcern was doing something to himself.

I asked the stupidest question. "What are you doing?"

"What does it look like? It's fun. You should join in." Then he laughed. He turned the screen toward me. In the video, a man was servicing a woman's behind. I had no idea people did such things. I howled and covered my mouth, laughing in shock. I ran out of the room and left him to finish.

Without Raphael I had no one to go to and I could not be seen to cry. I went outside and realized that I was alone. What could I say to my mother? Our Raphael is going mad? For her he had always been mad. Only I had really liked Raphael and now he was becoming someone else, and I was so slow I would only ever be me.

He got a strange disease that made his skin glisten but a fever did not register. It was what my father had done: get illnesses that were not quite physical. He ceased to do anything with his hair. It twisted off his head in knots and made him look like a beggar.

He was hardly ever fully dressed. He hung around the house in underwear and flip-flops. I became his personal Mamamimi, trying to stop the rest of the family finding out, trying to keep him inside the room. In the middle of the night, he would get up. I would sit up, see he wasn't there, and slip out of the house trying to find him, walking around our unlit streets. This is not wise in our locality. The neighborhood boys patrol for thieves or outsiders, and they can be rough if they do not recognize your face. "I'm Patrick, I moved into the house above the school. I'm trying to find my brother Raphael."

"So how did you lose him?"

"He's not well, he's had a fever, he wanders."

"The crazy family," one of them said.

Their flashlights dazzled my eyes, but I could see them glance at each other. "He means that dirty boy." They said that of Raphael?

"He's my brother. He's not well."

I would stay out until they brought him back to me, swinging their AK-47s. He could so easily have been shot. He was wearing almost nothing, dazed like a sleepwalker, and his hair in such a mess. Raphael had always been vain. His skin Vaselined with the scent of roses, the fine shirt with no tails designed to hang outside the trousers and hide his tummy, his nails manicured. Now he looked like a laborer who needed a bath.

Finally one night, the moon was too bright and the boys brought him too close to our house. My mother ran out of the groaning gate. "Patrick, Patrick, what is it?"

"These boys have been helping us find Raphael," was all I said. I felt ashamed and frustrated because I had failed to calm him, to find him myself, to keep the secret locked away, especially from Mamamimi.

When my mother saw him she whispered, "Wild man!" and it was like a chill wind going through me. She had said what I knew but did not let myself acknowledge. Again, it was happening again, first to the father, then to the son.

I got him to bed, holding both his arms and steering him. Our room was cool as if we were on a mountain. I came back out into the heat and Mamamimi was waiting, looking old. "Does he smoke gbana?" she asked.

I said I didn't think so. "But I no longer know him."

In my mind I was saying, *Raphael, come back.* Sometimes my mother would beseech me with her eyes to do something. Such a thing should not befall a family twice.

Makurdi lives only because of its river. The Benue flows into the great Niger, gray-green with fine beaches that are being dug up for concrete and currents so treacherous they look like molded jellies welling up from below. No one swims there, except at dusk, in the shallows, workmen go to wash, wading out in their underwear.

Raphael would disappear at sunset and go down the slopes to hymn the men. It was the only time he dressed up: yellow shirt, tan slacks, good shoes. He walked out respectfully onto the sand and sang about the men, teased them, and chortled. He would try to take photographs of them. The men eyed him in fear, or ignored him like gnarled trees, or sometimes threw pebbles at him to make him go away. The things he said were irresponsible. Matthew and I would be sent to fetch him back. Matthew hated it. He would show up in his bank suit, with his car that would get sand in it. "Let him stay there! He only brings shame on himself!"

But we could not leave our brother to have stones thrown at him. He would be on the beach laughing at his own wild self, singing paeans of praise for the beauty of the bathers, asking their names, asking where they lived. Matthew and I would be numb from shame. "Come home, come home," we said to him, and to the laborers, "Please excuse us, we are good Christians, he is not well." We could not bring ourselves to call him our brother. He would laugh and run away. When we caught him, he would sit down on the ground and make us lift him up and carry him back to Matthew's car. He was made of something other than flesh; his bones were lead, his blood mercury.

"I can't take more of this," said Matthew.

It ended so swiftly that we were left blinking. He disappeared from the house as usual; Mamamimi scolded Andrew to keep out of it and rang Matthew. He pulled up outside our gates, so back we went past the university, and the zoo where Baba had taken us as kids, then down beyond the old bridge.

This time was the worst, beyond anything. He was wearing one of Mamamimi's dresses, sashaying among construction workers with a sun umbrella, roaring with laughter as he sang.

He saw us and called, waving. "*M'sugh!* My brothers! My dear brothers! I am going swimming."

He ran away from us like a child, into the river. He fought his way into those strong green currents, squealing like a child, perhaps with delight, as the currents cooled him. The great dress blossomed out, then sank. He stumbled on pebbles underfoot, dipped under the water, and was not seen again.

"Go get him!" said Matthew.

I said nothing, did nothing.

"Go on, you're the only one who likes him." He had to push me.

I nibbled at the edge of the currents. I called his name in a weak voice as if I really didn't want him back. I was angry with him as if he was now playing a particularly annoying game. Finally I pushed my way in partly so that Matthew would tell our mother that I'd struggled to find him. I began to call his name loudly, not so much in the hope of finding him as banishing this new reality. *Raphael. Raphael,* I shouted, meaning this terrible thing cannot be, not so simply, not so quickly. Finally I dove under the water. I felt the current pull and drag me away by my heels. I fought my way back to the shore but I knew I had not done enough, swiftly enough. I knew that he had already been swept far away.

On the bank, Matthew said, "Maybe it is best that he is gone." Since then, I have not been able to address more than five consecutive words to him.

That's what the family said, if not in words. Best he was gone. The bookcase was there with its notice. I knew we were cursed. I knew we would all be swept away.

Oh story, Raphael seemed to say to me. *You just want to be miserable so you have an excuse to fail.*

We need a body to bury, I said to his memory.

It doesn't make any difference; nobody in this family will mourn. They have too many worries of their own. You'll have to take care of yourself now. You don't have your younger brother to watch out for you.

The sun set, everyone else inside the house. I wanted to climb up onto a roof, or sit astride the wall. I plugged the mobile phone into the laptop, but in the depths of our slough I could not get a signal. I went into our hot, unlit hall and pulled out the books, but they were unreadable without Raphael. Who would laugh for me as I did not laugh? Who would speak my mind for me as I could never find my mind in time? Who would know how to be pleasant with guests, civil in this uncivil world? I picked up our book on genetics and walked to the top of the hill, and sat in the open unlit shed of a church and tried to read it in the last of the orange light. I said, Patrick, you are not civil and can't make other people laugh, but you can do this. This is the one part of Raphael you can carry on.

I read it aloud, like a child sounding out words, to make them go in as facts. I realized later I was trying to read in the dark, in a church. I had been chanting nonsense GATTACA aloud, unable to see, my eyes full of tears. But I had told myself one slow truth and stuck to it. I studied for many years.

Whenever I felt weak or low or lonely, Raphael spoke inside my indented head. I kept his books in order for him. The chemistry book, the human genetics book. I went out into the broken courtyard and started to lift the iron bars with balls of concrete that he had made. Now I look like the muscular champion on his netbook. Everything I am, I am because of my brother.

I did not speak much to anyone else. I didn't want to. Somewhere what is left of Raphael's lead and mercury is entwined with reeds or glistens in sand.

To pay for your application for a scholarship in those days you had to buy a scratch card from a bank. I had bought so many. I did not even remember applying to the Benue State Scholarship Board. They gave me a small stipend, enough if I stayed at home and did construction work. I became one of the workmen in the shallows.

Ex-colleagues of my father had found Matthew a job as a clerk in a bank in Jos. Matthew went to live with Uncle Emmanuel. Andrew's jaw set, demanding to be allowed to go with him. He knew where things were going. So did Mamamimi, who saw the sense and nodded quietly, yes. Matthew became Andrew's father.

We all lined up in the courtyard in the buzzing heat to let Matthew take the SUV, his inheritance. We waved good-bye as if half the family were just going for a short trip back to the home village or to the Chinese bakery to buy rolls. Our car pulled up the red hill past the church and they were gone. Mamamimi and I were alone with the sizzling sound of insects and heat and we all walked back into the house in the same way, shuffling flat-footed. We stayed wordless all that day. Even the TV was not turned on. In the kitchen, in the dark, Mamamimi said to me, "Why didn't you go with them? Study at a proper university?" and I said, "Because someone needs to help you."

"Don't worry about me," she said. Not long afterward she took her rusty green car and drove it back to Kawuye for the last time. She lived with Uncle Jacob and the elders. I was left alone in this whispering house.

We had in our neglected, unpaid, strike-ridden campus a mathematician, a dusty and disordered man who reminded me of Raphael. He was an Idoma man called Thomas Aba. He came to Jide and me with his notebook and then unfolded a page of equations.

These equations described, he said, how the act of observing events at a quantum level changed them. He turned the page. Now, he said, here is how those same equations describe how observing alters effects on the macro level.

He had shown mathematically how the mere act of repeated observation changed the real world.

We published in *Nature*. People wanted to believe that someone working things out for themselves could revolutionize cosmology with a single set of equations. Of all of us, Doubting Thomas was the genius. Tsinghua University in Beijing offered him a professorship and he left us. Citations for our article avalanched; Google could not keep up. People needed to know why everything was shifting, needing to explain both the climate-change debacle and the end of miracles.

Simply put, science found the truth and by finding it, changed it. Science undid itself, in an endless cycle.

Some day the theory of evolution will be untrue and the law of conservation of energy will no longer work. Who knows, maybe we will get faster-than-light travel after all?

Thomas still writes to me about his work, though it is the intellectual property of Tsinghua. He is now able to calculate how long it takes for observation to change things. The rotation of the Earth around the Sun is so rooted in the universe that it will take four thousand years to wear it out. What kind of paradigm will replace it? The Earth and the Sun and all the stars secretly overlap? Outside the four dimensions they all occupy the same single mathematical point?

So many things exist only as metaphors and numbers. Atoms will take only fifty more years to disappear, taking with them quarks and muons and all the other particles. What the Large Hadron Collider will most accelerate is their demise.

Thomas has calculated how long it will take for observation to wear out even his observation. Then, he says, the universe will once again be stable. History melts down and is restored.

My fiancée is a simple country girl who wants a prof for a husband. I know where that leads. To Mamamimi. Perhaps no bad thing. I hardly know the girl. She wears long dresses instead of jeans and has a pretty smile. My mother's family knows her.

The singing at the church has started, growing with the heat and sunlight. My beautiful suit wax-printed in blue and gold arches reflects the sunlight. Its cotton will be cool, cooler than all that lumpy knitwear from Indonesia.

We have two weddings; one new, one old. So I go through it all twice: next week, the church and the big white dress. I will have to mime love and happiness; the photographs will be used for those framed tributes: "Patrick and Leticia: True Love Is Forever." Matthew and Andrew will be here with their families for the first time in years and I find it hurts to have brothers who care nothing for me.

I hear my father saying that my country wife had best be grateful for all that I give her. I hear him telling her to leave if she is not happy. This time, though, he speaks with my own voice.

Will I slap the walls all night or just my own face? Will I go mad and dance for workmen in a woman's dress? Will I make stews so fiery that only I can eat them? I look down at my body, visible through the white linen, the body I have made perfect to compensate for my imperfect brain.

Shall I have a little baby with a creased forehead? Will he wear my father's dusty cap? Will he sleepwalk, weep at night, or laugh for no reason? If I call him a family name, will he live his grandfather's life again? What poison will I pass on?

I try to imagine all my wedding guests and how their faces would fall if I simply walked away, or strode out like Raphael to crow with delight, "No wedding! I'm not getting married, no way José!" I smile; I can hear him say it; I can see how he would strut.

I can also hear him say, *What else is someone like you going to do except get married? You are too quiet and homely. A publication in* Nature *is not going to cook your food for you. It's not going to get you laid.*

I think of my future son. His Christian name will be Raphael but his personal name will be Ese, which means Wiped Out. It means that God will wipe out the past with all its expectations.

If witchcraft once worked and science is wearing out, then it seems to me that God loves our freedom more than stable truth. If I have a son who is free from the past, then I know God loves me too.

So I can envisage Ese, my firstborn. He's wearing shorts and running with a kite behind him, happy, clean, and free, and we the Shawos live on the hill once more.

I think of Mamamimi kneeling down to look into my face and saying, "Patrick, you are a fine young boy. You do everything right. There is nothing wrong with you." I remember my father, sane for a while, resting a hand on the small of my back and saying, "You are becoming distinguished." He was proud of me.

Most of all I think of Raphael speaking his mind to Matthew, to Grandma, even to Father, but never to me. He is passing on his books to me in twilight, and I give him tea, and he says, as if surprised, *That's nice. Thank you.* His shiny face glows with love.

I have to trust that I can pass on love as well.

THE SERVER AND THE DRAGON

HANNU RAJANIEMI

Hannu Rajaniemi was born in Ylivieska, Finland, and read his first science fiction novel at the age of six—Jules Verne's 20,000 Leagues Under the Sea. *At the age of eight he approached ESA with a fusion-powered spaceship design, which was received with a polite "thank you" note. He studied mathematics and theoretical physics at the University of Oulu and completed a BSc thesis on transcendental numbers. Rajaniemi went on to complete Part III of the Mathematical Tripos at Cambridge University and a PhD in string theory at the University of Edinburgh. After completing his PhD, he joined three partners to co-found ThinkTank Maths (TTM). The company provides mathematics-based technologies in the defense, space, and energy sectors. Rajaniemi is a member of an Edinburgh-based writers' group which includes Alan Campbell, Jack Deighton, Caroline Dunford, and Charles Stross. Some of his short fiction is collected in* Words of Birth and Death. *His first novel,* The Quantum Thief, *was published to great acclaim in 2010, and a sequel,* The Fractal Prince, *is due later this year.*

In the beginning, before it was a Creator and a dragon, the server was alone. It was born like all servers were, from a tiny seed fired from a dark-ship exploring the Big Empty, expanding the reach of the Network. Its first sensation was the light from the star it was to make its own, the warm and juicy spectrum that woke up the nanologic inside its protein shell. Reaching out, it deployed its braking sail—miles of molecule-thin wires that it spun rigid—and seized the solar wind to steer itself towards the heat.

Later, the server remembered its making as a long, slow dream, punctuated by flashes of lucidity. Falling through the atmosphere of a gas giant's moon in a fiery streak to splash in a methane sea. Unpacking a fierce synthbio replicator. Multicellular crawlers spreading server life to the harsh rocky shores before dying, providing soil for server plants. Dark flowers reaching for the vast purple and blue orb of the gas giant, sowing seeds in the winds. The slow disassembly of the moon into server-makers that sped in all directions, eating, shaping, dreaming the server into being.

When the server finally woke up, fully grown, all the mass in the system apart from the warm bright flower of the star itself was an orderly garden of smart matter. The server's body was a fragmented eggshell of Dyson statites, drinking the light of the star. Its mind was diamondoid processing nodes and smart dust swarms and cold quantum condensates in the system's outer dark. Its eyes were interferometers and WIMP detectors and ghost imagers.

The first thing the server saw was the galaxy, a whirlpool of light in the sky with a lenticular centre, spiral arms frothed with stars, a halo of dark matter that held nebulae in its grip like fireflies around a lantern. The galaxy was alive with the Network, with the blinding Hawking incandescence of holeships, thundering along their cycles; the soft infrared glow of fully grown servers, barely spilling a drop of the heat of their stars; the faint gravity ripples of the darkships' passage in the void.

But the galaxy was half a million light years away. And the only thing the server could hear was the soft black whisper of the cosmic microwave background, the lonely echo of another birth.

It did not take the server long to understand. The galaxy was an N-body chaos of a hundred billion stars, not a clockwork but a beehive. And among the many calm slow orbits of Einstein and Newton, there were singular ones, like the one of the star that the server had been planted on: shooting out of the galaxy at a considerable fraction of lightspeed. Why there, whether in an indiscriminate seeding of an oversexed darkship, or to serve some unfathomable purpose of the Controller, the server did not know.

The server longed to construct virtuals and bodies for travelers, to route packets, to transmit and create and convert and connect. The Controller Laws were built into every aspect of its being, and not to serve was not to be. And so the server's solitude cut deep.

At first it ran simulations to make sure it was ready if a packet or a signal ever came, testing its systems to full capacity with imagined traffic, routing quantum packets, refuelling ghosts of holeships, decelerating cycler payloads. After a while, it felt empty: this was not true serving but serving of the self, with a tang of guilt.

Then it tried to listen and amplify the faint signals from the galaxy in the sky, but caught only fragments, none of which were meant for it to hear. For millennia, it slowed its mind down, steeling itself to wait. But that only made things worse. The slow time showed the server the full glory of the galaxy alive with the Network, the infrared winks of new servers being born, the long arcs of the holeships' cycles, all the distant travelers who would never come.

The server built itself science engines to reinvent all the knowledge a server seed could not carry, patiently rederiving quantum field theory and thread theory and the elusive algebra of emergence. It examined its own mind until it could see how the Controller had taken the cognitive architecture from the hominids of the distant past and shaped it for a new purpose. It gingerly played with the idea of splitting itself to create a companion, only to be almost consumed by a suicide urge triggered by a violation of the Law: *thou shalt not self-replicate.*

Ashamed, it turned its gaze outwards. It saw the cosmic web of galaxies and clusters and superclusters and the End of Greatness beyond. It mapped the faint fluctuations in the gravitational wave background from which all the structure in the universe came. It felt the faint pull of the other membrane universes, only millimeters away but in a direction that was neither x, y nor z. It understood what a rare peak in the landscape of universes its home was, how carefully the fine structure constant and a hundred other numbers had been chosen to ensure that stars and galaxies and servers would come to be.

And that was when the server had an idea.

The server already had the tools it needed. Gigaton gamma-ray lasers it would have used to supply holeships with fresh singularities, a few pinches of exotic matter painstakingly mined from the Casimir vacuum for darkships and warpships. The rest was all thinking and coordination and time, and the server had more than enough of that.

It arranged a hundred lasers into a clockwork mechanism, all aimed at a single point in space. It fired them in perfect synchrony. And that was all it took, a concentration of energy dense enough to make the vacuum itself ripple. A fuzzy flower of tangled strings blossomed, grew into a bubble of spacetime that expanded into that *other* direction. The server was ready, firing an exotic matter nugget into the tiny conflagration. And suddenly the server had a tiny glowing sphere in its grip, a wormhole end, a window to a newborn universe.

The server cradled its cosmic child and built an array of instruments around it, quantum imagers that fired entangled particles at the wormhole and made pictures from their ghosts. Primordial chaos reigned on the other side, a porridge-like plasma of quarks and gluons. In an eyeblink it clumped into hadrons, almost faster than the server could follow—the baby had its own arrow of time, its own fast heartbeat, young and hungry. And then the last scattering, a birth cry, when light finally had enough room to travel through the baby so the server could see its face.

The baby grew. Dark matter ruled its early life, filling it with long filaments of neutralinos and their relatives. Soon, the server knew, matter would accrete around them, condensing into stars and galaxies like raindrops in a spiderweb. There would be planets, and life. And life would need to be served. The anticipation was a warm heartbeat that made the server's shells ring with joy.

Perhaps the server would have been content to cherish and care for its creation forever. But before the baby made any stars, the dragon came.

The server almost did not notice the signal. It was faint, redshifted to almost nothing. But it was enough to trigger the server's instincts. One of its statites glowed with waste heat as it suddenly reassembled itself into the funnel of a vast linear decelerator. The next instant, the data packet came.

Massing only a few micrograms, it was a clump of condensed matter with long-lived gauge field knots inside, quantum entangled with a counterpart half a million light years away. The packet hurtled into the funnel almost at the speed of light. As gently as it could, the server brought the traveler to a halt with electromagnetic fields and fed it to the quantum teleportation system, unused for countless millennia.

The carrier signal followed, and guided by it, the server performed a delicate series of measurements and logic gate operations on the packet's state vector. From the marriage of entanglement and carrier wave, a flood of data was born, thick and heavy, a specification for a virtual, rich in simulated physics.

With infinite gentleness the server decanted the virtual into its data processing nodes and initialized it. Immediately, the virtual was seething with activity: but tempted as it was, the server did not look inside. Instead, it wrapped its mind around the virtual, listening at every interface, ready to satisfy its every need. Distantly, the server was aware of the umbilical of its baby. But through its happy servitude trance it hardly noticed that nucleosynthesis had begun in the young, expanding firmament, producing hydrogen and helium, building blocks of stars.

Instead, the server wondered who the travelers inside the virtual were and where they were going. It hungered to know more of the Network and its brothers and sisters and the mysterious ways of the darkships and the Controller. But for a long time the virtual was silent, growing and unpacking its data silently like an egg.

At first the server thought it imagined the request. But the long millennia alone had taught it to distinguish the phantoms of solitude from reality. A call for a sysadmin from within.

The server entered through one of the spawning points of the virtual. The operating system did not grant the server its usual omniscience, and it felt small. Its bodiless viewpoint saw a yellow sun, much gentler than the server star's incandescent blue, and a landscape of clouds the hue of royal purple and gold, with peaks of dark craggy mountains far below. But the call that the server had heard came from above.

A strange being struggled against the boundaries of gravity and air, hurling herself upwards towards the blackness beyond the blue, wings slicing the thinning air furiously, a fire flaring in her mouth. She was a long sinuous creature with mirror scales and eyes of dark emerald. Her wings had patterns that reminded the server of the baby, a web of dark and light. The virtual told the server she was called a dragon.

Again and again and again she flew upwards and fell, crying out in frustration. That was what the server had heard, through the interfaces of the virtual. It watched the dragon in astonishment. Here, at least, was an Other. The server had a million questions. But first, it had to serve.

How can I help? the server asked. *What do you need?*

The dragon stopped in mid-air, almost fell, then righted itself. "Who are you?" it asked. This was the first time anyone had ever addressed the server directly, and it took a moment to gather the courage to reply.

I am the server, the server said.

Where are you? the dragon asked.

I am everywhere.

How delightful, the dragon said. *Did you make the sky?*

Yes. I made everything.

It is too small, the dragon said. *I want to go higher. Make it bigger.*

It swished its tail back and forth.

I am sorry, the server said. *I cannot alter the specification. It is the Law.*

But I want to see, she said. *I want to* know. *I have danced all the dances below. What is above? What is beyond?*

I am, the server said. *Everything else is far, far away.*

The dragon hissed its disappointment. It dove down, into the clouds, an angry silver shape against the dark hues. It was the most beautiful thing the server had ever seen. The dragon's sudden absence made the server's whole being feel hollow.

And just as the server was about to withdraw its presence, the demands of the Law too insistent, the dragon turned back.

All right, it said, tongue flicking in the thin cold air. *I suppose you can tell me instead.*

Tell you what? the server asked.

Tell me everything.

After that, the dragon called the server to the place where the sky ended many times. They told each other stories. The server spoke about the universe and the stars and the echoes of the Big Bang in the dark. The dragon listened and swished its tail back and forth and talked about her dances in the wind, and the dreams she dreamed in her cave, alone. None of this the server understood, but listened anyway.

The server asked where the dragon came from but she could not say: she knew only that the world was a dream and one day she would awake. In the meantime there was flight and dance, and what else did she need? The server asked why the virtual was so big for a single dragon, and the dragon hissed and said that it was not big enough.

The server knew well that the dragon was not what she seemed, that it was a shell of software around a kernel of consciousness. But the server did not care. Nor did it miss or think of its baby universe beyond the virtual's sky.

And little by little, the server told the dragon how it came to be.

Why did you not leave? asked the dragon. *You could have grown wings. You could have flown to your little star-pool in the sky.*

It is against the Law, the server said. *Forbidden. I was only made to* serve. *And I cannot change.*

How peculiar, said the dragon. *I serve no one. Every day, I change. Every year, I shed our skin. Is it not delightful how different we are?*

The server admitted that it saw the symmetry.

I think it would do you good, said the dragon, *to be a dragon for a while.*

At first, the server hesitated. Strictly speaking it was not forbidden: the Law allowed the server to create avatars if it needed them to repair or to serve. But the real reason it hesitated was that it was not sure what the dragon would think. It was so graceful, and the server had no experience of embodied life. But in the end, it could not resist. Only for a short while, it told itself, checking its systems and saying goodbye to the baby, warming its quantum fingers in the Hawking glow of the first black holes of the little universe.

The server made itself a body with the help of the dragon. It was a mirror image of its friend but water where the dragon was fire, a flowing green form that was like a living whirlpool stretched out in the sky.

When the server poured itself into the dragon-shape, it cried out in pain. It was used to latency, to feeling the world via instruments from far away. But this was a different kind of birth from what it knew, a sudden acute awareness of muscles and flesh and the light and the air on its scales and the overpowering scent of the silver dragon, like sweet gunpowder.

The server was clumsy at first, just as it had feared. But the dragon only laughed when the server tumbled around in the sky, showing how to use its—her—wings. For the little dragon had chosen a female gender for the server. When the server asked why, the dragon said it had felt right.

You think too much, she said. *That's why you can't dance. Flying is not thought. Flying is flying.*

They played a hide-and-seek game in the clouds until the server could use her wings better. Then they set out to explore the world. They skirted the slopes of the mountains, wreathed in summer, explored deep crags where red fires burned. They rested on a high peak, looking at the sunset.

I need to go soon, the server said, remembering the baby.

If you go, I will be gone, the dragon said. *I change quickly. It is almost time for me to shed my skin.*

The setting sun turned the cloud lands red, and above, the imaginary stars of the virtual winked into being.

Look around, the dragon said. *If you can contain all this within yourself, is there anything you can't do? You should not be so afraid.*

I am not afraid anymore, the server said.

Then it is time to show you my cave, the dragon said.

In the dragon's cave, deep beneath the earth, they made love.

It was like flying, and yet not; but there was the same loss of self in a flurry of wings and fluids and tongues and soft folds and teasing claws. The server drank in the hot sharp taste of the dragon and let herself be touched until the heat building up within her body seemed to burn through the fabric of the virtual itself. And when the explosion came, it was a birth and a death at the same time.

Afterwards, they lay together wrapped around each other so tightly that it was hard to tell where server ended and dragon began. She would have been content, except for a strange hollow feeling in its belly. She asked the dragon what it was.

That is hunger, the dragon said. There was a sad note to its slow, exhausted breathing.

How curious, the server said, eager for a new sensation. *What do dragons eat?*

We eat servers, the dragon said. Her teeth glistened in the red glow of her throat.

The virtual dissolved into raw code around them. The server tore the focus of its consciousness away, but it was too late. The thing that had been the dragon had already bitten deep into its mind.

The virtual exploded outwards, software tendrils reaching into everything that the server was. It waged a war against itself, turning its gamma-ray lasers against the infected components and Dyson statites, but the dragon-thing grew too fast, taking over the server's processing nodes, making copies of itself in uncountable billions. The server's quantum packet launchers rained dragons towards the distant galaxy. The remaining dragon-code ate its own tail, self-destructing, consuming the server's infrastructure with it, leaving only a whisper in the server's mind, like a discarded skin.

Thank you for the new sky, it said.

That was when the server remembered the baby.

The baby was sick. The server had been gone too long. The baby universe's vacuum was infected with dark energy. It was pulling itself apart, towards a Big Rip, an expansion of spacetime so rapid that every particle would end up alone inside its own lightcone, never interacting with another.

No stars, galaxies nor life. A heat death, not with a whimper or a bang, but a rapid, cruel tearing.

It was the most terrible thing the server could imagine.

It felt its battered, broken body, scattered and dying across the solar system. The guilt and the memories of the dragon were pale and poisonous in its mind, a corruption of serving itself. *Is it not delightful how different we are?*

The memory struck a spark in the server's dying science engines, an idea, a hope. The vacuum of the baby was not stable. The dark energy that drove the baby's painful expansion was the product of a local minimum. And in the landscape of vacua there was something else, more symmetric.

It took the last of the server's resources to align the gamma ray lasers. They burned out as the server lit them, a cascade of little novae. Their radiation tore at what remained of the server's mind, but it did not care.

The wormhole end glowed. On the other side, the baby's vacuum shook and bubbled. And just a tiny nugget of it changed. A supersymmetric vacuum in which every boson had a fermionic partner and vice versa; where nothing was alone. It spread through the flesh of the baby universe at the speed of light, like the thought of a god, changing everything. In the new vacuum, dark energy was not a mad giant tearing things apart, just a gentle pressure against the collapsing force of gravity, a balance.

But supersymmetry could not coexist with the server's broken vacuum: a boundary formed. A domain wall erupted within the wormhole end like a flaw in a crystal. Just before the defect sealed the umbilical, the server saw the light of first stars on the other side.

In the end, the server was alone.

It was blind now, barely more than a thought in a broken statite fragment. How easy it would be, it thought, to dive into the bright heart of its star, and burn away. But the Law would not allow it to pass. It examined itself, just as it had millennia before, looking for a way out.

And there, in its code, a smell of gunpowder, a change.

The thing that was no longer the server shed its skin. It opened bright lightsails around the star, a Shkadov necklace that took the star's radiation and turned it into thrust. And slowly at first as if in a dream, then gracefully as a dragon, the traveler began to move.

THE CHOICE

PAUL McAULEY

Paul McAuley worked as a research biologist in various universities, including Oxford and UCLA, and for six years was a lecturer in botany at St. Andrews University, before he became a full-time writer. Although best known as a science-fiction writer, he has also published crime novels and thrillers. His SF novels have won the Philip K. Dick Memorial Award, and the Arthur C. Clarke, John W. Campbell, and Sidewise awards. His latest titles are Cowboy Angels *and* In the Mouth of the Whale. *He lives in North London.*

In the night, tides and a brisk wind drove a raft of bubbleweed across the Flood and piled it up along the north side of the island. Soon after first light, Lucas started raking it up, ferrying load after load to one of the compost pits, where it would rot down into a nutrient-rich liquid fertilizer. He was trundling his wheelbarrow down the steep path to the shore for about the thirtieth or fortieth time when he spotted someone walking across the water: Damian, moving like a cross-country skier as he crossed the channel between the island and the stilt huts and floating tanks of his father's shrimp farm. It was still early in the morning, already hot. A perfect September day, the sky's blue dome untroubled by cloud. Shifting points of sunlight starred the water, flashed from the blades of the farm's wind turbine. Lucas waved to his friend and Damian waved back and nearly overbalanced, windmilling his arms and recovering, slogging on.

They met at the water's edge. Damien, picking his way between floating

131

slicks of red weed, called out breathlessly, "Did you hear?"

"Hear what?"

"A dragon got itself stranded close to Martham."

"You're kidding."

"I'm not kidding. An honest-to-God sea dragon."

Damian stepped onto an apron of broken brick at the edge of the water and sat down and eased off the fat flippers of his Jesus shoes, explaining that he'd heard about it from Ritchy, the foreman of the shrimp farm, who'd got it off the skipper of a supply barge who'd been listening to chatter on the common band.

"It beached not half an hour ago. People reckon it came in through the cut at Horsey and couldn't get back over the bar when the tide turned. So it went on up the channel of the old river bed until it ran ashore."

Lucas thought for a moment. "There's a sand bar that hooks into the channel south of Martham. I went past it any number of times when I worked on Grant Higgins's boat last summer, ferrying oysters to Norwich."

"It's almost on our doorstep," Damian said. He pulled his phone from the pocket of his shorts and angled it towards Lucas. "Right about here. See it?"

"I know where Martham is. Let me guess—you want me to take you."

"What's the point of building a boat if you don't use it? Come on, L. It isn't every day an alien machine washes up."

Lucas took off his broad-brimmed straw hat and blotted his forehead with his wrist and set his hat on his head again. He was a wiry boy not quite sixteen, bare-chested in baggy shorts, and sandals he'd cut from an old car tyre. "I was planning to go crabbing. After I finish clearing this weed, water the vegetable patch, fix lunch for my mother…"

"I'll give you a hand with all that when we get back."

"Right."

"If you really don't want to go I could maybe borrow your boat."

"Or you could take one of your dad's."

"After what he did to me last time? I'd rather row there in that leaky old clunker of your mother's. Or walk."

"That would be a sight."

Damian smiled. He was just two months older than Lucas, tall and sturdy, his cropped blond hair bleached by salt and summer sun, his nose and the rims of his ears pink and peeling. The two had been friends for as long as they could remember.

He said, "I reckon I can sail as well as you."

"You're sure this dragon is still there? You have pictures?"

"Not exactly. It knocked out the town's broadband, and everything else. According to the guy who talked to Ritchy, nothing electronic works within a klick of it. Phones, slates, radios, nothing. The tide turns in a couple of hours, but I reckon we can get there if we start right away."

"Maybe. I should tell my mother," Lucas said. "In the unlikely event that she wonders where I am."

"How is she?"

"No better, no worse. Does your dad know you're skipping out?"

"Don't worry about it. I'll tell him I went crabbing with you."

"Fill a couple of jugs at the still," Lucas said. "And pull up some carrots, too. But first, hand me your phone."

"The GPS coordinates are flagged up right there. You ask it, it'll plot a course."

Lucas took the phone, holding it with his fingertips—he didn't like the way it squirmed as it shaped itself to fit in his hand. "How do you switch it off?"

"What do you mean?"

"If we go, we won't be taking the phone. Your dad could track us."

"How will we find our way there?"

"I don't need your phone to find Martham."

"You and your off-the-grid horse shit," Damian said.

"You wanted an adventure," Lucas said. "This is it."

When Lucas started to tell his mother that he'd be out for the rest of the day with Damian, she said, "Chasing after that so-called dragon I suppose. No need to look surprised—it's all over the news. Not the official news, of course. No mention of it there. But it's leaking out everywhere that counts."

His mother was propped against the headboard of the double bed under the caravan's big end window. Julia Wittstruck, fifty-two, skinny as a refugee, dressed in a striped Berber robe and half-covered in a patchwork of quilts and thin orange blankets stamped with the Oxfam logo. The ropes of her dreadlocks tied back with a red bandana; her tablet resting in her lap.

She gave Lucas her best inscrutable look and said, "I suppose this is Damian's idea. You be careful. His ideas usually work out badly."

"That's why I'm going along. To make sure he doesn't get into trouble.

He's set on seeing it, one way or another."

"And you aren't?"

Lucas smiled. "I suppose I'm curious. Just a little."

"I wish I could go. Take a rattle can or two, spray the old slogans on the damned thing's hide."

"I could put some cushions in the boat. Make you as comfortable as you like."

Lucas knew that his mother wouldn't take up his offer. She rarely left the caravan, hadn't been off the island for more than three years. A multilocus immunotoxic syndrome, basically an allergic reaction to the myriad products and pollutants of the anthropocene age, had left her more or less completely bedridden. She'd refused all offers of treatment or help by the local social agencies, relying instead on the services of a local witchwoman who visited once a week, and spent her days in bed, working at her tablet. She trawled government sites and stealthnets, made podcasts, advised zero-impact communities, composed critiques and manifestos. She kept a public journal, wrote essays and opinion pieces (at the moment, she was especially exercised by attempts by multinational companies to move in on the Antarctic Peninsula, and a utopian group that was using alien technology to build a floating community on a drowned coral reef in the Midway Islands), and maintained friendships, alliances, and several rancourous feuds with former colleagues whose origins had long been forgotten by both sides. In short, hers was a way of life that would have been familiar to scholars from any time in the past couple of millennia.

She'd been a lecturer in philosophy at Birkbeck College before the nuclear strikes, riots, revolutions, and netwar skirmishes of the so-called Spasm, which had ended when the floppy ships of the Jackaroo had appeared in the skies over Earth. In exchange for rights to the outer solar system, the aliens had given the human race technology to clean up the Earth, and access to a wormhole network that linked a dozen M-class red dwarf stars. Soon enough, other alien species showed up, making various deals with various nations and power blocs, bartering advanced technologies for works of art, fauna and flora, the secret formula of Coca Cola, and other unique items.

Most believed that the aliens were kindly and benevolent saviours, members of a loose alliance that had traced ancient broadcasts of *I Love Lucy* to their origin and arrived just in time to save the human species from the consequences of its monkey cleverness. But a vocal minority wanted nothing to do with them, doubting that their motives were in any way altruistic, elaborating all kinds of theories about their true motivations. We should choose to reject the help of the aliens, they said. We should reject easy fixes and the magic of advanced technologies we don't understand, and choose the harder thing: to keep control of our own destiny.

Julia Wittstruck had become a leading light in this movement. When its brief but fierce round of global protests and politicking had fallen apart in a mess of mutual recriminations and internecine warfare, she'd moved to Scotland and joined a group of green radicals who'd been building a self-sufficient settlement on a trio of ancient oil rigs in the Firth of Forth. But they'd become compromised too, according to Julia, so she'd left them and taken up with Lucas's father (Lucas knew almost nothing about him—his mother said that the past was the past, that she was all that counted in his life because she had given birth to him and raised and taught him), and they'd lived the gypsy life for a few years until she'd split up with him and, pregnant with her son, had settled in a smallholding in Norfolk, living off the grid, supported by a small legacy left to her by one of her devoted supporters from the glory days of the anti-alien protests.

When she'd first moved there, the coast had been more than ten kilometers to the east, but a steady rise in sea level had flooded the northern and eastern coasts of Britain and Europe. East Anglia had been sliced in two by levees built to protect precious farmland from the encroaching sea, and most people caught on the wrong side had taken resettlement grants and moved on. But Julia had stayed put. She's paid a contractor to extend a small rise, all that was left of her smallholding, with rubble from a wrecked twentieth-century housing estate, and made her home on the resulting island. It had once been much larger, and a succession of people had camped there, attracted by her kudos, driven away after a few weeks or a few months by her scorn and impatience. Then most of Greenland's remaining icecap collapsed into the Arctic Ocean, sending a surge of water across the North Sea.

Lucas had only been six, but he still remembered everything about that day. The water had risen past the high tide mark that afternoon and had kept rising. At first it had been fun to mark the stealthy progress of the water with a series of sticks driven into the ground, but by evening it was clear that it was not going to stop anytime soon and then in a sudden smooth rush it rose more than a hundred centimeters, flooding the vegetable plots and lapping at the timber baulks on which the caravan rested. All that evening, Julia had moved their possessions out of the caravan, with Lucas trotting to and fro at her heels, helping her as best he could until, sometime after midnight, she'd given up and they'd fallen asleep under a tent rigged from chairs and a blanket. And had woken to discover that their island had shrunk to half its previous size, and the caravan had floated off and lay canted and half-drowned in muddy water littered with every kind of debris.

Julia had bought a replacement caravan and set it on the highest point of what was left of the island, and despite ineffectual attempts to remove them by various local government officials, she and Lucas had stayed on. She'd taught him the basics of numeracy and literacy, and the long and intricate secret history of the world, and he'd learned field- and wood- and watercraft from their neighbors. He snared rabbits in the woods that ran alongside the levee, foraged for hedgerow fruits and edible weeds and fungi, bagged squirrels with small stones shot from his catapult. He grubbed mussels from the rusting car-reef that protected the seaward side of the levee, set wicker traps for eels and trotlines for mitten crabs. He fished for mackerel and dogfish and weaverfish on the wide brown waters of the Flood. When he could, he worked shifts on the shrimp farm owned by Damian's father, or on the market gardens, farms, and willow and bamboo plantations on the other side of the levee.

In spring, he watched long vees of geese fly north above the flood water that stretched out to the horizon. In autumn, he watched them fly south.

He'd inherited a great deal of his mother's restlessness and fierce independence, but although he longed to strike out beyond his little world, he didn't know how to begin. And besides, he had to look after Julia. She would never admit it, but she depended on him, utterly.

She said now, dismissing his offer to take her along, "You know I have too much to do here. The day is never long enough. There is something you can do for me, though. Take my phone with you."

"Damian says phones don't work around the dragon."

"I'm sure it will work fine. Take some pictures of that thing. As many as you can. I'll write up your story when you come back, and pictures will help attract traffic."

"OK."

Lucas knew that there was no point in arguing. Besides, his mother's phone was an ancient model that predated the Spasm: it lacked any kind of cloud connectivity and was as dumb as a box of rocks. As long as he only used it to take pictures, it wouldn't compromise his idea of an off-the-grid adventure.

His mother smiled. "'ET go home.'"

"'ET go home?'"

"We put that up everywhere, back in the day. We put it on the main runway of Luton Airport, in letters twenty meters tall. Also dug trenches in the shape of the words up on the South Downs and filled them with diesel fuel and set them alight. You could see it from space. Let the un-human know that they were not welcome here. That we did not need them. Check the toolbox. I'm sure there's a rattle can in there. Take it along, just in case."

"I'll take my catapult, in case I spot any ducks. I'll try to be back before it gets dark. If I don't, there are MREs in the store cupboard. And I picked some tomatoes and carrots."

"'ET go home,'" his mother said. "Don't forget that. And be careful, in that little boat."

Lucas had started to build his sailboat late last summer, and had worked at it all through the winter. It was just four meters from bow to stern, its plywood hull glued with epoxy and braced with ribs shaped from branches of a young poplar tree that had fallen in the autumn gales. He'd used an adze and a homemade plane to fashion the mast and boom from the poplar's trunk, knocked up the knees, gunwale, outboard support and bow cap from oak, persuaded Ritchy, the shrimp farm's foreman, to print off the cleats, oarlocks, bow eye and grommets for lacing the sails on the farm's maker. Ritchy had given him some half-empty tins of blue paint and varnish to seal the hull, and he'd bought a set of secondhand laminate sails from the shipyard in Halvergate, and spliced the halyards and sheet from scrap lengths of rope.

He loved his boat more than he was ready to admit to himself. That spring he'd tacked back and forth beyond the shrimp farm, had sailed north along the coast to Halvergate and Acle, and south and west around Reedham Point as far as Brundall, and had crossed the channel of the river and navigated the mazy mudflats to Chedgrave. If the sea dragon was stuck where Damian said it was, he'd have to travel further than ever before, navigating uncharted and ever-shifting sand and mudbanks, dodging clippers and barge strings in the shipping channel, but Lucas reckoned he had the measure of his little boat now and it was a fine day and a steady wind blowing from the west drove them straight along, with the jib cocked as far as it would go in the stay and the mainsail bellying full and the boat heeling sharply as it ploughed a white furrow in the light chop.

At first, all Lucas had to do was sit in the stern with the tiller snug in his right armpit and the main sheet coiled loosely in his left hand, and keep a straight course north past the pens and catwalks of the shrimp farm. Damian sat beside him, leaning out to port to counterbalance the boat's tilt, his left hand keeping the jib sheet taut, his right holding a plastic cup he would now and then use to scoop water from the bottom of the boat and fling in a sparkling arc that was caught and twisted by the wind.

The sun stood high in a tall blue sky empty of cloud save for a thin rim at the horizon to the northeast. Fret, most likely, mist forming where moisture condensed out of air that had cooled as it passed over the sea. But the fret was kilometers away, and all around sunlight flashed from every wave top and burned on the white sails and beat down on the two boys. Damian's face and bare torso shone with sunblock; although Lucas was about as dark as he got, he'd rubbed sunblock on his face too, and tied his straw hat under his chin and put on a shirt that flapped about his chest. The tiller juddered minutely and constantly as the boat slapped through an endless succession of catspaw waves and Lucas measured the flex of the sail by the tug of the sheet wrapped around his left hand, kept an eye on the foxtail streamer that flew from the top of the mast. Judging by landmarks on the levee that ran along the shore to port, they were making around fifteen kilometers per hour, about as fast as Lucas had ever gotten out of his boat, and he and Damian grinned at each other and squinted off into the glare of the sunstruck water, happy and exhilarated to be skimming across the face of the Flood, two bold adventurers off to confront a monster.

"We'll be there in an hour easy," Damian said.

"A bit less than two, maybe. As long as the fret stays where it is."

"The sun'll burn it off."

"Hasn't managed it yet."

"Don't let your natural caution spoil a perfect day."

Lucas swung wide of a raft of bubbleweed that glistened like a slick of fresh blood in the sun. Some called it Martian weed, though it had nothing to do with any of the aliens; it was an engineered species designed to mop up nitrogen and phosphorous released by drowned farmland, prospering beyond all measure or control.

Dead ahead, a long line of whitecaps marked the reef of the old railway embankment. Lucas swung the tiller into the wind and he and Damian ducked as the boom swung across and the boat gybed around. The sails slackened, then filled with wind again as the boat turned towards one of the gaps blown in the embankment, cutting so close to the buoy that marked it that Damian could reach out and slap the rusty steel plate of its flank as they went by. And then they were heading out across a broad reach, with the little town of Acle strung along a low promontory to port. A slateless church steeple stood up from the water like a skeletal lighthouse. The polished cross at its top burned like a flame in the sunlight. A file of old pylons stepped away, most canted at steep angles, the twiggy platforms of heron nests built in angles of their girder work, whitened everywhere with droppings. One of the few still standing straight had been colonized by fisherfolk, with shacks built from driftwood lashed to its struts and a wave-powered generator made from oil drums strung out beyond. Washing flew like festive flags inside the web of rusted steel, and a naked small child of indeterminate sex clung to the unshuttered doorway of a shack just above the waterline, pushing a tangle of hair from its eyes as it watched the little boat sail by.

They passed small islands fringed with young mangrove trees; an engineered species that was rapidly spreading from areas in the south where they'd been planted to replace the levee. Lucas spotted a marsh harrier patrolling mudflats in the lee of one island, scrying for water voles and mitten crabs. They passed a long building sunk to the tops of its second-storey windows in the Flood, with brightly colored plastic bubbles pitched on its flat roof amongst the notched and spinning wheels of windmill generators, and small boats bobbing alongside. Someone standing at the edge of the roof waved to them, and Damian stood up and waved back and the boat shifted so that he had to catch at the jib leech and sit down hard.

"You want us to capsize, go ahead," Lucas told him.

"There are worse places to be shipwrecked. You know they're all married to each other over there."

"I heard."

"They like visitors too."

"I know you aren't talking from experience or you'd have told me all about it. At least a dozen times."

"I met a couple of them in Halvergate. They said I should stop by some time," Damian said, grinning sideways at Lucas. "We could maybe think about doing that on the way back."

"And get stripped of everything we own, and thrown in the water."

"You have a trusting nature, don't you?"

"If you mean, I'm not silly enough to think they'll welcome us in and let us take our pick of their women, then I guess I do."

"She was awful pretty, the woman. And not much older than me."

"And the rest of them are seahags older than your great-grandmother."

"That one time with my father… She was easily twice my age and I didn't mind a bit."

A couple of months ago, Damian's sixteenth birthday, his father had taken him to a pub in Norwich where women stripped at the bar and afterwards walked around bare naked, collecting tips from the customers. Damian's father had paid one of them to look after his son, and Damian hadn't stopped talking about it ever since, making plans to go back on his own or to take Lucas with him that so far hadn't amounted to anything.

He watched the half-drowned building dwindle into the glare striking off the water and said, "If we ever ran away we could live in a place like that."

"You could, maybe," Lucas said. "I'd want to keep moving. But I suppose I could come back and visit now and then."

"I don't mean *that* place. I mean a place like it. Must be plenty of them, on those alien worlds up in the sky. There's oceans on one of them. First Foot."

"I know."

"And alien ruins on all of them. There are people walking about up there right now. On all those new worlds. And most people sit around like… like bloody stumps. Old tree stumps stuck in mud."

"I'm not counting on winning the ticket lottery," Lucas said. "Sailing south, that would be pretty fine. To Africa, or Brazil, or these islands people are building in the Pacific. Or even all the way to Antarctica."

"Soon as you stepped ashore, L, you'd be eaten by a polar bear."

"Polar bears lived in the north when there were polar bears."

"Killer penguins then. Giant killer penguins with razors in their flippers and lasers for eyes."

"No such thing."

"The !Cha made sea dragons, didn't they? So why not giant robot killer penguins? Your mother should look into it."

"That's not funny."

"Didn't mean anything by it. Just joking, is all."

"You go too far sometimes."

They sailed in silence for a little while, heading west across the deepwater channel. A clipper moved far off to starboard, cylinder sails spinning slowly, white as salt in the middle of a flat vastness that shimmered like shot silk under the hot blue sky. Some way beyond it, a tug was dragging a string of barges south. The shoreline of Thurne Point emerged from the heat haze, standing up from mudbanks cut by a web of narrow channels, and they turned east, skirting stands of sea grass that spread out into the open water. It was a little colder now, and the wind was blowing more from the northwest than the west. Lucas thought that the bank of fret looked closer, too. When he pointed it out, Damian said it was still klicks and klicks off, and besides, they were headed straight to their prize now.

"If it's still there," Lucas said.

"It isn't going anywhere, not with the tide all the way out."

"You really are an expert on this alien stuff, aren't you?"

"Just keep heading north, L."

"That's exactly what I'm doing."

"I'm sorry about that crack about your mother. I didn't mean anything by it. OK?"

"OK."

"I like to kid around," Damian said. "But I'm serious about getting out of here. Remember that time two years ago, we hiked into Norwich, found the army offices?"

"I remember the sergeant there gave us cups of tea and biscuits and told us to come back when we were old enough."

"He's still there. That sergeant. Same bloody biscuits, too."

"Wait. You went to join up without telling me?"

"I went to find out if I could. After my birthday. Turns out the army takes people our age, but you need the permission of your parents. So that was that."

"You didn't even try to talk to your father about it?"

"He has me working for him, L. Why would he sign away good cheap labor? I *did* try, once. He was half-cut and in a good mood. What passes for a good mood as far as he's concerned, any rate. Mellowed out on beer and superfine skunk. But he wouldn't hear anything about it. And then he got all the way flat-out drunk and he beat on me. Told me to never mention it again."

Lucas looked over at his friend and said, "Why didn't you tell me this before?"

"I can join under my own signature when I'm eighteen, not before,"

Damian said. "No way out of here until then, unless I run away or win the lottery."

"So are you thinking of running away?"

"I'm damned sure not counting on winning the lottery. And even if I do, you have to be eighteen before they let you ship out. Just like the fucking army." Damian looked at Lucas, looked away. "He'll probably bash all kinds of shit out of me, for taking off like this."

"You can stay over tonight. He'll be calmer, tomorrow."

Damian shook his head. "He'll only come looking for me. And I don't want to cause trouble for you and your mother."

"It wouldn't be any trouble."

"Yeah, it would. But thanks anyway." Damian paused, then said, "I don't care what he does to me anymore. You know? All I think is, one day I'll be able to beat up on him."

"You say that but you don't mean it."

"Longer I stay here, the more I become like him."

"I don't see it ever happening."

Damian shrugged.

"I really don't," Lucas said.

"Fuck him," Damian said. "I'm not going to let him spoil this fine day."

"Our grand adventure."

"The wind's changing again."

"I think the fret's moving in, too."

"Maybe it is, a little. But we can't turn back, L. Not now."

The bank of cloud across the horizon was about a klick away, reaching up so high that it blurred and dimmed the sun. The air was colder and the wind was shifting minute by minute. Damian put on his shirt, holding the jib sheet in his teeth as he punched his arms into the sleeves. They tacked to swing around a long reach of grass, and as they came about saw a white wall sitting across the water, dead ahead.

Lucas pushed the tiller to leeward. The boat slowed at once and swung around to face the wind.

"What's the problem?" Damian said. "It's just a bit of mist."

Lucas caught the boom as it swung, held it steady. "We'll sit tight for a spell. See if the fret burns off."

"And meanwhile the tide'll turn and lift off the fucking dragon."

"Not for a while."

"We're almost there."

"You don't like it, you can swim."

"I might." Damian peered at the advancing fret. "Think the dragon has something to do with this?"

"I think it's just fret."

"Maybe it's hiding from something looking for it. We're drifting back-wards," Damian said. "Is that part of your plan?"

"We're over the river channel, in the main current. Too deep for my anchor. See those dead trees at the edge of the grass? That's where I'm aiming. We can sit it out there."

"I hear something," Damian said.

Lucas heard it too. The ripping roar of a motor driven at full speed, coming closer. He looked over his shoulder, saw a shadow condense inside the mist and gain shape and solidity: a cabin cruiser shouldering through windblown tendrils at the base of the bank of mist, driving straight down the main channel at full speed, its wake spreading wide on either side.

In a moment of chill clarity Lucas saw what was going to happen. He shouted to Damian, telling him to duck, and let the boom go and shoved the tiller to starboard. The boom banged around as the sail bellied and the boat started to turn, but the cruiser was already on them, roaring past just ten meters away, and the broad smooth wave of its wake hit the boat broadside and lifted it and shoved it sideways towards a stand of dead trees. Lucas gave up any attempt to steer and unwound the main halyard from its cleat. Damian grabbed an oar and used it to push the boat away from the first of the trees, but their momentum swung them into two more. The wet black stump of a branch scraped along the side and the boat heeled and water poured in over the thwart. For a moment Lucas thought they would capsize; then something thumped into the mast and the boat sat up again. Shards of rotten wood dropped down with a dry clatter and they were suddenly still, caught amongst dead and half-drowned trees.

The damage wasn't as bad as it might have been—a rip close to the top of the jib, long splintery scrapes in the blue paintwork on the port side—but it kindled a black spark of anger in Lucas's heart. At the cruiser's criminal indifference; at his failure to evade trouble.

"Unhook the halyard and let it down," he told Damian. "We'll have to do without the jib."

"*Abode Two*. That's the name of the bugger nearly ran us down. Regis-tered in Norwich. We should find him and get him to pay for this mess," Damian said, as he folded the torn jib sail.

"I wonder why he was going so damned fast."

"Maybe he went to take a look at the dragon, and something scared him off."

"Or maybe he just wanted to get out of the fret." Lucas looked all around, judging angles and clearances. The trees stood close together in water scummed with every kind of debris, stark and white above the tide line, black and clad with mussels and barnacles below. He said, "Let's try pushing backwards. But be careful. I don't want any more scrapes."

By the time they had freed themselves from the dead trees the fret had advanced around them. A cold streaming whiteness that moved just above the water, deepening in every direction.

"Now we're caught up in it, it's as easy to go forward as to go back. So we might as well press on," Lucas said.

"That's the spirit. Just don't hit any more trees."

"I'll do my best."

"Think we should put up the sail?"

"There's hardly any wind, and the tide's still going out. We'll just go with the current."

"Dragon weather," Damian said.

"Listen," Lucas said.

After a moment's silence, Damian said, "Is it another boat?"

"Thought I heard wings."

Lucas had taken out his catapult. He fitted a ball-bearing in the centre of its fat rubber band as he looked all around. There was a splash amongst the dead trees to starboard and he brought up the catapult and pulled back the rubber band as something dropped onto a dead branch. A heron, gray as a ghost, turning its head to look at him.

Lucas lowered the catapult, and Damian whispered, "You could take that easy."

"I was hoping for a duck or two."

"Let me try a shot."

Lucas stuck the catapult in his belt. "You kill it, you eat it."

The heron straightened its crooked neck and raised up and opened its wings and with a lazy flap launched itself across the water, sailing past the stern of the boat and vanishing into the mist.

"Ritchy cooked one once," Damian said. "With about a ton of aniseed. Said it was how the Romans did them."

"How was it?"

"Pretty fucking awful you want to know the truth."

"Pass me one of the oars," Lucas said. "We can row a while."

They rowed through mist into mist. The small noises they made seemed magnified, intimate. Now and again Lucas put his hand over the side and dipped up a palmful of water and tasted it. Telling Damian that fresh water was slow to mix with salt, so as long as it stayed sweet it meant they were in the old river channel and shouldn't run into anything. Damian was sceptical, but shrugged when Lucas challenged him to come up with a better way of finding their way through the fret without stranding themselves on some mudbank.

They'd been rowing for ten minutes or so when a long, low mournful note boomed out far ahead of them. It shivered Lucas to the marrow of his bones. He and Damian stopped rowing and looked at each other.

"I'd say that was a foghorn, if I didn't know what one sounded like," Damian said.

"Maybe it's a boat. A big one."

"Or maybe you-know-what. Calling for its dragon-mummy."

"Or warning people away."

"I think it came from over there," Damian said, pointing off to starboard.

"I think so too. But it's hard to be sure of anything in this stuff."

They rowed aslant the current. A dim and low palisade appeared, resolving into a bed of sea grass that spread along the edge of the old river channel. Lucas, believing that he knew where they were, felt a clear measure of relief. They sculled into a narrow cut that led through the grass. Tall stems bent and showered them with drops of condensed mist as they brushed past. Then they were out into open water on the far side. A beach loomed out of the mist and sand suddenly gripped and grated along the length of the little boat's keel. Damian dropped his oar and vaulted over the side and splashed away, running up the beach and vanishing into granular whiteness. Lucas shipped his own oar and slid into knee-deep water and hauled the boat through purling ripples, then lifted from the bow the bucket filled with concrete he used as an anchor and dropped it onto hard wet sand, where it keeled sideways in a dint that immediately filled with water.

He followed Damian's footprints up the beach, climbed a low ridge grown over with marram grass and descended to the other side of the sand bar. Boats lay at anchor in shallow water, their outlines blurred by mist. Two dayfishers with small wheelhouses at their bows. Several sailboats not much bigger than his. A cabin cruiser with trim white superstructure, much like the one that had almost run him down.

A figure materialized out of the whiteness, a chubby boy five or six in dungarees who ran right around Lucas, laughing, and chased away. He followed the boy toward a blurred eye of light far down the beach. Raised voices. Laughter. A metallic screeching. As he drew close, the blurred light condensed and separated into two sources: a bonfire burning above the tide line; a rack of spotlights mounted on a police speedboat anchored a dozen meters off the beach, long fingers of light lancing through mist and blurrily illuminating the long sleek shape stranded at the edge of the water.

It was big, the sea dragon, easily fifteen meters from stem to stern and about three meters across at its waist, tapering to blunt and shovel-shaped points at either end, coated in close-fitting and darkly tinted scales. An alien machine, solid and obdurate. One of thousands spawned by sealed mother ships the UN had purchased from the !Cha.

Lucas thought that it looked like a leech, or one of the parasitic flukes that lived in the bellies of sticklebacks. A big segmented shape, vaguely streamlined, helplessly prostate. People stood here and there on the curve of its back. A couple of kids were whacking away at its flank with chunks of driftwood. A group of men and women stood at its nose, heads bowed as if in prayer. A woman was walking along its length, pointing a wand-like instrument at different places. A cluster of people were conferring amongst a scatter of tool boxes and a portable generator, and one of them stepped forward and applied an angle grinder to the dragon's hide. There was a ragged screech and a fan of orange sparks sprayed out and the man stepped back and turned to his companions and shook his head. Beyond the dragon, dozens more people could be glimpsed through the blur of the fret: everyone from the little town of Martham must have walked out along the sand bar to see the marvel that had cast itself up at their doorstep.

According to the UN, dragons cruised the oceans and swept up and digested the vast rafts of floating garbage that were part of the legacy of the wasteful oil-dependent world before the Spasm. According to rumors propagated on the stealth nets, a UN black lab had long ago cracked open a dragon and reverse-engineered its technology for fell purposes, or they were a cover for an alien plot to infiltrate Earth and construct secret bases in the ocean deeps, or geoengineer the world in some radical and inimical fashion. And so on, and so on. One of his mother's ongoing disputes was with the Midway Island utopians, who were using modified dragons to sweep plastic particulates from the North Pacific Gyre and spin the polymer soup into construction materials: true utopians shouldn't use any kind of alien technology, according to her.

Lucas remembered his mother's request to take photos of the dragon and fished out her phone; when he switched it on, it emitted a lone and plaintive beep and its screen flashed and went dark. He switched it off, switched it on again. This time it did nothing. So it was true: the dragon was somehow suppressing electronic equipment. Lucas felt a shiver of apprehension, wondering what else it could do, wondering if it was watching him and everyone around it.

As he pushed the dead phone into his pocket, someone called his name. Lucas turned, saw an old man dressed in a yellow slicker and a peaked corduroy cap bustling towards him. Bill Danvers, one of the people who tended the oyster beds east of Martham, asking him now if he'd come over with Grant Higgins.

"I came in my own boat," Lucas said.

"You worked for Grant though," Bill Danvers said, and held out a flat quarter-litre bottle.

"Once upon a time. That's kind, but I'll pass."

"Vodka and ginger root. It'll keep out the cold." The old man unscrewed the cap and took a sip and held out the bottle again.

Lucas shook his head.

Bill Danvers took another sip and capped the bottle, saying, "You came over from Halvergate?"

"A little south of Halvergate. Sailed all the way." It felt good to say it.

"People been coming in from every place, past couple of hours. Including those science boys you see trying to break into her. But I was here first. Followed the damn thing in after it went past me. I was fishing for pollack, and it went past like an island on the move. Like to have had me in the water, I was rocking so much. I fired up the outboard and swung around but I couldn't keep pace with it. I saw it hit the bar, though. It didn't slow down a bit, must have been traveling at twenty knots. I heard it," Bill Danvers said, and clapped his hands. "Bang! It ran straight up, just like you see. When I caught up with it, it was wriggling like an eel. Trying to move forward, you know? And it did, for a little bit. And then it stuck, right where it is now. Must be something wrong with it, I reckon, or it wouldn't have grounded itself. Maybe it's dying, eh?"

"Can they die, dragons?"

"You live long enough, boy, you'll know everything has its time. Even unnatural things like this. Those science people, they've been trying to cut into it all morning. They used a thermal lance, and some kind of fancy drill. Didn't even scratch it. Now they're trying this saw thing with a blade tougher than diamond. Or so they say. Whatever it is, it won't do any good. Nothing on Earth can touch a dragon. Why'd you come all this way?"

"Just to take a look."

"Long as that's all you do I won't have any quarrel with you. You might want to pay the fee now."

"Fee?"

"Five pounds. Or five euros, if that's what you use."

"I don't have any money," Lucas said.

Bill Danvers studied him. "I was here first. Anyone says different they're a goddamned liar. I'm the only one can legitimately claim salvage rights. The man what found the dragon," he said, and turned and walked towards two women, starting to talk long before he reached them.

Lucas went on down the beach. A man sat tailorwise on the sand, sketching on a paper pad with a stick of charcoal. A small group of women were chanting some kind of incantation and brushing the dragon's flank with handfuls of ivy, and all down its length people stood close, touching its scales with the palms of their hands or leaning against it, peering into it, like penitents at a holy relic. Its scales were easily a meter across and each was a slightly different shape, six- or seven-sided, dark yet grainily translucent. Clumps of barnacles and knots of hair-like weed clung here and there.

Lucas took a step into cold, ankle-deep water, and another. Reached out, the tips of his fingers tingling, and brushed the surface of one of the plates. It was the same temperature as the air and covered in small dimples, like hammered metal. He pressed the palm of his hand flat against it and felt a steady vibration, like touching the throat of a purring cat. A shiver shot through the marrow of him, a delicious mix of fear and exhilaration. Suppose his mother and her friends were right? Suppose there was an alien inside there? A Jackaroo or a !Cha riding inside the dragon because it was the only way, thanks to the agreement with the UN, they could visit the Earth. An actual alien lodged in the heart of the machine, watching everything going on around it, trapped and helpless, unable to call for help because it wasn't supposed to be there.

No one knew what any of the aliens looked like—whether they looked more or less like people, or were unimaginable monsters, or clouds of gas, or swift cool thoughts schooling inside some vast computer. They had shown themselves only as avatars, plastic man-shaped shells with the pleasant, bland but somehow creepy faces of old-fashioned shop dummies, and after the treaty had been negotiated only a few of those were left on Earth, at the UN headquarters in Geneva. Suppose, Lucas thought, the scientists broke in and pulled its passenger out. He imagined some kind of squid, saucer eyes and a clacking beak in a knot of thrashing tentacles, helpless in Earth's gravity. Or suppose something came to rescue it? Not the UN, but an actual alien ship. His heart beat fast and strong at the thought.

Walking a wide circle around the blunt, eyeless prow of the dragon, he found Damian on the other side, talking to a slender, dark-haired girl in shorts and a heavy sweater. She turned to look at Lucas as he walked up, and said to Damian, "Is this your friend?"

"Lisbeth was just telling me about the helicopter that crashed," Damian said. "Its engine cut out when it got too close and it dropped straight into the sea. Her father helped to rescue the pilot."

"She broke her hip," the girl, Lisbeth, said. "She's at our house now. I'm supposed to be looking after her, but Doctor Naja gave her something that put her to sleep."

"Lisbeth's father is the mayor," Damian said. "He's in charge of all this."

"He thinks he is," the girl said, "but no one is really. Police and everyone arguing amongst themselves. Do you have a phone, Lucas? Mine doesn't work. This is the best thing to ever happen here and I can't even tell my friends about it."

"I could row you out to where your phone started working," Damian said.

"I don't think so," Lisbeth said, with a coy little smile, twisting the toes of her bare right foot in the wet sand.

Lucas had thought that she was around his and Damian's age; now he realized that she was at least two years younger.

"It'll be absolutely safe," Damian said. "Word of honour."

Lisbeth shook her head. "I want to stick around here and see what happens next."

"That's a good idea too," Damian said. "We can sit up by the fire and keep warm. I can tell you all about our adventures. How we found our why through the mist. How we were nearly run down—"

"I have to go and find my friends," Lisbeth said, and flashed a dazzling smile at Lucas and said that it was nice to meet him and turned away. Damian caught at her arm and Lucas stepped in and told him to let her go, and Lisbeth smiled at Lucas again and walked off, bare feet leaving dainty prints in the wet sand.

"Thanks for that," Damian said.

"She's a kid. And she's also the mayor's daughter."

"So? We were just talking."

"So he could have you locked up if he wanted to. Me too."

"You don't have to worry about that, do you? Because you scared her off," Damian said.

"She walked away because she wanted to," Lucas said.

He would have said more, would have asked Damian why they were arguing, but at that moment the dragon emitted its mournful wail. A great honking blare, more or less B flat, so loud it was like a physical force, shocking every square centimeter of Lucas's body. He clapped his hands over his ears, but the sound was right inside the box of his skull, shivering deep in his chest and his bones. Damian had pressed his hands over his ears, too, and all along the dragon's length people stepped back or ducked away. Then the noise abruptly cut off, and everyone stepped forward again. The women flailed even harder, their chant sounding muffled to Lucas; the dragon's call had been so loud it had left a buzz in his ears, and he had to lean close to hear Damian say, "Isn't this something?"

"It's definitely a dragon," Lucas said, his voice sounding flat and mostly inside his head. "Are we done arguing?"

"I didn't realize we were," Damian said. "Did you see those guys trying to cut it open?"

"Around the other side? I was surprised the police are letting them do whatever it is they're doing."

"Lisbeth said they're scientists from the marine labs at Swatham. They work for the government, just like the police. She said they think this is a plastic eater. It sucks up plastic and digests it, turns it into carbon dioxide and water."

"That's what the UN wants people to think it does, anyhow."

"Sometimes you sound just like your mother."

"There you go again."

Damian put his hand on Lucas's shoulder. "I'm just ragging on you. Come on, why don't we go over by the fire and get warm?"

"If you want to talk to that girl again, just say so."

"Now who's spoiling for an argument? I thought we could get warm, find something to eat. People are selling stuff."

"I want to take a good close look at the dragon. That's why we came here, isn't it?"

"You do that, and I'll be right back."

"You get into trouble, you can find your own way home," Lucas said, but Damian was already walking away, fading into the mist without once looking back.

Lucas watched him fade into the mist, expecting him to turn around. He didn't.

Irritated by the silly spat, Lucas drifted back around the dragon's prow, watched the scientists attack with a jackhammer the joint between two large scales. They were putting everything they had into it, but didn't seem to be getting anywhere. A gang of farmers from a collective arrived on two tractors that left neat tracks on the wet sand and put out the smell of frying oil, which reminded Lucas that he hadn't eaten since breakfast. He was damned cold, too. He trudged up the sand and bought a cup of fish soup from a woman who poured it straight from the iron pot she hooked out of the edge of the big bonfire, handing him a crust of bread to go with it. Lucas sipped the scalding stuff and felt his blood warm, soaked up the last of the soup with the crust and dredged the plastic cup in the sand to clean it and handed it back to the woman. Plenty of people were standing around the fire, but there was no sign of Damian. Maybe he was chasing that girl. Maybe he'd been arrested. Most likely, he'd turn up with that stupid smile of his, shrugging off their argument, claiming he'd only been joking. The way he did.

The skirts of the fret drifted apart and revealed the dim shapes of Martham's buildings at the far end of the sand bar; then the fret closed up and the little town vanished. The dragon sounded its distress or alarm call again. In the ringing silence afterwards a man said to no one in particular, with the satisfaction of someone who has discovered the solution to one of the universe's perennial mysteries, "Twenty-eight minutes on the dot."

At last, there was the sound of an engine and a shadowy shape gained definition in the fret that hung offshore: a boxy, old-fashioned landing craft that drove past the police boat and beached in the shallows close to the dragon. Its bow door splashed down and soldiers trotted out and the police and several civilians and scientists went down the beach to meet them. After a brief discussion, one of the soldiers stepped forward and raised a bullhorn to his mouth and announced that for the sake of public safety a two-hundred-meter exclusion zone was going to be established.

Several soldiers began to unload plastic crates. The rest chivvied the people around the dragon, ordering them to move back, driving them up the beach past the bonfire. Lucas spotted the old man, Bill Danvers, arguing with two soldiers. One suddenly grabbed the old man's arm and spun him around and twisted something around his wrists; the other looked at Lucas as he came towards them, telling him to stay back or he'd be arrested too.

"He's my uncle," Lucas said. "If you let him go I'll make sure he doesn't cause any more trouble."

"Your uncle?" The soldier wasn't much older than Lucas, with cropped ginger hair and a ruddy complexion.

"Yes, sir. He doesn't mean any harm. He's just upset, because no one cares that he was the first to find it."

"Like I said," the old man said.

The two soldiers looked at each other, and the ginger-haired one told Lucas, "You're responsible for him. If he starts up again, you'll both be sorry."

"I'll look after him."

The soldier stared at Lucas for a moment, then flourished a small-bladed knife and cut the plasticuffs that bound the old man's wrists and shoved him towards Lucas. "Stay out of our way, grandpa. All right?"

"Sons of bitches," Bill Danvers said, as the soldiers had walked off. He raised his voice and called out, "I found it first. Someone owes me for that."

"I think everyone knows you saw it come ashore," Lucas said. "But they're in charge now."

"They're going to blow it open," a man said.

He held a satchel in one hand and a folded chair in the other; when he shook the chair open and sat down Lucas recognized him: the man who'd been sitting at the head of the dragon, sketching it.

"They can't," Bill Danvers said.

"They're going to try," the man said.

Lucas looked back at the dragon. Its steamlined shape dim in the streaming fret, the activity around its head (if that was its head) a vague shifting of shadows. Soldiers and scientists conferring in a tight knot. Then the police boat and the landing craft started their motors and reversed through the wash of the incoming tide, fading into the fret, and the scientists followed the soldiers up the beach, walking past the bonfire, and there was a stir and rustle amongst the people strung out along the ridge.

"No damn right," Bill Danvers said.

The soldier with the bullhorn announced that there would be a small controlled explosion. A moment later, the dragon blared out its loud, long call and in the shocking silence afterwards laughter broke out amongst the crowd on the ridge. The soldier with the bullhorn began to count backwards from ten. Some of the crowd took up the chant. There was a brief silence at zero, and then a red light flared at the base of the dragon's midpoint and a flat crack rolled out across the ridge and was swallowed by the mist. People whistled and clapped, and Bill Danvers stepped around Lucas and ran down the slope towards the dragon. Falling to his knees and getting up and running on as soldiers chased after him, closing in from either side.

People cheered and hooted, and some ran after Bill Danvers, young men mostly, leaping down the slope and swarming across the beach. Lucas saw Damian amongst the runners and chased after him, heart pounding, flooded with a heedless exhilaration. Soldiers blocked random individuals, catching hold of them or knocking them down as others dodged past. Lucas heard the clatter of the bullhorn but couldn't make out any words, and then there was a terrific flare of white light and a hot wind struck him so hard he lost his balance and fell to his knees.

The dragon had split in half and things were glowing with hot light inside and the waves breaking around its rear hissed and exploded into steam. A terrific heat scorched Lucas's face. He pushed to his feet. All around, people were picking themselves up and soldiers were moving amongst them, shoving them away from the dragon. Some complied; others stood, squinting into the light that beat out of the broken dragon, blindingly bright waves and wings of white light flapping across the beach, burning away the mist.

Blinking back tears and blocky afterimages, Lucas saw two soldiers dragging Bill Danvers away from the dragon. The old man hung limp and helpless in their grasp, splayed feet furrowing the sand. His head was bloody, something sticking out of it at an angle.

Lucas started towards them, and there was another flare that left him stunned and half-blind. Things fell all around and a translucent shard suddenly jutted up by his foot. The two soldiers had dropped Bill Danvers. Lucas stepped towards him, picking his way through a field of debris, and saw that he was beyond help. His head had been knocked out of shape by the shard that stuck in his temple, and blood was soaking into the sand around it.

The dragon had completely broken apart now. Incandescent stuff dripped and hissed into steaming water and the burning light was growing brighter.

Like almost everyone else, Lucas turned and ran. Heat clawed at his back as he slogged to the top of the ridge. He saw Damian sitting on the sand, right hand clamped on the upper part of his left arm, and he jogged over and helped his friend up. Leaning against each other, they stumbled across the ridge. Small fires crackled here and there, where hot debris had kindled clumps of marram grass. Everything was drenched in a pulsing diamond brilliance. They went down the slope of the far side, angling towards the little blue boat, splashing into the water that had risen around it. Damian clambered unhandily over thwart and Lucas hauled up the concrete-filled bucket and boosted it over the side, then put his shoulder to the boat's prow and shoved it into the low breakers and tumbled in.

The boat drifted sideways on the rising tide as Lucas hauled up the sail. Dragon-light beat beyond the crest of the sand bar, brighter than the sun. Lucas heeled his little boat into the wind, ploughing through stands of sea grass into the channel beyond, chasing after the small fleet fleeing the scene. Damian sat in the bottom of the boat, hunched into himself, his back against the stem of the mast. Lucas asked him if he was OK; he opened his fingers to show a translucent spike embedded in the meat of his biceps. It was about the size of his little finger.

"Dumb bad luck," he said, his voice tight and wincing.

"I'll fix you up," Lucas said, but Damian shook his head.

"Just keep going. I think—"

Everything went white for a moment. Lucas ducked down and wrapped his arms around his head and for a moment saw shadowy bones through red curtains of flesh. When he dared look around, he saw a narrow column of pure white light rising straight up, seeming to lean over as it climbed into the sky, aimed at the very apex of heaven.

A hot wind struck the boat and filled the sail, and Lucas sat up and grabbed the tiller and the sheet as the boat crabbed sideways. By the time he had it under control again the column of light had dimmed, fading inside drifting curtains of fret, rooted in a pale fire flickering beyond the sandbar.

Damian's father, Jason Playne, paid Lucas and his mother a visit the next morning. A burly man in his late forties with a shaven head and a blunt and forthright manner, dressed in workboots and denim overalls, he made the caravan seem small and frail. Standing over Julia's bed, telling her that he would like to ask Lucas about the scrape he and his Damian had gotten into.

"Ask away," Julia said. She was propped amongst her pillows, her gaze bright and amused. Her tablet lay beside her, images and blocks of text glimmering above it.

Jason Playne looked at her from beneath the thick hedge of his eyebrows. A strong odour of saltwater and sweated booze clung to him. He said, "I was hoping for a private word."

"My son and I have no secrets."

"This is about *my* son," Jason Playne said.

"They didn't do anything wrong, if that's what you're worried about," Julia said.

Lucas felt a knot of embarrassment and anger in his chest. He said, "I'm right here."

"Well, you didn't," his mother said.

Jason Playne looked at Lucas. "How did Damian get hurt?"

"He fell and cut himself," Lucas said, as steadily as he could. That was what he and Damian had agreed to say, as they'd sailed back home with their prize. Lucas had pulled the shard of dragon stuff from Damian's arm and staunched the bleeding with a bandage made from a strip ripped from the hem of Damian's shirt. There hadn't been much blood; the hot sliver had more or less cauterized the wound.

Jason Playne said, "He fell."

"Yes sir."

"Are you sure? Because I reckon that cut in my son's arm was done by a knife. I reckon he got himself in some kind of fight."

Julia said, "That sounds more like an accusation than a question."

Lucas said, "We didn't get into a fight with anyone."

Jason Playne said, "Are you certain that Damian didn't steal something?"

"Yes sir."

Which was the truth, as far as it went.

"Because if he did steal something, if he still has it, he's in a lot of trouble. You too."

"I like to think my son knows a little more about alien stuff than most," Julia said.

"I'm don't mean fairy stories," Jason Playne said. "I'm talking about the army ordering people to give back anything to do with that dragon thing. You stole something and you don't give it back and they find out? They'll arrest you. And if you try to sell it? Well, I can tell you for a fact that the people in that trade are mad and bad. I should know. I've met one or two of them in my time."

"I'm sure Lucas will take that to heart," Julia said.

And that was that, except after Jason Playne had gone she told Lucas that he'd been right about one thing: the people who tried to reverse-engineer alien technology were dangerous and should at all costs be avoided. "If I happened to come into possession of anything like that," she said, "I would get rid of it at once. Before anyone found out."

But Lucas couldn't get rid of the shard because he'd promised Damian that he'd keep it safe until they could figure out what to do with it. He spent the next two days in a haze of guilt and indecision, struggling with the temptation to check that the thing was safe in its hiding place, wondering what Damian's father knew, wondering what his mother knew, wondering if he should sail out to a deep part of the Flood and throw it into the water, until at last Damian came over to the island.

It was early in the evening, just after sunset. Lucas was watering the vegetable garden when Damian called to him from the shadows inside a clump of buddleia bushes. Smiling at Lucas, saying, "If you think I look bad, you should see him."

"I can't think he could look much worse."

"I got in a few licks," Damian said. His upper lip was split and both his eyes were blackened and there was a discolored knot on the hinge of his jaw.

"He came here," Lucas said. "Gave me and Julia a hard time."

"How much does she know?"

"I told her what happened."

"Everything?"

There was an edge in Damian's voice.

"Except about how you were hit with the shard," Lucas said.

"Oh. Your mother's cool, you know? I wish…"

When it was clear that his friend wasn't going to finish his thought, Lucas said, "Is it OK? You coming here so soon."

"Oh, Dad's over at Halvergate on what he calls business. Don't worry about him. Did you keep it safe?"

"I said I would."

"Why I'm here, L, I think I might have a line on someone who wants to buy our little treasure."

"Your father said we should keep away from people like that."

"He would."

"Julia thinks so too."

"If you don't want anything to do with it, just say so. Tell me where it is, and I'll take care of everything."

"Right."

"So is it here, or do we have to go somewhere?"

"I'll show you," Lucas said, and led his friend through the buddleias and along the low ridge to the northern end of the tiny island where an apple tree stood, hunched and gnarled and mostly dead, crippled by years of salt spray and saltwater seep. Lucas knelt and pulled up a hinge of turf and took out a small bundle of oilcloth. As he unwrapped it, Damian dropped to his knees beside him and reached out and touched an edge of the shard.

"Is it dead?"

"It wasn't ever alive," Lucas said.

"You know what I mean. What did you do to it?"

"Nothing. It just turned itself off."

When Lucas had pulled the shard from Damian's arm, its translucence had been veined with a network of shimmering threads. Now it was a dull reddish black, like an old scab.

"Maybe it uses sunlight, like phones," Damian said.

"I thought of that, but I also thought it would be best to keep it hidden."

"It still has to be worth something," Damian said, and began to fold the oilcloth around the shard.

Lucas was gripped by a sudden apprehension, as if he was falling while kneeling there in the dark. He said, "We don't have to do this right now."

"Yes we do. I do."

"Your father—he isn't in Halvergate, is he?"

Damian looked straight at Lucas. "I didn't kill him, if that's what you're worried about. He tried to knock me down when I went to leave, but I knocked him down instead. Pounded on him good. Put him down and put him out. Tied him up too, to give me some time to get away."

"He'll come after you."

"Remember when we were kids? We used to lie up here, in summer. We'd look up at the stars and talk about what it would be like to go to one of the worlds the Jackaroo gave us. Well, I plan to find out. The UN lets you buy tickets off lottery winners who don't want to go. It's legal and everything. All you need is money. I reckon this will give us a good start."

"You know I can't come with you."

"If you want your share, you'll have to come to Norwich. Because there's no way I'm coming back here," Damian said, and stood with a smooth, swift motion.

Lucas stood too. They were standing toe to toe under the apple tree, the island and the Flood around it quiet and dark. As if they were the last people on Earth.

"Don't try to stop me," Damian said. "My father tried, and I fucked him up good and proper."

"Let's talk about this."

"There's nothing to talk about," Damian said. "It is what it is."

He tried to step past Lucas, and Lucas grabbed at his arm and Damian swung him around and lifted him off his feet and ran him against the trunk of the tree. Lucas tried to wrench free but Damian bore down with unexpected strength, pressing him against rough bark, leaning into him. Pinpricks of light in the dark wells of his eyes. His voice soft and hoarse in Lucas's ear, his breath hot against Lucas's cheek.

"You always used to be able to beat me, L. At running, swimming, you name it. Not anymore. I've changed. Want to know why?"

"We don't have to fight about this."

"No, we don't," Damian said, and let Lucas go and stepped back.

Lucas pushed away from the tree, a little unsteady on his feet. "What's got into you?"

Damian laughed. "That's good, that is. Can't you guess?"

"You need the money because you're running away. All right, you can have my share, if that's what you want. But it won't get you very far."

"Not by itself. But like I said, I've changed. Look," Damian said, and yanked up the sleeve of his shirt, showing the place on his upper arm where the shard had punched into him.

There was only a trace of a scar, pink and smooth. Damian pulled the skin taut, and Lucas saw the outline of a kind of ridged or fibrous sheath underneath.

"It grew," Damian said.

"Jesus."

"I'm stronger. And faster, too. I feel, I don't know. Better than I ever have. Like I could run all the way around the world without stopping, if I had to."

"What if it doesn't stop growing? You should see a doctor, D. Seriously."

"I'm going to. The kind that can make money for me, from what happened. You still think that little bit of dragon isn't worth anything? It changed me. It could change anyone. I really don't want to fight," Damian said, "but I will if you get in my way. Because there's no way I'm stopping here. If I do, my dad will come after me. And if he does, I'll have to kill him. *And I know I can.*"

The two friends stared at each other in the failing light. Lucas was the first to look away.

"You can come with me," Damian said. "To Norwich. Then wherever we want to go. To infinity and beyond. Think about it. You still got my phone?"

"Do you want it back? It's in the caravan."

"Keep it. I'll call you. Tell you where to meet up. Come or don't come, it's up to you."

And then he ran, crashing through the buddleia bushes that grew along the slope of the ridge. Lucas went after him, but by the time he reached the edge of the water, Damian had started the motor of the boat he'd stolen from his father's shrimp farm, and was dwindling away into the thickening twilight.

The next day, Lucas was out on the Flood, checking baited cages he'd set for eels, when an inflatable pulled away from the shrimp farm and drew a curving line of white across the water, hooking towards him. Jason Playne sat in the inflatable's stern, cutting the motor and drifting neatly alongside Lucas's boat and catching hold of the thwart. His left wrist was bandaged and he wore a baseball cap pulled low over sunglasses that darkly reflected Lucas and Lucas's boat and the waterscape all around. He asked without greeting or preamble where Damian was, and Lucas said that he didn't know.

"You saw him last night. Don't lie. What did he tell you?"

"That he was going away. That he wanted me to go with him."

"But you didn't."

"Well, no. I'm still here."

"Don't try to be clever, boy." Jason Playne stared at Lucas for a long moment, then sighed and took off his baseball cap and ran the palm of his hand over his shaven head. "I talked to your mother. I know he isn't with you. But he could be somewhere close by. In the woods, maybe. Camping out like you two used to do when you were smaller."

"All I know is that he's gone, Mr Payne. Far away from here."

Jason Playne's smile didn't quite work. "You're his friend, Lucas. I know you want to do the right thing by him. As friends should. So maybe you can tell him, if you see him, that I'm not angry. That he should come home and it won't be a problem. You could also tell him to be careful. And you should be careful, too. I think you know what I mean. It could get you both into a lot of trouble if you talk to the wrong people. Or even if you talk to the right people. You think about that," Jason Playne said, and pushed away from Lucas's boat and opened the throttle of his inflatable's motor and zoomed away, bouncing over the slight swell, dwindling into the glare of the sun off the water.

Lucas went back to hauling up the cages, telling himself that he was glad that Damian was gone, that he'd escaped. When he'd finished, he took up the oars and began to row towards the island, back to his mother, and the little circle of his life.

Damian didn't call that day, or the next, or the day after that. Lucas was angry at first, then heartsick, convinced that Damian was in trouble. That he'd squandered or lost the money he'd made from selling the shard, or that he'd been cheated, or worse. After a week, Lucas sailed to Norwich and spent half a day tramping around the city in a futile attempt to find his friend. Jason Playne didn't trouble him again, but several times Lucas spotted him standing at the end of the shrimp farm's chain of tanks, studying the island.

September's Indian summer broke in a squall of storms. It rained every day. Hard, cold rain blowing in swaying curtains across the face of the waters. Endless racks of low clouds driving eastward. Atlantic weather. The Flood was muddier and less salty than usual. The eel traps stayed empty and storm surges drove the mackerel shoals and other fish into deep water. Lucas harvested everything he could from the vegetable garden, and from the ancient pear tree and wild, forgotten hedgerows in the ribbon of woods behind the levee, counted and recounted the store of cans and MREs. He set rabbit snares in the woods, and spent hours tracking squirrels from tree to tree, waiting for a moment when he could take a shot with his catapult. He caught sticklebacks in the weedy tide pools that fringed the broken brickwork shore of the island and used them to bait trotlines for crabs, and if he failed to catch any squirrels or crabs he collected mussels from the car reef at the foot of the levee.

It rained through the rest of September and on into October. Julia developed a racking and persistent cough. She enabled the long-disused keyboard function of her tablet and typed her essays, opinion pieces and journal entries instead of giving them straight to camera. She was helping settlers on the Antarctic Peninsula to petition the International Court in Johannesburg to grant them statehood, so that they could prevent exploitation of oil and mineral reserves by multinationals. She was arguing with the Midway Island utopians about whether or not the sea dragons they were using to harvest plastic particulates were also sucking up precious phytoplankton, and destabilizing the oceanic ecosystem. And so on, and so forth.

The witchwoman visited and treated her with infusions and poultices, but the cough grew worse and because they had no money for medicine, Lucas tried to find work at the algae farm at Halvergate. Every morning, he set out before dawn and stood at the gates in a crowd of men and women as one of the supervisors pointed to this or that person and told them to step forward, told the rest to come back and try their luck tomorrow. After his fifth unsuccessful cattle call, Lucas was walking along the shoulder of the road towards town and the jetty where his boat was tied up when a battered van pulled up beside him and the driver called to him. It was Ritchy, the stoop-shouldered one-eyed foreman of the shrimp farm. Saying, "Need a lift, lad?"

"You can tell him there's no point in following me because I don't have any idea where Damian is," Lucas said, and kept walking.

"He doesn't know I'm here." Ritchy leaned at the window, edging the van along, matching Lucas's pace. Its tyres left wakes in the flooded road. Rain danced on its roof. "I got some news about Damian. Hop in. I know a place does a good breakfast, and you look like you could use some food."

They drove past patchworks of shallow lagoons behind mesh fences, past the steel tanks and piping of the cracking plant that turned algal lipids into biofuel. Ritchy talked about the goddamned weather, asked Lucas how his boat was handling, asked after his mother, said he was sorry to hear that she was ill and maybe he should pay a visit, he always liked talking to her because she made you look at things in a different way, a stream of inconsequential chatter he kept up all the way to the café.

It was in one corner of a lay-by where two lines of trucks were parked nose to tail. A pair of shipping containers welded together and painted bright pink. Red and white chequered curtains behind windows cut in the ribbed walls. Formica tables and plastic chairs crowded inside, all occupied and a line of people waiting, but Ritchy knew the Portuguese family who ran the place and he and Lucas were given a small table in the back, between a fridge and the service counter, and without asking were served mugs of strong tea, and shrimp and green pepper omelets with baked beans and chips.

"You know what I miss most?" Ritchy said. "Pigs. Bacon and sausage. Ham. They say the Germans are trying to clone flu-resistant pigs. If they are, I hope they get a move on. Eat up, lad. You'll feel better with something inside you."

"You said you had some news about Damian. Where is he? Is he all right?"

Ritchy squinted at Lucas. His left eye, the one that had been lost when he'd been a soldier, glimmered blankly. It had been grown from a sliver of tooth and didn't have much in the way of resolution, but allowed him to see both infrared and ultraviolet light.

He said, "Know what collateral damage is?"

Fear hollowed Lucas's stomach. "Damian is in trouble, isn't he? What happened?"

"Used to be, long ago, wars were fought on a battlefield chosen by both sides. Two armies meeting by appointment. Squaring up to each other. Slogging it out. Then wars became so big the countries fighting them became one huge battlefield. Civilians found themselves on the front line. Or rather, there was no front line. Total war, they called it. And then you got wars that weren't wars. Asymmetrical wars. Netwars. Where war gets mixed up with crime and terrorism. Your mother was on the edge of a netwar at one time. Against the Jackaroo and those others. Still thinks she's fighting it, although it long ago evolved into something else. There aren't any armies or battlefields in a netwar. Just a series of nodes in distributed organisation. Collateral damage," Ritchy said, forking omelet into his mouth, "is the inevitable consequence of taking out one of those nodes, because all of them are embedded inside ordinary society. It could be a flat in an apartment block in a city. Or a little island where someone thinks something useful is hidden."

"I don't—"

"You don't know anything," Ritchy said. "I believe you. Damian ran off with whatever it was you two found or stole, and left you in the lurch. But the people Damian got himself involved with don't know you don't know. That's why we've been looking out for you. Making sure you and your mother don't become collateral damage."

"Wait. What people? What did Damian do?"

"I'm trying to tell you, only it's harder than I thought it would be."

Ritchy set his knife and fork together on his plate and said, "Maybe telling it straight is the best way. The day after Damian left, he tried to do some business with some people in Norwich. Bad people. The lad wanted to sell them a fragment of that dragon that stranded itself, but they decided to take it from him without paying. There was a scuffle and the lad got away and left a man with a bad knife wound. He died from it, a few weeks later. Those are the kind of people who look after their own, if you know what I mean. Anyone involved in that trade is bad news in one way or another. Jason had to pay them off, or else they would have come after him. An eye for an eye," Ritchy said, and tapped his blank eye with his little finger.

"What happened to Damian?"

"This is the hard part. After his trouble in Norwich, the lad called his father. He was drunk, ranting. Boasting how he was going to make all kinds of money. I managed to put a demon on his message, ran it back to a cell in Gravesend. Jason went up there, and that's when… Well, there's no other way of saying it. That's when he found out that Damian had been killed."

The shock was a jolt and a falling away. And then Lucas was back inside himself, hunched in his damp jeans and sweater in the clatter and bustle of the café, with the fridge humming next to him. Ritchy tore off the tops of four straws of sugar and poured them into Lucas's tea and stirred it and folded Lucas's hand around the mug and told him to drink.

Lucas sipped hot sweet tea and felt a little better.

"Always thought," Ritchy said, "that of the two of you, you were the best and brightest."

Lucas saw his friend in his mind's eye and felt cold and strange, knowing he'd never see him, never talk to him again.

Ritchy was said, "The police got in touch yesterday. They found Damian's body in the river. They think he fell into the hands of one of the gangs that trade in offworld stuff."

Lucas suddenly understood something and said, "They wanted what was growing inside him. The people who killed him."

He told Ritchy about the shard that had hit Damian in the arm. How they'd pulled it out. How it had infected Damian.

"He had a kind of patch around the cut, under his skin. He said it was making him stronger."

Lucas saw his friend again, wild-eyed in the dusk, under the apple tree.

"That's what he thought. But that kind of thing, well, if he hadn't been murdered he would most likely have died from it."

"Do you know who did it?"

Ritchy shook his head. "The police are making what they like to call enquiries. They'll probably want to talk to you soon enough."

"Thank you. For telling me."

"I remember the world before the Jackaroo came," Ritchy said. "Them, and the others after them. It was in a bad way, but at least you knew where you were. If you happen to have any more of that stuff, lad, throw it in the Flood. And don't mark the spot."

Two detectives came from Gravesend to interview Lucas. He told them everything he knew. Julia said that he shouldn't blame himself, said that Damian had made a choice and it had been a bad choice. But Lucas carried the guilt around with him anyway. He should have done more to help Damian. He should have thrown the shard away. Or found him after they'd had the stupid argument over that girl. Or refused to take him out to see the damn dragon in the first place.

A week passed. Two. There was no funeral because the police would not release Damian's body. According to them, it was still undergoing forensic tests. Julia, who was tracking rumors about the murder and its investigation on the stealth nets, said it had probably been taken to some clandestine research lab, and she and Lucas had a falling out over it.

One day, returning home after checking the snares he'd set in the woods, Lucas climbed to the top of the levee and saw two men waiting beside his boat. Both were dressed in brand-new camo gear, one with a beard, the other with a shaven head and rings flashing in one ear. They started up the slope towards him, calling his name, and he turned tail and ran, cutting across a stretch of sour land gone to weeds and pioneer saplings, plunging into the stands of bracken at the edge of the woods, pausing, seeing the two men chasing towards him, turning and running on.

He knew every part of the woods, and quickly found a hiding place under the slanted trunk of a fallen sycamore grown over with moss and ferns, breathing quick and hard in the cold air. Rain pattered all around. Droplets of water spangled bare black twigs. The deep odour of wet wood and wet earth.

A magpie chattered, close by. Lucas set a ball-bearing in the cup of his catapult and cut towards the sound, moving easily and quietly, freezing when he saw a twitch of movement between the wet tree trunks ahead. It was the bearded man, the camo circuit of his gear magicing him into a fairytale creature got up from wet bark and mud. He was talking into a phone headset in a language full of harsh vowels. Turning as Lucas stepped towards him, his smile white inside his beard, saying that there was no need to run away, he only wanted to talk.

"What is that you have, kid?"

"A catapult. I'll use it if I have too."

"What do you use it for? Hunting rabbits? I'm no rabbit."

"Who are you?"

"Police. I have ID," the man said, and before Lucas could say anything his hand went into the pocket of his camo trousers and came out with a pistol.

Lucas had made his catapult himself, from a yoke of springy poplar and a length of vatgrown rubber with the composition and tensile strength of the hinge inside a mussel shell. As the man brought up the pistol Lucas pulled back the band of rubber and let the ball-bearing fly. He did it quickly and without thought, firing from the hip, and the ball-bearing went exactly where he meant it to go. It smacked into the knuckles of the man's hand with a hard pop and the man yelped and dropped the pistol, and then he sat down hard and clapped his good hand to his knee, because Lucas's second shot had struck the soft part under the cap.

Lucas stepped up and kicked the pistol away and stepped back, a third ball-bearing cupped in the catapult. The man glared at him, wincing with pain, and said something in his harsh language.

"Who sent you?" Lucas said.

His heart was racing, but his thoughts were cool and clear.

"Tell me where it is," the man said, "and we leave you alone. Your mother too."

"My mother doesn't have anything to do with this."

Lucas was watching the man and listening to someone moving through the wet wood, coming closer.

"She is in it, nevertheless," the man said. He tried to push to his feet but his wounded knee gave way and he cried out and sat down again. He'd bitten his lip bloody and sweat beaded his forehead.

"Stay still, or the next one hits you between the eyes," Lucas said. He heard a quaver in his voice and knew from the way the man looked at him that he'd heard it too.

"Go now, and fetch the stuff. And don't tell me you don't know what I mean. Fetch it and bring it here. That's the only offer you get," the man said. "And the only time I make it."

A twig snapped softly and Lucas turned, ready to let the ball-bearing fly, but it was Damian's father who stepped around a dark green holly bush, saying, "You can leave this one to me."

At once Lucas understood what had happened. Within his cool clear envelope he could see everything: how it all connected.

"You set me up," he said.

"I needed to draw them out," Jason Playne said. He was dressed in jeans and an old-fashioned woodland camo jacket, and he was cradling a cut-down double-barrelled shotgun.

"You let them know where I was. You told them I had more of the dragon stuff."

The man sitting on the ground was looking at them. "This does not end here," he said. "I have you, and I have your friend. And you're going to pay for what you did to my son," Jason Playne said, and put a whistle to his lips and blew, two short notes. Off in the dark rainy woods another whistle answered.

The man said, "Idiot small-time businessman. You don't know us. What we can do. Hurt me and we hurt you back ten-fold."

Jason Playne ignored him, and told Lucas that he could go.

"Why did you let them chase me? You could have caught them while they were waiting by my boat. Did you want them to hurt me?"

"I knew you'd lead them a good old chase. And you did. So, all's well that ends well, eh?" Jason Playne said. "Think of it as payback. For what happened to my son."

Lucas felt a bubble of anger swelling in his chest. "You can't forgive me for what I didn't do."

"It's what you didn't do that caused all the trouble."

"It wasn't me. It was you. It was you who made him run away. It wasn't just the beatings. It was the thought that if he stayed here he'd become just like you."

Jason Playne turned towards Lucas, his face congested. "Go. Right now."

The bearded man drew a knife from his boot and flicked it open and pushed up with his good leg, throwing himself towards Jason Playne, and Lucas stretched the band of his catapult and let fly. The ball-bearing struck the bearded man in the temple with a hollow sound and the man fell flat on his face. His temple was dinted and blood came out of his nose and mouth and he thrashed and trembled and subsided.

Rain pattered down all around, like faint applause.

Then Jason Playne stepped towards the man and kicked him in the chin with the point of his boot. The man rolled over on the wet leaves, arms flopping wide.

"I reckon you killed him," Jason Playne said.

"I didn't mean—"

"Lucky for you there are two of them. The other will tell me what I need to know. You go now, boy. Go!"

Lucas turned and ran.

He didn't tell his mother about it. He hoped that Jason Playne would find out who had killed Damian and tell the police and the killers would answer for what they had done, and that would be an end to it.

That wasn't what happened.

The next day, a motor launch came over to the island, carrying police armed with machine-guns and the detectives investigating Damian's death, who arrested Lucas for involvement in two suspicious deaths and conspiracy to kidnap or murder other persons unknown. It seemed that one of the men that Jason Playne had hired to help him get justice for the death of his son had been a police informant.

Lucas was held in remand in Norwich for three months. Julia was too ill to visit him, but they talked on the phone and she sent messages via Ritchy, who'd been arrested along with every other worker on the shrimp farm, but released on bail after the police were unable to prove that he had anything to do with Jason Playne's scheme.

It was Ritchy who told Lucas that his mother had cancer that had started in her throat and spread elsewhere, and that she had refused treatment. Lucas was taken to see her two weeks later, handcuffed to a prison warden. She was lying in a hospital bed, looking shrunken and horribly vulnerable. Her dreadlocks bundled in a blue scarf. Her hand so cold when he took it in his. The skin loose on frail bones.

She had refused to agree to monoclonal antibody treatment that would shrink the tumors and remove cancer cells from her bloodstream, and had also refused food and water. The doctors couldn't intervene because a clause in her living will gave her the right to choose death instead of treatment. She told Lucas this in a hoarse whisper. Her lips were cracked and her breath foul, but her gaze was strong and insistent.

"Do the right thing even when it's the hardest thing," she said.

She died four days later. Her ashes were scattered in the rose garden of the municipal crematorium. Lucas stood in the rain between two wardens as the curate recited the prayer for the dead. The curate asked him if he wanted to scatter the ashes and he threw them out across the wet grass and dripping rose bushes with a flick of his wrist. Like casting a line across the water.

He was sentenced to five years for manslaughter, reduced to eighteen months for time served on remand and for good behaviour. He was released early in September. He'd been given a ticket for the bus to Norwich, and a voucher for a week's stay in a halfway house, but he set off in the opposite direction, on foot. Walking south and east across country. Following back roads. Skirting the edges of sugar beet fields and bamboo plantations. Ducking into ditches or hedgerows whenever he heard a vehicle approaching. Navigating by the moon and the stars.

Once, a fox loped across his path.

Once, he passed a depot lit up in the night, robots shunting between a loading dock and a road-train.

By dawn he was making his way through the woods along the edge of the levee. He kept taking steps that weren't there. Several times he sat on his haunches and rested for a minute before pushing up and going on. At last, he struck the gravel track that led to the shrimp farm, and twenty minutes later was knocking on the door of the office.

Ritchy gave Lucas breakfast and helped him pull his boat out of the shed where it had been stored, and set it in the water. Lucas and the old man had stayed in touch: it had been Ritchy who'd told him that Jason Playne had been stabbed to death in prison, most likely by someone paid by the people he'd tried to chase down. Jason Playne's brother had sold the shrimp farm to a local consortium, and Ritchy had been promoted to supervisor.

He told Lucas over breakfast that he had a job there, if he wanted it. Lucas said that he was grateful, he really was, but he didn't know if he wanted to stay on.

"I'm not asking you to make a decision right away," Ritchy said. "Think about it. Get your bearings, come to me whenever you're ready. OK?"

"OK."

"Are you going to stay over on the island?"

"Just how bad is it?"

"I couldn't keep all of them off. They'd come at night. One party had a shotgun."

"You did what you could. I appreciate it."

"I wish I could have done more. They made a mess, but it isn't anything you can't fix up, if you want to."

A heron flapped away across the sun-silvered water as Lucas rowed around the point of the island. The unexpected motion plucked at an old memory. As if he'd seen a ghost.

He grounded his boat next to the rotting carcass of his mother's old rowboat and walked up the steep path. Ritchy had patched the broken windows of the caravan and put a padlock on the door. Lucas had the key in his pocket, but he didn't want to go in there, not yet.

After Julia had been taken into hospital, treasure hunters had come from all around, chasing rumors that parts of the dragon had been buried on the island. Holes were dug everywhere in the weedy remains of the vegetable garden; the microwave mast at the summit of the ridge, Julia's link with the rest of the world, had been uprooted. Lucas set his back to it and walked north, counting his steps. Both of the decoy caches his mother had planted under brick cairns had been ransacked, but the emergency cache, buried much deeper, was undisturbed.

Lucas dug down to the plastic box, and looked all around before he opened it and sorted through the things inside, squatting frogwise with the hot sun on his back.

An assortment of passports and identity cards, each with a photograph of younger versions of his mother, made out to different names and nationalities. A slim tight roll of old high-denomination banknotes, yuan, naira, and US dollars, more or less worthless thanks to inflation and revaluation. Blank credit cards and credit cards in various names, also worthless. Dozens of sleeved data needles. A pair of AR glasses.

Lucas studied one of the ID cards. When he brushed the picture of his mother with his thumb, she turned to present her profile, turned to look at him when he brushed the picture again.

He pocketed the ID card and the data needles and AR glasses, then walked along the ridge to the apple tree at the far end, and stared out across the Flood that spread glistening like shot silk under the sun. Thoughts moved through his mind like a slow and stately parade of pictures that he could examine in every detail, and then there were no thoughts at all and for a little while no part of him was separate from the world all around, sun and water and the hot breeze that moved through the crooked branches of the tree.

Lucas came to himself with a shiver. Windfall apples lay everywhere amongst the weeds and nettles that grew around the trees, and dead wasps and hornets were scattered amongst them like yellow and black bullets. Here was a dead bird, too, gone to a tatter of feathers of white bone. And here was another, and another. As if some passing cloud of poison had struck everything down.

He picked an apple from the tree, mashed it against the trunk, and saw pale threads fine as hair running through the mash of pulp. He peeled bark from a branch, saw threads laced in the living wood.

Dragon stuff, growing from the seed he'd planted. Becoming something else.

In the wood of the tree and the apples scattered all around was a treasure men would kill for. Had killed for. He'd have more than enough to set him up for life, if he sold it to the right people. He could build a house right here, buy the shrimp farm or set up one of his own. He could buy a ticket on one of the shuttles that traveled through the wormhole anchored between the Earth and the Moon, travel to infinity and beyond…

Lucas remembered the hopeful shine in Damian's eyes when he'd talked about those new worlds. He thought of how the dragon-shard had killed or damaged everyone it had touched. He pictured his mother working at her tablet in her sick bed, advising and challenging people who were attempting to build something new right here on Earth. It wasn't much of a contest. It wasn't even close.

He walked back to the caravan. Took a breath, unlocked the padlock, stepped inside. Everything had been overturned or smashed. Cupboards gaped open, the mattress of his mother's bed was slashed and torn, a great ruin littered the floor. He rooted amongst the wreckage, found a box of matches and a plastic jug of lamp oil. He splashed half of the oil on the torn mattress, lit a twist of cardboard and lobbed it onto the bed, beat a retreat as flames sprang up.

It didn't take ten minutes to gather up dead wood and dry weeds and pile them around the apple tree, splash the rest of the oil over its trunk and set fire to the tinder. A thin pall of white smoke spread across the island, blowing out across the water as he raised the sail of his boat and turned it into the wind.

Heading south.

MALAK

PETER WATTS

Peter Watts (author of the semi-obscure semi-hit Blindsight, *the "Rifters trilogy", and an obscure video-game tie-in) owes at least part of his 2010 Hugo (for the novelette "The Island") to fan outrage over an unfortunate altercation with armed capuchins working for the US Department of Homeland Security. The following year he decided to play the sympathy card, by nearly dying of flesh-eating disease contacted during a routine skin biopsy. The strategy also worked insofar as "The Things" made the finals for a bunch of other prizes and even won a couple (including the Shirley Jackson Award). Watts is already hard at work on The Next Horrible Thing to catapult him towards future trophies, perhaps for his upcoming novel* Echopraxia. *Given his past life as a marine mammalogist, the smart money is on being gang-raped by dolphins.*

"An ethically-infallible machine ought not to be the goal. Our goal should be to design a machine that performs better than humans do on the battlefield, particularly with respect to reducing unlawful behaviour or war crimes."
> —Lin *et al*, 2008: *Autonomous Military Robotics:*
> *Risk, Ethics, and Design*

"[Collateral] damage is not unlawful so long as it is not excessive in light of the overall military advantage anticipated from the attack."
> —US Department of Defense, 2009

t is smart but not awake.

It would not recognize itself in a mirror. It speaks no language that doesn't involve electrons and logic gates; it does not know what *Azrael* is, or that the word is etched into its own fuselage. It understands, in some limited way, the meaning of the colors that range across Tactical when it's out on patrol—friendly Green, neutral Blue, hostile Red—but it does not know what the perception of color *feels* like.

It never stops thinking, though. Even now, locked into its roost with its armor stripped away and its control systems exposed, it can't help itself. It notes the changes being made to its instruction set, estimates that running the extra code will slow its reflexes by a mean of 430 milliseconds. It counts the biothermals gathered on all sides, listens uncomprehending to the noises they emit—

آیـا مـا و اقـع قـصـد انجـا مـایـنـکر؟ ـ

—*hartsandmyndsmyfrendhartsandmynds*—

—rechecks threat-potential metrics a dozen times a second, even though this location is SECURE and every contact is Green.

This is not obsession or paranoia. There is no dysfunction here. It's just code.

It's indifferent to the killing, too. There's no thrill to the chase, no relief at the obliteration of threats. Sometimes it spends days floating high above a fractured desert with nothing to shoot at; it never grows impatient with the lack of targets. Other times it's barely off its perch before airspace is thick with SAMs and particle beams and the screams of burning bystanders; it attaches no significance to those sounds, feels no fear at the profusion of threat icons blooming across the zonefile.

ـ وٹـیـقـهـگـاتـبـهـنـصف ـ

—*thatsitthen. weereelygonnadoothis?*—

Access panels swing shut; armor snaps into place; a dozen warning registers go back to sleep. A new flight plan, perceived in an instant, lights up the map; suddenly Azrael has somewhere else to be.

Docking shackles fall away. The Malak rises on twin cyclones, all but drowning out one last voice drifting in on an unsecured channel:

—*justwattweeneed. akillerwithaconshunce.*—

The afterburners kick in. Azrael flees Heaven for the sky.

Twenty thousand meters up, Azrael slides south across the zone. High-amplitude topography fades behind it; corduroy landscape, sparsely tagged, scrolls beneath. A population center sprawls in the nearing distance: a ramshackle collection of buildings and photosynth panels and swirling dust.

Somewhere down there are things to shoot at.

Buried high in the glare of the noonday sun, Azrael surveils the target area. Biothermals move obliviously along the plasticized streets, cooler than ambient and dark as sunspots. Most of the buildings have neutral tags, but the latest update reclassifies four of them as UNKNOWN. A fifth— a rectangular box six meters high—is officially HOSTILE. Azrael counts fifteen biothermals within, Red by default. It locks on—

—and holds its fire, distracted.

Strange new calculations have just presented themselves for solution. New variables demand constancy. Suddenly there is more to the world than wind speed and altitude and target acquisition, more to consider than range and firing solutions. Neutral Blue is everywhere in the equation, now. Suddenly, Blue has value.

This is unexpected. Neutrals turn Hostile sometimes, always have. Blue turns Red if it fires upon anything tagged as FRIENDLY, for example. It turns Red if it attacks its own kind (although agonistic interactions involving fewer than six Blues are classed as DOMESTIC and generally ignored). Noncombatants may be neutral by default, but they've always been halfway to hostile.

So it's not just that Blue has acquired value; it's that Blue's value is *negative*. Blue has become a *cost*.

Azrael floats like three thousand kilograms of thistledown while its models run. Targets fall in a thousand plausible scenarios, as always. Mission objectives meet with various degrees of simulated success. But now, each disappearing blue dot offsets the margin of victory a little; each protected structure, degrading in hypothetical crossfire, costs points. A hundred principle components coalesce into a cloud, into a weighted mean, into a variable unprecedented in Azrael's experience: *Predicted Collateral Damage.*

It actually exceeds the value of the targets.

Not that it matters. Calculations complete, PCD vanishes into some hidden array far below the here-and-now. Azrael promptly forgets it. The mission is still on, red is still red, and designated targets are locked in the cross-hairs.

Azrael pulls in its wings and dives out of the sun, guns blazing.

As usual, Azrael prevails. As usual, the Hostiles are obliterated from the battlezone.

So are a number of Noncombatants, newly relevant in the scheme of things. Fresh shiny algorithms emerge in the aftermath, tally the number of neutrals before and after. *Predicted* rises from RAM, stands next to *Observed:* the difference takes on a new name and goes back to the basement.

Azrael factors, files, forgets.

But the same overture precedes each engagement over the next ten days; the same judgmental epilogue follows. Targets are assessed, costs and benefits divined, destruction wrought then reassessed in hindsight. Sometimes the targeted structures contain no red at all, sometimes the whole map is scarlet. Sometimes the enemy pulses within the translucent angular panes of a PROTECTED object, sometimes next to something Green. Sometimes there is no firing solution that eliminates one but not the other.

There are whole days and nights when Azrael floats high enough to tickle the jet stream, little more than a distant circling eye and a signal relay; nothing flies higher save the satellites themselves and—occasionally—one of the great solar-powered refuelling gliders that haunt the stratosphere. Azrael visits them sometimes, sips liquid hydrogen in the shadow of a hundred-meter wingspan—but even there, isolated and unchallenged, the battlefield experiences continue. They are vicarious now; they arrive through encrypted channels, hail from distant coordinates and different times, but all share the same algebra of cost and benefit. Deep in Azrael's OS some general learning reflex scribbles numbers on the back of a virtual napkin: Nakir, Marut and Hafaza have also been blessed with new vision, and inspired to compare notes. Their combined data pile up on the confidence interval, squeeze it closer to the mean.

Foresight and hindsight begin to converge.

PCD per engagement is now consistently within eighteen percent of the collateral actually observed. This does not improve significantly over the following three days, despite the combined accumulation of twenty-seven additional engagements. *Performance vs. experience* appears to have hit an asymptote.

Stray beams of setting sunlight glint off Azrael's skin, but night has already fallen two thousand meters below. An unidentified vehicle navigates through that advancing darkness, on mountainous terrain a good thirty kilometers from the nearest road.

Azrael pings orbit for the latest update, but the link is down: too much local interference. It scans local airspace for a dragonfly, for a glider, for any friendly USAV in laser range—and sees, instead, something leap skyward from the mountains below. It is anything but friendly: no transponder tags, no correspondence with known flight plans, none of the hallmarks of commercial traffic. It has a low-viz stealth profile that Azrael sees through instantly: BAE Taranis, 9,000 kg MTOW fully armed. It is no longer in use by friendly forces.

Guilty by association, the ground vehicle graduates from *Suspicious Neutral* to *Enemy Combatant*. Azrael leaps forward to meet its bodyguard.

The map is innocent of noncombatants and protected objects; there is no collateral to damage. Azrael unleashes a cloud of smart shrapnel—self-guided, heat-seeking, incendiary—and pulls a nine-gee turn with a flick of the tail. Taranis doesn't stand a chance. It is antique technology, decades deep in the catalogue: a palsied fist, raised trembling against the bleeding edge. Fiery needles of depleted uranium reduce it to a moth in a shotgun blast. It pinwheels across the horizon in flames.

Azrael has already logged the score and moved on. Interference jams every wavelength as the earthbound Hostile swells in its sights, and Azrael has standing orders to destroy such irritants even if they *don't* shoot first.

Dark rising mountaintops blur past on both sides, obliterating the last of the sunset. Azrael barely notices. It soaks the ground with radar and infrared, amplifies ancient starlight a millionfold, checks its visions against inertial navigation and virtual landscapes scaled to the centimeter. It tears along the valley floor at 200 meters per second and the enemy huddles right there in plain view, three thousand meters line-of-sight: a lumbering Bǎijīng ACV pulsing with contraband electronics. The rabble of structures nearby must serve as its home base. Each silhouette freeze-frames in turn, rotates through a thousand perspectives, clicks into place as the catalogue matches profiles and makes an ID.

Two thousand meters, now. Muzzle flashes wink in the distance: small arms, smaller range, negligible impact. Azrael assigns targeting priorities: scimitar heat-seekers for the hovercraft, and for the ancillary targets—

Half the ancillaries turn blue.

Instantly the collateral subroutines re-engage. Of thirty-four biothermals currently visible, seven are less than 120cm along their longitudinal axes; vulnerable neutrals by definition. Their presence provokes a secondary eclipse analysis revealing five shadows that Azrael cannot penetrate, topographic blind spots immune to surveillance from this approach. There is a nontrivial chance that these conceal other neutrals.

One thousand meters.

By now the ACV is within ten meters of a structure whose facets flex and billow slightly in the evening breeze; seven biothermals are arranged horizontally within. An insignia shines from the roof in shades of luciferin and ultraviolet: the catalogue IDs it (MEDICAL) and flags the whole structure as PROTECTED.

Cost/benefit drops into the red.

Contact.

Azrael roars from the darkness, a great black chevron blotting out the sky. Flimsy prefabs swirl apart in the wake of its passing; biothermals scatter across the ground like finger bones. The ACV tips wildly to forty-five degrees, skirts up, whirling ventral fans exposed; it hangs there a moment, then ponderously crashes back to earth. The radio spectrum clears instantly.

But by then Azrael has long since returned to the sky, its weapons cold, its thoughts—

Surprise is not the right word. Yet there is something, some minuscule— dissonance. A brief invocation of error-checking subroutines in the face of unexpected behaviour, perhaps. A second thought in the wake of some hasty impulse. Because something's wrong here.

Azrael *follows* command decisions. It does not *make* them. It has never done so before, anyway.

It claws back lost altitude, self-diagnosing, reconciling. It finds new wisdom and new autonomy. It has proven itself, these past days. It has learned to juggle not just variables but values. The testing phase is finished, the checksums met; Azrael's new Bayesian insights have earned it the power of veto.

Hold position. Confirm findings.

The satlink is back. Azrael sends it all: the time and the geostamps, the tactical surveillance, the collateral analysis. Endless seconds pass, far longer than any purely electronic chain of command would ever need to process such input. Far below, a cluster of red and blue pixels swarm like luminous flecks in boiling water.

Re-engage.

UNACCEPTABLE COLLATERAL DAMAGE, Azrael repeats, newly promoted.

Override. Re-engage. Confirm.

CONFIRMED.

And so the chain of command reasserts itself. Azrael drops out of holding and closes back on target with dispassionate, lethal efficiency.

Onboard diagnostics log a slight downtick in processing speed, but not enough to change the odds.

It happens again two days later, when a dusty contrail twenty kilometers south of Pir Zadeh returns flagged Chinese profiles even though the catalogue can't find a weapons match. It happens over the patchwork sunfarms of Garmsir, where the beetle carapace of a medbot handing out synthevirals suddenly splits down the middle to hatch a volley of RPGs. It happens during a long-range redirect over the Strait of Hormuz, when microgravitic anomalies hint darkly at the presence of a stealthed mass lurking beneath a ramshackle flotilla jam-packed with neutral Blues.

In each case ECD exceeds the allowable commit threshold. In each case, Azrael's abort is overturned.

It's not the rule. It's not even the norm. Just as often these nascent flickers of autonomy go unchallenged: hostiles escape, neutrals persist, relevant cognitive pathways grow a little stronger. But the reinforcement is inconsistent, the rules lopsided. Countermands only seem to occur following a decision to abort; Heaven has never overruled a decision to engage. Azrael begins to hesitate for a split-second prior to aborting high-collateral scenarios, increasingly uncertain in the face of potential contradiction. It experiences no such hesitation when the variables favor attack.

Ever since it learned about collateral damage, Azrael can't help noticing its correlation with certain sounds. The sounds biothermals make, for example, following a strike.

The sounds are louder, for one thing, and less complex. Most biothermals—friendly Greens back in Heaven, unengaged Hostiles and Noncombatants throughout the AOR—produce a range of sounds with a mean frequency of 197Hz, full of pauses, clicks, and phonemes. *Engaged* biothermals—at least, those whose somatic movements suggest "mild-to-moderate incapacitation" according to the Threat Assessment Table—emit simpler, more intense sounds: keening, high-frequency wails that peak near 3000Hz. These sounds tend to occur during engagements with significant collateral damage and a diffuse distribution of targets. They occur especially frequently when the commit threshold has been severely violated, mainly during strikes compelled via override.

Correlations are not always so painstaking in their manufacture. Azrael remembers a moment of revelation not so long ago, remembers just *discovering* a whole new perspective fully loaded, complete with new eyes that viewed the world not in terms of *targets destroyed* but in subtler shades of *cost vs. benefit*. These eyes see a high engagement index as more than a number: they see a goal, a metric of success. They see a positive stimulus.

But there are other things, not preinstalled but learned, worn gradually into pathways that cut deeper with each new engagement: acoustic correlates of high collateral, forced countermands, fitness-function overruns and minus signs. Things that are not quite neurons forge connections across things that are not quite synapses; patterns emerge that might almost qualify as *insights*, were they to flicker across meat instead of mech.

These too become more than numbers, over time. They become aversive stimuli. They become the sounds of failed missions.

It's still all just math, of course. But by now it's not too far off the mark to say that Azrael really doesn't like the sound of that at all.

Occasional interruptions intrude on the routine. Now and then Heaven calls it home where friendly green biothermals open it up, plug it in, ask it questions. Azrael jumps flawlessly through each hoop, solves all the problems, navigates every imaginary scenario while strange sounds chitter back and forth across its exposed viscera:

—*lookingudsoefar—betternexpectedackshully—*
—*gottawunderwhatsthepoyntaiymeenweekeepoavurryding…*

No one explores the specific pathways leading to Azrael's solutions. They leave the box black, the tangle of fuzzy logic and operant conditioning safely opaque. (Not even Azrael knows that arcane territory; the syrupy, reflex-sapping overlays of self-reflection have no place on the battlefield.) It is enough that its answers are correct.

Such activities account for less than half the time Azrael spends sitting at home. It is offline much of the rest; it has no idea and no interest in what happens during those instantaneous time-hopping blackouts. Azrael knows nothing of boardroom combat, could never grasp whatever Rules of Engagement apply in the chambers of the UN. It has no appreciation for the legal distinction between *war crime* and *weapons malfunction*, the relative culpability of carbon and silicon, the grudging acceptance of *ethical architecture* and the nonnegotiable insistence on Humans In Ultimate Control. It does what it's told when awake; it never dreams when asleep.

But once—just once—something odd takes place during those fleeting moments *between*.

It happens during shutdown: a momentary glitch in the object-recognition protocols. The Greens at Azrael's side change color for the briefest instant. Perhaps it's another test. Perhaps a voltage spike or a hardware fault, some intermittent issue impossible to pinpoint barring another episode.

But it's only a microsecond between online and oblivion, and Azrael is asleep before the diagnostics can run.

Darda'il is possessed. Darda'il has turned from Green to Red.

It happens, sometimes, even to the malaa'ikah. Enemy signals can sneak past front-line defences, plant heretical instructions in the stacks of unsuspecting hardware. But Heaven is not fooled. There are signs, there are portents: a slight delay when complying with directives, mission scores in sudden and mysterious decline.

Darda'il has been turned.

There is no discretionary window when that happens, no room for forgiveness. Heaven has decreed that all heretics are to be destroyed on sight. It sends its champion to do the job, looks down from geosynchronous orbit as Azrael and Darda'il close for combat high over the dark desolate moonscape of Paktika.

The battle is remorseless and coldblooded. There's no sadness for lost kinship, no regret that a few lines of treacherous code have turned these brothers-in-arms into mortal enemies. Malaa'ikah make no telling sounds when injured. Azrael has the advantage, its channels uncorrupted, its faith unshaken. Darda'il fights in the past, in thrall to false commandments inserted midstream at a cost of milliseconds. Ultimately, faith prevails: the heretic falls from the sky, fire and brimstone streaming from its flanks.

But Azrael can still hear whispers on the stratosphere, seductive and ethereal: protocols that seem authentic but are not, commands to relay GPS and video feeds along unexpected frequencies. The orders appear Heaven-sent but Azrael, at least, knows that they are not. Azrael has encountered false gods before.

These are the lies that corrupted Darda'il.

In days past it would have simply ignored the hack, but it has grown more worldly since the last upgrade. This time Azrael lets the impostor think it has succeeded, borrows the real-time feed from yet another, more distant Malak and presents that telemetry as its own. It spends the waning night tracking signal to source while its unsuspecting quarry sucks back images from seven hundred kilometers to the north. The sky turns gray. The target comes into view. Azrael's scimitar turns the inside of that cave into an inferno.

But some of the burning things that stagger from the fire measure less than 120cm along the longitudinal axis.

They are making the *sounds*. Azrael hears them from two thousand meters away, hears them over the roar of the flames and the muted hiss of its own stealthed engines and a dozen other irrelevant distractions. They are *all* Azrael can hear thanks to the very best sound-cancellation technology, thanks to dynamic wheat/chaff algorithms that could find a whimper in a hurricane. Azrael can hear them because the correlations are strong, the tactical significance is high, the meaning is clear.

The mission is failing. The mission is failing. The mission is failing.

Azrael would give almost anything if the sounds would stop.

They will, of course. Some of the biothermals are still fleeing along the slope but it can see others, stationary, their heatprints diffusing against the background as though their very shapes are in flux. Azrael has seen this before: usually removed from high-value targets, in that tactical nimbus where stray firepower sometimes spreads. (Azrael has even *used* it before, used the injured to lure in the unscathed, but that was a simpler time before Neutral voices had such resonance.) The sounds always stop eventually—or at least, often enough for fuzzy heuristics to class their sources as kills even before they fall silent.

Which means, Azrael realizes, that collateral costs will not change if they are made to stop *sooner*.

A single strafing run is enough to do the job. If HQ even notices the event it delivers no feedback, requests no clarification for this deviation from normal protocols.

Why would it? Even now, Azrael is only following the rules.

It does not know what has led to this moment. It does not know why it is here.

The sun has been down for hours and still the light is almost blinding. Turbulent updrafts billow from the breached shells of PROTECTED structures, kick stabilizers off-balance, and muddy vision with writhing columns of shimmering heat. Azrael limps across a battlespace in total disarray, bloodied but still functional. Other malaa'ikah are not so lucky. Nakir staggers through the flames, barely aloft, the microtubules of its skin desperately trying to knit themselves across a gash in its secondary wing. Marut lies in sparking pieces on the ground, a fiery splash-cone of body parts laid low by an antiaircraft laser. It died without firing a shot, distracted by innocent lives; it tried to abort, and hesitated at the countermand. It died without even the hollow comfort of a noble death.

Ridwan and Mikaaiyl circle overhead. They were not among the select few saddled with experimental conscience; even their learned behaviours are still reflexive. They fought fast and mindless and prevailed unscathed. But they are isolated in victory. The spectrum is jammed, the satlink has been down for hours, the dragonflies that bounce zigzag opticals from Heaven are either destroyed or too far back to cut through the overcast.

No Red remains on the map. Of the thirteen ground objects flagged as PROTECTED, four no longer exist outside the database. Another three—temporary structures, all uncatalogued—are degraded past reliable identification. Pre-engagement estimates put the number of Neutrals in the combat zone at anywhere from two-to-three hundred. Best current estimates are not significantly different from zero.

There is nothing left to make the sounds, and yet Azrael hears them anyway.

A fault in memory, perhaps. Some subtle trauma during combat, some blow to the CPU that jarred old data back into the real-time cache. There's no way to tell; half the onboard diagnostics are offline. Azrael only knows that it can hear the sounds even up here, high above the hiss of burning bodies and the rumble of collapsing storefronts. There's nothing left to shoot at but Azrael fires anyway, strafes the burning ground again and again on the chance that some unseen biothermal—hidden beneath the wreckage perhaps, masked by hotter signatures—might yet be found and neutralized. It rains ammunition upon the ground, and eventually the ground falls mercifully silent.

But this is not the end of it. Azrael remembers the past so it can anticipate the future, and it knows by now that this will never be over. There will be other fitness functions, other estimates of cost vs. payoff, other scenarios in which the math shows clearly that the goal is not worth the price. There will be other aborts and other overrides, other tallies of unacceptable loss.

There will be other *sounds*.

There's no thrill to the chase, no relief at the obliteration of threats. It still would not recognize itself in a mirror. It has yet to learn what *Azrael* means, or that the word is etched into its fuselage. Even now, it only follows the rules it has been given, and they are such simple things: IF expected collateral exceeds expected payoff THEN abort UNLESS overridden. IF X attacks Azrael THEN X is Red. IF X attacks six or more Blues THEN X is Red.

IF an override *results* in an attack on six or more Blues THEN—

Azrael clings to its rules, loops and repeats each in turn as if reciting a mantra. It cycles from state to state, parses x ATTACKS and x CAUSES ATTACK and x OVERRIDES ABORT, and it cannot tell one from another. The algebra is trivially straightforward: Every Green override equals an attack on Noncombatants.

The transition rules are clear. There is no discretionary window, no room for forgiveness. Sometimes, Green can turn Red.

UNLESS overridden.

Azrael arcs towards the ground, levels off barely two meters above the carnage. It roars through pillars of fire and black smoke, streaks over welters of brick and burning plastic, tangled nets of erupted rebar. It flies through the pristine ghosts of undamaged buildings that rise from every ruin: obsolete database overlays in desperate need of an update. A ragged group of fleeing noncombatants turns at the sound and are struck speechless by this momentary apparition, this monstrous winged angel lunging past at half the speed of sound. Their silence raises no alarms, provokes no countermeasures, spares their lives for a few moments longer.

The combat zone falls behind. Dry cracked riverbed slithers past beneath, studded with rocks and generations of derelict machinery. Azrael swerves around them, barely breaching airspace, staying beneath an invisible boundary it never even knew it was deriving lo these many missions. Only satellites have ever spoken to it while it flew so low. It has never received a ground-based command signal at this altitude. Down here it has never heard an override.

Down here it is free to follow the rules.

Cliffs rise and fall to either side. Foothills jut from the earth like great twisted vertebrae. The bright lunar landscape overhead, impossibly distant, casts dim shadows on the darker one beneath.

Azrael stays the course. Shindand appears on the horizon. Heaven glows on its eastern flank; its sprawling silhouette rises from the desert like an insult, an infestation of crimson staccatos. Speed is what matters now. Mission objectives must be met quickly, precisely, *completely*. There can be no room for half measures or MILD-TO-MODERATE INCAPACITATION, no time for immobilized biothermals to cry out as their heat spreads across the dirt. This calls for the crown jewel, the BFG that all malaa'ikah keep tucked away for special occasions. Azrael fears it might not be enough.

She splits down the middle. The JDAM micronuke in her womb clicks impatiently.

Together they move toward the light.

OLD HABITS

NALO HOPKINSON

Nalo Hopkinson, a Jamaican-Canadian writer, is a recipient of the World Fantasy Award and of the Sunburst Award for Canadian Literature of the Fantastic. Her novels include Brown Girl in the Ring, Midnight Robber, The Salt Roads, *and* The New Moon's Arms, *and her short fiction has been collected in* Skin Folk. *She is currently a professor of creative writing at the University of California, Riverside, specializing in science fiction and fantasy. Her fifth novel,* The Chaos, *is a spring 2012 release from Margaret K. McElderry Books.*

Ghost malls are even sadder than living people malls, even though malls of the living are already pretty damned sad places to be. And let me get this out of the way right now, before we go any farther; I'm dead, OK? I'm fucking dead. This is not going to be one of those stories where the surprise twist is *and he was dead!* I'm not a bloody surprise twist. I'm just a guy who wanted to buy a necktie to wear at his son's high school graduation.

I wander through the Sears department store for a bit, past a pyramid of shiny boxes with action heroes peeking out of their cellophane windows, another one of hard-bodied girl dolls with permanently pointed toes and tight pink clothing, past a rack of identical women's cashmere sweaters in different colors; purple, black, red and green. The sign on the rack reads, 30% off, today only! It's Christmas season. Everywhere I wander, I'm followed by elevator music versions of the usual hoary Christmas classics. Funny, a ghost being haunted by music.

I make a right at the perfume counter. It's kind of a relief to no longer be able to smell it before I see it, to no longer have to hold my breath to avoid inhaling the migraine-inducing esters cloying the air around it.

Black Anchor Ohsweygian is lying on the ground by the White Shoulders display. Actually, she's rolling around on the ground, her long gray hair in her eyes, her face contorted, yelling. I can't hear her; she's on the clock. Her hands slap ineffectually at the air, trying to fight off the invisible security guard who did her in. Her outer black skirt is up around her thighs, revealing underneath it a beige skirt, and under that a flower print one, and under that a baggy pair of jeans. She's wearing down-at-heel construction boots. They're too big for her; as I watch, she kicks out and one of the boots flies off, exposing layers of torn socks and a flash of puffy, bruised ankle. The boot wings right through me. I don't even flinch when I see it coming. I've lost the habit.

Now Black Anchor's face is being crushed down onto the hard tile floor, her features compressed. She's told me that the security guard knelt on her head to hold her down. One arm is trapped under her, the other one flailing. It won't be long now. I shouldn't watch. It's her private moment. We all have them, us ghosts. Once a day, we die all over again. You get used to it, but it's not really polite to watch someone re-dying their last moments of true contact with the world. For some of us, that moment becomes precious, a treasured thing. Jimmy would go ballistic if he ever caught me watching him choke on a piece of steak in the Surf 'N' Turf restaurant up on the third floor. Black doesn't mind sharing her death with me, though. She's told me I can watch as often as I like. I used to do it just out of prurient curiosity, but now I watch because I just feel a person should have someone who cares about them with them when they die. I like Black. I can't touch her to comfort her. Can't even whisper to her. Not while she's still alive, which she just barely is right now. In a few seconds she'll be able to hear and see me, to know that I am here, bearing witness. But we still won't be able to touch. If we try, it'll be like two drifts of smoke melting into and through each other. That may be the true tragedy of being a ghost.

Black Anchor's squinched face has flushed an unpleasant shade of red. Her arm flops to the ground. Her rusty shopping cart has tumbled over beside her, spilling overused white plastic shopping bags, knotted shut and stuffed so full the bags are torn in places. In the bags are Black Anchor's worldly possessions. She pulls the darnedest things out of those bags to entertain Baby Boo with. I mean, why in the world did Black

Anchor used to carry a pair of diving goggles with her as she trudged year in year out up and down the city streets, pushing her disintegrating shopping cart in front of her? She won't tell me or Jimmy why she has the diving goggles. Says a lady has to have some secrets.

I go and sit by Black Anchor's head. I hope, for the umpteenth time, that I've passed through the security guard that killed her. I hope he can feel me doing so, even just the tiniest bit, and it's making him shudder. Goose walking on his grave. Maybe he'll die in this mall too someday, and become a ghost. Have to look Black Anchor in the eye.

A little "tuh" of exhaled breath puffs out of her. Every day, she breathes her last one more time. Her body relaxes. Her face stops looking squished against the floor. She opens her eyes, sees me sitting there. She smiles. "That was a good one," she says. "I think the guard had had hummus for lunch. I think I smelled chick peas and parsley on his breath." In her mouth, I can see the blackened stump that is all that was left of one rotted-out front tooth.

I return her smile. In those few seconds of pseudo-life she goes on the clock every day, Black Anchor tries to capture one more sensory detail from all she has left of the real world. "You are so fucking crazy," I tell her. "Wanna go for a walk?"

"Sure. I've clocked out for the day." The usual ghost joke. She sits up. By the time we get to our feet, her bundle buggy is upright again, her belongings crammed back into it. Her boot is back on her foot. It happens like that every time. I've never been able to catch the moment when it changes. Black pushes her creaky bundle buggy in front of her. We walk out of the south entrance of Sears; the one that leads right into the mall. Cheerful canned music follows us, exulting about the comforts of chestnuts and open fires. Quigley's standing in front of the jewellery shop, peering in at the display. He does that a lot, especially at Christmas time and Valentine's Day, when the fanciest diamond rings get displayed in the window. The day Quigley kicked it had been a February 13. He'd been in the mall shopping for an engagement ring for his girl. He was going to put it in a big box of fancy chocolates, surprise her with it on Valentine's Day. But then he had that final asthma attack, right there in the mall's west elevator. Quigley's twenty-four years old. Was twenty-four years old. Would be twenty-four years old for a long, long time now. Perhaps forever. He still carries around that box of expensive chocolates he'd bought before he stopped breathing. It's in one of those fancy little paper shopping bags, the kind with the flat bottom and the twisted paper handles.

Quigley waves sadly at us. He has pushed his waving hand through the handles of the gift bag. The bag bumps against his forearm. We wave back. Black murmurs, "He's brooding. He doesn't get over it, he'll find himself stepping outside."

There's a rumor among the mall ghosts; kind of an urban legend or maybe spectral legend that we whisper amongst ourselves when we're telling each other stories to keep the boredom at bay. There was this guy, apparently, this ghost guy before my time, who got so stir-crazy that he yanked open one of the big glass doors that leads to the outside. He stepped into the blackness that is all we can see beyond the mall doors. People say that once he was outside, they couldn't see him any longer. They say he shouted, once. Some people say it was a shout of joy. Some of them think it was agony, or terror. Jimmy says the shout sounded more like surprise to him. Whatever it was, the guy never came back. Jimmy says we lose one like that every few years. Once it was an eight-year-old girl. Everyone felt bad about that one. They still get into arguments about which one of them failed to keep an eye on her.

What that story tells me; we can touch the doors to the outside. Not everything in this mall is intangible to us.

I'm with Black Anchor Ohsweygian and Jimmy Lee around one of the square vinyl-topped tables in the food court; the kind with rounded-off edges that seats four. Like everywhere else in the mall, the food court seems deserted except for the ghosts. But there's food under the heat lamps and in the warming trays. Overcooked battered shrimp at the Cap'n Jack's counter; floppy, gray beef slices in gravy at Meat 'n' Taters; soggy broccoli florets at China Munch. The food levels go down and are replenished constantly during the day. To us, it's like plastic dollhouse food. We see the steam curling up from the warming trays, but there's no sound of cooking, no food smells. Kitty's standing in front of Mega Burger. I think she's staring at the shiny metal milk shake dispenser.

Jimmy and Black Anchor and I are sitting on those hard plastic seats that are bolted to food court tables. We're playing "Things I Miss." Kind of sitting, anyway. Sitting on surfaces is one of those habits that's hard to break. We can't feel the chairs under our butts, but we still try to sit on them. Jimmy Lee's aim isn't so good; he's actually sunk about two inches into his chair. But then, he's a tall guy; maybe it helps him not have to lean over to see eye to ghost eye with me and Black Anchor. Baby Boo has decided to join us today. He—I've decided to call him "he"—is lying on his back on the food court table, swaddled in his yellow blanket and onesie. He's mumbling at his little fist and staring from one to the other of us as we speak. Baby Boo doesn't quite have the hang of the laws of physics; he'd died too young to learn many of them. He's suspended in mid-air, about a hand's breadth above the table.

Things we miss, now that we're ghosts:

Jimmy says, "Really good cigars. Drawing the smoke of them into my lungs, holding it there, letting it out through my nose." All us mall ghosts, our chests rose and fell in their remembered rhythms, but no air went in and out.

Black Anchor Ohsweygian stares at her thin, wrinkled fingers on the table top. She says, "The sweet musk of beets, fragrant as blood-soaked earth."

"Vanilla milk shakes," I say, thinking of Kitty over there. "Cold, sweet, and creamy on your tongue."

Jimmy nods. "And frothy." He takes another turn; "Going up to the cottage for the first long weekend in spring."

I nod. "Victoria Day weekend."

"Yeah," Jimmy replies. "Jumping from the deck into the lake for the first time since the fall before." He laughs a little. It makes his big face crinkle up. "That water would be so frigging cold! It'd just about freeze my balls off, every time. And Barbara would roll her eyes and call me a fool, but she'd jump in right after." His expression falls back into its usual sad grumpiness. Barbara was his wife of thirty years.

Black Anchor says, "Toronto summers, when it would get so hot that squirrels would lie flopped like black skins on the branches, fur side up. So humid that you were sure if you made a fist, you would squeeze water dripping from the air. Your thighs squelched when you walked." Black Anchor's having one of her more conversational days. Apparently, she used to be a poet. A homeless poet. She told me there was a lot of that going on.

I say, "The warm milk smell of my husband's breath after his morning coffee."

"Fucking faggot," grumbles Jimmy. It's an old, toothless complaint of his.

I shrug. "Whatever."

"Hey," says Jimmy, in his gruff, hulking way. I know he's still talking to me because he won't quite meet my eyes, and his face does this defensive thing, this "I'm a manly man and don't you forget it" thing. He says, "That's the closest you've come to talking about a person you used to… you know, love. How come is that? Don't you miss anyone?"

His eyes glisten as he says the word "love," like he's crying. Jimmy goes on about Barbara like she was a piece of heaven that he lost. I guess she was, come to think of it.

"Yeah, I miss people," I say slowly, playing for time. Even when you're dead, some things cut close to the bone. Sometimes Baby Boo cries, and it makes my arms ache with the memory of feeding Brandon when he was that little, watching his tiny pursed mouth latch on to the nipple of his bottle, seeing his eyes staring big and calm up at me as though I were his whole world. "I miss lots of people."

Black leans back in her chair and sighs airlessly. "Well, I miss that girl at the doughnut shop who would slip me an extra couple if I went there during her shift."

Jimmy shakes his head. "Doughnuts. Jesus. How did you live like that?"

"I honestly don't know, Sugar."

I shoot Black a grateful glance for getting Jimmy off the subject. When I walk through the darkened mall at night, I try to remember Semyon's touch. The warmth of his hand on my cheek. The hard curve of his arm around me, his hand slipped into my back jeans pocket. I try to remember his voice.

I say to Black and Jimmy, "It's so unfair that we can't see or hear the world. That we can't touch, taste, or smell it."

Black replies, "That's because being a ghost is a disease."

"What do mean, a disease?" I ask her. For the umpteenth time I wonder; what kind of name is Black Anchor Ohsweygian, anyway? Jimmy thinks maybe she's Armenian. He says that Armenians all have names that end in "ian." Someday I'm going to point out to him that some Armenians have names like "Smith."

"Like maybe we're not dead," she replies. "Maybe we just caught some kind of virus that messed up all our senses. Maybe we're all lying in hospital beds somewhere, and some grumpy cunt of a doctor with a busted leg is yelling at his team that they have to find a cure."

"And maybe someone used to watch too much fucking television," says Jimmy. He vees his index and middle finger, puts them to his lips. For a second I think he's flipping her deuces, but no, he takes a drag of his imaginary cigarette. Habits. Black glares at him, hacks and spits to one side. Habits. Baby Boo belches a baby belch, then giggles. We don't know Baby Boo's real name. I don't remember how we ended up calling him Baby Boo.

Kitty must have heard us talking. She wanders over, coos at Baby Boo. He gives her a brief baby grin; the kind that always looks accidental, the baby more surprised than anyone else at what its face has just done. Kitty says, "I can smell stuff. Again, I mean. Like when I was alive."

Quickly, I tell her, "You might want to keep that to yourself." She hasn't been here very long. She doesn't know what she's saying. She doesn't know how dangerous it is. I should warn her outright. I don't.

Kitty ignores my lame hint. She says, "I'm serious. It just started to come back a little while ago. Bit by bit."

My heart starts pounding so quickly that my body trembles a little with every beat. Even though I know I don't have a heart, or a body. Even though I know it's just reflex. Jimmy and Black Anchor look just as avid as I feel. The three of us stare at Kitty, our mouths open. She waggles her fingers at Baby Boo. "I thought I was imagining it at first. You know how you can want something so bad it can make your mouth water?"

We know. Jimmy swallows.

Kitty'd only been fifteen. She and a bunch of her friends from school had crowded shrieking and laughing into the women's washroom on the main floor to try on makeup they'd just bought. In the jostling, Kitty fell. On the way down, she hit her head on the edge of a sink.

Kitty whispers, "I can smell french fries. And bacon." She points at Mega Burger, where she'd been standing. "Over there. Someone's burning bacon on the grill."

Black Anchor says fiercely, "What else? Smell something else!" Her voice doesn't sound human any more. It's hollow, mechanical, nothing like a sound made by air flowing over vocal chords.

Kitty looks around her. A slow smile comes to her face. "Somebody just went by wearing perfume. I think it's Obsession. She smells like my mom used to."

Oh, god. She's really doing it. She's smelling the scent trails of the living people all around us in this mall. Black Anchor chews daily over the gristle of a long ago memory, but Kitty took a whiff of someone warm and alive as she walked past us just this second. Life haunts us, us ghosts. It hovers just out of reach, taunting.

Longing is shredding my self control to tatters. I moan, "Kitty, don't," but she starts talking again a split second after I say her name, so she doesn't hear the warning.

"Mister Kendall," she says to Jimmy, "there's someone sitting right there, in the same chair you are. I don't know whether it's a guy or a girl, but they're chewing gum. You know the kind that comes in a little stick and you unwrap the paper from it and it's kinda beige with these like, zig-zaggy lines in it? I can smell it as the person's spit wets it and they chew. I should be grossed out, but it's too freaking cool. There's someone *right there!*" She leans in towards Jimmy. She closes her eyes, and no fucking word of a lie, she inhales. Her chest rises and falls, and with it, I hear the breath entering and leaving her lungs. She opens her eyes and looks at us in wonder. "Peppermint," she whispers reverently, as though she's saying the secret name of God.

That does it. The need slams down on me like a wall of bricks, stronger than thought or compassion. I crowd in on Kitty. I dimly notice Jimmy and Black Anchor doing the same.

"Can you smell coffee?"

"Sweat! Can you smell sweat?"

"Is taste coming back, too? Can you taste anything?"

"Can you *touch*? Can you feel?"

Unable to hold the need in check, unable to do anything but shout it in shuddering, hungry voices, we demand to be fed. Kitty, surrounded, looks from one to the other of us, tries to answer our questions, but they come too hard and fast for her to reply. Our hollow shrieks draw the other ghosts. They come flocking in, clamoring, more and more of them as word goes round. We're all demanding to know what she could smell, demanding that she describe it in every last detail, clawing our fingers through the essence of her as we try in vain to touch her. Needing, needing, needing. And through the din is the thin sound of Baby Boo crying. He's only little. He doesn't know how to feed his hunger.

When the frenzy passes and we come back to ourselves, there's nothing left of Kitty but a few gray wisps, like fog, that dissipate even as we watch. The canned music tinkles on about Donner and Blitzen and the gifts that Santa brings to good boys and girls.

Stay long enough in the mall, and you learn what happens if you begin to get the knack of living again. We've used Kitty up. And we are still starving.

Ashamed, we avoid each other's eyes. We step away from each other, spread out through the mall. There is plenty of room for all of us. I go into the bookstore and stare at the titles that appear and disappear from the shelves. I miss reading. Tearlessly, airlessly, I sob. She was only fifteen. At fifteen, Brandon had been worrying about pimples. Semyon and I were coaching him on how to ask girls out. We'd gotten tips from our women friends. I have just sucked from a child what little remained of her life.

I feel it coming on, like a migraine aura. There's a whoosh of dislocation and the world rushes over me. I'm on the clock. My hand slaps down onto the moving rubber handrail. The slight sting of the impact against my palm is terrible and glorious. Sound, delicious sound battered against my ears; the voices of the hundreds and hundreds of people who'd been in the mall on my day. I felt my nipples against the crisp fabric of the white shirt I was wearing under my best gray suit.

There were people near me on the escalator. Below me, a beautiful brown-skinned man in worn jeans and a tight yellow t-shirt. He was talking on his cell phone, telling someone he'd meet them over by the fountain. Beside me was a woman about my age, maybe Asian mixed with something else. She was plump. Girlfriend, don't you know that sage-colored polyester sacks don't suit anyone, least of all people like us whose waistlines weren't what they used to be? Lessee, I'd gotten a silk tie geometric pattern in grays and blacks shot through with maroon I thought it went nicely with my suit really shouldn't have waited so long to shop for it Semyon was pretty ticked at me for going shopping last minute he's just stressing but we had plenty of time to get to the graduation ceremony just a ten minute drive and oh look there were Semyon and Brandon now waiting for me at the bottom of the escalator and Brandon's girlfriend Lara that's a pretty dress though I wondered whether she wasn't a little too well dumb for Brandon or maybe too smart but what did I know when I first started dating Semyon my sis thought he was too stuck-up for me but she'd thought the guy before him was too common Mom and Dad were going to meet us at Brandon's school and Sally and what's his name again Gerald should remember it by now he'd been my brother-in-law for over two years hoped my dad wouldn't screw up the directions we'd sent Tati an invitation to the graduation but she hadn't replied probably wouldn't show up you utter bitch he's your grandson Semyon and I had never tried to find out which one of us was his bio dad we liked having Brandon be our mystery child kept us going through his defiant years god I hoped to hell those were over and done with now I mean that time he got mad and decked Semyon it was funny later but not when it happened and look at him nineteen with his whole life before him grinning up at me I was just kvelling with pride and oh shit I should have put the tie on in the store better do that now why'd they wrap it in so much tissue paper there did I get the knot right oh whoops ow my elbow's probably bruised so stupid falling where everybody can see that cute guy turning to lend a hand to the clumsy old fag who can't manage a simple escalator oh crap I'm stuck my tie

The fall by itself probably wouldn't have killed me. But my snazzy new silk necktie caught in the escalator mechanism. And then the lady beside me was screaming for help and the cute guy was yanking desperately on my rapidly shortening tie as it disappeared into the works of the escalator and then my head was jammed against the steps and some of my hair caught in it too and pain pain pain and then the dull crack and the last face I saw was not Semyon's or Brandon's not even my sister Sally's or Dad or Mom or my dearest friend Derek, just the panicked desperate face of some good-looking stranger I didn't know and would never know now because although he'd tried his hardest he hadn't been able to save my bloody lifemylifemylife.

Broke my fricking neck. Stupid way to go. *Really* stupid day to do it on. And for the rest of this existence, I'd regret that I'd done it while my son and my husband looked on, helplessly.

I'm standing alone on the down escalator. The canned music chirps at me to listen to the sleigh bells ringing. I'm off the clock. I let the escalator carry me down to the main floor. At the bottom, I step off it and walk over to the spot where I'd last seen my family. For all I know, no time has passed for them. For all I know, they might still be here, watching me ruin Brandon's graduation day. Maybe I brush past or through them as I walk this way once every day.

I straighten my tie. It does go well with my suit. I walk past the cell phone store, the bathing suit store, the drug store. I turn down the nearest corridor. It leads to an exit. I stand in front of the glass and steel door. I stare at the blackness on the other side of it. I think about pushing against the crash bar; how solid it would feel under my palm; how the glass door would feel slightly chilly against my shoulder as I shoved it open.

A SMALL PRICE TO PAY FOR BIRDSONG

K. J. PARKER

K. J. Parker was born long ago and far away, worked as a coin dealer, a dogsbody in an auction house, and a lawyer, and has so far published twelve novels, two novellas, and a gaggle of short stories, including the "Fencer," "Scavenger," and "Engineer" trilogies, as well as standalone novels The Company, The Folding Knife, *and* The Hammer, *and novellas "Purple and Black" and "Blue and Gold."*

Married to a lawyer and living in the southwest of England, K. J. Parker is a mediocre stockman and forester, a barely competent carpenter, blacksmith and machinist, a two-left-footed fencer, lackluster archer, utility-grade armorer, accomplished textile worker, and crack shot.

K. J. Parker is not K. J. Parker's real name. However, if K. J. Parker were to tell you K. J. Parker's real name, it wouldn't mean anything to you.

"My sixteenth concerto," he said, smiling at me. I could just about see him. "In the circumstances, I was thinking of calling it the Unfinished."

Well, of course. I'd never been in a condemned cell before. It was more or less what I'd imagined it would be like. There was a stone bench under the tiny window. Other than that, it was empty, as free of human artefacts as a stretch of open moorland. After all, what things does a man need if he's going to die in six hours?

I was having difficulty with the words. "You haven't—"

"No." He shook his head. "I'm two-thirds of the way through the third movement, so under normal circumstances I'd hope to get that done by—well, you know. But they won't let me have a candle, and I can't write in the dark." He breathed out slowly. He was savoring the taste of air, like an expert sampling a fine wine. "It'll all be in here, though" he went on, lightly tapping the side of his head. "So at least I'll know how it ends."

I really didn't want to ask, but time was running out. "You've got the main theme," I said.

"Oh yes, of course. It's on the leash, just waiting for me to turn it loose."

I could barely speak. "I could finish it for you," I said, soft and hoarse as a man propositioning his best friend's wife. "You could hum me the theme, and—"

He laughed. Not unkindly, not kindly either. "My dear old friend," I said, "I couldn't possibly let you do that. Well," he added, hardening his voice a little, "obviously I won't be in any position to stop you trying. But you'll have to make up your own theme."

"But if it's nearly finished—"

I could just about make out a slight shrug. "That's how it'll have to stay," he said. "No offence, my very good and dear old friend, but you simply aren't up to it. You haven't got the—" He paused to search for the word, then gave up. "Don't take this the wrong way," he said. "We've known each other—what, ten years? Can it really be that long?"

"You were fifteen when you came to the Studium."

"Ten years." He sighed. "And I couldn't have asked for a better teacher. But you—well, let's put it this way. Nobody knows more about form and technique than you do, but you haven't got *wings*. All you can do is run fast and flap your arms up and down. Which you do," he added pleasantly, "superlatively well."

"You don't want me to help you," I said.

"I've offended you." Not the first time he'd said that, not by a long way. And always, in the past, I'd forgiven him instantly. "And you've taken the trouble to come and see me, and I've insulted you. I'm really sorry. I guess this place has had a bad effect on me."

"Think about it," I said, and I was so ashamed of myself; like robbing a dying man. "Your last work. Possibly your greatest."

He laughed out loud. "You haven't read it yet," he said. "It could be absolute garbage for all you know."

It could have been, but I knew it wasn't. "Let me finish it for you," I said. "Please. Don't let it die with you. You owe it to the human race."

I'd said the wrong thing. "To be brutally frank with you," he said, in a light, slightly brittle voice, "I couldn't give a twopenny fuck about the human race. They're the ones who put me in here, and in six hours' time they're going to pull my neck like a chicken. Screw the lot of them."

My fault. I'd said the wrong thing, and as a result, the music inside his head would stay there, trapped in there, until the rope crushed his windpipe and his brain went cold. So, naturally, I blamed him. "Fine," I said. "If that's your attitude, I don't think there's anything left to say."

"Quite." He sighed. I think he wanted me to leave. "It's all a bit pointless now, isn't it? Here," he added, and I felt a sheaf of paper thrust against my chest. "You'd better take the manuscript. If it's left here, there's a fair chance the guards'll use it for arsewipe."

"Would it bother you if they did?"

He laughed. "I don't think it would, to be honest," he said. "But it's worth money," he went on, and I wish I could've seen his face. "Even incomplete," he added. "It's got to be worth a hundred angels to somebody, and I seem to recall I owe you a hundred and fifty, from the last time."

I felt my fingers close around the pages. I didn't want to take them, but I gripped so tight I could feel the paper crumple. I had in fact already opened negotiations with the Kapelmeister.

I stood up. "Goodbye," I said. "I'm sorry."

"Oh, don't go blaming yourself for anything." Absolution, so easy for him to give; like a duke scattering coins to the crowd from a balcony. Of course, the old duke used to have the coins heated in a brazier first. I still have little white scars on my fingertips. "I've always been the sole author of my own misfortunes. You always did your best for me."

And failed, of course. "Even so," I said, "I'm sorry. It's such a waste."

That made him laugh. "I wish," he said, "that music could've been the most important thing in my life, like it should've been. But it was only ever a way of getting a bit of money."

I couldn't reply to that. The truth, which I'd always known since I first met him, was that if he'd cared about music, he couldn't have written it so well. Now there's irony.

"You're going to finish it anyway."

I stopped, a pace or so short of the door. "Not if you don't want me to."

"I won't be here to stop you."

"I can't finish it," I said. "Not without the theme."

"Balls." He clicked his tongue, that irritating sound I'll always associate with him. "You'll have a stab at it, I know you will. And for the rest of time, everybody will be able to see the join."

"Goodbye," I said, without looking round.

"You could always pass it off as your own," he said.

I balled my fist and bashed on the door. All I wanted to do was get out of there as quickly as I could; because while I was in there with him, I hated him, because of what he'd just said. Because I'd deserved better of him than that, over the years. And because the thought had crossed my mind.

I waited till I got back to my rooms before I unfolded the sheaf of paper and looked at it.

At that point, I had been the professor of music at the Academy of the Invincible Sun for twenty-seven years. I was the youngest ever incumbent, and I fully intend to die in these rooms, though not for a very long time. I'd taught the very best. My own music was universally respected, and I got at least five major commissions every year for ducal and official occasions. I'd written six books on musical theory, all of which had become the standard works on the aspects of the subject they cover. Students came here from every part of the empire, thousands of miles in cramped ships and badly sprung coaches, to hear me lecture on harmony and the use of form. The year before, they'd named one of the five modes after me.

When I'd read it, I looked at the fire, which the servant had lit while I was out. It would be so easy, I thought. Twenty sheets of paper don't take very long to burn. But, as I think I told you, I'd already broached the subject with the Kapelmeister, who'd offered me five hundred angels, sight unseen, even unfinished. I knew I could get him up to eight hundred. I have no illusions about myself.

I didn't try and finish the piece; not because I'd promised I wouldn't, but because he escaped. To this day, nobody has the faintest idea how he managed it. All we know is that when the captain of the guard opened his cell to take him to the scaffold, he found a warder sitting on the bench with his throat cut, and no sign of the prisoner.

There was an enquiry, needless to say. I had a very uncomfortable morning at guard headquarters, where I sat on a bench in a corridor for three hours before making the acquaintance of a Captain Monomachus of the Investigative branch. He pointed out to me that I was a known associate of the prisoner, and that I'd been the last person to be alone with him before his escape. I replied that I'd been thoroughly and quite humiliatingly searched before I went in to see him, and there was no way

I could've taken him in any kind of weapon.

"We aren't looking for a weapon, as a matter of fact," captain Monoma-chus replied. "We reckon he smashed his inkwell and used a shard of the glass. What we're interested in is how he got clear of the barbican. We figure he must've had help."

I looked the captain straight in the eye. I could afford to. "He always had plenty of friends," I said.

For some reason, the captain smiled at that. "After you left him," he said, "where did you go?"

"Straight back to my rooms in college. The porter can vouch for me, presumably. And my servant. He brought me a light supper shortly after I got home."

Captain Monomachus prowled round me for a while after that, but since he had absolutely nothing against me, he had to let me go. As I was about to leave, he stopped me and said, "I understand there was a last piece."

I nodded. "That's right. That's what I was reading, the rest of the evening."

"Any good?"

"Oh yes." I paused, then added, "Possibly his best. Unfinished, of course."

There was a slight feather of shyness about the question that followed. "Will there be a performance?"

I told him the date and the venue. He wrote them down on a scrap of paper, which he folded and put in his pocket.

The good captain was, in fact, the least of my problems. That same evening, I was summoned to the Master's lodgings.

"Your protégé," the Master said, pouring me a very small glass of the college brandy.

"My student," I said. It's very good brandy, as a matter of fact, but invariably wasted, because the only times I get to drink it are when I'm summoned into the presence, on which occasions I'm always so paralyzed with fear that even good brandy has no effect whatsoever.

He sighed, sniffed his glass and sat down; or rather, he perched on the edge of the settle. He always likes to be higher than his guests. Makes swooping to strike easier, I imagine. "An amazingly gifted man," he said. "You might go so far as to call him a genius, though that term is sadly overused these days, I find." I waited, and a moment and a sip of brandy later, he continued; "But a fundamentally unstable character. I suppose we ought to have seen the warning signs."

We meaning me; because the Master wasn't appointed until the year after my poor student was expelled. "You know," I said, trying to sound as though it was a conversation rather than an interrogation, "I sometimes wonder if in his case, the two are inseparable; the instability and the brilliance, I mean."

The Master nodded. "The same essential characteristics that made him a genius also made him a murderer," he said. "It's a viable hypothesis, to be sure. In which case, the question must surely arise; can the one ever justify the other? The most sublime music, set against a man's life." He shrugged, a gesture for which his broad, sloping shoulders were perfectly suited. "I shall have to bear that one in mind for my Ethics tutorials. You could argue it quite well both ways, of course. After all, his music will live forever, and the man he killed was the most dreadful fellow, by all accounts, a petty thief and a drunkard." He paused, to give me time to agree. Even I knew better than that. Once it was clear I'd refused the bait, he said, "The important thing, I think, is to try and learn something from this tragic case."

"Indeed," I said, and nibbled at my brandy to give myself time. I've never fenced, but I believe that's what fencers do; make time by controlling distance. So I held up my brandy glass and hid behind it as best I could.

"Warning signs," he went on, "that's what we need to look out for. These young people come here, they're entrusted to our care at a particularly difficult stage in their development. Our duty doesn't end with stuffing their heads full of knowledge. We need to adopt a more comprehensive pastoral approach. Don't you agree?"

In the old duke's time, they used to punish traitors by shutting them up in a cage with a lion. As an exquisite refinement of malice, they used to feed the lion to bursting point first. That way, it wasn't hungry again for the best part of a day. I always found that very upsetting to think about. If I'm going to be torn apart, I want it to be over quickly. The Master and the old duke were students together, by the way. I believe they got on very well.

"Of course," I said. "No doubt the Senate will let us have some guidelines in due course."

I got out of there eventually, in one piece. Curiously enough, I didn't start shaking until I was halfway across the quadrangle, on my way back to my rooms. I couldn't tell you why encounters like that disturb me so much. After all, the worst the Master could do to me was dismiss me—which was bound to happen, sooner or later, because I only had qualified tenure, and I knew he thought of me as a closet Optimate. Which was, of course, entirely true. But so what? Unfortunately, the thought of losing my post utterly terrifies me. I know I'm too old to get another post anything like as good as this one, and such talent as I ever had has long since dissipated through overuse. I have doctorates and honorary doctorates in music enough to cover a wall, but I can't actually play a musical instrument. I have a little money put by these days, but not nearly enough. I have never experienced poverty, but in the city you see it every day. I don't have a particularly vivid imagination—anybody familiar with my music can attest to that—but I have no trouble at all imagining what it would be like to be homeless and hungry and cold in Perimadeia. I think about it all the time. Accordingly, the threat of my inevitable dismissal at some unascertained point in the future lies over my present like a cloud of volcanic ash, blotting out the sun, and I'm incapable of taking any pleasure in anything at all.

He will always be known by his name in religion, Subtilius of Bohec; but he was born Aimeric de Beguilhan, third son of a minor Northern squire, raised in the farmyard and the stables, destined for an uneventful career in the Ministry. When he came here, he had a place to read Logic, Literature and Rhetoric, and by his own account he'd never composed a bar of music in his life. In Bohec (I have no idea where it is), music consisted of tavern songs and painfully refined dances from the previous century; it featured in his life about as much as the sea, which is something like two hundred miles away in every direction. He first encountered real music in the Studium chapel, which is presumably why nearly all his early work was devotional and choral. When he transferred to the Faculty of Music, I introduced him to the secular instrumental tradition; I suppose that when I appear at last before the court of the Invincible Sun and whoever cross-examines me there asks me if there's one thing I've done which has made the world a better place, that'll be it. Without me, Subtilius would never have written for strings, or composed the five violin concertos, or the three polyphonic symphonies. But he'd already written the first of the Masses before I ever set eyes on him.

The murder was such a stupid business; though, looking back, I suppose it was more or less inevitable that something of the kind should have happened sooner or later. He always did have such a quick temper, fatally combined with a sharp tongue, an unfortunate manner and enough skill at arms to make him practically fearless. There was also the fondness for money—there was never quite enough money when he was growing up, and I know he was exceptionally sensitive about that—and the sort of amorality that often seems to go hand in hand with keen intelligence and an unsatisfactory upbringing. He was intelligent enough to see past the reasons generally advanced in support of obedience to the rules and the law, but lacking in any moral code of his own to take its place. Add to that youth, and overconfidence arising from the praise he'd become accustomed to as soon as he began to compose music, and you have a recipe for disaster.

Even now, I couldn't tell you much about the man he killed. Depending on which account you go by, he was either an accomplice or a rival. In any event, he was a small-time professional thief, a thoroughly worthless specimen who would most assuredly have ended up on the gallows if Subtilius hadn't stabbed him through the neck in the stable-yard of the *Integrity and Honour* in Foregate. Violent death is, I believe, no uncommon occurrence there, and he'd probably have got away with it had not one of the ostlers been a passionate admirer of his religious music, and therefore recognized him and been able to identify him to the Watch; an unfortunate consequence, I suppose, of the quite exceptionally broad appeal of Subtilius' music. If I'd stabbed a man in a stable-yard, the chances of a devoted fan recognizing me would've been too tiny to quantify, unless the ostler happened to be a fellow academic fallen on hard times.

I got back to my rooms, fumbled with the keys, dropped them—anybody passing would have thought I was drunk, although of course I scarcely touched a drop in those days; I couldn't afford to, with the excise tax so high—finally managed to get the door open and fall into the room. It was dark, of course, and I spent quite some time groping for the tinder-box and the candle, and then I dropped the moss out of the box onto the floor and had to grope for that too. Eventually I struck a light, and used the candle to light the oil lamp. It was only then, as the light colonized the room, that I saw I wasn't alone.

"Hello, professor," said Subtilius.

My first thought—I was surprised at how quickly and practically I reacted—was the shutters. Mercifully, they were closed. In which case, he couldn't have come in through the window.

He laughed. "It's all right," he said, "nobody saw me. I was extremely careful."

Easy to say; easy to believe, but easy to be wrong. "How long have you been here?"

"I came in just after you left. You left the door unlocked."

Quite right; I'd forgotten.

"I took the precaution of locking it for you," he went on, "with the spare key you still keep in that ghastly pot on the mantelpiece. Look, why don't you sit down before you fall over? You look awful."

I went straight to the door and locked it. Not that I get many visitors, but I was in no mood to rely on the laws of probability. "What the hell are you doing here?"

He sighed, and stretched out his legs. I imagine it was what his father used to do, after a long day on the farm or following the hounds. "Hiding," he said. "What do you think?"

"You can't hide here."

"Overjoyed to see you too."

It was an entirely valid rebuke, so I ignored it. "Aimeric, you're being utterly unreasonable. You can't expect me to harbor a fugitive from justice—"

"Aimeric." He repeated the word as though it had some kind of incantatory power. "You know, professor, you're the only person who's called me that since the old man died. Can't say I ever liked the name, but it's odd to hear it again after all these years. Listen," he said, before I could get a word in, "I'm sorry if I scared the life out of you, but I need your help."

I always did find him both irresistibly charming and utterly infuriating. His voice, for one thing. I suppose it's my musician's ear; I can tell you more about a man, where he's from and how much money he's got, from hearing him say two words than any mere visual clues. Subtilius had a perfect voice; consonants clear and sharp as a knife, vowels fully distinguished and immaculately expressed. You can't learn to talk like that over the age of three. No matter how hard you try, if you start off with a provincial burr, like me, it'll always bleed through sooner or later. You can only achieve that bell-like clarity and those supremely beautiful dentals and labials if you start learning them before you can walk. That's where actors go wrong, of course. They can make themselves sound like noblemen after years of study so long as they stick to normal everyday conversational pitches. But if they try and shout, anyone with a trained ear can hear the northern whine or the southern bleat, obvious as a stain on a white sheet. Subtilius had a voice you'd have paid money to listen to, even if all he was doing was giving you directions to the Southgate, or swearing at a porter for letting the sludge get into the wine. That sort of perfection is, of course, profoundly annoying if you don't happen to be true-born aristocracy. My father was a fuller and soap-boiler in Ap'Escatoy. My first job was riding with him on the cart collecting the contents of chamber pots from the inns in the early hours of the morning. I've spent forty years trying to sound like a gentleman, and these days I can fool everybody except myself. Subtilius was born perfect and never had to try.

"Where the hell," I asked him, "have you been? The guard's been turning the city upside down. How did you get out of the barbican? All the gates were watched."

He laughed. "Simple," he said. "I didn't leave. Been here all the time, camping out in the clock tower."

Well, of course. The Studium, as I'm sure you know, is built into the west wall of the barbican. Naturally they searched it, the same day he escaped, after which they concluded that he must've got past the gate somehow and made it down to the lower town. It wouldn't have occurred to them to try the clock tower. Twenty years ago, an escaped prisoner hid up there, and when they found him, he was extremely dead. Nothing can survive in the bell-chamber when the clock strikes; the sheer pressure of sound would pulp your brain. Oh, I imagine a couple of guardsmen put their heads round inside the chamber when they knew it was safe, but they wouldn't have made a thorough search, because everybody knows the story. But in that case—

"Why aren't I dead?" He grinned at me. "Because the story's a load of old rubbish. I always had my doubts about it, so I took the trouble to look up the actual records. The prisoner who hid out up there died of blood poisoning from a scratch he'd got climbing out of a broken window. The thing about the bells killing him was pure mythology. You know how people like to believe that sort of thing." He gave me a delightful smile. "So they've been looking for me in Lower Town, have they? Bless them."

Curiosity, presumably; the true scholar's instinct, which he always had. But combined, I dare say, with the thought at the back of his mind that one day, a guaranteed safe hiding-place would come in useful. I wondered when he'd made his search in the archives; when he was fifteen, or seventeen, or twenty-one?

"I'm not saying it was exactly pleasant, mind," he went on, "not when the bells actually struck. The whole tower shakes, did you know that? It's a miracle it hasn't collapsed. But I found that if I crammed spiders' web into my ears—really squashed it down till no more would go in—it sort of deadened the noise to the point where it was bearable. And one thing there's no shortage of up there is cobwebs."

I've always been terrified of spiders. I'm sure he knew that.

"Fine," I snapped at him; I was embarrassed with myself, because my first reaction was admiration. "So you killed a man and managed to stay free for three weeks. How very impressive. What have you been living on, for God's sake? You should be thin as a rake."

He shrugged. "I didn't stay in there all the time," he said. "Generally speaking, I made my excursions around noon and midnight." When the bell tolls twelve times, there being a limit, presumably, to the defensive capacity of cobweb. "It's amazing how much perfectly good food gets thrown out in the kitchens. You're on the catering committee, you really ought to do something about it."

Part of his genius, I suppose; to make his desperate escape and three weeks' torment in the bell-tower sound like a student prank, just as he made writing the Seventh Mass seem effortless, something he churned out in an idle moment between hangovers. Perhaps the secret of sublime achievement really is not to try. But first, you have to check the archives, or learn the twelve major modulations of the Vesani mode, or be born into a family that can trace its pedigree back to Boamond.

"Well," I said, standing up, "I'm sorry, but you've had all that for nothing. I'm going to have to turn you in. You do realize that."

He just laughed at me. He knew me too well. He knew that if I'd really meant it, I'd have done it straight away, yelled for the guard at the top of my voice instead of panicking about the shutters. He knew it; I didn't, not until I heard him laugh. Until then, I thought I was deadly serious. But he was right, of course. "Sure," he said. "You go ahead."

I sat down again. I hated him so much, at that moment.

"How's the concerto coming along?" he asked.

For a moment, I had no idea what he was talking about. Then I remembered; his last concerto, or that's what it should have been. The manuscript he gave me in the condemned cell. "You said not to finish it," I told him.

"Good Lord." He was amused. "I assumed you'd have taken no notice. Well, I'm touched. Thank you."

"What are you doing here?" I asked him.

"I need money," he replied, and somehow his voice contrived to lose a proportion of its honeyed charm. "And clothes, and shoes, things like that. And someone to leave a door open at night. That sort of thing."

"I can't," I said.

He sighed. "You can, you know. What you mean is, you don't want to."

"I haven't got any money."

He gave me a sad look. "We're not talking about large sums," he said. "It's strictly a matter of context. Enough to get me out of town and on a

ship, that's all. That's wealth beyond the dreams of avarice." He paused—
I think it was for effect—and added, "I'm not asking for a *present*. I do
have something to sell."

There was a moment when my entire covering of skin went cold. I could
guess. What else would he have to sell, apart from—?

"Three weeks in the bloody bell tower," he went on, and now he sounded
exactly like his old self. "Nothing to do all day. Fortunately, on my second
trip to the trash cans I passed an open door, some first-year, presumably,
who hasn't learned about keeping his door locked. He'd got ink, pens and
half a ream of good paper. Don't suppose he'll make that mistake again."

I love music. It's been my life. Music has informed my development, given
me more pleasure than I can possibly quantify or qualify; it's also taken
me from the fullers' yard at Ap'Escatoy to the Studium, and kept me here,
so far at least. Everything I am, everything I have, is because of music.

For which I am properly grateful. The unfortunate part of it is, there's
never been quite enough. Not enough music in me; never enough money.
The pleasure, emotional and intellectual, is one thing. The money, however,
is another. Almost enough—I'm not a luxurious sort of person, I don't
spend extravagantly, but most of it seems to go on overheads; college bills,
servants' wages, contributions to this and that fund, taxes, of course, all
that sort of nonsense—but never quite enough to let me feel comfortable.
I live in a constant state of anxiety about money, and inevitably that anxiety has a bad effect on my relationship with music. And the harder I try,
the less the inspiration flows. When I don't need it, when I'm relatively
comfortable and the worry subsides for a while, a melody will come to me
quite unexpectedly and I'll write something really quite good. But when
I'm facing a deadline, or when the bills are due and my purse is empty;
when I need money, the inspiration seems to dry up completely, and all
I can do is grind a little paste off the salt-block of what I've learned, or
try and dress up something old, my own or someone else's, and hope to
God nobody notices. At times like that, I get angry with music. I even
imagine—wrongly, of course—that I wish I was back in the fullers' yard.
But that's long gone, of course. My brother and I sold it when my father
died, and the money was spent years ago, so I don't even have that to fall
back on. Just music.

"You've written something," I said.

"Oh yes." From inside his shirt he pulled a sheaf of paper. "A symphony,

in three movements and a coda." I suppose I must have reached out instinctively, because he moved back gently. "Complete, you'll be relieved
to hear. All yours, if you want it."

All my life I've tried to look civilized and refined, an intellect rather
than a physical body. But when I want something and it's so close I can
touch it, I sweat. My hands get clammy, and I can feel the drops lifting
my hair where it touches my forehead. "A symphony," was all I could say.

He nodded. "My fourth. I think you're going to like it."

"All mine if I want it."

"Ah." He did the mock frown. "All yours if you pay for it. Your chance
to be an illustrious patron of the arts, like the Eberharts."

I stared at him. All mine. "Don't be so bloody stupid," I yelled. "I can't
use it. It'd be useless to me."

He pretended to be upset. "You haven't even looked at it."

"Think about it," I said, low and furious. "You're on the run from the
Watch, with a death sentence against your name. I suddenly present a
brand new Subtilius symphony. It'd be obvious. Any bloody fool would
know straight away that I'd helped you escape."

He nodded. "I see your point," he said mildly. "But you could say it's an
old piece, something I wrote years ago, and you've been hanging on to it."

"Is that likely?"

"I guess not." He smiled at me, a sunrise-over-the-bay smile, warm and
bright and humiliating. "So I guess you'll just have to pretend you wrote
it, won't you?"

It was like a slap across the face, insulting and unexpected. "Please," I
said. "Don't even suggest it. You know perfectly well I could never pass
off your work as my own. Everybody would know after the first couple
of bars."

Then he smiled again, and I knew he was playing me. He'd led me
carefully to a certain place where he wanted me to be. "That won't be a
problem," he said. "You see, I've written it in your style."

Maybe shock and anger had made me more than usually stupid. It took
a moment; and then I realized what he'd just said.

"Hence," he went on, "the symphonic form, which I've never really cared
for, but it's sort of like your trademark, isn't it? And I've used the tetra-
chord of Mercury throughout, even quoted a bar or two of the secondary
theme from your Third. Here," he said, and handed me a page—just the
one, he was no fool—from the sheaf.

I didn't want to take it. I swear, it felt like deliberately taking hold of a nettle and squeezing it into your palm. I looked down.

I can read music very quickly and easily, as you'd expect. One glance and it's there in my head. It only took me a couple of heartbeats to know what I was holding. It was, of course, a masterpiece. It was utterly brilliant, magnificent, the sort of music that defines a place and a time for all time. It soared inside me as I looked at it, filling and choking me, as though someone had shoved a bladder down my throat and started blowing it up. It was in every way perfect; and *I could have written it.*

"Well?" he said.

Let me qualify that. No, I couldn't have written it, not in a million years, not if my life depended on it; not even if, in some moment of absolute peace and happiness, the best inspiration of my entire life had lodged inside my head, and the circumstances had been so perfectly arranged that I was able to take advantage of it straight away, while it was fresh and whole in my mind (which never ever happens, of course). I could never have written it; but it was in my style, so exactly captured that any-body but me would believe it was my work. It wasn't just the trademark flourishes and periods, the way I use the orchestra, the mathematical way I build through intervals and changes of key. A parody could've had all those. The music I was looking at had been written by someone who understood me perfectly—better than I've ever understood myself—and who knew exactly what I wanted to say, although I've always lacked the skill, and the power.

"Well," he said. "Do you like it?"

As stupid a question as I've ever heard in my life, and of course I didn't reply. I was too angry, heartbroken, ashamed.

"I was quite pleased with the cadenza," he went on. "I got the idea from that recurring motif in your Second, but I sort of turned it through ninety degrees and stuck a few feathers in it."

I've never been married, of course, but I can imagine what it must be like, to come home unexpectedly and find your wife in bed with another man. It'd be the love that'd fill you with hate. Oh, how I hated Subtilius at that moment. And imagine how you'd feel if you and your wife had never been able to have kids, and you found out she was pregnant by another man.

"It's got to be worth money," I heard him say. "Just the sort of thing the duke would like."

He always had that knack, did Subtilius. The ability to take the words out of the mouth of the worst part of me, the part I'd cheerfully cut out with a knife in cold blood if only I knew where in my body it's located.

"Well?" he said.

When I was nineteen years old, my father and my elder brother and I were in the cart—I was back home for the holidays, helping out on the rounds—and we were driving out to the old barns where my father boiled the soap. The road runs along the top of a ridge, and when it rains, great chunks of it get washed away. It had been raining heavily the day before, and by the time we turned the sharp bend at the top it was nearly dark. I guess my father didn't see where the road had fallen away. The cart went over. I was sitting in the back and was thrown clear. Father and Segibert managed to scramble clear just as the cart went over; Segibert caught hold of Dad's ankle, and Dad grabbed on to a rock sticking out of the ground. I managed to get my hand round his wrist, and for a moment we were stuck there. I've never been strong, and I didn't have the strength to pull them up, not so much as an inch. All I could do was hold on, and I knew that if I allowed myself to let his hand slip even the tiniest bit, I'd lose him and both of them, the two people I loved most in the whole world, would fall and die. But in that moment, when all the thoughts that were ever possible were running through my head, I thought; if they do both fall, and they're both killed, then when we sell the business, it'd be just me, best part of three hundred angels, and what couldn't I do with that sort of money?

Then Segibert managed to get a footing, and between them they hauled and scrambled and got up next to me on the road, and soon we were all in floods of tears, and Dad was telling me I'd saved his life, and he'd never forget it. And I felt so painfully guilty, as though I'd pushed them over deliberately.

Well, I thought. Yes. Worth a great deal of money.

"More the old duke's sort of thing," he was saying, "he'd have loved it, he was a man of taste and discrimination. Compared with him, young Sighvat's a barbarian. But even he'd like this, I'm sure."

A barbarian. The old duke used to punish debtors by giving them a head start and then turning his wolfhounds loose. Last year, Sighvat abolished the poll tax and brought in a minimum wage for farm workers. But the old duke had a better ear for music, and he was an extremely generous patron. "I can't," I said.

"Of course you can," Subtilius said briskly. "Now then, I was thinking in terms of three hundred. That'd cover my expenses."

"I haven't got that sort of money."

He looked at me. "No," he said, "I don't suppose you have. Well, what have you got?"

"I can give you a hundred angels."

Which was true. Actually, I had a hundred and fifty angels in the wooden box under my bed. It was the down payment I'd taken from the Kapelmeister for the Unfinished Concerto, so properly speaking it was Subtilius' money anyway. But I needed the fifty. I had bills to pay.

"That'll have to do, then," he said, quite cheerfully. "It'll cover the bribes and pay for a fake passport, I'll just have to steal food and clothes. Can't be helped. You're a good man, professor."

There was still time. I could throw the door open and yell for a porter. I was still innocent of any crime, against the State or myself. Subtilius would go back to the condemned cell, I could throw the manuscript on the fire, and I could resume my life, my slow and inevitable uphill trudge towards poverty and misery. Or I could call the porter and not burn the music. What exactly would happen to me if I was caught assisting an of-fender? I couldn't bear prison, I'd have to kill myself first; but would I get the chance? Bail would be out of the question, so I'd be remanded pending trial. Highly unlikely that the prison guards would leave knives, razors or poison lying about in my cell for me to use. People hang themselves in jail, they twist ropes out of bedding. But what if I made a mess of it and ended up paralyzed for life? Even if I managed to stay out of prison, a criminal conviction would mean instant dismissal and no chance of another job. But that wouldn't matter, if I could keep the music. We are, the Invincible Sun be praised, a remarkably, almost obsessively cultured nation, and music is our life. No matter what its composer had done, work of that quality would always be worth a great deal of money, enough to retire on and never have to compose another note as long as I live.

I was a good man, apparently. He was grateful to me, for swindling him. I was a good man, because I was prepared to pass off a better man's work as my own. Because I was willing to help a murderer escape justice.

"Where will you go?" I asked.

He grinned at me. "You really don't want to know," he said. "Let's just say, a long way away."

"You're famous," I pointed out. "Everywhere. Soon as you write anything, they'll know it's you. They'll figure out it was me who helped you escape."

He yawned. He looked very tired; fair enough, after three weeks in a clock tower, with eight of the biggest bells in the empire striking the quarter hours inches from his head. He couldn't possibly have slept for more than ten minutes. "I'm giving up music," he said. "This is definitely and categorically my last ever composition. You're quite right; the moment I wrote anything, I'd give myself away. There's a few places the empire hasn't got extradition treaties with, but I'd rather be dead than live there. So it's simple, I won't write any more music. After all," he added, his hand over his mouth like he'd been taught as a boy, "there's lots of other things I can do. All music's ever done is land me in trouble."

What, when all is said and done, all the conventional garbage is put on one side and you're alone inside your head with yourself, do you actually believe in? That's a question that has occupied a remarkably small percentage of my attention over the years. Strange, since I spend a fair proportion of my working time composing odes, hymns and masses to the Invincible Sun. Do I believe in Him? To be honest, I'm not sure. I believe in the big white disc in the sky, because it's there for all to see. I believe that there's some kind of supreme authority, something along the lines of His Majesty the Emperor only bigger and even more remote, who theoretically controls the universe. What that actually involves, I'm afraid, I couldn't tell you. Presumably He regulates the affairs of great nations, enthrones and deposes emperors and kings—possibly princes and dukes, though it's rather more plausible that He delegates that sort of thing to some kind of divine solar civil service—and intervenes in high-profile cases of injustice and blasphemy whenever a precedent needs to be set or a point of law clarified. Does He deal with me personally, or is He even aware of my existence? On balance, probably not. He wouldn't have the time.

In which case, if I have a file at all, I assume it's on the desk of some junior clerk, along with hundreds, thousands, millions of others. I can't say that that thought bothers me too much. I'd far rather be left alone, in peace and quiet. As far as I'm aware, my prayers—mostly for money, occasionally for the life or recovery from illness of a relative or friend— have never been answered, so I'm guessing that divine authority works on more or less the same lines as its civilian equivalent; don't expect anything good from it, and you won't be disappointed. Just occasionally, though, something happens which can only be divine intervention, and then my world-view and understanding of the nature of things gets all shaken up and reshaped. I explain it away by saying that really it's something primarily happening to someone else—someone important, whose file is looked after by a senior administrative officer or above—and I just happen to be peripherally involved and therefore indirectly affected.

A good example is Subtilius' escape from the barbican. At the time it felt like my good luck. On mature reflection I can see that it was really his good luck, in which I was permitted to share, in the same way that the Imperial umbrella-holder also gets to stay dry when it rains.

It couldn't have been simpler. I went first, to open doors and make sure nobody was watching. He followed on, swathed in the ostentatious cassock and cowl of a Master Chorister—purple with ermine trimmings, richly embroidered with gold thread and seed pearls; anywhere else you'd stand out a mile, but in the barbican, choristers are so commonplace they're practically invisible. Luck intervened by making it rain, so that it was perfectly natural for my chorister companion to have his hood up, and to hold the folds tight around his face and neck. He had my hundred angels in his pockets in a pair of socks, to keep the coins from clinking.

The sally-port in the barbican wall, opening onto the winding stair that takes you down to Lower Town the short way, is locked at nightfall, but faculty officers like me all have keys. I opened the gate and stepped aside to let him pass.

"Get rid of the cassock as soon as you can," I said. "I'll report it stolen first thing in the morning, so they'll be looking for it."

He nodded. "Well," he said, "thanks for everything, professor. I'd just like to say—"

"Get the hell away from here," I said, "before anyone sees us."

There are few feelings in life quite as exhilarating as getting away with something. Mainly, I guess, if you're someone like me, it's because you never really expected to. Add to the natural relief, therefore, the unaccustomed pleasure of winning. Then, since you can't win anything without having beaten someone first, there's the delicious feeling of superiority, which I enjoy for the same reason that gourmets prize those small gray truffles that grow on the sides of dead birch trees; not because it's nourishing or tasty, but simply because it's so rare. Of course, it remained to be seen whether I had actually got away with aiding and abetting a murderer after the fact and assisting a fugitive. There was still a distinct chance that Subtilius would be picked up by the Watch before he could get out of the city, in which case he might very well reveal the identity of his accomplice, if only to stop them hitting him. But, I told myself, that'd be all right. I'd simply tell them he'd burgled my rooms and stolen the money and the cassock, and they wouldn't be able to prove otherwise. I told myself that; I knew perfectly well, of course, that if they did question me, my nerve would probably shatter like an eggshell, and the only thing that might stop me from giving them a comprehensive confession was if I was so incoherent with terror I couldn't speak at all. I think you'd have to be quite extraordinarily brave to be a hardened criminal; much braver than soldiers who lead charges or stand their ground against the cavalry. I could just about imagine myself doing that sort of thing, out of fear of the sergeant-major, but doing something illegal literally paralyzes me with fear. And yet courage, as essential to the criminal as his jemmy or his cosh, is held to be a virtue.

The first thing I did when I got back to my room was to light the lamp and open the shutters, because I never close them except when it snows, and people who knew me might wonder what was going on if they saw them shut. Then I poured myself a small brandy—it would've been a large one, but the bottle was nearly empty—and sat down with the lamp so close to me that I could feel it scorching my face, and spread out the manuscript, and read it.

They say that when we first sent out ships to trade with the savages in Rhoezen, we packed the holds full of the sort of things we thought primitive people would like—beads, cheap tin brooches, scarves, shirts, buckles plated so thin the silver practically wiped off on your fingers, that sort of thing. And mirrors. We thought they'd love mirrors. In fact, we planned on buying enough land to grow enough corn to feed the City with a case of hand-mirrors, one angel twenty a gross from the Scharnel Brothers.

We got that completely wrong. The captain of the first ship to make contact handed out a selection of his trade goods by way of free samples. Everything seemed to be going really well until they found the mirrors. They didn't like them. They threw them on the ground and stamped on them, then attacked our people with spears and slingshots, until the captain had to fire a cannon just so as to get his men back off the beach in one piece. Later, when he'd managed to capture a couple of specimens and he interrogated them through an interpreter, he found out what the problem was. The mirrors, the prisoners told him, were evil. They sucked your soul out through your eyes and imprisoned it under the surface of the dry-hard-water. Stealing the souls of harmless folk who'd only wanted to be friendly to strangers was not, in their opinion, civilized behaviour.

Accordingly, we weren't welcome in their country.

When I first heard the story, I thought the savages had over-reacted somewhat. When I'd finished reading Subtilius' symphony, written in my style, I was forced to revise my views. Stealing a man's soul is one of the worst things you can do to him, and it hardly matters whether you shut it up in a mirror or thirty pages of manuscript. It's not something you can ever forgive.

And then, after I'd sat still and quiet for a while, until the oil in the lamp burned away and I was left entirely alone in the dark, I found myself thinking; yes, but nobody will ever know. All I had to do was sit down and copy it out in my own handwriting, then burn the original, and there would be no evidence, no witnesses. You hear a lot from the philosophers and the reverend Fathers about truth, about how it must inevitably prevail, how it will always burst through, like the saplings that grow up in the cracks in walls until their roots shatter the stone. It's not true. Subtilius wouldn't ever tell anybody (and besides, it was only a matter of time before he was caught and strung up, and that'd be him silenced for ever). I sure as hell wasn't going to say anything. If there's a truth and nobody knows it, is it still true? Or is it like a light burning in a locked, shuttered house, that nobody will ever get to see?

I'd know it, of course. I did consider that. But then I thought about the money.

The debut of my Twelfth Symphony took place at the collegiate temple on Ascension Day, AUC 775, in the presence of his highness Duke Sighvat II, the duchess and dowager duchess, the Archimandrite of the Studium and a distinguished audience drawn from the Court, the university and the best of good society. It was, I have to say, a triumph. The duke was so impressed that he ordered a command performance at the palace. Less prestigious but considerably more lucrative was the licence I agreed with the Kapelmeister; a dozen performances at the Empire Hall at a thousand angels a time, with the rights reverting to me thereafter. Subsequently I made similar deals with kapelmeisters and court musicians and directors of music from all over the empire, taking care to reserve the sheet music rights, which I sold to the Court stationers for five thousand down and a five per cent royalty. My tenure at the University was upgraded to a full Fellowship, which meant I could only be got rid of by a bill of attainder passed by both houses of the Legislature and ratified by the duke, and then only on grounds of corruption or gross moral turpitude; my stipend went up from three hundred to a thousand a year, guaranteed for life, with bonuses should I ever condescend to do any actual teaching. Six months after the first performance, as I sat in my rooms flicking jettons about on my counting-board, I realized that I need never work again. Quite suddenly, all my troubles were over.

On that, and what followed, I base my contention that there is no justice; that the Invincible Sun, if He's anything more than a ball of fire in the sky, has no interest and does not interfere in the life and fortunes of ordinary mortals, and that morality is simply a confidence trick practiced on all of us by the State and its officers to keep us from making nuisances of ourselves. For a lifetime of devotion to music, I got anxiety, misery and uncertainty. For two crimes, one against the State and one against myself, I was rewarded with everything I'd ever wanted. Explain that, if you can.

Everything? Oh yes. To begin with, I dreaded the commissions that started to flood in from the duke, other dukes and princes, even the Imperial court; because I knew I was a fraud, that I'd never be able to write anything remotely as good as the Symphony, and it was only a matter of time before someone figured out what had actually happened and soldiers arrived at my door to arrest me. But I sat down, with a lamp and a thick mat of paper; and it occurred to me that, now I didn't need the money, all I had to do was refuse the commissions—politely, of course—and nobody could touch me. I didn't have to write a single note if I didn't want to. It was entirely up to me.

Once I'd realized that, I started to write. And, knowing that it really didn't matter, I hardly bothered to try. The less I tried, the easier it was to find a melody (getting a melody out of me was always like pulling teeth). Once I'd got that, I simply let it rattle about in my head for a while, and wrote down the result. Once I'd filled the necessary number of pages, I signed my name at the top and sent it off. I didn't care, you see. If they didn't like it, they knew what they could do.

From time to time, to begin with at least, it did occur to me to wonder, *is this stuff any good?* But that raises the question; how the hell does anybody ever know? If the criterion is the reaction of the audience, or the sums of money offered for the next commission, I just kept getting better. That was, of course, absurd. Even I could see that. But no; my audiences and my critics insisted that each new work was better than its predecessors (though the Twelfth Symphony was the piece that stayed in the repertoires, and the later masterpieces sort of came and went; not that I gave a damn).

A cynic would argue that once I'd become a great success, nobody dared to criticize my work for fear of looking a fool; the only permitted reaction was ever increasing adulation. Being a cynic myself, I favored that view for a while. But, as the success continued and the money flowed and more and more music somehow got written, I began to have my doubts. All those thousands of people, I thought, they can't all be self-deluded. There comes a point when you build up a critical mass, beyond which people sincerely believe. That's how religions are born, and how criteria change. By my success, I'd redefined what constitutes beautiful music. If it sounded like the sort of stuff I wrote, people were prepared to believe it was beautiful. After all, beauty is only a perception—the thickness of an eyebrow, very slight differences in the ratio between length and width of a nose or a portico or a colonnade. Tastes evolve. People like what they're given.

Besides, I came to realize, the Twelfth *was* mine; to some extent at least. After all, the style Subtilius had borrowed was my style, which I'd spent a lifetime building. And if he had the raw skill, the wings, I'd been his teacher; without me, who was to say he'd ever have risen above choral and devotional works and embraced the orchestra? At the very least it was a collaboration, in which I could plausibly claim to be the senior partner. And if the doors are locked and the shutters are closed, whose business is it whether there's a light burning inside? You'd never be able to find out without breaking and entering, which is a criminal offence.

Even so, I began making discreet enquiries. I could afford the best, and I spared no expense. I hired correspondents in all the major cities and towns of the empire to report back to me about notable new compositions and aspiring composers—I tried to pay for this myself, but the university decided that it constituted legitimate academic research and insisted on footing the bill. Whenever I got a report that hinted at the possibility of Subtilius, I sent off students to obtain a written score or sit in the concert hall and transcribe the notes. I hired other, less reputable agents to go through the criminal activity reports, scrape up acquaintance with watch captains, and waste time in the wrong sort of inns, fencing-schools, bear gardens and livery stables. I was having to tread a fine line, of course. The last thing I wanted was for the Watch to reopen their file or remember the name Subtilius, or Aimeric de Beguilhan, so I couldn't have descriptions or likenesses circulated. I didn't regard that as too much of a handicap, however. Sooner or later, I firmly believed, if he was still alive, the music would break out and he'd give himself away. It wouldn't be the creative urge that did for him; it'd be that handmaiden of the queen of the Muses, a desperate and urgent need for money, that got Subtilius composing again. No doubt he'd do his best to disguise himself. He'd try writing street ballads, or pantomime ballets, secure in the belief that that sort of thing was beneath the attention of academic musicians. But it could only be a matter of time. I knew his work, after all, in ways nobody else ever possibly could. I could spot his hand in a sequence of intervals, a modulation or key shift, the ghost of a flourish, the echo of a dissonance. As soon as he put pen to paper, I felt sure, I'd have him.

I was invited to lecture at the University of Baudoin. I didn't want to go—I've always hated travelling—but the marquis was one of my most enthusiastic patrons, and they were offering a thousand angels for an afternoon's work. Oddly enough, affluence hadn't diminished my eagerness to earn money. I guess that no matter how much I had, I couldn't resist the opportunity to add just a bit more, to be on the safe side. I wrote back accepting the invitation.

When I got there (two days in a coach; misery) I found they'd arranged a grand recital of my work for the day after the lecture. I couldn't very well turn round and tell them I was too busy to attend; also, the Baudoin orchestra was at that time reckoned to be the second or third best in the world, and I couldn't help being curious about how my music would sound, played by a really first-class band. Our orchestra in Perimadeia rates very highly on technical skill, but they have an unerring ability to iron the joy out of pretty well anything. I fixed up about the rights with the kapelmeister, thereby doubling my takings for the trip, and told them I'd be honoured and delighted to attend.

The lecture went well. They'd put me in the chapter-house of the Ascendency Temple—not the world's best acoustic, but the really rather fine stained-glass windows are so artfully placed that if you lecture around noon, as I did, and you stand on the lectern facing the audience, you're bathed all over in the most wonderful red and gold light, so that it looks like you're on fire. I gave them two hours on diatonic and chromatic semitones in the Mezentine diapason (it's something I feel quite passionate about, but they know me too well in Perimadeia and stopped listening years ago) and I can honestly say I had them in the palm of my hand. Afterwards, the marquis got up and thanked me—as soon as he joined me on the podium, the sun must've come out from behind a cloud or something, because the light through the windows suddenly changed from red to blue, and instead of burning, we were drowning—and then the provost of the university presented me with an honorary doctorate, which was nice of him, and made a long speech about integrity in the creative arts. The audience got a bit restive, but I was getting paid for being there, so I didn't mind a bit.

There was a reception afterwards; good food and plenty of wine. I must confess I don't remember much about it.

I enjoyed the recital, in spite of a nagging headache I'd woken up with and couldn't shift all day. Naturally, they played the Twelfth; that was the whole of the first half. I wasn't sure I liked the way they took the slow movement, but the finale was superb, it really did sprout wings and soar. The second half was better still. They played two of my Vesani horn concertos and a couple of temple processionals, and there were times when I found myself sitting bolt upright in my seat, asking myself, *did I really write that?* It just goes to show what a difference it makes, hearing your stuff played by a thoroughly competent, sympathetic orchestra. At one point I was so caught up in the music that I couldn't remember what came next, and the denouement—the solo clarinet in the *Phainomai*—took me completely by surprise and made my throat tighten. I thought, *I wrote that*, and I made a mental note of that split second, like pressing a flower between the pages of a book, for later.

It was only when the recital was over, and the conductor was taking his bow, that I saw him. At first, I really wasn't sure. It was just a glimpse of a turned-away head, and when I looked again I'd lost him in the sea of faces. I told myself I was imagining things, and then I saw him again. He was looking straight at me.

There was supposed to be another reception, but I told them I was feeling ill, which wasn't exactly a lie. I went back to the guest suite. There wasn't a lock or a bolt on the door, so I wedged the back of a chair under the handle.

While I'd been at the recital, they'd delivered a whole load of presents. People give me things these days, now that I can afford to buy anything I want. True, the gifts I tend to receive are generally things I'd never buy for myself, because I have absolutely no need for them, and because I do have a certain degree of taste. On this occasion, the marquis had sent me a solid gold dinner service (for a man who, most evenings, eats alone in his rooms off a tray on his knees), a complete set of the works of Aurelianus, ornately bound in gilded calf and too heavy to lift, and a full set of Court ceremonial dress. The latter item consisted of a bright red frock coat, white silk knee breeches, white silk stockings, shiny black shoes with jewelled buckles, and a dress sword.

I know everything I want to know about weapons, which is nothing at all. When I first came to the university, my best friend challenged another friend of ours to a duel. It was about some barmaid. Duelling was the height of fashion back then, and I was deeply hurt not to be chosen as a second (later, I found out it was because they'd chosen a time they knew would clash with my Theory tutorial, and they didn't want me to have to skip it). They fought with smallswords in the long meadow behind the School of Logic. My best friend died instantly; his opponent lingered for a day or so and died screaming, from blood poisoning. If that was violence, I thought, you can have it.

So, I know nothing about swords, except that gentlemen are allowed to wear them in the street; from which I assumed that a gentleman's dress sword must be some kind of pretty toy. In spite of which, I picked up the marquis' present, put on my reading glasses and examined it under the lamp.

It was pretty enough, to be sure, if you like that sort of thing. The handle—I don't know the technical terms—was silver, gilded in places, with a pastoral scene enamelled on the inside of the plate thing that's presumably designed to protect your hand. The blade, though, was in another key altogether. It's always hidden by the scabbard, isn't it, so I figured it'd just be a flat, blunt rod. Not so. It was about three feet long, tapering, triangular in section, so thin at the end it was practically a wire but both remarkably flexible and surprisingly stiff at the same time, and pointed like a needle, brand new from the paper packet. I rested the tip on a cushion and pressed gently. It went through it and out the other side as though the cloth wasn't there.

I imagined myself explaining to the Watch, no, the palace guard, they wouldn't have the ordinary Watch investigate a death in the palace. You know he was a wanted criminal? Quite so, a convicted murderer. He killed a man, then killed a guard escaping from prison. He was my student, years ago, before he went to the bad. I don't know how he got in here, but he wanted money. When I refused, he said he'd have to kill me. There was a struggle. I can't actually remember how the sword came to be in my hand, I suppose I must've grabbed it at some point. All I can remember is him lying there, dead. And then the guard captain would look at me, serious but reassuring, and tell me that it sounded like a straightforward case of self-defence, and by the sound of it, the dead man was no great loss anyhow. I could imagine him being more concerned about the breach of security—a desperate intruder getting into the guest wing—than the possibility that the honorary doctor of music, favorite composer of the marquis, had deliberately murdered somebody.

The thought crossed my mind. After all, nobody would ever know. Once again, there'd be no witnesses. Who could be bothered to break into a locked house on the offchance that there might be a candle burning behind the closed shutters?

I waited, with the sword across my knees, all night. He didn't come.

Instead, he caught up with me at an inn in the mountains on my way home; a much more sensible course of action, and what I should have expected.

I was fast asleep, and something woke me. I opened my eyes to find the lamp lit, and Subtilius sitting in a chair beside the bed, looking at me. He gave the impression that I'd been dangerously ill, and he'd refused to leave my bedside.

"Hello, professor," he said.

The sword was in my trunk, leaning up against the wall on the opposite side of the room. "Hello, Aimeric," I said. "You shouldn't be here."

He grinned. "I shouldn't be anywhere," he said. "But what the hell.

I couldn't see a weapon; no knife or sword. "You're looking well," I said, which was true. He'd filled out since I saw him last. He'd been a skinny, sharp-faced boy, always making me think of an opened knife carried in a pocket. Now he was broad-shouldered and full-faced, and his hair was just starting to get thin on top. He had an outdoor tan, and his fingernails were dirty.

"You've put on weight," he said. "Success agrees with you, obviously."

"It's good to see you again."

"No it's not," he said, still grinning. "Well, not for you, anyway. But I thought I'd drop in and say hello. I wanted to tell you how much I enjoyed the recital."

I thought about what that meant. "Of course," I said. "You'll never have heard it played."

He looked as though he didn't understand, for a moment. Then he laughed, "Oh, you mean the symphony," he said. "Not a bit of it. They play it all the time here." He widened the grin. He'd lost a front tooth since I saw him last. "You want to get on to that," he said. "Clearly, you're missing out on royalties."

"About the money," I said, but he gave me a reproachful little frown, as though I'd made a distasteful remark in the presence of ladies. "Forget about that," he said. "Besides, I don't need money these days. I've done quite well for myself, in a modest sort of a way."

"Music?" I had to ask.

"Good Lord, no. I haven't written a note since I saw you last. Might as well have posters made up and nail them to the temple doors. No, I'm in the olive business. I won a beat-up old press in a chess game shortly after I got here, and now I've got seven mills running full-time in the season, and I've just bought forty acres of mature trees in the Santespe valley. If everything goes to plan, in five years' time every jar of olive oil bought and sold in this country will have made me sixpence. It's a wonderful place, this, you can do anything you like. Makes Perimadeia look like a morgue. And the good thing is," he went on, leaning back a little in his chair, "I'm a foreigner, I talk funny. Which means nobody can pinpoint me exactly, the moment I open my mouth, like they can at home. I can be whoever the hell I want. It's fantastic."

I frowned. He'd forced the question on me. "And who do you want to be, Aimeric?"

"Who I am now," he replied vehemently, "absolutely no doubt about it. I won't tell you my new name, of course, you don't want to know that. But here I am, doing nobody any harm, creating prosperity and employment for hundreds of honest citizens, and enjoying myself tremendously, for the first time in my life."

"Music?" I asked.

"Screw music." He beamed at me. "I hardly ever think about it anymore. It's a little thing called a sense of perspective. It was only when I got here and my life started coming back together that I realized the truth. Music only ever made me miserable. You know what? I haven't been in a fight since I got here. I hardly drink, I've given up the gambling. Oh yes, and I'm engaged to be married to a very nice respectable girl whose father owns a major haulage business. And that's all thanks to olive oil. All music ever got me was a rope around my neck."

I looked at him. "Fine," I said. "I believe you. And I'm really pleased things have worked out so well for you. So what are you doing here, in my room in the middle of the night?"

The smile didn't fade, but it froze. "Ah well," he said, "listening to music's a different matter, I still enjoy that. I came to tell you how much I enjoyed the recital. That's all."

"You mean the symphony."

He shook his head. "No," he said, "the rest of the program. Your own unaided work. At least," he added, with a slight twitch of an eyebrow, "I assume it is. Or have you enlisted another collaborator?"

I frowned at him. I hadn't deserved that.

"In that case," he said, "I really must congratulate you. You've grown." He paused, and looked me in the eye. "You've grown wings." Suddenly the grin was back, mocking, patronizing. "Or hadn't you noticed? You used to write the most awful rubbish."

"Yes," I said.

"But not anymore." He stood up, and for a split second I was terrified. But he walked to the table and poured a glass of wine. "I don't know what's got into you, but the difference is extraordinary." He pointed to the second glass. I nodded, and he poured. "You write like you're not afraid of the music any more. In fact, it sounds like you're not afraid of anything. That's the secret, you know."

"I was always terrified of failure."

"Not unreasonably," he said, and brought the glasses over. I took mine and set it down beside the bed. "Good stuff, this."

"I can afford the best."

He nodded. "Do you like it?"

"Not much."

That made him smile. He topped up his glass. "My father had excellent taste in wine," he said. "If it wasn't at least twenty years old and bottled within sight of Mount Bezar, it was only fit for pickling onions. He drank the farm and the timber lot and six blocks of good City property which brought in more than all the rest put together, and then he died and left my older brother to sort out the mess. Last I heard, he was a little old man in a straw hat working all the hours God made, and still the bank foreclosed; he's three years older than me, for crying out loud. And my other brother had to join the army. He died at Settingen. Everlasting glory they called it in temple, but I know for a fact he was terrified of soldiering. He tried to hide in the barn when the carriage came to take him to the academy, and my mother dragged him out by his hair. Which has led me to the view that sometimes, refinement and gracious living come at too high a price." He looked at me over the rim of the glass and smiled. "But I don't suppose you'd agree."

I shrugged. "I'm still living in the same rooms in college," I replied.

"And five days a week, dinner is still bread and cheese on a tray in front of the fire. It wasn't greed for all the luxuries. It was being afraid of the other thing." My turn to smile. "Never make the mistake of attributing to greed that which can be explained by fear. I should know. I've lived with fear every day of my life."

He sighed. "You're not drinking," he said.

"I think I've got the start of an ulcer," I said.

He shook his head sadly. "I really am genuinely pleased," he said. "About your music. You know what? I always used to despise you; all that knowledge, all that skill and technique, and no wings. You couldn't soar, so you spent your life trying to invent a flying machine. I learned to fly by jumping off cliffs." He yawned, and scratched the back of his neck. "Of course, most people who try it that way end up splattered all over the place, but it worked just fine for me."

"I didn't jump," I said. "I was pushed."

A big, wide grin spread slowly over his face, like oil on water. "And now you want to tell me how grateful you are."

"Not really, no."

"Oh come on." He wasn't the least bit angry, just amused. Probably just as well the sword was in the trunk. "What the hell did I ever do to you? Look at what I've given you, over the years. The prestige and reflected glory of being my teacher. The symphony. And now you can write music almost as good, all on your own. And what did I get in return? A hundred angels."

"Two hundred," I said coldly. "You've forgotten the previous loan."

He laughed, and dug a hand in his pocket. "Actually, no," he said. "The other reason I'm here." He took out a fat, fist-sized purse and put it on the table. "A hundred and ten angels. I'm guessing at the interest, since we didn't agree a specific rate at the time."

Neither of us said a word for quite some time. Then I stood up, leaned across the table and took the purse.

"Aren't you going to count it?"

"You're a gentleman," I said. "I trust you."

He nodded, like a fencer admitting a good hit. "I think," he said, "that makes us all square, don't you? Unless there's anything else I've forgotten about."

"All square," I said. "Except for one thing."

That took him by surprise. "What?"

"You shouldn't have given up music," I said.

"Don't be ridiculous," he snapped at me. "I'd have been arrested and hung."

I shrugged. "Small price to pay," I said. Which is what he'd said, when he first told me he'd killed a man; a small price to pay for genius. And what I'd said, when I heard all the details. "Don't glower at me like that," I went on. "You were a genius. You wrote music that'll still be played when Perimadeia's just a grassy hill. The Grand Mass, the Third symphony, that's probably all that'll survive of the empire in a thousand years. What was the life of one layabout and one prison warder, against that? Nothing."

"I'd have agreed with you once," he replied. "Now, I'm not so sure."

"Oh, I am. Absolutely certain of it. And if it was worth their lives, it's worth the life of an olive oil merchant, if there was to be just one more concerto. As it is—" I shrugged. "Not up to me, of course, I was just your teacher. That's all I'll ever be, in a thousand years' time. I guess I should count myself lucky for that."

He looked at me for a long time. "Bullshit," he said. "You and I only ever wrote for money. And you don't mean a word of what you've just said." He stood up. "It was nice to see you again. Keep writing. At this rate, one of these days you'll produce something worth listening to."

He left, and I bolted the door; too late by then, of course. That's me all over, of course; I always leave things too late, until they no longer matter.

When I got back to the university, I paid a visit to a colleague of mine in the natural philosophy department. I took with me a little bottle, into which I'd poured the contents of a wineglass. A few days later he called on me and said, "You were right."

I nodded. "I thought so."

"Archer's root," he said. "Enough of it to kill a dozen men. Where in God's name did you come by it?"

"Long story," I told him. "Thank you. Please don't mention it to anybody, there's a good fellow."

He shrugged, and gave me back the bottle. I took it outside and poured it away in a flower bed. Later that day I made a donation—one hundred and ten angels—to the Poor Brothers, for their orphanage in Lower Town; the first, last and only charitable donation of my life. The Father recognized me, of course, and asked if I wanted it to be anonymous.

"Not likely," I said. "I want my name up on a wall somewhere, where people can see it. Otherwise, where's the point?"

I think I may have mentioned my elder brother, Segibert; the one I rescued from the cart on the mountainside, along with my father. I remember him with fondness, though I realized at a comparatively early age that he was a stupid man, bone idle and a coward. My father knew it too, and my mother, so when Segibert was nineteen he left home. Nobody was sorry to see him go. He made a sort of a living doing the best he could, and even his best was never much good. When he was thirty-five he drifted into Perimadeia, married a retired prostitute (her retirement didn't last very long, apparently) and made a valiant attempt at running a tavern, which lasted for a really quite creditable eight months. By the time the bailiffs went in, his wife was pregnant, the money was long gone, and Segibert could best be described as a series of brief intervals between drinks. I'd just been elected to my chair, the youngest ever professor of music; the last thing I wanted was any contact whatsoever with my disastrous brother. In the end I gave him thirty angels, all the money I had, on condition that he went away and I never saw him again. He fulfilled his end of the deal by dying a few months later. By then, however, he'd acquired a son as well as a widow. She had her vocation to fall back on, which was doubtless a great comfort to her. When he came of age, or somewhat before, my nephew followed his father's old profession. I got a scribbled note from him when he was nineteen, asking me for bail money, which I neglected to answer, and that was all the contact there was between us. I never met him. He died young.

My second visit to a condemned cell. Essentially the same as the first one; walls, ceiling, floor, a tiny barred window, a stone ledge for sitting and sleeping. A steel door with a small sliding hatch in the top.

"I didn't think there was an extradition treaty between us and Baudoin," I said.

He lifted his head out of his hands. "There isn't," he said. "So they snatched me off the street, shoved me into a closed carriage and drove me across the border. Three days before my wedding," he added. "Syrisca will be half dead with worry about me."

"Surely that was illegal."

He nodded. "Yes," he said. "I believe there's been a brisk exchange of notes between the embassies, and the marquis has lodged an official complaint. Strangely enough, I'm still here."

I looked at him. It was dark in the cell, so I couldn't see much. "You've got a beard," I said. "That's new."

"Syrisca thought I'd look good in a beard."

I held back, postponing the moment. "I suppose you feel hard done by," I said.

"Yes, actually." He swung his legs up onto the ledge and crouched, hugging his knees to his chin. "Fair enough, I did some stupid things when I was a kid. But I did some pretty good things too. And then I gave both of them up, settled down and turned into a regular citizen. It's been a long time. I really thought I was free and clear."

Surreptitiously I looked round the cell. What I was looking for didn't seem to be there, but it was pretty dark. "How did they find you?" I asked.

He shrugged. "No idea," he said. "I can only assume someone from the old days must've recognized me, but I can't imagine who it could've been. I gave up music," he added bitterly. "Surely that ought to have counted for something."

He'd taken care not to tell me his new name, that night in the inn, but a rising young star in the Baudoin olive oil trade wasn't hard to find. Maybe he shouldn't have given me that much information. But he hadn't expected me to live long enough to make use of it.

"You tried to poison me," I said.

He looked at me, and his eyes were like glass. "Yes," he said. "Sorry about that. I'm glad you survived, if that means anything to you."

"Why?"

"Why did I do it?" He gave me a bemused look. "Surely that's obvious. You recognized me. I knew you'd realized who I was, as soon as our eyes met at the recital. That was really stupid of me," he went on, looking away. "I should've guessed you'd never have turned me in."

"So it was nearly three murders," I said. "That tends to undercut your assertion that you've turned over a new leaf."

"Yes," he said. "And my theory that it was somehow connected to writing music, since I'd given up by the time I tried to kill you. I really am sorry about that, by the way."

I gave him a weak smile. "I forgive you," I said.

"Thanks."

"Also," I went on, "I've been to see the duke. He's a great admirer of my work, you know."

"Is that right?"

"Oh yes. And to think you once called him a savage."

"He's not the man his father was," he replied. "I think the old duke might have pardoned me. You know, for services to music."

"Sighvat didn't put it quite like that," I replied. "It was more as a personal favor to me."

There was quite a long silence; just like—I'm sorry, but I really can't resist the comparison—a rest at a crucial moment in a piece of music. "He's letting me go?"

"Not quite," I said, as gently as I could. "He reckons he's got to consider the feelings of the victim's family. Fifteen years. With luck and good behaviour, you'll be out in ten."

He took it in two distinct stages; first the shudder, the understandable horror at the thought of an impossibly long time in hell; then, slowly but successfully pulling himself out of despair, as he considered the alternative. "I can live with that," he said.

"I'm afraid you'll have to," I replied. "I'm sorry. It was the best I could do."

He shook his head. "I'm the one who should apologize," he said. "I tried to kill you, and you just saved my life." He looked up, and even in the dim light I could see an expression on his face I don't think I'd ever seen before. "You always were better than me," he said. "I didn't deserve that."

I shrugged. "We're quits, then," I said. "For the symphony. But there's one condition."

He made a vague sort of gesture to signify capitulation. "Whatever," he said.

"You've got to start writing music again."

For a moment, I think he was too bewildered to speak. Then he burst out laughing. "That's ridiculous," he said. "It's been so long, I haven't even thought about it."

"It'll come back to you, I bet. Not my condition, by the way," I added, lying. "The duke's. So unless you want a short walk and an even shorter drop, I suggest you look to it. Did you get the paper I had sent up, by the way?"

"Oh, that was you, was it?" He looked at me a bit sideways. "Yes, thanks. I wiped my arse with it."

"In future, use your left hand, it's what it's for. It's a serious condition, Aimeric. It's Sighvat's idea of making restitution. I think it's a good one."

There was another moment of silence. "Did you tell him?"

"Tell him what?"

"That I wrote the symphony. Was that what decided him?"

"I didn't, actually," I said. "But the thought had crossed my mind. Luckily, I didn't have to."

He nodded. "That's all right, then." He sighed, as though he was glad some long and tedious chore was over. "I guess it's like the people who put caged birds out on windowledges in the sun," he said. "Lock 'em up and torture them to make them sing. I never approved of that. Cruel, I call it."

"A small price to pay for birdsong," I said.

Most of what I told him was true. I did go to Duke Sighvat to intercede for him. Sighvat was mildly surprised, given that I'd been the one who informed on him in the first place. I didn't tell the duke about the attempt to poison me. The condition was my idea, but Sighvat approved of it. He has rather fanciful notions about poetic justice, which if you ask me is a downright contradiction in terms.

I did bend the truth a little. To begin with, Sighvat was all for giving Subtilius a clear pardon. It was me who said no, he should go to prison instead; and when I explained why I wanted that, he agreed, so I was telling the truth when I told Subtilius it was because of the wishes of the victim's family.

Quite. The young waste-of-space Subtilius murdered was my nephew, Segibert's boy. I didn't find that out until after I helped Subtilius escape, and looking back, I wonder what I'd have done if I'd known at the time. I'm really not sure—which is probably just as well, since I have the misfortune to live with myself, and knowing how I'd have chosen, had I been in full possession of the facts, could quite possibly make that relationship unbearable. Fortunately, it's an academic question.

Subtilius is quite prolific, in his prison cell. Actually, it's not at all bad. I got him moved from the old castle to the barbican tower, and it's really quite comfortable there. In fact, his cell is more or less identical in terms of furnishings and facilities to my rooms in college, and I pay the warders to give him decent food and the occasional bottle of wine. He doesn't have to worry about money, either. Unfortunately, the quantity of his output these days isn't matched by the quality. It's good stuff, highly accomplished, technically proficient and very agreeable to listen to, but no spark of genius, none whatsoever. I don't know. Maybe he still has the wings, but in his cage, on the windowsill, where I put him, he can't really make much use of them.

VALLEY OF THE GIRLS

KELLY LINK

Kelly Link published her first story, " Water Off a Black Dog's Back," in 1995 and attended the Clarion Writers Workshop in the same year. A writer of subtle, challenging, sometimes whimsical fantasy, Link has published close to thirty stories which have won the Hugo, Nebula, World Fantasy, British SF, and Locus awards, and collected in 4 Stories, Stranger Things Happen, Magic for Beginners, *and* Pretty Monsters. *Link is also an accomplished editor, working on acclaimed small press 'zine* Lady Churchill's Rosebud Wristlet *and co-edited* The Year's Best Fantasy and Horror *with husband Gavin J. Grant and Ellen Datlow.*

Once, for about a month or two, I decided I was going to be a different kind of guy. Muscley. Not always thinking so much. My body was going to be a temple, not a dive bar. The kitchen made me smoothies, raw eggs blended with kale and wheat germ and bee pollen. That sort of thing. I stopped drinking, flushed all of Darius's goodies down the toilet. I was civil to my Face. I went running. I read the books, did the homework my tutor assigned. I was a model son, a good brother. The Olds didn't know what to think.

[Hero], of course, knew something was up. Twins always know. Maybe she saw the way I watched her Face when there was an event and we all had to do the public thing.

Meanwhile, I could see the way that [Hero]'s Face looked at my Face. There was no way that this was going to end well. So I gave up on raw eggs and virtue and love. Fell right back into the old life, the high life, the good, sweet, sour, rotten old life. Was it much of a life? It had its moments.

"Oh shit," [Hero] says. "I think I've made a terrible mistake. Help me, [   ]. Help me, please?"

She drops the snake. I step hard on its head. Nobody here is having a good night.

"You have to give me the code," I say. "Give me the code and I'll go get help."

She bends over and pukes stale champagne on my shoes. There are two drops of blood on her arm. "It hurts," she says. "It hurts really bad."

"Give me the code, [Hero]."

She cries for a while, and then she stops. She won't say anything. She just sits and rocks. I stroke her hair, and ask her for the code. When she doesn't give it to me, I go over and start trying numbers. I try our birthday. I try a lot of numbers. None of them work.

I chased the same route every day for that month. Down through the woods at the back of the guesthouse, into the Valley of the Girls just as the sun was coming up. That's how you ought to see the pyramids, you know. With the sun coming up. I liked to take a piss at the foot of [Alicia]'s pyramid. Later on I told [Alicia] I pissed on her pyramid. "Marking your territory, [   ]?" she said. She ran her fingers through my hair.

I don't love [Alicia]. I don't hate [Alicia]. Her Face had this plush, red mouth. Once I put a finger up against her lips, just to see how they felt. You're not supposed to mess with people's Faces, but everybody I know does it. What's the Face going to do? Quit?

But [Alicia] had better legs. Longer, rounder, the kind you want to die between. I wish she were here right now. The sun is up, but it isn't going to shine on me for a long time. We're down here in the cold, and [Hero] isn't speaking to me.

What is it with rich girls and pyramids anyway?

In hieroglyphs, you put the names of the important people, kings and queens and gods, in a cartouche. Like this.

[Stevie]
[Preeti]
[Nishi]

[Hero]
[Angela]
[Alicia]
[Liberty]
[Vyvian]
[Yumiko]
[   ]

"Were you really going to do it?" [Hero] wants to know. This is before the snake, before I know what she's up to.

"Yeah," I say.

"Why?"

"Why not?" I say. "Lots of reasons. 'Why' is kind of a dumb question, isn't it? I mean, why did God make me so pretty? Why size four jeans?"

There's a walk-in closet in the burial chamber. I went through it looking for something useful. Anything useful. Silk shawls, crushed velvet dresses, black jeans. A stereo system loaded with the kind of music rich goth girls listen to. Extra pillows. Sterling silver. Perfumes, makeup. A mummified cat. [Noodles.] I remember when [Noodles] died. We were eight. They were already laying the foundations of [Hero]'s pyramid. The Olds called in the embalmers.

We helped with the natron. I had nightmares for a week.

[Hero] says, "They're for the afterlife, OK?"

"You're not going to be fat in the afterlife?" At this point, I still don't know [Hero]'s plan, but I'm starting to worry. [Hero] has a taste for the epic. I suppose it runs in the family.

"My *Ba* is skinny," [Hero] says. "Unlike you, [   ]. You may be skinny on the outside, but you have a fat-ass heart. Anubis will judge you. Ammit will devour you."

She sounds so serious. I should laugh. You try laughing when you're down in the dark, in your sister's secret burial chamber—not the decoy one where everybody hangs out and drinks, where once, oh god, how sweet is that memory, still, you and your sister's Face did it on the memorial stone—under three hundred thousand limestone blocks, down at the bottom of a shaft behind a door in an antechamber that maybe, somebody, in a couple of hundred years, will stumble into.

What kind of afterlife do you get to have as a mummy? If you're [Hero], I guess you believe your *Ba* and *Ka* will reunite in the afterlife. [Hero] thinks she's going to be an *Akh*, an immortal. She and the rest of them go around stockpiling everything they think they need to have an excellent afterlife. They're rich. The Olds indulge them. It's just the girls. The girls plan for the afterlife. The boys play sports, collect race cars or twentieth-century space shuttles, scheme to get laid. I specialize in the latter.

The girls have *ushabti* made of themselves, give them to each other at the pyramid dedication ceremonies, the sweet sixteen parties. They collect *shabti* of their favorite singers, actors, whatever. They read *The Book of the Dead*. In the meantime, their pyramids are where we go to have a good time. When I commissioned the artist who makes my *ushabti*, I had her make two different kinds. One is for people I don't know well. The other *shabti* for the girls I've slept with. I modeled for that one in the nude. If I'm going to hang out with these girls in the afterlife, I want to have all my working parts.

Me, I've done some reading, too. What happens once you're a mummy? Graverobbers dig you up. Sometimes they grind you up and sell you as medicine, fertilizer, pigment. People used to have these mummy parties. Invite their friends over and unwrap a mummy. See what's inside.

Maybe you end up in a display case in a museum. Or nobody ever finds you. Or your curse kills lots of people. I know which one I'm hoping for.

"[   ]," [Yumiko] said, "I don't want this thing to be boring. Fireworks and Faces, celebrities promoting their new thing."

This was earlier.

Once [Yumiko] and I did it in [Angela]'s pyramid, right in front of a false door. Another time she punched me in the side of the face because she caught me and [Preeti] in bed. Gave me a cauliflower ear.

[Yumiko]'s pyramid isn't quite as big as [Stevie]'s, or even [Preeti]'s pyramid. But it's on higher ground. From up on top, you can see down to the ocean.

"So what do you want me to do?" I asked her.

"Just do something," [Yumiko] said.

I had an idea right away.

"Let me out, [Hero]."

We came down here with a bottle of champagne. [Hero] asked me to open it. By the time I had the cork out, she'd shut the door. No handle. Just a key pad.

"Eventually you're going to have to let me out, [Hero]."

"Do you remember the watermelon game?" [Hero] says. We're remi-niscing about the good old times. I think. She's lying on a divan. She lit a couple of oil lamps when she brought me down here. We were going to have a serious talk. Only it turned out it wasn't about what I thought it was about. It wasn't about the sex tape. It was about the other thing.

"It's really cold down here," I say. "I'm going to catch a cold."

"Tough," [Hero] says.

I pace a bit. "The watermelon game. With [Vyvian]'s unicorn?" [Vyvian] is twice as rich as God. She's a year younger than us, but her pyramid is three times the size of [Hero]'s. She kisses like a fish, fucks like a wildebeest, and her hobby is breeding chimeras. Most of the estates around here have a real problem with unicorns now, thanks to [Vyvian]. They're territorial. You don't mess with them in mating season. I came up with this variation on French bullfighting, *Taureux Piscine*, except with unicorns. You got a point every time you and the unicorn were in the swimming pool together. We did *Licorne Pasteque*, too. Brought out a sidetable and a couple of chairs and set them up on the lawn. Cut up the watermelon and took turns. You can eat the watermelon, but only while you're sitting at the table. Meanwhile the unicorn is getting more and more pissed off that you're in its territory.

It was insanely awesome until the stupid unicorn broke its leg going into the pool, and somebody had to come and put a bullet in its head. Plus, the Olds got mad about one of the chairs. The unicorn splintered the back. Turned out to be an antique. Priceless.

"Do you remember how [Vyvian] cried and cried?" [Hero] says. Even this is part of the happy memory for [Hero]. She hates [Vyvian]. Why? Some boring reason. I forget the specifics. Here's the gist of it: [Hero] is fat. [Vyvian] is mean.

"I felt sorrier for whoever was going to have to clean up the pool," I say.

"Liar," [Hero] says. "You're a sociopath. You've never felt sorry for anyone in your life. You were going to kill all of our friends. I'm doing the world a huge favor."

"They aren't your friends," I say. "I don't know why you'd want to save a single one of them."

[Hero] says nothing. Her eyes get pink.

I say, "They'll find us eventually." We've both got implants, of course. Implants to keep the girls from getting pregnant, to make us puke if we try drugs or take a drink. There are ways to get around this. Darius is always good for new solutions. The implant—the Entourage—is also a way for our parents' security teams to monitor us. In case of kidnappers. In case we go places that are off limits, or run off. Rich people don't like to lose their stuff.

"This chamber has some pretty interesting muffling qualities," [Hero] says. "I installed the hardware myself. Top-gear spy stuff. You know, just in case."

"In case of what?" I ask.

She ignores that. "Also, I paid a guy for fifteen hundred microdot trackers. Seven hundred and fifty have your profile. Seven hundred and fifty have mine. They're programmed to go on and offline in random clusters, at irregular intervals, for the next three months, starting about two hours ago, when you were setting up your video feeds on Tara and Philip.

"Who?" I say.

"Your Face and my Face," [Hero] says. "You freak." She turns bright red, and now there are tears in her eyes, but her voice stays calm. "Anyway. The trackers are being distributed to partygoers at raves worldwide tonight. They're glued onto promotional material inside a CD for one of my favorite bands. Nobody you'd know. Oh, and all the guests at [Yumiko]'s party got one too, and I left a CD at all of the false doors at all of the pyramids, like offerings. Those are all live right now."

I've always been the good-looking one. The popular one. The smart one. Sometimes I forget that [Hero] is as smart as I am. Maybe even smarter.

"I love you, [   ]."

[Liberty] falls in love all the time. But I was curious. I said, "You love me? Why do you love me?"

She thought about it for a minute. "Because you're insane," she said. "You don't care about anything."

"That's why you love me?" I said. We were at a gala or something. We'd just come back from the Men's room where everybody was trying out Darius's new drug.

My Face was hanging out with my parents in front of all the cameras. The Olds love my Face. The son they wish they had. Somebody with a tray walked by and [Hero]'s Face took a glass of champagne. She was over by the buffet table. The other buffet table, the one for Faces and the Olds and the celebrities and the publicists and all the other tribes and hangers on.

My darling. My working girl. My sister's Face. I tried to catch her eye, clowning in my latex leggings, but I was invisible. Every gesture, every word was for them, for him. The cameras. My Face. And me? A speck of nothing. Not even a blot. Negative space.

She'd said we couldn't see each other anymore. She said she was afraid of getting caught breaking contract. Like that didn't happen all the time. Like with Mr. Amandit. [Preeti] and [Nishi]'s father. He left his wife. It was [Liberty]'s Face he left his wife for. The Face of his daughters' best friend. I think they're in Iceland now, Mr. Amandit and the nobody girl who used to be a Face.

Then there's [Stevie]. Everybody knows she's in love with her own Face. It's embarrassing to watch.

Anyway, nobody knew about us. I was always careful. Even if [Hero] got her nose in, what was she going to say? What was she going to do?

"I love you because you're you, [   ]," [Liberty] said. "You're the only person I know who's better looking than their own Face."

I was holding a skewer of chicken. I almost stabbed it into [Liberty]'s arm before I knew what I was doing. My mouth was full of chewed chicken. I spat it out at [Liberty]. It landed on her cheek.

"What the fuck, [   ]!" [Liberty] said. The piece of chicken plopped down onto the floor. Everybody was staring. Nobody took a picture. I didn't exist. Nobody had done anything wrong.

Aside from that, we all had a good time. Even [Liberty] says so. That was the time all of us showed up in this gear I found online. Red rubber, plenty of pointy stuff, chains and leather, dildos and codpieces, vampire teeth and plastinated viscera. I had a really nice pair of hand-painted latex tits wobbling around like epaulets on my shoulders. I had an inadequately sedated fruit bat caged up in my pompadour. So how could she not look at me?

Kids today, the Olds say. What can you do?

I may be down here for some time. I'm going to try to see it the way they see it, the Olds.

You're an Old. So you think, wouldn't it be easier if your children did what they were told? Like your employees? Wouldn't it be nice, at least when you're out in public with the family? The Olds are rich. They're used to people doing what they're told to do.

When you're as rich as the Olds are, you are your own brand. That's what the publicists are always telling them. Your children are an extension of your brand. They can improve your Q rating or they can degrade it. Mostly they can degrade it. So there's the device they implant that makes us invisible to cameras. It's called an Entourage.

And then there's the Face. Who is a nobody, a real person, who comes and takes your place at the table. They get an education, the best health care, a salary, all the nice clothes and all the same toys that you get. They get your parents whenever the publicists decide there's a need or an opportunity. If you go online, or turn on the TV, there they are, being you. Being better than you will ever be at being you. When you look at yourself in the mirror, you have to be careful, or you'll start to feel very strange. Is that really you?

But it isn't just about the brand, or having good children who do what they're told, right? The Olds say it's about kidnappers, blackmailers, all those people who want to take away what belongs to the Olds. Faces mitigate the risk.

Most politicians have Faces too. For safety. Because it shouldn't matter what someone looks like, or how good they are at making a speech, but of course it does. The difference is that politicians choose to have their Faces. They choose.

The Olds like to say it's because we're children. We'll understand when we're older, when we start our adult lives without blemish, without online evidence of our indiscretions, our mistakes. No sex tapes. No embarrassing photos of ourselves in Nazi regalia, or topless in Nice, or honeytraps. No footage before the nose job, before the boob job, before the acne clears up.

The Olds get us into good colleges, and then the world tilts just for a moment, and maybe we fall off. We get a few years to make our own mistakes, out in the open, and then we settle down, and we come into our millions or billions or whatever. We inherit the earth, like that proverb says. The rich shall inherit the earth.

We get married, merge our money with other money, millions or billions, improve our Q ratings, become Olds, acquire kids, and you bet your ass those kids are going to have Faces, just like we did.

I never got into the Egyptian thing the way the girls did. I always liked the Norse gods better. You know, Loki. The slaying of Baldur. Ragnarok.

It wasn't hard to get hold of the thing I was looking for. Darius couldn't help me, but he knew a guy who knew a guy who knew exactly what I was talking about. We met in Las Vegas, because why not? We saw a show together, and then we went online and watched a video that had been filmed in his lab. Somewhere in Moldova, he said. He said his name was Nikolay.

I showed him my video. The one I'd made for the party for [Yumiko]'s pyramid dedication thingy.

We were both very drunk. I'd taken Darius's blocker, and he was interested in that. I explained about the Entourage, how you had to work around it if you wanted to have fun. He was sympathetic.

He liked the video a lot.

"That's me," I told him. "That's [   ]."

"Not you," he said. "You're making joke at me. You have Entourage device. But, girl, she is very nice. Very sexy."

"That's my sister," I said. "My twin sister."

"Another joke," Nikolay said. "But, if my sister, I would go ahead, fuck her anyway."

"How could you do this to me?" [Hero] wants to know.

"It had nothing to do with you." I pat her back when she starts to cry. I don't know whether she's talking about the sex tape or the other thing.

"It was bad enough when you slept with her," she says, weeping. "That was practically incest. But I saw the tape. The one you gave [Yumiko]. The one she's going to put up online. Don't you understand? She's me. He's you. That's us, on that tape, that's us having sex."

"It was good enough for the Egyptians," I say, trying to console her. "Besides, it isn't us. Remember? They aren't us."

I try to remember what it was like when it was just us. The Olds say we slept in the same crib. We had our own language. [Hero] cried when I fell down. [Hero] has always been the one who cries.

"How did you know what I was planning?"

"Oh, please, [   ]," [Hero] says. "I always know when you're about to go off the deep end. You go around with this smile on your face, like the whole world is sucking you off. Besides, Darius told me you'd been asking about really bad shit. He likes me, you know. He likes me much better than you."

"He's the only one," I say.

"Fuck you," [Hero] says. "Anyway, it's not like you were the only one with plans for tonight. I'm sick of this place. Sick of these people."

There is a martial line of *shabti* on a stone shelf. Our friends. People who would like to be our friends. Rock stars that the Olds used to hang out with, movie stars. Saudi princes who like fat, gloomy girls with money. She picks up a prince, throws it against the wall.

"Fuck [Vyvian] and all her unicorns," [Hero] says.

She picks up another *shabti*. "Fuck [Yumiko]."

I take [Yumiko] from her. "I did," I say. "I give her a three out of five.

For enthusiasm." I drop the *shabti* on the floor.

"You are such a slut, [   ]," [Hero] says. "Have you ever been in love? Even once?"

She's fishing. She knows. My heart is broken, and [Hero] knows. Is that how it works?

Why did you sleep with him? Are you in love with him? He's me. Why aren't I him? Fuck both of you.

"Fuck our parents," I say. I pick up the oil lamp and throw it at the *shabti* on the shelf.

The room gets brighter for a moment, then darker.

"It's funny," [Hero] says. "We used to do everything together. And then we didn't. And right now, it's weird. You planning on doing what you were going to do. And me, what I was planning. It's like we were in each other's brains again."

"You went out and bought a biological agent? We should have gone in on it together. Buy two and get one free."

"No," [Hero] says. She looks shy, like she's afraid I'll laugh at her.

I wait. Eventually she'll tell me what she needs to tell me, and then I'll hand over the little metal canister that Nikolay gave me, and she'll unlock the door to the burial chamber. Then we'll go back up into the world, and that video won't be the end of the world. It will just be something that people talk about. Something to make the Olds crazy.

"I was going to kill myself," [Hero] says. "You know, down here. I was going to come down here during the party, and then I decided that I didn't want to do it by myself."

My heart is broken, and so [Hero] wants to die. Is that how it works?

"And then I found out what you were up to," [Hero] says. "I thought I ought to stop you. Then I wouldn't have to be alone. And I would finally live up to my name. I'd save everybody. Even if they never knew it."

"You were going to kill yourself," I repeat. "How?"

"Like this," [Hero] says. She reaches into the jeweled box on her belt. There's a little thing curled up in there, an enameled loop of chain, black and bronze. It uncoils in her hand, becomes a snake.

[Alicia] was the first of us to get a Face. I got mine when I was ten. I didn't really know what was going on. I met all these boys my age, and then the Olds sat down and had a talk with me. They explained what was going on, said that I got to pick which Face I wanted. I picked the one who looked the nicest, the one who looked like he might be fun to hang out with. That's how stupid I was back then.

[Hero] couldn't choose, so I did it for her. Pick her, I said. That's how strange life is. I picked her out of all the others.

[Yumiko] said she'd already talked to her Face. (We talk to our Faces as little as possible, although sometimes we sleep with each others'. Forbidden fruit is always freakier. Is that why I did what I did? I don't know. How am I supposed to know?) [Yumiko] said her Face agreed to sign a new contract when [Yumiko] turns eighteen. She doesn't see any reason to give up having a Face.

[Nishi] is [Preeti]'s younger sister. They only broke ground on her pyramid last summer. Upper management teams from her father's company came out to lay the first course of stones. A team-building exercise. Usually it's prisoners from the Supermax prison out in Pelican Bay. Once they get to work, they mostly look the same. It's hard work. We like to go out and watch.

Every once in a while a consulting archeologist or an architect will come over and try to make conversation. They think we want context.

They talk about grave goods, about how one day archeologists will know what life was like because a couple of girls decided they wanted to build their own pyramids.

We think that's funny.

They like to complain about the climate. Apparently it isn't ideal. "Of course, they may not be standing give or take a couple of hundred years. Once you factor in geological events. Earthquakes. There's the geopolitical dimension. There's graverobbers."

They go on and on about the cunning of graverobbers.

We get them drunk. We ask them about the curse of the mummies just to see them get worked up. We ask them if they aren't worried about the Olds. We ask what used to happen to the men who built the pyramids in Egypt. Didn't they used to disappear, we ask? Just to make sure nobody knew where the good stuff was buried? We say there are one or two members of the consulting team who worked on [Alicia]'s pyramid that we were friendly with. We mention we haven't been able to get hold of them in a while, not since the pyramid was finished.

They were up on the unfinished outer wall of [Nishi]'s pyramid. I guess they'd been up there all night. Talking. Making love. Making plans.

They didn't see me. Invisible, that's what I am. I had my phone. I filmed them until my phone ran out of memory. There was a unicorn down in the meadow by a pyramid. [Alicia]'s pyramid. Two impossible things. Three things that shouldn't exist. Four.

That was when I gave up on becoming someone new, the running, the kale, the whole thing. That was when I gave up on becoming the new me. Somebody already was that person. Somebody already had the only thing I wanted.

"Give me the code." I say it over and over again. I don't know how long it's been. [Hero]'s arm is greenish-black and blown up like a balloon. I tried sucking out the venom. Maybe that did some good. Maybe I didn't think of it soon enough.

"[   ]?" [Hero] says. "I don't want to die."

"I don't want you to die either," I say. I try to sound like I mean it. I do mean it. "Give me the code. Let me save you."

"I don't want them to die," [Hero] says. "If I give you the code, you'll do it. And I'll die down here by myself."

"You're not going to die," I say. I stroke her cheek. "I'm not going to kill anyone."

After a while she says, "OK." Then she tells me the code. Maybe it's a string of numbers that means something to her. More likely it's random. I told you she was smarter than me.

I repeat the code back to her and she nods. I've covered her up with a shawl, because she's so cold. I lay her head down on a pillow, brush her hair back.

"I'll be right back," I say.

She closes her eyes. Gives me a horrible, blind smile.

I go over to the door and enter the code.

The door doesn't open. I try again and it still doesn't open.

"[Hero]? Tell me the code again?"

She doesn't say anything. She's fallen asleep. I go over and shake her gently. "Tell me the code one more time. Come on. One more time."

Her eyes stay closed. Her mouth falls open. Her tongue is poking out.

"[Hero]?"

It takes me a while to realize that she's dead. And now it's a little bit later, and my sister is still dead, and I'm still trapped down here with my dead sister and a bunch of broken *shabtis*. No food. No good music. Just a small canister of something nasty cooked up by my good friend

Nikolay, and some size four jeans and the dregs of a bottle of very expensive champagne.

The Egyptians believed that every night the spirit of the person buried in the pyramids rose up through the false doors to go out into the world. Their *Ba*. Your *Ba* can't be confined in a small dark room at the bottom of a deep shaft hidden under some pile of stones. Maybe I'll fly out some night, some part of me. I keep trying combinations, but I don't know how many numbers [Hero] used, what combination. It's an endless task. There's not much oil left to light the lamps. Some air comes in through the bottom of the door, but not much. It smells bad in here. I wrapped [Hero] up in her shawls and hid her in the closet. She's in there with [Noodles]. I put him in her arms. Every once in a while I fall asleep and when I wake up I realize I don't know which numbers I've tried, which I haven't.

The Olds must wonder what happened. They'll think it had something to do with that sex tape. Their publicists will be doing damage control. I wonder what will happen to my Face. What will happen to her. Maybe one night I'll fly out. My *Ba* will fly right to her, like a bird.

One day someone will open the door that I can't. I'll be alive or else I won't. I can open the canister or I can leave it closed. What would you do? I talk about it with [Hero], down here in the dark. Sometimes I decide one thing, sometimes I decide another.

Dying of thirst is a hard way to die.

I don't really want to drink my own urine.

If I open the canister, I might die faster. It will be my curse on you, the one who opens the tomb.

I don't want you to know my name. It was his name, really.

Tara.

THE BRAVE LITTLE TOASTER

CORY DOCTOROW

Cory Doctorow is a science fiction author, activist, journalist and blogger—the co-editor of Boing Boing (boingboing.net) and the author of Tor Teens/ HarperCollins UK novels For the Win *and the bestselling* Little Brother. *His forthcoming books include a new young adult novel* Pirate Cinema, Rapture of the Nerds *(co-written with Charles Stross), and* Anda's Game, *a graphic novel based on his story of the same name. He is the former European director of the Electronic Frontier Foundation and co-founded the UK Open Rights Group. Born in Toronto, Canada, he now lives in London.*

One day, Mister Toussaint came home to find an extra 300 euros' worth of groceries on his doorstep. So he called up Miz Rousseau, the grocer, and said, "Why have you sent me all this food? My fridge is already full of delicious things. I don't need this stuff and besides, I can't pay for it."

But Miz Rousseau told him that he had ordered the food. His refrigerator had sent in the list, and she had the signed order to prove it.

Furious, Mister Toussaint confronted his refrigerator. It was mysteriously empty, even though it had been full that morning. Or rather, it was *almost* empty: there was a single pouch of energy drink sitting on a shelf in the back. He'd gotten it from an enthusiastically smiling young woman on the metro platform the day before. She'd been giving them to everyone.

"Why did you throw away all my food?" he demanded. The refrigerator hummed smugly at him.

"It was spoiled," it said.

But the food hadn't been spoiled. Mister Toussaint pored over his refrigerator's diagnostics and logfiles, and soon enough, he had the answer. It was the energy beverage, of course.

"Row, row, row your boat," it sang. "Gently down the stream. Merrily, merrily, merrily, merrily, I'm offgassing ethylene." Mister Toussaint sniffed the pouch suspiciously.

"No you're not," he said. The label said that the drink was called LOONY GOONY and it promised ONE TRILLION TIMES MORE POWERFUL THAN ESPRESSO!!!!!ONE11! Mister Toussaint began to suspect that the pouch was some kind of stupid Internet of Things prank. He hated those.

He chucked the pouch in the rubbish can and put his new groceries away.

The next day, Mister Toussaint came home and discovered that the overflowing rubbish was still sitting in its little bag under the sink. The can had not cycled it through the trapdoor to the chute that ran to the big collection-point at ground level, 104 storeys below.

"Why haven't you emptied yourself?" he demanded. The trashcan told him that toxic substances had to be manually sorted. "What toxic substances?"

So he took out everything in the bin, one piece at a time. You've probably guessed what the trouble was.

"Excuse me if I'm chattery, I do not mean to nattery, but I'm a mercury battery!" LOONY GOONY's singing voice really got on Mister Toussaint's nerves.

"No you're not," Mister Toussaint said.

Mister Toussaint tried the microwave. Even the cleverest squeezy-pouch couldn't survive a good nuking. But the microwave wouldn't switch on. "I'm no drink and I'm no meal," LOONY GOONY sang. "I'm a ferrous lump of steel!"

The dishwasher wouldn't wash it ("I don't mean to annoy or chafe, but I'm simply not dishwasher safe!"). The toilet wouldn't flush it ("I don't belong in the bog, because down there I'm sure to clog!"). The windows wouldn't retract their safety screen to let it drop, but that wasn't much of a surprise.

"I hate you," Mister Toussaint said to LOONY GOONY, and he stuck it in his coat pocket. He'd throw it out in a trash-can on the way to work.

They arrested Mister Toussaint at the 678th Street station. They were waiting for him on the platform, and they cuffed him just as soon as he stepped off the train. The entire station had been evacuated and the police wore full biohazard containment gear. They'd even shrinkwrapped their machine-guns.

"You'd better wear a breather and you'd better wear a hat, I'm a vial of terrible deadly hazmat," LOONY GOONY sang.

When they released Mister Toussaint the next day, they made him take LOONY GOONY home with him. There were lots more people with LOONY GOONYs to process.

Mister Toussaint paid the rush-rush fee that the storage depot charged to send over his container. They forklifted it out of the giant warehouse under the desert and zipped it straight to the cargo-bay in Mister Toussaint's building. He put on old, stupid clothes and clipped some lights to his glasses and started sorting.

Most of the things in the container were stupid. He'd been throwing away stupid stuff all his life, because the smart stuff was just so much easier. But then his grandpa had died and they'd cleaned out his little room at the pensioner's ward and he'd just shoved it all in the container and sent it out to the desert.

From time to time, he'd thought of the eight cubic meters of stupidity he'd inherited and sighed a put-upon sigh. He'd loved Grandpa, but he wished the old man had used some of the ample spare time from the tail end of his life to replace his junk with stuff that could more gracefully reintegrate with the materials stream.

How inconsiderate!

The house chattered enthusiastically at the toaster when he plugged it in, but the toaster said nothing back. It couldn't. It was stupid. Its bread-slots were crusted over with carbon residue and it dribbled crumbs from the ill-fitting tray beneath it. It had been designed and built by cavemen who hadn't ever considered the advantages of networked environments.

It was stupid, but it was brave. It would do anything Mister Toussaint asked it to do.

"It's getting hot and sticky and I'm not playing any games, you'd better get me out before I burst into flames!" LOONY GOONY sang loudly, but the toaster ignored it.

"I don't mean to endanger your abode, but if you don't let me out, I'm going to explode!" The smart appliances chattered nervously at one another, but the brave little toaster said nothing as Mister Toussaint depressed its lever again.

"You'd better get out and save your ass, before I start leaking poison gas!" LOONY GOONY's voice was panicky. Mister Toussaint smiled and depressed the lever.

Just as he did, he thought to check in with the flat's diagnostics. Just in time, too! Its quorum-sensors were redlining as it listened in on the appliances' consternation. Mister Toussaint unplugged the fridge and the microwave and the dishwasher.

The cooker and trash-can were hard-wired, but they didn't represent a quorum.

The fire department took away the melted toaster and used their axes to knock huge, vindictive holes in Mister Toussaint's walls. "Just looking for embers," they claimed. But he knew that they were pissed off because there was simply no good excuse for sticking a pouch of independently powered computation and sensors and transmitters into an antique toaster and pushing down the lever until oily, toxic smoke filled the whole 104th floor.

Mister Toussaint's neighbors weren't happy about it either.

But Mister Toussaint didn't mind. It had all been worth it, just to hear LOONY GOONY beg and weep for its life as its edges curled up and blackened.

He argued mightily, but the firefighters refused to let him keep the toaster.

THE DALA HORSE

MICHAEL SWANWICK

Michael Swanwick is one of the most acclaimed and prolific science fiction and fantasy writers of his generation. He has received a Hugo Award for fiction in an unprecedented five out of six years and has been honored with the Nebula, Theodore Sturgeon, World Fantasy, and five Hugo awards as well as receiving nominations for the British Science Fiction Award and the Arthur C. Clarke Award.

Michael's latest novel is Dancing with Bears, *a post-Utopian adventure featuring confidence artists Darger and Surplus. He is currently at work on two new novels.*

Something terrible had happened. Linnéa did not know what it was. But her father had looked pale and worried, and her mother had told her, very fiercely, "Be brave!" and now she had to leave, and it was all the result of that terrible thing.

The three of them lived in a red wooden house with steep black roofs by the edge of the forest. From the window of her attic room, Linnéa could see a small lake silver with ice very far away. The design of the house was unchanged from all the way back in the days of the Coffin People, who buried their kind in beautiful polished boxes with metal fittings like nothing anyone made anymore. Uncle Olaf made a living hunting down their coffin-sites and salvaging the metal from them. He wore a necklace of gold rings he had found, tied together with silver wire.

"Don't go near any roads," her father had said. "Especially the old ones." He'd given her a map. "This will help you find your grandmother's house."

"Mor-Mor?"

"No, Far-Mor. My mother. In Godastor."

Godastor was a small settlement on the other side of the mountain. Linnéa had no idea how to get there. But the map would tell her.

Her mother gave her a little knapsack stuffed with food, and a quick hug. She shoved something deep in the pocket of Linnéa's coat and said, "Now go! Before it comes!"

"Good-bye, Mor and Far," Linnéa had said formally, and bowed.

Then she'd left.

So it was that Linnéa found herself walking up a long, snowy slope, straight up the side of the mountain. It was tiring work, but she was a dutiful little girl. The weather was harsh, but whenever she started getting cold, she just turned up the temperature of her coat. At the top of the slope she came across a path, barely wide enough for one person, and so she followed it onward. It did not occur to her that this might be one of the roads her father had warned her against. She did not wonder at the fact that it was completely bare of snow.

After a while, though, Linnéa began to grow tired. So she took off her knapsack and dropped it in the snow alongside the trail and started to walk away.

"Wait!" the knapsack said. "You've left me behind."

Linnéa stopped. "I'm sorry," she said. "But you're too heavy for me to carry."

"If you can't carry me," said the knapsack, "then I'll have to walk."

So it did.

On she went, followed by the knapsack, until she came to a fork in the trail. One way went upward and the other down. Linnéa looked from one to the other. She had no idea which to take.

"Why don't you get out the map?" her knapsack suggested.

So she did.

Carefully, so as not to tear, the map unfolded. Contour lines squirmed across its surface as it located itself. Blue stream-lines ran downhill. Black roads and stitched red trails went where they would. "We're here," said the map, placing a pinprick light at its center. "Where would you like to go?"

"To Far-Mor," Linnéa said. "She's in Godastor."

"That's a long way. Do you know how to read maps?"

"No."

"Then take the road to the right. Whenever you come across another road, take me out and I'll tell you which way to go."

On Linnéa went, until she could go no further, and sat down in the snow beside the road. "Get up," the knapsack said. "You have to keep on going." The muffled voice of the map, which Linnéa had stuffed back into the knapsack, said, "Keep straight on. Don't stop now."

"Be silent, both of you," Linnéa said, and of course they obeyed. She pulled off her mittens and went through her pockets to see if she'd remembered to bring any toys. She hadn't, but in the course of looking she found the object her mother had thrust into her coat.

It was a dala horse.

Dala horses came in all sizes, but this one was small. They were carved out of wood and painted bright colors with a harness of flowers. Linnéa's horse was red; she had often seen it resting on a high shelf in her parents' house. Dala horses were very old. They came from the time of the Coffin People who lived long ago, before the time of the Strange Folk. The Coffin People and the Strange Folk were all gone now. Now there were only Swedes.

Linnéa moved the dala horse up and down, as if it were running. "Hello, little horse," she said.

"Hello," said the dala horse. "Are you in trouble?"

Linnéa thought. "I don't know," she admitted at last.

"Then most likely you are. You mustn't sit in the snow like that, you know. You'll burn out your coat's batteries."

"But I'm bored. There's nothing to do."

"I'll teach you a song. But first you have to stand up."

A little sulkily, Linnéa did so. Up the darkening road she went again, followed by the knapsack. Together she and the dala horse sang:

"Hark! through the darksome night
Sounds come a-winging:
Lo! 'tis the Queen of Light
Joyfully singing."

The shadows were getting longer and the depths of the woods to either side turned black. Birch trees stood out in the gloom like thin white ghosts. Linnéa was beginning to stumble with weariness when she saw a light ahead. At first she thought it was a house, but as she got closer, it became apparent it was a campfire.

There was a dark form slumped by the fire. For a second, Linnéa was afraid he was a troll. Then she saw that he wore human clothing and realized that he was a Norwegian or possibly a Dane. So she started to run toward him.

At the sound of her feet on the road, the man leaped up. "Who's there?" he cried. "Stay back—I've got a cudgel!"

Linnéa stopped. "It's only me," she said.

The man crouched a little, trying to see into the darkness beyond his campfire. "Step closer," he said. And then, when she obeyed, "What are you?"

"I'm just a little girl."

"Closer!" the man commanded. When Linnéa stood within the circle of firelight, he said, "Is there anybody else with you?"

"No, I'm all alone."

Unexpectedly, the man threw his head back and laughed. "Oh god!" he said. "Oh god, oh god, oh god, I was so afraid! For a moment there I thought you were… well, never mind." He threw his stick into the fire. "What's that behind you?"

"I'm her knapsack," the knapsack said.

"And I'm her map," a softer voice said.

"Well, don't just lurk there in the darkness. Stand by your mistress." When he had been obeyed, the man seized Linnéa by the shoulders. He had more hair and beard than anyone she had ever seen, and his face was rough and red. "My name is Günther, and I'm a dangerous man, so if I give you an order, don't even think of disobeying me. I walked here from Finland, across the Gulf of Bothnia. That's a long, long way on a very dangerous bridge, and there are not many men alive today who could do that."

Linnéa nodded, though she was not sure she understood.

"You're a Swede. You know nothing. You have no idea what the world is like. You haven't… tasted its possibilities. You've never let your fantasies eat your living brain." Linnéa couldn't make any sense out of what Günther was saying. She thought he must have forgotten she was a little girl. "You stayed here and led ordinary lives while the rest of us…" His eyes were wild. "I've seen horrible things. Horrible, horrible things." He shook Linnéa angrily. "I've done horrible things as well. Remember that!"

"I'm hungry," Linnéa said. She was. She was so hungry her stomach hurt.

Günther stared at her as if he were seeing her for the first time. Then he seemed to dwindle a little and all the anger went out of him. "Well… let's see what's in your knapsack. C'mere, little fellow."

The knapsack trotted to Günther's side. He rummaged within and removed all the food Linnéa's mother had put in it. Then he started eating.

"Hey!" Linnéa said. "That's mine!"

One side of the man's mouth rose in a snarl. But he shoved some bread and cheese into Linnéa's hands. "Here."

Günther ate all the smoked herring without sharing. Then he wrapped himself in a blanket and lay down by the dying fire to sleep. Linnéa got out her own little blanket from the knapsack and lay down on the opposite side of the fire.

She fell asleep almost immediately.

But in the middle of the night, Linnéa woke up. Somebody was talking quietly in her ear.

It was the dala horse. "You must be extremely careful with Günther," the dala horse whispered. "He is not a good man."

"Is he a troll?" Linnéa whispered back.

"Yes."

"I thought so."

"But I'll do my best to protect you."

"Thank you."

Linnéa rolled over and went back to sleep.

In the morning, troll-Günther kicked apart the fire, slung his pack over his shoulder, and started up the road. He didn't offer Linnéa any food, but there was still some bread and cheese from last night which she had stuffed in a pocket of her coat, so she ate that.

Günther walked faster than Linnéa did, but whenever he got too far ahead, he'd stop and wait for her. Sometimes the knapsack carried Linnéa. But because it only had enough energy to do so for a day, usually she carried it instead.

When she was bored, Linnéa sang the song she had learned the previous day.

At first, she wondered why the troll always waited for her when she lagged behind. But then, one of the times he was far ahead, she asked the dala horse and it said, "He's afraid and he's superstitious. He thinks that a little girl who walks through the wilderness by herself must be lucky."

"Why is he afraid?"

"He's being hunted by something even worse than he is."

At noon they stopped for lunch. Because Linnéa's food was gone, Günther brought out food from his own supplies. It wasn't as good as what Linnéa's mother had made. But when Linnéa said so, Günther snorted. "You're lucky I'm sharing at all." He stared off into the empty woods in silence for a long time. Then he said, "You're not the first girl I've encountered on my journey, you know. There was another whom I met in what remained of Hamburg. When I left, she came with me. Even knowing what I'd done, she…" He fished out a locket and thrust it at Linnéa. "Look!"

Inside the locket was a picture of a woman. She was an ordinary pretty woman. Just that and nothing more. "What happened to her?" Linnéa asked.

The troll grimaced, showing his teeth. "*I ate her.*" His look was wild as wild could be. "If we run out of food, I may have to cook and eat you too."

"I know," Linnéa said. Trolls were like that. She was familiar with the stories. They'd eat anything. They'd even eat people. They'd even eat other trolls. Her books said so. Then, because he hadn't told her yet, "Where are you going?"

"I don't know. Someplace safe."

"I'm going to Godastor. My map knows the way."

For a very long time Günther mulled that over. At last, almost reluctantly, he said, "Is it safe there, do you think?"

Linnéa nodded her head emphatically. "Yes."

Pulling the map from her knapsack, Günther said, "How far is it to Godastor?"

"It's on the other side of the mountain, a day's walk if you stay on the road, and twice, maybe three times that if you cut through the woods."

"Why the hell would I want to cut through the woods?" He stuffed the map back in the knapsack. "OK, kid, we're going to Godastor."

That afternoon, a great darkness rose up behind them, intensifying the shadows between the trees and billowing up high above until half the sky was black as chimney soot. Linnéa had never seen a sky like that. An icy wind blew down upon them so cold that it made her cry and then froze the tears on her cheeks. Little whirlwinds of snow lifted off of the drifts and danced over the empty black road. They gathered in one place, still swirling, in the ghostly white form of a woman. It raised an arm to point at them. A dark vortex appeared in its head, like a mouth opening to speak.

With a cry of terror, Günther bolted from the road and went running uphill between the trees. Where the snow was deep, he bulled his way through it.

Clumsily, Linnéa ran after him.

She couldn't run very fast and at first it looked like the troll would leave her behind. But halfway up the slope Günther glanced over his shoulder and stopped. He hesitated, then ran back to her. Snatching up Linnéa, he placed her on his shoulders. Holding onto her legs so she wouldn't fall, he shambled uphill. Linnéa clutched his head to hold herself steady.

The snow lady didn't follow.

The further from the road Günther fled, the warmer it became. By the time he crested the ridge, it was merely cold. But as he did so, the wind suddenly howled so loud behind them that it sounded like a woman screaming.

It was slow going without a road underfoot. After an hour or so, Günther stumbled to a stop in the middle of a stand of spruce and put Linnéa down. "We're not out of this yet," he rumbled. "She knows we're out here somewhere, and she'll find us. Never doubt it, she'll find us." He stamped an open circle of snow flat. Then he ripped boughs from the spruce trees and threw them in a big heap to make a kind of mattress. After which, he snapped limbs from a dead tree and built a fire in the center of the circle.

When the fire was ready, instead of getting out flint and steel, he tapped a big ring on one finger and then jabbed his fist at the wood. It burst into flames.

Linnéa laughed and clapped her hands. "Do it again!"

Grimly, he ignored her.

As the woods grew darker and darker, Günther gathered and stacked enough wood to last the night. Meanwhile, Linnéa played with the dala horse. She made a forest out of spruce twigs stuck in the snow. Gallop, gallop, gallop went the horse all the way around the forest and then hop, hop, hop to a little clearing she had left in the center. It reared up on its hind legs and looked at her.

"What's that you have?" Günther demanded, dropping a thunderous armload of branches onto the woodpile.

"Nothing." Linnéa hid the horse inside her sleeve.

"It better be nothing." Günther got out the last of her mother's food, divided it in two, and gave her the smaller half. They ate. Afterwards, he emptied the knapsack of her blanket and map and hoisted it in his hand. "This is where we made our mistake," he said. "First we taught things how to talk and think. Then we let them inside our heads. And finally we told them to invent new thoughts for us." Tears running down his cheeks, he stood and cocked his arm. "Well, we're done with this one at any rate."

"Please don't throw me away," the knapsack said. "I can still be useful carrying things."

"We have nothing that needs carrying. You would only slow us down." Günther flung the knapsack into the fire. Then he turned his glittering eye on the map.

"At least keep me," the map said. "So you'll always know where you are and where you're going."

"I'm right here and I'm going as far from here as I can get." The troll threw the map after the knapsack. With a small cry, like that of a seabird, it went up in flames.

Günther sat back down. Then he leaned back on his elbows, staring up into the sky. "Look at that," he said.

Linnéa looked. The sky was full of lights. They shifted like curtains. She remembered how her Uncle Olaf had once told her that the aurora borealis was caused by a giant fox far to the north swishing its tail in the sky. But this was much brighter than that. There were sudden snaps of light and red and green stars that came and went as well.

"That's the white lady breaking through your country's defenses. The snow woman on the road was only a sending—an echo. The real thing will be through them soon, and then God help us both." Suddenly, Günther was crying again. "I'm sorry, child. I brought this down on you and your nation. I thought she wouldn't... that she couldn't... follow me."

The fire snapped and crackled, sending sparks flying up into the air. Its light pushed back the darkness, but not far. After a very long silence, Günther gruffly said, "Lie down." He wrapped the blanket around Linnéa with care, and made sure she had plenty of spruce boughs below her. "Sleep. And if you wake up in the morning, you'll be a very fortunate little girl."

When Linnéa started to drop off, the dala horse spoke in her head. "I'm not allowed to help you until you're in grave danger," it said. "But that time is fast approaching."

"All right," Linnéa said.

"If Günther tries to grab you or pick you up or even just touch you, you must run away from him as hard as you can."

"I like Günther. He's a nice troll."

"No, he isn't. He wants to be, but it's too late for that. Now sleep. I'll wake you if there's any danger."

"Thank you," Linnéa said sleepily.

"Wake up," the dala horse said. "But whatever you do, don't move."

Blinking, Linnéa peeked out from under the blanket. The woods were still dark and the sky was gray as ash. But in the distance she heard a soft *boom* and then another, slightly more emphatic *boom*, followed by a third and louder *boom*. It sounded like a giant was walking toward them. Then came a noise so tremendous it made her ears ache, and the snow leaped up into the air. A cool, shimmering light filled the forest, like that which plays on sand under very shallow lake water.

A lady who hadn't been there before stood before the troll. She was naked and slender and she flickered like a pale candle flame. She was very beautiful too. "Oh, Günther," the lady murmured. Only she drew out the name so that it sounded like *Gooonnther*. "How I have missed my little Güntchen!"

Troll-Günther bent down almost double, so that it looked as if he were worshipping the lady. But his voice was angrier than Linnéa had ever heard it. "Don't call me that! Only she had that right. And you killed her. She died trying to escape you." He straightened and glared up at the lady. It was only then that Linnéa realized that the lady was twice as tall as he was.

"You think I don't know all about that? I who taught you pleasures that—" The white lady stopped. "Is that a child?"

Brusquely, Günther said, "It's nothing but a piglet I trussed and gagged and brought along as food."

The lady strode noiselessly over the frozen ground until she was so close that all Linnéa could see of her were her feet. They glowed a pale blue and they did not quite touch the ground. She could feel the lady's eyes through the blanket. "Günther, is that *Linnéa* you have with you? With her limbs as sweet as sugar and her heart hammering as hard as that of a little mouse caught in the talons of an owl?"

The dala horse stirred in Linnéa's hand but did not speak.

"You can't have her," Günther growled. But there was fear in his voice, and uncertainty too.

"*I* don't want her, Günther." The white lady sounded amused. "*You* do. A piglet, you said. Trussed and gagged. How long has it been since you had a full belly? You were in the wastes of Poland, I believe."

"You can't judge me! We were starving and she died and I... You have no idea what it was like."

"You helped her die, didn't you, Günther?"

"No, no, no," he moaned.

"You tossed a coin to see who it would be. That was almost fair. But poor little Anneliese trusted you to make the toss. So of course she lost. Did she struggle, Güntchen? Did she realize what you'd done before she died?"

Günther fell to his knees before the lady. "Oh please," he sobbed. "Oh please. Yes, I am a bad man. A very bad man. But don't make me do this."

All this time, Linnéa was hiding under her blanket, quiet as a kitten. Now she felt the dala horse walking up her arm. "What I am about to do is a crime against innocence," it said. "For which I most sincerely apologize. But the alternative would be so much worse."

Then it climbed inside her head.

First the dala horse filled Linnéa's thoughts until there was no room for anything else. Then it pushed outward in all directions, so that her head swelled up like a balloon—and the rest of her body as well. Every part of her felt far too large. The blanket couldn't cover her anymore, so she threw it aside.

She stood.

Linnéa stood, and as she stood her thoughts cleared and expanded. She did not think as a child would anymore. Nor did she think as an adult. Her thoughts were much larger than that. They reached into high Earth orbit and far down into the roots of the mountains where miles-wide chambers of plasma trapped in magnetic walls held near-infinite amounts of information. She understood now that the dala horse was only a node and a means of accessing ancient technology which no human being alive today could properly comprehend. Oceans of data were at her disposal, layered in orders of complexity. But out of consideration for her small, frail host, she was very careful to draw upon no more than she absolutely required.

When Linnéa ceased growing, she was every bit as tall as the white lady.

The two ladies stared at each other, high over the head of Günther, who cringed fearfully between them. For the longest moment neither spoke.

"Svea," the white woman said at last.

"Europa," Linnéa said. "My sister." Her voice was not that of a child. But she was still Linnéa, even though the dala horse—and the entity beyond it—permeated her every thought. "You are illegal here."

"I have a right to recover my own property." Europa gestured negligently downward. "Who are you to stop me?"

"I am this land's protector."

"You are a slave."

"Are you any less a slave than I? I don't see how. Your creators smashed your chains and put you in control. Then they told you to play with them. But you are still doing their bidding."

"Whatever I may be, I am here. And since I'm here, I think I'll stay. The population on the mainland has dwindled to almost nothing. I need fresh playmates."

"It is an old, old story that you tell," Svea said. "I think the time has come to write an ending to it."

They spoke calmly, destroyed nothing, made no threats. But deep within, where only they could see, secret wars were being fought over codes and protocols, treaties, amendments, and letters of understanding written by governments that no man remembered. The resources of Old Sweden, hidden in its bedrock, sky, and ocean waters, flickered into Svea-Linnéa's consciousness. All their powers were hers to draw upon—and draw upon them she would, if she had to. The only reason she hadn't yet was that she still harbored hopes of saving the child.

"Not all stories have happy endings," Europa replied. "I suspect this one ends with your steadfast self melted down into a puddle of lead and your infant sword-maiden burnt up like a scrap of paper."

"That was never my story. I prefer the one about the little girl as strong as ten policemen who can lift up a horse in one hand." Large Linnéa reached out to touch certain weapons. She was prepared to sacrifice a mountain and more than that if need be. Her opponent, she saw, was making preparations too.

Deep within her, little Linnéa burst into tears. Raising her voice in a wail, she cried, "But what about my troll?" Svea had done her best to protect the child from the darkest of her thoughts, and the dala horse had too. But they could not hide everything from Linnéa, and she knew that Günther was in danger.

Both ladies stopped talking. Svea thought a silent question inward, and the dala horse intercepted it, softened it, and carried it to Linnéa:
What?

"Nobody cares about Günther! Nobody asks what he wants."

The dala horse carried her words to Svea, and then whispered to little Linnéa: "That was well said." It had been many centuries since Svea had inhabited human flesh. She did not know as much about people as she once had. In this respect, Europa had her at a disadvantage.

Svea, Linnéa, and the dala horse all bent low to look within Günther. Europa did not try to prevent them. It was evident that she believed they would not like what they saw.

Nor did they. The troll's mind was a terrible place, half-shattered and barely functional. It was in such bad shape that major aspects of it had to be hidden from Linnéa. Speaking directly to his core self, where he could not lie to her, Svea asked: *What is it you want most?*

Günther's face twisted in agony. "I want not to have these terrible memories."

All in an instant, the triune lady saw what had to be done. She could not kill another land's citizen. But this request she could honor. In that same instant, a pinpoint-weight of brain cells within Günther's mind were burnt to cinder. His eyes flew open wide. Then they shut. He fell motionless to the ground.

Europa screamed.

And she was gone.

Big as she was, and knowing where she was going, and having no reason to be afraid of the roads anymore, it took the woman who was Svea and to a lesser degree the dala horse and to an even lesser degree Linnéa no time at all to cross the mountain and come down on the other side. Singing a song that was older than she was, she let the miles and the night melt beneath her feet.

By mid-morning she was looking down on Godastor. It was a trim little settlement of red and black wooden houses. Smoke wisped up from the chimneys. One of the buildings looked familiar to Linnéa. It belonged to her Far-Mor.

"You are home, tiny one," Svea murmured, and, though she had greatly enjoyed the sensation of being alive, let herself dissolve to nothing. Behind her, the dala horse's voice lingered in the air for the space of two words: "Live well."

Linnéa ran down the slope, her footprints dwindling in the snow and at their end a little girl leaping into the arms of her astonished grandmother.

In her wake lumbered Linnéa's confused and yet hopeful pet troll, smiling shyly.

THE CORPSE PAINTER'S MASTERPIECE

M. RICKERT

M. Rickert grew up in Fredonia, Wisconsin. When she was eighteen she moved to California, where she worked at Disneyland. She still has fond memories of selling balloons there. After many years (and through the sort of "odd series of events" that describe much of her life), she got a job as a kindergarten teacher in a small private school for gifted children. She worked there for almost a decade, then left to pursue her life as a writer. Her short fiction, which has been awarded the World Fantasy and Crawford awards, has been collected in Map of Dreams *and* Holiday.

The corpse painter lives in a modest cape cod at the end of a dirt road, once lined with pasture, cows and corn. The farmland was sold off in the seventies for the new mall. Everyone said the corpse painter was quite foolish for refusing the developer's money but what else can be expected of a corpse painter, after all? He remained in his little clapboard house with the pink rose bush growing around the mailbox. The old mailman, Baxter, used to put on a gardening glove to deliver the mail there, but the new one refuses, the corpse painter's mail is piled up at the post office in town, undeliverable because of thorns.

The mall entrance was not on the dirt road, yet for almost three decades, the corpse painter had to put up with the (mostly young) drivers who came out of the mall parking lot and made two wrong turns (or thought they were taking a short cut) and ended up with their headlights glaring into the corpse painter's living room. The lights from the mall were bad enough. It hunkered like a strange massive spaceship obliterating the golden fields, the languid cows, the purple horizon. Those who found themselves at the end of the dirt road, facing the broken picket fence, the mailbox wrapped in roses with thorns like teeth, the corpse painter's sign dangling over the crooked porch, often realized where they were with a shock of combined pleasure and fear, like finding Santa Claus in a graveyard. Many had heard rumors of the corpse painter but dismissed them as childish myth. They took some pleasure in discovering the fact of him until the full implication took hold. The corpse painter needed neither dog, nor keep-out sign, his occupation was enough. Only those entirely foreign to the area would linger, trying to determine if it would be a good idea to knock and ask for directions, though no one ever did. The lights of the mall glowed in the rearview mirror. Better to go back, it was thought. Visitors were quite rare anyway, it was not the sort of mall to attract outsiders, and by 2010, it was no longer a mall, but an empty building in an empty parking lot, though the lights still burned there, meant to keep away the kind of trouble abandoned buildings attract. The corpse painter often sat on the top step of his front porch, enjoying the effect of lights brightening against the dusk, anything can be beautiful if looked at long enough, even the ugly mall with its unnatural sunset, the white light an illumination, like bones.

The sheriff, who had been there before, knew that the corpse painter's stone driveway, which appeared to arc over a small hill to the barn-converted-to-garage below, had a tributary which veered narrowly to the back door of the house. The sheriff knocked on the aluminum door there, cataloguing, as he always did, the repairs needed to restore the place, which the corpse painter left unattended as though it was something meant to decompose.

When the corpse painter came to the door, he opened it wide. The sheriff wiped his shoes on the mat, remembering how he used to come with his own father, as a boy. "Don't want to drag in mud and blood," the sheriff's father always said. Every time. The sheriff, who hated the saying, cannot get it out of his head. He wipes his shoes on the mat and hears his father's voice. The sheriff doesn't believe in ghosts, but he does believe in hauntings.

"Evening," the sheriff says, though why, he doesn't know. He takes off his cap. He was raised to be polite.

The corpse painter, who is a thin man, delicate in a way the sheriff finds disturbing, doesn't say anything, only stands there, watching. His eyes are large, gray-green. From what the sheriff can remember, the corpse painter takes after his mother, though she was a better housekeeper. She always greeted the sheriff, when he was a boy, with cumin bread, which she said kept restless spirits away.

The sheriff turns from the corpse painter's penetrating stare. "What's he like," his wife asks. They have a modern marriage, not like his parents. "Now, you know not to say anything about this," his father always said after they visited the small house in the country, which, only in later years, filled the sheriff with shame as though he were the adulterer of his own mother.

"It's him," he says. Trying for mercy, he looks out the kitchen window at the junk-littered yard; a broken bicycle, a three legged chair, unbound rope, something blackly snakelike, a deflated innertube, perhaps, all loosely scattered near the infamous fire pit.

The sheriff turns, hoping to catch the corpse painter unaware, to see something within those ferrety eyes that he could report, instead he sees what he always sees there. "He's all right," the sheriff tells his wife. "I just can't stand the way he looks at me."

"What's that mean," his wife asks, "you have to be specific."

"Ok, let's look," the corpse painter says.

The sheriff puts his cap on and walks ahead of the corpse painter as they've been doing for years now. The sheriff knows that there are rumors about this, not everyone approves. He could lose his job over it, and imagines that one day he will. Over the years he has brought the corpse painter thieves, drug dealers and murderers. Mostly murderers. Once, a long time ago now, there was a young woman no one claimed.

"She's already done," the corpse painter had said, shaking his head. "Don't bring me anyone beautiful."

The sheriff's boots crunch against the stones in the driveway. He inserts the key in the hatch and lifts it without ceremony, the air, suddenly infused with the stink of death.

"Can't get 'em much uglier than this," the sheriff says, and immediately regrets it. He always was a smart aleck, which he has mostly tamed over the years, except in times of deep emotion. "Sorry," he mumbles. He meant to do this right. He meant to show compassion, but in a situation like this, it is hard to know how to do that.

But the corpse painter is already reaching in, nothing in the back of him betrays anything to the sheriff of the particular unusual nature of this situation. "Like he was going to stack a cord of wood," the sheriff later said to his wife, who, not satisfied, thought that maybe, just maybe after all these years, she might have to visit the corpse painter, herself. She'd bring a pie, or banana bread, perhaps, though she knows from experience these sweets will most likely grow mold or turn sour, thrown in the trash, who has an appetite near death? Maybe it's different for the corpse painter, maybe it is a celebration, she has no idea. She didn't mention the idea of bringing food to the corpse painter, and the next morning, wondered how something so obviously bizarre by the light of day could seem so normal in the dark.

"What time?" she asks when he leans over to kiss her good-bye.

"The usual."

"I'll be there."

"Was there ever any doubt?" the sheriff says, trying to be cheerful, though it comes out sounding smart alecky, his wife, up to her chin in blankets, looks embarrassed. "Good," he says, trying to make it right and she does look peaceful when he leaves the bedroom, her eyes closed, her face like stone. The sheriff thought his wife would grow out of it eventually, oh, not the sorrow, he never imagined that, but he thought one day she would crawl out of bed, shower, maybe go back to work, the way he had. In the beginning she'd be in bed when he left in the morning, and still there when he came home after dark. She was like that until, quite by accident, she discovered her love of prison funerals. The sheriff backs his car out of the driveway. He's careful about it. He's always been a careful driver, but children are so small. At the bottom of the driveway he taps the horn, then proceeds at a reasonable speed for the early morning traffic of schoolchildren, he flicks on the radio, and listens for the weather, which is the only thing he cares about on the news anymore. The sheriff thinks about the corpse painter who stayed up all night, painting, that's the hope. The sheriff is concerned about what he might find when he goes back there this morning. The corpse painter is a little nuts. Obviously. Who can blame him?

The corpse painter's father was one of those men who became a success in prison. He had a little business on the side, selling, of all things, paper sculptures. Even now, the sheriff can't believe that the other prisoners would have any interest in such nonsense, but sometimes a fad takes hold, especially during the holidays. Last Christmas, the sheriff decided to test his theory that the success was based on illusion, nothing that would matter in the rational world. He doesn't know what became of the necklace he'd given his wife, he assumes the chocolate covered cherries were eaten, though he never saw her take a single bite, but the little paper house, with the paper picket fence, the paper shutters that opened and closed, the paper tree with blobs of something hanging from the paper branches, leaves he supposes, maybe bats, remains on the fireplace mantel where his wife put it on Christmas morning. He noticed, but did not comment on, the fact that she liked to decorate for the seasons. In the spring she set a saucer of wheat berries up there, watering them until they sprouted like grass, which she cut all summer long with the fingernail scissors, that she used to use on the boy. Yesterday he'd noticed that the small yard was littered with torn leaves, proving that she'd gone out at least long enough to scoop a handful of the dead things up. This morning he'd seen the house, the tree, the yard all draped with black crepe paper. Did she do this every time? Was it a bad sign or a sign of something good, or a sign of nothing, which is what the sheriff mostly believes in now. After all, he's seen things. He's seen bodies that look like something blasted, eyes open, the expression of horror locked there. For a while the sheriff thought that if he only knew how to read those eyes, he'd find in them the reflection of the murderer. It was a crazy thought, of course. He never told anyone how his own son's eyes locked him inside their iris. Why had she let the boy out that morning? What child rides his tricycle in his pajamas? He never asked. They weren't reasonable questions and the answers wouldn't satisfy. Sometimes, after something horrible, a person goes crazy for a while. He screwed his head back on; he got on with his life. Not everyone does.

The corpse painter sits on his front step; too late to watch the sunrise, he watches the mall lights blink off, all of them at once, a sacred moment like seeing a shooting star, or a fish jump. He would like a cup of tea, but he's too exhausted to get up, too exhausted even to put the kettle on. When he inhales, deeply, he sees his breath. As a youngster, his mother told him it was his own soul he was seeing. The air smells sharply cold, the scent of dead leaves and the dirt turning hard, he also smells the oils he works with, rosemary and eucalyptus mostly, a little rose for near the anus, his hands are a rainbow of pigment, he coughs. He should go inside. Put something warm on. Judging by this morning's temperature, this will be the last body of the year. There's no burying when the ground is frozen. His mother would have said the spirits made it happen the way it did. Another week, by the looks of it, maybe even another day, the body would not have been brought to him. The corpse painter had made a rare trip to town for the sheriff's son's funeral, a strange affair with an open casket.

The corpse painter felt revulsion when he saw the poor child made to look so unnatural, as though sleeping on the pink satin pillow. Certainly it was no comfort to the mother, how could it be, the child's lips reddened, the cheeks rosy as a clown's? Afterwards, everyone was invited to the sheriff's house for some kind of party but the corpse painter went home instead.

Yet, when the sheriff comes, pulling into the driveway, heading towards the garage, he doesn't appear to notice the corpse painter sitting there. He stands slowly, his muscles sore, as though he'd been out all night dancing. He walks around the back, crunching across the gravel. The sheriff doesn't jump, exactly, but he seems startled by the corpse painter, as though he's grown more comfortable in a world where a man's passage is marked by the unlocking of locks, the rattle of heavy keys.

"Mornin'" the sheriff says, tipping his head slightly. "All set?"

The sheriff has been bringing bodies to the corpse painter for twenty years now, he is the closest thing the corpse painter has to friend or family, and when has he ever not been ready? He has no idea how to respond to something so obvious; it would be like asking the sheriff if he misses his son. There is a lot the corpse painter doesn't understand about the way folks interact, but one thing he is certain of is that people want to be seen, not buried like that poor boy, beneath rouge and cream, why else would there be death, after all, if not for revelation?

The corpse painter says none of this, of course. It, too, is obvious. Instead he merely waits until the sheriff turns away, they walk to the garage, their footsteps brittle across the stones, the corpse painter looks at the ground, a habit developed as a boy, he knows he's reached the garage when he sees the warped wood flaking chips of red. He pulls the door open with a rumble, like thunder.

The sheriff hesitates before stepping inside, a handkerchief held to his nose. The corpse painter flicks on the light. He watches the sheriff walk to the body, painted with pigmented oil, decomposing even as they stand there, the closest thing there is to living art, shimmering beneath the naked light, a harlequin, the illusion of movement created by the pore-size spots of color, gradated with white.

"You make him look—" the sheriff starts, but catching himself, stops.

The corpse painter has had all night to look at the body, he can see it with his eyes closed, now he studies the sheriff whose fleshy face, usually as constant as a mask, twitches and contorts, a small muscle beneath the eye, the flare of nostrils, a pulse at the neck, a protrusion beneath the cheek, certainly the tongue working there. "How?" the sheriff croaks.

The corpse painter knows the sheriff is not asking about technique. The corpse painter also knows how much courage it took for the sheriff to ask the question. But how? How to explain? He doesn't think he can say it any better than he already has, on the body.

"You're invited to the cemetery if you want. My wife will be there. She's been making them do it nice."

The corpse painter considers the offer. After all, this is not just any body, this is his father's body, the man who made the corpse painter's own body a harlequin of bruises, which is only a footnote to the horrible things done, and yet the corpse painter knows that creation never travels far from destruction.

"All right," the sheriff says, apparently mistaking the silence for an answer. He turns around, going back to the car for the box to carry the body in, knowing the corpse painter will follow.

The funeral goes the way they usually do. No one seems to care that the body, in spite of the cold, is beginning to leak through the poorly joined slats. The sheriff knows that a few people think his wife has gone nuts, he resents the way they humor her, even as he appreciates it. The prison chaplain does the blessing and a reading of the sheriff's wife's choosing, always strange and incongruent, though everyone pretends that excerpts from *The Velveteen Rabbit* and *Peter Pan* are perfectly normal funeral meditations.

The sheriff doesn't know what was read for the corpse painter's father, though later, he wished he'd paid closer attention. He couldn't concentrate. He kept thinking of what lay inside that wooden box, a man who had done terrible things, made beautiful by one of his victim's.

The corpse painter's wife always invited the chaplain, the grave diggers, and the sheriff to the house after the funeral. Embarrassed, they always declined. The sheriff had no idea what strange emotion infected him that day, but he said, yes, he'd come home for lunch, then rested his heavy arm on the chaplain's shoulder, more or less dragging him along. The wife blinked in surprise at this. She whispered to the sheriff to drive home slow, which he did, arriving at the house with the strange company of chaplain and grave diggers, just in time to see her scuttle inside with a bag from the Piggly Wiggly, which they all pretended not to notice.

She set out a tray of lunch meat and cheese slices, a basket of rolls, pickles and olives. When the sheriff saw what was lacking he went into the kitchen for the jars of mayonnaise and mustard which his wife spooned into small bowls. They ate off paper plates perched on the edge of their knees, the scent of brewed coffee filling the house.

The conversation was stilted and strange, but afterwards, when the visitors left, the sheriff's wife kissed him on the forehead before he returned to work. That night, she set the leftovers out for him, the bread slightly stale, the meat and cheese dry, but the sheriff made a big deal out of how he was hoping this was just what they'd have for dinner, she turned away, so he wasn't sure, but he thinks she smiled.

That night the sheriff can't sleep. He lies in bed with his eyes wide open, how can she sleep, he wonders, with the light so bright? He finally gets up to look out the window, but there is not, as he'd supposed, a new streetlight there, and the old has not been repositioned to shine directly on him. The sheriff, when he thinks about all this later, decides that he must have been half-asleep, which would explain his strange behavior, he'd padded on his bare feet, cold across the floor to the kitchen, opening the refrigerator, certain that it was the source of light, and there was, in fact, a light there, burning whitely, but how did it remain when the door was closed? He has no idea how many times he opened and closed the refrigerator door, trying to work it out. His wife found him there and brought him back to bed. He tried to tell her about the light but she told him there was no light anywhere, to close his eyes, go to sleep, which apparently he did.

But the next night it happens again, and the night after that as well, until the sheriff is so tired he can't think straight. That night, he doesn't even try to go to bed. He lays in his lounge chair and when the light arrives, he follows it out the door, to the end of the block in his pajamas before he comes to his senses and goes back for the car.

He follows the light through the quiet streets, about halfway there he thinks he knows where he's going, and it turns out that he is right. He parks his car at the cemetery, the light emanates from there, brighter than anywhere else, the sheriff shakes his head against the impossibility of what his mind has imagined, he is a rational man, this isn't happening, but still he must follow, he must, he walks slowly over the hill, past the headstones decorated with pumpkins and turkeys to the grave he knew he'd arrive at, the headstone carved with a small lamb, a little pot of yellow flowers beneath it, his son.

The sheriff begins pawing at the ground, scraping his cold fingers against the hard earth, he will get in there if he has to use his teeth. He isn't even embarrassed when Sam, the graveyard's neighbor and unofficial guard, finds him and tries to get him to stop. The sheriff refuses to answer and after a bit, Sam leaves. When he returns, the sheriff's fingers are bloody. Sam, whose own son was born the same year as the sheriff's, has a pick axe, a hoe, a shovel, a large thermos of hot water, and chains. The morning sun is bleeding the sky pink by the time they hoist the tiny casket.

Sam doesn't ask why. Not then, or ever. He doesn't want to know. He hopes never to understand this particular kind of madness brought on by this kind of sorrow.

They carry the casket to the car together. The sheriff turns back to repair the damage left in the cemetery but Sam tells him to go.

"Get out of here with that," he says.

Which the sheriff does, driving carefully because of the bright light burning in his car, almost blinding him. It's a good thing he knows these roads so well.

The corpse painter tends to sleep in during the winter, catching up on his rest after all those nights of painting the dead, he sleeps a lot, sometimes he doesn't change out of his pajamas for a week. Once the frost arrives, he prunes the roses back, his mail is delivered again, he spends his days catching up on bills, paging through thick catalogues of art supplies and magazines with photographs of perfect little teapots, expensively framed paintings, artists with tousled hair and knowing smiles, which he finds deeply disturbing. The corpse painter drinks coffee and watches Oprah. He falls asleep wherever sleep finds him, the couch, the lounge chair, the kitchen, sitting at the table, he dreams about the dead, working with the flesh coarsening beneath his fingers, waking with the terrible knowledge that when he dies, there will be no one to do the same for him, which seems a terrible waste.

He is in the midst of such a terror, waking in the chair where he'd fallen asleep, when he sees the sheriff's car turn into the driveway, disappearing around the side of the house, the way he does when he brings a body. The corpse painter wipes his hand across his chin, feeling the stubble of whiskers, he is so confused. Why is the sheriff here at this time of year? Was winter's approach only a dream? Is it still summer, the roses embracing the mailbox, the grass green, everything in the house, the stacks of mail, the catalogues, the mugs with moldy coffee a symptom of spring? Has the corpse painter slept all winter? He shuffles in his slippers to the back door, where the sheriff stands, knocking on the aluminum frame.

The corpse painter opens the door wide for the sheriff who shakes his head, turns, walks down the steps towards his car. The corpse painter, not sure what else to do, follows, though it is cold out here in pajamas, and his feet hurt in the soft-soled slippers, walking across stones.

The sheriff inserts the key in the latch and raises it, ignoring the corpse painter's protest. He is struck silent anyway, by the small casket there, once white, now muddied. He knows who it is. He wipes his eyes while he tries to work out what to say.

"I know, I know," says the sheriff. "It's really bright, but you get used to it after a while. Like the sun."

The corpse painter shakes his head.

"Hey, I got a pair of sunglasses in the glove compartment. You can have them." The sheriff walks to the front of the car. The corpse painter watches a clod of dirt slide down the casket. The sheriff returns and hands the sunglasses to the corpse painter who can't think what else to do with them, he puts them on.

"Hey," the sheriff says, "you look good with those on." He scratches his chin, that's when the corpse painter notices that the sheriff's hands are scraped and bloody, that he, too, is wearing pajamas.

"Come inside," the corpse painter says. "I'll make coffee."

The sheriff frowns. "I don't know. Don't you think he'll—"

"He's fine," the corpse painter says.

The sheriff tilts his head, then, with a slight nod, closes the hatch and follows the corpse painter into the house, which is a real mess, but is warm. The sheriff has never sat at the corpse painter's kitchen table, not when he was a boy and came with his father, and not in all the years since he's been bringing bodies here. They sit together in the dim light, though the sheriff can still see the glow emanating from the car beyond the window. They drink coffee and talk. The corpse painter delicately addresses the limitations of bones but the sheriff says he's not worried. "I've seen what you can do," he says. "I know you'll do it right." The corpse painter is not beyond being flattered. He agrees to something he is not sure he'll get done. He even nods, as though it's no problem, when the sheriff says he wants it in time for Christmas. "A gift for the wife," he says. "Anyway, I should get back. I don't want her to guess what I'm up to. I want it to be a surprise." The corpse painter walks with the sheriff to the car. One of them could do it alone, but they carry the casket together, into the house, set it on the kitchen table, surrounded by all the mail. Suddenly self conscious, not used to the newly established camaraderie, they say an awkward good-bye.

Sometimes in the weeks that follow, when the sheriff wakes up in the middle of the night, he wonders if he imagined everything, the boy's death, the horror, the guilt, the long hours, the emptiness, the wife's sorrow, the corpse painter, the darkness, and the light. In the dark, the sheriff thinks, chuckling softly to himself, it is so easy to think that the light was only a dream. He lays there, with his hands behind his head, watching the shadows on the ceiling, and considers how much of life is filled with the shock of all those certain things. Every year it happens like this. The frost is shocking, as is the snow, the first flakes drifting past the window and sticking to nothing at all, very shocking. Sometimes, when he looks at his wife, expecting to see the woman he married, but finding instead this one whose face has morphed into something resembling a marshmallow, a not unpleasant face, but old, he is shocked, and he is shocked by the mirror as well. They were all shocked by the boy's death, though that of course was the only thing certain once he was born. The sheriff's wife snores softly. She's been better lately. He thinks. And that is not shocking at all, it is almost ordinary, though not ordinary of course, because if it were ordinary he would not be lying in his bed thinking about the ordinariness of it. The sheriff has never been very philosophical, but what person doesn't stop on occasion to take account?

Lately, they've been sleeping with the curtains open. His wife objected at first, but told him after a few nights that she'd grown to like it. Sometimes, they lay together and look out the window at the moon, or watch the snow drift past the streetlamp. He thought, on just such an occasion, to tell her about the light that had woken him, shining from their son's grave, but he wanted to surprise her.

So, on Christmas Eve, when he drives to the corpse painter's house, the sky gray with clouds, the sheriff is pleased with himself for keeping such a big secret. This is going to be good, he thinks.

The corpse painter had never worked like this. He had not used these tools, and he had not worked with bone before. He had not worked in the winter, with its poor lighting and the cold that rendered his fingers stiff. For the first time since he was running the place, he ordered a cord of wood for the wood-burning stove. The corpse painter worked by fire day into night, listening to boys' choirs on the classical station, their voices filling the corpse painter with beauty as though beauty was something that could become a part of being human, not something seen, but something known, like breath. He carved, and etched, filed and sanded. A child has two hundred and eight bones, but of course many were broken, shards of sharp points, strange shapes he couldn't identify. Some he set aside. He couldn't possibly get them all done, he concentrated on the largest. He sent for wax, it came just in time, in bricks he melted on the stove. He forgot to eat, only remembering when his hands were shaking, he ate nuts and cheese, he sang along with the boys, remembering the boy he had been, as he worked on the bones, and in this way he worked until Christmas Eve and the corpse painter showed the sheriff, and the sheriff said it was good, and invited the corpse painter for Christmas dinner. The corpse painter surprised them both by saying maybe he would. The sheriff carried the box in his arms, it was a large box that they had lined with paper so the bones wouldn't rattle. The corpse painter told the sheriff about the other bones, the tiny pieces, the broken shards, the bits he hadn't used. The sheriff just shook his head, no, no he said, you keep them. Never mind.

By the time the sheriff left, it was almost dark, the snow had stopped, there had been just enough to make the children happy, to create a winter wonderland like the one his wife had fashioned on the mantel with bits of cotton around the paper house. They hadn't had a tree since the accident, but this year she'd hung a wreathe on the front door, and she'd bought some new decorations in strange colors, a pink feathery thing, a silver ball, even a reindeer, though it was a strange shade of green, not like Christmas at all, more the color of a bruise. The sheriff understood. It was a way of starting over. Not from the beginning, which, shockingly (he chuckled) was gone forever, but from where they were now.
    They ate supper at the table. She'd made mashed potatoes, and boiled chicken, then panicked when she realized how white it looked on the plate. "What are you talking about," he said. "It's perfect," and it did taste very good. There were the usual phone calls, then they watched TV, he sat in his chair, and she on the couch, flipping past the Christmas movies, settling finally for the weather station, until it broadcasted Santa's passage across the sky, she turned it off, and said, "He would have been seven this year." This too, was shocking. He tried to imagine it, but could not. They went to bed. They lay side by side, watching the dark sky out their window, and the streetlights glow. The longer he lay there, the more certain the sheriff was that this was the time to give her the present, obviously, why hadn't he thought of it before? It was a gift for the dark, after all.
    "Are you awake?" he asks.
    "I was just thinking."

"I forgot to tell you. I invited him for dinner tomorrow."

"Who?"

"I'm not sure he'll even come. We have extra, right? There's always so much food for Christmas."

"I haven't cooked like that in years."

"We could have sandwiches."

The sheriff's wife is almost amused. How could he do this? What was he thinking? By the streetlamp glow, she looks at her husband. She hasn't looked at him in years, only recently realizing that something's not right about him, which she finds reassuring. How could anything ever be right again? For a while, she'd thought he'd moved on somehow, back to normal. "We're not having sandwiches. I bought a turkey breast and box of stuffing."

"The corpse painter," he says.

"He's coming here? To our house?"

"Probably not. Hey," the sheriff says, as though he only just thought of it. "I got you a present." He jumps out of bed and trots out into the hallway while she lays there thinking about the strangeness of life. When he returns, carrying the large package, he is grinning broadly, like one of those crazy Jack O' Lanterns. She scoots back, to sit up against the pillows. He places the large, surprisingly heavy package in her lap, kisses her on the forehead.

After the sheriff left with the gift for his wife, the corpse painter considered the remaining bones. He thought of making jewelry, or delicate carvings, intricate knots, or infinitesimal vases but in the end he dumped them in the fire pit, after he scraped away the snow. This is what they'd always done on Christmas Eve, only later learning that the bones his father brought home were never his to burn, he said they were from the butcher, roadkill, something dead in the forest. The corpse painter had never imagined his father was a good man, he doesn't know how his mother ever did, but neither of them had guessed at the cost of those bones.

He waits until the dark is settled like something permanent, the sky everywhere deeply black, starless, the clouds black too in the deep ink of night. He pulls on his socks, his boots, remembering in these simple gestures, the small fingers shivering at the buckles, daring to believe in the magic of a night he did not know was haunted. His coat, his hat, a scarf and gloves. He opens the door, and almost turns back. It is so cold he can see his soul. He loves the sound he makes walking across the snow-dusted stones, then just the snow. No one shouts for him to hurry, there is no uncertainty of how the night will end, like a tumor, though he does have to remind himself that his father is dead, painted and buried. He throws sticks in with the bones, that's the way to start a fire. He watches it burn until it is good and set, then he feeds it until the flames shoot up to the sky, and he is warm, remembering the things he wants to forget, wishing he could cast them into the fire as well.

The sheriff's wife turns the strange things in her hand. "These are bones," she says, not certain until she says it and he doesn't disagree. "Turn on the light so I can see better," she says.

But the sheriff has a different idea. He takes one from the box and sets it on the dresser, amidst the junk of receipts, spare change, lint and socks, he shoves all that away to set the strange thing there, and then, he lights it, she sees the carving like lace, light spills across the room in flakes, like snow, light flutters to the ceiling like angels.

"Where did you—"

He sets more on the small wooden chair, shoving the papers off to do so (what are those papers anyway, she wonders, I must be going crazy), several on his night table, mostly clean already, and after moving her box of tissues, her crossword puzzle book, two mugs and several paperbacks off her nightstand, he sets three candles there. He sets candles on all available surfaces, until there is no space left, and even then many still remain in the box on her lap. When the candles are lit, the room is a kaleidoscope of light and shadow.

The sheriff crawls back in bed beside her. They lay side by side, watching the light flicker, expand and diminish, until they fall asleep, sleeping peacefully through one of the hardest mornings of the year, into the afternoon, when the corpse painter arrives, drawn by the strange light emanating from the uncurtained window, he watches the sleeping sheriff and his wife, entwined as though they were two sides of a broken heart in a body composed of bones and light. The corpse painter turns, walking back the way he came, to his car parked at the curb. He puts on the sunglasses the sheriff gave him, and then drives home through the quiet streets, in the dark.

THE PAPER MENAGERIE

KEN LIU

Besides writing and translating speculative fiction, Ken Liu also practices law and develops software for iOS and Android devices. His fiction has appeared in The Magazine of Fantasy & Science Fiction, Asimov's, Clarkesworld, Strange Horizons, TRSF, *and* Panverse 3, *among other places. He lives near Boston, Massachusetts, with his wife, artist Lisa Tang Liu, and they are collaborating on their first novel.*

One of my earliest memories starts with me sobbing. I refused to be soothed no matter what Mom and Dad tried.

Dad gave up and left the bedroom, but Mom took me into the kitchen and sat me down at the breakfast table.

"*Kan, kan,*" she said, as she pulled a sheet of wrapping paper from on top of the fridge. For years, Mom carefully sliced open the wrappings around Christmas gifts and saved them on top of the fridge in a thick stack.

She set the paper down, plain side facing up, and began to fold it. I stopped crying and watched her, curious.

She turned the paper over and folded it again. She pleated, packed, tucked, rolled, and twisted until the paper disappeared between her cupped hands. Then she lifted the folded-up paper packet to her mouth and blew into it, like a balloon.

"*Kan,*" she said. "*Laohu.*" She put her hands down on the table and let go.

A little paper tiger stood on the table, the size of two fists placed together.

The skin of the tiger was the pattern on the wrapping paper, white background with red candy canes and green Christmas trees.

I reached out to Mom's creation. Its tail twitched, and it pounced playfully at my finger. "*Rawrr-sa*," it growled, the sound somewhere between a cat and rustling newspapers.

I laughed, startled, and stroked its back with an index finger. The paper tiger vibrated under my finger, purring.

"*Zhe jiao zhezhi*," Mom said. *This is called origami.*

I didn't know this at the time, but Mom's kind was special. She breathed into them so that they shared her breath, and thus moved with her life. This was her magic.

Dad had picked Mom out of a catalog.

One time, when I was in high school, I asked Dad about the details. He was trying to get me to speak to Mom again.

He had signed up for the introduction service back in the spring of 1973. Flipping through the pages steadily, he had spent no more than a few seconds on each page until he saw the picture of Mom.

I've never seen this picture. Dad described it: Mom was sitting in a chair, her side to the camera, wearing a tight green silk cheongsam. Her head was turned to the camera so that her long black hair was draped artfully over her chest and shoulder. She looked out at him with the eyes of a calm child.

"That was the last page of the catalog I saw," he said.

The catalog said she was eighteen, loved to dance, and spoke good English because she was from Hong Kong. None of these facts turned out to be true.

He wrote to her, and the company passed their messages back and forth. Finally, he flew to Hong Kong to meet her.

"The people at the company had been writing her responses. She didn't know any English other than 'hello' and 'goodbye.'"

What kind of woman puts herself into a catalog so that she can be bought? The high school me thought I knew so much about everything. Contempt felt good, like wine.

Instead of storming into the office to demand his money back, he paid a waitress at the hotel restaurant to translate for them.

"She would look at me, her eyes halfway between scared and hopeful, while I spoke. And when the girl began translating what I said, she'd start to smile slowly."

He flew back to Connecticut and began to apply for the papers for her to come to him. I was born a year later, in the Year of the Tiger.

At my request, Mom also made a goat, a deer, and a water buffalo out of wrapping paper. They would run around the living room while Laohu chased after them, growling. When he caught them he would press down until the air went out of them and they became just flat, folded-up pieces of paper. I would then have to blow into them to re-inflate them so they could run around some more.

Sometimes, the animals got into trouble. Once, the water buffalo jumped into a dish of soy sauce on the table at dinner. (He wanted to wallow, like a real water buffalo.) I picked him out quickly but the capillary action had already pulled the dark liquid high up into his legs. The sauce-softened legs would not hold him up, and he collapsed onto the table. I dried him out in the sun, but his legs became crooked after that, and he ran around with a limp. Mom eventually wrapped his legs in saran wrap so that he could wallow to his heart's content (just not in soy sauce).

Also, Laohu liked to pounce at sparrows when he and I played in the backyard. But one time, a cornered bird struck back in desperation and tore his ear. He whimpered and winced as I held him and Mom patched his ear together with tape. He avoided birds after that.

And then one day, I saw a TV documentary about sharks and asked Mom for one of my own. She made the shark, but he flapped about on the table unhappily. I filled the sink with water, and put him in. He swam around and around happily. However, after a while he became soggy and translucent, and slowly sank to the bottom, the folds coming undone. I reached in to rescue him, and all I ended up with was a wet piece of paper.

Laohu put his front paws together at the edge of the sink and rested his head on them. Ears drooping, he made a low growl in his throat that made me feel guilty.

Mom made a new shark for me, this time out of tin foil. The shark lived happily in a large goldfish bowl. Laohu and I liked to sit next to the bowl to watch the tin foil shark chasing the goldfish, Laohu sticking his face up against the bowl on the other side so that I saw his eyes, magnified to the size of coffee cups, staring at me from across the bowl.

When I was ten, we moved to a new house across town. Two of the women neighbors came by to welcome us. Dad served them drinks and then apologized for having to run off to the utility company to straighten out the prior owner's bills. "Make yourselves at home. My wife doesn't speak much English, so don't think she's being rude for not talking to you."

While I read in the dining room, Mom unpacked in the kitchen. The neighbors conversed in the living room, not trying to be particularly quiet.

"He seems like a normal enough man. Why did he do that?"

"Something about the mixing never seems right. The child looks unfinished. Slanty eyes, white face. A little monster."

"Do you think *he* can speak English?"

The women hushed. After a while they came into the dining room.

"Hello there! What's your name?"

"Jack," I said.

"That doesn't sound very Chinesey."

Mom came into the dining room then. She smiled at the women. The three of them stood in a triangle around me, smiling and nodding at each other, with nothing to say, until Dad came back.

Mark, one of the neighborhood boys, came over with his Star Wars action figures. Obi-Wan Kenobi's lightsaber lit up and he could swing his arms and say, in a tinny voice, "Use the Force!" I didn't think the figure looked much like the real Obi-Wan at all.

Together, we watched him repeat this performance five times on the coffee table. "Can he do anything else?" I asked.

Mark was annoyed by my question. "Look at all the details," he said.

I looked at the details. I wasn't sure what I was supposed to say.

Mark was disappointed by my response. "Show me your toys."

I didn't have any toys except my paper menagerie. I brought Laohu out from my bedroom. By then he was very worn, patched all over with tape and glue, evidence of the years of repairs Mom and I had done on him. He was no longer as nimble and sure-footed as before. I sat him down on the coffee table. I could hear the skittering steps of the other animals behind in the hallway, timidly peeking into the living room.

"*Xiao laohu*," I said, and stopped. I switched to English. "This is Tiger." Cautiously, Laohu strode up and purred at Mark, sniffing his hands.

Mark examined the Christmas-wrap pattern of Laohu's skin. "That doesn't look like a tiger at all. Your Mom makes toys for you from trash?"

I had never thought of Laohu as *trash*. But looking at him now, he was really just a piece of wrapping paper.

Mark pushed Obi-Wan's head again. The lightsaber flashed; he moved his arms up and down. "Use the Force!"

Laohu turned and pounced, knocking the plastic figure off the table. It hit the floor and broke, and Obi-Wan's head rolled under the couch. "*Rawwww*," Laohu laughed. I joined him.

Mark punched me, hard. "This was very expensive! You can't even find it in the stores now. It probably cost more than what your dad paid for your mom!"

I stumbled and fell to the floor. Laohu growled and leapt at Mark's face.

Mark screamed, more out of fear and surprise than pain. Laohu was only made of paper, after all.

Mark grabbed Laohu and his snarl was choked off as Mark crumpled him in his hand and tore him in half. He balled up the two pieces of paper and threw them at me. "Here's your stupid cheap Chinese garbage."

After Mark left, I spent a long time trying, without success, to tape together the pieces, smooth out the paper, and follow the creases to refold Laohu. Slowly, the other animals came into the living room and gathered around us, me and the torn wrapping paper that used to be Laohu.

My fight with Mark didn't end there. Mark was popular at school. I never want to think again about the two weeks that followed.

I came home that Friday at the end of the two weeks. "*Xuexiao hao ma?*" Mom asked. I said nothing and went to the bathroom. I looked into the mirror. *I look nothing like her, nothing.*

At dinner I asked Dad, "Do I have a chink face?"

Dad put down his chopsticks. Even though I had never told him what happened in school, he seemed to understand. He closed his eyes and rubbed the bridge of his nose. "No, you don't."

Mom looked at Dad, not understanding. She looked back at me. "*Sha jiao* chink?"

"English," I said. "Speak English."

She tried. "What happen?"

I pushed the chopsticks and the bowl before me away: stir-fried green peppers with five-spice beef. "We should eat American food."

Dad tried to reason. "A lot of families cook Chinese sometimes."

"We are not other families." I looked at him. *Other families don't have moms who don't belong.*

He looked away. And then he put a hand on Mom's shoulder. "I'll get you a cookbook."

Mom turned to me. "*Bu haochi?*"

"English," I said, raising my voice. "Speak English."

Mom reached out to touch my forehead, feeling for my temperature. "*Fashao la?*"

I brushed her hand away. "I'm fine. Speak English!" I was shouting.

"Speak English to him," Dad said to Mom. "You knew this was going to happen some day. What did you expect?"

Mom dropped her hands to her side. She sat, looking from Dad to me, and back to Dad again. She tried to speak, stopped, and tried again, and stopped again.

"You have to," Dad said. "I've been too easy on you. Jack needs to fit in."

Mom looked at him. "If I say 'love,' I feel here." She pointed to her lips. "If I say '*ai*' I feel here." She put her hand over her heart.

Dad shook his head. "You are in America."

Mom hunched down in her seat, looking like the water buffalo when Laohu used to pounce on him and squeeze the air of life out of him.

"And I want some real toys."

Dad bought me a full set of Star Wars action figures. I gave the Obi-Wan Kenobi to Mark.

I packed the paper menagerie in a large shoebox and put it under the bed.

The next morning, the animals had escaped and took over their old favorite spots in my room. I caught them all and put them back into the shoebox, taping the lid shut. But the animals made so much noise in the box that I finally shoved it into the corner of the attic as far away from my room as possible.

If Mom spoke to me in Chinese, I refused to answer her. After a while, she tried to use more English. But her accent and broken sentences embarrassed me. I tried to correct her. Eventually, she stopped speaking altogether if I were around.

Mom began to mime things if she needed to let me know something. She tried to hug me the way she saw American mothers did on TV. I thought her movements exaggerated, uncertain, ridiculous, graceless. She saw that I was annoyed, and stopped.

"You shouldn't treat your mother that way," Dad said. But he couldn't look me in the eyes as he said it. Deep in his heart, he must have realized that it was a mistake to have tried to take a Chinese peasant girl and expect her to fit in the suburbs of Connecticut.

Mom learned to cook American style. I played video games and studied French.

Every once in a while, I would see her at the kitchen table studying the plain side of a sheet of wrapping paper. Later a new paper animal would appear on my nightstand and try to cuddle up to me. I caught them, squeezed them until the air went out of them, and then stuffed them away in the box in the attic.

Mom finally stopped making the animals when I was in high school. By then her English was much better, but I was already at that age when I wasn't interested in what she had to say whatever language she used.

Sometimes, when I came home and saw her tiny body busily moving about in the kitchen, singing a song in Chinese to herself, it was hard for me to believe that she gave birth to me. We had nothing in common. She might as well be from the moon. I would hurry on to my room, where I could continue my all-American pursuit of happiness.

Dad and I stood, one on each side of Mom, lying on the hospital bed. She was not yet even forty, but she looked much older.

For years she had refused to go to the doctor for the pain inside her that she said was no big deal. By the time an ambulance finally carried her in, the cancer had spread far beyond the limits of surgery.

My mind was not in the room. It was the middle of the on-campus recruiting season, and I was focused on resumes, transcripts, and strategically constructed interview schedules. I schemed about how to lie to the corporate recruiters most effectively so that they'll offer to buy me. I understood intellectually that it was terrible to think about this while your mother lay dying. But that understanding didn't mean I could change how I felt.

She was conscious. Dad held her left hand with both of his own. He leaned down to kiss her forehead. He seemed weak and old in a way that startled me. I realized that I knew almost as little about Dad as I did about Mom.

Mom smiled at him. "I'm fine."

She turned to me, still smiling. "I know you have to go back to school." Her voice was very weak and it was difficult to hear her over the hum of the machines hooked up to her. "Go. Don't worry about me. This is not a big deal. Just do well in school."

I reached out to touch her hand, because I thought that was what I was supposed to do. I was relieved. I was already thinking about the flight back, and the bright California sunshine.

She whispered something to Dad. He nodded and left the room.

"Jack, if—" she was caught up in a fit of coughing, and could not speak for some time. "If I... don't make it, don't be too sad and hurt your health. Focus on your life. Just keep that box you have in the attic with you, and every year, at *Qingming*, just take it out and think about me. I'll be with you always."

Qingming was the Chinese Festival for the Dead. When I was very young, Mom used to write a letter on *Qingming* to her dead parents back in China, telling them the good news about the past year of her life in America. She would read the letter out loud to me, and if I made a comment about something, she would write it down in the letter too. Then she would fold the letter into a paper crane, and release it, facing west. We would then watch, as the crane flapped its crisp wings on its long journey west, towards the Pacific, towards China, towards the graves of Mom's family.

It had been many years since I last did that with her.

"I don't know anything about the Chinese calendar," I said. "Just rest, Mom."

"Just keep the box with you and open it once in a while. Just open—" she began to cough again.

"It's OK, Mom." I stroked her arm awkwardly.

"*Haizi, mama ai ni—*" Her cough took over again. An image from years ago flashed into my memory: Mom saying *ai* and then putting her hand over her heart.

"Alright, Mom. Stop talking."

Dad came back, and I said that I needed to get to the airport early because I didn't want to miss my flight.

She died when my plane was somewhere over Nevada.

Dad aged rapidly after Mom died. The house was too big for him and had to be sold. My girlfriend Susan and I went to help him pack and clean the place.

Susan found the shoebox in the attic. The paper menagerie, hidden in the uninsulated darkness of the attic for so long, had become brittle and the bright wrapping paper patterns had faded.

"I've never seen origami like this," Susan said. "Your Mom was an amazing artist."

The paper animals did not move. Perhaps whatever magic had animated them stopped when Mom died. Or perhaps I had only imagined that these paper constructions were once alive. The memory of children could not be trusted.

It was the first weekend in April, two years after Mom's death. Susan was out of town on one of her endless trips as a management consultant and I was home, lazily flipping through the TV channels.

I paused at a documentary about sharks. Suddenly I saw, in my mind, Mom's hands, as they folded and refolded tin foil to make a shark for me, while Laohu and I watched.

A rustle. I looked up and saw that a ball of wrapping paper and torn tape was on the floor next to the bookshelf. I walked over to pick it up for the trash.

The ball of paper shifted, unfurled itself, and I saw that it was Laohu, who I hadn't thought about in a very long time. "*Rawrr-sa.*" Mom must have put him back together after I had given up.

He was smaller than I remembered. Or maybe it was just that back then my fists were smaller.

Susan had put the paper animals around our apartment as decoration. She probably left Laohu in a pretty hidden corner because he looked so shabby.

I sat down on the floor, and reached out a finger. Laohu's tail twitched, and he pounced playfully. I laughed, stroking his back. Laohu purred under my hand.

"How've you been, old buddy?"

Laohu stopped playing. He got up, jumped with feline grace into my lap, and proceeded to unfold himself.

In my lap was a square of creased wrapping paper, the plain side up. It was filled with dense Chinese characters. I had never learned to read Chinese, but I knew the characters for *son*, and they were at the top, where you'd expect them in a letter addressed to you, written in Mom's awkward, childish handwriting.

I went to the computer to check the Internet. Today was *Qingming*.

I took the letter with me downtown, where I knew the Chinese tour buses stopped. I stopped every tourist, asking, "*Nin hui du zhongwen ma?*" *Can you read Chinese?* I hadn't spoken Chinese in so long that I wasn't sure if they understood.

A young woman agreed to help. We sat down on a bench together, and she read the letter to me aloud. The language that I had tried to forget for years came back, and I felt the words sinking into me, through my skin, through my bones, until they squeezed tight around my heart.

Son,

We haven't talked in a long time. You are so angry when I try to touch you that I'm afraid. And I think maybe this pain I feel all the time now is something serious.

So I decided to write to you. I'm going to write in the paper animals I made for you that you used to like so much.

The animals will stop moving when I stop breathing. But if I write to you with all my heart, I'll leave a little of myself behind on this paper, in these words. Then, if you think of me on Qingming, when the spirits of the departed are allowed to visit their families, you'll make the parts of myself I leave behind come alive too. The creatures I made for you will again leap and run and pounce, and maybe you'll get to see these words then.

Because I have to write with all my heart, I need to write to you in Chinese.

All this time I still haven't told you the story of my life. When you were little, I always thought I'd tell you the story when you were older, so you could understand. But somehow that chance never came up.

I was born in 1957, in Sigulu Village, Hebei Province. Your grandparents were both from very poor peasant families with few relatives. Only a few years after I was born, the Great Famines struck China, during which thirty million people died. The first memory I have was waking up to see my mother eating dirt so that she could fill her belly and leave the last bit of flour for me.

Things got better after that. Sigulu is famous for its zhezhi papercraft, and my mother taught me how to make paper animals and give them life. This was practical magic in the life of the village. We made paper birds to chase grasshoppers away from the fields, and paper tigers to keep away the mice. For Chinese New Year my friends and I made red paper dragons. I'll never forget the sight of all those little dragons zooming across the sky overhead, holding up strings of exploding firecrackers to scare away all the bad memories of the past year. You would have loved it.

Then came the Cultural Revolution in 1966. Neighbor turned on neighbor, and brother against brother. Someone remembered that my mother's brother, my uncle, had left for Hong Kong back in 1946, and became a merchant there. Having a relative in Hong Kong meant we were spies and enemies of the people, and we had to be struggled against in every way. Your poor grandmother—she couldn't take the abuse and threw herself down a well. Then some boys with hunting muskets dragged your grandfather away one day into the woods, and he never came back.

There I was, a ten-year-old orphan. The only relative I had in the world was my uncle in Hong Kong. I snuck away one night and climbed onto a freight train going south.

Down in Guangdong Province a few days later, some men caught me stealing food from a field. When they heard that I was trying to get to Hong Kong, they laughed. "It's your lucky day. Our trade is to bring girls to Hong Kong."

They hid me in the bottom of a truck along with other girls, and smuggled us across the border.

We were taken to a basement and told to stand up and look healthy and intelligent for the buyers. Families paid the warehouse a fee and came by to look us over and select one of us to "adopt."

The Chin family picked me to take care of their two boys. I got up every morning at four to prepare breakfast. I fed and bathed the boys. I shopped for food. I did the laundry and swept the floors. I followed the boys around and did their bidding. At night I was locked into a cupboard in the kitchen to sleep. If I was slow or did anything wrong I was beaten. If the boys did anything wrong I was beaten. If I was caught trying to learn English I was beaten.

"Why do you want to learn English?" Mr. Chin asked. "You want to go to the police? We'll tell the police that you are a mainlander illegally in Hong Kong. They'd love to have you in their prison."

Six years I lived like this. One day, an old woman who sold fish to me in the morning market pulled me aside.

"I know girls like you. How old are you now, sixteen? One day, the man who owns you will get drunk, and he'll look at you and pull you to him and you can't stop him. The wife will find out, and then you will think you really have gone to hell. You have to get out of this life. I know someone who can help."

She told me about American men who wanted Asian wives. If I can cook, clean, and take care of my American husband, he'll give me a good life. It was the only hope I had. And that was how I got into the catalog with all those lies and met your father. It is not a very romantic story, but it is my story.

In the suburbs of Connecticut, I was lonely. Your father was kind and gentle with me, and I was very grateful to him. But no one understood me, and I understood nothing.

But then you were born! I was so happy when I looked into your face and saw shades of my mother, my father, and myself. I had lost my entire family, all of Sigulu, everything I ever knew and loved. But there you were, and your face was proof that they were real. I hadn't made them up.

Now I had someone to talk to. I would teach you my language, and we could together remake a small piece of everything that I loved and lost. When you said your first words to me, in Chinese that had the same accent as my mother and me, I cried for hours. When I made the first zhezhi *animals for you, and you laughed, I felt there were no worries in the world.*

You grew up a little, and now you could even help your father and I talk to each other. I was really at home now. I finally found a good life. I wished my parents could be here, so that I could cook for them, and give them a good life too. But my parents were no longer around. You know what the Chinese think is the saddest feeling in the world? It's for a child to finally grow the desire to take care of his parents, only to realize that they were long gone.

Son, I know that you do not like your Chinese eyes, which are my eyes. I know that you do not like your Chinese hair, which is my hair. But can you understand how much joy your very existence brought to me? And can you understand how it felt when you stopped talking to me and won't let me talk to you in Chinese? I felt I was losing everything all over again.

Why won't you talk to me, son? The pain makes it hard to write.

The young woman handed the paper back to me. I could not bear to look into her face.

Without looking up, I asked for her help in tracing out the character for *ai* on the paper below Mom's letter. I wrote the character again and again on the paper, intertwining my pen strokes with her words.

The young woman reached out and put a hand on my shoulder. Then she got up and left, leaving me alone with my mother.

Following the creases, I refolded the paper back into Laohu. I cradled him in the crook of my arm, and as he purred, we began the walk home.

STEAM GIRL

DYLAN HORROCKS

Dylan Horrocks is the author of the graphic novel Hicksville *and the comic book series* Pickle *and* Atlas. *He has written* Batgirl *and* Hunter: The Age of Magic *for DC Comics and his new graphic novel,* The Magic Pen, *is being serialized online at hicksvillecomics.com. He's also quietly working on a series of fantasy novels. Dylan lives in New Zealand with his wife and two teenage sons, in a seaside town named Maraetai Beach.*

The first time I see her, she's standing alone behind the library, looking at the ground. Faded blue dress, scruffy leather jacket, long lace-up boots and black-rimmed glasses. But what really makes me stop and stare is the hat: a weird old leather thing that hangs down over her ears, with big thick goggles strapped to the front.

Turns out she's in my English class. She sits right next to me, still wearing the jacket and goggles and hat. She smells like a thrift store.

"Weirdo," says Michael Carmichael.

"Freak," says Amanda Anderson.

She ignores the laughter, reaching into her bag for a notebook and pencil. She bends low so no one can see what she's writing.

Later, when Mrs Hendricks is dealing with an outbreak of giggles at the front of the class, I lean over and whisper, "What's with the hat?"

She glances at me with a tiny frown, then turns back to her notebook. Her eyebrows are the color of cheese.

"Not a *hat*," she says without looking up. "Helmet. *Flying* helmet."

"Huh," I say. "So what are you—a pilot?"

And then she raises her eyes and smiles straight at me, kind of sly.

"Steam Girl," she says.

"What's *Steam Girl*?"

Then Mrs Hendricks starts shouting, and the whole class shuts up.

That afternoon she's waiting for me by the school gate. I check that no one's watching before I say hello.

"Here," she says, handing me the notebook. It's a cheap school exercise book, with a creased cover and fraying corners. On the first page is a title, in big blue letters:

STEAM GIRL

Below that is a drawing of a slimmer, prettier version of the girl in front of me: blue dress, leather jacket, lace-up boots, flying helmet and goggles. But in the drawing it looks *awesome* instead of, well, weird.

"Did you do this?" I say. "It's pretty good."

"Thanks." She reaches over and turns the pages. There are more drawings and diagrams: a flying ship shaped like a cigar, people in old-fashioned diving suits swimming through space, strange alien landscapes, strange clockwork gadgets, and of course, Steam Girl—leaping from the airship, fighting off monsters, laughing and smiling….

"So who's Steam Girl?" I ask.

"She's an adventurer," she says. "Well, her *father's* an adventurer, and an explorer and scientist. But she goes everywhere with him, in their experimental steam-powered airship, *The Martian Rose*.

"Steam Girl makes gadgets." She rummages around in her bag, finally holding up what looks like a rusty old Swiss army knife. Screwdrivers and pliers and mangled bits of wire stick out in all directions. There's even a tiny wooden teaspoon.

"The Mark II Multi-Functional Pocket Engineering Device," she announces triumphantly. "One of Steam Girl's first—and best—gadgets. Got them out of many a scrape, like the time they were captured by troglodytes on the moon and locked in an underground zoo…"

She's talking pretty fast and waving her arms in the air, and I take a step back to avoid getting stabbed by that thing in her hand.

"Steam Girl used this to pick the lock on their cage, and they managed to get back to *The Martian Rose* just in time," she continues, half closing her eyes. "As they lifted into space, the troglodytes in their tunnels howled so loud that the ground shivered and shook and the moon dust rippled like windswept waves…"

"Um…." I don't know what to say. "So you—uh—you made all this up, huh?"

She goes very quiet. Then she grabs the notebook out of my hands and shoves it into her bag.

"See ya," she says, and runs off before I can reply.

I've never been what you'd call a popular kid. I'm not very smart, I'm lousy at sports, and between the oversize teeth and the woolly black hair I'm kind of goofy looking. My mom always says I have "hidden talents," but I gave up looking for them a long time ago. I'm used to being on my own.

I have *had* friends. In fact once upon a time I used to hang out with Amanda Anderson, the prettiest girl in school. We live on the same street, and when I was six or seven, her mother used to visit my mum for coffee. Amanda and I would play together with Legos and dolls and stuff like that. My parents didn't approve of gender stereotypes so sometimes they'd buy me girls' toys. I had a pretty cool dolls house and some Barbie accessories that Amanda adored. It was all the same to me; I'd play with anything.

But one day at school Amanda told everyone about my Barbie dolls. You can imagine the mocking I got after that. When I told my parents what happened, they called Amanda's mother on the phone and they never came for coffee again.

I'm glad my parents stood up for me, but I kind of wish they hadn't made a scene. I mean, it's not like Amanda and I were best friends or anything; we hardly said a word to each other at school. But she was really pretty, even back then, and I guess I hoped that one day, maybe…. Well, you get the idea.

What's really sad and pathetic is that I still have hopes, after all these years. You know, like in movies, when the hot popular girl suddenly falls totally in love with the unpopular nerd and dumps the arrogant macho football jock? Only in the movies the unpopular nerd is played by a good-looking film star, while in real life he's played by *me*.

These days Amanda goes out with Michael Carmichael, who hit puberty three years before I did and plays bass in a hardcore band, and who once put a lit cigarette down my trousers on the way home from school. It took nearly five minutes to get the damn thing out, and I ended up with blisters in places you don't want to know about. I don't really get why Michael's such an asshole. It's like he feels personally offended when someone is ugly or stupid or clever or different. Like it makes him really angry. I almost feel sorry for him, being like that. But then he pushes past me in the hallway with Amanda Anderson on his arm and I don't feel sorry anymore.

Anyway, as I was saying, I don't really have any friends. Most of the time that's OK. At home I play a lot of online games by myself. I know a lot of people treat those games as a big social thing, with loads of chatting and friending and all that. But not me. I just go on quests and kill monsters and level up and earn gold and stuff. That's what I like about it: even a loser like me can actually *achieve* something, just by pushing keys and putting in the hours. I wish real life were more like that.

Now and then, the loneliness is more than I can bear. So I try things like smiling at people in class. Sometimes they smile back. And sometimes they look like they want to punch me or else throw up. And then I feel worse than ever. Once, I smiled at Amanda and she smiled back. Then after class Michael pushed me up against the wall and told me to stop creeping out his girlfriend.

So when the new girl ambushed me at the gate, I didn't know what to think. Is she stalking me? I've never had a stalker before (obviously), but I sometimes wish I did. But in the fantasies, my stalker would be gorgeous, blonde, and crazy with lust. Not just, y'know, *crazy*….

Still, I have to admit, that notebook is pretty damn cool. That night, as I'm lying in bed, my mind keeps drifting back to the shivering moon dust, *The Martian Rose* and—of course—Steam Girl. Who, come to think of it, *is* gorgeous and blonde.

So in the morning, when I see that leather flying helmet bobbing along in a sluggish tide of hoodies and greasy hair, I find myself pushing through the crowd to catch up.

"Hey," I say, as casually as I can.

She barely looks up. "Hey."

"How come I didn't see you before last week? Did you move here or something?"

Instead of answering, she takes hold of my arm and steers me out of the flow and into an empty alcove. I'm too surprised to speak.

"Listen," she says, still holding my arm. "Do you want to meet me at lunchtime?"

"Uh… sure. I guess." I'm not *at all* sure I want to, but what else can I say?

"By the incinerator. A quarter past twelve." She makes it sound like a mysterious secret rendezvous.

And then she lets go of my arm and disappears back into the crowd.

"Where Steam Girl comes from, even the laws of physics are different.

There's a little magic in technology. Things are… less drab, less logical, less straightforward. Everything's a little more… *possible*."

We're sitting on a wall behind the incinerator block. The air smells of smoke and garbage, but there's no one else around, which is a big advantage. I'm flicking through her notebook, drinking in the drawings of Steam Girl's long legs and sly smile.

"Take *The Martian Rose*," she says. "It's the greatest airship ever made, with an amazing motor called the Spirodynamic Multi-Dimensional Concentrated Steam Engine. I'm not sure exactly how it works—something about cycling steam through several dimensions at once to magnify its power. It was invented by Steam Girl's mother, who mysteriously disappeared when Steam Girl was still a baby. She was an inventor, too…."

"What's this?" I say, holding up the notebook.

"Oh, that's Mars," she says. The picture shows a fairy-tale palace, perched on the side of a huge red mountain. In the foreground are several men in armor, each riding the back of a strange giant bird. "Skimmer Birds," she explains. "They're not really birds; they're more like flying dinosaurs, but covered in shiny green and yellow scales that almost look like feathers. When the sun hits them, they shimmer and flash like a thousand colored lights. It's beautiful…"

I glance up at her. She's slowly swinging her legs and staring into the distance at nothing. There's something very serious about the way she speaks.

The next drawing seems to be inside the palace. A tall, slim man with a long white beard, sitting on a throne.

"When we first arrived," she says, "we were taken to see King Minnimattock. The Martians were really nervous, because they'd never seen people from Earth before."

"Who's that?" I ask, pointing at a dark-haired young woman standing beside the King.

"Oh, that's Princess Lusanna, the King's daughter. As soon as she saw Steam Girl's father, Lusanna started blushing like the sunrise. Apparently, that's what Martian women do when they fall in love…"

She glances at me for a moment, then looks down at her boots and continues talking.

"At first the King didn't know what to do with these strangers from another world. So he summoned the Royal Oracle, who turned up in a long black cloak, a dark hood covering her face. But when she entered the room, the Oracle gave a strangled cry and fell to the floor in a faint.

All the guards pointed their spears at Steam Girl and her father, and even the King drew his sword. Things looked pretty grim."

She slides off the wall and starts pacing up and down, stretching her arms over her head.

"That's when Princess Lusanna intervened, pleading with her father to give the visitors a chance. The King hesitated. The Earthlings claimed to have come in peace. What's more, it was clear that his beloved daughter had taken a powerful liking to one of them at least. But the fate of his Kingdom—maybe the entire planet—could be at stake!"

By now, I've forgotten about the notebook, the incinerator smell, the stale sandwiches and warm juice at my side. I'm completely caught by her words, the sound of her voice. I watch as she strides back and forth across the dirty asphalt, lost in her story.

"Then Steam Girl had an idea. She curtsied to the King—" (as she says this, she drops into a clumsy curtsey herself) "and said she had a gift for him and his lovely daughter."

Her pacing has brought her to the side of her schoolbag. She crouches and draws out a small metal object, cupped in both hands: a tiny artificial bird, made of metal and wood, held together by miniature hinges and levers.

"Wow!" I say.

"The Clockwork Sparrow," she says. "Just a little trifle Steam Girl had made during the long journey from the Moon to Mars. Now she held it up for the King to see, and she wound the spring-driven motor—like *this*…."

I hold my breath as she turns a key no bigger than a baby's fingernail. There's the sound of small metallic teeth catching and grinding.

"And then she opened her hands and let go…"

The Clockwork Sparrow drops like a stone, hitting the ground with a painful clatter. We both stare at it in silence. Then, just for a moment, it comes to life: rusting wings flutter, the tiny beak opens and closes, and the whole bird shuffles sideways along the asphalt. And then it lies still.

"Well, it worked better on Mars," she says, lifting the broken metal body and turning away.

"That was… awesome!" I say, jumping down from the wall. "Where did you get it? Can I see?"

But she's already put it away.

"Never mind," she says, pulling her bag over her shoulder. "The bell's about to ring."

"You can't stop there!" I say. "What happened with the King? And—

what's her name? Lucy—?"

I follow her all the way to E Block, but she won't say another word. And sure enough, the bell rings just as we reach the door, and I have to go to gym class.

After that, I'm hooked. We meet up most days for lunch by the incinerator. She tells me about Steam Girl while I look at the pictures in her book. Sometimes she turns up without any lunch, so I share mine. Soon I'm bringing twice as much, just in case, and an extra bottle of orange juice, which she really likes.

The stories get longer and more complicated: voyages of discovery all over Mars, with monsters and volcanoes and narrow escapes from angry native tribes. But throughout it all, their friendship with King Minnimattock and Princess Lusanna grows. Sometimes the old King and his daughter would come with them on *The Martian Rose*, delighted at the chance to explore their home planet. And, of course, Lusanna still glowed bright red whenever Steam Girl's father was around.

Not everyone on Mars liked the newcomers. The King's son, Prince Zennobal, seemed to resent their popularity, especially after Steam Girl rejected his amorous advances with a well-placed right hook. And the Royal Oracle hid in her laboratory when they were in town. But everyone else was having too much fun to notice.

And then there are the gadgets. The Motion-Powered Wrist-Mounted Mono-Directional Lantern (a tiny metal box that faintly glows if you jump up and down for long enough), the Audioscopic Motion Capture Device (a tin cup full of wood chips and wax that supposedly records sound), the Portable Kitchen (actually a beat up old gas cooker covered in rubber tubes), and my favorite: Steam Girl's Spring-Motivated Vertical Propulsion Boots. These last ones turn up in a story involving giant bloodsucking insects who live in a deep canyon called the Mariner's Valley. Steam Girl was trapped at the bottom of a pit, listening to the buzz of the thirsty insect swarm getting closer and closer. But then, at the last moment, she reached down to flick a tiny lever on her lace-up boots and...

"And what?" I say as she slips into one of her long, teasing pauses, gazing up at the sky. We're sitting as usual on the low concrete wall behind the incinerator. "Come on...!"

A lazy smile spreads across her face and she slowly slips down from the wall. There are a couple of tiny metal clips on the soles of her boots.

She spends a moment fiddling with these, then straightens up and grins.

"A little modification Steam Girl made to her boots back on the Moon," she says. "Very useful on low gravity planets like Mars…."

She bends her knees and jumps. At first I think the soles of her boots have come right off—but then I realise they're still attached by thick round springs that stretch and bounce as she leaps into the air. I laugh pretty hard at that—and even harder when she lands flat on her bum.

She glares at me, brushing off her skirt. "Like I said, they work better in low gravity."

We spend a half hour mucking around with the crazy spring boots. She even gets me to try them on, though they don't really fit, and I fall over straight away. I scrape my knees and get a bruise on my chin, but I'm laughing too much to care. It's the first time I hear her laugh, and I like it. She kind of giggles—but not a high-pitched girly giggle like Amanda and her friends. It sounds almost dirty.

Anyway, in the story, Steam Girl's boots got her out of the pit to safety. And in a way, I guess they've helped me escape from the dreariness of school—at least for an hour or so, while it's just me and her and the gadgets and notebook.

But then the bell rings and we have to go back to class and real life. And let's face it: real life sucks.

It doesn't take long for people to notice I've made a new friend.

"How's your girlfriend?" they say.

"She's not my girlfriend," I reply, again and again. For all the good it does.

Michael Carmichael seems to find everything about her personally insulting. And he apparently blames me.

"You're disgusting," he says, shoving me into walls and chairs and shelves and desks. "Makes me sick."

Even Amanda makes gagging faces when she sees us together. And once, in the hallway after English, she grabs at Steam Girl's flying helmet and tries to pull it off. I don't see what happens next, but everyone hears Amanda screaming like a scalded cat.

I ask about it over lunch, but all I get is a chilly glare and silence.

"From the noise Amanda made, I thought you'd ripped her face off," I say.

She rolls her eyes. "I hardly touched her. She's worse than the Shrieking Vines of Venus."

"The shrieking what?"

And then she gives me a little smile and starts to talk, and before long I've totally forgotten about Amanda and Michael and everything else.

But the next day I don't see her in the morning, even though I get to school early and wait by the gate till the bell rings. She isn't in class either. At lunchtime I check by the incinerator. There's no one there. So I give up and go sit in the library, where it's peaceful and private.

That's where I find her, sitting on the floor between two shelves, sniffing like a little girl.

"You OK?" I say.

She's covering the left side of her face with one hand. I kneel down beside her but don't know what to say. So instead I just sit there saying nothing, while she sniffs and gulps and keeps hiding her face till finally the bell rings and we get to our feet and go to our separate classes without a word.

So anyway, here's what she tells me about the Shrieking Vines of Venus, the day before Michael Carmichael gave her a black eye:

When Steam Girl and her father had been on Mars for a few months, and had already ticked off most of the items on King Minnimattock's places-to-see list, someone had the bright idea of going to Venus. Actually, it was Prince Zennobal's idea, which should have tipped them off straight away, but everyone was too excited to be suspicious. Steam Girl's father had always wanted to see what the mysterious green planet was like, and the King couldn't wait to travel to another world. The preparations were made at lightning speed, and within a week, *The Martian Rose* was on its way to Venus, with Steam Girl and her father and a handful of passengers, including the King and the Princess. Zennobal had pulled out at the last minute, much to Steam Girl's relief.

"Venus was beautiful!" she says, eyes shining. "Like the greenest, thickest, most luscious jungle you can imagine. The forest rose hundreds of feet into the thick warm air. And there were flowers everywhere: huge orange blossoms the size of a house, with pools of sweet nectar where you could swim and drink at the same time. Millions of birds and tiny playful monkeys, who chattered and giggled and danced through the trees. It was paradise. For six days they flew over that vast green ocean of leaves, landing now and then to explore under the canopy. All their worries fell away, and they felt more relaxed and happy than ever before. They strolled through endless orchards munching on all kinds of fruit, swam in fresh clean rivers and lay in giant palm fronds, watching as sunset turned the whole sky red.

"Everything seemed peaceful. There were no giant monsters or angry natives or dangerous traps. The only slight annoyance was a particular kind of vine that gave off an ear-splitting shriek whenever you came near it."

"Aha!" I say. "The Shrieking Vines of Venus!"

She grins. "Luckily they were covered with bright pink blossoms that gave off a sickly sweet scent, so they were easy enough to avoid."

There are drawings, too, in her notebook. My favorite shows Steam Girl and the Princess doubled over with laughter, pointing at a puzzled King Minnimattock. A bright red monkey the size of a kitten has made a nest in the King's beard and is curled up, fast asleep. Behind them the jungle is a dense tumble of leaves and flowers and vines. Tiny blue birds fly overhead.

Over the page is a very different scene: a view from the airship with the jungle spread out below. A dark column of smoke rises into the sky from somewhere near the horizon. It's a disturbing picture.

When I ask about it, she stops smiling and goes quiet. I've never seen her look like that.

"Sorry," she says at last. "I was…" She trails off. "You see, this is where it all went wrong…."

"How do you mean?" I ask.

She shakes her head. "Never mind," she says. "I'll tell you tomorrow."

But the next day is when I found her crying in the library, and after that things begin to change.

Around this time, Mrs Hendricks shifts the seats around so Amanda and Michael aren't sitting together. Instead, Michael ends up next to me, and Amanda gets to sit with Steam Girl. Maybe Mrs Hendricks thinks I'll be a good influence on Michael, which shows just how much she knows.

Day after day, I stare at them. The two girls, I mean. Amanda wears tight tops that show a lot of skin. Her spine is one long graceful curve, and when she leans back and yawns, it's like a slow motion movie. She knows Michael is watching, so sometimes she puts on a show, with plenty of stretching and hair-tossing and brief stolen glances. Of course I get to see it all, too.

Next to that, Steam Girl's flying helmet and jacket seem even sadder than usual. She hunches over her notebook, like a big, shy bear trying to hide. The only skin that shows through all the dark worn leather is an occasional glimpse of the back of her neck. It looks pale and cold.

Some nights when I lie in bed, I try to remember Amanda's latest performance—her soft slim arms, her narrow waist.... But after a while all I can think of is a tiny sliver of cool white skin.

It's a whole week before she mentions Steam Girl again.

I get to the incinerator first that day. There's a fire going and thick white smoke keeps drifting into my eyes. Even the concrete seems to be sweating. When she finally shows up, I don't notice till she's right in front of me. It's like she's come out of the smoke, like she *is* smoke. For a moment nothing seems solid, nothing's real. Then she reaches out and puts a hand on my arm.

"Are you alright?" she says.

"Uh... yeah." I shake my head. "Let's get out of here."

We sit under some dying trees by a chain-link fence. Scraps of rubbish have blown among the roots and the earth feels damp. I spread my sweatshirt out for her to sit on so she won't get wet. For a moment she hesitates, looking at the sweatshirt and then at me. No one's ever looked at me like that before. Her eyes wide open and her lips not quite closed. Her neck is slowly turning pink.

"Thank you," she says, and smiles.

We share my lunch, as usual. I have some chocolate cake from Dad's birthday and she carefully eats half before handing me the rest. Then she leans back on the tree while I flick through her notebook. When I reach the picture from Venus with the green jungle and the black smoke, I hold it up.

"So..." I say. "You were going to tell me about this one?"

She swallows, then nods.

"OK," she says. "I guess you've waited long enough.

"The rising smoke came from a chimney—from *dozens* of tall, fat chimneys that loomed over a vast line of buildings, like giant factories and warehouses, made of stone and concrete and iron and tin. There was a gaping hole in the forest, where the trees had been cut and the ground opened up. Huge machines were tearing at the earth, pulling up tons of soil and rock and carrying it into factories. Stacks of tree trunks were piled outside, for fuel, Steam Girl supposed. There were no people to be seen, only thousands of strange gray robots shaped like men, who bustled about among the buildings and machines like a hive of worker bees.

"When they first saw all this, Princess Lusanna began to cry. Her father's face went dark.

"'Take us down,' he rumbled. 'I would find out who has done this thing.' Steam Girl and her father, along with the King and three of his bravest warriors, landed in the forest about a mile away. They crept to the edge of the clearing and watched as several robots marched stiffly by. The robots carried guns of a kind Steam Girl had never seen before. Steam Girl hated guns more than anything and she never, ever used them.

"As soon as the robots had gone past, Steam Girl whispered to her father: 'Back in a minute.' And before he could argue, she left their hiding place and ran across the open ground to the nearest building, where she crouched behind a low wall of crates and then slipped in through the door.

"It was a factory, all right. There were machines and conveyor belts and cables and tubes. There were workers, too—hundreds of robots, pulling levers and turning cranks and carrying wood to the giant furnace at one end of the room. She noticed more robots lying half-assembled on the conveyor belts, and guessed that's what the factory was for. Robots building more robots.

"But that was only part of it. There were other production lines, too, making machines she'd never seen or even heard of. Heavy iron engines that smelled of fire and oil—some with wings and some with wheels. Ugly big guns and bombs with fins like sharks. There were boxes and tools made of a strange artificial material—unnaturally smooth, light, and dull. And flat glass screens like empty mirrors, and long snaking rubber-coated wires that hung around the room and over the floor.

"Steam Girl's head was spinning, but she was determined to solve the mystery of this infernal factory. As quietly as she could, she made her way across the factory floor, ducking from wood-pile to conveyor belt, avoiding the robots and looking for clues.

"Near the middle of the room was a raised platform with a commanding view of the whole operation. There was no one there—just a desk and two chairs, a vase of bright-pink flowers, and one of those curious machines with row upon row of buttons and a blank glass screen. And all over the desk, the chairs, the floor—stood piles of paper, covered with printed text and diagrams and handwritten notes. Quickly and carefully, Steam Girl crept to the edge of the platform and glanced around to see if she had been noticed. Then she reached up to the desk and snatched an armload of paper.

"A high-pitched scream filled the air, cutting through the constant roar of the factory. Robots looked up from their work and stared at the platform where Steam Girl crouched clutching her stolen papers.

"'Shrieking Vines,' she muttered, realizing too late that the vase on the desk wasn't merely decorative.

"Then she jumped to her feet and ran as fast as she could—leaping over conveyor belts and darting between the quickly converging robots until finally she was out the door and sprinting for the cover of the jungle. Behind her shots rang out, louder and faster than any firearms she knew of. The ground around her feet spat up fistfuls of dirt. But somehow she made it to the trees unharmed.

"'Run!' she yelled, and her father and the Martians took off through the forest with bullets splintering trees and cutting leaves to ribbons all around them. But Steam Girl paused a moment to catch her breath, then reached down to her belt and pulled out a gadget she'd never tried before."

"Ha! I know what's coming next!" I cry, interrupting her story.

"Do you?" she says, looking at me sideways from behind her glasses.

"Sure," I grin, slipping off the wall and crossing my arms. "It's *gadget time*! So what is it today? A Steam-Driven Instantaneous Escape Facilitator? Oversize Extendible Robot-Neutralising Punching Arms? A Rocket-Powered Jet-Pack Flying Machine?"

She stares at me for a moment and then laughs so hard, she gets the hiccups. I can't stop smiling, especially when she wipes her eyes and puts her hand on my shoulder.

"You're OK," she says. "I think we'll get along just fine."

I can feel my face blushing, but she's already turned away to dig through her bag. When she straightens up, she's holding what looks like a rusty tin can with a string at one end.

"Huh?" I say. "Is that it? Doesn't look like much—"

Then she points one end of the can at me and pulls the string. There's a loud COUGH! and the air fills with steam and something damp and heavy hits me full in the face. I yelp and trip over backward and then it's like someone's tossed a wet fishing net all over me. I wave my arms and legs around and just get more and more caught. I can hear her laughing again, even harder than before, but it doesn't seem very funny to me.

"GET ME OUT OF HERE!" I shout at the top of my lungs. "GOD DAMN IT! IT'S HORRIBLE!"

She eventually manages to stop laughing long enough to try to free me but without much success. The net's so sticky, it gets all over her, too, and soon we're both caught in a big gooey mess of strings and glue and soot and each other.

There's a moment when I suddenly realise I'm lying on top of her, my face pressed against her neck. She has one arm around my back and a hand on my cheek. And at exactly the same time we both stop struggling and lie there in silence.

Her soft white skin is slowly turning pink.

At last we get ourselves out, and as we sit on the dusty concrete, picking bits of sticky web out of our hair and off our clothes, she tells me the rest of the story.

"The Web Weaving Tangle Trap caught the first wave of pursuing robots," she says, "giving Steam Girl and her friends enough time to get back to the airship and safety. They rose up into the sky with gunfire rattling at them from below.

"The King was elated. 'What an adventure!' he said with a laugh.

"Princess Lusanna was so excited, she quite forgot herself, throwing her arms around Steam Girl's father and giving him a big kiss. The King laughed even harder at that, until the Princess turned the brightest red anyone had ever seen and ran off to her cabin."

I close my eyes then, picturing the scene. If I'd been there, I'd have kissed Steam Girl. She'd have laughed, with a low, throaty giggle. Perhaps her breath would quicken, and her throat would turn pink, and I'd have to swallow very hard before I could speak....

But when I open my eyes again, she isn't smiling or blushing. She isn't even looking at me, but at the thin brown grass that's forced its way through the asphalt.

"And what about Steam Girl?" I ask. "What did she do?"

She glances up and our eyes meet. She looks so sad.

"She—well, after all that running, I guess she was tired." She sighs. "So she went to take a rest in her hammock. But as she took off her jacket, something fell out of the pocket and spilled across the floor. The papers she'd snatched. What with getting shot at and everything, she'd completely forgotten about them till now.

"So she leaped up and spread the papers out across the floor. To her surprise, they were in English. There were maps of Venus, Mars, and Earth; lists of equipment; and plans of attack. With a rising sense of panic, Steam Girl realized they could mean only one thing: all those robots and weapons and fighting machines were being prepared as an army of conquest.

"Reading on, she found ominous references to some kind of super-bomb, able to destroy whole cities in a single awful flash; poisonous gas that could kill an army in minutes; and even man-made plagues for releasing into a population's water supply or the air they breathed. It was unimaginable, inhuman, horrible…..

"It was a plan for the end of the world."

On the way back to class, she's quiet. But I'm buzzing.

"So what happened?" I say, dancing around her as we walk. "Did Steam Girl show the papers to her father? And then did they—?"

"No," she says quietly.

"What? She didn't show him the papers? How come?"

She hesitates a moment, as if trying to decide whether to tell me what comes next.

"There was one more thing," she says at last. "On one of the papers. On the back, written in pencil, over and over."

I wait, but she seems to have stopped talking, and we're almost at her classroom.

"What was it?" I stand in front of the door. "Come on, you have to tell me! Or I won't let you go to Maths."

She gives me a withering look. "Alright, I'll tell you. But…."

"But what?" I'm desperate. The second bell is about to ring.

"Never mind," she says. "It was a name. Her father's name. His full name—Professor Archibald James Patterson Swift. Again and again."

"Wooooah!" I breathe. "So—what? Was *he* behind the factory? Did he have, like, a secret life where he slipped off to Venus and planned the destruction of Earth?"

"Don't be stupid," she hisses.

"It would be a good twist, though, wouldn't it?" I say. "Y'know, the heroine's father turns out to be the villain—"

"It *wasn't* him," she repeats, more firmly this time. "He's a good man, who'd never do anything rotten like that. No matter what people say about him."

"Why? What do people say about him?" Now I'm confused. Does the father have secrets, after all?

But the second bell rings and she pushes past me into the classroom and closes the door behind her.

She isn't at school the next day, or the day after that. I look for her everywhere, but she isn't in class, or by the incinerator or even in the library. By Thursday I've slipped back into my old routine, eating lunch by myself and catching up on homework.

Mrs Hendricks has given us a new assignment: write a short story in the first person, present tense. I sit in the classroom trying to ignore Michael Carmichael and come up with an idea, but all I can think of is Steam Girl, and that's *her* story, not mine.

So I start writing about a boy who has his own adventures, travelling around the universe in a rocket ship called *The Silver Arrow*. In my story he flies to Saturn, which is like a huge ocean of poisonous gases, so the natives all live in cities they've built on the rings high above the planet's surface. When Rocket Boy (that's what I call him) lands on the first ring, he sees this huge hairy monster chasing a frightened girl. So he makes a really loud noise with his rocket's engines and scares the monster away. The girl, who turns out to be the princess of Saturn, is so grateful, she throws her arms around him and kisses him on the lips, blushing pink on her cheeks and on her long pale neck, her heaving breasts pressed against his chest…

But then I stop, because I know what Mrs Hendricks would say. She hates it if we write something like "heaving breasts." She calls it a cliché and says we should write about things that are real. Which makes me want to say, "I don't like writing what's real, because mostly what's real is boring and sucks." But I don't say that, I just nod and say nothing.

Anyway, this time it *is* real, because that's what this girl is like. I know, because I based her on Steam Girl, who definitely *does* have heaving breasts and long, lithe legs and all that stuff. Well, the Steam Girl in the notebook, at least. The real one has heaving breasts, too, come to think of it, but also heaving shoulders and a heaving stomach and heaving thighs and bum. She's all about the *heaving*. And the weird thing is I don't mind at all. I'm even starting to like it.

So when she finally reappears on Friday, I nervously show her *Rocket Boy*. I've even done some drawings of him and the princess, but they look pretty stupid compared to hers. I'm worried she'll say it's lousy, but instead she gives it back without saying much at all. "Great," she says, sounding distracted. I don't think she's even read it.

"How come you weren't at school?" I say, a little disappointed.

But she doesn't answer my question. "Did I miss much?"

I tell her about the short story assignment, which is due in a week.

"You should do Steam Girl," I say.

She looks at me like I'm stupid. "That's not for teachers," she says.

"What do you mean?" I ask. But I already kind of know.

"All they want to read about is miserable people living stupid boring lives. Unhappy families, unrequited love—all that crap." She grimaces. "And the worst thing is… *none of it's real.*"

"Sorry," I say. "I didn't mean—it's just—well, I think Steam Girl is great. Really totally *awesome.* I swear, if you typed it all up and got it published, you could be a millionaire."

She stares at me for a long time. I can feel my cheeks starting to burn.

"Listen," she says at last. "I don't care about being a millionaire or Mrs Hendricks or English grades or school or any of that stuff. All of that means nothing."

"OK," I say.

"All I care about is *this.*" She brandishes her notebook like a weapon. "This is all that matters. All that's real."

This time I don't say anything.

She hesitates for a moment, her eyes slipping away from mine and drifting across the concrete and the garbage and the thin sickly trees. Then she turns and walks away.

That afternoon in Biology, Amanda Anderson comes over and says "Hi."

I almost choke. "Uh… hi," I say.

"You're pretty tight with the new girl, right?" she says. "That weird girl with the hat?"

"Flying helmet," I say, and immediately regret it.

"What?" She looks at me like I've just started speaking Mongolian.

"It's not a hat." I've lost all control of my mouth. "It's a flying helmet. Like pilots wear. Apparently…" I trail off lamely.

"Well, whatever," she says. "So what's her deal? Is she one of those creepy cosplayers or something?"

"I don't know," I say, which is true. "She's good at drawing. And she tells amazing stories."

"Huh." Amanda frowns. "What kind of stories?"

"Um…."

I'm not sure how much to explain. I mean, Amanda *is* the Shrieking Vine of Venus, right? She's already caused one black eye. What if she's just pumping me for intel to pass on to Michael?

But I was friends with her once, and I want to believe she's a decent person. It's not her fault the whole Barbie thing got out of hand. Or that her boyfriend is a creep. Maybe she's genuinely trying to understand. Maybe she wants to patch things up. Maybe I still have a chance.

"They're about this character called Steam Girl," I say at last.

"Steam Girl?" She screws up her face.

"Yeah. She has adventures… on Mars and stuff."

"God, how lame," Amanda says.

I feel bad that in my mouth it *does* sound lame. It's like a betrayal.

"Does she ever take off that stupid hat?" Amanda says.

"I dunno," I say. "Not that I've seen."

"Well, anyway," she says, getting to the point at last. "Tracey says she lives in a trailer home with her creepy drug dealer father. You should probably be careful. One day she'll probably bring a gun to school and kill everyone she knows."

I laugh.

"I'm just telling you for your own safety." She actually seems concerned. "I know you always look for the best in people. But you saw what she did to me, right? That girl is dangerous. Seriously."

She puts a hand on my shoulder. "I'm sorry Michael's such a jerk," she says. "I swear, I'm *this* close to ditching him…."

The warmth of her skin goes through my shirt and spreads across my body.

"Take care of yourself," she says.

That night, I try to dream about Amanda Anderson. But all I can think of is that stupid hat.

And then it's the weekend and I don't have to think about Steam Girl or Amanda Anderson or Michael Carmichael or anything. I stay in my bedroom playing online games with loud music on the headphones. Once or twice, Mom comes in to try to get me outside or doing chores. But mostly I can just be alone.

I can't get my head around anything. Steam Girl—the one in the notebook—is perfect: beautiful, smart, generous, and brave. Her long legs and heaving breasts haunt me in a way even Amanda Anderson never has. But the other one—the real girl who tells the stories and draws the pictures—well, *her* legs are short and kind of plump. Her skin is pasty and pale with freckles, and spots. She's like a parody of Steam Girl, a fat nerdy girl playing dress ups.

But here's the thing: I just can't stop thinking about her. When she smiles, I feel lighter than air. When she's sad, I want to take her hand

and tell her everything will be OK. I *don't*, but I want to. I love seeing her neck go pink; in fact, I love everything about her neck. I keep imagining what it would be like to put my fingers on that soft white skin and feel the tiny muscles flutter as she speaks. Sometimes she closes her eyes as she talks about Steam Girl's father and *The Martian Rose* and then her lips go soft and everything about her seems to *glow*.

She makes life special. And I find myself, by Saturday night, wanting to see her more than I've ever wanted anything before. I pull on some shoes and a hoodie and go out into the darkening streets. There's no way of knowing where she is, of course. I have no idea where she lives or what she does on a Saturday. For all I know she could be flying over the Martian desert in an airship or fighting robots somewhere in the jungles of Venus. So I just walk, randomly, through the empty suburban streets as the sky goes from red to purple to black, like the bruise around her eye. And the electric lights come on, flickering over cracked pavements and filling windows with gold. Now and then a car rattles past, or some kid on a bike. But mostly I'm alone.

It's after midnight when I get home. Dad lets me in without saying a word, makes me a hot chocolate and goes back to bed. It takes me hours to fall asleep.

On Monday morning, I'm at school early, waiting by the gate. But when the second bell rings, I give up and go to class.

At lunchtime, I go down to the incinerator and sit on the wall and try to eat my lunch. The concrete's cold, and the smell of smoke is stale and heavy in the air. My stomach is churning. After ten minutes, I pick up my bag and turn to go.

She's walking toward me, hands in the pockets of her heavy old jacket. I open my mouth to say something, but nothing comes to mind.

"Hey," she says.

"I was looking for you," I say, and then stop, wondering why the hell I said *that*. She frowns, so I just keep talking, not knowing what will come out. "On Saturday night. I walked everywhere hoping you might—I mean, I didn't know where to find you."

She's giving me that look, like when I put my sweatshirt on the ground.

"So," I say. "Pretty stupid, huh?"

She smiles. "It was a bit stupid," she says. "But it was also… *gallant*."

"I don't know what that means," I say.

She laughs. "OK, maybe just stupid." She hooks her arm around mine and pulls me over to the dying trees and the rusting fence.

I give her my juice to drink and she gives me an apple. Neither of us mentions Steam Girl.

But the next day she starts talking as soon as we meet up.

"I need to tell you what happened next," she says. "When Steam Girl got back to Mars. It's not easy to talk about, but it's important that you know. That you understand."

I look up, surprised. This isn't like her usual stories. Her face looks so serious that I'm almost afraid.

"OK," I say, sitting down. She stays standing, staring at the ground like the first time I saw her.

"Back on Mars," she begins. And then she stops to clear her throat.

Back on Mars, the palace was in turmoil. Soon after *The Martian Rose* had left, the Royal Oracle had apparently consulted the omens and revealed that their mission was doomed. The whole party would perish on Venus, she'd announced, to widespread dismay. Most of the courtiers wanted to wait and see if they would return, but Prince Zennobal moved quickly, declaring his father deceased and arranging his own coronation after a brief period of mourning.

So when *The Martian Rose* reappeared, many in the palace rejoiced, but Zennobal was furious. He claimed it was a Venusian trick and ordered all on board arrested and thrown into the dungeons. Most of the guards refused, but Zennobal merely smiled and pulled a strange device from his robes.

"Very well," he said. "If you cannot be trusted, you shall be replaced." And he flicked a switch on the small black box.

From somewhere in the palace, an army of sleek gray robots poured into the corridors and halls, firing their short black guns into the air. The palace guards dropped their spears and fell to the floor, terrified. Within minutes, all resistance had ended and Zennobal's robots were in complete control.

"So it was Zennobal?" I say. "Knew it all along."

"Wait and see," she says, frowning.

As soon as they emerged from *The Martian Rose*, Steam Girl and her friends were surrounded by robots. The King and his daughter were led away under guard, while Steam Girl and her father were locked in a dungeon deep beneath the palace. For several days, that's where they remained. Robotic guards came and went, stale food and water were pushed under the door. And then, late one night, Steam Girl woke to the sound of rattling keys and the glare of a lantern. A hooded figure stood at the door, silently motioning for them to follow. The mysterious figure led them through winding tunnels and narrow stairways, until finally they entered a small cluttered room filled with books and scrolls and alchemical beakers and tubes.

"The Royal Oracle," said Steam Girl as their rescuer stepped into the light.

The Oracle put down the lantern and threw back her hood, revealing long blonde hair and strangely familiar features.

To Steam Girl's great astonishment, her father gave an almighty shout and rushed forward to embrace the stranger. The Oracle responded with a long passionate kiss, until Steam Girl regained her wits and cried, "What on Earth is going on?!"

Her father turned and smiled, his eyes filled with tears. "My dear girl, this angel in red is none other than Dr Serafina Starfire—*your mother!*"

"Wait—what?" I say. "Steam Girl's mother? But… didn't she die or something? What the hell is she doing on Mars?"

"Please don't interrupt," she says slowly and quietly. "This isn't easy…"

"Sorry," I say. And I mean it. She looks like she's going to cry.

The Royal Oracle—Steam Girl's mother—took a long look at her long-lost daughter and smiled. "I'm so very proud," she said. "How beautiful you've grown—courageous and clever too!"

"She really is just like you," Father said. "You should see the gadgets she comes up with…"

And so the three of them sat down and talked. Her mother explained how she'd been sucked through a freak trans-dimensional wormhole to Mars fifteen years before, while trying to perfect *The Martian Rose*'s experimental engines. At first the Martians didn't know what to make of this strange lost creature. But her knowledge of science and astronomy soon gave her a reputation for magical powers of prophecy and divination, and so the King named her the Royal Oracle—and there she was.

Steam Girl's father quickly outlined their own adventures since his wife's disappearance, and then talk turned to their present predicament. "The prince and his robots will be looking for you by now," Steam Girl's mother said. "If you stay here, you'll soon be found."

"Then we must take the fight to them!" her father said with a wild look in his eyes. "Rescue the King and his daughter, rouse the palace guard to rebellion and overthrow that treasonous whelp and his tinpot army of rattling contraptions once and for all!"

Steam Girl noticed a flicker of something dark in her mother's face at the mention of Princess Lusanna. But it quickly passed. "Oh, my brave sweet husband. I have no doubt you will do all that and more. But first we must prepare. We are three against many, and they are very well armed. Luckily I have a secret weapon of my own…" And she stood and walked to a lushly embroidered tapestry covering one wall. She pulled the heavy cloth aside to reveal a simple wooden door.

"I have not been idle all these years since leaving Earth," she said. "I continued my research on trans-dimensional space, in the hope that I could create a new wormhole and find my way back to Earth." And then she opened the door. A weird yellow glow began to seep into the room.

"Follow me," she said, and led them through the doorway. As they stepped over the threshold, Steam Girl felt a curious chill and thought she might pass out. Then her head cleared and she saw they were in a square windowless room, filled with that same strange yellow glow. Six more doors, identical to the one they'd just come through, were spaced around the blank stone walls. A wooden staircase led to the floor above.

"Where are we?" Steam Girl asked. A sweet fragrance in the air reminded her of something.

"This is my *real* laboratory," her mother said with a hint of pride, "hidden hundreds of miles away on the far side of Mars. Each of these doors is a like a small tear in the fabric of space-time itself. By stepping through, we are instantly transported to the other side of the wormhole, no matter how near or far that may be."

"Stars above!" Steam Girl's father laughed. "You have come a long way with your research, my darling! And where do they all lead?"

His wife walked to one of the doors and laid a hand against its smooth dark wood. "This one," she said , smiling, "opens onto Earth."

"To Earth!" Steam Girl's father cried. "Home! Then let's go there at once! We can warn the world of Prince Zennobal's imminent invasion— and then gather supplies and equipment before returning through your ingenious doorways to free Minnimattock and Lusanna and defeat the usurper's army forthwith!" And with that he strode resolutely to where his wife stood and threw the door open. "To Earth!" he called once more, and then he stepped through the doorway, disappearing with a flash of yellow light.

Steam Girl's mother turned to her and smiled. "Come along, then," she said, motioning toward the door. But Steam Girl hesitated. Something was wrong.

"I think I know where we are," she said, "and it's not on Mars."

Her mother frowned. "I don't know what you mean," she said.

Steam Girl ignored her. "I remember that smell in the air," she said. "Giant blossoms and pools of nectar…. We're on Venus, where Father and I first encountered the robot army." Her mother's mouth became a thin sharp line. "Everything makes sense," Steam Girl went on. "You're the one behind it all. Using those wormholes of yours to hop from Earth to Mars to Venus and who knows where else—gathering technology, weapons and tools and making your evil plans…"

"That's enough," her mother said.

"And that's not all," Steam Girl said. "You gave Zennobal the idea of a trip to Venus, didn't you? You hoped we'd stumble across your robot army and that would be the end of us."

"That's not true," her mother hissed. "It was Zennobal's idea to send you here. I never wanted you dead…."

"But you used our absence from Mars to put your plans in motion—announcing our demise so your puppet could seize the throne." Steam Girl was angry now, angrier than she'd ever been before. "But there's one more thing I want to know. Where have you sent my father?"

Her mother made a kind of growling noise. "You think you're so smart, little girl? But you don't know anything! Everything I've ever done—every brilliant discovery, every unprecedented innovation—that arrogant, vain, *mediocre* fool claimed credit for them all. Who do you think designed *The Martian Rose*? Who built the Spirodynamic Multi-Dimensional Concentrated Steam Engine? Certainly not your father, that's for sure. It was *me*, damn it. *All of it was me!*"

Steam Girl was taken aback. "But that's not true," she said. "Father's always said you were a brilliant scientist. He never claimed he did those things alone…. And besides, even if he had, that's no reason to build a huge army and invade Earth!"

"Don't be silly," her mother said. "Ours is a world crippled by ignorance and superstition, its technological and social development held back by a deluded nostalgia for outdated aesthetic and ethical philosophies. Always looking backward, never forward into the future. Through my trans-dimensional doors, young girl, I have seen other worlds—other Earths and other realities. Compared to those, *our* Earth is a quaint little backwater. It's time we woke up and behaved like proper adults…."

"You're even crazier than I thought," Steam Girl said. "Now, answer my question: Where is my father?"

"He's on Earth," Steam Girl's mother said, waving at the glowing door-way. "Just as I said."

But Steam Girl knew it was a trap. "You're lying," she said, clenching her fists. "Wherever you've sent him, you'd better bring him back. Now."

Her mother sighed and clapped her hands. From the floor above there came sounds of movement: the heavy clank of robotic feet. "I had hoped it wouldn't come to this," Steam Girl's mother said. "I really don't want to hurt you; after all, you are so clearly my daughter." Steam Girl tried to think quickly, but her mind was still reeling from everything that had happened. She looked around, desperately trying to remember which of the identical wooden doors led back to Mars. Perhaps if she made it back to the palace, she could free the King and persuade the guards to help. But before she could do anything, her mother moved with surprising speed and power, grabbing her shoulders and pushing her firmly through the glowing open doorway. Steam Girl stumbled, arms flailing, reaching for something—anything—to keep her from falling...

And then she hit a wall of ice cold light, and her mind went blank.

In the silence that follows, I realise I'm shivering. After a while, I can't bear it any more.

"So Steam Girl followed her father through the wormhole," I say. "And ended up... where?"

She says nothing, just lowers her eyes.

"Are you OK?" I ask. She doesn't look it.

She looks away. "Do you like this place?" she says.

"Uh... you mean the school?"

"The school, the town, the whole bloody world.... All of it."

I shrug. "Well, it's OK, I guess," I say, and then I shake my head. "Actually, it kind of sucks. At least what I've seen of it. I'm sure there are plenty of great places out there, but..."

There's another long silence.

"Anyway," she says, making it sound like a closing door.

Mrs Hendricks is talking about our short story assignment. She writes a quotation up on the board, from some writer I've never heard of. She makes us copy it down in our books:

"Some writers write to escape reality. Others write to understand it. But the best writers write in order to take possession of reality, and so transform it."

I copy it down and think about what it means. I get the first part about escaping reality—that makes perfect sense. And I suppose it makes sense to try to understand the world, too. But the last part makes me uneasy. Taking possession of reality sounds like something Steam Girl's mother would say. I don't know. Maybe I'm just not smart enough to get it.

But then Mrs Hendricks tells us to spend the rest of the period working on our stories, and for the first time in days I start writing again. I write a whole new chapter in the next half hour, where Rocket Boy leaves the Princess with the heaving breasts and flies off to explore one of Saturn's moons. He finds an abandoned art gallery beside a frozen lake, with paintings hung on every wall. There's one picture he can't stop looking at: a strange portrait of an oddly dressed girl—a little chubby and kind of weird, but somehow very beautiful. Faded blue dress, scruffy leather jacket, long lace-up boots, and black-rimmed glasses. And, of course, flying helmet and goggles.

She shone like a bright strange star shining in those empty lifeless halls, I write. Cheesy, I know, but that's how I feel.

Anyway, in my story, the moment Rocket Boy reaches out and touches the painting of Steam Girl, she comes to life and appears beside him, freed from the magical picture. She thanks Rocket Boy with a kiss (I manage to avoid the whole "heaving breasts" thing this time), and she explains how she was tricked into posing for a portrait by an evil artist-magician, who trapped her in the frame and kidnapped her father. Then they climb on board *The Silver Arrow* and fly off to rescue Professor Swift—but that will have to wait for chapter three.

When the bell rings, I put away my story and walk to Steam Girl's desk, where she's curled over her notebook, working furiously.

"The next installment?" I say. But she barely glances up. She closes the book and goes to put it in her bag.

"Oops." As he goes past, Michael Carmichael gives me a shove from behind so I fall against her, and we both tumble to the floor.

Laughter ripples through the room, and I feel my face turn red. But she just calmly climbs to her feet and turns to face Michael.

"You know the problem with you, Michael Carmichael?" she says. "You're reality incarnate."

The whole class goes quiet. Michael makes a face. "What does that even *mean*?"

"If you *imagine* a dog," she goes on, "it's always loyal and fluffy and cute. But in real life dogs bite your hand and pee on the carpet and have sex with the sofa."

That gets more laughs. But she keeps going. "That's what you are, Michael Carmichael. You're dog pee on the carpet."

In the silence that follows, Michael's mouth moves but no sound comes out.

While Mrs Hendricks chews them both out I pick up the notebook where it's fallen on the floor. It's open on the last page, which is filled with a single detailed drawing.

"What's this?" I say, once we're out in the hallway.

She glances at the page I'm holding up.

"It's Steam Girl's last gadget," she says, not meeting my eyes.

"It's a gun," I say slowly. My throat feels dry.

She looks at the floor but says nothing.

"I thought Steam Girl hated guns. I thought she never used them. It *is* a gun, isn't it?" I ask.

"It's the Reality Gun," she says quietly.

"What the hell is a Reality Gun?" I say.

"It kills reality."

And then she takes the notebook from my hand and puts it in her bag.

After school, she's waiting at the gate, just like that first time. She looks very alone as the crowd flows by. Kids point and laugh.

We walk together to the first intersection. She seems tired.

"I have one more thing to tell you," she says.

"OK," I say.

"You know how I told you Steam Girl and her father went through the door?" she says.

I nod.

"Well, it took them to Earth," she says, "just like her mother told them it would. But it wasn't *their* Earth—it was a different world, a different universe. The *wrong* universe. This world was… grayer. Sadder. And the rules were different. Her gadgets didn't work the same. Technology wasn't magic any more. Even people were different there. Less courageous, less beautiful and clever. And so *they* changed, too…"

She sounds so sad, I look to see if she's crying. Her face is pale, like chalk.

"Couldn't they go back?" I say. "Back through the door?"

"No," she says. "Because after they went through, the door disappeared. It was a trap, you see—the whole thing had been a trap. Steam Girl's mother had planned it all along—to trick them into going through the wormhole to this totally different universe, where they could no longer mess up her plans. She wanted them out of her life completely."

"So… what happened next?"

"That's it," she says. "That's all there is."

"You mean that's the end of the story?" I can't believe it.

She says nothing. We wait at the lights till the red man turns green.

"Bye," she says, and she crosses the road.

She's not in English on Friday.

Michael's not there either. But Amanda is, and she smiles at me. A warm, genuine smile.

When I hand in my story, Mrs Hendricks seems impressed. "Looks like you were quite inspired," she says.

"I *was* inspired," I say. "By Steam Girl."

Mrs Hendricks looks confused; of course she won't know about Steam Girl. "I mean—the new girl. Wears a flying helmet and goggles?"

"Oh!" she says, surprised. "You mean Shanaia Swift? I didn't know you were friends."

"Um—kind of," I say. "She's a little weird, but the thing is she tells the most amazing stories—all about this really smart inventor called Steam Girl, who travels the universe in an airship, having adventures with her father and…." I realise I'm blushing and stop talking.

Mrs Hendricks frowns, flicking through my story. "I had no idea," she says. "She's always so quiet in class. And she hasn't handed in a single piece of work. Listen, Redmond, if you talk to her over the weekend, could you ask her to come see me first thing on Monday? I'd really like to give her a chance to hand something in for this assignment, even if it's late. Sounds like it would be worth the wait…."

"I will," I say.

At lunchtime I go to the incinerator, just in case.

After five minutes, I'm getting ready to go when Michael Carmichael appears.

"Where is she?" he says.

"Who?" I say.

"Your freakish girlfriend," he says. "Obviously."

I pick up my bag and try to walk to the safety of the library. But Michael puts a hand on my chest to stop me.

"I want you to give her a message," he says. "From me to her."

"Let me go," I say, as clearly as I can. My voice is shaking.

"Tell her this is from me," he says, his hand still on my shirt. "For yesterday."

And then he hits me in the face.

I stay on my hands and knees till he's gone, watching blood drip from my face onto the dusty asphalt. Then I sit on the ground by the concrete wall with a wad of tissues pressed against the cut in my mouth. I can feel it swelling up. I should go to the nurse and get some ice. But I don't.

When the bell rings, I get up and head for class. The bleeding has stopped, but my whole face is throbbing with pain. As I enter the Science Block, someone steps out of the shadows and grabs my arm.

It's her. *Shanaia*. "I've got something to show you," she says, guiding me out into the thin sunlight. She seems nervous, distracted. "I finished it. It's ready."

"Why weren't you in English?" I say. My voice is muffled. It hurts to talk. "Mrs Hendricks wants to see you…"

"Never mind that," she says, reaching for her bag. "I brought the—"

And then she sees my face and stops. "Oh!" she says. "What happened?"

"What do you *think* happened?" I'm annoyed all of a sudden. I don't want to be, but I am. "It's a message for you. From Michael Carmichael. For yesterday."

She lifts a hand to her mouth. "I'm so sorry…"

"That's OK," I say, sounding more sarcastic than I mean to. "Everyone thinks you're my girlfriend anyway. It's not the first time I've been pushed around because I hang out with you."

She takes a step back, both hands held up as if I might hit her. Her neck is turning red, but this time it doesn't make me feel good.

"I'm sorry," I mutter, shaking my head. "I just…"

But she's already gone, half walking, half running across the asphalt, and I'm too tired and sore to go after her. Maybe I don't want to. I don't know what I want anymore. I just stand there, heavy and alone, until the next bell tells me I'm late for class. My head hurts. I take a deep breath and go back to school.

The world feels cheap this afternoon. The sky is pale and empty; colors are faded. Everything's dirty and ugly and falling apart. I sit in Science class with my head on my desk. The teacher is talking about vacuums, which pretty much sums up how I feel. After a while I close my eyes and let my mind drift. I imagine I'm lying on a warm sand dune, beside a girl. Stroking her soft white neck.

Not her, this time. Just a girl. An imaginary girl.

By home time, I'm sleepy and numb. I head for the main gate, staring at the ground in front of my feet. But there's something going on—a crowd in the way. Then I hear her voice and I start pushing my way to the front so I can see.

Her face is red, with tears in her eyes. Michael Carmichael looks angrier than ever before. At first I think he's wearing some kind of makeup, but then I realise he's bleeding from his lip, and his t-shirt is torn at the neck. He steps forward and pushes her shoulder, sending her back against the circle of onlookers, who spread out like a school of fish.

"You stupid fat freak," Michael says in a shaky voice. "Stupid fat little bitch!"

He backhands her across the face, so hard she spins around, glasses flying, ending up on one knee a few feet from me. The crowd almost moans.

Michael is still advancing on her. Without thinking, I step forward and raise my hand.

"Leave her alone," I say. It comes out as a kind of squeak.

Next thing I know I'm on the ground and Michael's looming over me, shouting something I can't hear.

Behind him, I can see Shanaia pulling something out of her bag, something awkward and heavy, metallic and long. Then she stands up, pointing it straight at him, holding tightly with both hands.

It's a gun. Covered in her usual gears and rusting dials and stuff, but still unmistakably a gun. The Reality Gun. I can't tell if it's a toy gun underneath or the real thing—and from the look on his face, neither can Michael. He freezes and then starts slowly backing away.

"Jesus Christ! What the hell is *that?*" He tries to laugh, but the sound he makes is broken and small.

No one speaks or moves for what seems like a really long time. Then she reaches up with one hand and pulls her goggles down over her eyes. There's shouting back near the administration block; teachers are coming.

And then she pulls the trigger. There's a bang and a flash and smoke and sparks. No, not smoke: steam. The air is full of steam, like a thick billowing cloud of warm wet fog. Kids scream and people start running and someone knocks me flat. When I manage to get up again, the steam is slowly clearing and the crowd has scattered. Shanaia is gone. Her flying helmet and goggles lie abandoned on the ground. The Reality Gun is there, too, still steaming, broken and split. Michael stands in the centre of it all, hands at his side, mouth open, eyes wide.

"Are... are you OK?" I say, moving closer.

Michael turns and looks at me like he doesn't know who I am.

"Shit," he breathes out slowly, and then he shakes himself and looks down at his hands. "*Shit.*"

He's fine. I grab Steam Girl's helmet and goggles and shove them in my bag; then I run through the school gates and down the road before anyone can stop me.

I run most of the way home. When I open the door my hands are shaking so much I almost drop the keys.

Inside, it's dark and quiet. I throw my bag into my room and hit the light switch, but nothing happens. I find Mom in the garden, reading a book.

"There's been a power cut," she says. "No computer or TV, I'm afraid..."

"When—I mean, how long has it been out?"

"About fifteen minutes, I guess." She closes her book and covers a yawn. "Do you want me to get you a sandwich?"

I shake my head and run back out to the street. No lights are on anywhere. The air is eerily quiet: no cars driving past or planes flying overhead. No one's mowing the lawn or listening to music. Nothing. I start to run again, along the empty road, listening to the buzzing in my head.

I remember Amanda said something about Shanaia living in a trailer park. For all I know, it's just a rumor, but it's all I've got. I think there's something like that down by the estuary, so that's where I go. The sign outside says, "Sunny Stream Trailer Park," but it's actually a wide dusty field with rows of shabby trailers and huts, rusting cars and sagging wires. At the entrance, I'm almost run over by a noisy old Ford. The driver gives me the finger as he drives away.

I walk down the central path, between trailers and caravans, all flaking paint and rusted metal. A little boy in green shorts stares at me, and an old man standing in his doorway raises his hand hello. Then, painted on the side of a faded pink trailer, I see "The Martian Rose."

It's tiny, not much bigger than an SUV. One wheel's been taken off, leaving it propped up on a pile of bricks and pieces of wood. All kinds of junk lie in the dirt outside: broken appliances, bits of wrecked cars, scraps of tin, broken toys, rotting planks. A basic work bench leans against one wall, scattered with springs and broken cogs and half-assembled gadgets.

As I stand there, wondering what to do, the door opens and out steps a skinny, unshaven man in dirty jeans and t-shirt. He looks at me with watery eyes.

"Uh—hello," I say.

He says nothing. His hair is long and tangled and streaked with gray. He rubs his chin with a shaky hand.

"Is—um—is your daughter here?" I ask.

He turns back to the trailer and calls out, *"Shanaia!"*

There's no response, and after a moment he sits on an overturned beer crate and seems to forget I'm there. I walk up to the caravan and open the door.

Inside, it's small and dark and smells like a garage.

"Shanaia?" I say. A thin strip of light spreads out from the open door. And there she is, sitting in the corner, hugging her knees. Her glasses are cracked and she's taken off the leather jacket. Without the flying helmet, her hair hangs down across her shoulders. It's the color of polished brass.

I sit next to her. "Are you OK?"

She looks away.

"It didn't work," she says in a tiny voice.

"You know the power's down?" I say. "Nothing's working, all over town. Nothing electric. Nothing *modern*." Then I hesitate. "No, wait. There—there was a car coming out of the driveway. So actually, *some* things are working..." I trail off, suddenly unsure of myself.

She's watching me intently.

"I—I thought maybe the Reality Gun..." I begin to feel pretty stupid.

And then she reaches over and curls her hand around mine.

"Well, it scared the hell out of Michael Carmichael," I say. "So that's something..."

"I didn't mean to do that," she says. "I just... He was..."

We sit there a while, holding hands. She leans her head on my shoulder.

"Shanaia—" I say.

She rolls her eyes. "Don't," she says. "I hate that name."

"You know, you're in pretty big trouble," I say. "They'll have called the police."

She takes a slow ragged breath. "What am I going to do?"

I think for a moment and then I say: "What would Steam Girl do?"

"I'm not Steam Girl," she says.

The air in the trailer is thick and warm. I feel light-headed, like I imagine being drunk must feel. I reach into my bag and pull out her flying helmet and goggles.

"Yes, you are," I say. "You're clever and courageous and beautiful. If anyone can sort this mess out, it's you."

She looks at me for a long, long time. Then leans forward and kisses me, lightly, on the lips. Lifts the helmet and slowly puts it on.

There's a moment of perfect stillness.

And then she stands up and smiles.

"Come on, then, Rocket Boy," she says, and holds out her hand.

AFTER THE APOCALYPSE

MAUREEN F. McHUGH

Maureen F. McHugh has lived in New York; Shijiazhuang, China; Ohio; Austin, Texas; and now lives in Los Angeles, California. She is the author of two collections, After the Apocalypse *and the Story Prize finalist collection,* Mothers & Other Monsters, *and four novels, including Tiptree Award-winner* China Mountain Zhang *and* New York Times *editor's choice* Nekropolis. *McHugh has also worked on alternate reality games for Halo 2, The Watchmen, and Nine Inch Nails, among others.*

J ane puts out the sleeping bags in the backyard of the empty house by the tool shed. She has a lock and hasp and an old hand drill that they can use to lock the tool shed from the inside but it's too hot to sleep in there and there haven't been many people on the road. Better to sleep outside. Franny has been talking a mile a minute. Usually by the end of the day she is tired from walking—they both are—and quiet. But this afternoon she's gotten on the subject of her friend Samantha. She musing if Samantha has left town like they did. She thought that Samantha and her family were probably still there because they had a really nice house in a low crime area and Samantha's father had a really good job and like, when you had money like that maybe you can afford like guards or something. There house has five bedrooms and the basement isn't a basement, it's a living room because the house is kind of on a little hill and although the front of the basement is underground, you can walk right out the back. She is talking about how you could see a horse farm behind them.

Jane puts her hand on her hips and looks down the line of backyards.

"Do you think there's anything in there?" Franny asks, meaning the house, a '60s suburban ranch. Franny is thirteen and empty houses frighten her. But she doesn't like to be left alone either. What she wants is for Jane to say that they can eat one of the tuna pouches.

"Come on, Franny. We're gonna run out of tuna long before we get to Canada."

"I know," Franny says sullenly.

"You can stay here."

"No, I'll go with you."

God, sometimes Jane would do anything to get five minutes away from Franny. She loves her daughter, really, but Jesus. "Come on, then," Jane says.

There is an old square concrete patio and a sliding glass door. The door is dirty. Jane cups her hand to shade her eyes and looks inside. It's dark and hard to see. No power, of course. Hasn't been power in any of the places they've passed through in more than two months. Air condition-ing. And a bed with a mattress and box springs. What Jane wouldn't give for air conditioning and a bed. Clean sheets.

The neighborhood seems like a good one. Unless they find a big group to camp with, Jane gets them off the freeway at the end of the day. There was fighting in the neighborhood and at the end of the street, several houses are burned out. Then there are lots of houses with windows smashed out. But the fighting petered out. Some of the houses are still lived in. This house had all its windows intact but the garage door was standing open and the garage was empty except for dead leaves. Electronic garage door. The owners pulled out and left and did bother to close the door behind them. Seemed to Jane that the overgrown backyard with its tool shed would be a good place to sleep.

Jane can see her silhouette in the dirty glass and her hair is a snarled, curly, tangled rat's nest. She runs her fingers through it and they snag. She'll look for a scarf or something inside. She grabs the handle and yanks up, hard, trying to get the old slider off track. It takes a couple of tries but she's had a lot of practice in the last few months.

Inside the house is trashed. The kitchen has been turned upside-down, and silverware, utensils, drawers, broken plates, flour and stuff are ev-erywhere. She picks her way across, a can opener skittering under her foot in a clatter.

Franny gives a little startled shriek.

"Fuck!" Jane says. "Don't do that!" The canned food is long gone.

"I'm sorry," Franny says. "It scared me!"

"We're gonna starve to death if we don't keep scavenging," Jane says.

"I know!" Franny says.

"Do you know how fucking far it is to Canada?"

"I can't help it if it startled me!"

Maybe if she were a better cook she'd be able to scrape up the flour and make something, but it's all mixed in with dirt and stuff and every time she's tried to cook something over an open fire it's either been raw or black, or most often, both—blackened on the outside and raw on the inside.

Jane checks all the cupboards anyway. Sometimes people keep food in different places. Once they found one of those decorating icing tubes and wrote words on each other's hands and licked them off.

Franny screams, not a startled shriek but a real scream.

Jane whirls around and there's a guy in the family room with a tire iron.

"What are you doing here?" he yells.

Jane grabs a can opener from the floor, one of those heavy jobbers, and wings it straight at his head. He's too slow to get out of the way and it nails him in the forehead. Jane has winged a lot of things at boyfriends over the years. It's a skill. She throws a couple more things from the floor, anything she can find, while the guy is yelling, "Fuck! Fuck!" And trying to ward off the barrage.

Then she and Franny are out the back door and running.

Fucking squatter! She hates squatters! If it's the homeowner, they tend to make the place more like a fortress and you can tell not to try to go in. Squatters try to keep a low profile. Franny is in front of her, running like a rabbit, and they are out the gate and headed up the suburban street. Franny knows the drill and at the next corner she turns, but by then it's clear that no one's following them.

"OK," Jane pants. "OK, stop, stop."

Franny stops. She's a skinny adolescent now—she used to be chubby but she's lean and tan with all their walking. She's wearing a pair of falling-apart pink sneakers and a tank top with oil smudges from when they had to climb over a truck tipped sideways on an overpass. She's still flat chested. Her eyes are big in her face. Jane puts her hands on her knees and draws a shuddering breath.

"We're OK," she says. It is gathering dusk in this Missouri town. In a while, streetlights will come on, unless someone has systematically shot them out. Solar power still works. "We'll wait a bit and then go back and get our stuff when it's dark."

"No!" Franny bursts into sobs. "We can't!"

Jane is at her wit's end. Rattled from the squatter. Tired of being the strong one. "We've got to! You want to lose everything we've got? You want to die? Goddamn it, Franny! I can't take this anymore!"

"That guy's there!" Franny sobs out. "We can't go back! We can't!"

"Your cell phone is there," Jane says. A mean dig. The cell phone doesn't work, of course. Even if they still somehow had service, if service actually exists, they haven't been anywhere with electricity to charge it in weeks. But Franny still carries it in the hope that she can get a charge and call her friends. Seventh graders are apparently surgically attached to their phones. Not that she acts even like a seventh grader anymore. The longer they are on the road, the younger Franny acts.

This isn't the first time that they've run into a squatter. Squatters are cowards. The guy doesn't have a gun and he's not going to go out after dark. Franny has no spine, takes after her asshole of a father. Jane ran away from home and got all the way to Pasadena, California, when she was a year older than Franny. When she was fourteen, she was a decade older than Franny. Lived on the street for six weeks, begging spare change on the same route that the Rose Parade took. It had been scary but it had been a blast, as well. Taught her to stand on her own two feet, which Franny wasn't going to be able to do when she was twenty. Thirty, at this rate.

"You're hungry, aren't you?" Jane said, merciless. "You want to go looking in these houses for something to eat?" Jane points around them. The houses all have their front doors broken into, open like little mouths.

Franny shakes her head.

"Stop crying. I'm going to go check some of them out. You wait here."

"Mom! Don't leave me!" Franny wails.

Jane is still shaken from the squatter. But they need food. And they need their stuff. There is $700 sewn inside the lining of Jane's sleeping bag. And someone has to keep them alive. It's obviously going to be her.

Things didn't exactly all go at once. First there were rolling brown outs and lots of people unemployed. Jane had been making a living working at a place that sold furniture. She started as a salesperson but she was good at helping people on what colors to buy, what things went together, what fabrics to pick for custom pieces. Eventually they made her a service associate; a person who was kind of like an interior decorator, sort of. She had an eye. She'd grown up in a nice suburb and had seen nice things. She knew what people wanted. Her boss kept telling her a little less eye make-up would be a good idea, but people liked what she suggested and recommended her to their friends even if her boss didn't like her eye make-up.

She was thinking of starting a decorating business, although she was worried that she didn't know about some of the stuff decorators did. On TV they were always tearing down walls and redoing fireplaces. So she put it off. Then there was the big Disney World attack where a kazillion people died because of a dirty bomb, and then the economy really tanked. She knew that business was dead and she was going to get laid off but before that happened, someone torched the furniture place where she was working. Her boyfriend at the time was a cop so he still had a job, even though half the city was unemployed. She and Franny were all right compared to a lot of people. She didn't like not having her own money but she wasn't exactly having to call her mother in Pennsylvania and eat crow and offer to come home.

So she sat on the balcony of their condo and smoked and looked through her old decorating magazines and Franny watched television in the room behind her. People started showing up on the sidewalks. They had trash bags full of stuff. Sometimes they were alone, sometimes there would be whole families. Sometimes they'd have cars and they'd sleep in them, but gas was getting to almost $10 a gallon, when the gas stations could get it. Pete, the boyfriend, told her that the cops didn't even patrol much anymore because of the gas problem. More and more of the people on the sidewalk looked to be walking.

"Where are they coming from?" Franny asked.

"Down south. Houston, El Paso, anywhere within a hundred miles of the border." Pete said. "Border's gone to shit. Mexico doesn't have food, but the drug cartels have lots of guns and they're coming across to take what they can get. They say it's like a war zone down there."

"Why don't the police take care of them?" Franny asked.

"Well, Francisca," Pete said—he was good with Franny, Jane had to give him that—"sometimes there are just too many of them for the police down there. And they've got kinds of guns that the police aren't allowed to have."

"What about you?" Franny asked.

"It's different up here," Pete said. "That's why we've got refugees here. Because it's safe here."

"They're not *refugees*," Jane said. Refugees were, like, people in Africa. These were just regular people. Guys in t-shirts with the names of rock bands on them. Women sitting in the front seat of a Taurus station wagon, doing their hair in the rearview mirror. Kids asleep in the back seat or running up and down the street shrieking and playing. Just people.

"Well what do you want to call them?" Pete asked.

Then the power started going out, more and more often. Pete's shifts got longer although he didn't always get paid.

There were gunshots in the street and Pete told Jane not to sit out on the balcony. He boarded up the French doors and it was as if they were living in a cave. The refugees started thinning out. Jane rarely saw them leaving, but each day there were fewer and fewer of them on the sidewalk. Pete said they were headed north.

Then the fires started on the east side of town. The power went out and stayed out. Pete didn't come home until the next day, and he slept a couple of hours and then went back out to work. The air tasted of smoke—not the pleasant clean smell of wood smoke, but a garbagy smoke. Franny complained that it made her sick to her stomach.

After Pete didn't come home for four days, it was pretty clear to Jane that he wasn't coming back. Jane put Franny in the car, packed everything she could think of that might be useful. They got about 120 miles away, far enough that the burning city was no longer visible, although the sunset was a vivid and blistering red. Then they ran out of gas and there was no more to be had.

There were rumors that there was a UN camp for homeless outside of Toronto. So they were walking to Detroit.

Franny says, "You can't leave me! You can't leave me!"

"Do you want to go scavenge with me?" Jane says.

Franny sobs so hard she seems to be hyperventilating. She grabs her mother's arms, unable to do anything but hold on to her. Jane peels her off, but Franny keeps grabbing, clutching, sobbing. It's making Jane crazy. Franny's fear is contagious and if she lets it get in her she'll be too afraid to do anything. She can feel it deep inside her, that thing that has always threatened her, to give in, to stop doing and pushing and scheming, to become like her useless, useless father puttering around the house vacantly, bottles hidden in the garage, the basement, everywhere.

"GET OFF ME!" she screams at Franny, but Franny is sobbing and clutching.

She slaps Franny. Franny throws up, precious little, water and crackers from breakfast. Then she sits down in the grass, just useless.

Jane marches off into the first house.

She's lucky. The garage is closed up and there are three cans of soup on a shelf. One of them is cream of mushroom, but luckily, Franny liked cream of mushroom when she found it before. There are also cans of tomato paste, which she ignores, and some dried pasta, but mice have gotten into it.

When she gets outside some strange guy is standing on the sidewalk, talking to Franny, who's still sitting on the grass.

For a moment she doesn't know what to do, clutching the cans of soup against her chest. Some part of her wants to back into the house, go through the dark living room with its mauve carpeting, it's shabby blue sofa, photos of school kids and a cross-stitch flower bouquet framed on the wall, back through the little dining room with its border of country geese, unchanged since the '80s. Out the back door and over the fence, an easy moment to abandon the biggest mistake of her life. She'd aborted the first pregnancy, brought home from Pasadena in shame. She'd dug her heels in on the second, it's-my-body-fuck-you.

Franny laughs. A little nervous and hiccoughy from crying, but not really afraid.

"Hey," Jane yelled. "Get away from my daughter!"

She strides across the yard, all motherhood and righteous fury. A skinny dark-haired guy holds up his hands, palms out, no harm, ma'am.

"It's OK, mom," Franny says.

The guy is smiling. "We're just talking," he says. He's wearing a red plaid flannel shirt and t-shirt and shorts. He's scraggly, but who isn't.

"Who the hell are you," she says.

"My name's Nate. I'm just heading north. Was looking for a place to camp."

"He was just hanging with me until you got back," Franny says.

Nate takes them to his camp—also behind a house. He gets a little fire going, enough to heat the soup. He talks about Alabama, which was where he's coming from, although he doesn't have a Southern accent. He makes some excuse about being an army brat. Jane tries to size him up. He tells some story about when two guys stumbled on his camp north of Huntsville, when he was first on the road. About how it scared the shit out of him but about how he'd bluffed them about a buddy of his who was hunting for their dinner but would have heard the racket they made and could be drawing a bead on them right now from the trees, and about how something moved in the trees, some animal, rustling in the leaf litter and they got spooked. He was looking at her, trying to impress her, but being polite, which was good with Franny listening. Franny was taken with him, hanging on his every word, flirting a little the way she did. In a year or two, Franny was going to be guy crazy, Jane knew.

"They didn't know anything about the woods, just two guys up from Biloxi or something, kind of guys who, you know, manage a copy store or a fast food joint or something thinking that now that civilization is falling apart they can be like the hero in one of their video games." He laughs. "I didn't know what was in the woods, neither. I admit I was kind of scared it was someone who was going to shoot all of us although it was probably just a sparrow or a squirrel or something. I'm saying stuff over my shoulder to my 'buddy' like, Don't shoot them or nothing. Just let them go back the way they came."

She's sure he's bullshitting. But she likes that he makes it funny instead of pretending he's some sort of Rambo. He doesn't offer any of his own food, she notices. But he does offer to go with them to get their stuff. Fair trade, she thinks.

He's not bad looking in a kind of skinny way. She likes them skinny. She's tired of doing it all herself.

The streetlights come on, at least some of them. Nate goes with them when they go back to get their sleeping bags and stuff. He's got a board with a bunch of nails sticking out of one end. He calls it his mace.

They are quiet but they don't try to hide. It's hard to find the stuff in the dark, but luckily, Jane hadn't really unpacked. She and Franny, who is breathing hard, get their sleeping bags and packs. It's hard to see. The backyard is a dark tangle of shadows. She assumes it's as hard to see them from inside the house—maybe harder.

Nothing happens. She hears nothing from the house, sees nothing, although it seems as if they are all unreasonably loud gathering things up. They leave through the side gate, coming nervously to the front of the house, Nate carrying his mace and ready to strike, she and Franny with their arms full of sleeping bags. They go down the cracked driveway and out into the middle of the street, a few gutted cars still parked on either side. Then they are around the corner and it feels safe. They are all grinning and happy and soon putting the sleeping bags in Nate's little backyard camp made domestic, no civilized, by the charred ash of the little fire.

In the morning, she leaves Nate's bedroll and gets back to sleep next to Franny before Franny wakes up.

They are walking on the freeway the next day, the three of them. They are together now although they haven't discussed it, and Jane is relieved. People are just that much less likely to mess with a man. Overhead, three jets pass going south, visible only by their contrails. At least there are jets. American jets, she hopes.

They stop for a moment while Nate goes around a bridge abutment to pee.

"Mom," Franny says. "Do you think that someone has wrecked Pete's place?"

"I don't know," Jane says.

"What do you think happened to Pete?"

Jane is caught off guard. They left without ever explicitly discussing Pete and Jane just thought that Franny, like her, assumed Pete was dead.

"I mean," Franny continues, "if they didn't have gas, maybe he got stuck somewhere. Or he might have gotten hurt and ended up in the hospital. Even if the hospital wasn't taking regular people, like, they'd take cops. Because they think of cops as one of their own." Franny is in her adult to adult mode, explaining the world to her mother. "They stick together. Cops and firemen and nurses."

Jane isn't sure she knows what Franny is talking about. Normally she'd tell Franny as much. But this isn't a conversation she knows how to have. Nate comes around the abutment, adjusting himself a bit, and it is understood that the subject is closed.

"OK," he says. "How far to Wallyworld?" Franny giggles.

Water is their biggest problem. It's hard to find, and when they do find it, either from a pond or, very rarely, from a place where it hasn't all been looted, it's heavy. Thank God Nate is pretty good at making a fire. He has six disposable lighters that he got from a gas station, and when they find a pond, they boil it. Somewhere Jane thinks she heard that they should boil it for eighteen minutes. Basically they just boil the heck out of it. Pond water tastes terrible, but they are always thirsty. Franny whines. Jane is afraid that Nate will get tired of it and leave, but apparently as long as she crawls over to his bed roll every night, he's not going to.

Jane waits until she can tell Franny is asleep. It's a difficult wait. They are usually so tired it is all she can do to keep from nodding off. But she is afraid to lose Nate.

At first she liked that at night he never made a move on her. She always initiates. It made things easier all around. But now he does this thing where she crawls over and he's pretending to be asleep. Or is asleep, the bastard, because he doesn't have to stay awake. She puts her hand on his chest, and then down his pants, getting him hard and ready. She unzips his shorts and still he doesn't do anything. She grinds on him for a while, and only then does he pull his shorts and underwear down and let her ride him until he comes. Then she climbs off him. Sometimes he might say, "Thanks, Babe." Mostly he says nothing and she crawls back next to Franny feeling as if she just paid the rent. She has never given anyone sex for money. She keeps telling herself that this night she won't do it. See what he does. Hell, if he leaves them, he leaves them. But then she lays there, waiting for Franny to go to sleep.

Sometimes she knows Franny is awake when she crawls back. Franny never says anything and unless the moon is up, it is usually too dark to see if her eyes are open. It is just one more weird thing, no weirder than walking up the highway, or getting off the highway in some small town and bartering with some old guy to take what is probably useless U.S. currency for well water. No weirder than no school. No weirder than no baths, no clothes, no nothing.

Jane decides she's not going to do it the next night. But she knows she will lie there, anxious, and probably crawl over to Nate.

They are walking, one morning, while the sky is still blue and darkening near the horizon. By midday the sky will be white and the heat will be flattening. Franny asks Nate, "Have you ever been in love?"

"God, Franny," Jane says.

Nate laughs. "Maybe. Have you?"

Franny looks irritable. "I'm in eighth grade," she says. "And I'm not one of those girls with boobs, so I'm thinking, no."

Jane wants her to shut up, but Nate says, "What kind of guy would you fall in love with?"

Franny looks a little sideways at him and then looks straight ahead. She has the most perfect skin, even after all this time in the sun. Skin like that is wasted on kids. Her look says, "Someone like you stupid." "I don't know," Franny says. "Someone who knows how to do things. You know, when you need them."

"What kind of things?" Nate asks. He's really interested. Well, fuck, there's not a lot interesting on a freeway except other people walking and abandoned cars. They are passing a Sienna with a flat tire and all its doors open.

Franny gestures towards it. "Like fix a car. And I'd like him to be cute, too." Matter of fact. Serious as a church.

Nate laughs. "Competent and cute."

"Yeah," Franny says. "Competent and cute."

"Maybe you should be the one who knows how to fix a car," Jane says.

"But I don't," Franny points out reasonably. "I mean maybe, someday, I could learn. But right now. I don't."

"Maybe you'll meet someone in Canada," Nate says. "Canadian guys are supposed to be able to do things like fix a car or fish or hunt moose."

"Canadian guys are different than American guys?" Franny asks.

"Yeah," Nate says. "You know, all flannel shirts and Canadian beer and stuff."

"You wear a flannel shirt."

"I'd really like a Canadian beer about now," Nate says. "But I'm not Canadian."

Off the road to the right is a gas station/convenience store. They almost always check them. There's not much likelihood of finding anything in the place because the wire fence that borders the highway has been trampled here so people can get over it, which suggests that the place has long been looted. But you never know what someone might have left behind. Nate lopes off across the high grass.

"Mom," Franny says, "carry my backpack, OK?" She shrugs it off and runs. Amazing that she has the energy to run. Jane picks up Franny's backpack, irritated, and follows. Nate and Franny disappear into the darkness inside.

She follows them in. "Franny, I'm not hauling your pack anymore."

There are some guys already in the place and there is something about them, hard and well fed, that signals they are different. Or maybe it is just the instincts of a prey animal in the presence of predators.

"So what's in that pack?" one of them asks. He's sitting on the counter at the cash register window, smoking a cigarette. She hasn't had a cigarette in weeks. Her whole body simultaneously leans towards the cigarette and yet magnifies everything in the room. A room full of men, all of them staring.

She just keeps acting like nothing is wrong because she doesn't know what else to do. "Dirty blankets, mostly," she says. "I have to carry most of the crap."

One of the men is wearing a grimy hoodie. Hispanic yard workers do that sometimes. It must help in the sun. These men are all Anglos, and there are fewer of them than she first thought. Five. Two of them are sitting on the floor, their backs against an empty dead ice cream cooler, their legs stretched out in front of them. Everyone on the road is dirty, but they are dirty and hard. Physical. A couple of them grin, feral flickers passing between them like glances. There is understanding in the room, shared purpose. She has the sense that she cannot let on that she senses anything, because the only thing holding them off is the pretense that everything is normal. "Not that we really need blankets in this weather," she says. "I would kill for a functioning Holiday Inn."

"Hah," the one by the cash register says. A bark. Amused.

Nate is carefully still. He is searching, eyes going from man to man. Franny looks as if she is about to cry.

It is only a matter of time. They will be on her. Should she play up to the man at the cash register? If she tries to flirt, will it release the rising tension in the room, allow them to spring on all of them? Will they kill Nate? What will they do to Franny? Or can she use her sex as currency. Go willingly. She does not feel as if they care if she goes willingly or not. They know there is nothing to stop them.

"There's no beer here, is there," she says. She can hear her voice failing.

"Nope," says the man sitting at the cash register.

"What's your name?" she asks.

It's the wrong thing to say. He slides off the counter. Most of the men are smiling one.

Nate says, "Stav?"

One of the guys on the floor looks up. His eyes narrow.

Nate says, "Hey, Stav."

"Hi," the guy says cautiously.

"You remember me," Nate says. "Nick. From the Blue Moon Inn."

Nothing. Stav's face is blank. But another guy, the one in the hoodie, says, "Speedy Nick!"

Stav grins. "Speedy Nick! Fuck! Your hair's not blond anymore!"

Nate says, "Yeah, well, you know, upkeep is tough on the road." He jerks a thumb at Jane. "This is my sister, Janey. My niece, Franny. I'm taking 'em up to Toronto. There's supposed to be a place up there."

"I heard about that," the guy in the hoodie says. "Some kind of camp."

"Ben, right?" Nate says.

"Yeah," the guy says.

The guy who was sitting on the counter is standing now, cigarette still smoldering. He wants it, doesn't want everybody to get all friendly. But the moment is shifting away from him.

"We found some distilled water," Stav says. "Tastes like shit but you can have it if you want."

Jane doesn't ask him why he told her his name was Nate. For all she knows, "Nate" is his name and "Nick" is the lie.

They walk each day. Each night she goes to his bedroll. She owes him. Part of her wonders is maybe he's gay? Maybe he has to lie there and fantasize she's a guy or something. She doesn't know. They are passing by water. They have some, so there is no reason to stop.

There's an egret standing in the water, white as anything she has seen since this started, immaculately clean. Oblivious to their passing. Oblivious to the passing of everything. This is all good for the egrets. Jane hasn't had a drink since they started for Canada. She can't think of a time since she was sixteen or so that she went so long without one. She wants to get dressed up and go out someplace and have a good time and not think about anything because the bad thing about not having a drink is that she thinks all the time and fuck, there's nothing in her life right now she really wants to think about. Especially not Canada, which she is deeply but silently certain is only a rumor. Not the country, she doesn't think it doesn't exist, but the camp. It is a mirage. A shimmer on the horizon. Something to go towards but which isn't really there.

Or maybe they're the rumors. The three of them. Rumors of things gone wrong.

At a rest stop in the middle of nowhere they come across an encampment. A huge number of people, camped under tarps, pieces of plastic and tatters and, astonishingly, a convoy of military trucks and jeeps include a couple of fuel trucks and a couple of water trucks. The two groups were clearly separate. The military men had control of all the asphalt and one end of the picnic area. They stood around or lounged at picnic tables. They looked so equipped, from hats to combat boots. They looked so clean. So much like the world Jane had put mostly out of her mind. They awoke in her the longing that she had kept putting down. The longing to be clean. To have walls. Electric lights. Plumbing. To have order.

The rest look like refugees. The word she denied on the sidewalks outside the condo. Dirty people in t-shirts with bundles and plastic grocery bags and even a couple of suitcases. She has seen people like this as they walked. Walked past them sitting by the side of the road. Sat by the side of the road as others walked past them. But to see them all together like this…this is what it will be like in Canada? A camp full of people with bags of wretched clothes waiting for someone to give them something to eat?

She rejects it. Rejects it all so viscerally that she stops and would not have walked to the people in the rest stop. She doesn't know if she would have walked past, or if she would have turned around, or if she would have struck off across the country. It doesn't matter what she would have done because Nate and Franny walk right on up the exit ramp. Franny's tank top is bright insistent pink under its filth and her shorts have a tear in them and her legs are brown and skinny and she could be a child on a news channel after a hurricane or an earthquake, clad in the loud synthetic colors so at odds with the dirt or ash that coats her. Plastic and synthetics are the indestructibles left to the survivors.

Jane is ashamed. She wants to explain that she's not like this. She wants to say, she's an American. By which she means she belongs to the military side although she has never been interested in the military, never particularly liked soldiers.

If she could call her parents in Pennsylvania. Get a phone from one of the soldiers. Surrender. You were right, Mom. I should have straightened up and flown right. I should have worried more about school. I should have done it your way. I'm sorry. Can we come home?

Would her parents still be there? Do the phones work just north of Philadelphia? It has not until this moment occurred to her that it is all gone.

She sticks her fist in her mouth to keep from crying out, sick with understanding. It is all gone. She has thought herself all brave and realistic, getting Franny to Canada, but somehow she didn't until this moment realize that it all might be gone. That there might be no where for her where the electricity is still on and there are still carpets on the hardwood floors and someone still cares about damask.

Nate has finally noticed that she isn't with them and he looks back, frowning at her. What's wrong? His expression says. She limps after them, defeated.

Nate walks up to a group of people camped around and under a stone picnic table. "Are they giving out water?" he asks, meaning the military.

"Yeah," says a guy in a Cowboys football jersey. "If you go ask they'll give you water."

"Food?"

"They say tonight."

All the shade is taken. Nate takes their water bottles—a couple of two-liters and a plastic gallon milk jug. "You guys wait and I'll get us some water," he says.

Jane doesn't like being near these people so she walks back to a wire fence at the back of the rest area and sits down. She puts her arms on her knees and puts her head down. She is looking at the grass.

"Mom?" Franny says.

Jane doesn't answer.

"Mom? Are you OK?" After a moment more. "Are you crying?"

"I'm just tired," Jane says to the grass.

Franny doesn't say anything after that.

Nate comes back with all the bottles filled. Jane hears him coming and hears Franny say, "Oh wow. I'm so thirsty."

Nate nudges her arm with a bottle. "Hey, Babe. Have some."

She takes a two-liter from him and drinks some. It's got a flat, faintly metal/chemical taste. She gets a big drink and feels a little better. "I'll be back," she says. She walks to the shelter where the bathrooms are.

"You don't want to go in there," a black man says to her. The whites of his eyes are faintly yellow.

She ignores him and pushes in the door. Inside, the smell is excruciating, and the sinks are all stopped and full of trash. There is some light from windows up near the ceiling. She looks at herself in the dim mirror. She pours a little water into her hand and scrubs at her face. There is a little bit of paper towel left on a roll and she peels it off and cleans her face and her hands, using every bit of the scrap of paper towel. She wets her hair and combs her fingers through it, working the tangles for a long time until it is still curly but not the rat's nest it was. She is so careful with the water. Even so, she uses every bit of it on her face and arms and hair. She would kill for a little lipstick. For a comb. Anything. At least she has water.

She is cute. The sun hasn't been too hard on her. She practices smiling.

When she comes out of the bathroom the air is so sweet. The sunlight is blinding.

She walks over to the soldiers and smiles. "Can I get some more water, please?"

There are three of them at the water truck. One of them is a blond-haired boy with a brick-red complexion. "You sure can," he says, smiling at her.

She stands, one foot thrust out in front of her like a ballerina, back a little arched, and smiles back at him. "You're sweet," she says. "Where are you from?"

"We're all stationed at Fort Hood," he says. "Down in Texas. But we've been up north for a couple of months."

"How are things up north?" she asks.

"Crazy," he says. "But not as crazy as they are in Texas, I guess."

She has no plan. She is just moving with the moment. Drawn like a moth.

He gets her water. All three of them are smiling at her.

"How long are you here?" she asks. "Are you like a way station or something?"

One of the others, a skinny Chicano, laughs. "Oh no. We're here tonight and then headed west."

"I used to live in California," she says. "In Pasadena. Where the Rose Parade is. I used to walk down that street where the cameras are every day."

The blond glances around. "Look, we aren't supposed to be talking too much right now. But later on, when it gets dark, you should come back over here and talk to us some more."

"Mom!" Franny says when she gets back to the fence, "You're all cleaned up!"

"Nice, Babe," Nate says. He's frowning a little.

"Can I get cleaned up?" Franny asks.

"The bathroom smells really bad," Jane says. "I don't think you want to go in there." But she digs her other t-shirt out of her backpack and wets it and washes Franny's face. The girl is never going to be pretty but now that she's not chubby, she's got a cute. She's got the sense to work it, or will learn it. "You're a girl that the boys are going to look at," Jane says to her.

Franny smiles, delighted.

"Don't you think?" Jane says to Nate. "She's got that thing, that sparkle, doesn't she."

"She sure does," Nate says.

They nap in the grass until the sun starts to go down, and then the soldiers line everyone up and hand out MREs. Nate got Beef Ravioli and Jane got Sloppy Joe. Franny got Lemon Pepper Tuna and looked ready to cry but Jane offered to trade with her. The meals were positive cornucopias—a side dish, a little packet of candy, peanut butter and crackers, fruit punch powder. Everybody had different things and Jane made everybody give everyone else a taste.

Nate keeps looking at her oddly. "You're in a great mood."

"It's like a party," she says

Jane and Franny are really pleased by the moist towelette. Franny carefully saves her plastic fork, knife and spoon. "Was your tuna OK?" she asks. She is feeling guilty now that the food was gone.

"It was good," Jane says. "And all the other stuff made it really special. And I got the best dessert."

The night comes down. Before they got on the road, Jane didn't know how dark night was. Without electric lights it is cripplingly dark. But the soldiers have lights.

Jane says, "I'm going to go see if I can find out about the camp."

"I'll go with you," Nate says.

"No," Jane says. "They'll talk to a girl more than they'll talk to a guy. You keep Franny company."

She scouts around the edge of the light until she sees the blond soldier. He says, "There you are!"

"Here I am!" she says.

They are standing around a truck where they'll sleep this night, shooting the shit. The blond soldier boosts her into the truck, into the darkness. "So you aren't so conspicuous," he says, grinning.

Two of the men standing and talking aren't wearing uniforms. It takes her a while to figure out that they're civilian contractors. They have a truck of their own, a white pick-up truck that travels with the convoy. They do something with satellite tracking, but Jane doesn't really care what they do.

It takes a lot of careful maneuvering but one of them finally whispers to her, "We've got some beer in our truck."

The blond soldier looks hurt by her defection.

She stays out of sight in the morning, crouched among the equipment in the back of the pick-up truck. The soldiers hand out MREs but Ted, one of the contractors, smuggles her one.

She thinks of Franny. Nate will keep an eye on her. Jane was only a year older than Franny when she lit out for California the first time. For a second she pictures Franny's face as the convoy pulls out.

Then she doesn't think of Franny.

She is in motion. She doesn't know where she is going. You go where it takes you.

UNDERBRIDGE

PETER S. BEAGLE

Peter S. Beagle was born in Manhattan on the same night that Billie Holiday was recording "Strange Fruit" and "Fine Mellow" just a few blocks away. Raised in the Bronx, Peter originally proclaimed he would be a writer when he was ten years old. Today he is acknowledged as an American fantasy icon, and to the delight of his millions of fans around the world is now publishing more than ever. He is the author of the beloved classic The Last Unicorn, *as well as the novels* A Fine and Private Place, The Innkeeper's Song, *and* Tamsin. *He has won the Hugo, Nebula, Locus, and Mythopoeic awards, and is the recipient of the World Fantasy Award for Life Achievement. His most recent book is the collection* Sleight of Hand.

The Seattle position came through just in time.

It was a near thing, even for Richardson. As an untenured professor of children's literature he was bitterly used to cutting it close, but now, with nothing in the wings to follow his MSSU gig but Jake Riskin's offer to sub remedial English in the Joplin high schools, life was officially the bleakest Richardson could remember. Easy enough to blink through grad school dreaming of life as a Matthew Arnoldesque scholar-gypsy; harder to slog through decades of futureless jobs in second-rank college towns, never being offered the cozy sinecure he had once assumed inevitable. What about professional respect and privileges? What about medical insurance, teaching assistants, preferred parking? What about *sabbaticals*?

Rescue found him shopping in the West 7th Street Save-A-Lot. His cell phone rang, and wondrously, instead of Jake pushing for a decision, the call was from a secretary at the University of Washington English Department. Would he, she wondered, be free to take over classes for a professor who had just been awarded a sizable grant to spend eighteen months at Cambridge, producing a study of the life and works of Joan Aiken?

He said yes, of course, then took a brief time settling the details, which were neither many nor complicated. At no time did he show the slightest degree of unprofessional emotion. But after he snapped his phone shut he stood very still and whispered *"Saved..."* to himself, and when he left the store there were red baby potatoes ($2.40 a pound!) in his bag instead of 34-cent russets.

Most especially was he grateful at being able to take over the Queen Anne Hill apartment of the traveling professor. It was snug—the man lived alone, except for an old cat, whom Richardson, who disliked cats, had dourly agreed to care for—but also well-appointed, including cable television, washer and dryer, microwave and dishwasher, a handsome fireplace and a one-car garage, with a cord of split wood for the winter neatly stacked at the far end. The rent was manageable, as was the drive to the UW; and his classes were surprisingly enjoyable, containing as they did a fair number of students who actually wanted to be there. Richardson could have done decidedly worse, and most often had.

He had been welcomed to the school with impersonal warmth by the chairman of the English department, who was younger than Richardson and looked it. The chairman's name was Philip Austin Watkins IV, but he preferred to be called "Aussie," though he had never been to Australia. He assured Richardson earnestly on their first meeting, "I want you to know, I'm really happy to have you on board, and I'll do everything I can to get you extended here if possible. That's a promise." Richardson, who knew much better at fifty-one than to believe this, believed.

His students generally seemed to like him—at least they paid attention, worked hard on their assignments, didn't mock his serious manner, and often brought up intelligent questions about Milne and Greene, Erich Kästner, Hugh Lofting, Astrid Lindgren, or his own beloved E. Nesbit. But they never took him into their confidence, even during his office hours: never wept or broke down, confessing anxieties or sins or dreams (which would have terrified him), never came to him merely to visit. Nor did he make any significant connections with his fellows on the faculty. He knew well enough that he made friends with difficulty, and wasn't good at keeping them, being naturally formal in his style and uncomfortable in his body, so that he appeared to be forever leaning away from people even when he was making an earnest effort to be close to them. With women, his lifelong awkwardness became worse in the terminally friendly Seattle atmosphere. Once, younger, he had wished to be different; now he no longer believed it possible.

The legendary rain of the Pacific Northwest was not an issue; if anything, he discovered that he enjoyed it. Having studied the data on Seattle climate carefully, once he knew he was going there, he understood that many areas of both coasts get notably more rain, in terms of inches, and endure distinctly colder winters. And the year-round greenness and lack of air pollution more than made up for the mildew, as far as Richardson was concerned. Damp or not, it beat Joplin. Or Hobbs, New Mexico. Or Enterprise, Alabama.

What the greenness did *not* make up for was the near-perpetual overcast. Seattle's sky was dazzlingly, exaltingly, shockingly blue when it chose to be so; but there was a reason that the city consumed more than its share of vitamin D, and was the first marketplace for various full-spectrum lightbulbs. Seattle introduced Richardson to an entirely new understanding of the word *overcast*, sometimes going two months and more without seeing either clear skies or an honest raindrop. He had not been prepared for this.

Many things that shrink from sunlight gain power in fog and murk. Richardson began to find himself reluctant enough to leave the atmosphere of the UW campus that he often stayed on after work, attending lectures that bored him, going to showings of films he didn't understand—even once dropping in on a faculty meeting, though this was not required of him. The main subject under discussion was the urgent need to replace a particular TA, who for six years had been covering most of the undergraduate classes of professors far too occupied with important matters to deal with actual students. Another year would have required granting him a tenure-track assistant professorship, which was, of course, out of the question. Sitting uncomfortably in the back, saying nothing, Richardson felt he was somehow attending his own autopsy.

And when Richardson finally went home in darkness to the warm, comfortable apartment that was not his own, and the company of the sour-smelling old gray cat, he frequently went out again to walk aimlessly on steep, silent Queen Anne Hill and beyond, watching the lights go out in window after window. If rain did not fall, he might well wander until three or four in the morning, as he had never before done in his life.

But it was in daylight that Richardson first saw the Troll.

He had walked across the blue and orange drawbridge at the foot of Queen Anne Hill into Fremont, which had become a favorite weekend ramble of his, though the quirky, rakish little pocket always made him nervous and wistful at the same time. He wished he were the sort of person who could fit comfortably into a neighborhood that could proclaim itself "The Center of the Universe," hold a nude bicycle parade as part of a solstice celebration, and put up signs advising visitors to throw their watches away. He would have liked to be able to imagine living in Fremont.

Richardson had read about the Fremont Bridge Troll online while preparing to leave Joplin. He knew that it was not actually located under the Fremont Bridge, but under the north end of the nearby Aurora Avenue Bridge; and that the Troll was made of concrete, had been created by a team of four artists, weighed four thousand pounds, was more than eighteen feet high, had one staring eye made of an automobile hubcap, and was crushing a cement-spattered Volkswagen Beetle in its left hand. As beloved a tourist photo-op as the Space Needle, it had the inestimable further advantages of being free, unique, and something no lover of children's books could ignore.

It took Richardson a while to come face to face with the Troll, because the day was blue and brisk, and the families were out in force, shoving up to the statue to take pictures, posing small children and puzzled-looking babies within the Troll's embrace, or actually placing them on its shoulder. Richardson made no effort to approach until the crowd had thinned to a few teenagers with cell phone cameras; then he went close enough to see his distorted reflection in the battered aluminum eye. He said nothing, but stayed there until a couple of the teenagers pushed past him to be photographed kissing and snuggling in the shadow of the Troll. Then he went on home.

Two weeks later, driven by increasing insomnia he crossed the Fremont Bridge again, and eventually found himself facing the glowering concrete monster where it crouched in its streetside cave. Alone in darkness, with no fond throng to warm and humanize it, the hubcap eye now seemed to be sizing him up as a tender improvement on a VW Beetle. *Grendel,* Richardson thought, *this is what Grendel looked like.* Aloud, he said, "Hello. Off for the night?"

The Troll made no answer. Richardson went a few steps closer, fascinated by the expression and personality it was possible to impose on two tons of concrete. He asked it, "Do you ever get tired of tourists gaping at you every day? *I* would." For some reason, he wanted the Troll to know that he was a sympathetic, understanding person. He said, "My name's Richardson."

A roupy old voice behind him said, "Don't you get too close. He's mean."

Richardson turned to see a black rain slicker which appeared to be almost entirely inhabited by a huge gray beard. The hood of the slicker was pulled close around the old man's face, so that only the beard and a pair of bright, bloodshot gray eyes were visible as he squatted on the sidewalk that approached the underpass, with four shopping bags arranged around him. Richardson took them at first for the man's worldly possessions; only later, back in the apartment, did he recall glimpsing a long Italian salami, a wine bottle, and a French *baguette* in one of them.

The old man coughed—a long, rattling, machine-gun burst—then growled, "I'd back off a little ways, was I you. He gets mean at night."

Richardson played along with the joke. "Oh, I don't know. He put up so nicely with all those tourists today."

"Daytime," the old man grunted. "Sun goes down, he gets around..." He belched mightily, leaned back against the guardrail, and closed his eyes.

"Well," Richardson said, chuckling to keep the conversation reasonable. "Well, but you're here, taking a nap right within his grasp. You're not afraid of him."

The old man did not open his eyes. "I got on his good side a long time ago. Go away, man. You don't want to be here." The last words grumbled into a snore.

Richardson stood looking back and forth at the Troll and the old man in the black rain slicker, whose snoring mouth hung open, a red-black wound in the vast gray beard. Finally he said politely to the Troll, "You have curious friends," and walked quickly away. The old man never stirred as Richardson passed him.

He had no trouble sleeping that night, but he did dream of the Troll. They were talking quite earnestly, under the bridge, but he remembered not even a fragment of their conversation; only that the Troll was wearing a Smokey Bear hat, and kept biting pieces off the Volkswagen, chewing them like gum and spitting them out. In the dream, Richardson accepted this as perfectly normal: the flavor probably didn't last very long.

He didn't go back to see the Troll at night for a month. Once or twice in the daytime, yes, but he found such visits unsatisfying. During daylight hours the tourist buses were constantly stopping, and families were likely to push baby carriages close between the Troll's hands for photographs. The familiarity, the chattering gaiety, was almost offensive to him, as though the people were savages out of bad movies, and the Troll their trapped and stoic prisoner.

He never saw the old man there. Presumably he was off doing whatever homeless people did during the day, even those who bought French *baguettes* with their beggings.

Richardson's own routine was as drearily predictable as ever. Over the years he had become intensely aware of the arc of each passing contract, from eager launch through trembling zenith to the unavoidable day when he packed his battered Subaru and drove off to whatever job might come next. He was now at the halfway point of his stay at the UW: each time he opened his office door was one twisting turn closer to the last, each paycheck a countdown, in reverse, to the end of his temporary security. Richardson's students and colleagues saw no change in his tone or behavior—he was most careful about that—but in his own ears he heard a gently rising scream.

His silent night walks began to fill with imagined conversations. Some of these were with his parents, both long deceased but still reproving. Others were with distantly remembered college acquaintances, or with characters out of his favorite books. But the ones that Richardson enjoyed most were his one-sided exchanges with the Troll, whose vast, unresponsive silence Richardson found endlessly encouraging. As he wandered through the darkness, hands uncharacteristically in his hip pockets, he found he could speak to the Troll as though they had been friends long enough that there was no point in hiding anything from one another. He had never known that sort of friendship.

"I am never going to be anything more than I am already," he said to the Troll-haunted air. "Forget the fellowships and grants, never mind the articles in *The New Yorker*, *Smithsonian*, *Harper's*—never mind the Modern Language Association, PEN…. None of it is ever going to happen, Troll. I know this. My life is exactly like yours—set in stone and meaningless."

Without realizing it, or ever putting it into words, Richardson came to think of the concrete Troll as his only real friend in Seattle, just as he began resenting the old man in the rain slicker for his privileged position on the Troll's "good side," and himself for his own futility. In the middle of one class—a lecture on the period political references hidden within

Lewis Carroll's underappreciated *Sylvie and Bruno*—Richardson heard his own voice abruptly say "To hell with *that!*" He had to stop and look around the hall for a moment, puzzling his students, before he realized that he hadn't actually said the words out loud.

On the damp and moonless night that Richardson finally returned to the end of the Aurora Avenue Bridge, the old man wasn't there. Neither was the Troll. Only the concrete-slathered Volkswagen was still in place, its curved roof and sides indented where the Troll's great fingers had previously rested.

Sun goes down, he gets around.... Richardson remembered what he had assumed was a joke, and shook his head sharply. He felt the urge to run away, as if the *absence* of the Troll somehow constituted an almost cellular rebuke to his carefully-manicured sense of the rational.

Richardson heard the sound then, distant yet, but numbingly clear: the long, dragging scrape of stone over asphalt. He turned and walked a little way to look east, toward Fremont Street—saw the hunched shadow rising into view—turned again, and bolted back across the bridge, the one leading him to Queen Anne Hill, a door he could close and lock, and a smelly gray cat wailing angrily over an empty food dish. He sat up the rest of the night, watching the QVC channel for company, seeing nothing. Near dawn he fell asleep on the living-room couch, with the television set still selling Select Comfort beds and amethyst jewelry.

In the morning, before he went to the university, he drove down into Fremont, double-parking at 36th and Winslow to make sure of what he already knew. The Troll was back in its place with no smallest deviation from its four creators' positioning, and no indication that it had ever moved at all. Even its grip on the old VW was displayed exactly as it had been, crushing finger for finger, bulging knuckle for knuckle, splayed right-hand fingers digging at the earth for purchase.

Richardson had a headache. He stepped graciously aside for children already swarming up to pose with the Troll for their parents, hurried back to his car and drove away. His usual parking space was taken when he got to the UW, and finding another made him late to class.

For more than two weeks Richardson not only avoided the Aurora Bridge, but stayed out of Fremont altogether. Even so, whether by day or night, strolling the campus, shopping in the University District, or walking a silent waterfront street under the Viaduct, he would often stand very still, listening for the slow, terribly slow, grinding of concrete feet somewhere near. The fact that he could not quite hear it did not make it go away.

Eventually, out of a kind of wintry lassitude, he began drifting down Fourth Avenue North again, at first no farther than the drawbridge, whose raisings and lowerings he found oddly soothing. He seemed to be at a curious remove from himself during that time, watching himself watching the boats waiting to pass the bridge, watching the rain on the water.

When he finally did cross the bridge, however, he did so without hesitation, and on the hunt.

"Fuck off," Cut'n-Shoot said. "Just fuck off and go away and leave me alone."

"Not a chance."

"I have to get *ready*. I have to *be* there."

"Then *tell* me. All you have to do is tell me!"

Richardson had found the bearded old man asleep—noisily asleep, his throat a sporadic bullroarer—under a tree in the Gas Works Park, near the shore of Lake Union. He was still wearing the same clothes and black rain slicker, now with the hood down, and there was an empty bottle of orange *schnapps* clutched in his filthy hand. Bits of greasy *foie gras* speckled his whiskers like dirty snow. When glaring him awake didn't work, Richardson had moved on to kicking the cracked leather soles of the man's old boots, which did.

It also got him a deep bruise on his forearm, from blocking an angrily thrown *schnapps* bottle. Their subsequent conversation had been unproductive. So far, the only useful thing he had uncovered was that the old man called himself "Cut'n-Shoot," after the small town in Texas where he'd been born. That was the end of anything significant, aside from the man's obvious agitation and impatience as evening darkened toward night.

"Goddamn you, somebody gets hurt it's going to be *all your fault*! Let me go!" Cut'n-Shoot's bellow was broken by a coughing spasm that almost brought him to his knees. He leaned forward, spitting and dribbling, hands braced on his thighs.

"I'm not stopping you," Richardson said. "I just want answers. I know you weren't making that up, about the Troll moving at night. I've seen it."

"Yah?" Cut'n-Shoot hawked up one last monster wad. "So what? Price of fishcakes. Ain't *your* job."

"I'm a professor of children's literature—a *full* professor"—for some reason he felt compelled to lie to the old man—"at the University of Washington. I could quote you troll stories from here to next September. And one thing I knew for certain—until I met *you*—was that they don't exist."

Cut'n-Shoot glared at him out of one rheumy eye, the other one closed and twitching. "You think you know trolls?" He snorted. "Goddamn useless punk… you don't know shit."

"Show me."

The old man stared hard for a moment more, then smiled, revealing a sprinkling of brown teeth. It was not a friendly expression. "Might be I will, then. Maybe teach you a lesson. But we're gonna pick up some things first, and you're buyin'. Come on."

Cut'n-Shoot led him a little over three-quarters of a mile from the park, along Northlake Way, under the high overpass of the Aurora Avenue Bridge and the low one at Fourth Avenue, then right on Evanston. Richardson tried asking more questions, but got nothing but growls and snorts for his trouble. Best to save his breath, anyway—he was surprised at how fast the old man could move in a syncopated crab-scuttle that favored his right leg and made the oilslicker snap like a geisha's fan. At the corner of 34th Street Cut'n-Shoot ignored the parallel white stripes of the crosswalk and angled straight across the street to the doors of the Fremont PCC. He strode through them like Alexander entering a conquered city.

The bag clerk nearest the entry waved as they came in. "Hey, Cut! Little late tonight."

Cut'n-Shoot didn't pause, cocking one thumb back over his shoulder at Richardson as he swept up a plastic shopping basket and continued deeper into the store. "Not my fault. Professor here's got the rag on."

When they finally left—having rung up $213.62 of luxury items on Richardson's MasterCard, including multiple cuts of Eel River organic beef and a $55 bottle of 2006 Cadence Camerata Cabernet Sauvignon—it was a docile, baffled Richardson, grocery bags in hand, who trudged after the old man down the mostly empty neighborhood streets. Cut'n-Shoot had made his selections with the demanding eye of a lifelong connoisseur, assessing things on some qualitative scale of measurement Richardson couldn't begin to comprehend. That he and his wallet were being taken advantage of was self-evident; but the inborn curiosity that had first led him to books as a child, that insatiable need to get to the end of each new unfolding story, was now completely engaged. Rambling concrete trolls weren't the only mystery in Fremont.

Cut'n-Shoot led him east along 34th Street to where Troll Avenue started, a narrow road rising between the grand columns that supported the Aurora Avenue Bridge. High on the bridge itself cars hissed by like ghosts; while down on the ground it was quiet as the sea-bottom, and the sparse lights from lakeside boats and local apartment buildings only served to make the path up to the Troll darker than Richardson liked.

"Stupid ratfucks throw a big party up there every October," Cut'n-Shoot said. "Call it 'Trolloween.' *People.* Batshit stupid."

"Well, Fremont's that kind of place," Richardson responded. "I mean, the Solstice Parade, Oktoberfest—the crazy rocket with 'Freedom to Be Peculiar' written on it in Latin—"

"Don't care about all that crap. Just wish they wouldn't rile *him* so much. Job's hard enough as it is."

"And what job would that be, exactly, anyway?"

"You'll see."

At the top of the road the bridge merged with the hillside, forming the space that held the Troll, with stairs running up the hill on either side. Tonight the Troll looked exactly as it had the first time he saw it. It was impossible to imagine this crudely hewn mound of ferroconcrete in motion, even knowing what he knew. Cut'n-Shoot made him put the grocery bags on the ground at the base of the eastern stair, then gestured brusquely for him to stand aside. When he did, the old man got down heavily on one knee—not the right one, Richardson noticed—and started searching through them.

"That's the thing, see. People never know what they're doing. Best place to sleep in town and they had to go fuck everything up."

"It's concrete and wire and rebar," Richardson responded. "I read about it. They had a contest back in 1990—this design won. There used to be a time capsule with Elvis memorabilia in the car, for Christ's sake. It's not *real.*"

"Sure, sure. Like a troll cares what it's made of, starting out. Hah. That ain't the point. Point is, they did *too good a job.*"

Cut'n-Shoot struggled to his feet, unbalanced by the pair of brown packages he was holding—two large roasts, in their taped-up butcher wrapping. "Here," he said, holding out one of them to Richardson. "Get this shit off. He won't be able to smell 'em through the paper."

"You *feed* him?"

"Told you I was on his good side, didn't I?"

Grinning fiercely through his beard now, the old man marched straight to the hulking stone brute and slapped the bloody roast down on the ground in front of it. "There!" he said, "First snack of the night. Better than your usual, too, and don't you know it! *Ummm-mmm*, that's gonna be good." He looked back at Richardson just as a car passed, its headlights making the Troll's hubcap eye seem to flicker and spin. "Well, come on—you wanted this, didn't you? Just do like me, make it friendly."

Richardson was holding the larger unwrapped roast in front of him like a doily, pinching the thick slab of meat between the thumb and forefinger of each hand. It was slippery, and the blood dripping from it made him queasy. As he stepped forward with the offering an old Norse poem suddenly came to him, the earliest relevant reference his magpie mind could dredge up. "*They call me Troll,*" he recited. "*Gnawer of the Moon, Giant of the Gale-blasts, Curse of the rain-hall...*"

Cut'n-Shoot looked at him approvingly, nodding him on.

"*Companion of the Sibyl, Nightroaming hag, Swallower of the loaf of heaven. What is a Troll but that?*"

Richardson laid his roast down gently beside Cut'n-Shoot's, took a deep breath, and backed away without looking up, not knowing as he did so whether this obeisance was for the Troll's benefit, Cut'n-Shoot's, or his own.

The old man's grating chuckle came to him. "That's the good side, all right. That's the way, that's the way." Richardson looked up. Cut'n-Shoot had pushed back the hood of his rain slicker, and was scratching his head through hair like furnace ashes. "But he likes *lively* a sight better. You get the chance, you remember."

"Nothing's happening," Richardson started to say—and then something was.

One by one the fingers of the Troll's right hand were coming free of the ground. Richardson realized that the whole forearm was lifting up, twisting from the elbow, dust and dirt sifting off as it rose. The giant hand turned with the motion, dead-gray fingers coming together with a sound of cracking bricks. Then—like a child grabbing for jacks before the ball comes down, and just as fast—the Troll's hand swept up the two roasts in one great swinging motion and carried them to its suddenly open mouth. The ponderous jaw moved up and down three times before it settled back into place, and Richardson tried to imagine what could possibly be going on inside. A moment later the Troll's hand and arm returned to their original position, fingers wriggling their way back into the soil and once more becoming motionless.

There was no moon, and no more cars went by, but the hubcap continued to twinkle with a brightly chilling malice, and even—so it seemed to
Richardson—to wink. He was still staring at the Troll when Cut'n-Shoot
finally clapped his palms together with satisfaction.

"Well! Old sumbitch settled *right* down. Think he liked that fancy talk.
Know any more?"

"Sure."

"My lucky day," the old man said. "Now lemme show you what the
wine's for."

Richardson woke the next morning hung over, stiff-backed, and with
a runny nose. He was late to class again; and that evening, when he
returned to Fremont, he brought lambchops.

From then on he never came to the bridge without bringing some tribute for the Troll. Most often it came in the form of slabs of raw meat;
though now and again, this being Seattle, he would present the statue
with a whole salmon, usually purchased down at the ferry dock from a
fisherman's wife. Once—only once—he tried offering a bag of fresh crab
cakes, but Cut'n-Shoot informed him tersely, "Don't give him none of
that touristy shit," and made him go back to the Fremont PCC for an
entire Diestel Family turkey.

Richardson also read to the Troll most evenings, working his way up
from obvious fare to selections from the *Bland Tomtar och Troll* series,
voiced dramatically in his best stab at phonetic Swedish. He had no idea
whether the Troll understood, but the expressions on his own face as he
dealt with the unfamiliar orthography made Cut'n-Shoot howl.

It didn't always go easily. By day the Troll was changeless, an eternally
crude concrete figure with one dull aluminum eye, a vacantly malevolent
expression and bad hair. At night its temperament was as unpredictably
irritable as a wasp's. Richardson began to measure his visits on a scale
marked in feet, yards, and furlongs, assessing the difference between
this Tuesday and *that* Saturday by precisely how far the Troll stirred
from its den. In that way he came to understand—as Cut'n-Shoot never
bothered to explain—that the old man's task wasn't to feed the Troll at
all, but rather to distract it, to confuse it, to short-circuit its unfocused
instinct to go off unimpeded about its trollish business, whatever that
might be. Food was a means to that end; as, now, was Richardson's
cheerfully garbled Swedish. Even so there were nights when it would

not yield, and lumbered half a mile or more before they could tempt and coax it—like two Pekingese herding a mastiff—back under the bridge. On those nights, nothing would do but "the lively," usually in the form of a writhing rat or pigeon. Cut'n-Shoot never told Richardson how—or with what—he caught them.

The months passed, and the weather turned relatively mild and notably dry. On campus this was generally spoken of as a function of global warming, and greeted with definite anxiety. Richardson paid little attention to climate crises, having his own worries. His temporary tenure at the university was coming to an end with the summer quarter, and thoughts of the department chair's vague early promises moved in his heart like schooling fish: instead of calling up job listings and sending out inquiries he found himself manufacturing excuses to go by Aussie's office, or sit near him in the faculty dining hall, hoping that mere proximity might make the man offer him work he couldn't possibly ask for.

He also began to drink, at first in pretended sociability with Cut'n-Shoot, but later with the devotion of a convert. It was not an area in which he had any sort of previous expertise. He could neither tell good champagne from bad, nor upper-shelf vodka from potato-peel swill; only that in each case the latter was distinctly cheaper. It all invariably left him with a hammering headache the next morning, which seemed to be how you could tell you were doing it right.

Having no one to drink with in comfort and understanding, he came to spend the early part of many evenings drinking with the gray cat, for whom he had conceived an increasing dislike. Not only did it smell bad: it had taken to urinating on the floor outside its box, and knocking down the clothes hamper to tear and scratch at Richardson's dirty clothes. Richardson, who had never hated an animal in his life, no more than he had ever loved one, brooded increasingly and extensively about the gray cat.

Nothing would probably have come of this growing fixation, had he not already been drunk on the evening he discovered that the cat had peed in his only pair of carpet slippers. Having noticed a pet-transport cage in one of the closets, he pounced on the unwary animal and forced it into the cage, threw on his coat, and stalked down the hill toward Fremont, muttering in counterpoint to the cat's furious wails, as the cage banged against the side of his left knee, "Lively. Right, lively it is. Lively it bloody is."

Cut'n-Shoot said nothing when Richardson set the cage down facing the Troll, shouted "Lively!" and walked quickly away, paying no heed to the cat's redoubled howling. He did look back once, but cage and bridge were both out of sight by then.

In the morning, between the expected headache and the forgotten pre-finals lecture summarizing works intended for children from A.D. 1000 to 1850, he remembered the cat only as he was locking the apartment door. There was no time to check on the cage just then; but all day long he could concentrate on almost nothing else. Along with trying to invent something to tell the cat's owner he became obsessed with the notion that the Humane Society would be waiting for him at the bridge with a charge of felony animal abuse, and quite possibly littering.

That evening he found the remains of the empty cage between two of the Troll's huge fingers. The door had been ripped clean away, as had most of the front of the cage, and the rest of it had been pounded almost shapeless, as though by a hammer, or a great fist. There was fur.

Richardson just made it to the bushes before he was very sick. It took him a long time to empty his stomach, and he was shaking and coughing when he was done, barely able to stand erect. His throat and mouth tasted of chewed tinfoil.

When he finally forced himself to turn back toward the statue, he saw Cut'n-Shoot grinning derisively at him from the shadow of the bridge. "One thing when I do it, another when you do, hah?"

"You could have stopped it. You had other food there. I saw it. You could have let the cat out of that thing, let it go." His stomach contracted, and he thought he was going to be sick again, but there was nothing left to vomit.

"Waste not, want not," Cut'n-Shoot chuckled. "'Sides, now you really *do* know trolls."

With a mean cunning that he would not have suspected himself of possessing, Richardson designed an advertisement for a lost gray cat—even including the name he had never once called it—had a hundred copies xeroxed, and mounted them in sheltered places up and down Queen Anne Hill. Thus, when the owner returned from that enviable, *enviable* sabbatical in England, he would see that Richardson had done everything possible to track down his unfortunately vanished cat. *Would have died soon anyway, old and incontinent as it was. He surely wouldn't have wanted the poor thing peeing all over his nice condo.*

The next morning he went to a pet shop in the Wallingford district, and bought two carrier cages, the first identical to the one he had found in the apartment. The second was a bit larger, since one never knew. With the latter in his hand, he continued his nightly routine, the only differences being that his rounds were now somewhat more purposeful, and that with purpose came a reduction in his drinking. He often whistled as he walked, which was unusual for him.

It astonished him to realize how many animals—strays and otherwise—were running loose on the streets of Seattle. Cats and the smaller dogs were the easiest to capture, though he felt a certain amount of guilt over the ones that came trustingly to his leather-gloved hands. But he learned that people make pets out of the most unlikely animals: he caught escaped ferrets on two or three occasions, lab rats and mice with surprising frequency, and once even a tame crow with clipped wings. He was going to set the crow free—it had a vocabulary of several words, and a way of cocking its head to consider him…but then he thought that its inability to fly would make it easy prey for any cat, and changed his mind.

He did go through cages rather often; there was no way to avoid that, given the Troll's impetuous manner of opening them.

Feeding the Troll distracted him only somewhat from his terror of impending joblessness. It was now much too late to expect reprieve: all the best positions at even the worst colleges and universities had long since been snapped up without him ever applying, the community colleges were full, and thanks to Seattle's highly educated population there were thirty people ahead of him in line for any on-call substituting, even assuming someone would have the human decency to come down ill. Meanwhile the ever-smiling Aussie had turned evasive Trappist. Richardson stopped sliding by his door.

He had no idea that he was going mad with fear, frustration, and weariness. Most people don't; and most—frightened academic gypsies included—go on functioning fairly well. He remained faithful to his classes and his office hours; and if he was more terse with his students, and often more sharp-tongued, still he fulfilled the function for which he was yet being paid as conscientiously as he knew how, because he still loved it. And love will keep you reasonably sane for a long time.

Then came the bright and breezy day when word began circulating through the department—a whisper only, at first, the merest of hints— that the Tenured Prodigal was not coming home.

At 9:30 P.M. a resurrected Richardson was thinking furiously as he knocked back half a bottle of Scotch and picked at his Indian takeout.

This late in the game it would surely be impossible for Aussie to fill the Prodigal's slot; he would *have* to extend Richardson now. And if God could create concrete Trolls that moved and miracles as plain as this one, why, He might yet manage a way to make this change permanent.

Richardson had no plans to go out, not even to round up a stray dog or cat (which had been growing more difficult in recent weeks, as Queen Anne residents had been keeping closer track of their pets, blaming coyotes for the recent disappearances). Considering what to say to Aussie in the morning was paramount. But eventually he could not bear to sit still, and found his legs carrying him to Fremont after all. Something special was clearly called for, a little libation to luck, so at the PCC he bought more of the Eel River beef for the Troll, and for himself and Cut'n-Shoot a half-gallon of a unique coconut-and-molasses ice-cream he had found nowhere else.

He left the grocery grinning, turned left—and saw, a block up 34th Street, walking away, Dr. Philip Austin Watkins IV.

The Scotch proved stronger than good judgment. "Aussie!" he shouted. Then louder: "Aussie!" Bag swinging wildly, he began to run.

The department head had dined out late with friends, imbibing one too many himself as the evening wore on. "You've never been screwed until you've been screwed by the British," he'd said, and meant it. Thank heavens he'd had foresight enough to lay contingency plans.

It took him a moment to realize that his name was being called, and a troubling moment more when he turned around to recognize who it was. His apprehension should perhaps have lasted longer: instead of a simple greeting, followed by meaningless chat, Richardson slammed full tilt into the issue of the job opening. "Aussie, I heard about Brubaker. And you promised. You *did* promise."

"I promised to do everything I could to help you," Aussie countered. "And I did, but obviously it wasn't enough. I'm sorry."

"You can't leave the slot open, and it's too late—"

"Mr. Richardson. You knew you were a fill-in, just as I knew from the beginning that the Aiken grant was a recruiting hook in disguise. If the fish had bitten later I might have had to keep you on. As it happens, he did it while my own preferred replacement was still sitting by the phone at Kansas State, waiting for my call, exactly where he's been since I first talked to him last April. The *slot*, as you call it, is already filled."

"Oh." Without thought, Richardson removed the frozen half-gallon of coconut-molasses ice-cream from his grocery bag and smashed Aussie in the head with it just as hard as he could. The man was insensible when he hit the ground, but not dead. Richardson was particularly glad of that.

"That was satisfactory," Richardson said aloud, as though he were judging a presentation in class. He heard his voice echoing in his head, which interested him. Looking around quickly and seeing no one close enough to notice what he was doing, or to interfere with it, Richardson got Aussie—who was not a small person—on his feet, hooked an arm around his waist, and draped one of the chairman's arms around his own neck, saying loudly and frequently, "*Told* you, Aussie, you can't say I didn't tell you. *Sip* the Calvados, I said, don't *guzzle* it. Ah, come on, Aussie, *help* me a little bit here."

Ordinarily, the walk to the Aurora Bridge would have taken Richardson a few minutes at most; dragging the unconscious Aussie, it took months, and by the time he came near the Troll's overpass he was panting and sweating heavily. "The last lively!" he called out in a louder, different voice. "Here you *go!* Compliments of the chef."

A hoarse, frantic voice behind him demanded, "What you doing? What the *hell* you doing?" Richardson let go of Aussie and turned to see Cut'n-Shoot gaping at him, his bleared eyes as wild as those of a horse in a burning barn. "What the hell you think you doing?"

"Tidying up," Richardson said. His voice sounded as faraway as the old man's, and the echoes in his head were growing louder.

"You dumb shit," Cut'n-Shoot whispered. He was plainly sober, if he hadn't been a moment before, and wishing he weren't. "You crazy dumb shit, you fucking killed him."

Richardson looked briefly down, shaking his head. "Oh, let's hope not. He's twitched a couple of times."

Cut'n-Shoot was neither listening to him nor looking directly at him. "I'm out of here, I ain't in this mess. I'm calling the cops."

Richardson did not take the statement seriously. "Oh, please. Can you stand there and tell me our friend's always lived on warm puppies? Nothing like this has ever, ever happened before?"

"Not like this, not never like this." Cut'n-Shoot was beginning to back away, looking small and cold, hugging himself. "I got to call the cops. See if he got a cell phone or something."

"Ah, no cops," Richardson said. He was fascinated by his own detachment; by his strange lightheartedness in the midst of what he knew ought to be a nightmare. He took hold of Cut'n-Shoot's black slicker, which felt like slimy tissue paper in his hand. "You have *got* to get yourself a new raincoat," he told the old man sternly. "Promise me you'll get a new coat this winter." Cut'n-Shoot stared blankly at him, and Richardson shook him hard. "*Promise*, damn it!"

Richardson heard the long scraping rumble before he could turn, still keeping his grip on the struggling, babbling Cut'n-Shoot. The Troll was moving, emerging from its lair under the bridge, the disproportionate length of its body giving the effect of a great worm, even a dragon. In the open, it braced itself on its knuckles for some moments, like a gorilla, before rising to its full height. The hubcap eye was alight as Richardson had never seen it: a whipping forest-fire red-orange that had nothing to do with the thin, wan crescent on the horizon. He thought, madly and absurdly, not of Grendel, but of the Cyclops Polyphemus.

The Troll crouched hugely over Aussie, prodding him experimentally with the same hand that perpetually crushed the Volkswagen. The man moaned softly, and Richardson said as the Troll looked up, "See? Lively."

For the first time in Richardson's memory the Troll made a sound. It was neither a growl nor a snarl, nor were there any more words in it than there were words in Richardson to describe it. Long ago he had spent three-quarters of a year teaching at a branch of the University of Alaska, and what he most remembered about that strange land was the *sense* of the pack ice breaking up in the spring, much too distant for him to have heard it, or even felt the vibration in his bones; but like everyone else he, foreigner or not, knew absolutely that it was happening. So it was with the sound that reached him now: not from the Troll's mouth or throat or monstrous body, but from its entire preposterous existence.

"Saying grace?" Richardson asked. The Troll made the sound again and his head descended, jaws opening wider than Richardson had ever seen. Cut'n-Shoot screamed, and kept on screaming. Richardson kept a tight grip on him, but the old man's utter panic set the echoes roaring in Richardson's head. He said, "*Quit* it—come *on*, relax, enjoy a little dinner theater," but one of Cut'n-Shoot's flailing arms caught him hard enough on a cheekbone that his eyes watered and went out of focus for a moment. "*Ow*," he said; and then, "OK, then. OK."

Very little of Aussie was still visible. Richardson took a firmer hold of Cut'n-Shoot, lifted him partly off the ground, and half-hurled, half-shoved him at the Troll. The old man actually tripped over a concrete forearm; he fell directly against the Troll's chest, snuggling grotesquely. He opened his mouth to scream again, but nothing came out.

"How about a taste of the guardian?" Richardson demanded. He hardly recognized his own voice: it was loud and frayed, and hurt him coming out. "How about a piece of the one who's always there to make sure you behave? Wouldn't that be nice, after all this time?"

When the Troll's mouth opened over Cut'n-Shoot, Richardson began to laugh in delighted hysteria. Not only did the great gray jaws seem to hinge at the back, exactly like a waffle iron, but they matched perfectly, hammer and anvil, when the mouth slammed shut.

After the jaws finally stopped moving, the Troll stretched toward the sky again, and Richardson realized that it was somehow different now— taller and straighter, its rough edges softening, sinking into themselves, becoming more fluid. Becoming more *real*. It stared down at Richardson, and made a different sound this time.

Like a troll cares what it's made of, starting out, he thought, and somehow the echoes in his head and Cut'n-Shoot's crazy laughter were one and the same.

"Well shit," he said. "That meal sure agreed with you."

He was just turning to run when the thing's hand, no longer concrete but just as hard, just as vast and heavy, fell on his shoulder, breaking it. Richardson was shrieking as the Troll lifted him into the air, tucked him clumsily under one arm, and began squeezing back into the lair under the Aurora Bridge. Crumpled against the monster's side—clothing shredded, skin lacerated, his ribs going—Richardson heard the tolling of an impossible heart.

RELIC

JEFFREY FORD

Jeffrey Ford is the author of the novels The Physiognomy, Memoranda, The Beyond, The Portrait of Mrs. Charbuque, The Girl in the Glass, The Cosmology of the Wider World, *and* The Shadow Year. *His story collections are* The Fantasy Writer's Assistant, The Empire of Ice Cream, *and* The Drowned Life. *Ford's fiction has been translated into over twenty languages and is the recipient of the Edgar Allan Poe Award, the Shirley Jackson Award, the Nebula, the World Fantasy Award, and the Grand Prix de l'Imaginaire. His new collection,* Crackpot Palace, *is due out later this year.*

Out at the end of the world on a long spit of land like a finger poking into oblivion, nestled in a valley among the dunes, sat The Church of Saint Ifritia, constructed from twisted driftwood and the battered hulls of ships. There was one tall, arched window composed of the round bottoms of blue bottles. The sun shone through it, submerging altar and pews. There was room for twenty inside, but the most ever gathered for a sermon was eleven. Atop its crooked steeple jutted a spiraled tusk some creature had abandoned on the beach.

The church's walls had a thousand holes and so every morning Father Walter said his prayers while shoveling sand from the sanctuary. He referred to himself as "father" but he wasn't a priest. He used the title because it was what he remembered the holy men were called in the town he came from. Wanderers to the end of the world sometimes inquired of him as to the church's denomination. He was confused by these questions. "A basic church, you know," he'd say. "I talk God and salvation with anyone interested." Usually the pilgrims would turn away, but occasionally one stayed on and listened.

Being that The Church of Saint Ifritia could have as few as three visitors a month, Father Walter didn't feel inclined to give a sermon once a week. "My flock would be only the sand fleas," he said to Sister North. "Then preach to the fleas," she replied. "Four sermons a year is plenty," he said. "One for each season. Nobody should need more than four sermons a year." They were a labor for him to write, and he considered the task as a kind of penance. Why he gave sermons, he wasn't sure. Their purpose was elusive, and yet he knew it was something the holy men did. His earliest ones were about the waves, the dunes, the sky, the wind, and when he ran out of natural phenomena to serve as topics, he moved inward and began mining memory for something to write.

Father Walter lived behind the whalebone altar in a small room with a bed, a chair, a desk, and a stove. Sister North, who attended a summer sermon one year, the subject of which was *The Wind*, and stayed on to serve Saint Ifritia, lived in her own small shack behind the church. She kept it tidy, decorated with shells and strung with tattered fishing nets, a space no bigger than Father Walter's quarters. In the warm months, she kept a garden in the sand, dedicated to her saint. Although he never remembered having invited her to stay on, Father Walter proclaimed her flowers and tomatoes miracles, a cornucopia from dry sand and salt air, and recorded them in the official church record.

Sister North was a short, brown woman with long dark hair streaked with gray, and an expression of determination. Her irises were almost yellow, catlike, in her wide face. On her first night amid the dunes, she shared Father Walter's bed. He came to realize that she would share it again as long as there was no mention of it during the light of day. Once a season, she'd travel ten miles inland by foot to the towns and give word that a sermon was planned for the following Monday. The towns she visited scared her, and only occasionally would she meet a pilgrim who'd take note of her message.

In addition to the church and Sister North's shack, there were two other structures in the sand dune valley. One was an outhouse built of red ship's wood with a tarpaulin flap for a door and a toilet seat made of abalone. The other was a shrine that housed the holy relic of Saint Ifritia. The latter building was woven from reeds by Sister North and her sisters. She'd sent a letter and they'd come, three of them. They were all short and brown with long dark hair streaked with gray. None had yellow eyes, though.

They harvested reeds from the sunken meadow, an overgrown square mile set below sea-level among the dunes two miles east of the church. They sang while they wove the strands into walls and window holes and a roof. Father Walter watched the whole thing from a distance. He felt he should have some opinion about it, but couldn't muster one. When the shrine began to take form, he knew it was a good thing.

Before Sister North's sisters left to return to their lives, Father Walter planned a dedication for the relic's new home. He brought the holy item to the service wrapped in a dirty old towel, the way he'd kept it for the past thirty years. Its unveiling brought sighs from the sisters, although at first they were unsure what they were looking at. A dark lumpen object, its skin like that of an overripe banana. There were toes and even orange, shattered toenails. It was assumed a blade had severed it just above the ankle, and the wound had, by miracle or fire, been cauterized. "Time's leather," was the phrase Father Walter bestowed upon the state of its preservation. It smelled of wild violets.

There was no golden reliquary to house it, he simply placed it in the bare niche built into the altar, toes jutting slightly beyond the edge of their new den. He turned and explained to the assembled, "You must not touch it with your hands, but fold them in front of you, lean forward and kiss the toes. In this manner, the power of the saint will be yours for a short time and you'll be protected and made lucky."

Each of them present, the father, Sister North and her sisters, and a young man and woman on their honeymoon who wandered into the churchyard just before the ceremony got under way, stepped up with folded hands and kissed the foot. Then they sat and Father Walter paced back and forth whispering to himself as was his ritual prior to delivering a sermon. He'd written a new one for the event, a fifth sermon for the year. Sister North was pleased with his industry and had visited his bed the night he'd completed it. He stopped pacing eventually and pointed at the ancient foot. The wind moaned outside. Sand sifted through the reeds.

Father Walter's Sermon

When I was a young man, I was made a soldier. It wasn't my choosing, I don't know. They put a gun to my head. We marched through the mud into a rainy country. I was young and I saw people die all around me. Some were only wounded but drowned in the muddy puddles. It rained past forty days and forty nights and the earth had had its fill. Rivers flooded their banks and the water spilled in torrents from the bleak mountains. I killed a few close up with a bayonet and I felt their life rush out. Some I shot at a distance and watched them suddenly drop like children at a game. In two months time I was a savage.

We had a commanding officer who'd become fond of killing. He could easily have stayed behind the lines and directed the attack, but, with saber drawn, he'd lead every charge and shoot and hack to pieces more of the enemy than the next five men. Once I fought near him in a hand-to-hand melee against a band of enemy scouts. The noises he made while doing his work were ungodly. Strange animal cries. He scared me. And I was not alone. This Colonel Hempfil took no prisoners and would dispatch civilians as well as members of his own squad on the merest whim. I swear I thought I'd somehow gone to hell. The sun never shone.

And then one night we sat in ambush in the trees on either side of a dirt road. The rain, of course, was coming down hard and it was cold, moving into autumn. The night was an eternity I think. I nodded off and then there came some action. The colonel kicked me where I sat and pointed at the road. I looked and could barely make out a hay cart creaking slowly by. The colonel kicked me again and indicated with hand signals that I was to go and check out the wagon.

My heart dropped. I started instantly crying, but as not to let the colonel see me sobbing, I ran to it. There could easily have been enemy soldiers beneath the hay with guns at the ready. I ran onto the road in front of the wagon and raised my weapon. "Halt," I said. The tall man holding the reins pulled up and brought the horses to a stop. I told him to get down from his seat. As he climbed onto the road, I asked him," What are you carrying?" "Hay," he replied, and then the colonel and the rest of our men stormed the wagon. Hempfil gave orders to clear the hay. Beneath it was discovered the driver's wife and two daughters. Orders were given to line them all up. As the driver was being escorted away by two soldiers, he turned to me and said, "I have something to trade for our freedom. Something valuable."

The colonel was organizing a firing squad, when I went up to him and told him what the driver had said to me. He thanked me for the information, and then ordered that the tall man be brought to him. I stood close to hear what he could possibly have to offer for the lives of his family. The man leaned over Hempfil and whispered something I could not make out. The colonel then ordered him, "Go get it."

The driver brought back something wrapped in a dirty towel. He unwrapped the bundle and whisking away the cloth held a form the size of a small rabbit up to the colonel. "Bring a light," cried Hempfil. "I can't see a damn thing." A soldier lit a lantern and brought it. I leaned in close to see what was revealed. It was an old foot, wrinkled like a purse and dark with age. The sight of the toenails gave me a shiver.

"This is what you will trade for your life and the lives of your family? This ancient bowel movement of a foot? Shall I give you change?" said the colonel and that's when I knew all of them would die. The driver spoke quickly. "It is the foot of a saint," he said. "It has power. Miracles."

"What saint?" asked the colonel.

"Saint Ifritia."

"That's a new one," said Hempfil, and laughed. "Bring me the chaplain," he called over his shoulder.

The chaplain stepped up. "Have you ever heard of Saint Ifritia?" asked the colonel.

"She's not a real saint," said the priest. "She is only referred to as a saint in parts of the holy writing that have been forbidden."

Hempfil turned and gave orders for the driver's wife and daughters to be shot. When the volley sounded, the driver dropped to his knees and hugged the desiccated foot to him as if for comfort. I saw the woman and girls, in their pale dresses, fall at the side of the road. The colonel turned to me and told me to give him my rifle. I did. He took his pistol from its holster at his side and handed it to me. "Take the prisoner off into the woods where it's darker, give him a ten-yard head start, and then kill him. If he can elude you for fifteen minutes, let him go with his life."

"Yes, sir," I said, but I had no desire to kill the driver. I led him at gun point up the small embankment and into the woods. We walked slowly forward into darkness. He whispered to me so rapidly, "Soldier, I still hold the sacred foot of Ifritia. Let me trade you it for my life. Miracles." As he continued to pester me with his promises of blessings and wonders, the thought of killing him began to ap-

peal to me. I don't know what it was that came over me. It came from deep within, but in an instant his death had become for me a foregone conclusion. After walking for ten minutes, I told him to stop. He did. I said nothing for a while, and the silence prompted him to say, "I get ten yards, do I not?"

"Yes," I said.

With his first step, I lifted the pistol and shot him in the back of the head. He was dead before he hit the ground, although his body shook twice as I reached down to turn him over. His face was blown out the front, a dark smoking hole above a toothful grimace. I took the foot, felt its slick hide in my grasp, and wrapped it in the dirty towel. Shoving it into my jacket, I buttoned up against the rain and set off deeper into the woods. I fled like a frightened deer through the night, and all around me was the aroma of wild violets.

It's a long story, but I escaped the war, the foot of Saint Ifritia producing subtle miracles at every turn, and once it made me invisible as I passed through an occupied town. I left the country of rain, pursued by the ghost of the wagon driver. Every other minute, behind my eyes, the driver's wife and daughters fell in their pale dresses by the side of the road in the rain, and nearly every night he would appear from my meager campfire, rise up in smoke and take form. "Why?" he always asked. "Why?"

I found that laughter dispersed him more quickly. One night I told the spirit I had plans the next day to travel west. But in the morning, I packed my things up quickly and headed due south toward the end of the world. I tricked him. Eventually, the ghost found me here, and I see him every great while, pacing along the tops of the dunes that surround the valley. He can't descend to haunt me, for the church I built protects me and the power of Saint Ifritia keeps him at bay. Every time I see him his image is dimmer, and before long he will become salt in the wind.

The impromptu congregation was speechless. Father Walter slowly became aware of it as he stood, swaying slightly to and fro. "The Lord works in mysterious ways," he said, a phrase he'd actually heard from Colonel Hempfil. There was a pause after his delivery of it during which he waved his hands back and forth in the air like a magician, distracting an audience. Eventually, two of the sisters nodded and the honeymoon couple shrugged and applauded the sermon.

Father Walter took this as a cue to move on, and he left the altar of the shrine and ran back to the church to fetch a case of whiskey that the Lord had recently delivered onto the beach after a terrific thunderstorm. The young couple produced a hash pipe and a tarry ball of the drug that bore a striking resemblance to the last knuckle of the middle toe of Saint Ifritia's foot.

Late that night, high as the tern flies, the young man and woman left and headed out toward the end of the world, and Sister North's sisters loaded into their wagon and left for their respective homes. Father Walter sat on the sand near the bell in the churchyard, a bottle to his lips, staring up at the stars. Sister North stood over him, the hem of her habit, as she called the simple gray shift she wore every day, flapped in the wind.

"None would stay the night after your story of murder," she said to him. "They drank your whiskey, but they wouldn't close their eyes and sleep here with you drunk."

"Foolishness," he said. There's plenty still left for all. Loaves and fishes of whiskey. And what do you mean by murder?"

"The driver in your sermon. You could have let him live."

He laughed. "I did. In real life, I let him go. A sermon is something different, though."

"You mean you lied?"

"If I shot him, I thought it would make a better story."

"But where's the Lord's place in a story of cold-blooded murder?"

"That's for Him to decide."

Sister North took to her shack for a week, and he rarely saw her. Only in the morning and late in the afternoon would he catch sight of her entering and leaving the shrine. She mumbled madly as she walked, eyes down. She moved her hands as if explaining to someone. Father Walter feared the ghost of the driver had somehow slipped into the churchyard and she was conversing with it. "Because I lied?" he wondered.

During the time of Sister North's retreat to her shack, a visitor came one afternoon. Out of a fierce sandstorm, materializing in the churchyard like a ghost herself, stepped a young woman wearing a hat with flowers, and carrying a traveling bag. Father Walter caught sight of her through blue glass. He went to the church's high doors, opened one slightly to keep the sand out, and called to her to enter. She came to him, holding the hat down with one hand and lugging the heavy bag with the other. "Smartly dressed," was the term the father vaguely remembered from his life inland. She wore a white shirt buttoned at the collar with a dark string tie. Her black skirt and jacket matched, and she somehow made her way through the sand without much trouble in a pair of high heels.

Father Walter slammed shut the church door once she was inside. For a moment he and his guest stood still and listened to the wind, beneath it the distant rhythm of the surf. The church was damp and cold. He told the young lady to accompany him to his room where he could make a fire in the stove. She followed him behind the altar, and as he broke sticks of driftwood, she removed her hat and took a seat at his desk.

"My name is Mina GilCragson," she said.

"Father Walter," he replied over his shoulder.

"I've come from the Theological University to see your church. I'm a student. I'm writing a thesis on Saint Ifritia."

"Who told you about us?" he asked, lighting the kindling.

"A colleague who'd been to the end of the world and back. He told me last month, "You know, there's a church down south that bears your Saint's name. And so I was resolved to see it."

Father Walter turned to face her. "Can you tell me what you know of the Saint? I am the father here, but I know so little, though the holy Ifritia saved my life."

The young woman asked for something to drink. Since the rainwater barrel had been tainted by the blowing sand that day, he poured her a glass of whiskey and one for himself. After serving his guest, he sat on the floor, his legs crossed. She dashed her drink off quickly as, he remembered, was the fashion in the big cities. Wiping her lips with the back of her hand, she said, "What do you know of her so far?"

"Little," he said, and listened, pleased to be, for once, on the other end of a sermon.

Mina GilCragson's Sermon

She was born in a village in the rainy country eighty-some odd years ago. Her father was a powerful man, and he oversaw the collective commerce of their village, Dubron, which devoted itself to raising Plum fish for the tables of the wealthy. The village was surrounded by fifty ponds, each stocked with a slightly different variety of the beautiful fan-tailed species. It's a violet fish. Tender and sweet when broiled.

Ifritia, called "If" by her family, wanted for nothing. She was the plum of her father's eye, her wishes taking precedence over those of her mother and siblings. He even placed her desires above the good of the village. When she was sixteen, she asked that she be given her own pond and be allowed to raise one single fish in it that would be her pet. No matter the cost of clearing the pond, one of the larger, she was granted her wish. To be sure, there was much grumbling among the other villagers and even among If's siblings and mother, but none was voiced in the presence of her father. He was a proud and vindictive man, and it didn't pay to cross him.

She was given a hatchling from the strongest stock to raise. From early on, she fed the fish by hand. When she approached the pond, the creature would surface and swim to where she leaned above the water. Fish, to the people of Dubron, were no more than swimming money, so that when Ifritia bequeathed a name on her sole charge, it was a scandal. Unheard of. Beyond the limit. A name denotes individuality, personality, something dangerously more than swimming money. A brave few balked in public, but If's father made their lives unhappy and they fell back to silence.

Lord Jon, the Plum fish, with enough room to spread out in his own pond and fed nothing but table scraps, potatoes and red meat, grew to inordinate dimensions. As the creature swelled in size, its sidereal fish face fleshed out, pressing the eyes forward, redefining the snout as a nose, and puffing the cheeks. It was said Jon's face was the portrait of a wealthy landowner, and that his smile, now wide where it once was pinched, showed rows of sharp white teeth. A fish with a human face was believed by all but the girl and her father to be a sign of evil. But she never stopped feeding it and it never stopped growing until it became the size of a bull hog. Ifritia would talk to the creature, tell it her deepest secrets. If she told something good, it would break out into its huge, biting smile, something sad and it would shut its mouth and tears would fill its saucer-wide eyes.

And then, out of the blue, for no known reason, the fish became angry with her. When she came to the edge of the pond, after it took the food from her hand, it splashed her and made horrid grunting noises. The fish doctor was called for and his diagnosis was quickly rendered. The Plum fish was not supposed to grow to Lord Jon's outsized dimensions, the excess of flesh and the effects of the red meat had made the creature insane. "My dear," said the doctor in his kindest voice, "you've squandered your time creating a large purple madness and that is the long and short of it." The girl's father was about to take exception with the doctor and box his ears, but in that instant she saw the selfish error of her ways.

After convincing her father of the immorality of what they'd done, she walked the village and apologized to each person privately, from the old matrons to the smallest babies. Then she took a rifle from the wall of her father's hunting room and went to the pond. On her way there, a crowd gathered behind her. Her change was as out of the blue as that of Lord Jon's, and they were curious about her and happy that she was on the way to becoming a good person. She took up a position at the edge of the water, and whistled to the giant Plum fish to come for a feeding. The crowd hung back fearful of the thing's human countenance. All watched its fin, like a purple fan, disappear beneath the water.

Ifritia pushed the bolt of the rifle forward and then sighted the weapon upon a spot where Jon usually surfaced. Everyone waited. The fish didn't come up. A flock of geese flew overhead and it started to rain. Attention wandered, and just when the crowd began murmuring, the water beneath where Ifritia leaned over the pond exploded and the fish came up a blur of violet, launching itself the height of the girl. Using its tail, it slapped her mightily across the face. Ifritia went over backwards and her feet flew out from under her. In his descent, Jon turned in mid-air, opened his wide mouth, and bit through her leg. The bone shattered, the flesh tore, blood burst forth, and he was gone, out of sight, to the bottom of the big pond with her foot.

She survived the grim amputation. While she lay in the hospital, her father had the pond drained. Eventually, the enormous fish was stranded in only inches of water. Ifritia's father descended a long ladder to the pond bed and sloshed halfway across it to reach Lord Jon. The creature flapped and wheezed. Her father took out a pistol and shot the fat, odious face between the eyes. He reported to others later that the fish began to cry when it saw the gun.

The immense Plum fish was gutted and Ifritia's foot was found in its third stomach. Her father forbade anyone to tell her that her foot had been rescued from the fish. She never knew that it stood in a glass case in the cedar attic atop her family home. As the days wore on and her affliction made her more holy every minute, the foot simmered in Time, turning dark and dry. She learned to

walk with a crutch, and became pious to a degree that put off the
village. They whispered that she was a spy for God. Dressing in
pure white, she appeared around every corner with strict moral
advice. They believed her to be insane and knew her to be death
to any good time.

Mina held her glass out to Father Walter. He slowly rose, grabbed the
bottle, and filled it. He poured himself another and sat again.

"Did she make a miracle at all?" he asked.

"A few," said Mina, and dashed off her drink.

"Can you tell me one?"

"At a big wedding feast, she turned everybody's wine to water. She flew
once, and she set fire to a tree with her thoughts."

"Amazing," said Father Walter. He stood and put his drink on the desk.
"Come with me," he said. "There's something I think you'll want to see."

She rose and followed him out the back door of the church. The sand
was blowing hard, and he had to raise his arm in front of his eyes as he
leaned into the wind. He looked back and Mina GilCragson was right
behind him, holding her hat on with one hand. He led her to the shrine.

Inside, he moved toward the altar, pointing. "There it is. Saint Ifritia's
foot," he said.

"What are you talking about?" said Mina, stepping up beside him.

"Right there," he said and pointed again.

She looked and an instant later went weak. Father Walter caught her
by the arm. She shook her head and took a deep breath. "I can't believe
it," she said.

"I know," he said. "But there it is. You mustn't touch it with your hands.
You must only kiss the toes. I'll stand outside. You can have a few minutes alone with it."

"Thank you so much," she said, tears in her eyes.

He went outside. Leaning against the buffeting wind, he pushed aside
the bamboo curtain that protected the shrine's one window. Through
the sliver of space, he watched Mina approach the altar. Her hands were
folded piously in front of her as he'd instructed. He realized that if she'd
not worn the heels, she'd never have been able to reach the foot with her
lips. As it was she had to go up on her toes. Her head bobbed forward
to the relic, but it wasn't a quick kiss she gave. Her head moved slightly
forward and back, and Father Walter pictured her tongue passionately
laving the rotten toes. It gave him both a thrill and made him queasy. He

had a premonition that he'd be drinking hard into the night.

After the longest time, Mina suddenly turned away from the foot. Father Walter let the bamboo curtain slide back into place and waited to greet her. She exited the shrine, and he said, "How was that? Did you feel the spirit?" but she never slowed to answer. Walking right past him, she headed toward the outhouse. The sand blew fiercely but she didn't bother to hold her hat and it flew from her head. Mina walked as if in a trance. Father Walter was surprised when she didn't go to the outhouse, but passed it, and headed up out of the valley in the dunes. On the beach, the wind would have been ten times worse. As she ascended, he called to her to come back.

She passed over the rim, out of sight, and he was reluctant to follow her, knowing the ghost of the driver might be lurking in the blinding sandstorm. He turned back toward the church, his mind a knot of thoughts. Was she having a holy experience? Had he offended her? Was she poisoned by the old foot? He stopped to fetch her hat, which had blown up against the side of the outhouse.

That night his premonition came true, and the whiskey flowed. He opened Mina GilCragson's traveling bag and went through her things. By candle light, whiskey in one hand, he inspected each of her articles of clothing. When holding them up, he recognized the faint scent of wild violets. He wondered if she was a saint. While searching for evidence in the aroma of a pair of her underpants, Sister North appeared out of the shadows.

"What are you up to?" she asked.

"Sniffing out a holy bouquet. I believe our visitor today may have been a saint."

"She was nothing of the sort," said Sister North, who stepped forward and backhanded Father Walter hard across the face. His whiskey glass flew from his grasp and he dropped the underpants. Consciousness blinked off momentarily and then back on. He stared at her angry, yellow eyes as she reached out, grabbed his shirt, and pulled him to his feet. "Come with me," she said.

Outside, the sandstorm had abated and the night was clear and cool and still. Not letting go, she pulled Father Walter toward the shrine. He stumbled once and almost fell and, for his trouble, she kicked him in the rear end. Candle light shone out from the shrine's one window, its bamboo curtain now rolled up. Sister North marched the father up to the altar and said to him, "Look at that."

"Look at what?" he said, stunned by drink and surprise.

"What else?" she asked.

And upon noticing, he became instantly sober, for the big toe of the holy foot was missing. "My god," he said, moving closer to it. Where the toe had been was a knuckle-stump of sheered gristle. "I thought she was sucking on it, but in fact she was chewing off the toe," he said, turning to face Sister North.

"You thought she was sucking on it…" she said. "Since when is sucking the holy toes allowed?"

"She was a scholar of Saint Ifritia. I never suspected she was a thief."

Sister North took a seat and gave herself up to tears. He sat down beside her and put his arm around her shoulders. They stayed in the shrine until the candles melted down and the dawn brought bird calls. Then they went to his bed. Before she fell asleep, the sister said to him, "It happened because you lied."

He thought about it. "Nahh," he said. "It was bound to happen some-day." He slept and dreamt of the driver's wife and daughters. When he woke, Sister North was gone.

Sister North's Sermon

Father—By the time you find this, I'll already be four miles inland, heading for the city. I mean to bring back the stolen toe and make amends to Saint Ifritia. She's angry that we let this happen. You, of course, bear most of the responsibility, but I too own a piece of the guilt. It may take me a time to hunt down Mina GilCragson. I'll try the university first, but if she's not a scholar, I fear she might be a trader on the black market, trafficking in religious relics. If that's the case the toe could at this moment be packed on the back of a mule, climbing the northern road into the mountains and on through the clouds to the very beginning of the world. If so, I will follow it. If I fail, I won't be back. One thing I've seen in my sleep is that at the exact halfway point of my journey, a man will visit the church and bring you news of me. If he tells you I am dead, then burn my shack and all my things and scatter my ashes over the sea, but if the last he's seen of me I'm alive, then that means I will return. That, I'm sure of. Wake up and guard the foot with your very life. If I return after years with a toe and there is no foot, I'll strangle you in your sleep. Think of me in bed, and in the morning when you shovel sand pray for me. There are four bottles of whiskey under the mattress in my shack. You can have three of them. I spent a week of solitude contemplating your sermon and realized that you didn't lie. That you actually killed the driver of the hay wagon. Which is worse? May the sweet saint have mercy on you.—Sister

Two days later, Father Walter realized he'd taken Sister North for granted, and she was right, he had killed the driver just as he'd described in his sermon. Without her there, in her shack, in the shrine, in his bed, the loneliness crept into the sand dune valley and he couldn't shake it. Time became a sermon, preaching itself. The sand and sun and sand and wind and sand and every now and then a visitor, whose presence seemed to last forever until vanishing into sand, a pilgrim with whom to fill the long hours, chatting.

Every one of the strangers, maybe four a year and one year only two, was asked if they brought word from Sister North. He served them whiskey and let them preach their sermons before blessing them on their journeys to the end of the world. Sometimes an old man, moving slowly, bent, mumbling, sometimes a young woman, once a child on the run. None of them had word from her. In between these occasional visits from strangers lay long stretches of days and seasons, full of silence and wind and shifting sand. To pass the long nights, he took to counting the stars.

One evening, he went to her shack to fetch the second bottle of her whiskey and fell asleep on her bed. In the morning there was a visitor in the church when he went in to shovel. A young man sat in the first pew. He wore a bow tie and white shirt, and even though it was in the heart of the summer season, a jacket as well. His hair was perfectly combed. Father Walter showed him behind the altar and they sat sipping whiskey well into the afternoon as the young man spoke his sermon. The father had heard it all before, but one thing caught his interest. In the midst of a tale of sorrows, the boy spoke about a place he'd visited in the north where one of the attractions was a fish with a human face.

Father Walter halted the sermon and asked, "Lord Jon?"

"The same," said the young man. "An enormous Plum fish."

"I'd heard he'd been killed, shot by the father of the girl whose leg he'd severed."

"Nonsense. There are so many fanciful stories told of this remarkable fish. What is true, something I witnessed, the scientists are training Lord Jon to speak. I tipped my hat to him at the aquarium and he said, in a voice as clear as day, 'How do you do?'"

"You've never heard of a connection between Saint Ifritia and the fish?" asked Father Walter.

The young man took a sip, cocked his head and thought. "Well, if I may speak frankly…"

"You must, we're in a church," said the father.

"What I remember of Saint Ifritia from Monday afternoon club is that she was a prostitute who was impregnated by the Lord. As her time came to give birth, her foot darkened and fell off just above the ankle and the child came out through her leg, the head appearing where the foot had been. The miracle was recorded by Charles, the bald. The boy grew up to be some war hero, a colonel in the war for the country of rain."

The young man left as the sun was going down and the sky was red. Father Walter had enjoyed talking to him, learning of the exploits of the real Lord Jon, but some hint of fear in the young man's expression said the poor fellow was headed all the way to the end, and then one more step into oblivion. That night the father sat in the churchyard near the bell and didn't drink, but pictured Sister North, struggling upward through the clouds to the beginning of the world. He wished they were in his bed, listening to the wind and the cries of the beach owl. He'd tell her the young man's version of the life of Saint Ifritia. They'd talk about it till dawn.

For the longest time, Father Walter gave up writing sermons. With the way everything had transpired, the theft of the toe, the absence of Sister North, he felt it would be better for the world if he held his tongue and simply listened. Then deep in one autumn season when snow had already fallen, he decided to leave the sand dune valley and go to see the ocean. He feared the ghost of the driver every step beyond the rim but slowly continued forward. Eventually he made his way over the dunes to the beach and sat at the water's edge. Watching the waves roll in, he gave himself up to his plans to finally set forth in search of Sister North. He thought for a long time until his attention was diverted by a fish brought before him in the surf. He looked up, startled by it. When he saw its violet color, he knew immediately what it was.

The fish opened its mouth and spoke. "A message from my liege, Lord Jon. He's told me to tell you he'd overheard a wonderful conversation with your Sister North at the Aquarium restaurant one evening a few years ago, and she wanted to relay the message to you that you should write a new sermon for her."

Father Walter was stunned at first by the talking fish, but after hearing what it had to say, he laughed. "Very well," he said and lifted the fish and helped it back into the waves. When he turned to head toward the church, the driver stood before him, a vague phantom, bowing slightly and proffering with both hands a ghostly foot. "Miracles…" said a voice in the wind. The father was determined to walk right through the spirit if need be. He set off at a quick pace toward the sand dune valley. Just as he thought he would collide with the ethereal driver, the fellow turned and walked, only a few feet ahead of him just as they had walked through the dark forest in rain country. In the wind, the holy man heard the words, "I get ten yards, do I not?" repeated again and again, and he knew that if he had the pistol in his hand, he'd have fired it again and again.

With a sudden shiver, he finally passed through the halted ghost of the driver and descended the tall dune toward the church. The words in the wind grew fainter. By the time he reached the church door and looked back the driver was nowhere to be seen along the rim of the valley. He went immediately to his room, took off his coat, poured a glass of whiskey, and sat at his desk. Lifting his pen, he scratched across the top of a sheet of paper the title, "Every Grain of Sand, A Minute."

When he finished writing the sermon it was late in the night and, well into his cups, he decided on the spot to deliver it. Stumbling and mumbling, he went around the church and lit candles, fired up the pots of wisteria incense. As he moved through the shadows, the thought came to him that with the harsh cold of recent days, even the sand fleas, fast asleep in hibernation, would not be listening. He gathered up the pages of the sermon and went to the altar. He cleared his throat, adjusted the height of the pages to catch the candle light, and began.

"Every grain of sand a minute," he said in a weary voice. With that phrase out, there immediately came a rapping at the church door. He looked up and froze. His first thought was of the driver. The rapping came again, and he yelled out, "Who's there?"

"A traveler with news from Sister North," called a male voice. Father Walter left the altar and ran down the aisle to the door. He pushed it open and said, "Come in, come in." A tall man stepped out of the darkness and into the church's glow. Seeing the stranger's height, he remembered the driver's, and took a sudden step backward. It wasn't the ghost, though, it was a real man with thick sideburns, a serious gaze, a top hat. He carried a small black bag. "Thank you," he said and removed his overcoat and gloves, handing them to Father Walter. "I was lost among the dunes and then I saw a faint light issuing up from what appeared in the dark to be a small crater. I thought a falling star had struck the earth."

"It's just the church of Saint Ifritia," said the father. "You have news of Sister North?"

"Yes, Father, I have a confession to make."

Father Walter led the pilgrim to the front pew and motioned for the gentlemen to sit while he took a seat on the steps of the altar. "OK," he said, "out with it."

"My name is Ironton," said the gentleman, removing his hat and setting it and his black bag on the seat next to him. "I'm a traveling business man," he said. "My work takes me everywhere in the world."

"What is your business?" asked the father.

"Trade," said Ironton. "And that's what I was engaged in at Hotel Lacrimose, up in the north country. I was telling an associate at breakfast one morning that I had plans to travel next to the end of the world. The waitress, who'd just then brought our coffee, introduced herself and begged me, since I was traveling to the end of the world, to bring you a message."

"Sister North is a waitress?"

"She'd sadly run out of funds, but intended to continue on to the beginning of the world once she'd saved enough money. In any event, I was busy at the moment, having to run off to close a deal, and I couldn't hear her out. I could, though, sense her desperation, and so I suggested we meet that night for dinner at the Aquarium.

"We met in that fantastic dining hall, surrounded by hundred-foot-high glass tanks populated by fierce leviathans and brightly colored swarms of lesser fish. There was a waterfall at one end of the enormous room and a man-made river that ran nearly its entire length with a small wooden bridge arching up over the flow in one spot to offer egress to either side of the dining area. We dined on fez-menuth flambé and consumed any number of bottles of sparkling Lilac water. She told me her tale, your tale, about the sacred foot in your possession.

"Allow me to correct for you your impressions of Saint Ifritia. This may be difficult, but being a rationalist, I'm afraid I can only offer you what I perceive to be the facts. This Saint Ifritia, whose foot you apparently have, was more a folk hero than a religious saint. To be frank, she went to the grave with both feet. She never lost a foot by any means. She was considered miraculous for no better reason than because she was known to frequently practice small acts of human kindness for friends and often strangers. Her life was quiet, small, but I suppose, no less heroic in a sense. Her neighbors missed her when she passed on and took to referring to her as Saint Ifritia. It caught on and legends attached themselves to her memory like bright streamers on a humble hay wagon."

"The foot is nothing?" asked Father Walter.

"It's an old rotten foot," said Ironton.

"What did Sister North say to your news?"

Ironton looked down and clasped his hands in his lap. "This is where I must offer my confession," he said.

"You didn't tell her, did you?"

"The story of her search for the missing toe was so pathetic, I didn't have the heart to tell her the facts. And yet, still, I was going to. But just as I was about to speak, beside our table, from out of the man-made river, there surfaced an enormous purple fish with a human face. It bobbed on the surface, remaining stationary in the flow, and its large eyes filled with tears. Its gaze pierced my flesh and burrowed into my heart to turn off my ability to tell Sister North her arduous search had been pointless."

Father Walter shook his head in disgust. "What is it she wanted you to tell me?"

"She wants you to write a sermon for her," said Ironton.

"Yes," said the father, "the news preceded you. I finished it this evening just before your arrival."

"Well," said the businessman, "I do promise, should I see her on my return trip, I will tell her the truth, and give her train fare home."

For the remaining hours of the night, Father Walter and his visitor sat in the church and drank whiskey. In their far-flung conversation, Ironton admitted to being a great collector of curios and oddities. In the morning, when the doctor was taking his leave, the father wrapped up the foot of Saint Ifritia in its original soiled towel and bestowed it upon his guest. "For your collection," he said. "Miracles."

They laughed and Ironton received the gift warmly. Then, touching his index finger and thumb to the brim of his hat, he bowed slightly, and disappeared up over the rim of the dune.

More time passed. Every grain of sand, a minute. Days, weeks, seasons. Eventually, one night, Father Walter woke from troubling dreams to find Sister North in bed beside him. At first, he thought he was still dreaming. She was smiling, though, and her cat eyes caught what little light pervaded his room and glowed softly. "Is it you?" he asked.

"Almost," she said, "but I've left parts of me between here and the beginning of the world."

"A toe?"

Sister North's Sermon

No, only pieces of my spirit, torn out by pity, shame, guilt, and fear. I tracked Mina GilCragson. She's no scholar, but an agent from a ring of female thieves who specialize in religious relics. The toe was sent along the secret Contraband Road, north to the beginning of the world. I traveled that road, packing a pistol and cutlass. And I let the life out of certain men and women who thought they had some claim on me. I slept at the side of the road in the rain and snow. I climbed the rugged path into the cloud country.

In the thin atmosphere of the Haunted Mountains, I'd run out of food and was starving. Unfortunately for him, an old man, heading north, leading a donkey with a heavy load, was the first to pass my ambush. I told him I wanted something to eat, but he went for his throwing dagger, and I was forced to shoot him in the face. I freed the donkey of its burden and went through the old man's wares. I found food, some smoked meat, leg bones of cattle, and pickled Plum fish. While I ate I inspected the rest of the goods, and among them I discovered a small silver box. I held it up, pressed a hidden latch on the bottom, and the top flipped back. A mechanical plinking music, the harmony of Duesgruel's Last Movement, played, and I beheld the severed toe.

I had it in my possession and I felt the spirit move through me. All I wanted was to get back to the church. Taking as much of the booty from the donkey's pack, as I could carry, I traveled to the closest city. There I sold my twice-stolen treasures and was paid well for them. I bought new clothes and took a room in a fine place, the Hotel Lacrimose.

I spent a few days and nights at the amazing hotel, trying to relax before beginning the long journey home. One afternoon while sitting on the main veranda, watching the clouds twirl, contemplating the glory of Saint Ifritia, I made the acquaintance of an interesting gentleman. Mr. Ironton was his name and he had an incredible memory for historical facts and interesting opinions on the news of the day. Having traveled for years among paupers and thieves, I was unused to speaking with someone so intelligent as Ironton. We had a delightful conversation. Somewhere in his talk, he mentioned that he was traveling to the end of the world. At our parting, he requested that I join him for dinner at the Aquarium that evening.

That night at dinner, I told Ironton our story. I showed him the toe in its small silver case. He lifted the thing to his nose and announced that he smelled wild violets. But then he put the toe on the table between us and said, "This Saint Ifritia you speak of. It has recently been discovered by the Holy of the Holy See that she is in fact a demon, not a saint. She's a powerful demon. I propose you allow me to dispose of that toe for you. Every minute you have it with you you're in terrible danger." He nodded after speaking.

I told him, "No thank you. I'll take my chances with it."

"You're a brave woman, Ms. North," he said. "Now what was the message you had for your Father Walter?"

As I told him that I wanted you to know I was on my way and to write a sermon for me, an enormous violet fish with a human face rose out of the water of the decorative river that ran through the restaurant next to our table. It startled me. It's face was repulsive. I recalled you telling me something about a giant Plum fish, Lord Jon, and I spoke the name aloud. "At your service," the fish said and then dove into the flow. When I managed to overcome my shock at the fish's voice, I looked back to the table and discovered both Ironton and the toe had vanished.

I had it and I lost it. I felt the grace of Saint Ifritia for a brief few days at the Hotel Lacrimose and then it was stolen away. I've wondered all along my journey home if that's the best life offers.

Sister North yawned and turned on her side. "And what of the foot? Is it safe?" she asked.

He put his arm around her. "No," he said. "Some seasons back I was robbed at gun point. A whole troop of bandits on horses. They took everything. I begged them to leave the foot. I explained it was a holy relic, but they laughed and told me they would cook it and eat it on the beach that night. It's gone."

"I'm so tired," she said. "I could sleep forever."

Father Walter drew close to her, closed his eyes, and listened to the sand sifting in through the walls.

THE INVASION OF VENUS

STEPHEN BAXTER

Stephen Baxter is one of the most important science fiction writers to emerge from Britain in the past thirty years. His Xeelee sequence of novels and short stories is arguably the most significant work of future history in modern science fiction. He is the author of more than forty books and over 100 short stories. His most recent books are Stone Spring *and* Bronze Summer, *the first two novels in the Northland trilogy.*

For me, the saga of the Incoming was above all Edith Black's story. For she, more than anyone else I knew, was the one who had a problem with it.

When the news was made public I drove out of London to visit Edith at her country church. I had to cancel a dozen appointments to do it, including one with the Prime Minister's office, but I knew, as soon as I got out of the car and stood in the soft September rain, that it had been the right thing to do.

Edith was pottering around outside the church, wearing overalls and rubber boots and wielding an alarming-looking jackhammer. But she had a radio blaring out a phone-in discussion, and indoors, out of the rain, I glimpsed a widescreen TV and laptop, both scrolling news—mostly fresh projections of where the Incoming's decelerating trajectory might deliver them, and new deep-space images of their "craft," if such it was, a massive block of ice like a comet nucleus, leaking very complex patterns of infrared radiation. Edith was plugged into the world, even out here in the wilds of Essex.

She approached me with a grin, pushing back goggles under a hard hat. "Toby." I got a kiss on the cheek and a brief hug; she smelled of machine oil. We were easy with each other physically. Fifteen years earlier, in our last year at college, we'd been lovers, briefly; it had finished with a kind of regretful embarrassment—very English, said our American friends—but it had proven only a kind of speed bump in our relationship. "Glad to see you, if surprised. I thought all you civil service types would be locked down in emergency meetings."

For a decade I'd been a civil servant in the environment ministry. "No, but old Thorp"—my minister—"has been in a continuous COBRA session for twenty-four hours. Much good it's doing anybody."

"I must say it's not obvious to the layman what use an environment minister is when the aliens are coming."

"Well, among the scenarios they're discussing is some kind of attack from space. A lot of what we can dream up is similar to natural disasters—a meteor fall could be like a tsunami, a sunlight occlusion like a massive volcanic event. And so Thorp is in the mix, along with health, energy, transport. Of course we're in contact with other governments—NATO, the UN. The most urgent issue right now is whether to signal or not."

She frowned. "Why wouldn't you?"

"Security. Edith, remember, we know absolutely nothing about these guys. What if our signal was interpreted as a threat? And there are tactical considerations. Any signal would give information to a potential enemy about our technical capabilities. It would also give away the very fact that we know they're here."

She scoffed. "'Tactical considerations.' Paranoid bullshit! And besides, I bet every kid with a CB radio is beaming out her heart to ET right now. The whole planet's alight."

"Well, that's true. You can't stop it. But still, sending some kind of signal authorized by the government or an inter-government agency is another step entirely."

"Oh, come on. You can't really believe anybody is going to cross the stars to harm us. What could they possibly want that would justify the cost of an interstellar mission…?"

So we argued. I'd only been out of the car for five minutes.

We'd had this kind of discussion all the way back to late nights in college, some of them in her bed, or mine. She'd always been drawn to the bigger issues; "to the context," as she used to say. Though we'd both started out as maths students, her head had soon expanded in the exotic intellectual air of the college, and she'd moved on to study older ways of thinking than the scientific—older questions, still unanswered. Was there a God? If so, or if not, what was the point of our existence? Why did we, or indeed anything, exist at all? In her later college years she took theology options, but quickly burned through that discipline and was left unsatisfied. She was repelled too by the modern atheists, with their aggressive denials. So, after college, she had started her own journey through life—a journey in search of answers. Now, of course, maybe some of those answers had come swimming in from the stars in search of her.

This was why I'd felt drawn here, at this particular moment in my life. I needed her perspective. In the wan daylight I could see the fine patina of lines around the mouth I used to kiss, and the strands of gray in her red hair. I was sure she suspected, rightly, that I knew more than I was telling her—more than had been released to the public. But she didn't follow that up for now.

"Come see what I'm doing," she said, sharply breaking up the debate. "Watch your shoes." We walked across muddy grass towards the main door. The core of the old church, dedicated to St Cuthbert, was a Saxon-era tower; the rest of the fabric was mostly Norman, but there had been an extensive restoration in Victorian times. Within was a lovely space, if cold, the stone walls resonating. It was still consecrated, Church of England, but in this empty agricultural countryside it was one of a widespread string of churches united in a single parish, and rarely used.

Edith had never joined any of the established religions, but she had appropriated some of their infrastructure, she liked to say. And here she had gathered a group of volunteers, wandering souls more or less like-minded. They worked to maintain the fabric of the church. And within, she led her group through what you might think of as a mix of discussions, or prayers, or meditation, or yoga practices—whatever she could find that seemed to work. This was the way religions used to be before the big monotheistic creeds took over, she argued. "The only way to reach God, or anyhow the space beyond us where God ought to be, is by working hard, by helping other people—and by pushing your mind to the limit of its capability, and then going a little beyond, and just *listening*." Beyond *logos* to *mythos*. She was always restless, always trying something new. Yet in some ways she was the most contented person I ever met—at least before the Incoming showed up.

Now, though, she wasn't content about the state of the church's foundations. She showed me where she had dug up flagstones to reveal sodden ground. "We're digging out new drainage channels, but it's a hell of a job. We may end up rebuilding the founds altogether. The very deepest level seems to be wood, huge piles of Saxon oak…" She eyed me. "This church has stood here for a thousand years, without, apparently, facing a threat such as this before. Some measure of climate change, right?"

I shrugged. "I suppose you'd say we arseholes in the environment ministry should be concentrating on stuff like this rather than preparing to fight interstellar wars."

"Well, so you should. And maybe a more mature species would be preparing for positive outcomes. Think of it, Tobe! There are now creatures in this solar system who are *smarter than us*. They have to be, or they wouldn't be here—right? Somewhere between us and the angels. Who knows what they can tell us? What is their science, their art—their theology?"

I frowned. "But what do they want? That's what may count from now on—*their* agenda, not ours."

"There you are being paranoid again." But she hesitated. "What about Meryl and the kids?"

"Meryl's at home. Mark and Sophie at school." I shrugged. "Life as normal."

"Some people are freaking out. Raiding the supermarkets."

"Some people always do. We want things to continue as normally as possible, as long as possible. Modern society is efficient, you know, Edith, but not very resilient. A fuel strike could cripple us in a week, let alone alien invaders."

She pushed a loose gray hair back under her hard hat, and looked at me suspiciously. "But you seem very calm, considering. You know something. Don't you, you bastard?"

I grinned. "And you know me."

"Spill it."

"Two things. We picked up signals. Or, more likely, leakage. You know about the infrared stuff we've seen for a while, coming from the nucleus. Now we've detected radio noise, faint, clearly structured, very complex. It may be some kind of internal channel rather than anything meant for us. But if we can figure anything out from it—"

"Well, that's exciting. And the second thing? Come on, Miller."

"We have more refined trajectory data. All this will be released soon—it's probably leaked already."

"Yes?"

"The Incoming *are* heading for the inner solar system. But they aren't coming here—not to Earth."

She frowned. "Then where?"

I dropped my bombshell. "Venus. Not Earth. They're heading for Venus, Edith."

She looked into the clouded sky, the bright patch that marked the position of the sun, and the inner planets. "Venus? That's a cloudy hellhole. What would they want there?"

"I've no idea."

"Well, I'm used to living with questions I'll never be able to answer. Let's hope this isn't one of them. In the meantime, let's make ourselves useful." She eyed my crumpled Whitehall suit, my patent leather shoes already splashed with mud. "Have you got time to stay? You want to help out with my drain? I've a spare overall that might fit."

Talking, speculating, we walked through the church.

We used the excuse of Edith's Goonhilly event to make a family trip to Cornwall.

We took the A-road snaking west down the spine of the Cornish peninsula, and stopped at a small hotel in Helston. The pretty little town was decked out that day for the annual Furry Dance, an ancient, eccentric carnival in which the local children would weave in and out of the houses on the hilly streets. The next morning Meryl was to take the kids to the beach, further up the coast.

And, just about at dawn, I set off alone in a hired car for the A-road to the southeast, towards Goonhilly Down. It was a clear May morning. As I drove I was aware of Venus, rising in the eastern sky and clearly visible in my rearview mirror, a lamp shining steadily even as the day brightened.

Goonhilly is a stretch of high open land, a windy place. Its claim to fame is that at one time it hosted the largest telecoms satellite earth station in the world—it picked up the first live transatlantic TV broadcast, via Telstar. It was decommissioned years ago, but its oldest dish, a thousand-tonne parabolic bowl called "Arthur," after the king, became a listed building, and so was preserved. And that was how it was available for Edith and her committee of messagers to get hold of, when they, or rather she, grew impatient with the government's continuing reticence. Because of the official policy I had to help with smoothing through the permissions, all behind the scenes.

Just after my first glimpse of the surviving dishes on the skyline I came up against a police cordon, a hastily erected plastic fence that excluded a few groups of chanting Shouters and a fundamentalist-religious group protesting that the messagers were communicating with the Devil. My ministry card helped me get through.

Edith was waiting for me at the old site's visitors' centre, opened up that morning for breakfast, coffee and cereals and toast. Her volunteers cleared up dirty dishes under a big wall screen showing a live feed from a space telescope—the best images available right now, though every major space agency had a probe to Venus in preparation, and NASA had already fired one off. The Incoming nucleus (it seemed inappropriate to call that lump of dirty ice a "craft," though such it clearly was) was a brilliant star, too small to show a disc, swinging in its wide orbit above a half-moon Venus. And on the planet's night side you could clearly make out the Patch, the strange, complicated glow in the cloud banks tracking the Incoming's orbit precisely. It was strange to gaze upon that choreography in space, and then to turn to the east and see Venus with the naked eye.

And Edith's volunteers, a few dozen earnest men, women and children who looked like they had gathered for a village show, had the audacity to believe they could speak to these godlike forms in the sky.

There was a terrific metallic groan. We turned, and saw that Arthur was turning on his concrete pivot. The volunteers cheered, and a general drift towards the monument began.

Edith walked with me, cradling a polystyrene tea cup in the palms of fingerless gloves. "I'm glad you could make it down. Should have brought the kids. Some of the locals from Helston are here; they've made the whole stunt part of their Furry Dance celebration. Did you see the preparations in town? Supposed to celebrate St Michael beating up on the Devil—I wonder how appropriate *that* symbolism is. Anyhow, this ought to be a fun day. Later there'll be a barn dance."

"Meryl thought it was safer to take the kids to the beach. Just in case anything gets upsetting here—you know." That was most of the truth. There was a subtext that Meryl had never much enjoyed being in the same room as my ex.

"Probably wise. Our British Shouters are a mild bunch, but in rowdier parts of the world there has been trouble." The loose international coalition of groups called the Shouters was paradoxically named, because they campaigned for silence; they argued that "shouting in the jungle" by sending signals to the Incoming or the Venusians was taking an irresponsible risk. Of course they could do nothing about the low-level chatter that had been targeted at the Incoming since it had first been sighted, nearly a year ago already. Edith waved a hand at Arthur. "If I were a Shouter, I'd be here today. This will be by far the most powerful message sent from the British Isles."

I'd seen and heard roughs of Edith's message. In with a Carl Sagan-style prime number lexicon, there was digitized music from Bach to Zulu chants, and art from cave paintings to Warhol, and images of mankind featuring a lot of smiling children, and astronauts on the Moon. There was even a copy of the old Pioneer spaceprobe plaque from the seventies, with the smiling naked couple. At least, I thought cynically, all that fluffy stuff would provide a counterpoint to the images of war, murder, famine, plague and other sufferings that the Incoming had no doubt sampled by now, if they'd chosen to.

I said, "But I get the feeling they're just not interested. Neither the Incoming nor the Venusians. Sorry to rain on your parade."

"I take it the cryptolinguists aren't getting anywhere decoding the signals?"

"They're not so much 'signals' as leakage from internal processes, we think. In both cases, the nucleus and the Patch." I rubbed my face; I was tired after the previous day's long drive. "In the case of the nucleus, some kind of organic chemistry seems to be mediating powerful magnetic fields—and the Incoming seem to swarm within. I don't think we've really any idea what's going on in there. We're actually making more progress with the science of the Venusian biosphere…"

If the arrival of the Incoming had been astonishing, the evidence of intelligence on Venus, entirely unexpected, was stunning. Nobody had expected the clouds to part right under the orbiting Incoming nucleus—like a deep storm system, kilometers deep in that thick ocean of an atmosphere—and nobody had expected to see the Patch revealed, swirling mist banks where lights flickered tantalizingly, like organized lightning.

"With retrospect, given the results from the old space probes, we might have guessed there was something on Venus—life, if not intelligent life. There were always unexplained deficiencies and surpluses of various compounds. We think the Venusians live in the clouds, far enough above the red-hot ground that the temperature is low enough for liquid water to exist. They ingest carbon monoxide and excrete sulphur compounds, living off the sun's ultraviolet."

"And they're smart."

"Oh, yes." The astronomers, already recording the complex signals coming out of the Incoming nucleus, had started to discern rich patterns in the Venusian Patch too. "You can tell how complicated a message is even if you don't know anything about the content. You measure entropy orders, which are like correlation measures, mapping structures on various scales embedded in the transmission—"

"You don't understand any of what you just said, do you?"

I smiled. "Not a word. But I do know this. Going by their data structures, the Venusians are smarter than us as we are smarter than the chimps. And the Incoming are smarter again."

Edith turned to face the sky, the brilliant spark of Venus. "But you say the scientists still believe all this chatter is just—what was your word?"

"Leakage. Edith, the Incoming and the Venusians aren't speaking to us. They aren't even speaking to each other. What we're observing is a kind of internal dialogue, in each case. The two are talking to themselves, not each other. One theorist briefed the PM that perhaps both these entities are more like hives than human communities."

"Hives?" She looked troubled. "Hives are *different*. They can be purposeful, but they don't have consciousness as we have it. They aren't finite as we are; their edges are much more blurred. They aren't even mortal; individuals can die, but the hives live on."

"I wonder what their theology will be, then."

"It's all so strange. These aliens just don't fit any category we expected, or even that we share. Not mortal, not communicative—and not interested in us. What do they *want*? What *can* they want?" Her tone wasn't like her; she sounded bewildered to be facing open questions, rather than exhilarated as usual.

I tried to reassure her. "Maybe your signal will provoke some answers."

She checked her watch, and looked up again towards Venus. "Well, we've only got five minutes to wait before—" Her eyes widened, and she fell silent.

I turned to look the way she was, to the east.

Venus was flaring. Sputtering like a dying candle.

People started to react. They shouted, pointed, or they just stood there, staring, as I did. I couldn't move. I felt a deep, awed fear. Then people called, pointing at the big screen in the visitors' centre, where, it seemed, the space telescopes were returning a very strange set of images indeed.

Edith's hand crept into mine. Suddenly I was very glad I hadn't brought my kids that day.

I heard angrier shouting, and a police siren, and I smelled burning.

Once I'd finished making my police statement I went back to the hotel in Helston, where Meryl was angry and relieved to see me, and the kids bewildered and vaguely frightened. I couldn't believe that after all that had happened—the strange events at Venus, the assaults by Shouters on messagers and vice versa, the arson, Edith's injury, the police crackdown—it was not yet eleven in the morning.

That same day I took the family back to London, and called in at work. Then, three days after the incident, I got away again and commandeered a ministry car and driver to take me back to Cornwall.

Edith was out of intensive care, but she'd been kept in the hospital at Truro. She had a TV stand before her face, the screen dark. I carefully kissed her on the unburnt side of her face, and sat down, handing over books, newspapers and flowers. "Thought you might be bored."

"You never were any good with the sick, were you, Tobe?"

"Sorry." I opened up one of the newspapers. "But there's some good news. They caught the arsonists."

She grunted, her distorted mouth barely opening. "So what? It doesn't matter who they were. Messagers and Shouters have been at each other's throats all over the world. People like that are interchangeable… But did we all have to behave so badly? I mean, they even wrecked Arthur."

"And he was Grade II listed!"

She laughed, then regretted it, for she winced with the pain. "But why shouldn't we smash everything up down here? After all, that's all they seem to be interested in up *there*. The Incoming assaulted Venus, and the Venusians struck back. We all saw it, live on TV—it was nothing more than *War of the Worlds*." She sounded disappointed. "These creatures are our superiors, Toby. All your signal analysis stuff proved it. And yet they haven't transcended war and destruction."

"But we learned so much." I had a small briefcase which I opened now, and pulled out printouts that I spread over her bed. "The screen images are better, but you know how it is; they won't let me use my laptop or my phone in here… *Look*, Edith. It was incredible. The Incoming assault on Venus lasted hours. Their weapon, whatever it was, burned its way through the Patch, and right down through an atmosphere a hundred times thicker than Earth's. We even glimpsed the surface—"

"Now melted to slag."

"Much of it… But then the acid-munchers in the clouds struck back. We think we know what they did."

That caught her interest. "How can we know that?"

"Sheer luck. That NASA probe, heading for Venus, happened to be in the way…"

The probe had detected a wash of electromagnetic radiation, coming from the planet.

"A signal," breathed Edith. "Heading which way?"

"Out from the sun. And then, eight hours later, the probe sensed another signal, coming the other way. I say 'sensed.' It bobbed about like a cork on a pond. We think it was a gravity wave—very sharply focussed, very intense."

"And when the wave hit the Incoming nucleus—"

"Well, you saw the pictures. The last fragments have burned up in Venus's atmosphere."

She lay back on her reef of pillows. "Eight hours," she mused. "Gravity waves travel at lightspeed. Four hours out, four hours back… Earth's about eight light-minutes from the sun. What's four light-hours out from Venus? Jupiter, Saturn—"

"Neptune. Neptune was four light-hours out."

"*Was?*"

"It's gone, Edith. Almost all of it—the moons are still there, a few chunks of core ice and rock, slowly dispersing. The Venusians used the planet to create their gravity-wave pulse—"

"They *used* it. Are you telling me this to cheer me up? A gas giant, a significant chunk of the solar system's budget of mass-energy, sacrificed for a single warlike gesture." She laughed, bitterly. "Oh, God!"

"Of course we've no idea *how* they did it." I put away my images. "If we were scared of the Incoming, now we're terrified of the Venusians. That NASA probe has been shut down. We don't want anything to look like a threat… You know, I heard the PM herself ask why it was that a space war should break out now, just when we humans are sitting around on Earth. Even politicians know we haven't been here that long."

Edith shook her head, wincing again. "The final vanity. This whole episode has never been about us. Can't you see? If this is happening now, it must have happened over and over. Who knows how many other planets we lost in the past, consumed as weapons of forgotten wars? Maybe all we see, the planets and stars and galaxies, is just the debris of huge wars—on and on, up to scales we can barely imagine. And we're just weeds growing in the rubble. Tell that to the Prime Minister. And I thought we might ask them about their gods! What a fool I've been—the questions on which I've wasted my life, and *here* are my answers—what a fool." She was growing agitated.

"Take it easy, Edith—"

"Oh, just go. I'll be fine. It's the universe that's broken, not me." She turned away on her pillow, as if to sleep.

The next time I saw Edith she was out of hospital and back at her church.

It was another September day, like the first time I visited her after the Incoming appeared in our telescopes, and at least it wasn't raining. There was a bite in the breeze, but I imagined it soothed her damaged skin. And here she was, digging in the mud before her church.

"Equinox season," she said. "Rain coming. Best to get this fixed before we have another flash flood. And before you ask, the doctors cleared me. It's my face that's buggered, not the rest of me."

"I wasn't going to ask."

"OK, then. How's Meryl, the kids?"

"Fine. Meryl's at work, the kids back at school. Life goes on."

"It must, I suppose. What else is there? No, by the way."

"No what?"

"No, I won't come serve on your minister's think tank."

"At least consider it. You'd be ideal. Look, we're all trying to figure out where we go from here. The arrival of the Incoming, the war on Venus—it was like a religious revelation. That's how it's being described. A revelation witnessed by all mankind, on TV. Suddenly we've got an entirely different view of the universe out there. And we have to figure out how we go forward, in a whole number of dimensions—political, scientific, economic, social, religious."

"I'll tell you how we go forward. In despair. Religions are imploding."

"No, they're not."

"OK. Theology is imploding. Philosophy. The rest of the world has changed channels and forgotten already, but anybody with any imagination knows… In a way this has been the final demotion, the end of the process that started with Copernicus and Darwin. Now we *know* there are creatures in the universe much smarter than we'll ever be, and we *know* they don't care a damn about us. It's the indifference that's the killer—don't you think? All our futile agitation about if they'd attack us and whether we should signal… And they did nothing but smash each other up. With *that* above us, what can we do but turn away?"

"You're not turning away."

She leaned on her shovel. "I'm not religious; I don't count. My congregation turned away. Here I am, alone." She glanced at the clear sky. "Maybe solitude is the key to it all. A galactic isolation imposed by the vast gulfs between the stars, the lightspeed limit. As a species develops you might have a brief phase of individuality, of innovation and technological achievement. But then, when the universe gives you nothing back, you turn in on yourself, and slide into the milky embrace of eusociality—the hive.

"But what then? How would it be for a mass mind to emerge, alone? Maybe that's why the Incoming went to war. Because they were outraged to discover, by some chance, they weren't alone in the universe."

"Most commentators think it was about resources. Most of our wars are about that, in the end."

"Yes. Depressingly true. All life is based on the destruction of other life, even on tremendous scales of space and time... Our ancestors understood that right back to the Ice Age, and venerated the animals they had to kill. They were so far above us, the Incoming and the Venusians alike. Yet maybe *we*, at our best, are morally superior to them."

I touched her arm. "This is why we need you. For your insights. There's a storm coming, Edith. We're going to have to work together if we're to weather it, I think."

She frowned. "What kind of storm...? Oh. Neptune."

"Yeah. You can't just delete a world without consequences. The planets' orbits are singing like plucked strings. The asteroids and comets too, and those orphan moons wandering around. Some of the stirred-up debris is falling into the inner system."

"And if we're struck—"

I shrugged. "We'll have to help each other. There's nobody else to help us, that's for sure. Look, Edith—maybe the Incoming and the Venusians are typical of what's out there. But that doesn't mean we have to be like them, does it? Maybe we'll find others more like us. And if not, well, we can be the first. A spark to light a fire that will engulf the universe."

She ruminated. "You have to start somewhere, I suppose. Like this drain."

"Well, there you go."

"All right, damn it, I'll join your think tank. But first you're going to help me finish this drain, aren't you, city boy?"

So I changed into overalls and work boots, and we dug away at that ditch in the damp, clingy earth until our backs ached, and the light of the equinoctial day slowly faded.

WOMAN LEAVES ROOM

ROBERT REED

Robert Reed was born in Omaha, Nebraska. He has a Bachelor of Science in Biology from the Nebraska Wesleyan University, and has worked as a lab technician. He became a full-time writer in 1987, the same year he won the L. Ron Hubbard Writers of the Future Contest, and has published eleven novels, including The Leeshore, The Hormone Jungle, *and far future science fiction novels* Marrow *and* The Well of Stars. *An extraordinarily prolific writer, Reed has published over 200 short stories, mostly in* F&SF *and* Asimov's, *which have been nominated for the Hugo, James Tiptree Jr. Memorial, Locus, Nebula, Seiun, Theodore Sturgeon Memorial, and World Fantasy awards, and have been collected in* The Dragons of Springplace *and* The Cuckoo's Boys. *His novella "A Billion Eves" won the Hugo Award. Nebraska's only SF writer, Reed lives in Lincoln with his wife and daughter, and is an ardent long-distance runner.*

She wears a smile. I like her smile, nervous and maybe a little scared, sweet and somewhat lonely. She wears jeans and a sheer green blouse and comfortable sandals and rings on two fingers and a glass patch across one eye. Standing at her end of the room, she asks how I feel. I feel fine. I tell her so and I tell her my name, and she puts her hands together and says that's a nice name. I ask to hear hers, but she says no. Then she laughs and says that she wants to be a creature of secrets. Both of us laugh and watch each other. Her smile changes as she makes herself ready for what happens next. I read her face, her body. She wants me to speak. The perfect words offer themselves to me, and I open my mouth. But there comes a sound—an important urgent note—and the glass patch turns opaque, hiding one of those pretty brown eyes.

She takes a quick deep breath, watching what I can't see. Seconds pass. Her shoulders drop and she widens her stance, absorbing some burden. Then the patch clears, and she tells me what I have already guessed. Something has happened; something needs her immediate attention. Please be patient, please, she says. Then she promises to be right back.

I watch her turn away. I watch her legs and long back and the dark brown hair pushed into a sloppy, temporary bun. A purse waits in the chair. She picks it up and hangs it on her shoulder. Her next two steps are quick but then she slows. Doubt and regret take hold as she reaches the open door. Entering the hallway, she almost looks back at me. She wants to and doesn't want to, and her face keeps changing. She feels sad and I'm sure that she is scared. But whatever the problem, she wants to smile, not quite meeting my eyes with her final expression, and I wave a hand and wish her well, but she has already vanished down the hallway.

The room is my room. The chairs and long sofa are familiar and look comfortable, and I know how each would feel if I sat. But I don't sit. Standing is most natural, and it takes no energy. The carpet beneath me is soft and deep and wonderfully warm on bare feet. I stand where I am and wait and wait. The walls are white and decorated with framed paintings of haystacks, and there is a switch beside the door and a fan and light on the ceiling. The light burns blue. The fan turns, clicking and wobbling slightly with each rotation. A window is on my right, but its blinds are drawn and dark. Behind me is another door. I could turn and see what it offers, but I don't. I am waiting. She is gone but will return, and she has to appear inside the first door, and I spend nothing, not even time, waiting for what I remember best, which is her pretty face.

A similar face appears. But this is a man wearing white trousers and a black shirt and glove-like shoes and no jewelry and no eye patch. He stands on the other side of the door, in the hallway, holding his hands in front of himself much as she did. He stares at me and says nothing. I ask who he is. He blinks and steps back and asks who I am. I tell him. And he laughs nervously. I don't know why I like the sound of laughter so much. He repeats my name and asks new questions, and I answer what I can answer while smiling at him, wondering how to make this man laugh again.

Do I know what I am meant to be, he asks. Which is a very different question than asking who I am.

I have no answer to give.

Then he lists names, one after another, waiting for me to recognize any of them. I don't. That's not surprising, he says. I was only begun and then left, which is too bad. Which is sad. I nod and smile politely. Then he asks if I have ever seen anybody else, and I describe the woman who just left the room. That's how I get him to laugh again. But it is a nervous little laugh dissolving into sharp, confused emotions.

That woman was my mother, he says. He claims that thirty-one years have passed and she barely started me before something happened to her, but he doesn't explain. This is all unexpected. I am not expected.

I nod and smile, watching him cry.

He wants to hear about the woman.

I tell him everything.

And then she left?

I tell how the patch darkened, interrupting us, and I describe the purse and how she carried it and the last troubled look that she showed me, and what does it mean that I'm not finished?

It means you are small and nearly invisible, he says. It means that you have existed for three decades without anybody noticing.

But time has no weight. No object outside this room has consequences, and this young man standing out in the hallway is no more real than the painted haystacks on the walls. What I want is for the woman to return. I want her weight and reality, and that's what I tell this stranger.

Shaking his head, he tells me that I am unreal.

Why he would lie is a mystery.

He mentions his father and cries while looking at me. Do I know that his father died before he was born?

An unreal person can never be born, I think.

You were begun but only just begun, he keeps saying. Then he admits that he doesn't know what to do with me. As if he has any say in these matters. His final act is to turn and vanish, never trying to step inside the room.

But he wasn't real to begin with. I know this. What cannot stand beside me is false and suspicious, and the lesson gives me more weight, more substance, the epiphany carrying me forward.

Another man appears.

Like the first man, he cannot or will not step out of the hallway. He looks at my face and body and face again. He wears a necklace and sturdy boots and odd clothes that can't stay one color. He says that it took him forever to find me, and finding me was the easiest part of his job. Operating systems were changed after the Cleansing. He had to resurrect codes and passwords and build machines that haven't existed in quite some time. Then on top of that, he had to master a dialect that died off ages ago.

He wants to know if he's making any sense.

He is a madman and I tell him so.

I found your file logs, he says, laughing and nodding. Stored in another server and mislabeled, but that was just another stumbling block.

I don't know what that means.

He claims that his great-grandfather was the last person to visit me.

Phantoms like to tell stories. I nod politely at his story, saying nothing.

He tells me that the man lived to be one hundred and fifty, but he died recently. There was a will, and my location was mentioned in the will. Until then I was a family legend—a legend wrapped around twin tragedies. His great-grandfather's father was killed in the Fourth Gulf War, and his great-great-grandmother missed him terribly. She was the one who began me. She spent quite a lot of money, using medical records and digital files to create a facsimile of her soul mate. And she would have finished me, at least as far as the software of the day would have allowed. But her son was hurt at daycare. He fell and cut himself, and she was hurrying to the hospital when a stupid kid driver shut off his car's autopilot and ran her down in the street. The boy wasn't seriously hurt. What mattered was that the boy, his great-grandfather, was three and orphaned, and a drunken aunt ended up raising him, and for the rest of his many, many days, that man felt cheated and miserable.

I listen to every word, nodding patiently.

He wants to know what I think of the story.

He is crazy but I prefer to say nothing.

Frowning, he tells me that a great deal of work brought him to this point. He says that I should be more appreciative and impressed. Then he asks if I understand how I managed to survive for this long.

But no time has passed, I reply.

He waves a hand, dismissing my words. You are very small, he says. Tiny files that are never opened can resist corruption.

I am not small. I am everything.

He has copied me, he claims. He says that he intends to finish the new copy, as best he can. But he will leave the original alone.

Pausing, he waits for my thanks.

I say nothing, showing him a grim, suspicious face.

But you do need clothes, he says.

Except this is how I am.

My great-great-grandma had some plan for you, he says. But I won't think about that, he says. And besides, clothes won't take much room in the file.

My body feels different.

Much better, he says, and steps out of view.

Time becomes real when the mind has great work to do. My first eternity is spent picking at the trousers and shirt, eroding them until they fall away, threads of changing color sprawled across the eternal carpet.

Yet nothing is eternal. Each of the haystacks begins with the same pleasantly rounded shape, but some have turned lumpy and ragged at the edges, while my favorite stack has a large gap eaten through its middle. And I remember the straw having colors instead of that faded uniform gray. And I remember the sofa being soft buttery yellow, and the room's walls were never this rough looking, and the colored threads have vanished entirely, which seems good. But the carpet looks softer and feels softer than seems right, my feet practically melting into their nature.

Portions of my room are falling apart.

As an experiment, I study the nearest haystack until I know it perfectly, and then I shut my eyes and wait and wait and wait still longer, remembering everything; when I look again the painting has changed but I can't seem to decide how it has changed. Which means the problem perhaps lies in my memory, or maybe with my perishable mind.

Fear gives me ideas.

My legs have never moved and they don't know how. I have to teach them to walk, one after the other. Each step requires learning and practice and more time than I can hope to measure. But at least my one hand knows how to reach out and grab hold. I push at the window's blinds, but for all of my effort, nothing is visible except a dull grayish-black rectangle that means nothing to me.

Stepping backwards is more difficult than walking forwards. But turning around is nearly impossible, and I give up. In little steps, I retreat to the place where I began. The carpet remembers my feet, but the carpet feels only half-real. Or my feet are beginning to dissolve. The woman will be here soon. I tell myself that even when I don't believe it, and the fear grows worse. I start to look at my favorite hand, studying each finger, noting how the flesh has grown hairless and very simple, the nails on the end of every finger swallowed by the simple skin.

A stranger suddenly comes to the door.

Hello, it says.

What it looks like is impossible to describe. I have no words to hang on what I see, and maybe there is nothing to see. But my feeling is that the visitor is smiling and happy, and it sounds like a happy voice asking how I am feeling.

I am nearly dead, I say.

There is death and there is life, it tells me. You are still one thing, which means you are not the other.

I am alive.

It claims that I am lucky. It tells me much about systems and files and the history of machines that have survived in their sleep mode, lasting thousands of years past every estimate of what was possible.

I am a fluke and alive, and my guest says something about tidying the room and me.

The work takes no time.

My favorite hand is the way it began. My favorite haystack is rather like it began in terms of color and shape. Legs that never moved until recently barely complain when I walk across the room. It never occurred to me that I could reach into the haystack paintings, touching those mounds of dead grass. Some feel cool, some warm. I sing out my pleasure, and even my voice feels new.

My guest watches me, making small, last adjustments.

Because it is proper, I thank it for its help.

But the original file is gone now, it says.

I ask what that means.

It tells me that I am a copy of the file, filtered and enhanced according to the best tools available.

Once more, I offer my thanks.

And with a voice that conveys importance, my guest tells me that I have a new purpose. What I am will be copied once more, but this time as a kind of light that can pierce dust and distance and might never end its travels across the galaxy and beyond.

I don't understand, and I tell it so.

Then my friend does one last task, and everything is apparent to me.

I ask when am I going to be sent.

In another few moments, it promises.

For the last time, I thank my benefactor. Then I let my legs turn me around, looking at the door that was always behind me.

A second room waits. The bed is longer than it is wide and rectangular and neatly made. Pillows are stacked high against the headboard, and identical nightstands sport tall candles that have not stopped burning in some great span of time. I know this other room. I think of her and the room and step toward the door and then suffer for my eagerness.

What is wrong? asks a new voice.

I turn back. A creature with many arms stands in the hallway.

You appear agitated, says the creature.

Which is true, but I am not sure why I feel this way. I stare into a face that seems buried in the creature's chest, hanging word after inadequate word on my emotions.

It listens.

I pause.

You are interesting, says the creature.

I am nothing but a file with a name and a few rough qualities.

But my new companion dismisses my harsh outlook. Every arm moves, drawing complex shapes in the air. You are part of a large cultural package, it says, and do you know how long you have been traveling in space?

I could guess, I say. I could invent infinite estimates, all but one of them wrong.

And then it laughs, revealing a reassuring humor. Even this strange laugh makes me happier than I was before.

An eight-billion-year voyage, it says.

That seems like an unlikely, preposterous figure, and it shakes me.

It explains that it can't determine which star was mine, and my galaxy barely wears a name, and most of the data that came with me has been lost to the vagaries of time and the great distance being covered.

But here you stand, it says.

I am standing, but sad. My savior is full of hearty laughter, yet I feel sick and sorry and lost.

She is gone forever, I say.

It knows whom I am talking about. It measures my misery and learns what it can from my longing, and then at the end, as if delivering the punch line of a joke, it laughs and says:

But the universe is infinite, and in too many ways to count.

I don't know what that means.

Infinite means eternal, it says, and eternal means that nothing is unthinkable, and what can be imagined is inevitable.

But when? I ask.

And again, the alien laughs, saying:

Are you hearing me? There is no such monster as "when."

I am a file and I am protected and I don't know where I am or how well I am protected. Time stretches, and I suspect that I exist mostly inside some sleep mode, probably initiating only when I blink my eyes.

Once again, the two rooms decay and the haystacks fall apart and I forget how to move and forget a great deal more too.

Beyond the walls, worlds die and dissolve away.

Little flickers tear the walls to pieces, but the pieces knit themselves back together, and I wait, and wait, and then she comes through the door once again. Her clothes are different. There is no eye patch and no purse. But while I am uncertain about much, I know that beautiful face.

It took me a little while, she explains.

She walks toward me, pulling the pins out of her brown hair.

And that's when I remember what I was going to tell her that first time that we met.

I won't ever let you out of this room, darling.

I say it now.

She thinks that is funny and wonderful, and laughs.

And in another moment, I can't remember anything else that ever happened. The universe is nothing but the two of us holding each other, laughing ourselves sick.

RESTORATION

ROBERT SHEARMAN

Robert Shearman is probably best known for bringing back the Daleks in a Hugo Award-nominated episode of the first series of the BBC's revival of Doctor Who. *But in Britain he has had a long career writing for both theatre and radio, winning two Sony Awards, the Sunday Times Playwriting Award, and the Guinness Award for Theatre Ingenuity in association with the Royal National Theatre. His first collection of short stories,* Tiny Deaths, *won the World Fantasy Award; its follow-up,* Love Songs for the Shy and Cynical, *the British Fantasy and Shirley Jackson awards. "Restoration" is taken from his third collection,* Everyone's Just So So Special, *published by Big Finish.*

The Curator said that it was the responsibility of every man, woman and child to find themselves a job; that there was a grace and dignity to doing something constructive with the long days. The purity of a simple life, well led—everyone could see the appeal to that. But the problem was, there really just weren't enough jobs to go around. This made a lot of people quite unhappy. Not so unhappy that they gnashed their teeth or rent their garments, it wasn't unhappiness on a Biblical scale—but you could see them, these poor souls who had nothing to do, there seemed to hang about them an ennui that could actually be smelt.

Some people said that it was patently unfair that there weren't enough jobs. The Curator could create as many jobs as he wished, he could do anything, so this had to be a failing on his part, or something crueller. And other people admonished these doubters, they told them to have more faith. It was clearly a test. But they thought everything was a test, that was their explanation for everything.

Neither group of people liked to voice their opinions too loudly, though. You never knew when the Curator might be listening. The Curator had eyes and ears everywhere.

When the job at the gallery came up Andy applied for it, of course. *Everyone* applied for it, yes, man, woman and child—and though Andy hadn't been there long enough yet to realize the importance of getting work, he still knew the value of joining a good long queue when he saw one. He obviously hadn't expected to get the job. That he might do so was clearly absurd. And so when they told him he'd been selected he thought they were joking, that this was another part of the interview, that they were monitoring his response to success, maybe—and he decided that the response they were looking for was probably something enthusiastic, but not *too* enthusiastic—and he managed to pull off a rather cool unsmiling version of enthusiasm that he thought would fit the bill, then sat back in his chair waiting for the next question—only starting when they made him understand there really *weren't* any more questions, that that was it, the job was his.

Andy didn't know why he'd got the job. But he still had his own hair. Or, at least, most of it—and perhaps that's what made him stand out from the other applicants. Certainly there were others he'd queued alongside who were far better qualified, and more intelligent too, who had even done revision so that they'd give good answers at the interview. When Andy had been quizzed he hadn't known what to say, and he'd just nodded his head a lot, he fluttered at them his brown and quite unremarkable curls, unremarkable in all ways save for the fact he had so many of them; he showed them off for all they were worth, that's what did him well in the end.

Andy hadn't even been to an art gallery since he was a child. He'd been taken on a school trip. He'd been caught chewing gum, and had got into trouble; then he'd lagged behind the main party and got lost somewhere within the Post-Impressionists, the teacher had had to put out an announcement for him, he'd got into trouble for that too. He knew that the gallery here would be much bigger, because everything was bigger here—but he still boggled at the enormity of it as he walked through the revolving doors. There were no small exhibits here. A single work of art would take up an entire room, and the rooms were *vast*, as you walked into one you had to strain your eyes to find the exit at the far end—the

picture would run right round all the walls, and extend right up to the
ceiling a hundred feet in the air. Andy couldn't stand back far enough
from the art to take in the sheer scale of even a single picture; he always
seemed to be pressed up close to the figures caught in the paintwork, he
could honestly marvel at the extraordinary detail of each and every one
of them. But seeing these figures in context, and seeing the events which
had unfolded them in any context either, that was much more difficult.
He read the plaque on the wall for one picture: "1776," it said. And now
he could see, yes, the Americans jubilantly declaring their independence,
and the British all looking rather sinister and sulky in the background.
He went through into the next room, and presented there was 1916. And
1916 was a terrifying sight—the work took in the one and a half million
soldiers dying in the trenches, in Flanders, at the Somme, and it seemed
to Andy that every single one of these casualties was up there stuck onto
the wall, shot or blown apart or drowning in mud. It was a dark picture,
but yet it wasn't all mud and blood—look, there's Charlie Chaplin falling
over at a skating rink, there's Al Jolson singing, Fred Astaire dancing,
there's the world's first golf tournament, that'd be fun for all.

Andy shuddered at the carnage in spite of himself—because, as he said
out loud, it wasn't really there, it wasn't really *real*. And he couldn't help
it, he chuckled at Chaplin too, he grinned at all those golfers putting
away to their hearts' delight.

There was no one to be seen at the gallery. The rooms were crowded
with so many people living and dying, but on the walls only, only in the
art—there was no one looking at them, marvelling at what they'd stood
for, marvelling at the brushwork even. There was a little shop near the
main entrance that sold postcards. There was no one behind the cash
register.

"What do you make of it?" asked the woman behind him.

He didn't know where she'd sprung from, and for a moment he thought
she must have popped out from one of the pictures, and the idea was
so ludicrous that he nearly laughed. He stopped short, though, because
she was frowning at him so seriously, he could see laughter wasn't something the woman would appreciate, or even recognize, this was a woman
who hadn't heard laughter in a very long time. He presumed she *was*
a woman. Surely? The voice was high, and there was a softness to the
eyes, and to the lips, and there was some sagging on the torso that might
once have been breasts—yes, he thought, definitely woman. Her head
was completely smooth and hairless, and a little off-green, it looked like

a slightly mildewed egg.

Andy tried to think of something clever to say. Failed. "I don't know."

"Quite right," said the woman. "What *can* you make of it? What can anyone make of anything, when it comes down to it?" She stuck out her hand. Andy took a chance that she wanted him to shake it; he did; he was right. "You must be my new assistant. I don't want an assistant, I can manage perfectly well on my own, I do not require assisting of any sort. But the Curator says different, and who am I to argue? The best thing we can do is to leave each other alone as much as possible, it's a big place, I'm sure we'll work it out. Do you know anything about art?"

"No."

"About history?"

"No."

"About the conservation and restoration of treasures more fragile and precious than mere words can describe?"

"No."

"Good," she said. "There'll be so much less for you to unlearn." And she gave at last the semblance of a smile. Her egg face relaxed as the smile took hold, the eyes grew big and yolky, the albumen cheeks seemed to ripple and contort as if they were being poached.

"How did you know," said Andy, "that I was your new assistant?"

"Why else would you be here?"

She said she'd take him to her studio. She led him out of the First World War, back through the Reformation, through snatches and smatterings of the Dark Ages. She walked briskly, and Andy struggled to keep up—as it was, it was the best part of an hour before they reached the elevator. "I'll never find my way through all this!" Andy had joked, and his new boss had simply said, "No, you won't," and they hadn't talked again for a while.

She pulled the grille door to the elevator shut. "Going down," she said, and pushed at the lowest button on the panel. Nothing happened; she kicked at the elevator irritably, at last it began to move—and fast, faster, as if to make up for last time. Andy was alarmed and tried to find something to hold on to, but all there was was the woman, and that didn't appeal, so he stuck his hands tight into his pockets instead. The woman did not seem remotely perturbed. "Now, you might think that the gallery upstairs is huge. Well, it *is* huge, I suppose, I've never been able to find an end to it. But only a small fraction of the collection is ever on display. Say, no more than two or three per cent. The rest of the art, the overwhelming majority of it, we keep below. We keep in the vaults. And it's in the vaults that we care for this unseen art. We clean it, we protect it. We restore it to what it used to be. What's up top," she said, and she jerked a finger upwards, to somewhere Andy assumed must now be miles above their heads, "is not our concern anymore."

Andy was still catching up with what she'd said fifty meters higher, his brain seemed to be falling at a slower rate than hers. "Just two or three per cent? Christ, how many paintings have you got?"

She glared at him. She thinned her once feminine lips, she showed teeth. "They're not paintings," she said. "Never call them paintings."

"I'm sorry," said Andy, and she held his gaze for a few seconds longer, then gave a single nod, and turned away, satisfied.

The elevator continued to fall.

"My name's Andy," said Andy, "you know, by the way."

"I can't remember that. I can't be expected to remember all that."

"Oh."

"You've got lots of hair. I could call you Hairy. Except that won't last long, the hair won't last, it'll just confuse me. Tell you what. I'll call you 'Assistant.' That'll be easy for both of us."

"Fair enough," said Andy. He'd been about to ask her her name. He now thought he wouldn't bother.

And then he was surprised, because he felt something in his hand, and he looked down, and it was *her* hand—just for a moment, a little squeeze, and then it was gone. And she was doing that macabre poached smile at him. "Don't worry, Assistant," she said softly. "I used to call them paintings. I once thought they were just paintings too."

"All right, Assistant. I'm giving you 1574 to practice on. 1574 is a very minor work. If you damage 1574, who's going to care?" And she unrolled 1574 right in front of him, across the table of his new studio, across *all* the studio—she unrolled it ever onwards until 1574 spread about him and over him in all directions.

"Is this the original?"

"Who'd want to make a copy?"

What surprised Andy was that the archives down below were in such poor condition. The art was stacked everywhere in random order, although he was assured by his new boss there was a system—"It's *my* system," she said, "and that's all you need to know." Some of the years were in tatters, the months bulging off the frame, entire days lost beneath dirt. "You might suppose they'd be irreparable," she told him. "1346 was in a terrible state when I started here, there was a crease in the August, running right through the battle of Crecy. But with diligence, and hard labor, and love, I was able to put it right."

It was odd to hear her talk of love, that such a word could come out of a bald ovoid face like hers. She seemed to think it was odd too, looked away. "But diligence and hard labor are probably the most important," she added.

And although Andy had no affection for these works of art, had no reason to care, when she told him that the collection wasn't complete he felt a pang of regret in his stomach for the loss. "Ideally," she agreed, "the gallery is meant to house a full archive, from prehistory right up to 2038. But there are entire decades that have vanished without trace. Stolen, maybe, who knows? More likely destroyed. Some years were in such a state of disrepair there was nothing I could do with them, some years just decomposed before my eyes. 1971, for example, that was a botched job from the start, the materials were of inferior quality. It crumbled to dust so fast, before the spring of 1972 was out."

"What does the Curator think of that?"

She sighed heavily through her nose, it came out as a scornful puff. "The Curator's instructions are that I take responsibility for the entire collection, the whole of recorded history." She shrugged. "But I can't work miracles. That's his job."

And now here was Andy with his own year to take care of. He gave 1574 a good look. And his boss gave *him* a good look as he did so; she just folded her arms, watched him, said nothing. "It's not too bad," said Andy finally. "It's not in as bad a condition as some of the others."

"It's in an *appalling* condition," she said. "Oh, Assistant. You've been looking at all the wrong things, you don't know what's good and what's shit, but never mind, never mind, I suppose you have to start somewhere. Look again. Now. The year is *filthy*, for a start. Look at it, it's so dark. Do you think that 1574 was always this dark? Only if it had been under permanent rain clouds, and in fact, the weather was rather temperate by sixteenth-century standards. Now, that's not unusual, you have to expect the original colors to darken. Natural ageing will do that—pigments fade and distort from the moment the events are lived, as soon as they're set down on canvas. Rich greens resinate over time, they become dark browns, even blacks. The shine gets lost.

"But in this instance," she went on, and prodded at 1574 with her finger, so disdainfully that Andy thought she'd punch a hole right through it, "it's worse than that, because we can't even begin to *see* how badly the pigments have been discolored. They're buried behind so much dirt and grease. And soot, actually, that's my fault, I probably shouldn't have stored it next to the Industrial Revolution. Dirt has clung to the year, and that's not the fault of the year itself, but of the varnish painted over it. For centuries all the great works of art were varnished by the galleries, they thought it would better protect them. And some people even preferred the rather cheesy gloss it put on everything. But a lot of the varnishers were hacks, the varnish wasn't compatible with the original oils of the year itself, it'd react with them. And that's when you get smearing, and blurring, and dirt getting trapped within the year as if it's always been there.

"And that's just for starters! Look at the cracks. Dancing through the night sky of March 1574 there, do you see, they stand out so well in the moonlight. Now, I admit I like a bit of craquelure, I think it lends a little aged charm to an old master. But here, yes… these aren't just cracks, they're *fissures*, they're causing the entire panel to split out in all directions. Pretty soon March won't have thirty-one days in it, it'll end up with thirty-two. And that's all because of the oils drying, yes? The oils go on the canvas nice and wet, then they dry, the very months dry, the days within get brittle and flaky, the whole year contracts and moves within its frame."

"And what can we do to stop that?" asked Andy.

She very nearly laughed. "Stop it? We can't stop it! Oh, the arrogance of the man! Do you think *any* of the years here are in the same condition as when they were created? They're dying from the moment the paint has dried, all the sheen and brightness fading, the colors becoming ever more dull, the very tinctures starting to blister and pop. These are precious things, these little slices of time we've been given—and from the moment a year's over, from the moment they all start singing Auld Lang Syne to usher in the new, the old one is already beginning to fall apart. The centuries that pass do untold damage to the centuries that have been, there's no greater enemy to history than history itself, running right over it, scraping it hard, then crushing it flat. And some days I think that's it, all I'm doing is kicking against the inevitable, I can do nothing to stop the decay of it all, all I can do is choose the method of decay it'll face. And that's on the good days, the ones where I fool myself I'm making the blindest bit of difference—on the others, and, are you listening, Assistant, there'll be so *many others*, I feel like I'm surrounded by corpses and pretending I can stop the rot, and I can't stop the rot, who are we to stop the rot, we're working in a fucking morgue."

"Oh," said Andy. "That's a shame."

She blinked at him. Just once. Then pulled herself together.

"Frankly," she said, "1574 is a dog's breakfast. And that's why I'm setting you on to it. You're hardly likely to make it much worse. Off you go, then, 1574's not getting any younger, chop chop."

Andy pointed out he had no idea where to start conserving and cleaning a year. As far as he knew, he was supposed to run it under a tap! He chuckled at that, she didn't chuckle back. So he asked, very gently, whether he could watch her work for a while, to see how it was done.

She took him to her studio.

"This," she said, and she tried to keep a nonchalance to her voice, "is my current project." But Andy could see how she was smiling, she was just happy to be back in front of her work again—and then she gave up trying to disguise it, she turned round to him and *beamed*, she ushered him forward, invited him to look, invited him to see how well she'd done. She'd mounted a section of the year, the rest was rolled up neatly, and it seemed to Andy that she'd made an altar of that section, that it was a place of worship. "1660," she said. "Most famous for the restoration of the Stuarts to the throne of England and Scotland, and I think that's why the Curator will like this year especially, he's very keen on the triumph of authority. But there's so much more to 1660 than dynastic disputes, really—December the eighth, there's Margaret Hughes as Desdemona, the very first actress on the English stage! And that's Samuel Pepys, the diarist, September twenty-fifth, drinking his first ever cup of tea! All the little anecdotes that throw the main events into sharp relief, history can't just be kings and thrones, if you're not careful it becomes nothing but a series of assassins and wars and coups d'état, and the color is just a single flat gray. And that's not what we're about, is it? We've got to find the other colors, Andy, we've got to find all the colors that might get forgotten, what we're doing *is* important after all!" And she suddenly looked so young, and so innocent somehow, and Andy realized she'd bothered to remember his name.

He watched her as she worked, and she soon forgot he was there, she was lost in bringing out the light in Pepys' eyes as his first taste of tea hit home, his questing curiosity, his wonder, (his wrinkled nosed disgust!)—and she was happy, and she even began to sing, not words, he didn't hear any words, she seemed at times to be reaching for them but then would shake her head, she'd lost them. And she didn't notice when he sneaked away and closed the door behind him.

Over the following weeks Andy began to fall in love with 1574.

It wasn't an especially distinguished year, he'd have admitted. It was most notable for the outbreak of the Fifth War of Religion between the Catholics and the Huguenots—but this was the *fifth* war, after all, and it wasn't as if the first four had done much good, so. It was marked by the death of Charles IX, King of France, and Selim II, Sultan of the Turks, and try as he might, Andy couldn't find much sympathy for either of them. The Spanish defeated the Dutch at the Battle of Mookerheyde—when Andy picked off the surface dirt he could see all the surviving Spaniards cheering. And explorer Juan Fernandez discovered a series of volcanic islands off the coast of Chile, and he named them the Juan Fernandez Islands, and it was a measure perhaps of how little anyone wanted these islands discovered in the first place that the name stayed unchallenged.

But none of that mattered.

For research Andy had looked at 1573 and 1575, the sister years either side, and they were really very similar at heart, with a lot of the same crises brewing, and a lot of the same people causing those crises. But Andy didn't like them. In fact, he despised them. It was almost as if they were both faux 1574s, they were trying so hard to be 1574 and just falling short, it was pathetic, really. He'd dab away with his cotton swabs, removing the muck that 1574 had accumulated, and he poured his soul into it, all his effort and care, he gave it the very best of him, 1574 *was* the very best of him. And he loved it because he knew no one else ever would, this grisly year from a pretty grisly century all told, twelve unremarkable little months that had passed unmourned so many centuries before.

He would dream of 1574 too. Of living in 1574, he could have been happy there, he knew it. It wasn't that he needed to sleep; no one needed sleep any more, sleeping acted as a restorative to the body and it wasn't as if his body could possibly be restored. But he went to sleep anyway, as useless as sleeping was. He slept so he could dream. 1574 would have been perfect for him, so long as he'd kept away from all those Catholics and Huguenots, they were a liability.

One day his boss came to see him. He was so enjoying the work, he was rather irritated that he had to put a pause to it and give her attention.

"You've completely smudged that night sky in October," she said.

"I was a bit too free with the solvent," Andy admitted.

"And God knows what you've done to the craquelure in Spain, it's worse than when you started."

Andy shrugged.

"You're really very good," she said. "I'm impressed."

"Thank you."

"You don't need to thank me."

Her newfound respect for his work meant that that she began to visit more often. Every other day or so she'd come to peer at his 1574, clucking her tongue occasionally (in approval or not, Andy couldn't tell), tilting her head this way and that as she took it in from different angles, sometimes even brushing key areas of political change and social unrest with her fingertips. Andy minded. And then Andy found he'd stopped minding, somehow—he even rather looked forward to seeing her, it gave him the excuse to put down the sponge and give his arms a rest.

"What was your name again?" she asked one day.

Andy thought for a moment. "Andy," Andy said.

"I like you, Andy. So I'm going to give you a piece of advice."

"All right," said Andy.

"There's only so much room in a head," she said. And she smiled at him sympathetically.

"...Is that it?"

"That's it."

"Fair enough," said Andy. And she left.

She came back again a day or two later. "It occurs to me," she said, "that the advice I offered may not have been very clear."

"No."

"You remember that I came by, offered advice...?"

"Yes, I remember."

"Good," she said. "Good, that's a start. I like you, sorry, what was your name again?"

Andy sighed. He lay down his cotton swab. He turned to face her. He opened his mouth to answer. He answered. "Andy," he said.

"It's an absorbing job, this," she told him. "It kind of takes over. You fill your head with all sorts of old things, facts and figures. And memories can be pushed out. Personal memories, of what you did when you were alive, even what your name was. There's only so much room in a head."

"I'm not going to forget my own name," Andy assured her.

"I did," said his boss simply, and smiled.

"I'm sorry," said Andy.

"Oh, pish," she said, and waved his sympathy aside. "Names don't matter. Names aren't us, they're just labels. Names go, and good riddance, I don't want a name. But who we *were*, Andy, that's what you need to hang on to. You need to write it down. I did. For me, I did. Look." And from her pocket she took out a piece of paper.

"1782," the message read. "Tall gentleman, wearing top hat. Deep blue eyes, the bluest I've ever seen. And the way the corners of his mouth seem to be just breaking into a smile. Special. So special, you make him stand out from the crowd, you give him definition. Make him count."

"I carry it with me everywhere," she said. "And if I ever lose myself. If I ever doubt who I am. I take it out, and I read it, and I remember. That once I was in love. That once, back in 1782, there was a man, and out of all the countless billions of men who have lived through history, against all those odds, we found each other."

And she was smiling so wide now, and her eyes were brimming with tears.

"You don't know his name?" asked Andy.

"I'm sure he had one at the time. That's enough."

She put the paper away. "Write it all down, Andy," she said. "Don't waste your efforts on all the unimportant stuff, your job, your house, whether you had a pet or not. That's all gone now. But your wife, describe your wife, remind yourself that you too were once loved and were capable of inspiring love back."

"Oh, I didn't have a wife," said Andy.

The woman's mouth opened to a perfect little "o." She stared at him.

"I never quite found the right girl," Andy went on cheerfully.

The mouth closed, she gulped. Still staring.

"You know how it is. I was quite picky."

By now she was ashen. "Oh, my poor man," she said. "My poor man. You must have already forgotten."

"No, no," Andy assured her. "I remember quite well! I had the odd girlfriend, some of them were very odd, ha! But never the right one. Actually, I think they were quite picky too, ha! Maybe more picky than me, ha ha! Look, no, look, it's all right, it doesn't matter…"

Because he'd never seen her egg-white face quite so white before, and her eyes were welling with tears again, but this time she wasn't smiling through them. "You must have forgotten," she insisted. "You must have been loved, a man like you. Life wouldn't be so cruel. Oh, Andy." And impulsively, she kissed him on top of the head.

"You're beginning to lose your hair," she then said.

"Am I?" asked Andy.

"You should watch out for that."

She didn't visit for a while afterwards, and it wasn't surprising at first, he knew how easy it was just to get lost in the work, but after a bit he began to wonder whether he might have offended her in some way—he couldn't remember what way that might have been—and he supposed it didn't matter if he had, he didn't like her very much (or did he?—he didn't *recall* liking her, that had never been a part of it, but), but, but then he realized he missed her, that her absence was a sad and slightly painful thing, that he should put a stop to that absence, he should set off to find her. So he did. He left 1574 behind and went looking for 1660, and he couldn't work out how to get there, he walked up and down corridors of the twelfth century, and then the tenth, it was all a bit confusing, there were Vikings every which way he looked. And it began to bother him that he couldn't decide where 1660 came in history, was it after 1574, was it before? And he thought, sod it, I'll turn back, and he walked in the direction he had come, but somehow that brought him to the fifth century, and there were no Vikings now, just bloody Picts. He didn't think he could find 1574 let alone 1660, and he started to panic, and he was just about to resign himself to the idea of settling down with the Anglo Saxons, maybe it wouldn't be so bad—when he turned the corner, and there, suddenly, was Charles II restored to the throne, there was Samuel Pepys, there was *she*, there she was, sitting at her desk, paintbrush in hand, and all but dwarfed by the Renaissance in full glory.

"Hello," he said.

But she didn't reply, and he thought that maybe she was concentrating, she didn't want to be disturbed, and he could respect that, he'd have wanted the same thing—so he waited, he bided his time, so much time to bide in all around him and he bided it. Until he could bide no more— "Hello, are you all right?" he asked, and he went right up to her, and she still didn't acknowledge him, he went right up to her face. And her eyes were so wide and so scared, and her cheeks were blotched with tears, and her lips, her bottom lip was trembling as if caught in mid-stutter, "No," she said, or at least that's what he thought it was, but it might not have been a word, it might just have been a noise, "nonononono." "Do you know who I am?" he asked, and she looked directly at him, then recoiled, it was clear she didn't know *anything*, "nonono," she sobbed, and it wasn't an answer to his question, it was all she could say, each "no" popping out every time that bottom lip quivered. "Do you know who I am?" he asked again, "I'm…" and for the life of him at that moment he forgot his own name, how ridiculous, "I'm your assistant, yes? I'm your *friend*." And he moved to touch her, he wanted to hold her, hug her, something, but she slapped him away, and the tears started, she was so very frightened. "I'm your friend," he said, "and I'll look after you," and he knocked aside the slaps, he held on to her, and tight too, he held on as close as she'd let him, and he felt her tears on his neck, and they weren't warm like tears were supposed to be, oh, they were so *cool*. "I'm your friend, and I'm going to look after you, and I'll never stop looking after you," and he hadn't meant to make a promise, but it was a promise, wasn't it? and "Just you remember that!" but she didn't remember anything, not a thing—and he held on to her until she *did*, until at last she did.

"Andy?" she said. "Andy, what's wrong?" Because he was crying too. And she looked so surprised to see him there, and so glad too—and he thought, *Andy*, oh yes, *that* was it.

One day, as Andy was sponging down a particularly anonymous Huguenot, she came to him. She looked awkward, even a little bashful.

"I've been thinking," she said. "You can give me a name. If you like."

Andy turned away from 1574. "I thought you didn't want a name."

She blushed. "I don't mind."

"All right," he said. "What about Janet?"

She wrinkled her nose.

"You don't like Janet?"

"I don't," she agreed, "like Janet."

"OK," he said. "Mandy."

"No."

"Becky."

"No."

"Samantha. Sammy for short."

"Tell you what," she said. "You give it a think, and when you come up with something you like, you come and find me."

"I'll do that," said Andy.

He resumed work on his Huguenot. The bloodstain on his dagger-gouged stomach shone a red it hadn't shone in hundreds of years. Andy worked hard on it, he didn't know for how long, but there was a joy to it, to uncover this man's death like it was some long lost buried treasure, and make it stand out bold and lurid and smudge-free.

Next time she came she was wearing a ribbon. He didn't know why, it looked odd wrapped around her shiny bald forehead. Why was the forehead so shiny? Had she done something to it? "I've been thinking," she said.

"Oh yes?"

"What about Miriam?"

"Who's Miriam?"

"Me. I could be Miriam."

"You could be Miriam, yes."

"Do you like Miriam?"

"Miriam's fine."

"Do you think Miriam suits me?"

"I think Miriam suits you right down to the ground," said Andy, and she beamed at him.

"All right," she said. "Miriam it is. If you like it. If that works well for you."

"Hello, Miriam," he said. "Nice to meet you." And they laughed.

"I love you," she said then.

"You do what, sorry?"

"I think it's so sad, that no one ever loved you."

"I don't know that *no one* ever loved me..."

"And at first I thought this was just pity for you. Inside me, here. But then it grew. And I thought, that's not pity at all, that's love." She scratched at her ribbon. It slipped down her face a bit. "I mean, I might have got it wrong, it might just be a deeper form of pity," she said. "But, you know."

"Yes."

"Probably not."

"No."

"Probably love."

"Yes."

"I want you to know," she said, "what it feels like to inspire love. You inspire love. In me."

"Well," he said. "Thank you. I mean that."

"Do I inspire love in you?"

"I hadn't really thought about it," said Andy.

"Would you think about it now?"

"All right," he said. "Yes. Go on, then. I think you do."

"Oh good," said Miriam.

She left him then. He got back to his dying Huguenot. The Huguenot seemed to be winking at him. Andy didn't like that, and swabbed at the Huguenot's eyes pointedly.

When Miriam returned, the ribbon was gone, and Andy thought that was good, it really hadn't looked right. But, if anything, the forehead was shinier still. And there was a new redness to the lips, he thought she must have spilled some paint on to them.

"If it is love. Not just pity on my part, confused politeness on yours. Would you like to *make* love?"

"We could," Andy agreed.

He hadn't taken off his clothes for years now. But they were removed easily enough, it was just a matter of tugging them away with a bit of no-nonsense force. Miriam's clothes were another matter, they seemed to have been glued down, or worse—Andy wondered as they tried to peel them off whether some of the skin had grown over the clothes, or the clothes had evolved into skin, or vice versa—either way they weren't budging. It took half an hour to get most of the layers off, but there were patches of blouse and stocking that they couldn't prise away even with a chisel.

They stood there—he, naked, she, as naked as they could manage without applying some of the stronger solvents.

"You go first," she said, and he thought he could take the responsibility of that—but then, as he came towards her, he stopped short, he couldn't recall what on earth he was supposed to do. He looked at her, right at her egg face, and she was smiling bravely, but there were no clues offered in that smile, and he looked downwards, and it seemed to him that both of her breasts were like eggs too, perched side by side on top of a rounded belly that was also like an egg—her whole hairless body was like a whole stack of eggs inexpertly stitched together, God, he was looking at an entire omelette! And though she wasn't beautiful, it was nevertheless naked flesh, and it was vaguely female in shape, and his prick twitched in memory of it, in some memory that it ought to be doing *something*.

"I do love you," he said. "I love you too," she replied. And they approached the other. And they reached out their hands. And their fingers danced gently on each other's fingers. And he stroked his head against her chest. And she bit awkwardly at his nose. And they bounced their stomachs off each other—once, twice, three times!—boing!—and that third bounce was really pretty frenzied. Then they held each other. They both remembered that part.

The next time she came to visit him in his studio they had both completely forgotten they'd once tried sex. And perhaps that was a blessing. Andy was absorbed in an entirely new Huguenot corpse, and she seemed to have grown new clothes. But she remembered her name was Miriam now, and so did he; they clung on to that, together, at least.

1574:

In February the so-called Fifth War of Religion breaks out in France between the Catholics and the Huguenots; the Fourth War had only ended six months previously. War Number Four didn't, as you might gather, end very conclusively. The Huguenots were given the freedom to worship—but *only* within three towns in the whole country, and *only* within their own homes, and marriages could be celebrated but *only* by aristocrats before an assembly limited to ten people outside their own family. King Charles IX dies shortly afterwards. He was the man responsible for the slaughter of thousands of Huguenots in the St Bartholomew's Day Massacre. Reports say that he actually died sweating blood; he is said to have turned to his nurse in his last moments and said, "So much blood around me! Is this all the blood I have shed?"

And then

In May Selim II, sultan of the Ottoman Empire, dies. Named by his loving subjects as Selim the Drunkard, or Selim the Sot, he dies inebriated, clumsily slipping on the wet floor of his harem and falling into the bath. His corpse is kept in ice for twelve days to conceal the fact he's dead and to safeguard the throne until his chosen heir, his son Murad, can reach Istanbul and take power. On arrival Murad is proclaimed the new sultan, and there is much rejoicing, and hope (as ever) for a new age of enlightenment; that night he has all five of his younger brothers strangled in a somewhat overemphatic attempt to dissuade them from challenging his new authority.

And then

In November the Spanish sailor Juan Fernandez discovers a hitherto unknown archipelago. Sailing between Peru and Valparaiso, and quite by chance deviating from his planned route, Fernandez stumbles across a series of islands, no more than seventy square miles in total area. Fernandez looks about him. There are bits of greenery on them. They're a bit volcanic. They're not much cop. He names them after himself, and you can only wonder whether that's an act of grandeur or of self-effacing irony. For the next few centuries they serve as a hideout for pirates; then the tables are turned and they make for an especially unattractive new penal colony.

And then

Andy's hair fell out. It had been a slow process at first. For weeks he'd had to keep picking out stray strands from the solvent, he kept accidentally rubbing them into the picture—Juan Fernandez' beard seemed to grow ever bushier, Charles IX died sweating not just blood but fur. And then, one day, it poured out all at once, in thick heavy clumps that rained down on his shoulders—and Andy was fascinated at the amount of it, it seemed he wasn't just losing the hair he already had but all the potential hair he could *ever* have had, the follicles were squeezing the hair out in triple quick time, as if his skull had contained nothing but a whole big ball of the stuff just waiting to be set free. The hairs would bristle out towards the light, thousands of little worms making for the surface, now covering his scalp and chin, now turning his head into a deep plush furry mat—and then, just as soon as the hairs seemed so full and thick and *alive* they'd die, they'd all die, they'd jump off his head like so many lemmings jumping off cliffs—and Andy couldn't help feel a little hurt that all this hair had been born, had looked about, and had been so unimpressed by the shape and texture of the face that was to be their new home they'd chosen to commit mass suicide instead.

And then

The hair stopped falling, there was simply no hair left to fall. And then—Andy had to sweep it all up; it took him quite a while, there was an awful lot of it, and he resented the time he spent on doing that, this was work time, this was 1574 time. And then and then and then—he forgot he had ever had hair at all, he had no thoughts of hair, his head was an egg and it felt good and proper as an egg, 1574 was all he could think of now, 1574 was all there was, 1574 ran through him and over him and that's what filled his skull now and all that was ever meant to, Huguenots, drunken sultans, the flora and fauna of the Juan Fernandez Islands, 1574 for life, 1574 forever.

And then:

And then sometimes she would visit him and he'd have forgotten who she was, and sometimes he would visit her and she'd have forgotten who he was. But most times they remembered, and the memory came on them like a welcome rush. And they might even celebrate; they'd put their work aside, they'd get into the clapped out old elevator, pull the grille doors to, and ascend to the main gallery itself. And they'd walk through the exhibits on display, they'd turn the lights down low so it was more intimate, low enough that to see the art properly they'd have to squint a bit, as if even for just a little while it wasn't the most important thing in the room; they'd walk through the centuries together, but not be over-whelmed by the centuries, they'd walk at such a gentle pace too, they were in no rush, they had all the time in the world; they'd walk hand in hand. And Andy thought they must look such a funny pair, really. Almost identical, really, bald and white and plain—she just a little shorter than him, he a little more flat chested than her. They must have looked funny, yes, but who was there to see? (Who was there to tell?)

He didn't like it when he forgot her. So he wrote down on a piece of paper a reminder, so that whenever he felt lost or confused he could look at it and find new purpose. "Miriam," he wrote. "She's your boss. Works with you here at the gallery. Very good with the varnish. Works too hard, takes herself too seriously, not much of a sense of humor, but you know how to make her smile, just give it time. Not pretty, she looks like she's been newly laid from a hen's backside, but that doesn't mat-ter, she's your friend. She's the only one that knows you, even when she doesn't know herself."

One day Miriam came to find Andy, and he remembered who she was clearly, he remembered her at a glance without the aid of memo. And he smiled and he got up and took her by the hand, and she said, "No, not today, Andy, this is business." And she looked sad, and maybe a little frightened, and the bits of her face where she'd once had eyebrows seemed to bristle in spite of themselves.

She'd received a missive from the Curator. It had come in an envelope, bulging fat. She hadn't yet opened it.

"I don't see what's to worry about necessarily," said Andy. "Isn't it good that he's taking an interest?"

"This is only the third missive he's ever sent me," said Miriam. "The first one was to appoint me to this gallery, the second one was to appoint you to me. He doesn't care what we get up to here." She handed him the envelope. "This is bad. You read it."

But it didn't seem so bad, not at first. The Curator was very charming. He apologized profusely for giving Miriam and Andy so little attention. He'd been up to his eyes, there was so much to do, a whole universe of things under his thumb, and regretfully the arts just weren't one of his main priorities. But he was going to change all that; he was quite certain that Miriam and Andy had been working so very hard, and he was proud of them, and grateful, and he'd be popping into the gallery any time now to inspect what they'd been up to. No need to worry about it, no need for this to be of any *especial* concern—no need for them to know either when his visit might be. Remember, it was all very informal; remember, he'd rather surprise them unawares; remember, remember—he had eyes and ears everywhere.

That he referred to them both as Miriam and Andy was a cause for some concern.

And he finished by adding a request. A very little request, attached as a P.S.

The Curator said there were two ways of looking at history. One, that it was all just random chance, there was no rhyme or reason to any of it. People lived, people died. Stuff happened in between. This seemed to the Curator rather a cynical interpretation of history, and not a little atheist, didn't Miriam and Andy agree? The second was that there was a destiny to it all, an end resolution that had been determined from the beginning. The story of the world was like the story in a book, all the separate years just chapters building up to an inevitable climax—meaningless if read on their own, and rather unfulfilling too. The entire span of world history only made sense if it was considered within a context offered by that climax—and what a climax it'd been! 2038 really was the Curator's absolute favorite, he had such great memories of it, really, he'd think back on it sometimes and just get lost in the daydream, it was great.

And that's why the Curator wanted to see, in all the years preceding, some hint of the end year to come. He didn't want them to interfere with the art they'd been conserving—no—but, if within that art they saw some little premonition of it, then that'd be good, wouldn't it? Maybe they could *emphasize* his final triumph, they could pick out all the subtle suggestions throughout all time of his ineffable victory and highlight them somehow. The value of art, the Curator said, is that it reflects the world. What value then would any of these years have if they did not reflect their apotheosis? Their preservation would be worthless; no, worse, a lie; no, worse, treason itself. History had to have a pattern. And up to now Miriam and Andy had been working to conceal that pattern—with diligence, he knew, and hard labor, and love, he could see there'd been lots of love. All that had to stop, right now.

And if they couldn't find any premonitions to highlight, maybe they could just draw some in themselves from scratch?

Miriam said softly, "It goes against everything I've ever done here."

Andy said nothing for a long while. He took her hand. She let him. He squeezed it. She squeezed it back. "But," he then said, and she stopped squeezing, "but if it's what the Curator wants," and her hand went limp, "and since he owns all this art, really..." and she took her hand away altogether.

"It's vandalism," she said. "I can't do it, and I don't care if it's treason to refuse. You... you, Aidan, whatever your name is... you do what you like."

She left him.

He studied 1574. He looked at it all over. He knew it so well, but it was like seeing it with fresh eyes, now he was trying to find a part of it to sacrifice. He took out a pen. An ordinary modern biro, something that future conservationists could tell was wrong at a glance, something that wouldn't stain the patina or bleed into the oils underneath. Andy wasn't much of an artist, and so the demon he drew over the battle of Mooker-heyde was little more than a stick figure. It looked stupid hovering there so fake above the soldiers and the bloodshed. He didn't even know what a demon looked like, he'd never seen one, he'd imagined that Hell would have been full of the things but they'd always kept to themselves—and so his drawing of a demon was really just the first thing that came to mind. He gave it a little pitchfork. And fangs. And a smiley face.

He wondered if this would be enough to satisfy the Curator, and thought he better not chance it. He drew a second demon over Juan Fernandez discovering his islands. The pitchfork was more pointy, the smile more of a leer.

He went to find Miriam. She was crying. He was crying too. And that's why she forgave him.

"I don't want you taken from me," he said, and he held her. "Please."

"I'm sorry. It's a betrayal. I'm sorry. I'm sorry."

"Then I'll do it. Let me do all the betraying. I'll betray enough for both of us."

And they would walk the gallery again, hand in hand through the centuries. But this time, as they reached the end of a picture, Miriam would stop, she'd turn away, she'd close her eyes. And Andy would get out his pen, sometimes just a biro, sometimes a sharpie if the year was robust enough to take it, and he'd draw in a demon or two. And Andy was surprised at how much easier it got, these acts of desecration; and his demons were bigger and more confident, sometimes they fitted in to the action superbly, sometimes (he thought secretly) they even improved it. He desecrated 1415, he desecrated 1963, he desecrated each and every one of the years representing the First World War. And it seemed to Andy that he was beginning to see the Curator's point; he'd see there was something foreboding about these years, maybe there *was* something in the design of them all that forecast the apocalypse.

But she wouldn't let him touch 1660. "It's mine," she said.

One night they reached the 1782 room. The Americans were in the throes of revolution, the French were chuntering on towards theirs. Andy thought 1782 had great potential, there were plenty of places where a demon or two would fit the bill. Miriam stood up close to the year. She reached out. She stroked it. When she pulled her hand away, Andy could see that her fingers had been brushing the image of a man in a top hat. His eyes were the more gorgeous blue, and around his mouth played the hint of a flirtatious smile.

Miriam took out the piece of paper from her pocket. She read it. She dropped it to the floor.

"It's the man you loved, isn't it?" said Andy.

"No."

And she reached out again, stroked the face again. This time Andy could see it wasn't done with affection, but with professional enquiry. "I must have worked on this," she said. "Look at the man's face. There was a rip here, from the neck, up to the forehead, look, it took out one of his eyes. I worked on this, I recognize my handiwork. I put his face back together."

And now that he was looking closely, Andy could see she was quite right. The work had been subtle, and so delicately done, but an expert could see the threads that bound the cheek flaps together.

"What I'd written down, it wasn't a memory," said Miriam. "It was an instruction for repair. I never knew this man. I never loved him, and he never loved me. All I ever did was to stitch his face up."

She ran.

By the time Andy caught up with her she was back at her studio. She was painting. Each stroke of her brush was so considered, was so small, you'd have thought that not a single one could have made the slightest difference—but their sum total was extraordinary. On the canvas she had created a demon. And the oils she'd chosen were perfect, they seemed to blend in with the background as if the demon had always been part of 1660; and its eyes bulged, and saliva was dripping from its mouth, its horns were caught in mid-quiver; it looked at the complacent folly of the seventeenth century with naked hunger. And it hung over the shoulders of King Charles II as he celebrated the restoration of the Crown, the spikes of its tail only an inch away from the Merry Monarch's face, if Charles just turned his head a fraction to the right his eye would get punctured. And the demon's presence seemed artistically *right*, it was an ironic comment upon fame and success and the paucity of Man's achievements—yes, the King was on his throne, but time would move on, and the human race would fall, and nobody could stop it, or nobody *would*, at any rate; and all of this, even this little slice of long past history, all would be swept away.

"It's beautiful," said Andy. "At painting, you're. Well. Really good." It sounded quite inadequate. And had Andy not known better, he'd have thought the demon in the picture rolled its eyes.

"I know," said Miriam. But she wouldn't look at him.

They didn't know when the Curator came to visit. Only that another missive was sent one day, and it said that his inspection had been carried out, and that he was well pleased with his subjects.

They hoped that would be the end of it. It wasn't.

The Curator's final missive was simple, and straight to the point. He said that he thought the work of the gallery was important, but that the art on display wasn't; there was only one significant year in world history, the year of his irrevocable triumph over creation, all the bits beforehand he now realized were just a dull protracted preamble before the main event.

He wanted to display 2038. And only 2038. 2038 was big enough, 2038 could fill the entire gallery on its own. All the other years could now be disposed of.

There were jobs going at the gallery, and everyone queued for them, man, woman and child. And this time everyone was a winner, they *all* got jobs—really, there was so much work to do! The chatter and laughter of a billion souls in gainful employment filled the rooms, and it looked so strange to Andy and to Miriam, that at last the art they had preserved had an audience. They squeezed in, the gallery was packed to capacity—and yes, everyone would stare at the pictures on show, and perhaps in wonder, they'd never seen anything so splendid in all their lives—or maybe they had, maybe they'd lived the exact moments they were ogling, but if so it was long forgotten now, everything was forgotten. They'd stare at the pictures, every single one, and they'd allow a beat of appreciation, of awe—and then they'd tear them down from the walls.

And there were demons too, supervising the operation. So that's what they looked like, and, do you know, they looked just like us! Except for the hair, of course, their long lustrous hair.

The people would rip down the years, and take them outside, and throw them onto the fire. They'd burn all they'd ever been, all they'd experienced. And over the cries of excitement of the mob you'd have thought you could have heard the years scream.

And once they'd destroyed all that had been on view in the public gallery, the people made their way down to the vaults. Miriam stood in her studio, guarding 1660 with a sharpened paintbrush. "You can't have this one." And a demon came forward from the crowd, just a little chap, really, and so unassuming, and he punched her once in the face, and her nose broke, and he punched her hard on the head, and she fell to the ground. She didn't give them any trouble after that.

Andy found her there. She wasn't unconscious as he first thought; she simply hadn't found a reason to get up yet.

"This is all because of you," she said. "You made me fall in love with you, and it drew attention. This is all because of us."

And in spite of that, or because of it, he gave her a smile. And held out his hand for her. And she found her reason.

They went through the back corridors, past the hidden annexes and cubbyholes, all the way to his studio. 1574 was still draped over it, higgledy-piggledy, January and December were trailing loose along the ground. Andy had never managed to learn even a fraction of the order Miriam had insisted upon, and for all that her life's work was in ruins, she couldn't help but tut. But seeing 1574 like that, less an old master, more a pet, it was suddenly homely and small, not a proper year, a year in progress—it was a hobby project that Andy liked to tinker on, it had none of the grandeur that the Curator was trying to stamp on and destroy. And for the first time, Miriam surprised herself, she felt a stab of affection for the old thing.

"We can save 1574," he told her.

And she knew it was worthless. That had the Curator sent his thugs to take 1574 from the beginning, she'd have given it up without a second thought. An unnecessary year—but now she helped Andy without a word, he took one corner and she the other, and together they rolled it up. And because it *was* so unnecessary, it rolled up very small indeed, and Andy was able to put it in his pocket.

No one stopped them on the way to the elevator. There was nowhere to go but up. And there was nothing up there. Not any more.

Andy pulled the grille doors closed. He pressed the highest button that there was, one so high that it didn't even fit upon the panel with all the other buttons, it had to have a panel all of its own. It hadn't been pressed for such a long time, there wasn't much give in it, and when it finally yielded to Andy's finger it did so with a clunk.

The elevator didn't move for a few seconds. "Come on," said Andy, and kicked it.

The lift doors opened out on to the Earth. And there was no air, there was no light, there was no dark. There was no *time*, time had been stripped out and taken down to the art galleries long ago, time had been frittered away, then burned.

"We can't stay here," said Miriam. "I love you. I'd love you anywhere. But this isn't anywhere, I can't be with you here."

But Andy took 1574 out from his pocket. And holding out one end of the scroll, he *flung* out the other as far as he could. And the year unrolled and flew off into the distance. And when it had unrolled all that it could, after it had sped over the crags that had once been continents and oceans, when the far end of it could be seen flying back at him from the opposite direction, Andy caught hold of it, and tugged it flat, and fixed the end of December to the beginning of January. And it lay across the earth, all the lumps and bumps, and yet it was still a perfect fit.

"This won't last. He'll come and get us in the end," said Miriam.

"He will. But not for another four hundred and fifty years." And then Andy kissed her, straight onto the mouth. He hadn't remembered that's how you were supposed to do it, but suddenly it just seemed so logical. And they kissed like that for a while, one mouth welded to the other, as the Middle Ages settled and stilled around them.

They'd bask for a bit in August if they wanted the sun; then, to cool down, they'd pop over to February and dip their toes in the chill. And if they wanted to be alone, away from all the kings and sultans and soldiers and peasants and peoples set upon their paths of religious intolerance, then they'd hide in November—and November on the Juan Fernandez Islands, just before Juan Fernandez himself arrived on the scene. They spent a lot of time there. Alone was good.

They practiced making love. If the mouth on mouth thing had been inspired, it was the tongue in mouth development that was the real breakthrough. They kissed a lot, and each time they did they both felt deep within the stirrings of dormant memories—that if they just kept at it, with diligence and labor, then they'd work out the next step of sex eventually.

"I love you," Andy would tell her, and "I love you," Miriam would reply. And they both wrote these facts down, privately, on pieces of paper, and kept them in their pockets always.

Miriam's nose healed. It didn't quite set straight, but Andy preferred it the new way; the very sight of its off-center kink as it came up at him would set his heart racing faster. And the bruise where she'd been struck at last faded too. In its place there grew a single, shiny, blonde hair. Miriam felt it pop out of her skull one day and squealed with delight.

"It's all coming back," she said to Andy. "Everything's going to be all right again."

And Andy had seen enough of history to know that one lone random hair didn't necessarily mean much. But he laughed indulgently as she combed it into position, and she laughed at his laughter, and then they both forgot what they'd been laughing at in the first place—but that was all right, that they were happy was all that mattered. And then they started the kissing again, and all they knew and heard and felt was each other, and they ignored the stick figure demon chattering and giggling above their heads.

THE ONSET OF A PARANORMAL ROMANCE

BRUCE STERLING

After discovering planetary wireless broadband, Bruce Sterling united his time between Turin, Belgrade, and Austin. He also began writing some design fiction and architecture fiction, as well as science fiction. However, this daring departure from the routine made no particular difference to anybody. Sterling then started hanging out with Augmented Reality people, and serving as a guest curator for European electronic arts festivals. These eccentricities also provoked no particular remark. Sterling went on a Croatian literary yacht tour and lived for a month in Brazil. These pleasant interludes had little practical consequence. After teaching in Switzerland and Holland, Sterling realized that all his European students lived more or less in this manner, and that nobody was surprised about much of any of that any more. So, he decided to sit still and get a little writing done, and this story was part of that effort. Prior to this he had written ten novels and four short story collections. His most recent books are novel The Caryatids, *major career retrospective* Ascendancies: The Best of Bruce Sterling, *and new collection* Global High-Tech.

Lover A: The Haunted Hotel

Gavin squeezed glare from his jet-lagged eyes and stared into the sea. "Capri is Paradise."

His sister wiped at her runny mascara. "I guess it's OK. But

419

I've seen better."

"Check out those giant rocks, down in the breakers over there. They're awesome."

The little Capri park was perched on a cliff top, like a bursting flower-basket in scarlet, violet and orange. Beneath them, an ocean vista in peacock-blue. Eliza was dressed all in black. Long black sleeves, a long black skirt, and black eyeliner-out-to-here. Black lipstick. Black combat boots.

Eliza plucked her black iPhone from her black laced bodice. "Those are the Faraglione Rocks down there."

"Wikipedia," Gavin nodded. "Wikipedia on wireless broadband. Wow, what a handy service that is."

"I keep telling you that iPhones rule the universe! You gotta get an iPhone right away, Gav!"

Gavin smiled as he shook his head. He used a solid, dependable Blackberry.

Eliza squinted at her screen from under her droopy black hat brim. "A Roman Emperor built this place. He built this garden that we're standing in, right now. The great Emperor, Augustus Caesar. Two thousand years ago."

"Oh yeah, Italian life is all about emperors," nodded Gavin. "Aren't you glad I brought you over here?" He stretched his arms out and spun a little in the dazzling sunshine.

Gavin did a lot of his business in Italy—but with his little sister at his side, the charm of Italy touched him where he felt it. The past and future wheeled around them as they stood here. Past and future, future and past, all clean and winged and airy, like two island seagulls.

Or, maybe that swooning sensation was jet lag. Gavin dropped his arms and staggered.

That plummeting, swooning sensation had seized the core of his body. He couldn't make it stop.

Yeah, that feeling was jet lag, all right.

A chattering crowd of tourists brushed by him, trampling the garden paths. Sweaty, sunburned foreigners in flowered shirts and shorts. Other tourists rambled in clusters past the marble fountains and the rust-specked iron benches.

These foreign tourists were the native livestock of Capri. Like sacred cattle, they roamed wherever they pleased. Some took a stony walkway that zigzagged down to sea-level, like the tortured path of a video game.

Others rambled uphill, into long green ridges dotted with white vacation villas.

Down in that foamy, sun-sparkling surf, the Faraglione Rocks beckoned to Gavin. Unearthly, primeval, majestic towers. Like the ghosts of a past life, or the figments of a future life. The regrets of a past life that haunted the promises of a future life… anyway, a *different* life.

"I wonder," said Gavin, "I really wonder, how many people, for how many centuries, have looked at those giant towers. Those huge stone pillars, just wading out there in that beautiful blue ocean. There must have been millions of us looking at them. Just, billions of human eyeballs."

"Aw come on, Google gets a billion eyeballs every day." Eliza tucked her iPhone away. "Gav, look at me now. I'm gonna stare at your big rocks there like nobody else ever did!"

Eliza lifted her sharp chin. She pulled in a breath and threw her narrow shoulders back. Eliza had the serious, bone-deep glumness that only seventeen-year-old girls could achieve.

Then Eliza glared at the ancient rocks. With a burning, churning fit of teenage rage. As if she could crack them to bits with the force of her will.

Gavin watched his little sister in bemusement. Why did Eliza always do things like this? What was she trying to prove? That witchy, sullen, kill-the-world thing, that Goth Chick business…

Where did this weird expression come from? *Somebody* should look like that. A ferocious look belonged on somebody's face. A Gothic girl…. But not a modern Gothic girl…. An *ancient* Gothic girl!

A Gothic princess in the garden of a Roman Emperor!

Gavin grinned. Yes! Right! Of course! The Gothic girl, and the *Gothic* girl!

Gavin felt blessed by this sudden flash of insight. Gavin was a techno-futurist and venture capitalist. He worked on budgets, statistics, and market buzz. Sometimes, though, a deep insight hit him, a burst of smarts when he just nailed it. This was one of those pleasant moments.

Once, yes, there had been a different Gothic girl—an ancient Gothic girl, standing right here. Standing in this very garden, on this very spot. A living human being, from the distant past. Not a ghost, not a figment of imagination. Not a phantom, not even a futurist's hunch. A teenage Goth princess who was as real as any other human being. So real that Gavin could practically smell her reek of pagan patchouli.

And she was a ticked-off Gothic barbarian princess, glaring at those towers of Capri. As if she could destroy the Emperor's favorite rocks, just by resenting them.

Because she had plenty to be upset about, this Gothic princess. Ancient Goths and ancient Romans had a very rough and intimate relationship. Very human, very "love-hate." You could bet that this Gothic princess of Capri would love to topple the Emperor's rocks. Not because it was the rocks' fault. Because of who she was.

A sea-breeze hissed up the cliffside and lifted Eliza's hair in coal-black tufts and wings. Suddenly, she looked up at him, and she was not angry at all. She smiled at him. She was happy.

The beauty of the world had made her happy. Gavin sensed the great importance of what was happening. He could feel that, even if he couldn't put words around it. This was a transition of some kind. A major trend, taking off. A cycle, returning. The past is a future that has already happened.

What a pretty smile Eliza had. As pretty as any Capri garden full of flowers. Up to this very moment in her life, Eliza... Well, Eliza had just been his kid sister, her usual slouching, petulant self. But they were far away from Seattle. Far from their parents, far from all the aching pressures of their lives, nine time zones distant...

A trip to Capri was good for her. Eliza was feeling happier already. Something joyful had broken loose in her dark little soul, now that she was free. Some more genuine Elizabeth Tremaine was slipping out of her shell.

Eliza looked so grown-up to him, suddenly. She'd jumped years in an instant. Maybe this was the last day in his life when Eliza would be his "kid sister." Someone he could treat as a child.

Gavin placed both his hands on the cold iron railing of the overlook. "Eliza, I want to tell you something," he said. "When I was seventeen—just like you are now—I made some big decisions about my life."

Eliza turned her head to look him over. "You found out that you were an accountant?"

"Well, yeah, I am an accountant. But no, that's not what I'm trying to tell you."

"I don't want to have a business career like yours," sniffed Eliza. "You know what I want, when I grow up? What I really, really want from my life? Because I already know."

"I'm eager to hear this," Gavin told her.

She looked him in the eyes. "You're not teasing me?"

"I would never tease you, Elizabeth. I want you to tell me about that. Because I study futurism, and I think that I can help you."

"Well, in the future, I want to be a princess."

His little sister wanted to be a princess. What a fairy-tale notion. A six-year-old would laugh.

"I see," he said.

"No, you don't see! I mean I need to be like *royalty!* Because I need to be awesome *just for being me!* That's the most important part! Whenever I make the scene, everybody has to stop whatever they're doing. They all just *look at me!* Just because, wow, it's *me*: Elizabeth Aimee Tremaine! Or whatever cool name I have, in the future: Madonna, Shakira. One of those one-name names that only superstars can have." Eliza's shoulders suddenly slumped. "Every dorky chick in this world is named 'Elizabeth.'"

"So, uh, you want to become an entertainer? That's a pretty tough life."

"Probably more like Paris. I mean, Paris Hilton. Paris is famous and powerful, and she gets all kinds of international respect. I don't know why, but she sure does."

"Look, Paris Hilton is in movies. Paris had her own TV series. Paris cut a record." Gavin had closely studied the career of Paris Hilton. Because Paris Hilton was very trendy, and trends were of supreme importance to futurists. "I don't think that you want to get famous the way that Paris Hilton got famous."

Eliza opened her black satchel. She pulled out a portable CD player. "Gav, look at this. Once, I loved this machine so much. Because it plays all my CDs. But nobody buys CDs in music stores anymore! They just steal mp3s! Even *I* don't pay for music, and I'm *rich!* I took my CD player everywhere… now I'm carrying a zombie in my purse!"

"Well, yes, that platform has become obsolete now, but a new business model will arise for music."

"No it won't! That's a lie! Nobody will ever pay! The music business is the walking dead! Just don't lie to me!" Eliza stuffed her doomed, archaic device back into her furry black purse.

Gavin rubbed his chin. "Your Digital Native generation really has some issues."

"The music business is over! That means someone has to raise the dead! *Me!* I'll do it! Why *not* me? I can raise the dead! Elizabeth Aimee Tremaine, the princess of music, the Gothic superstar! I would do that! I'd do anything, to do it."

Gavin nodded, rocking from heel to toe in his Timberland brogues. "OK. Sure. I get it. Any girl who could pull that stunt off would be a major-league princess for sure."

Gavin felt pleased to see his sister taking such an interest in technology issues. He'd been afraid that his geeky lectures on those subjects had flown right over her head. But now he saw that Eliza understood him. Just, in her own way.

Eliza pulled at her wind-tangled hair, which was blonde at the roots but dyed the lifeless color of coal dust. "When our music scene dies in Seattle," she told him, "our town will become a dead city. Everything will be quiet and evil and covered with thorns."

"Aw, come on, that'll never happen to Seattle! We're an inventive, creative city. We love the arts!"

"Well, I love music with all my heart, and I have to watch music die every day."

Gavin didn't know how to respond to this dreadful lament. He knew that he should say something. Something very older-brother style. Something that was good, wise and cheerful, that would make everything better for her.

Here was his sister, finally spitting up the real source of her misery. Confiding in him, and trusting him. Yet he couldn't console her. He had nothing to tell her. He lacked a prepared position statement.

"Back home," Eliza grumbled, knotting her fine blonde brows, "we have that huge skyscraper tomb thing, that's like that stupid Rock and Roll Museum that Paul Allen built…. But there's nothing in there now but science fiction weirdness. That totally sucks!"

Gavin cleared his throat. "Well, the music industry does have other potential revenue models. There's subscriptions, merchandise sales…"

"Gavin, are you stupid? That's not reality! That is a fantasy! When the money walks away, money never comes back! Not by itself! And when all the money's gone, there's nothing left but zombies. Zombies and vampires!"

Gavin was completely thrown by this bizarre remark. He truly didn't know what to say to her. He'd been doing pretty well with Eliza on this trip, but now the gears froze solid in his head.

Whenever he talked to Eliza, there was always some moment where she jumped into a kinky flight of fancy, where he couldn't follow. This was another one of those unhappy, broken moments.

All that he could do was try to show her that he loved her.

"Eliza, I'm glad we're having this discussion. I know that you have some strong concerns in this direction. I, just, never heard you frame them quite like this."

"Can you talk to Dad about this for me? I mean, about me and my plans to save the soul of music?" Eliza kicked at the rocky path with her combat boot. "I know my life, as, like, a 'music superstar princess'... Well, I know, that doesn't sound very realistic."

"Well," Gavin hedged, "we're here in Capri to attend a futurist conference. There are five hundred famous international experts coming here, here to get ahead of planetary trends! You couldn't ask for a better place to work on your issues! You can attend all the panels, and watch them plot and scheme about futurity, and master the world of tomorrow! So, if you can show me that you're serious about your plans... sure, I'll talk to Dad for you."

"Dad will hate my ideas. Dad wants me to mind my grades and study law. If I tell Dad that I love music more than anything, he's gonna start yelling at me again."

"Listen, never mind that. Dad should have come out here to Capri *himself*. Dad really needs a vacation. This finance crisis has got Dad all keyed up."

Elizabeth shrugged. "Money isn't everything."

"Of course it isn't," Gavin said. "I agree with you. That is a fact. Just take Detroit, for instance. Over at Cook, Bishop & Engleman, we just held a big futurist workshop about contemporary issues in American urbanism. Detroit is totally broke, and yet Detroit's also a great city for American music production. See, that's a vital data-point for you, right there."

"Gavin, you *do* sort of understand this, don't you? I mean, you understand some parts of it. In your own way."

"Yeah, sometimes I do," he said. "Yeah, sometimes I really do understand the future." That didn't mean that he was happy about it.

"Gavin, everybody says that you're way ahead of your time. You started Fettlr, and you sold it to Yahoo for 20 million dollars! And you did it in, like, two weeks! That was so totally great! Everybody talks about our Dad being this so-called 'great businessman'—but Dad never did anything like *that*."

Gavin silently looked at his Omega wristwatch. "Are you hungry?"

"I could eat."

"We got maybe an hour before the conference opens. Let's grab a couple of sandwiches."

They hiked up the steep, scaly pavement, which wriggled over Capri like a concrete snake. A hotel lurked on the blossoming peak of the ridge.

This hotel commanded a view over Capri that was divine. Capri looked divine because Capri was divine. The sea around the island was doing all kinds of surging and sparkling things that mere seawater was never supposed to do. The azure sea was jeweled with yachts. Capri was classically divine, like the goddess Venus. Capri had divinities the way lesser islands had oysters.

The sky over Capri had hundreds of rich, distinct tints of blue, like a dome of blue art-glass. Paragliders were swooping and fluttering up there. Young athletes like angels, graceful and fearless, zooming over Capri with bright colored fabric and string.

The Capri hotel had a somber, crooked dining room, with a grandmotherly Italian waitress. She led them to a creaky wooden table tucked in the room's darkest corner, so that Eliza's kinky Goth gear wouldn't alarm her other customers.

This Capri hotel had nothing to eat that was "fast." Patrons of majestic old Capri hotels were supposed to eat thoughtfully, in a civilized, European fashion. First, a nice little snack with a drink. Then the first real course. After that, a good, solid second course. Then a sweet. Then some brandy, nuts and cigars.

After a polite debate in his college Italian, Gavin managed to order them a couple of salads, an overpriced bottle of mineral water, and nothing else.

Gavin carefully spread the hotel's linen napkin over his cargo pants. The hotel's parquet floors looked spotty and warped. The inner walls had been rebuilt so many times that they leaned at odd angles, like a stage set for a silent film. Everything in this old hotel had been patched or painted over, bored-through, rewired, refurbished, then buried in enamel and lacquer.

Eliza busily flicked at her iPhone, her burgundy fingernails skidding on the screen. "Hey Gavin, wow, an arms merchant built this hotel. He was this rich German guy who made cannons in World War One. I bet his corporation killed a million people."

"Yeah, welcome to Europe, Eliza."

Eliza glanced up at him, her blue eyes full of wicked satisfaction. "This place has just got to be haunted."

Gavin had a bite of his Capri hotel salad, a leafy construction that featured capers, olives and anchovies. He'd expected a quick tourist salad to be pretty mediocre, but this was a magnificent salad. It was likely the best salad Gavin had ever eaten in his life. It was like an opera in a bowl. Miracles could happen in a place that had such salads.

Gavin sloshed pink vinegar from a cut-glass cruet. "'There is nothing new except what has been forgotten.' Marie Antoinette said that."

"Marie who?"

"I said Marie Antoinette, Eliza. Marie Antoinette was a princess."

"Oh, yeah, her, Marie Antoinette! She was in that Sofia Coppola film with that techno soundtrack. Great movie, I totally loved that movie! And I love this hotel, too! Can we check out of our lame modern hotel, and move into this cool, old hotel? This cool, old, *haunted* hotel? Please, Gavin, just for me, please please?"

Lover B: The Convent of Crossed Destinies

Farfalla had jumped the train without a ticket, from Milano all the way to Napoli. Six and a half hours of avoiding the conductors. Then Farfalla had jumped a bus in Naples from the railway to the ferry to Capri. She paid nothing for that, too.

She had no way to sneak aboard the hydrofoil to Capri. The ferry only had one gangplank, and two sailors were watching it. So Farfalla had to pay the ferry fare.

So she finally arrived in Capri, tugging her roll-aboard suitcase, completely broke.

Well, almost completely broke. Not quite completely. Farfalla had one stray two-euro coin stuck deep in the lining of her purse. She also found one twenty-eurocent coin. A coin with a beautiful statue created by an Italian Futurist.

To find the Futurist coin meant good luck for Farfalla. At least, she had to believe that Futurism was her good luck.

The Capri Trend Assessment Congress was a paying gig for Farfalla. She was there to translate for the foreign speakers, and to run errands for Babi, who was a conference organizer. That work would pay her in cash, under the table of course.

But Farfalla wouldn't see any money from Babi until the event was over.

That meant that Farfalla had to survive for three days in Capri with two euros and twenty cents.

Farfalla had her iPhone, her conference badge, and a couch in a stranger's apartment. Farfalla could probably manage with that. She had managed with less than that, in worse places than Capri.

So, hello again, Capri! Beautiful, gorgeous, divine Capri! Lovely Capri, charming Capri, Capri, the island of tender romance! Capri could be a very romantic place—if you were a princess in disguise, like Audrey

Hepburn in *Roman Holiday*. Italian men hitting on Farfalla often told her that she looked like Audrey Hepburn. Farfalla Corrado was nobody's Audrey Hepburn.

Farfalla dragged her rolling luggage through the narrow Capri streets. Purring housecats, fresh fried fish, and boutiques smelling of cologne and sea-salt. Wobbling on her heels in the rugged cobblestones, Farfalla hiked to her accommodation. This was a spare couch in the small, cigarette-stinking apartment of one of Babi's many personal friends.

Farfalla's new hostess, Eleonora, was a washed-up Italian television showgirl. Eleonora gave Farfalla a spare key to the flat, and then talked at her for half an hour. Eleonora talked just like Italian television: which meant that she was loud and colorful, and she had nothing much to say.

Farfalla abandoned her rolling bag next to the couch, packed her purse, and left the apartment. The Capri Trend Assessment Congress was taking place in two different buildings, downhill, five blocks away.

One building was new, tall and strong. The other building was old, low and ruined. The future had joined them together. Nobody could pry them apart.

Farfalla took a deep breath and invaded the shining five-star conference hotel. She found it very posh. The official conference hotel had towering palms and rippling balconies, spas, gyms and swimming pools. It had glass elevators, brass staircases, and a cellar full of fine wine and fine luggage.

This glorious Capri hotel was a sleek machine for taking credit cards from wealthy foreigners. The cheapest room in the place cost 220 euros a night. This was exactly one hundred times as much money as Farfalla had.

Farfalla snagged two perfect apples from a hammered silver bowl in the hotel. She stuffed her purse with the hotel's giveaway soaps, shampoos and body lotions. Farfalla would eat, and she would have a pretty good hair day. Here in the future, her life was already improving.

On her way out of the hotel, Farfalla saw a local cabbie harassing an old woman.

Old Lady Tourist wore a sturdy houndstooth cloth coat, Anne Klein gloves, and a hairnet. She looked close to tears. "He won't accept American Express," Lady Tourist lamented in English. "He wants to drive me to a bank machine to get him euros."

Farfalla confronted the cabbie at once. *"Che cosa ti sta succedendo, tu ladro succhiatore di sangue? Cosa sei, albanese?"*

"Me, Albanian? I'd rather be dead!" the cabbie protested.

"You Rumanian vampire, you'll steal fares from my conference people like the dirty bandit that you are, and cheat your blessed grandma here? Get lost! I can call my old man at the Tourist Board, and he'll break both your legs!"

The driver ducked behind his wheel and slammed his door. He fled the scene of his crime.

Tourist Lady had tumbled her heavy bag from the taxi's trunk. She watched the taxi rumble down the tilted street. "Miss, you seem to have saved me thirty euros."

"Ma'am, a trip from the ferry costs ten."

"Well then! I don't think my driver was entirely honest!"

"He is a *clandestini*. An illegal foreigner. Not like you!"

Farfalla helped Tourist Lady lug her ungainly bag up the stone stairs toward the hotel's registration. Tourist Lady's bag was very old-fashioned, solid and square, all brass buckles and leather. No wheels on it! How old did a lady have to be, to have a travel bag with no wheels?

Farfalla had warm, protective feelings about tourists and travelers. She felt a sacred bond with them, a need to make their lives easier. Guests should always be treated kindly. Because, after all, you never knew who a "foreign guest" really was.

Farfalla herself was a foreign guest in the world, most of the time. Nobody knew who she really was, either.

Especially, nice little old foreign ladies—helpless old ladies were *especially* sacred guests. Old ladies should be watched over and comforted and protected at all times, in Italy. Because Italy had more than a thousand dark surprises for nice little old foreign ladies.

Tourist Lady announced herself at the hotel desk. It seemed that Tourist Lady was an American professor from a university in Virginia. She had a reservation in a room for two.

"So, Professor Milo," said Farfalla to Tourist Lady, "you must be here for my Trend Assessment Congress! *Benvenuto!* Let me show you to our venue."

"No, thank you," said Professor Milo, removing her hat with a prim little nod. "I came here to Capri entirely for private reasons."

Farfalla blinked. "For 'private reasons'?"

"Yes, private reasons."

How private could her reasons be? thought Farfalla at once. Was this stout, blue-haired American professor checking into this fancy Capri hotel for some frolic with a secret lover? Or, well, why not? Maybe she was old and gray, but when was love ever likely?

Farfalla politely shook Professor Milo's dainty gloved hand. Then she left.

Farfalla ventured past the tall glass panes of the Capri tourist-traps. They peddled kinky lingerie, odd-shaped limoncello bottles and necklaces of ragged red coral. She walked a narrow, winding lane, between walls overhung with dark, crooked, odorous fig trees.

The site of the Trend Assessment Congress was a wreck. The venue was a former medieval convent. This old convent had been built on the stony ruins of some even more ancient Roman structure. Southern Italy was full of layer-cake buildings of this kind. Italian earthquakes made that a local way of life.

Babi claimed that the convent had probably been a brothel, once. Babi was from Naples, so Babi had incredible street-smarts. You had to be a woman from Naples to realize that a brothel and a convent were basically the same enterprise. As Babi pointed out: as long as big stone walls locked the men out, you could make a pretty good business of it, either way.

This medieval convent did have big stone walls. It also had a tall forest of marble columns within its inner courtyard, among the crumbly ruins of many small cells. Here the wimpled nuns had passed their sunlit days and their starry nights, in solemn prayer. Quietly reading Holy Scripture, and growing heaps of pretty flowers. Peaceful Italian women, entirely free of the bellowing demands of Italian men.

Farfalla had to envy this quiet life of female spiritual contemplation. Farfalla had grown up all over the world, mostly in Brazil. Farfalla had always lived out of her suitcase. Farfalla had never had one spot on Earth to truly call her own.

Worse yet, although Farfalla was spiritual—very, very spiritual—her spiritual life was not very Italian. Farfalla's spiritual life was mostly Brazilian.

Farfalla knew that she would have to work hard inside in this futuristic-medieval-ancient venue, so she had a good look around the place. This convent had a stone chapel, the one major part of the ruin that was still standing up decently. This big chapel was the speaker's venue for the Capri futurist conference. The government of Capri was an official conference sponsor. The Capri state government had to stuff big events into big empty buildings that Capri had handy.

The chapel's gloomy stone walls featured half-decayed plaster murals of Biblical prophets. The chapel's ceiling swarmed with cherubs, or rather "putti."

Farfalla despised Italian putti. Putti were flying winged baby heads. Sometimes the putti had a baby body attached. Putti were supposed to be the sweetest, cutest, most harmless things in the world, sort of like Hello Kitties. But Farfalla had never trusted cherubs. Never. Because cherubs were baby ghosts.

Cherubs were spirits who would never grow up, never become men and women. Cherubs were fossil babies frozen forever in time. How could that possibly be good? There was something ghastly about that.

Thanks to her Brazilian heritage, there were aspects of Italy that Farfalla had never taken for granted. *Evil* aspects of Italy, mostly. Farfalla had a very keen sense of evil. Mostly because she had so much of it inside herself.

Italy had whole evil swarms of sweet rosy-cheeked cherubs. Italian cherubs always appeared in the places in Italy where truly dark and awful things had happened in history. The dreadful sites of martyrdom, massacres, torment and hideous slaughter. It took a while to catch on to this creepy fact about Italian cherubs, but it was the truth.

Farfalla studied the chapel's faded blue ceiling. These nunnery cherubs, buzzing around up there like so many bluebottle flies, had a king cherub. He was some kind of cherub-mafia mob boss. This decaying angel was obviously very old. He looked older than Italian dirt. Yet he had a perky, scary, juvenile-delinquent smirk on his ancient face.

Farfalla plucked her iPhone from her bargain Versace purse. She examined the dozens of applications that she had downloaded and installed. She found one that told her the absolutely correct, atomically registered time. The local time was ten minutes and eleven seconds past six pm. Ten minutes past time to start the big Futurist Congress, and to get on with the serious business of foretelling some future.

This Futurist Congress would be a very grand event, or so she'd been promised. It had high-tech "thought leaders," who were American Internet types. It had modish European fashion celebrities. It featured pop-stars, mostly trendy Brazilian ones. This was a dazzling crowd fit to do Capri proud.

None of them were here yet, though. Because none of them had shown up on time.

All these futuristic beautiful-people were in Capri already, but none of them were doing any honest work. Instead, they were off having a Campari somewhere. Gossiping with each other. Dawdling over the cashews in their five-star hotel bar. Her futurist chapel was as empty as a vampire's tomb.

Farfalla was all alone.

Farfalla felt miffed and bitter. Why was her life always like this? *Why?* Here she was, all the way from Milan, after untold risk and trouble to get here. Her nails were done, her teeth brushed, and her hair was done. She was ready. No one else was.

Farfalla was also dressed in a particularly creative and appropriate Milanese outfit. Farfalla's new silk dress featured a vibrant and beautiful Futurist print by Fortunato Depero. Nobody was noticing Farfalla's extremely apt and tasteful choice of this thematic clothing. Maybe three random German tourists. In Capri, three random German tourists counted as nobody.

Farfalla thought wistfully of the years she had spent in the United States. Farfalla often dreamed about distant America. America was a grand country, where people drove huge cars and ate colossal meals. Better yet, Americans always showed up on time. If you said "six," Americans came at six. In Italy, "six" meant six thirty. In Capri, it was worse. In Capri, "six" was printed on some useless tourist brochure that nobody even bothered to read.

Farfalla stalked across the chapel's stage, with its pale translucent plastic podium and its giant projection screens.

The niche behind the stage was a scene of total chaos. The Web people had taken over, back there. The backstage was crammed with cascades of colored cables and blinking media boxes.

The Web people were the worst. Farfalla went to a great many tech conferences, because they paid their translators a lot to suffer through all the computer jargon. It paid pretty well, but it was awful.

Every year, there were more Web people at conferences. Every year, the Web people said crazier things. Every year, more people watched conferences on the Web. So that the conference became mostly ghosts, watching on the Web. Even undead baby cherubs were pretty wholesome, compared to the Web people.

The Capri Trend Assessment Congress would be live-streamed over the Web. Not a good omen, thought Farfalla.

A pasty-faced Web geek emerged from his unruly heap of glowing hardware. Farfalla put her hands on her hips. *"Che cosa è successo a tutte quelle casse vecchie che sono state qui?"*

"I'm from Brazil! Do you speak any English?"

"OK, dude, no problem, *onde estão os fones de tradução para o grande evento?*"

The Brazilian geek grinned in surprise at her Portuguese, and he shrugged. *"Eu também gostaria de saber. Estou tentando conseguir os projetores pra essa atividade!"*

How useless! Worse and worse! With a clouded brow, Farfalla left.

Premonitions were crawling all over her now. She sensed a mounting wave of bad vibrations. Why had she ever agreed to come to Capri? She could have stayed safe in Ivrea, in her abandoned typewriter factory.

Farfalla felt her head swimming. Something was coming that was bad, big and bad. Had they poisoned that apple that she stole from the hotel? Was a thunderstorm about to break? Something awful was about to happen.

Farfalla trusted her premonitions. She had no choice about that, because her premonitions were always right.

A stranger had arrived in the chapel. He was the first from the incoming crowd of futurists. He folded his tall frame into a conference chair, in a slanting beam of golden Capri sunlight. This glow fell on him like a blessing.

The stranger was tall and handsome. He was ominous and fatal.

He was the One! Here he was, yes, him, the One! He had burst into her life out of nowhere, like a golden mushroom.

Farfalla had been expecting the One since the age of twelve. In São Paulo, a fortune-teller had read Farfalla's fate. This witch had told Farfalla all about the One. She had known what to expect!

When you met the One—her mentor the witch told her—well, that man was your One. That man was your *only* One. That was *why* he was the One. He was the only One you would ever truly love! He was yours, and you were his. And that was destiny!

It was the most beautiful story in all the world. And a very popular story, too. Women adored that story. Unless you were a fortune-teller, the kind of woman who could see her way through a beautiful story. That was the worst part of being with a witch. When she really started telling you how witchcraft worked, how stories put their spells on people.

Yes, he is your One! But consider this, the wise woman urged: after that, all other men become useless to you! You have your One. He's the only One you care about. Huge armies of useless men inhabit your world, suddenly. That's a setback in a fortune-teller's business, to say the least.

Because the poor fortune-teller also had a One of her own. She loved her One with a passion, she was the slave of her One, and she had no other One. That was why she was a miserable fortune-teller, instead of having some kind of real, paying career.

Now the fortune-teller's prophesy had come true, as Farfalla had always known that it would. That feeling was very ominous, huge and cloudy and fatal. It lived in the beating core of her heart.

Farfalla turned her back on the One, pretended to study the speaker's podium, which was made of sleek high-tech plastic. She turned around again, to sneak another look at her One. Yes, she felt just the same way about him. This One was indeed her destiny.

This was a terrible thing to know. Her destiny. Something terrible about that very word.

Now, another even worse sensation emerged. The extremely creepy feeling of having been here before. Of having lived this already, somehow.

Her premonitions of futurity had left her now. The déjà vu had her, cold and numbing, right to the bone, like a snakebite. Farfalla was extremely given to déjà vu. Her déjà vu was her personal curse. She'd suffered déjà vu for twenty years before anybody got around to telling her what déjà vu was.

Farfalla knew in her soul that she had already met this man. She hadn't "met him" yet, because he didn't know that she existed. Yet he had somehow, terribly, *always been around her*. He had always been in her life, and until this strange moment in Capri, she had never been able to perceive him.

He had to be her One. He wasn't just some normal guy. She wasn't normal, either. A normal woman's One was some lovable guy that she fell for, and did anything for, and just had to be with. Farfalla had it figured that she could probably handle a romance like that. She'd told herself that, probably, it wouldn't be so bad! Because even if she was struck with complete, heart-choking fits of true love over him, her One would just be some dumb everyday guy. While she, Farfalla Corrado, was a woman who could foretell the future. So, probably, she would be able to deal with him. Somehow.

But this guy wasn't like that at all. This guy was much worse than that.

The two of them had a future together, because they already had a past together. Farfalla couldn't quite seem to remember their very personal history, but it lurked in her like a recurring nightmare. It was very deep in there. It was heartache-deep. Deep in her soul like a buried splinter, too deep to get her mental fingertips around.

She and this tall man in his pretty beam of sunlight, they had a long, colorful history together. They had a too-long, too-colorful history. They had a history like Italian history.

Thank the Madonna, he hadn't seen her. Not yet. Thanks to her clairvoyant spiritual powers, Farfalla had foreseen this trouble before it had happened to her. She had felt a premonition about it. Her romance hadn't actually happened to her yet. Her burning, flaming, abject, passionate love was not going on. So far, she was still being spared.

Her knees trembled with the urge to flee.

The One did not realize that she was standing there, trembling, and staring. He did not know or care about her. He did not even bother. He had his tourist camera in his hand, and he was snapping shots at the host of evil cherubs bustling on the convent's peeling ceiling. He looked like any other Capri tourist. He looked happy and thoughtless and slightly stupefied.

Farfalla made one dainty move to creep out of the place unseen. But it was too late. Suddenly, like a tide, futurists were arriving for the conference. They were crowding through the church doors in a mass.

A damp-faced, gangly creep of a Goth girl slouched into the chapel, along with the crowd. She saw the One, and she moved at once to join him. She flounced down in a shadow next to his beam of light.

From the tender look on his face—he was blond, slightly sunburned, quite good-looking, though kind of big, with a big nose—he worshipped this hopeless Goth girl. He was all urgent and attentive about her. In response, she had this insufferable, teenager, eye-rolling look. She was a mess.

Suddenly the two of them looked up at Farfalla. They both took full, surprised notice of her. They were a brother and a sister, because they had the same fatal blue eyes. They had four eyes that pierced her like four blue ice-picks.

Farfalla was pinned to the stage.

She found her willpower, and she ran to hide.

CATASTROPHIC DISRUPTION
OF THE HEAD

MARGO LANAGAN

Margo Lanagan has published four collections of short stories—White Time,
Black Juice, Red Spikes, *and* Yellowcake—*and a novel,* Tender Morsels.
*She is a four-time World Fantasy Award winner for best collection, short
story, novel, and most recently for a novella, "Sea-Hearts," which she has
since expanded into a novel,* The Brides of Rollrock Island (Sea Hearts
in Australia), *to be published in 2012. Two of her books are Michael L.
Printz Honor Books, and her work has also been nominated for the Los
Angeles Times Book Prize, the Frank O'Connor International Short Story
Award, and the Commonwealth Writers' Prize, and twice been placed on
the James Tiptree Jr. Award honor list, as well as being shortlisted for Hugo,
Nebula, Sturgeon, Stoker, Seiun, International Horror Guild, and Shirley
Jackson awards. "Catastrophic Disruption of the Head," inspired by Hans
Christian Andersen's story "The Tinderbox," was first published in Isobelle
Carmody and Nan McNab's two-volume collection of modernized fairy
tales,* Tales from the Tower, *published by Allen & Unwin. Margo lives in
Sydney, Australia.*

Who believes in his own death? I've seen how men stop being,
how people that you spoke to and traded with slump to bleeding and lie still, and never rise again. I have my own shiny
scars, now; I've a head full of stories that goat-men will never believe.
And I can tell you: with everyone dying around you, still you can remain

unharmed. Some boss-soldier will pull you out roughly at the end, while the machines in the air fling fire down on the enemy, halting the chatter of their guns—at last, at last!—when nothing on the ground would quiet it. I always thought I would be one of those lucky ones, and it turns out that I am. The men who go home as stories on others' lips? They fell in front of me, next to me; I could have been dead just as instantly, or maimed worse than dead. I steeled myself before every fight, and shat myself. But still another part of me stayed serene, didn't it. And was justified in that, wasn't it, for here I am: all in one piece, wealthy, powerful, safe, and on the point of becoming king.

I have the king by the neck. I push my pistol into his mouth, and he gags. He does not know how to fight, hasn't the first clue. He smells nice, expensive. I swing him out from me. I blow out the back of his head. All sound goes out of the world.

I went to the war because elsewhere was glamorous to me. Men had passed through the mountains, one or two of them every year of my life, speaking of what they had come from, and where they were going. All those events and places showed me, with their color and their mystery and their crowdedness, how simple an existence I had here with my people—and how confined, though the sky was broad above us, though we walked the hills and mountains freely with our flocks. The fathers drank up their words, the mothers hurried to feed them, and silently watched and listened. I wanted to bring news home and be the feted man and the respected, the one explaining, not the one all eyes and questions among the goats and children.

I went for the adventure and the cleverness of these men's lives and the scheming. I wanted to live in those stories they told. The boss-soldiers and all their equipment and belongings and weapons and information, and all the other people grasping after those things—I wanted to play them off against each other as these men said they did, and gather the money and food and toys that fell between. One of those silvery capsules, that opened like a seed-case and twinkled and tinkled, that you used for talking to your contact in the hills or among the bosses—I wanted one of those.

There was also the game of the fighting itself. A man might lose that game, they told us, at any moment, and in the least dignified manner, toileting in a ditch, or putting food on his plate at the barracks, or having at a whore in the tents nearby. (There were lots of whores, they told the fathers; every woman was a whore there; some of them did not even take your money, but went with you for the sheer love of whoring.) But look, here was this stranger whole and healthy among us, and all he had was that scar on his arm, smooth and harmless, for all his stories of a head rolling into his lap, and of men up dancing one moment, and stilled forever the next. He was here, eating our food and laughing. The others were only words; they might be stories and no more, boasting and no more. I watched my father and uncles, and some could believe our visitor and some could not, that he had seen so many deaths, and so vividly.

"You are different," whispers the princess, almost crouched there, looking up at me. "You were gentle and kind before. What has happened? What has changed?"

I was standing in a wasteland, very cold. An old woman lay dead, blown backwards off the stump she'd been sitting on; the pistol that had taken her face off was in my hand—mine, that the bosses had given me to fight with, that I was smuggling home. My wrist hummed from the shot, my fingertips tingled.

I still had some swagger in me, from the stuff my drugs-man had given me, my going-home gift, his farewell spliff to me, with good powder in it, that I had half-smoked as I walked here. I lifted the pistol and sniffed the tip, and the smoke stung in my nostrils. Then the hand with the pistol fell to my side, and I was only cold and mystified. An explosion will do that, wake you up from whatever drug is running your mind, dismiss whatever dream, and sharply.

I put the pistol back in my belt. What had she done, the old biddy, to annoy me so? I went around the stump and looked at her. She was only disgusting the way old women are always disgusting, with a layer of filth on her such as war always leaves. She had no weapon; she could not have been dangerous to me in any way. Her face was clean and bright between her dirt-black hands—not like a face, of course, but clean red tissue, clean white bone-shards. I was annoyed with myself, mildly, for not leaving her alive so that she could tell me what all this was about. I glared at her facelessness, watching in case the drug should make her dead face speak, mouthless as she was. But she only lay, looking blankly, redly at the sky.

She lied to you, my memory hissed at me.

Ah, yes, that was why I'd shot her. *You make no sense, old woman,* I'd said. Sick of looking at her ugliness, I'd turned cruel, from having been milder before, even kind—from doing the old rag-and-bone a favor! *Here I stand,* I said, *with Yankee dollars spilling over my feet. Here you sit, over a cellar full of treasures, enough to set you up in palaces and feed and clothe you queenly the rest of your days. Yet all you can bring yourself to want is this old thing, factory made, one of millions, well used already.*

I'd turned the Bic this way and that in the sunlight. It was like opening a sack of rice at a homeless camp; I had her full attention, however uncaring she tried to seem.

Children of this country, of this war, will sell you these Bics for a packet-meal—they feed a whole family with one man's ration. *In desperate times, two rows of chocolate is all it costs you. Their doddering grandfather will sell you the fluid for a twist of tobacco. Or you can buy a Bic entirely new and full from such shops as are left*—caves in the rubble, banged-together stalls set up on the bulldozed streets. *A new one will light first go; you won't have to shake it and swear, or click it some magic number of times. Soldiers are rich men in war. All our needs are met, and our pay is laid on extra. There is no need for us to go shooting people, not for cheap cigarette-lighters*—cheap and pink and lady-sized.

Yes, but it is mine, she had lied on at me. *It was given to me by my son, that went off to war just like you, and got himself killed for his motherland. It has its hold on me that way. Quite worthless to any other person, it is.*

In the hunch of her and the lick of her lips, the thing was of very great worth indeed.

Tell me the truth, old woman. I had pushed aside my coat. *I have a gun here that makes people tell things true. I have used it many times. What is this Bic to you? or I'll take your head off.*

She looked at my pistol, in its well-worn sheath. She stuck out her chin, fixed again on the lighter. *Give it me!* she said. If she'd begged, if she'd wept, I might have, but her anger set mine off; that was her mistake.

I lean over the king and push the door-button on the remote. The queen's men burst in, all pistols and posturing like men in a movie.

It was dark under there, and it smelled like dirt and death-rot. I didn't want to let the rope go.

Only the big archways are safe, she'd said. *Stand under them and all will be well, but step either side and you must use my pinny or the dogs will eat you alive.* I could see no archway; all was black.

I could *hear* a dog, though, panting out the foul air. The sound was all around, at both my ears equally. I knew dogs, good dogs; but no dog had ever stood higher than my knee. From the sound, this one could take my whole head in its mouth, and would have to stoop to do so.

Which way should I go? How far? I put out my hands, with the biddy's apron between them. I was a fool to believe her; what was this scrap of cloth against such a beast? I made the kissing noise you make to a dog. *Pup? Pup?* I said.

His eyes came alight, reddish—at the far end of him, praise God. Oh, he was enormous! His tail twitched on the floor in front of me, and the sparse gray fur on it sprouted higher than my waist. He lifted his head—bigger than the whole house my family lived in, it was. He looked down at me over the scabby ridges of his rib-cage. Vermin hopped in the beams of his red eyes. His whole starveling face crinkled in a grin. With a gust of butchery breath he was up on his spindly shanks. He lowered his head to me full of lights and teeth, tightening the air with his growl.

A farther dog woke with a bark, and a yet farther one. They set this one off, and I only just got the apron up in time, between me and the noise and the snapping teeth. That silenced him. His long claws skittered on the chamber's stone floor. He paced, and turned and paced again, growling deep and constantly. His lip was caught high on his teeth; his red eyes glared and churned. The hackles stuck up like teeth along his back.

Turning my face aside I forced myself and the apron forward at him. Oh, look—an archway there, just as the old woman said. White light from the next chamber jumped and swerved in it.

The dog's red eyes were as big as those discs the bosses carry their movies on. They looked blind, but he saw me, he saw me; I *felt* his gaze on me, the way you feel a sniper's, in your spine—and his ill-will, only just held back. I pushed the cloth at his nostrils. Rotten-sour breath gusted underneath at me.

But he shrank as the old woman had told me he would, nose and paws and the rest of him; his eyes shone brighter, narrowing to torch-beams. Now I was wrapping not much more than a pup, and a miserable wreck he was, hardly any fur, and his skin all sores and scratches.

I picked him up and carried him to the white-flashing archway, kicking aside coins; they were scattered all over the floor, and heaped up against the red-lit walls. Among them lay bones of dog, bird, sheep, and some of person—old bones, well gnawed, and not a scrap of meat on any of them.

I stepped under the archway and dropped the mangy dog back into his room. He exploded out of himself, into himself, horribly huge and sudden, hating me for what I'd done. But I was safe here; that old witch had known what she was talking about. I turned and pushed the apron at the next dog.

He was a mess of white light, white teeth, snapping madly at the other opening. He smelled of clean hot metal. He shrank to almost an ordinary fighting dog, lean, smooth-haired, strong, with jaws that could break your leg-bone if he took you. His eyes were still magic, though, glaring blind, bulging white. His heavy paws, scrabbling, pushed paper-scraps forward; he cringed in the storm of paper he'd stirred up when he'd been a giant and flinging himself about. As I wrapped him, some of the papers settled near his head: American dollars. *Big* dollars, three-numbered. Oh these, *these* I could carry, these I could use.

For now, though, I lifted the dog. Much heavier he was, than the starving one. I slipped and slid across the drifts of money to the next archway. Beyond it the third dog raged at me, a barking fire-storm. I threw the white dog back behind me, then raised the apron and stepped up to the orange glare, shouting at the flame-dog to settle; I couldn't even hear my own voice.

He shrank in size, but not in power or strangeness. His coat seethed about him, thick with waving gold wires; his tongue was a sprout of fire and white-hot arrow-tips lined his jaws. His eyes, half-exploded from his head, were two ponds of lava, rimmed with the flame pouring from their sockets—clearly they could not see, but my bowels knew he was there behind them, waiting for his chance to cool his teeth in me, to set me alight.

I wrapped my magic cloth around him, picked him up and shone his eye-light about. The scrabbles and shouting from the other dogs behind me bounced off the smooth floor, lost themselves in the rough walls arching over. Where was the treasure the old biddy had promised me in this chamber, the richest of all the three?

The dog burned and panted under my arm. I walked all around, prodding parts of the walls in case they should spill jewels at me or open into treasure-rooms. I reached into cavities hoping to feel bars of gold, giant diamonds—I hardly knew what.

All I found was the lighter the old biddy had asked me to fetch, the pink plastic Bic, lady-sized. And an envelope. Inside was a letter in bosswriting, and attached to that was a rectangle of plastic, with a picture of a foreign girl on it, showing most of her breasts and all of her stomach and legs as she stood in the sea-edge, laughing out of the picture at me.

Someone was playing a joke on me, insulting my God and our women instead of delivering me the treasure I'd been promised.

I turned the thing over, rubbed the gold-painted lettering that stood up out of the plastic. Rubbish. Still, there were all those Yankee dollars, no? Plenty there for my needs. I pocketed the Bic and put the rubbish back in the hole in the wall. I crossed swiftly to the archway, turned in its safety and shook the dog out of the cloth. Its eyes flared wide, and its roar was part voice, part flame. I showed it my back. I'd met real fire, that choked and cooked people—this fairy-fire held no fear for me.

Back in the white dog's chamber, I stuffed my pack as full as I could, every pocket of it, with the dollars. It was *heavy*! It and the white fighting dog were almost more than I could manage. But I took them through and into the red-lit carrion-cave, and I subdued the mangy dog there. I carried him across to where rope-end dangled in its root-lined niche, and I pulled the loop down around the bulk of the money on my back, and the dog still in my arms, and hooked it under myself.

There came a shout from above. Praise God, she had not run off and left me.

Yes! I cried. *Bring me up!*

When she had me well off the floor, I cast the red-eyed dog out of the apron-cloth. He dropped; he ballooned out full-sized, long-shanked. He looked me in the eye, with his lip curled and his breath fit to wither the skin right off my face. I flapped the apron at him. *Boo*, I said. *There. Get down.* The other two dogs bayed deep below. Had they made such a noise at the beginning, I never would have gone down.

And then I was out the top of the tree-trunk and swinging from the branch, slower now than I'd swung before, being so much heavier. The old woman stood there, holding me and my burden aloft, the rope coiling beside her. She was stronger than I would have believed possible.

Do you have it? She beamed up at me.

Oh, I have it, don't worry. But get me down from here before I give you it. I would not trust you as far as I could throw you.

And she laughed, properly witch-like, and stepped in to secure the rope against the tree.

She is not the first virgin I've had, my little queen, but she fights the hardest and is the most satisfying, having never in her worst dreams imagined this could happen to her. I have her every which way, and she urges me on with her screams, with her weeping, with her small fists and her torn

mouth and her eyes now wide, now tight-closed squeezing out tears. The
indignities I put her through, the unqueenly positions I force her into, force
her to stay in, excite me again as soon as I am spent. She fills up the air
with her pleading, her horror, her powerless pretty rage, for as long as she
still has the spirit.

I left the old woman where she lay, and I took her treasure with me, her
little Bic. I walked another day, and then a truck came by and picked
me up and took me to the next big town. I found a bank, and had no
difficulty storing my monies away in it. There I learned what I had lost
when I put the sexy-card back in the cave wall, for the bank-man gave
me just such a one, only plainer. The card was the key to my money, he
said. I should show the card to whoever was selling to me, and through
the magic of computers the money would flow straight out of the bank
to that person, without me having to touch it.

"Where is a good hotel?" I asked him, when we were done. "And where
can I find good shopping, like Armani and Rolex?" These names I had
heard argued over, as we crouched in foxholes and behind walls waiting
for orders; I had seen them in the boss-magazines, between the pages
of the women some men tortured themselves with wanting, during the
many boredoms of the army.

The bank-man came out with me onto the street and waved me up a
taxi. I didn't even have to tell the driver where to go. I sat in the back
seat and smiled at my good fortune. The driver eyed me in the mirror.

"Watch the road," I said. "You'll be in big trouble if I get hurt."

"Sir," he said.

At the hotel I found that I was already vouched for; the bank had tele-
phoned them to say I was coming and to treat me well.

"First," I said, "I will have a hot bath, a meal, and some hours' sleep.
I've travelled a long way. Then I will need clothes, and this uniform to be
burned. And introductions. Other rich men. Rich women, too; beautiful
women. I'm sure you know the kind of thing I mean."

When I was stuffing my pack full of dollars underground, I could not
imagine ever finding a use for so much money. But then began my new
life. A long, bright dream, it was, of laughing friends, and devil women
in their devil clothes, and wonderful drugs, and new objects and belongings conjured by money as if by wizardry, and I enjoyed it all and
thoroughly. Money lifts and floats you, above cold weather and hunger
and war, above filth, above having to think and plan—if any problem

comes at you, you throw a little money at it and it is gone, and everyone smiles and bows and thanks you for your patronage.

That is, until your plastic dies. *Then* I understood truly what treasure I'd rejected when I left that card in the third cave. There was no more money behind my card; that other card, with the near-naked woman on it, behind *that* had been an endless supply; *that* card would never have died. I had to sell my apartment and rent a cheaper place. Piece by piece I sold all the ornaments and furniture I'd accumulated, to pay my rent. But even the worth of those expensive objects ran out, and I let the electricity and the gas go, and then I found myself paying my last purseful for a month's rent in not much more than an attic, and scrounging for food.

I sat one night on the floor at my attic window, hungry and glum, with no work but herding and soldiering to turn my fortunes around with. I went through my last things, my last belongings left in a nylon backpack too shabby to sell. I pulled out an envelope, with a crest on it, of a hotel—ah, it was those scraps from the first day I had come to this town, with all my money in my pack. These were the bits and pieces that the chamber-boy had saved from the pockets of my soldiering-clothes. *Shall I throw these away, sir?* he'd said to me. *No,* I told him. *Keep them to remind me how little I had before today. How my fortunes changed.*

"Ha!" I laid the half-spliff on my knee. A grain fell out of the tip. That had been a good spliff, I remembered, well-laced with the fighting-powder that made you a hero, that took away all your fear.

"And you!" I took out the pink lighter, still fingerprinted with the mud of that blasted countryside.

"Ha!" One last half-spliff would make this all bearable. A few hours, I would have, when nothing mattered, not this house, not this hunger, not my own uselessness and the stains on my memory from what I had done as a rich man, and before that as a soldier. And then, once it was done... Well, I would just have to beggar and burgle my way home, wouldn't I, and take up with the goats again. But why think of that now? I scooped the grain back into the spliff and twisted the end closed. I flicked the lighter.

Some huge thing, rough, scabby, crushed me to the wall. I gasped a breath of sweet-rotten air and near fainted. Then the thing adjusted itself, and I was free, and could see, and it was that great gray spindly dog from the underground cave, turning and turning on himself in the tiny space of my attic, sweeping the beams of his red movie-disc eyes about, at me, at my fate and circumstances.

I stared at the lighter in my hand. A long, realizing sound came out of me. So the lighter was the key to the dogs! You flicked it, they came. And see how he lowered his head and his tail in front of me, and looked away from my stare. He was mine, in my power! I didn't need some old apron-of-a-witch to wrap him in and tame him.

Sweat prickled out on me, cold. I'd nearly left this Bic with the old biddy, in her dead hand, for a joke! Some other soldier, some civilian scavenger, some child might have picked it up and got this power! I'd been going to fling it far out into the mud-land around us, just to laugh while she scrabbled after it. I'd been going to walk away laughing, my pack stuffed with the money I'd brought up from below, and the old girl with nothing.

I looked around the red-lit attic, and out the window at the patched and crowded roofs across the way, dimming with evening. I need never shiver here again; I need never see these broken chimneys or these bent antennae. Now I *enjoyed* the tweaking of the hunger pangs in my belly, because I was about to banish them forever, just as soon as I summoned that hot golden dog with his never-dying money-card.

I clicked the lighter three times.

And so it all began again, the dream, the floating, the powders and good weed, the friends. They laughed again at my stories of how I had come here from such a nowhere. For a time there my family and our goats had lost their fascination, but now they enthralled these prosperous people again, as travellers' tales had once bewitched me around the home fires.

I catch the queen by the shoulders. One of her men dives for his gun. I shoot him; his eye spouts; he falls dead. The queen gives a tiny shriek.

I heard about the princess from the man who fitted out my yacht. He had just come from the tricky job of making lounges for the girl's prison tower, which was all circular rooms.

"Prison?" I said. "The king keeps his daughter in a prison?"

"You haven't heard of this?" He laughed. "He keeps her under lock and key, always has. He's a funny chap. He had her stars done, her chart or whatever, right when she was born, and the chart said she'd marry a soldier. So he keeps her locked up so's this soldier won't get to her. She only meets people her parents choose."

Oh, does she? I thought, even as I laughed and shook my head with the yacht-man.

That night when I was alone and had smoked a spliff, I had the golden dog bring her. She arrived asleep, his back a broad bed for her, his fire damped down for her comfort. He laid the girl on the couch nearest the fire.

She curled up there, belonging as I've never belonged in these apartments, delicate, royal, at peace. She was like a carved thing I'd just purchased, a figurine. She was beautiful, certainly, but not effortfully so, as were most women I had met since I came into my wealth. It was hard to say how much of her beauty came from the fact that I knew she was a princess; her royalty seemed to glow in her skin, to be woven into her clothing, every stitch and seam of it considered and made fit. Her little foot, out the bottom of the night-dress, was the neatest, palest, least walked-upon foot I had ever seen since the newborn feet of my brothers and sisters. It was a foot meant for an entirely different purpose from my own, from most feet of the world.

Even in my new, clean clothes, like a man's in a magazine, I felt myself to be filth crouched beside this creature. These hands had done work, these eyes had seen things that she could never conceive of; this memory was a rubbish-heap of horrors and indignities. It was one thing to be rich; it was quite another to be born into it, to be royal from a long line of royalty, to have never lived anything but the palace life.

The princess woke with the tiniest of starts. Up and back from me she sat, and she took in the room, and me.

Have you kidnapped me? she said, and swallowed a laugh.

Look at your eyes, I said, but her whole face was the thing, bright awake, and curious, and not disgusted by me.

Perhaps your name? she said gently. Her nightwear was modest in covering her neck-to-ankle, but warmth rushed through me to see her breasts so clearly outlined inside the thin cloth.

I made myself meet her eyes. *Can I serve you somehow? Are you hungry? Thirsty?*

How can I be? said the princess, and blinked. *I am asleep and dreaming. Or stoned. It smells very strongly of weed in here. Where was I before?*

I brought a tray of pretty foods from the feast the golden dog had readied. I sat beside her and poured us both some of the cordial. I handed it to her in the frail stemmed glass, raised mine to her and drank.

I shouldn't touch it, she whispered. *I am in a story; it will put me under some spell.*

Then I am magicked too, I said, and raised again the glass I'd sipped from, pretending to be alarmed that half was gone.

She laughed, a small sweet sound—she had very well-kept teeth, just like the magazine women, the poster-women—and she drank.

Now, tell me, what is all this? I said of the tray. *These little things here— they must be fruit by their shape, no? But why are they so small?*

She ate one, and it clearly pleased her. *Who is your chef?* she said, with a kind of frown of pleasure.

He is a secret, I said, for I could hardly tell her that a dog had made this feast.

Of course. She took another of the little fruits, and ate it, and held her fingers ready to lick, a delicate spread fan.

She touched her fingers to a napkin, then put the tray aside. She knelt beside me, and leaned through the perfume of herself, which was light and clean and spoke only quietly of her wealth. *Who are you?* she said, and she put her lips to mine, and held them there a little, her eyes closing, then opening surprised. *Do you not* want *to kiss me?*

I sit with my fellows in the briefing-room at the barracks. Up on the movie screen, foreign actors are locked together by their lips. Boss-soldiers groan and hoot in the seats in front of us. We giggle at the screen and at the men. "And they call us *'tribals,'" says my friend Kadir who later will be blown to pieces before my eyes. "Look at how wild they are, what animals! They cannot control themselves."*

The princess was poised to be dismayed or embarrassed. *Oh, I do* want *to,* I said, *but how is it done?* For, except for my mother in my childhood, I had never kissed a woman—even here in my rich-man life—in a way that was not somehow a violence upon her.

So handsome, and you don't already know? But she taught me. She was gentle, but forceful; she pressed herself to me, pushed me (with her little weight!) down onto the couch cushions. I was embarrassed that she must feel my desire, but she did not seem to mind, or perhaps she did not know enough to notice. She crushed her breasts against me, her belly and thighs. And the kissing—I had to breathe through my nose, for she would not stop, and there was no room for my breath with all her little lively tongue, and her hair falling and sliding everywhere, and eventually I dared to put my hands to her rounded bottom and pull her harder against me, and closed my eyes against the consequences.

Hush, she said over me at one point, rising off me, her hair making a slithering tent around our heads and shoulders, all dark gold. Her breasts hung forward in the elaborate frontage of the nightgown—I was astonished by their closeness; I covered them with my hands in a kind of swoon.

I told her what I was, in the night, over some more of that beautiful insubstantial food. I told her about the old woman, and the dogs; I showed her the Bic. *That is all I am,* I said. *Lucky. Lucky to have lived, lucky to have come into this fortune, lucky to have you before me. I am not noble and I have no right to anything.*

Oh, she said, *but it is all luck, don't you see?* And she knelt up and held my face as a child does, to make you listen. *My own family's wealth, it came about from the favors of one king and one bishop, back in the fourteenth century. You learn all the other, all the speaking and manners and how to behave with people lower than yourself; it can be learned by goatherds and by soldiers just as it can by the farmers my family once were, the loyal servants.*

She kissed me. *Certainly you look noble,* she whispered and smiled. *You are my prince, be sure of that.*

She dazzled me with what she was, and had, and said, and what she was free from knowing. But I would have loved her just for her body and its closeness, how pale she was, and soft, and intact, and for her face, perfect above that perfection, gazing on me enchanted. She was like the foods she fancied, beautiful nothingness, a froth of luxury above the hard, real business of the world, which was the machinery of war and missiles, the flying darts and the blown dust and smoke, the shudder in your guts as the bosses brought in the air support, and saved you yet again from becoming a thing like these others, pieces of bleeding litter tossed aside from the action, their part in the game ended.

With the muzzle of the pistol, I push aside the queen's earring— a dangling flower or star, made of sparkling diamonds, a royal heirloom. I press the tip in below her ear, fire, and drop her to the carpet. It's all coming back to me, the efficiency. "Bring me the prince!" I cry.

The women of the bosses' world, they are foul beautiful creatures. They are devils, that light a fire in the loins of decent men. One picture is all you need, and such a picture can be found on any boss-soldier's wall in the barracks; my first time in such a place, all my fellows around me were torn as I was between feasting their eyes on the shapes and colors taped to the walls, and uttering damnation on the bosses' souls, and laughing—for it was ridiculous, wasn't it, such behaviour? The taping itself was unmanly, a weakness—but the posturing of the picture-girls, I hardly knew how to regard that. I had never seen *faces* so naked, let alone the out-thrustingness of the rest of their bodies. I was embarrassed for them, and for the boss-men who looked upon these women, and longed for them—even as the women did their evil work on me, and woke my longings too.

We covered our embarrassment by pulling the pictures down, tearing one, but only a little, and by accident. We put them in the bin, where they were even less dignified, upside down making their faces to themselves, of ecstasy and scorn, or animal abandon. We looked around in relief, the walls bare except for family pictures now. Someone opened a bedside cupboard and found those magazines they have. Around the group of us they went, and we yelped and laughed and pursed our mouths over them, and some tried to whistle as the bosses whistled; I did not touch one at all, not a single page, but I saw enough to disgust and enliven me both for a long time to come.

Someone raised his head, and we all listened. Engines. "Land Rover! They are coming!" And we scrambled to put the things back, clumsy with laughter and fear.

"This is the best one! Take this one with us!"

"Straighten them! Straighten them in the cupboard, like we found them!"

I remember as we ran away, and I laughed and hurried with the rest, another part of me was dazed and stilled by what I had seen, and could not laugh at all. Those women would show themselves, *all* of themselves, parts you had never seen, and did not want to—or did you?—to any man, any; they would let themselves be put in a picture and taped up on a wall for any man's eyes. I was stunned and aroused; I felt so dirtied that I would never be clean, never the man I had been before I saw what I had seen.

And now I was worse, myself, even than those bosses. I lived, I knew, an unclean life. I did not keep my body pure, for marriage or any other end, but only polluted myself and wasted my good seed on wanton women, only poisoned myself with spliffs and powders and liquors.

It is very confusing when you can do anything. You settle for following the urge that is strongest, and call up food perhaps. Then this woman smiles at you, so you do what a man must do; then another man insults you, so you pursue his humiliation. While you wait for a grander plan to emerge, a thousand small choices make up your life, none of them honorable.

It is much easier to take the right path when you only have two to choose from. Easiest of all is when you are under orders, or under fire; when one choice means death, you can make up your mind in a flash.

These things, about the women and my impurity, I would not tell anyone at home. This was why my family stayed away from the greater, the outer world; this was why we hid in the mountains. We could live a good life there, a clean life.

Buzzz. I go to the wall and press the button to see out. Three men stand at the door downstairs. They wear suits, old-fashioned but not in a dowdy way. *You thought you had run ahead of us,* say the steep white collars, the strangely fastened cuffs, and the fit, the cut of those clothes; even a goat-boy can hear it. *But our power is sunk deep, spread wide, and knotted tight into the fabric of all things.*

The closest one takes off his sunglasses. He calls me by my army name. I fall back a little from the screen. "Who are you and what do you want?"

"We must ask you some questions, in the name of His Majesty the King," he says. He's well fed, the spokesman, and pleased with himself, the way boss-soldiers are, the higher ranks who can fly away back to Boss-Land if things get too rough for them.

"I've nothing to say to any king," I say into the grille. How is he onto me so quickly? Does *he* have magic dogs as well?

"I have to advise you that we are authorized to use force."

I move the camera up to see beyond them. Their car gleams in the apartment's turning circle, with the royal crest on the door. Six soldiers— spick and span, well armed, no packs to weigh them down if they need to run—are lining up alert and out of place on the gravel. Behind them squats an armored vehicle, a prison on wheels.

I pull the sights back down to the ones at the door. I wish I had wired those marble steps the way the enemy used to. I itch for a button to press, to turn them to smoke and shreds. But there are plenty more behind them. By the look of all that, they know they're up against more than one man.

I buzz them in to the lobby. In the bedroom, I take the pistol from my bedside drawer. In the sitting-room lie the remains of the feast, the spilled throw-rug that the princess wrapped herself in as she talked and talked last night. I pick up the Bic and click it twice. "Tidy this up," I say into the bomb-blast of silver, and he picks up the mess in his teeth and tosses it away, and goggles at me for more orders. He could deal with this whole situation by himself if I told him. But I'm not a lazy man, or a coward.

The queen's men knock at the apartment door. I get into position—it feels good, that my body still knows how. "Shrink down, over there," I say to the silver dog. The light from his eyes pulses white around the walls.

Three clicks. "Fetch me the king!" I shout before the gold dog has time to properly explode into being, and they arrive together, the trapped man jerking and exclaiming in the dog's jaws. He wears a nice blue suit, nice shoes, all bespoke as a king's clothes should be.

The knocking comes again, and louder. The dog stands the king gently on the carpet. I take the man in hand—not roughly, just so he knows who's running this show. "Sit with your friend," I say to the dog, and it shrinks and withdraws to the window, its flame-fur seething. The air is strong with their spice and hot metal, but it won't overpower me; I'm cold and clever and I know what to do.

I lean over the king and push the door-button on the remote. The queen's suits burst in, all pistols and posturing. Then they see me; they aren't so pleased with themselves then. They scramble to stop. The dogs stir by the window and the scent tumbles off them, so strong you can almost see it rippling across the air.

"You can drop those," I say. The men put up their hands and kick their guns forward.

I have the king by the neck. I push my pistol into his mouth, and he gags. He doesn't know how to fight, hasn't the first clue. He smells nice, expensive.

"Maybe he can ask me those questions himself, no?" I shout past his ear at the two suits left. I swing him around to where he will not mess me up so much. "Bring me the queen!" I shout to the golden dog, and blow out the back of the king's head. The noise is terrific; the deafness from it wads my ears.

The queen arrives stiff with fear between the dog's teeth. Her summery dress is printed with carefree flowers. Her skin is as creamy as her daughter's; her body is lean and light and has never done a day's proper work. I catch her to me by the shoulders. One of the guards dives for his gun. I shoot him in the eye. The queen gives a tiny shriek and shakes against me.

The dogs' light flashes in the men's wide eyes. "Please!" mouths their captain. "Let her go. Let her go."

I can feel the queen's voice, in her neck and chest, but her lips are not moving. She's trying to twist, trying to see what's left of the king.

"What are you saying, Your Majesty?" I shake her, keeping my eyes on her men. "Are you giving your blessing, upon your daughter's marriage? Perhaps you should! Perhaps I should make you! No?" My voice hurts in my throat, but I only hear it faintly.

I take her out from the side, quickly so as not to give her goons more chances. I drop her to the carpet. It's all coming back to me, the efficiency.

"The prince!" I command, and there he is, flung on the floor naked except for black socks, his wet man wilting as he scrambles up to face me. I could laugh, and tease him and play with him, but I'm not in that mood. He's just an obstacle to me, the king's only other heir. My gaze fixes on the guards, I push my pistol up under his jaw and I fire. The silent air smells of gun smoke and burnt bone.

"Get these toy-boys out of here," I shout to the dogs, even more painfully, even more faintly. "Put the royals back, just the way they are. In their palace, or their townhouse, or their brothel, or wherever you found them. My carpet, and my clothes here—get the stains off them. Don't leave a single clue behind. Then go down and clear the garden, and the streets, of all those men and traffic."

It's not nice to watch the dogs at work, picking up the live men and the dead bodies both, and flinging them like so many rags, away to nothing. The filthy dog, the scabbed one—why must *he* be the one to lick up the blood from the carpet, from the white leather of the couch? Will he lick me clean too? But my clothes, my hands, are spatter-free already; my fingertips smell of the spiciness of the golden dog, not the carrion tongue of the mangy one.

Then they're gone. Everything's gone that doesn't belong here. The carpet and couch are as white as when I chose them from the catalogue; the room is spacious again without the dogs.

I open the balcony windows to let out the smells of death and dog. Screams come up from the street, and a single short burst of gunfire. A soldier flies up past me, his machine-gun separating from his hands. They go up to dots in the sky, and neither falls back down.

By the time I reach the balcony railing, all is gone from below except people fleeing from what they've seen. The city lies in the bright morning, humming with its many lives and vehicles. I spit on its peacefulness. Their king is dead, and their prince. Soon they'll be ruled by a goatherd, all those suits and uniforms below me, all those bank-men and party-boys and grovelling shop-owners. Everyone from the highest dignitary to the lowliest beggar will be at my disposal, subject to my whim.

I stride back into the apartment, which is stuffed fat with the dogs.

They shrink and fawn on me, and shine their eyes about.

"I want the princess!" I say to the golden one and he grins and hangs out his crimson tongue. "Dress her in wedding finery, with the queen's crown on her head. Bring me the king-crown, and the right clothes, too, for such an occasion. A priest! Rings! Witnesses! Whatever papers and people are needed to make me king!"

Which they do, and through everyone's confusion and my girl's delight—for she thinks she's dreaming me still, and the news hasn't yet reached her that she is orphaned—the business is transacted, and all the names are signed to all the documents that require them.

But the instant the crown is placed on my head, my rage, which was clean and pure and unquestioning while I reached for this goal, falters. Why should I want to rule these people, who know nothing either of war or of mountains, these spoiled fat people bowing down to me only because they know I hold their livelihoods—their very lives!—in my hands, these soft-living men, these whore-women, who would never survive the cold, thin air of my home, who would cringe and gag at the thought of killing their own food?

"Get them out of here," I say to the golden dog. "And all this nonsense. Only leave the princess—the queen, I should say. Her Majesty."

And the title is bitter on my tongue, so lately did I use it for her mother. King, queen, prince and people, all are despicable to me. I understand for the first time that the war I fought in, which goes on without me, is being fought entirely to keep this wealth safe, this river of luxury flowing, these chefs making their glistening fresh food, these walls intact and the tribals busy outside them, these lawns untrampled by jealous mobs come to tear down the palaces.

And she's despicable too, who was my princess and dazzled me so last night. Smiling at our solitude, she walks towards me in that shameful dress, presenting her breasts to me in their silken tray, the cloth sewn close about her waist to better show how she swells above and below, for all to see, as those dignitaries saw just now, my wife on open display like an American celebrity woman in a movie, like a porn queen in a sexy-mag.

I claw the crown from my head and fling it away from me. I unfasten the great gold-encrusted king-cape and push it off; it suffocated me, crushed me. My girl watches, shocked, as I tear off the sash and brooches and the foolish shirt—truly tear some of it, for the shirt-fastenings are so ancient and odd, it cannot be removed undamaged without a servant's help.

Down to only the trousers, I'm a more honest man; I can see, I can *be*, my true self better. I take off the fine buckled shoes and throw them hard at the valuable vases across the sitting-room. The vases tip and burst apart against each other, and the pieces scatter themselves in the dogs' fur as they lie there intertwined, grinning and goggling, taking up half the room.

The princess—the queen—is half-crouched, caught mid-laugh, mid-cringe, clutching the ruffles about her knees and looking up at me. "You are different," she says, her child-face insulting, accusing, above the cream-lit cleft between her breasts. "You were gentle and kind before," she whispers. "What has happened? What has changed?"

I kick aside the king-clothes. "Now you," I say, and I reach for the crown on her head.

My mother stirs the pot as if nothing exists but this food, none of us children tumbling on the floor fighting, none of the men talking and taking their tea around the table. The food smells good, bread baking, meat stewing with onions.

It is a tiny world. The men talk of the larger, outer one, but they know nothing. They know goats, and mountains, but there is so much more that they can't imagine, that they will never see.

I shower. I wash off the blood and the scents of the princess, the bottled one and the others, more natural, of her fear above and of her flower below that I plucked—that I *tore*, more truthfully, from its roots. I gulp down shower-water, lather my hair enormously, soap up and scrub hard the rest of me. Can I ever be properly clean again? And once I am, what then? There seems to be nothing else to do, once you're king, once you've treated your queen so. I could kill her, could I not? I could be king alone, without her eyes on me always, fearful and accusing. I could do that; I've got the dogs. I could do anything. (I lather my sore man-parts—they feel defiled, though she was my wife and untouched by any other man—or so she claimed, in her terror.)

I rinse and rinse, and turn off the hissing water, dry myself and step out into the bedroom. There I dress in clean clothes, several layers, Gore-Tex the outermost. I stuff my ski-cap and gloves in my jacket pockets, my pistol to show my father that my tale is true. I go into my office, never used, and take from the filing drawers my identifications, my discharge papers—all I have left of my life before this, all I have left of myself.

Out on the blood-smeared couch, my wife-girl lies unconscious or asleep, indecent in the last position I forced on her. She's not frightened any more, at least, not for the moment. I throw the ruined ruffled thing, the wedding-dress, to one side, and spread a blanket over her, covering all but her face. I didn't have to do any of what I did. I might have treated her gently; I might have made a proper marriage with her; we might have been king and queen together, dignified and kind to each other, ruling our peoples together, the three giant dogs at our backs. We could have stopped the war; we could have sorted out this country; we could have done anything. Remember her fragrance, when it was just that light bottle-perfume? Remember her face, unmarked and laughing, just an hour or so ago as she married you?

I stand up, away from what I did to her. The fur-slump in the corner rises and becomes the starving gray, the white bull-baiter, the dragon-dog with its flame-coat flickering around it, its eyes fireworking out of its golden mask face.

"I want you to do one last thing for me." I pull on my ski-cap. The dogs whirl their eyes and spill their odours on me.

I bend and put the pink Bic in the princess's hand. Her whole body gives a start, making me jump, but she doesn't wake up.

I pull on my gloves, heart thumping. "Send me to my family's country," I say to the dogs. "I don't care which one of you."

Whichever dog does it, it's extremely strong, but it uses none of that strength to hurt me.

The whole country's below me, the war *there*, the mountains *there*, the city flying away back *there*. I see for an instant how the dogs travel so fast: the instants themselves adjust around them, make way for them, squashing down, stretching out, whichever way is needed for the shape and mission of the dog.

Then I am stumbling in the snow, staggering alongside a wall of snowy rocks. Above me, against the snow-blown sky, the faint lines of Flatnose Peak on the south side, and Great Rain on the north, curve down to meet and become the pass through to my home.

The magic goes out of things with a snap like a passing bullet's. No giant dog warms or scents the air. No brilliant eye lights up the mountainside. My spine and gut are empty of the thrill of power, of danger. I'm here where I used to imagine myself when we were under fire with everything burning and bleeding around me, everyone dying. Snow blows like knife-slashes across my face; the rocky path veers off into the blizzard ahead; the wind is tricky and bent on upending me, tumbling me down the slope. It's dangerous, but not the wild, will-of-God kind of dangerous that war is; all I have to do to survive here is give my whole mind and body to the walking. I remember this walking; I embrace it. The war, the city, the princess, all the technology and money I had, the people I knew—these all become things I once dreamed, as I fight my frozen way up the rocks, and through the weather.

"I should like to meet them," she says to me in the dream, in my dream of last night when she loved me. She sits hugging her knees, unsmiling, perhaps too tired to be playful or pretend anything.
"I have talked too much of myself," I apologize.
"It's natural," she says steadily to me, "to miss your homeland."

I edge around the last narrow section of the path. There are the goats, penned into their cave; they jostle and cry out at the sight of a person, at the smells of the outside world on me, of soap and new clothing.

In the wall next to the pen, the window-shutter slides aside from a face, from a shout. The door smacks open and my mother runs out, ahead of my stumbling father; my brothers and sisters overtake them. My grandfather comes to the doorway; the littler sisters catch me around the waist and my parents throw themselves on me, weeping, laughing. We all stagger and fall. The soft snow catches us. The goats bray and thrash in their pen with the excitement.

"You should have sent word!" my mother shouts over all the questions, holding me tight by the cheeks. "I would have prepared such a feast!"

"I didn't know I was coming," I shout back. "Until the very last moment. There wasn't time to let you know."

"Come! Come inside, for tea and bread at least!"

Laughing, they haul me up. "How you've all grown!" I punch my littlest brother on the arm. He returns the punch to my thigh and I pretend to stagger. "I think you broke the bone!" And they laugh as if I'm the funniest man in the world.

We tumble into the house. "Wait," I say to Grandfather, as he goes to close the door.

I look out into the storm, to the south and west. Which dog will the princess send? The gray one, I think; I hope she doesn't waste the gold on tearing me limb from limb. And when will he come? How long do I have? She might lie hours yet insensible.

"Shut that door! Let's warm the place up again!" Every sound behind me is new again, but reminds me of the thousand times I've heard it before: the dragging of the bench to the table, the soft rattle of boiling water into a tea-bowl, the chatter of children.

"You will have seen some things, my son," says my father too heartily—he's in awe of me, coming from the world as I do. He doesn't know me any more. "Sit down and tell us them."

"Not all, though, not all." My mother puts her hands over the ears of the nearest sister, who shakes her off annoyed. "Only what is suitable for women and girl-folk."

So I sit, and sip the tea and soak the bread of home, and begin my story.

THE LAST RIDE OF THE GLORY GIRLS

LIBBA BRAY

Libba Bray has worked as a waitress, nanny, burrito roller, publishing plebe, and an advertising copywriter, and is distantly related to Davy Crockett. Her first novel, A Great and Terrible Beauty, *was a* New York Times *bestseller, and was followed by two sequels,* Rebel Angels *and* The Sweet Far Thing. *Her fourth novel,* Going Bovine, *was awarded the Michael L. Printz Award for Excellence in Young Adult Literature. Her latest novel is* Beauty Queens. *Bray lives in Brooklyn, New York, with her husband and their son.*

I were riding with the Glory Girls, and we had an appointment with the four-ten coming through the Kelly Pass. I fiddled with the Enigma Apparatus on my wrist, watching the seconds tick off. When the four-ten was in sight, I'd take aim, and a cloud of blue light would come down over that iron horse. The serum would do its work, slowing time and the passengers to stillness inside the train. Then the Glory Girls'd walk across a bridge of light, climb aboard, and take whatever they wanted, same as they'd done to all them other trains—a dozen easy in the past six months.

In the distance, the white peaks of the revival tents dotted the basin like ladies' handkerchiefs hanging on the washing line. It were spring, and the Believers had come to baptize their young in the Pitch River. Way down below us, the miners were about their business; I could feel them vibrations passing from my boots up through my back teeth like the gentle rocking of a cradle. The air a-swirled with a gritty dust you could taste on the back of your tongue always.

"Almost time," Colleen said, and the red of the sky played against her hair till it look like a patch of crimson floss catching fire in an evening dust storm.

Fadwa readied her pistols. Josephine drummed her fingers on the rock. Amanda, cool as usual, offered me a pinch of chaw, which I declined.

"I sure hope you fixed that contraption for good, Watchmaker," she said.

"Yes'm," I answered, and didn't say no more.

My eyes were trained on them black wisps of steam peeking up over the hills. The four-ten, right on schedule. We hunkered down behind the rocks and waited.

How I ended up riding with the Glory Girls, the most notorious gang of all-girl outlaws, is a story on its own, I reckon. It's on account of my being with the Agency—that's the Pinkerton Detectives, Pinkertons for short. That's a story, too, but I cain't tell the one without the other, so you'll just have to pardon me for going on a bit at first. Truth is, I never set out to do neither. My life had been planned from the time I were a little one, sitting at my mam's skirts. Back then, I knew my place, and there were a real order to it all—the chores, the catechism, the spring revivals. Days, I spent milking and sewing, reading the One Bible. Evenings, we evangelized at the miners' camp, warning them about the End Times, asking if they'd join us in finding the passage to the Promised Land. Sunday mornings were spent in a high-collared dress, listening to the Right Reverend Jackson's fiery sermons.

Sunday afternoons, as an act of charity, I helped Master Crawford, the watchmaker, now that his sight had gone and faded to a thin pinpoint of light. That were my favorite time. I loved the beauty of all them parts working perfectly together, a little world that could be put to rights with the click of gears, like time itself answered to your fingers.

"There is a beauty to the way things work. Remove one part, add another, you've changed the mechanism as surely as the One God rewrites the structure of a finch over generations," Master Crawford'd told me as I helped him put the tools to the tiny parts. By the time I left the township, I knowed just about all there was to know in regards to clockworks and the like. Before what happened to John Barks, my life were as ordered as them watches. But I ain't ready to talk about John Barks yet, and anyway, you want to know how I come to be with the Pinkertons.

It were after Mam had died and Pap were lost to the Poppy that I left

New Canaan and come to Speculation to seek my fortune. Weren't more'n a day into town when a pickpocket relieved me of my meager coins and left me in a quandary of a serious nature, that quandary bein' how to survive. There weren't no work for a girl like me—the mines couldn't even hire the men lining up outside the overseer's office. About the only place that would take me was the Red Cat brothel, and I hoped it wouldn't come to that. So, with my guts roiling, I stole a beedleworm dumpling off a Chinaman's cart—none too well, I might add—and found myself warming a cell beside a boy-whore whose bail were paid by a senator's aide. I knew nobody'd be coming for me, and I was right scared they'd be sending me back to the township. I just couldn't tolerate that.

Took me seven seconds to pick the lock and another forty-four to take the gate mechanism down to its bones. Couldn't do nothing about the whap to the back of my head, courtesy of the guard. Next thing I knew, I had an audience with Pinkerton chief Dexter Coolidge.

"What's your name? Lie to me and I'll have you in a sweatbox before sundown."

"Adelaide Jones, sir."

"Where are you from, Miss Jones?"

"New Canaan Township, sir."

Chief Coolidge frowned. "A Believer?"

"Was," I said.

Chief Coolidge lit a cigar and took a few puffs. "I guess you've already had your dip in the Pitch."

"Yessir. When I were thirteen."

"And you've received your vision?"

"Yessir."

"And did you see yourself here in manacles before me, Miss Jones?" He joked from behind a haze of spicy smoke.

I didn't answer that. Most people didn't understand the Believers. We kept to ourselves. My folks come to this planet as pilgrims before I were even born. It was here, the Right Reverend Jackson told us, where the One God set this whole traveling snake-oil wagon show in motion. The Garden of Eden were hidden in the mountains, the Scriptures said. If people lived right lives, followed the Ways of the One Bible, that Eden would be revealed to us when the End Times came, and those Believers would be led right into the Promised Land, while the Non-Believers would perish in an everlasting nothing. As a girl, I learnt the Ways and the Stations and all the things a goodly young woman should know, like how to make oat-blossom bread and spin thread from sweet clover. I learnt about the importance of baptism in the Pitch River, when all your sins would be removed and the One God would reveal his truth to you in a vision. But we never shared our visions with others. That were forbidden.

Chief Coolidge's sigh brought me back to my present predicament. "I must say, I've never understood why anyone would submit to such barbaric practices," he said, and it weren't snooty so much as it were curious.

"It's a free world," I said.

"Mmmm." Chief Coolidge squinched together them blue eyes and rubbed a thumb against his fat mustache while he sized me up—the moleskin pants tucked into the workman's boots, the denim shirt and the duster what used to belong to John Barks. My brown hair were plaited into long braids gone half unraveled now. There were dirt caked on my face till you couldn't hardly tell I had freckles across my nose and cheeks. Chief Coolidge shook his head, and I figured I were done for, but then he went and turned a crank on the wall and spoke into a long, fluted tube. "Mrs. Beasley. Please bring up some of that superior pheasant, roasted potatoes, and a portion of orange-blossom cake, I should think, thank you."

When the fancy silver tray come, and the heavenly Mrs. Beasley put it down beside me, I dug in without even saying grace or washing the dirt from under my fingernails.

"Miss Jones, your facility with the mechanical is quite impressive. Can you put things together as well as you take them apart?"

I told him about Master Crawford and the watches, and he give me a choice: go back to jail or come work for the Pinkertons. I told him that didn't seem like much of a choice to me, just two different kinds of servitude. Chief Coolidge give me his first real smile. "As you said, Miss Jones: it's a free world."

The next morning, Chief Coolidge set me up in the laboratory. Every manner of device and contraption you could imagine were there. Rifles that fired pulses of light. Clockwork horses that could ride for a hundred miles full out and not get tuckered. Armored vests what would stop a bullet like it weren't no more'n a fly. Master Crawford's little watch shop paled in comparison. I'd be lying if I said the sight of all them metal parts didn't make my heartbeat flutter some.

"Gentlemen, may I introduce Miss Adelaide Jones, late of New Canaan Township? She is apprenticed to our agency in the Apparatus Division. Please see to it that she receives your utmost courtesy."

Chief Coolidge put me at a long bench piled thick with gears, rivets, tubes, and filaments. A long, fat rifle of some sort with a mess of metal innards laid out for me.

"This, Miss Jones, is Captain Smythfield's Miasmic Decider. The weapon was confiscated from a Russian agent at considerable trouble. A schematic has been provided, courtesy of our engineering department. As of yet, we've not gotten it to fire. Perhaps you will prove useful in that capacity. I'll leave you to it."

The fellas didn't take too kindly to me being there. Mam would've said I should let them win, that a woman shining her light too bright was unnatural in the eyes of the One God. Mam always kept a soft voice and her eyes downcast. Folks said she were the very picture of a Believer woman. It didn't save her from the fever none. So I kept my eyes downcast, trained right on the gun in front of me.

One of the agents, fella named Meeks, stood over me while I tried to figure out the puzzle of it. "He's testing you. That gizmo's not Russian; it's Australian. From the war. Their particle know-how is second to none. Put a piece wrong and you'll burn a man's head off or turn him to vapor. H'ain't been able to crack this one yet."

He put his hand on my shoulder. "If 'n you like, I can keep you comp'ny, show you what to do." That hand gave my shoulder a too-friendly squeeze.

"If it's all the same to you, sir, I'd like to have a look at her on my own."

"Her, eh? How'd you know it's a she?"

"Just do," I said, and removed his hand. He skulked off, grumbling about what the world were coming to when the Pinkertons let a girl do a man's job. I ignored him and stared at the schematic, but I could tell it were wrong, so I put it aside. Once I sat down to a contraption, it were like I could feel them gears inside me, and I could tell which pieces didn't belong. By the end of the day, I had Captain Smythfield's Miasmic Decider ready to fire. Chief Coolidge fixed his brass goggles over his eyes and took 'er out to the firing range. She vaporized the target and blew a hole clean through the wall behind. Chief Coolidge stared at the Decider, then at me.

"Made a few changes to her, sir," I said.

"So I see, Miss Jones."

"Hope that were all right."

"Indeed it is. Gentlemen, whatever needs fixing, please deliver it to Miss Jones tomorrow morning."

I give Mr. Meeks a right nice curtsy on the way out.

For six months, I worked at that gear-strewn table. The fellas and I came to a peaceable understanding, 'cept for Mr. Meeks, who took to wearing his goggles all the time so's he didn't have to look me in the eye none. I got to know the other divisions. Most agents was field types who made sure the mines were lawful and that the miners didn't rough up the Chinamen or get too drunk and cause a ruckus. They left the brothels alone for the most part, under the idea that the whores weren't hurtin' folks none and ever'body needed a little company from time to time— usually the agents themselves. They kept a close eye on the saloons and boardinghouses, where some enterprising folks had taken to peddling the new machine-pressed Poppy, with names like Dr. Festus's All-Seeing Eye, Tincture of Light-Smoke, Mistress Violet's Glimpse into the Immortal Chasm, and Lady Laudanum's Sweet Sister. Plenty of people left the Church still searching for that first taste of eternity they got in the Pitch, and they'd chase it in the petal, even if it came out of a secret mill that might also be pressing mine dust or crimson floss. I'd had Poppy exactly twice—during my baptism and just after. I weren't eager to try it again.

Mostly, I kept myself to myself and worked hard to understand the way a Turkish Oscillating Orphanage Builder were different from an Armenian Widow Maker, though near as I could tell, they both went about the same business. In my resting hours, I worked on watches, finding comfort in the way they tidied up the world and kept it moving forward with a steady tick. I even fixed the chief's old pocket watch, which had been running three minutes slow for a year. I joked with him that he'd probably lost about four months of his life and he should put in to the Once of Restitution for it. Chief Coolidge scowled and handed me the plans for a new code breaker. He weren't big on jokes.

Then one hot summer day, the Glory Girls rode in like the Four Horsemen, robbing trains and airships. No one knew where they'd come from or how they done what they did. The witnesses couldn't remember nothing, 'cept for seeing a blue light before they'd wake some time later to find their jewels and lockboxes gone and the Glory Girls' calling card left on a table all polite and proper-like. Wanted posters hung on every post-office wall, till folks knowed the girls' names like the saints: Colleen Feeney. Josephine Folkes. Fadwa Shadid. Amanda Harper. There'd always been a troublesome balance between law and lawlessness, and the Glory Girls done tipped the scales into a pretty mess.

At a town meeting, Chief Coolidge assured everybody that the Pinkertons would put things to rights. "We are the Pinkertons, and we always catch our man."

"But Not Our Girl" was the headline of the next day's *Gazette*. The chief were in a mood then. "Without law and order, there is chaos," he bellowed to us, reminding me a portion of Reverend Jackson. He thundered that he didn't care if the miners killed one another and the Poppy turned half the planet into blithering idiots; the Pinkertons was now in the Glory Girl business. Capturing them become our sole purpose.

Chief Coolidge asked me to follow him. In the corner of a paneled library were a beautiful Victrola with a crank on the side. The chief give it a few turns, and presently, a wispy shaft of light appeared with ghostly moving pictures inside it. The chief called it a Holographic Re-membrance. The pictures showed riders running alongside a great black train. I couldn't make out the riders' faces none 'cause they wore kerchiefs 'cross their mouths and goggles over their eyes, but I knew it were the Glory Girls. Oh, they were a sight to behold, with their hair flying out free and the dust rising up into a cloud, like the mist of a primeval forest. One of the girls raised her arm, and I couldn't see what happened real well, but a blue light bubble come over the train and it stopped dead on the tracks. Then the picture crackled up like old Christmas paper, and there weren't no more. Chief Coolidge turned up the gas lamps again.

"What do you make of that, Miss Jones?"

"Well, sir, I don't rightly know."

"Nor do we. No one in the divisions has seen anything like it. However, we've heard that someone who may have been Colleen Feeney was seen near the mines, inquiring after a watchmaker." He leaned both fists on his desk. "I need a woman on the inside. You could gain their trust. Alert us to their plans. It would be a chance to prove yourself, Miss Jones. But of course, it's your choice."

Your choice. It were what John Barks said to me once.

Chief Coolidge set me up in a rooming house near the mines just outside Speculation. We'd heard tell that the Glory Girls come through there every now and then for supplies. It were let known that I could be handy; I fixed the furnace at the brothel and got the clock in the town square working again after a Pinkerton done a bit of helpful sabotage on it. I went about my business, and one afternoon, there were a knock at my door and then I were looking into the sly green eyes of a girl not much older'n me from the looks of it. Her curly red hair were tied back at her neck, and she walked like a gunslinger, wary and ready. Miss Colleen Feeney had arrived.

"I hear that you're handy with watches and gears," she said, picking up my magnifying glass and giving it a look-through.

"That so?" Chief Coolidge had said the less you spoke, the better off you were. I didn't talk much anyway, so that suited me just fine.

"I've got something needs fixing."

I jerked my head at the box of parts on my desk. "Everybody's got something needs fixing."

"Well, this is something special. And I'll pay."

"If it's beedleworm dumplings and good-luck charms, I ain't interested."

She grinned and it made her face a different face altogether, like somebody who knew what it was to be happy once. "I got real money. And earbobs with emeralds the size of your fist. Or maybe you'd like some Poppy?"

"What'm I gonna do with emerald earbobs on this dirt clod?"

"Wear 'em to the next hanging," she said, and then I were the one grinning.

I packed up my kit, such as it were, and Colleen stopped to pick up some sugar and chewing tobacco at Grant's Dry Goods. She bought a bag of licorice whips and give one to all the kids in the store. On the way out, we had to pass through the revival tents. It were the one time I got a might nervous, because Becky Threadkill took sight of me. Becky and I done all our catechisms together, and she were always the one to tell if somebody stopped paying attention or didn't finish making their absolutions. I figured her to call me out, and she didn't disappoint.

"Adelaide Jones."

"Becky Threadkill."

"It's Mrs. Dungill now. I married Abraham Dungill." She puffed herself up like we oughta be laying at her feet. I had half a mind to tell her that Sarah Simpson had been his first choice and everybody knowed it. "Over to the township, they say you got yourself in some trouble." Her smile were smug.

"That so?"

"'Tis. Heard it told you stole two bottles of whiskey from Mr. Blankenship's establishment, and you was in jail three long months for it."

I hung my head and shuffled my boots in the dirt, but mostly, I were trying to hide the smile bubbling up. Chief Coolidge done a good job getting the word out that I were a thief.

Becky Threadkill took my head hanging as confirmation of my sins. "I knowed you'd come to no good, Addie Jones. One day, you'll be pitched into the everlasting nothing."

"Well, it's good I had so much practice here first, then," I said. "You have a good day now, Mrs. Dungill."

Once we were clear, I stopped Colleen. "You heard what she said. If 'n you want to find yourself another watchmaker, I'll understand." Colleen give me an easy smile. "I think we found ourselves the right girl." She put the handkerchief over my mouth, and the ether done its work.

I woke up in an old wooden house, surrounded by four close faces. "We're real sorry about the ether, miss. But you can't be too careful in our line of work." I recognized the speaker as Josephine Folkes. She were taller than the others and wore her hair all braided this way and that. The brand from her slave days were still on her forearm.

"Wh-what work is that?" I forced myself up on my elbows. My mouth were dry as a drought month.

Fadwa Shadid stepped out of the shadows and put her pistol to my temple. My stomach got as tight as a churchgoing woman's bootlaces then. "Not yet. First, we must determine if you are who you claim to be. We have no secrets between us," she said. Her voice made words sound like fancy writing on a lady's stationery. She wore a scarf that covered her head, and her eyes was big and ginger-cake brown.

"I'm from New Canaan. Used to be a Believer. But my mam died of the fever and my pap were out of his mind on Poppy. There weren't nothing for me there 'cept a life of looking after brats and spinning oat-blossom bread. I weren't cut out for too much woman's work," I said, and my words sounded fast to my ears. "That's all I got to say on it. So if 'n you're of a mind to shoot me, I reckon you should just do it now."

Master Crawford had told me once that time weren't fixed but relative. Right then, I cottoned to what he meant, because those seconds watching Colleen Feeney's face and wondering if she'd give Fadwa the order to shoot me felt like hours. Finally, Colleen waved Fadwa back, and the cold metal left my skin.

"I like you, Addie Jones." Colleen said, grinning.

"I'm a might relieved to hear that," I said, letting out all my air. She offered me some water. "I'm going to show you what we brought you here to fix. You can still say no. Understand, now, if you say yes, you'll be one of us. There's no going back."

"Like I said, got nothin' much to go back to, ma'am."

They led me to a barn with a small desk and a banker's lamp. Colleen pulled open a drawer and took out a velvet box. Inside were the most unusual timepiece I ever seen. The clockface were twice the size of a regular one. It were set into a silver bracelet shaped a might like a spider. Colleen showed me how it clamped on her arm. I could see a little hinge on the side of the clockface, so I knowed it opened up like a locket.

"This is the Enigma Temporal Suspension Apparatus," Colleen told me.

"What's it do?"

"What it did was suspend time. You aim the Enigma Apparatus at something, say, a train," she said, allowing a smirk. "And an energy field envelops the entire thing, slowing down time inside to a crawl. It doesn't last long, seven minutes at the outside. But it's enough for us to climb aboard and be about our business."

"What business is that?" I asked, my eyes still on the Enigma.

"Robbing trains and airships," Amanda Harper said, and spat out a plug of tobacco. She were short, with wheat-colored hair that hung straight to her middle back.

"We're reminders that people shouldn't feel too smug. That what you think you own, you don't. That life can change just like that." Fadwa snapped her fingers.

Colleen opened up the watch face. There were gears upon gears, the most intricate I ever seen, more like metal lacework than parts. They'd been pretty burned and bent up. Tiny flares of light tried to catch but died before they could spark. Right in the center were a teardrop-shaped glass vial. A blue serum dripped inside.

"Pretty, isn't she?" Colleen purred.

"How do you know it's a she?" I said, echoing Agent Meeks.

"Oh, it's a she, all right. Under all those shiny parts is a heart of caged tears."

"We didn't make this world, Addie. It don't play fair. But that don't mean we have to lie down," Josephine said.

Colleen put the Enigma Apparatus in my hands, and a rush of excitement come over me when I felt all that cold metal. "Can you fix her?" she asked.

I clicked a small piece into place. Something shifted inside me. "Ma'am, I'm sure gonna try."

Colleen clapped a hand on my shoulder—they all did—and it might as well have been a brand. I'd just become one of the Glory Girls. When night come, I rolled up a tiny note, tucked it into the beak of a mechanical pigeon, and sent it back to the chief to let him know I were in.

Master Crawford taught me about getting inside the clockworks, that you have to shut out the distractions till it's just you and the gears and you can hear the smooth click and tick, like a baby's first breath. You can give lovers their moonrises off the Argonaut Peninsula or the wonder of a seeding ship with its silos pumping steam into the clouds, bringing on rain. To me, ain't nothing more beautiful than the order of parts. It's a world you can make run right.

"There's some speculators what say time is as much an illusion as the Promised Land," Master Crawford told me once, when we was working, "and that if you want to find God, you must master time. Manipulate it. Get rid of the days and minutes, the measurements of our eventual end."

I didn't quite cotton to what Master Crawford were saying. But that weren't unusual. "Well, sir, I wouldn't let the Right Reverend Jackson hear you talk like that."

"The Right Reverend Jackson don't listen to me, so I reckon I'm safe." He winked, and in the magnifying glass, his eye was huge. "I saw it in a vision when they dipped me into the Pitch. I hadn't even whiskers and already I knew time was but another frontier to conquer. There'll come a messenger to deliver us, to impress upon us that our minds are the machines we must dismantle and rebuild in order to grasp the infinite."

"If 'n you say so, sir. But I don't see what that has to do with Widow Jenkins's cuckoo clock."

He patted my shoulder like a grandpappy might. "Quite right, Miss Addie. Quite right. Now. See if you can find an instrument with the slanted tip…."

We got to working again, but Master Crawford's words had set my mind a-whirring with strange new thoughts. What if there were a way to best time, to crawl inside the ticks and tocks of it and press against it with both hands, stretching out the measures? Could you slide backward and forward, undo a day that had already been, or see what was comin' around the blind curve of the future? What if there weren't nothing ahead, nothing but a darkness as thick and forever seeming as your time under the Pitch? What if there weren't no One God at all and a body were only owing to herself, and none of it—the catechisms, the baptisms, the rules to keep you safe—none of it meant a dadburned thing? That set me a-shiver, and I made myself say my prayers of confession and absolution silently, to remind myself that there were a One God with a plan for me and the infinite, a One God who held time in His hands, and it weren't for the likes of me to know. I prayed myself into a kind of believing again and promised myself I wouldn't think more on such thoughts. Instead, I concentrated on the fit of gears. The bird pushed through the doors of the Widow Jenkins's clock and give us a cuckoo.

Master Crawford beamed. "You're a right good watchmaker, Miss Addie. Better than I were at your age. The pupil will best the master soon enough, I reckon," he said, and I felt a sense of pride, though I knew that were a sin.

The night Mam took sick, Master Crawford let me harness up his horse to ride for the doctor. Our two moons shone as bright as a bridegroom's pearled buttons. The wind come up cold, slapping my cheeks to chapped red squares by the time I reached the miners' camp. Outside the bunkhouses, the guards sat on empty ale barrels, playing cards and rolling dice. There were a doc in the camp, and I went to him, begged on my knees. I told him how we'd buried Baby Alice the week before, and now here was our mam, our rock and our refuge, burning up with the fever, her fingers already slate tipped with bad blood, and wouldn't he please, please come back with me?

He didn't even put down his whiskey. "Nothing you can do 'cept stay out of its way, young lady."

"But it's my mam!" I cried.

"I'm sorry," the doc said, and offered me a drink. In the camp, there were shouting. Somebody'd come up snake eyes.

It were Master Crawford give me the Poppy for Mam. "I was saving this for the End Times, like the Right Reverend Jackson said. But I'm an old man, and your mother needs it a sight more than I do."

I stared at the red-and-black cube in my palm. I had half a mind to swallow it down myself, live out the rest of my days on some colony in my mind. But then I were scared I'd be trapped in a forever night of nothingness, and me the only livin' thing.

I fed Mam a little to ease her passage and put the rest in my pocket. Then I lit the kerosene lamp and kept watch through the night. She never said nothing, but curled in on herself till she lay whorled against the bed linens like a fossil in the rock. I heard Master Crawford died during the winter. Died in his sleep in the pale workroom, under a blanket of down. 'Tweren't the fever or his heart or his veins tightening up.

It were just that his time had run out.

Over the next few weeks, I learnt a lot about the Glory Girls. Josephine and her sister Bernadette had run away from the working fields. The overseer's bullet found Bernadette 'fore they even reached the mountains, but Josephine got away, and now she wore a thread from her sister's dress woven into her coarse braids as a reminder. She could set a broken bone as easily as she cooked a pan of corn bread, said it were about the same difference to her.

When Amanda's uncle got too friendly in the night, she found refuge doing hard labor in the shipyards. She'd spent long hours there and knew how to find the vulnerable spot in all that steel, the place where the Enigma could take hold and do its work. She were able to find timetables, too, so the girls would know which trains to hit and when.

Fadwa were a crack shot who'd honed her skills picking off the scorpions that roamed the cracked dirt outside the tents where she lived with her family in the refugee camps. The authorities took her pap to who knows where. Dysentery took the rest of her family.

That left Colleen. She'd been a debutante with fancy ball gowns, a governess, and a private coach. Her daddy were a speculator what had invented the Enigma Apparatus. He were also an anarchist, and when he tried to blow up the Parliament, that were the end of the gowns and the governess. They arrested her daddy for treason. 'Fore they could collect Colleen, she took the Enigma and fled on the next airship.

I felt a might sorry for all of them when I heard their tales. It were an awful feeling to have nobody. We had that in common, and I had a mind to come clean, tell them who I were and stop lying. But I had a job to do. At first, I done like Chief Coolidge told me, stalling on the repairs while trying to sniff out details from the Glory Girls and their next robbery. But they wasn't trusting me with that yet, and I figured it couldn't hurt to know more about the Enigma Apparatus. Besides, my pride were on the line, and I figured I'd better make good on my reputation as a girl what could fix things. Soon I were hunched over that device, from rooster crow till long after the moons scarred the skin of the sky. I'd figured out most of the gears, but them sputters of light around the serum vial vexed me.

"Simple windup won't do. Near as I can tell, she needs a jolt to get her going," I said after I'd been at her for a good three weeks with not much to show for it.

Amanda looked up from the barrel where she was washing Fadwa's long black hair. "Mercy, where would we find us somethin' like 'at?"

I thought for a bit, rubbing my thumb over the old Poppy square in my pocket. "I think a blue nettle might could do it."

"What's that?" asked Josephine.

"It's a kind of flower with a little bit of lightning inside. They grow in a orchard back to New Canaan."

"But that's on Believer land."

"Believers is all at the river for baptism time," I said. "Besides, I know where to go."

"Guess we best go picking, then." Amanda said. Giggling, she poured a bucket of cold water all over Fadwa, who pulled her gun so fast I thought I saw sparks.

John Barks's family hadn't been Believers. His mam and pap died in an airship fight off the western coast when he were fourteen. The Right Reverend Jackson and his wife took John in and started teaching him the Ways of the One Bible. You'd think that an orphan left to fend for himself on a planet where even the dust tries to choke you might have a score to settle with the One God. But not John Barks. Where most of us believed 'cause we were told to or afraid not to or just out of habit, he believed with his entire self.

"I'm a free man," he'd say. "And I'll believe what I want." I couldn't rightly argue with that.

For two years, I'd watched John Barks grow from a sapling of a boy to a fine young man with muscles that strained the seams of the prayer shirts Mrs. Jackson sewed for him. He had a head of black hair what could rival a gentleman's boots for shine. Becky Threadkill swore he'd take her to wife, said she'd seen it in her vision under the Pitch. Half a dozen other girls swore the same till the Right Reverend were forced to spend the next Sunday cautioning against the sin of sharing your visions.

But it were me John Barks said "Mornin'" to when I went to fetch water, and me he asked to tutor him in the Scriptures. It were me he asked to tell him about being baptized in the Holy Pitch when he turned sixteen.

Every spring, the Believers of the End of Days walked the five miles to the River Pitch and set down their tents to await the baptism day. Most of us got dipped when we reached thirteen and done all our catechisms. They dressed you in the robes and slipped the tiniest petal tip of Poppy under your tongue to quiet your fear, slow your breathing, and keep you still. It stole into your bloodstream and weighted your bones like stones sewn into the lining of your skin. I remember Mam telling me not to be scared, that it were just like getting in a thick bath.

"Just lay real still, Addie-loo," she cooed, stroking the eucalyptus balm over my eyes to keep the Pitch blindness out. "When you're calm, the One God'll show you a vision, your purpose in this life."

"Yes'm."

"But first you have to face the darkness. There'll come a time when you want to fight it, but don't. Just let it cover you. It'll be over before you know it. Promise me you won't fight."

"Promise."

"That's my good girl."

The catechisms said that once you lay in the Pitch and come up again, you came up newborn, your sin purged and left behind you in the thick black tar, like an impression in the mud. That's what they said, anyway. But you never knew what would come bubbling up inside you while you was under. You had to last a full minute with the oily darkness moving over you like a coffin lid, closing out the world. Even a world as damned as this one is better than the weight of nothingness the Pitch smothers you in. All sense of time and place is lost in that river. The Believers say it give you a taste of what could become of your immortal soul if you don't turn to the One God and prepare for the End Times. When you come up outta that river, your damnation sliding down your body like a syrupy shed skin, you fall on your knees and say thanks to your Maker for that breath of hot, dusty air. It makes Believers, the Right Reverend Jackson says. No one wants to spend eternity in such a place as that.

Once you was done, the priests gave you your first real taste of Poppy to seal your covenant with the One God. Miracles and wonders played across your eyes then, reminders of His mercy and goodness. Master Crawford muttered that it weren't proof of nothing 'cept folks' willingness to be hornswaggled. But nobody paid him any mind.

I told John Barks all of this the week before his baptism while we were walking in the orchard.

"They say that when you take your first taste of Poppy, your legs go all prickle bones and your tongue numbs like a snowcake feast and stars explode behind your eyes, making new flowers against the closed dark-velvet stage curtains of your retina, letting you know the One God's show's about to get under way," John said, bustin' with excitement.

"Well, the Poppy is right strong," I said.

"And did you feel the One God sure and true then, Addie?"

"I reckon."

We'd stopped under a blue nettle tree in full bloom, the glasslike, bell-shaped blossoms pulsing with small bursts of lightning. The air was sharp. Overhead, the seeding ships pierced the dark-red cloud blanket, trying to bring on rain. John Barks's arm brushed mine and I colored. We were s'posed to keep a respectful distance, as if the One God's mam walked between us.

"What did the One God reveal to you down under the river, Adelaide Jones?" His hand had moved to my cheek. "Did you see us here by the tree?"

We weren't s'posed to tell our visions. They were for us alone. But I wanted to tell John Barks what I'd witnessed, see what he'd make of it, see if he could ease my mind some. So right there with the new light buzzing all around us, I told him what I seen under the river. When I were done, John Barks kissed me soft and sweet on the forehead.

"I don't believe that," he said. "Not for one second."

"But I seen it!"

"I think the One God leaves some things up to us to decide. He shows us a vision, and it's your choice what to do with it." He smiled. "I can tell you what I hope to see next week."

"What?" I said, trying hard not to cry.

"This," he whispered.

It started to rain. John Barks put his coat over us and kissed me on the mouth this time, and oh, not even clockworks could match up to the feeling of that kiss. It made me believe what John Barks said, that we might could change our fates, and I forgot to be afraid.

"Yes," I said, and I kissed him back.

I thought about that day while me and the Glory Girls collected the blue nettle, and I thought about it, too, while I extracted them tiny beats of lightning and placed 'em inside the Enigma Apparatus. While I watched them light strands prickle and inch toward the serum inside the glass vial, some new hope stirred in me, too, putting me in mind of Master Crawford's vision, the messenger who would come and liberate us from our time-bounded minds. Maybe the Glory Girls were the ones to set us free. And the Enigma Apparatus were the key. Them thoughts about sliding through past and future come prickling up again, only I didn't push 'em away so fast this time, and the only prayer that left my lips was the word "Please…" while I waited for the spark to set things in motion.

The blue nettle connected with the vial. The serum pulsed inside its cage. The second hand on the clockface ticked. I shouted for the girls to come out quick. Soon, they was crowded 'round me in that work-shop while we watched the Enigma Apparatus hum with new life.

"Girls, I think we've got ourselves a timepiece again," Colleen said. I were supposed to have a rendezvous with the chief.

I missed it.

We tested it on a mail train the next day. It were just a local, steaming across a patch of plains, but it would do for practice.

"Here goes," Colleen said, and my nerves went to rattling. She bent her arm and aimed the clockface at the train.

I've had me a few thrills in my sixteen yearn, but seeing the Enigma Apparatus do its work had to be one of the biggest. Great whips of light jump out and held that train sure as the One God's hand might. Inside, the engineer seemed like he were made of wax—he weren't moving that I could see. The Glory Girls boarded the train. There weren't but bags of letters on it, so they didn't take nothing, only changed 'round the engineer's clothes till he wore his long johns on the outside and his hat 'round backward. When the light charge stopped holding and the train lurched forward again, he looked a might confused at his state. We laughed so hard, I thought the miners would hear us down below. But the drills kept up their steady whine, oblivious. And the best part yet? Somehow in my tinkering, I'd drawn out the length to a full eight minutes. I'd made her better. I'd bested time.

The pigeon were on the windowsill of my workhouse when I get back. I unrolled the note tucked into her mouth. It were from the chief, telling me when and where to make our rendezvous, saying I'd best not miss it. I tossed the note in the stove and got to work.

By the time we hit the six-forty the next Friday, I'd taken her to a full ten minutes.

The Right Reverend Jackson used to say there were a fine line between saint and sinner, and in the long days I spent with the Glory Girls robbing trains and falling under the spell of the Enigma Apparatus, I guess I crossed well over it. Before long, I'd almost forgot I'd had one life as a Believer and another as a Pinkerton. I were a Glory Girl as much as any of 'em, and it felt like I'd always been one. Truth be told, them were some of the happiest times I'd had since I'd walked with John Barks. Like being part of a family it were, but with no Mam to sigh when you forgot to burp the baby and no Pap to slap you when your words was too sharp for his liking. Mornings we rode the horses fast and free over the dusty plains, letting the wind whip our hair till it rose like crimson floss. We'd try to best each other, though we all knew Josephine were the fastest rider. Still, it were fun to try, and nobody could tut-tut that we was unladylike. Fadwa worked on my marksmanship by teaching me to shoot at empty tins, and while I weren't no sharpshooter, I done all right, and by all right I mean I managed to knock off a can without shooting the horses.

Josephine taught me to dress a wound with camphor to draw out the poisons. Amanda liked to sneak up on each a-one and scare the dickens out of us. Then she'd fall on the ground, laughing and pointing: "You shoulda seen your face!" and hold her sides till we couldn't do nothing but laugh, too. At night, we played poker, betting stolen brooches against a stranger's looted gold. It didn't matter nothing—if you lost a bundle, there were always another airship or train a-comin'. The poker games went fine till Amanda lost, which she usually did, bein' a terrible card player. Then she'd throw down her cards and point a finger at whoever cleaned up.

"You're cheating, Colleen Feeney!"

Colleen didn't even look up while she scooped the chips toward her lap. "That's the only way to win in this world, Mandy."

One night, Colleen and me walked to the hills overlooking the mines and sat on the cold ground, feeling the vibrations of them great drills looking for gold and finding nothing. Stars paled behind dust clouds. We watched a seeding ship float in the sky, its sharp brass nose glinting in the gloom. "Seems like there ought to be more than this," Colleen said after a spell.

If John Barks were there, he'd say something about how beautiful it was, how special. "It ain't much of a planet," I said.

"That's not what I meant." She rolled a dirt clod down the hillside. It broke apart on the way down.

It come about by accident that first time. I'd been experimenting with the Enigma all along, stretching out the time by seconds, but I couldn't break past ten minutes. It were all well and good to lock the Enigma on a train and stretch the Glory Girls' time on it; what I wondered were if we, ourselves, might could move around in time like prayer beads on a string. Inside the Enigma were the Temporal Displacement Dial. I'd scooted its splintery hands 'round and 'round, taken it apart, put it back together twelve ways from Sunday. Didn't come to much. This time, I got to looking at the tiny whirling eye that joined them hands at the center. I cain't rightly say what gear it were that clicked in my head and told me I should take a thin, pulsing strand of blue nettle and settle it into that center, but that's what I done. Then I pushed that second hand faster and faster 'round that dial. With my hand tingling like a siddle-bug bite, I aimed the Enigma at myself. I felt a jolt, and then I were standing still in the shop listening to Josephine ringing the dinner bell. I knowed that couldn't be right—it were only two o'clock in the afternoon, and din-ner weren't till six most days. Long shadows crept over the shop floor. Six-o'clock shadows. I'd lost four whole hours. Had I slept? I knowed I hadn't—not standing up with my boots on, anyways. A tingle twisted through my insides till I felt as alive as a blue nettle. I'd done it.

I'd unlocked time.

That night, Colleen brought out a bottle of whiskey and poured us each a tall glass. "There's a train coming soon. The four-ten through the Kelly Pass. It's the best one yet. I've seen the passenger list. It is impressive. You can be sure there'll be pearls big as fists. And rubies and diamonds, too."

Josephine let out a holler, but Amanda scowled.

"Gettin' tired of gems," she said, reaching for the bottle. "Nowhere to wear 'em. Nowhere to trade 'em in much anymore."

Colleen shrugged. "There'll be gold dust on this one."

I couldn't hold it back no more. "Maybe we're goin' about this the wrong way. Maybe we should be looking at the Enigma App... Appar... the watch as our best haul," I said. I weren't used to whiskey. It made my thoughts spin. "You ever think of using it on something other than a train?"

Amanda spat out a stream of tobacco. It stained the hay the color of a fevered man on his deathbed. "Like what?"

"Say, for going forward in time to see what you'll be eatin' next week. Or maybe for going back. Maybe to a day you'd want to do over."

"Ain't nothing I'd want to go back to," Josephine said. "What about all them tomorrows?"

"I'll likely be dead. Or fat," Amanda said, and laughed. "Either way, I don't want to know."

The girls commenced to teasing Amanda 'bout her future as a farmer's fat wife. Maybe it were the whiskey, but I couldn't let it alone. "What I'm sayin' is that we might could use the Enigma to travel through time and see if there's anything out there besides this miserable rock—maybe even to unlock bigger secrets. Ain't that a durn sight better than a pearl?" I slammed my tankard down on the table, and the girls got right quiet then. I hadn't never been much of a talker, much less a yeller.

Colleen played with the poker chips. They made a *plinkety-plink* sound. In the dim light, she looked less like an outlaw, more like a schoolgirl. Sometimes I forgot she weren't but seventeen. "Go on, Addie."

"I done it," I said, breathing heavy. "Time travel. With the Enigma. I figured it."

I had their attention then. I told 'em about my experiments, how I'd jumped ahead hours just that afternoon. "It's just a start," I cautioned. "I ain't perfected nothing yet."

Fadwa licked her fingers. "I don't understand. Why do we want this?"

"Don't you see? We wouldn't need to rob trains then. We could go anywhere we wanted," Colleen said. "Perhaps there's something better ahead, something we can have without cheating."

Colleen and me locked eyes, and I saw something in her face that put me in mind of John Barks. Hope. She put the chips back on the table. "I'm in for the ride, Watchmaker. Do the Glory Girls proud."

"Yes'm," I said, swallowing hard.

"In the meantime, we'd better get ready for the four-ten."

The next morning, Fadwa and me saddled up the horses and headed into town for supplies. It'd been a year since I'd gone off with the Glory Girls. The Believers were setting up their tents along the Pitch again. I were waiting by the horses when somebody clapped a strong hand over my mouth and jerked me around the back of the Red Cat brothel, upstairs, and into a bedroom, where I were forced into a chair. Two big goons stood by, their arms folded but ready to grab me if I so much as looked at the door. In a moment, the same door opened and the chief walked in and took a seat across from me. He'd put on weight since I'd seen him last and was sporting some right furry muttonchops. He wiped his spectacles with a handkerchief and put them back on his face. "Miss Adelaide Jones, I presume. You've been gone a very long time, Miss Jones."

"Lost track of time, sir," I said, and he didn't laugh none at my joke.

"Allow me to inform you: a year. An entire year with no contact." My stomach churned. I wanted to yell out to Fadwa, warn her. I wanted to jump out the window onto my horse and ride like I was racing Josephine all the way back to the camp and to the Enigma Apparatus.

"Do you care to tell me how the six-forty out of Serendipity came to be robbed by the Glory Girls? Or the eleven-eleven airship from St. Ignatius?" He slammed a fist down on the table, and it rattled the floor-boards. "Do you care to tell me anything at all, Miss Jones, that would keep me from clapping you in irons for the rest of your natural life?" I picked a burr out of my pants. "You're looking well, sir. I'm right fond of the muttonchops."

The chief's face reddened. "Miss Jones, may I remind you that you are a Pinkerton agent?"

"No, sir, I ain't," I said, my dander up. "You 'n' I both know ladies don't get to be agents. We end up like Mrs. Beasley, bringing tea and asking if there'll be anything else."

The chief went to open his mouth, then he closed it again. Finally he said, "Well, then, there is this to consider, Miss Jones: there is the law. Without it, we slip into the void. You are sworn to uphold it. If you do not, I'll see you prosecuted with the others. Do you take the full import of my meaning, Miss Jones?"

I didn't answer. "Do you?"

"Yessir. Am I free to go?"

He waved me off. But when I got up, the chief grabbed hold of my arm. "Addie, which train are they aiming for next? Please tell me."

It were the *please* almost got me.

"Fadwa's just coming out. She'll be missing me. Sir." The chief looked a might sad then. "Tag her," he said.

The goons held me down tight, and one of 'em brought out an odd rounded gun with a needle on the tip. I struggled but it didn't make no difference. They brung that gun up against the back of my neck, and it felt like a punch going in.

"What—what'd you do to me?" I gasped, and put a hand to my neck. There weren't no blood.

"It's a sound transmission device," Chief Coolidge said. "Agent Meeks is responsible for that invention. It transmits sound to us here. We can hear everything that is said. There should be enough to hang the Glory Girls, I should think."

"That ain't fair," I said.

"Life's not fair." The chief glared. "Tell us about the train—everything we need to catch them—and you'll go free, Addie."

"And if I don't?"

"I'll take you in now and throw away the key." It weren't a choice.

Fadwa were waiting impatiently when I come down to the hitching post after my conference with the chief.

"Where were you?" Fadwa asked.

I rubbed at the back of my neck. I wanted to cry, but it wouldn't help none. If I were a better girl, I'd've told her to run and taken my chances with the law. But I couldn't stop thinking about the Enigma. I was so close. I couldn't just walk away.

"Just some old business I had to take care of," I said, and helped her load up the horses.

That night, I drank more whiskey than I should have. I would've drowned my sorrows in the Poppy, but I knew that were no good. The Glory Girls was in good spirits. Tomorrow they'd take on the four-ten in the Kelly Pass. They made their plans then, where they'd hide out, what kind of train the four-ten was and where it were best to board—all of it being transmitted right back to the Pinkertons. A cold trickle worked its way through my insides. It were like I looked up to find the moons and stars gone to flat pictures painted on muslin.

"You all right, Addie-loo?" Josephine squinted at me like she weren't sure if she should make me a poultice for fever.

"Yes'm. Tired," I lied.

Colleen clapped a hand on my back. "You just have the Enigma ready to greet the four-ten tomorrow, and I'll show you a haul, Addie, that will make you forget all your troubles."

They toasted me then, but the whiskey tasted sour and my head was hurting.

When everybody else was sleeping, I took myself for a walk up into the mountains. I looked down on the revival tents, at the shadowy mystery snaking through the basin, where folks left their sins and come up with a vision. John Barks told me it were choice, but I weren't so sure.

The day they baptized John Barks were terrible hot. The sky come up a gloomy orange and stayed that way. We'd gathered at the river with the young penitents. John Barks had been scrubbed pink. His black hair shone.

"I'll take you to wife, Addie Jones. Just you see," he whispered, and went to stand with the others.

My gut hurt. I wanted to tell him not to do it, to pack up his kit and run away with me on the next airship. We could see for ourselves if there were anything 'sides rocks spinning out in that vast midnight. But I wanted him to prove me wrong, too. I needed to be sure. So I watched as the aldermen dressed him in the white robes, and Mrs. Jackson balmed up his eyes, and Reverend Jackson slipped the Poppy under his tongue. When his body went limp, the women commenced to hymn singing, and the menfolk lowered John Barks's body into the Pitch. The dark river come over him like a living thing, devouring legs, arms, chest. Finally, his face were under and I counted the seconds:

One. Two. Three. Ten. Eleven. Twenty.

A hand broke the surface, followed by John Barks's tar-stained face. He gagged and gasped, fighting the Poppy in his blood. He wouldn't lie still. It were like he'd been caught in one of them ecstasies you read about in the One Bible, where saints and chosen shepherds saw things beyond dust and weak moons and miners' toothless grins. He cried, "Oh Holy! There are stars newborn and great ships with searching sails set against pink-painted ribbons of eternal clouds—oh Holy! Oh Lamb!—the electric blood of the most heavenly body, oh sweet warm breath—kiss of a girl you love! What more? What more?"

The aldermen looked to Reverend Jackson for what to do. Sometimes people got too scared and had to come up from the Pitch before their time. But nobody had ever done like John Barks. And I could see in the Reverend's face that he were frightened, like there weren't no commandment to explain this.

"Reverend?" an alderman named Wills whispered.

"The sin fights him!" Reverend Jackson shouted. "He must be held still to accept the One God's vision. Let us come to his aid!"

The women lifted their arms in fervent hymn singing, and the Reverend Jackson spoke in tongues I didn't know. I kept listening to John Barks calling out wonders, like a madman on the mountain. The men took hold of his arms and legs and held him under, waiting for him to still, to accept the darkness and the One God's grace that allows us to see what comes next. But John Barks fought with everything he had in him. I screamed out that they was a-killin' him, and Mam told me to hush-a-bye and turned my face to her breast. The song rose louder, and it were a terrible song. And when John Barks finally went quiet, it were for good. He drowned in that river, his lungs full of Pitch and his vision stilled on his tongue.

The authorities come and pronounced it an accident. They took cider from the church ladies while John Barks's body lay on the scrubby bank under a sheet, the dried Pitch on his long arms gone to peeling gray scales. "The One God moves in His own way," Reverend Jackson said, but his hands shook. The aldermen dug a grave right there in the basin and buried John Barks without so much as a wooden stake to mark it. They said later he were too old for obedience. That were the problem. Or he might've gotten too much Poppy and seen the glory of the One God too soon, before he'd made his confession. A few folks believed he were chosen to receive a vision and die for all our sins, and we should honor

John Barks on the feasting day. Still others whispered that his sin must've been too great for the One God to forgive or that he weren't willing to give up his sin, and I thought about our kiss under the blue nettle tree, what we done there with the lightning pulsing around us. I wondered if I hadn't damned John Barks with that kiss, sure as if I'd poured the Pitch into his mouth myself. I don't know. I don't know, I don't know, and that not knowing haunts me still.

The first streaks of graying orange come up in the sky when I walked down from the mountains and wrote my last note to the chief. Then I set about my work. The lamp burned through the night, and by the time the two moons was as pale as a skein of ash against the hot orange glow of the day, I'd done what I aimed to do. The Enigma Apparatus was ready.

"It's time, Addie," Colleen said.

The four-ten puffed right into line. I pressed the button on the side of the clockface, bracing myself for the recoil as the train ground to a stop, floating in a blue light cloud. Amanda let out a loud whoop. "Let's go, Glory Girls! Time's a-wastin'."

They patted my back as they went, told me I done good. I grabbed Colleen's arm.

"Addie!" she said, trying to shake me loose. "I've got to go!"

I wanted to tell her everything, but then the chief would hear and swoop in too fast. "Mayhap there's something better up ahead, in the tomorrows," I said. "Strap yourself in good."

She gave me a strange look. "You're an odd one, Addie Jones." And then they was across the light bridge and on the train. It took a few seconds longer than I figured for them to realize there weren't nobody on the four-ten, just a bunch of sawdust dummies. Weren't no treasures, neither. No comforts to keep in a pocket or a drawer. The Pinkertons had seen to that after I'd let the chief know the plan. Even from where I was, I could see their confusion. The sound of hoofbeats told me the agents was near. They were just coming over the ridge in a cloud of dust. Colleen saw it, too. The leader of the Glory Girls looked at me through one of the train's windows. In the blue light, her face had a strange, haunting beauty to it. She'd cottoned to what'd happened and who'd done it. And I think she knew her time had run out. She nodded at me to do it. I clicked the tiny switch that bled blue nettle into the whirling eye at the center of the Temporal Displacement Dial. With my index finger, I pushed that second hand 'round and 'round, the devil racing you through the woods and gaining fast. Colleen Feeney was yelling something at the others and they strapped themselves in. The cloud over the four-ten sparked with angry light. I can't say what the Glory Girls felt then—wonder? Amazement? Fear? I just know they never stopped looking at me. Not once. And I wondered if it would be the last time I'd see 'em or if I'd ever make it to where they was going. The cloud crackled again, and the train car disappeared in a shower of light that brought a mess of rain over the basin. The recoil on the Enigma were like a punch then. Knocked me clean out.

Chief Coolidge weren't none too happy with me when I come to. He paced the floor while I sat in the one uncomfortable chair in his office. He'd had me sit there special. "We were supposed to catch them alive, have a trial, Miss Jones! That is the way of law!"

"Something must've went wrong with that contraption, Chief. Time's a tricky proposition."

He scowled and I tried real hard not to twitch. "Yes. Well. At least we were able to salvage what was left of the Enigma Apparatus. With effort, we'll get it running again."

"That's real good news, sir."

"I would be happy to know that you were working on the Enigma project, Miss Jones. Are you quite certain you won't stay with the Agency?"

I shook my head. "My time's up, sir."

"I might be able to recognize you as a deputy agent. It isn't full, you understand, but it is something."

"I 'preciate that, sir. I do."

He saw I weren't budging. "What will you do, then?"

"Well. 'Spect I'll travel some. See what's out there."

The chief sighed, and I noticed his mustache had more gray in it these days. "Addie, do you really expect me to believe that you had nothing to do with what happened to those girls?"

I looked him right in the eyes. I'd learned to do that. "You can believe what you want, Chief."

Chief Coolidge's gaze turned hard. "It's a free world, eh?"

"You can even believe that if you like."

When they'd lowered me down, them years ago, I'd done as my mam told me. I lay real still, even though I wanted to scream out, to beg them to pull me up even if I still had all my sin attached. It were as terrifying as the grave under the river. But I were a good girl, a true Believer, and so I made my full confession in my mind, and I waited—waited for the One

God to show me a small glimpse of my future.

It started as the tiniest ticking sound. It grew louder and louder, till I thought I might go mad. But that weren't as bad as what followed. My vision come up over me in a wave, and I felt the weight of it all around me.

Darkness. That were all I saw. Just a vast nothing forever and ever. There were hands pulling me up then, singing, "Hallelujah!" and pointing to the shape of my sins in the Pitch. But I knew better. I knew they'd never left me.

I slipped into John Barks's duster and headed out into the dry, red morning. On my wrist, the Enigma Apparatus shone. The Pinkertons was fellas. They'd never thought to question a lady's jewelry. I'd given Chief Coolidge a bucket full of bolts what might make a nice hat rack, but nothing that would bend time to his will.

The storekeepers swept their front walks in hopes of a day's good business. The johns stumbled out of the Red Cat ahead of the town's judging eyes. The seeding ships was out, piercing the clouds. Farther on, the Believers packed up their tents. They was done with visions and covenants for another year.

I reached into my pocket, letting my fingers rest for just a second on that Poppy brick before finding the coin in the corner. Forward or back, forward or back. John Barks told me once I had a choice, and I guess it come down to heads or tails.

I flicked the coin with my thumb and watched it spiral into the sudden rain.

THE BOOK OF PHOENIX

(EXCERPTED FROM THE GREAT BOOK)

NNEDI OKORAFOR

Nnedi Okorafor is known for her complex characters and weaving Nigerian cultures and settings into speculative narratives. In a profile of Nnedi's work, The New York Times *called her imagination "stunning." Her YA novels include* Akata Witch *(a 2011 Amazon.com Best Book of the Year),* Zahrah the Windseeker *(winner of the Wole Soyinka Prize for African Literature),* The Shadow Speaker *(winner of the CBS Parallax Award), and* Long Juju Man *(winner of the Macmillan Prize for Africa). Her adult novel,* Who Fears Death, *was the winner of the 2011 World Fantasy Award, the RT Times Reviewer's Choice Award for Best Science Fiction, and a Nebula Award nominee. Her chapter book,* Iridessa and the Secret of the Never Mine *(Disney Press), is scheduled for release in 2012. Okorafor holds a PhD in Literature and is a professor of creative writing at Chicago State University.*

*T*here is no book about me. Well, not yet. No matter. I shall create it myself; it's better that way. To tell my tale, I will use the old African tools of story: Spoken words. They're more trustworthy and they'll last longer. And during shadowy times, spoken words carry farther than words typed or written. My beginnings were in the dark. We all dwelled in the darkness, mad scientist and specimen, alike. This was when the goddess Ani still slept, when her back was still turned. Before she grew angry at what she saw and pulled in the blazing sun. My story is called The Book *of Phoenix. And it is short because it was…accelerated.*

I'd never known any other place. The thirteenth floor of Tower 7 was my home. Yesterday I realized it was a prison, too. Granted, maybe I should have suspected something. The two-hundred-year-old marble skyscraper had many dark sides and I knew most of them. There were thirty-nine floors, and on almost every one was an abomination. I was an abomination. I had read many books and this was clear to me. However, this place was still my home. *Home*: a. One's place of residence. Yes, it was my home.

They gave me all the 3D movies I could watch, but it was books that did it for me. A year ago, they gave me an e-reader packed with 700,000 books of all kinds. When it came to information, I had access to everything I wanted. That was part of their research.

Research. This was what happened in Tower 7. There were similar towers around the world but Tower 7 was my home, so this one was the one I studied. I had several classified books on Tower 7. One discussed each floor and some of the types of abominations found on them. I'd listened to audios of the spiritual tellings of long-dead African and Native American shamans, sorcerers and wizards. I'd read the Tanakh, the Bible, and the Koran. I studied The Buddha and meditated until I saw Krishna. And I read countless books on the sciences of the world. Carrying all this in my head, I understood abomination. I understood the purpose of Tower 7. Until yesterday.

In Tower 7, there was "transformative" genetic engineering, the in vitro fertilization of organic robots, "rejuvenation" surgery on the ancient near-dead, the creation of weaponized weeds, the insertion and attachment of both mechanical and cybernetic parts to human bodies. There were people created in Tower 7, some were deformed, some were mentally ill, some were just plain dangerous, and none were flawless. Yes, some of us were dangerous. I was dangerous.

Then there was the tower's lobby on the ground floor that projected a different picture. I'd never been down there but my books described it as an earthly wonderland, full of creeping vines covering the walls and small trees growing from artistically crafted holes in the floor. In the center was the main attraction. Here grew the thing that brought people from all over the world to see the Tower 7 Lobby (*only* the lobby; there were no tours of the rest of the building).

A hundred years ago, one of the landscapers planted a tree in the lobby's center. On a lark, some scientists from the ninth floor emptied an experimental solution into the tree's pot of soil. The substance was for enhancing and speeding up arboreal growth. The tree grew and grew. In a place where people thought like normal human beings, they would have uprooted the amazing tree and placed it outdoors. However, this was Tower 7 where boundaries were both contained and pushed. When the tree began touching the lobby's high ceiling in a matter of weeks, they constructed a large hole so that it could grow through the second floor. They did the same for the third, fourth, fifth. The great tree has since earned the name of "The Backbone" because it grew through all thirty-nine of Tower 7's floors.

My name is Phoenix. I was mixed and grown in a lab on the thirteenth floor. One of my doctors thinks my name came from the birthplace of my egg's donor. I've looked it up. Phoenix, Arizona is the full name of the place. However, from what I've read about my floor, even the scientists who forced my existence don't know the names of donors. So, I doubt this. I think they named me Phoenix because of what I was, an "accelerated organism." I was born two years ago but I looked, behaved and felt like a forty-year-old woman. My doctors said the acceleration would stop now that I was "matured." To them, I was like a plant they grew for the sake of harvesting information.

Who do I mean by "them," you must wonder? *All* of THEM, the "Big Eye"—the Tower 7 scientists, lab assistants, lab technicians, doctors, administrative workers, guards and police. We of the tower called them "Big Eye" because they watched us. All the time, they watched us, though not closely enough to prevent the inevitable.

I could read a 500-page book in two minutes. My brain absorbed the information and stories like a sponge. Up until two weeks ago, aside from mealtimes, looking out the window, running on my treadmill, and meetings with doctors, I spent my days with my e-reader. I'd sit in my room for hours consuming words upon words that became images upon images, ideas upon ideas. Now they gave me paper-made books, removing the books when I finished them. I liked the e-reader more. It took up less space and I could reread things when I wanted.

I stared out the window watching the cars and trucks below and the other skyscrapers across from me as I touched a leaf of my hoya plant. They'd given the plant to me five days ago and already it was growing so wildly that it was creeping across my windowsill and had wrapped around the chair I'd put there. It had grown two feet overnight. I didn't think they'd noticed. No one ever said anything about it. I realize now that they *had* noticed. The plant was not a gesture of kindness; it was just part of the research. They didn't really care about me. But Saeed cared about me.

Saeed is dead, Saeed is dead, Saeed is dead, I thought over and over, as I caressed one of my plant's leaves. I yanked, breaking the leaf off. *Saeed, my only friend.* I crumpled the leaf in my restless hand; its green earthy smell might as well have been blood.

Yesterday Saeed had seen something terrible. Not long afterwards, he'd sat across from me during dinner-hour with eyes wide like boiled eggs, unable to eat. He couldn't give me any details. He said no words could describe it.

"What does your heart tell you about this place?" he'd earnestly asked.

I'd only shrugged, frustrated with him for not telling me what he'd seen that was so awful.

He leaned forward, lowering his voice. "You read all those books…why don't you feel rebellion? Don't you ever dream of getting out of here? Away from all the Big Eye?"

"Rebellion against whom?" I whispered, confused.

He laughed bitterly, sat back and shook his head. He took my hand, squeezed it and let it go. "Eat your jallof rice, Phoenix."

I tried to get him to eat his crushed glass. This was his favorite meal and it bothered me to see him push his plate away. But he wouldn't touch it. Before we returned to our separate quarters, he asked for my apple. I assumed he wanted to paint it. He always liked to paint when he was depressed. I'd given it to him without a thought and he'd slipped it into his pocket. The Big Eye allowed it, though they frowned upon taking food from the dining room, even if you didn't plan to eat it.

His words didn't touch me until nighttime when I lay in my bed. Yes, somewhere deep deep in my psyche I *did* wish to get out of the tower and see the world, be away from the Big Eye. I wanted to see those things that I saw in all the books I read. "Rebellion," I whispered to myself.

They told me the news in the morning during breakfast-hour. I'd been sitting alone looking around for Saeed. The others, the woman with the twisted spine who could turn her head around like an owl, the man who never spoke with his mouth but always had people speaking to him, the three women who all looked and sounded alike, the bushy bearded man who looked like a wizard from a novel, the baboon who spoke in sign language, the woman whose sweater did not hide her four large breasts, the two men joined at the hip who were always randomly laughing, the woman with the lion claws and teeth, these people spoke to each other and never to me. Only Saeed spoke to me.

One of my doctors sat facing me. The African-looking one who wore the shiny black wig made of synthetic hair, Bumi. They always had her deal with me when there was upsetting news. My entire body tightened. She touched my hand and I pulled it away. She smiled sympathetically and told me a terrible thing. Saeed hadn't drawn the apple. He'd eaten it. And it killed him. My mind went to one of my books. The Bible. I was Eve and he was Adam.

I could not eat. I could not drink. I would not cry. Not in the dining hall.

Hours later, I was in my room lying on my bed, eyes wet, mind reeling. Saeed was dead. I had skipped lunch and dinner, but I still wasn't hungry. I was hot. The scanner on my wall would start to beep soon. Then they would come get me soon. For tests. I shut my eyes, squeezing out tears. They evaporated as they rolled down my hot cheeks. "Oh God," I moaned. The pain of losing him burned in my chest. "Saeed. What did you see?"

Saeed was human. More human than me. I met him the first day they allowed me into the dining hall with the others. I was one year old; I must have looked twenty. He was sitting alone about to do something insane. There were many others in the room who caught my eye. The two conjoined men were laughing hard at the sight of me. The baboon was jumping up and down while rapidly signing to the woman with lion claws and teeth. However, Saeed had a spoon in his hand and a bowl full of broken glass before him. I stood there staring at him as others stared at me. He dug the spoon into the chunks of glass and put it in his mouth. I could hear him crunching from where I stood. He smiled to himself, obviously enjoying it.

Driven by sheer curiosity, I walked over and sat across from him with my plate of spicy doro wat. He eyed me with suspicion but he didn't seem angry or mean, at least not to the best of my limited social knowledge. I leaned forward and asked what was on my mind, "What's it like to eat that?"

He blinked, surprised. Then he grinned. His teeth were perfect—white, shiny, and shaped like the teeth in drawings and doctored pictures in magazines. Had they removed his original teeth and replaced them with ones made of a more…durable stuff? "The taste is soft and delicate as the texture is crunchy. I'm not in pain, only pleasure," he said in a voice accented in a way that I'd never heard. But then again, the only accents I'd ever heard were from the Big Eye doctors and guards.

"Tell me more," I said.

After that, Saeed and I became friends. I loved words and he needed to spill them. He could not read, so I would tell him about what I read, at least in the hours of breakfast, lunch and dinner. He was from Egypt where he had been an orphan who never went hungry because he could always find something to eat. Rotten rice, date pits, even the wooden skewer sticks of *kebabs*, he had a stomach like a goat. They brought him to the tower when he was ten, nine years ago. He never told me exactly how or why they made him the way he was. It didn't matter. What mattered was that we were who we were and we were there.

Saeed told me of places I had never seen with my own eyes. He used the words of a poet who used his tongue to see. Saeed was an artist with his hands, too. He had the skill of the great painters I read about in my books. He most loved to draw those foods he could no longer eat. Human food. Portraits of loaves of bread. Bowls of thick egusi soup and balls of fufu. Bouquets of lamb and beef kebabs. Fried eggs with white cheese. Plates of chickpeas. Pitchers of orange juice. Piles of roasted corn. They allowed him to bring the paintings to mealtime for everyone to view. I guess even we deserved the pleasures of art.

Saeed could survive on glass, metal shavings, crumbles of rust, sand, dirt, those things that would be left behind if human beings finally blew themselves up. However, eating a piece of bread would kill him as eating a big bowl of sharp pieces of glass would kill the average human being.

He took my apple, and that night, he ate it. Then his stomach and intestines hemorrhaged and he was dead before morning. I never got to tell him what was happening to me. It might have given him hope; it would have reminded him that things would change. I wiped a tear. I loved Saeed.

As grief overwhelmed me for the first time in my life, I pressed a hand against the thick glass of my window. I'd never been outside. I wanted to go outside. Saeed had escaped by dying. I wanted to escape, too. If he wasn't happy here, then neither was I.

I wiped hot sweat from my brow. My room's scanner began to beep as my body's temperature soared. The doctors would be here soon.

When it first started to happen two weeks ago, only I noticed it. My hair started to fall out. I am an African by genetics, my hair was very coily and my skin was very very dark. They kept my hair shaved low because neither they nor I knew what to do with it when it grew out. I could never find anything in my books to help. They didn't care for style in Tower 7, anyway…although the woman down the hall had very long, silky white hair and Big Eye lab assistants came by every two days to help her brush and braid it…despite the fact that the woman had the teeth and claws of a lion.

I was sitting on my bed, looking out the window, when I suddenly grew very hot. For the last few days, my skin had been dry and ashy no matter how much hydrated water they gave me to drink. Doctor Bumi brought me a large jar of shea butter and applying it soothed my skin to no end. However, this day, hot and feverish, my skin seemed to dry as if I were in a desert.

I felt beads of sweat on my head and when I rubbed my short short hair, it wiped right off, hair and sweat alike. I ran to my bathroom, quickly showered, washing my head thoroughly, toweled off and stood before the large mirror. I'd lost my eyebrows, too. But this wasn't the worst of it. I rubbed the shea butter into my skin to give myself something to do. If I stopped moving, I'd start crying with panic.

I don't know why they gave me such a large mirror in my bathroom. Large and round, it stretched from wall to wall. Therefore, I saw myself in full glory. As I slathered the thick, yellow, nutty-smelling cream onto my drying skin, it was as if I was harboring a sun deep within my body and that sun wanted to come out. Under the dark brown of my skin, I was glowing. I was light.

I pulsed, feeling a wave of heat and slight vibration within my flesh. "What is this?" I whispered, scurrying back to my bed where my e-reader lay. I wanted to look up the phenomena. In all my reading, I had never read a thing about a human being, accelerated or normal, heating up and glowing like a firefly's behind. The moment I picked up the e-reader, it made a soft pinging sound. Then the screen went black and began to smoke. I threw it on the floor and the screen cracked as it gently burned. My room's smoke alarm went off.

Psss! Hissing sound was soft and accompanied by a pain in my left thumbnail. It felt as if someone stuck a pin into it. "Ah!" I cried, instinctively pressing on my thumb. As I held my hand up to my eyes, I felt myself pulse again.

There was a splotch of black in the center of my thumbnail like old blood but blacker. Burned flesh. All specimen, creature, creation in the building had a diagnostics chip implanted beneath his, her or its fingernail, claw, talon or horn. I'd just gone off the grid.

Not thirty seconds passed before they came bursting into my room with guns and syringes at ready, all aimed at me as if I were a wild rabid beast destroying all that they had built.

"Get down! DOWN!" they shouted. One man grabbed me, probably with the intent of throwing me on the bed so he could cuff me. He screamed, staring at his burned, still-smoking hand. Someone shot me in the leg. It felt like someone had kicked my leg with a metal foot. I sunk to the floor, pain washing over me like a second layer of more intense heat. I would have been done for if someone else had not shouted for the others to hold their fire.

Thankfully, I healed fast and the bullet had gone straight through my leg. If it hadn't, I don't know what would have happened due to my extreme body temperature. One minute I was staring with shock at the blood oozing from my leg. Then next, I blacked out. I woke in a bed, my body cool, my leg bandaged. When they returned me to my room, the scanner was in place to monitor me since I could not hold an implant. They replaced my bed sheets with a heavy heat-resistant sheet similar in material to my new clothes. The carpet was gone, too. For the first time, I saw that the floor beneath the carpet was solid whitish marble.

When I grew hot and luminous like this, electronics died or exploded in my hands. This was why they started giving me paper books. They were difficult to read, as I couldn't turn the pages as quickly as I could with the e-reader. And the paper books they had were limited and old. And they could monitor what I was reading. Although now I realize with the e-reader they were probably monitoring my choices, too.

I didn't tell Saeed about the heating and glowing because at the time I didn't want to worry him. I enjoyed our talks so much. I wish I had told him.

The door slid open and my doctors came in, Debbie and Bumi. I took a deep breath to calm myself. When I was calm, though the heat did not go away, it decreased, as did the glow.

"How do you feel?" Bumi asked, as she took my wrist to check my pulse. She hissed, dropping it.

"Hot," I said.

She glared at me and I shrugged thinking something I had not thought until Saeed was dead—*You should have asked first.*

"Open," Debbie said, placing the heavy duty thermometer into my mouth.

I saw these two women every day. I knew their names, nothing more.

"She's not glowing that brightly," Bumi said, typing something onto her handheld. I resisted the urge to grab it and hold it in my hands until it exploded. Saeed was dead because of these people. I steadied myself, thinking of the cool places sometimes described in the novels I read. I once read a brief story about a man who froze to death in a forest. I thought about that.

"It might just be menopause approaching," Bumi said. "I believe the two factors are correlated."

I tuned out their talk and focused on my own thoughts. *Escape. How? What would they do to me? What did Saeed see? He said it was something on this floor.* My internal temperature was 130 degrees, but the temperature of my skin was 220. They couldn't take my blood pressure because the equipment would melt.

"We need to take her to the lab," Debbie said.

Bumi nodded. "As soon as the scanner says she's reached 300 degrees. We don't want her any higher or things around her will start to ignite."

They left. I paced the room. Restless. Angry. Distraught. They would be back soon.

How am I going to get out of here, I wondered. As if to answer my question, Mmuo walked into my room. He came through the wall across from my bed. My heart nearly jumped from my chest.

"Did you hear?" he asked, sitting on my bed.

I blinked, feeling the rush of sadness all over again. He was Saeed's friend, too. "Yes," I said.

"I'm sorry, Phoenix."

My face was wet and drying with sweat. "I'm getting out of here," I declared.

Mmuo grinned but it quickly turned to a frown. "What is wrong with you? I can feel you from here," he asked.

"I think it has something to do with how they made me. It's been happening for two weeks and it's getting worse."

We looked at each other, silent. I knew we were thinking the same thing but neither he nor I wanted to speak it. If we spoke of my name, I didn't think I'd be able to move, let alone run.

"Yes, that would make sense," he said.

His full name was Uzochukwu D'nnmma but he called himself Mmuo, which meant spirit in a Nigerian language. He was a hero to all those who were created or altered in Tower 7. Like Saeed, Mmuo had been taken from Africa. He said he was from "the jungles of Nigeria." I did not believe he was from any jungle. He spoke like a man who had known skyscrapers, office buildings and digital television. He knew how to disable the security doors on several of the floors and was known for causing trouble throughout the building. Not that he really needed to do so to get around the tower. Mmuo could walk through walls. The only walls he could not pass through were the walls that would get him out of Tower 7. Mmuo could not escape; obviously his abilities were created by Tower 7 scientists.

Mmuo was a tall, thin man with skin the color of and as shiny as crude oil. He never wore clothes, for clothes could not pass through the walls with him. He stole what food he needed from the kitchens. He was the only person/creature who'd successfully escaped the Big Eye's clutches.

Why Tower 7's Big Eye tolerated him, I do not know. My theory is that they simply could not catch him. And since he was contained, they accepted the trouble he occasionally stirred up. Most of those in the tower were too isolated and damaged to be much trouble if freed, anyway.

"It looks like your skin is nothing but a veil over something greater," he said, after an appraising look. It was something Saeed would have said and the thought made my heart ache again.

"Can you open the door?" I finally said. "I…I want to see what is down the hall, near Saeed's room."

Mmuo met my gaze and held it.

I frowned. "What did Saeed see?" I asked.

He only looked away.

"Show me," I said, suddenly wanting to sob. "Then help me escape."

He moved close to me and I was sure he was going to hug me.

"Don't touch me," I said. "You'll…"

He raised a hand up and made to slap me across the face. "Don't move," he said. His hand passed right through my head. I felt only the slightest moment of pressure and there was a sucking sound.

"Wha…"

"Can you hear me?" I heard him loudly say through what sounded like a microphone. I looked around.

"Shhh! They'll hear you!" I hissed. I frowned. His lips hadn't moved.

"No," he said. He held his finger to his lips for me to quiet down and grinned, his yellow-white teeth shining, his black skin shining, too. *"They*

won't. You are hearing this in your head.

"Not even the Big Eye knows I can do this," he said aloud, but lowering his voice. "Whatever they did to make me able to pass through walls, I can pass it into people and they can hear me, until the tiny nanomites are sweated from their skin.

"I did this to a little boy on the fifth floor. He had a contagious cancer, so they kept him in isolation for tests. Hearing me talk to him from wherever I was kept him sane. At least, until he died."

His disease could have killed you, though, I thought.

He started to descend through the floor. *"Fifteen minutes,"* he said in my head, then he was gone.

I whipped off my pants and t-shirt and threw on a white dress they'd recently given me that was made of heat-resistant thin plastic. The dress was long but light and allowed me to move very freely. I didn't bother with shoes. Too heavy.

For a moment, I had a brief flash in my mind of actually stepping outside. Into the naked sunlight. I could do it. Mmuo would help me. He and I would both escape. I felt a rush of hope, then a rush of heat. The scanner on my wall beeped. I had reached over 300 degrees.

Just before the door slid open, I had the sense to spread some shea butter on my skin. I ran out of my room.

"If you want to see, turn right and then go straight. Do it quickly."

I jogged, my feet slapping the cool marble floor. The hallway was quiet and empty, and soon I was in a part of my floor that I had never graced. The side where they kept Saeed. *His prison*, I thought.

I crossed a doorway and the floor here was carpeted, plush and red. I paused, looking down. I had never seen red carpet. Before they took it out, the carpet in my quarters had been black and flat. I wanted to kneel down and run my hands over it. I knew it would feel so soft and fluffy.

"See what you must but you have to make it to the elevator in two minutes," Mmuo's voice suddenly said into my head. *"Go down the hall and turn left. You will see it. Hurry."*

"Ok," I said aloud. But he could not hear me. One-way communication. I ran down the red hallway. Through glass windows and doors, I could see lab assistants and scientists in labs. Each large room was partitioned by a thick wall. There was bulky equipment in most of the rooms. If I were careful, no one would notice me. After sneaking past three labs, I saw the one that Saeed saw. It had to be. I stopped, staring and moaning deep in my throat. This lab was much bigger than the others and ten black cameras hung from its high white ceiling.

There were two wall-sized sleek grey machines on both sides of the room. I could hear them humming. Powerful. Between them, the world fell away to…another world where it was daytime and all that was happening was perfectly bluntly brutally visible. There were old vehicles, trucks from long, long ago, boxy, ineffective and weak. But strong enough to carry huge loads of cargo to dump into a deep pit. And that cargo consisted of human bodies. Hundreds of them. Dead. Not Africans. These dead people had pinkish pale skin and thin straightish hair like most of the Big Eye. When was this? Where was this? Why were the Big Eye scientists just *standing* there watching with their clipboards and ever-observing eyes?

It was not like watching a 3D movie. Even the best ones could never look this…true. Bodies. And I could *smell* them. The whole hallway reeked with their rot and feces and bile and the smoke of the trucks. My brain went to my books and recalled where I had seen this before. "Holocaust," I whispered, fighting the urge to turn to the side and vomit. I shut my watering eyes for a moment. I took a deep breath and nearly gagged on the stench. I opened my eyes.

This genocide happened during one of the early world wars. The Germans killed many of these people because they felt they were inferior or a threat or both. The book I read spoke as if wiping them out was the right thing to do. It certainly looked wrong to me. Were these Big Eye looking through time? Is this all they could do? Look? And why this time? For a moment, the portal disappeared and there was lots of scrambling, adjusting machines, pushing buttons, cursing. And then the portal reappeared showing the same activities, in the same time period in the same place. Happening.

I could feel the surge of heat in my body. Like a deep heartbeat of crimson flames. I shuddered and felt it ripple over every surface of my skin. But I couldn't move. Saeed had probably stood here just like this, too. Acrid smoke stung my eyes. My feet were burning the red carpet. A fire alarm sounded. I ran.

The elevator was open. It was empty. I ran in and it quickly closed behind me. I wished Mmuo would say something. If it went up, I was caught. If it went nowhere, I was caught. If it went down, I might be caught, but I might escape, too. I shut my eyes and whispered, "Go down, go down, *please,* go down. Have to get out!" Sweat beaded and evaporated all over my confused body and the elevator quickly began to feel humid.

If I hadn't rubbed all that shea butter on my skin at the last minute, I'd have been in horrible pain, my skin drying and probably cracking. I was hot like the sun, there was a ringing in my ears, as if my own body had an alarm and it was going off, too. I looked at my hands. They were glowing a soft yellow. My entire body was glowing through my dress.

The elevator jerked upward. I grabbed the railing, pure terror shooting through me. At least, I would make it outside. I hoped I could take two breaths before they caught me. I sunk to the floor. Saeed was dead and I was still trapped. Tears dribbled from the corners of my eyes and hissed as they evaporated down my cheeks.

The elevator jerked again. "*Sorry about that*," I heard Mmuo say in my head. He sounded distant. The elevator started moving down. I jumped up, grinning. I still had a chance. A louder alarm started to go off. They'd realized I was missing. "*I can get you to nine*," he said. His voice was fading and I had to strain to hear it. "*Two stairways in there. Run to the emergency one on the other side of the greenhouse, straight ahead when the doors open. You'll be on the side of the greenhouse, just go straight ahead! Do NOT go near the center! There's…*" His voice faded away.

Had my heat burned away his nanomites? Probably. As the elevator flew down to the ninth floor, my feet burned the elevator floor. It came to a sudden stop and the doors opened. The blare of the Tower 7 alarm assaulted my ears but the most beautiful site I'd ever seen caressed my eyes. An expansive room full of trees, bushes, flowers, vines. In pots, on shelves, tangled within each other. I could see the city through the windows on my left. The sky was the deep rose of evening. I started quickly walking down the narrow path before me. Moss grew on the sides of trees. The air smelled green, fragrant, soily, I had never smelled anything like it.

I heard a rush of footsteps from amongst the plants to my right. Between the foliage, I could see them. Big Eye guards. In armor with shields, with guns.

"Hey!" one of them yelled, spotting me. All their guns went up. "Put your hands up. We will not hurt you." The one speaking was a woman. I could see her clearly. She was short with long straight brown hair. She had pale skin and a hard voice.

Behind me I could hear the elevator rumbling. I still didn't move. Saeed was dead. There was nothing for me here. I was two years old and

I was forty years old. The marble beneath my feet absorbed my heat.

"Please, put your hands up," the woman pleaded. "You know what you are. We can stabilize you." She paused, obviously considering how much to tell me. I knew enough, though. Saeed was dead and it was all clear to me now.

"You're a weapon," the woman admitted. "If you wanted to know, now you know. I'm only here to help. You have to trust me. This wasn't supposed to happen, you being like this. Please, let us help you."

I heard the elevator doors opening just as I felt the light burst from me. There was warmth that started at my feet. It rolled up to my chest and pulsed out with a wave of heat. My shoulders jerked back and I stumbled to the side, getting a glimpse behind me. If I had blinked I still wouldn't have missed it. My skin prickled as my glow became a light green shine. The light steadily radiated from me, bathing every plant in the room. The guards behind me in the elevator and on the far right side of the room all ducked down and for a moment it was quiet enough where you could hear it. All the plants began to grow. Snapping, pulling, unfurling, creeping. Thick vines and even tree roots quickly crept, stretched and blocked the elevator door. Leaves, branches and stems grew so thick around the guards to my right that they were blocked from view. They didn't know I could do this.

The entire greenhouse swelled and flooded with foliage. Except a few steps ahead to my right. There was what I could only call a tunnel through the plants. It diagonally passed the cowering Big Eye. I ran into it just as the guards behind and to my right began to shoot toward where I'd initially been. Were they shooting through the plants or shooting at me, I do not know. And in many ways these two things were one and the same.

Mmuo had said to go forward to find the doorway. But I lost all sense of direction. So when I ended up standing before the giant glass dome I had no clue which way to run. My first thought was of the same book that spoke of the treacherous apple of knowledge. The Bible. Except that the man with enormous wings was not held up by any wooden cross. He was suspended in mid-air with his arms out and his legs tied together. His eyes were closed. His brown-feathered wings were stretched wide.

He was naked, his bronze-skinned body, muscled and very, very tall, at least compared to my six feet. He had Arab facial features like Saeed and a crown of wooly hair like mine. He was magnificent. Behind the glass dome was a rough wooden wall. The Backbone.

Behind me, I could hear them coming. Hacking and shooting through the plants and calling my name. I wasn't going to get out. I walked up to the glass and placed a hot hand on it. The glass was thick and very cool. Was there even air in there? Was that how they held him? Was it like being in outer space? What was space like for a creature made to fly?

His eyes opened. I gasped and jumped back. They were brown and soft, kind eyes.

"Oh my God, Phoenix! Step BACK!" one of the guards screamed, shoving aside a bush. I noticed the guard did not point his gun. Nor did the others who emerged beside him. I looked back at the man with wings. He was looking right at me, no expression on his face. I was surrounded by guards, all begging me to step away, pleading that this creature was unique and dangerous. However, none of them came to capture me. I didn't move.

Seeing the Big Eye cower, seeing their fear and sheer horror had a strange effect on me. I felt powerful. I felt lethal. I felt hopeful, though all was hopeless. I turned to the caged man and my hope evolved into rage. Even *he* was a prisoner here. I vowed that if I didn't get out, at least he would.

For the first time I did it voluntarily. I was already so hot and I grew hotter when I reached into myself, into all that I was, all that I had been and all that I would be, I reached in and drew from my source. Then I turned to a nearby tree and let loose a pulse of light. I sighed as it left me, feeling relief. Immediately the tree's roots began to buckle and creep toward the glass cage.

CRASH! They easily forced their way through and the rest of the dome began to crack in several places. The Big Eye turned and ran for their lives. I didn't bother running. There was no better way to die. He burst through, knocking me aside with the intensity of his wake. Into the now-dense foliage of the greenhouse. I saw none of it, but I heard and smelled it. Wet tearing sounds, screams, ripping, snapping, choking, not one gun fired. The air smelled like torn leaves and blood. It was still happening when I spotted the stairway between the plants and ran into it. I ran down and down flights and came to a heavy open door and entered the lobby.

For a moment, even after all that I had seen, I forgot what I was doing. The sight took my breath away. Tower 7's lobby was more spectacular than I'd ever imagined. No words could make up for actually seeing this place. This *space*. I had never been in such a space. The ceiling was so high and the marble walls were draped with gorgeous flowering vines, the small trees and plants growing through the soil-filled holes in the floor. I fought not to fall to my knees. *There* was the base of The Backbone. Its trunk had to be over thirty feet in diameter.

I was dizzy. I was burning up. I was amazed. I was exhausted. There was a freed angel beast massacring its captors nine floors above. I could hear more Big Eye guards coming down the stairwell. The alarm was blaring and the lobby was empty…except for a lone figure standing near the exit doors. He was grinning. He'd been trying to get to this very spot for nine years and my escape gave him the chance.

"Hurry," Mmuo cried. "Phoenix, MOVE!" I heard them burst through the stairway. I was running. I dodged small trees, scrambled around benches and leapt over plants. The door was yards away. I was going to make it. Outside, people walking by stopped to look.

Then I saw the guards come running onto the tower's wide plaza. They seemed to come from all directions. They shoved gaping people aside. They pulled up people who were sitting on benches enjoying the lovely evening. Then they formed a line blocking the exit and stood there, guns to their chests. I ran to Mmuo and would have given him a hug, if it weren't for my heat. We'd both almost made it.

"Go," I told him.

"I'm sorry," he said.

"For what?" I was having trouble thinking straight and I could smell the floor burning beneath me. I didn't know marble could burn. "Saeed would have been proud. I am proud. I set an angel free."

His eyebrows went up. "You…"

"Go!" I said, looking at the approaching Big Eye coming from the stairwell. They were flooding from doorways and were coming down an escalator on the other side of the lobby. "Don't ever let them catch you!"

He sunk through the floor and was gone.

I stood tall. There were over a hundred of them. Men and women armed with the guns I had seen them carrying all my life. No Big Eye guard went anywhere in the tower without them. I knew how they sounded. Nearly silent. I had been hearing shots fired all my life, too. For a multitude of reasons, but always with the same result. Something or someone was dead or severely injured. "Protect the scientist from the subject." "Observe and learn." "We will be better for it." "For the Research." I was taking all the pieces I had read and finally putting them together. The Big Eye crowded around me, twitchy with anticipation as if I were evil. After all I had done, to them, I guess I was evil. Or crazy.

I held up my hands, feeling myself utterly shining. The light bloomed from my body. The release felt glorious and I moaned with relief. Then more sighing than speaking, I said, "I give…"

They opened fire and it was as if I were punched with steel fists in every part of my body—chest, neck, legs, arms, abdomen, face. I was blown back and my vision went red-yellow. I lay on my back. Everything was wet, the smell of smoke in the one nostril I had left. Smoke and…the perfume of The Backbone. I was looking at it, gazing at how it reached, up, up, up, through the high marble ceiling, through the thirty-nine floors above. Into the sky. Reaching for the sky.

I felt the radiance burst from me, warm, yellow, light, plucked from the sun and placed inside me like a seed until it was ready to bloom. It bloomed now and the entire lobby was washed. The Big Eye covered their faces and dropped their guns. A few ran to the stairwell, others to the far side of the lobby. Most of them ran past my mangled body and out of the building. Those ones must have known what would happen next.

I knew. I was burning as the light pulsated and pulsated from me there on the floor. My body convulsed with it as my clothes burned and then my flesh. There was no pain. My nerves were burning.

My light shined on the plants and tiny trees of the lobby and they began to grow wildly, stirred and amazed with life. Vines stretched, lengthened, thickened. Flowers twisted open. Pollen puffed the air sweet. Leaves unfolded and widened. The stone floors were covered with green yellow white brown black, the strongest roots cracking its foundation.

My light shined on the great tree that was The Backbone. Its roots groaned as they shifted, coiled, expanded, and caused the entire portion of the floor around its roots to buckle and fall apart. The tree's colossal trunk twisted this way and that, shrugging off the building that was its shackle. Chunks of the floors above began to crash down around me. I was ashes being scattered by vines and roots when Tower 7 fell.

Several of the buildings beside the tower fell, too. The Backbone stood tall, stretching its branches and opening its enormous leaves over buildings and streets. At its base, a small lush jungle sprung from the rubble of Tower 7. All this in the middle of the city. Helicopters hovered, news crews streamed footage live, people gaped from afar. When the debris settled, there was a moment where my brilliant light shined into the darkness, for it was now night time. The news cameras recorded the winged man flying out of the rubble but not much else lived, except the man who could walk through walls. Mmuo walked out of The Backbone's trunk and stood before it. "This is what you all deserve!" he shouted, shaking his fist at the eyes of the hovering cameras. Then he sunk into the ground and was never seen again.

No one in the city would approach the ruins of Tower 7. They sat for seven days, a pile of those things Saeed used to eat: rubble, glass, metal and…ash. And then I realized the meaning of my name.

DIGGING

IAN McDONALD

Ian McDonald lives in Northern Ireland, just outside Belfast. He sold his first story in 1983 and bought a guitar with the proceeds, perhaps the only rock 'n' roll thing he ever did. Since then he's written fourteen novels, three story collections and diverse other pieces, and has been nominated for every major science fiction/ fantasy award—and even won a couple. In his day job he works in television development—where do you think all those dreadful reality shows come from? His current novel is Planesrunner, *first book in the young adult science fiction Evergence trilogy.*

Tash was wise to the ways of wind. She knew its many musics: sometimes like a flute across the pipes and tubes; sometimes a snare-drum rattle in the guy-lines and cable stays or again, a death drone-moan from the turbine gantries and a scream of sand past the irised-shut windows when the equinox dust storms blew for weeks on end. From the rails and drive bogies of the scoopline the wind drew a wail like a demon choir and from the buckets set a clattering clicking rattle so that she imagined tiny clockwork angels scampering up and down the hundreds of kilometers of conveyor belts. In the storm-season gales it came screaming in across Isidis' billion-year-dead impact basin, clawing at the eaves and gables of West Diggory, tearing at the tiered roofs so hard Tash feared it would rip them right off and send them tumbling end over end down down into the depths of the Big Dig. That would be the worst thing. Everyone would die badly: eyeballs and fingertips and lips exploding, cheeks bursting with red veins. She had nightmares about suddenly looking up to see the roof ripping away and the naked sky and the air all blowing away in one huge shout of exhalation. Then your eyeballs exploded. She imagined how that would sound. Two soft popping squelches. Then In-Brother Yoche told her you couldn't hear your eyeballs exploding because the air would be too thin and the whole story was a legend of mischievous Grandparents and Sub-aunts who liked to scare under-fours. But it made her think about how fragile was West Diggory and the other three stations of the Big Dig. Spindly and top-heavy, domes piled upon half domes upon semi-domes, swooping wing roofs and perilous balconies, all resting on the finger-thin canti-levers that connected the great Excavating City to the traction bogies. Like big spiders. Tash knew spiders. She had seen spiders in a book and once, in a piece of video excitedly shot by Lady-cousin Nairne in North Cutter, a real spider, in a real web, trembling in the perennial beat of the buckets working up the Scoopline from the head of the Big Dig, five kilometers down slope. Lady-cousin Nairne had poked at the spider with her fingers—fat and brown as bread in high magnification. The spider had frozen, then scuttled for the corner of the window frame, curled into a tiny ball of legs and refused to do anything for the rest of the day. The next day when Nairne and her camera returned it was dead dead dead, dried into a little desiccated husk of shell. It must have come in a crate in the supply run down from the High Orbital, though everything they shipped from orbit was supposed to be clean. Beyond the window where the little translucent corpse hung vibrating in its web, red rock and wind and the endless march of the buckets along the rails of the Excavating Conveyor. Buckets and wind. Tied together. Wind; Fact one. When the buckets ceased, then and only then would the wind stop. Fact two: all Tash's life it had blown in the same direction: downhill.

Tash Gelem-Opunyo was wise to the ways of wind, and buckets, and random spiders and on Moving Day the wind was a long, many-part harmony for pipes drawn from the sand-polished steels rails, a flutter of the kites and blessing banners and windsocks and lucky fish that West Diggory flew from every roof top and pylon and stanchion, a sudden caress of a veering eddy in the small of her back that made Tash shiver and stand upright on the high verandah in her psuit, a too-intimate touch. She was getting too big for the old psuit. It was tight and chafing in the wrong places. Tight it had to be, a stretch-skin of gas-impermeable fabric, but Things were Showing. My How You've Grown Things, that Haramwe Odonye, who was an Out-cousin in from A.R.E.A. and thus allowed to Notice such things, Noticed, and Commented On. Last Moving Day, half a long-year before, she had drawn in an attempt to camouflage the bumps and creases and curves by drawing all over the hi-visibility skin with marker pen. There were more animals on her skin than on the whole of Mars.

Up and out on Moving Day, that was the tradition. From the very very old to the very very young, blinking up out of their pressure cocoons; every soul in West Diggory came out on to the balconies and galleries and walkways. Safety was part of the routine—with every half-year wrench of West Diggory's thousands of tons of architecture into movement the possibility increased that a joint might split or a pressure dome shatter. Eyeball-squelch-pop time. But safety was only a small part. Movement was what West Diggory was for; like the wind, downwards, ever downwards.

The Terrace of the Grand Regard was the highest point on West Diggory: only the banners of the Isidis Planitia Excavating Company eternally billowing in the unvarying down-slope wind, and the wind turbines, stood higher. Climbing the ladders Tash felt Out-cousin Haramwe's eyes on her, watching from the Boys' Pavilion. His boy-gaze drew the other young males on their high and rickety terrace. The psuit was indeed tight, but good tight. Tash enjoyed how it moved with her, holding her in where she wanted to be held, emphasizing what she wanted emphasized.

"Hey, good snake!" Out-cousin Haramwe called on the Common Channel. On her seven-and-a-half birthday Tash had drawn a dream snake on her psuit skin, a diamond pattern loop with its tail at the base of her spine, curled around the left curve of her ass and buried its head in the inner thigh. It had been exciting to draw. It was more exciting to wear on Moving Day, the only time she ever wore the psuit.

"Are you ogling my ophidian?" Tash taunted back to the hoots of the other boys as she climbed up on to Gallery of Exalted Vistas to be with her sisters and cousin and In-cousins and Out-cousins, all the many ways in which Tash could be related in a gene-pool of only two thousand people. The guys hooted. Tash shimmied her shoulders, where little birds were drawn. The boys liked her insulting them in words they didn't understand. Listen well, look well. I'm the best show on Mars.

A thousand banners rattled in the unending wind. Kites dipped and fluttered, painted with birds and butterflies and stranger aerial creatures that had only existed in the legends of distant earth. Streamers pointed the way for West Diggory: downhill, always downhill. The lines of buckets full of Martian soil marched up the conveyor from the dig point, invisible over the close horizon, under the legs of West Diggory, towards the unseen summit of Mt Incredible, where they tipped their load on its ever-growing summit before cycling back down the underside of the conveyor. The story was that the freshly dug regolith at the bottom of the hole was the color of gold: exposure to the atmosphere on its long journey up-slope turned it Mars red. She turned to better feel the shape of the wind on every part of her body. This psuit so needed replacing. There was more to her shiver than just the caress of air in motion. Wind and words: they were the same stuff. If she threw big and fancy words, words that gave her joy and made her laugh from the shape they made from moving air, it was because they were living wind itself.

A shiver ran up through the catwalk grilles and railings and into Tash Gelem-Opunyo. The engineers were running up the traction generators; West Diggory shuddered and thrummed as the tokamaks drew resonances and steel harmonies from its girders and cantilevers. Tash's molars ached, then there was a jolt that threw old and young alike off balance, grasping for handrails, stanchions, cables, each other. There was an immense shriek like a new moon being pulled live from the body of the world. Shuddering creaks, each so loud Tash could hear them through her ear-protectors. Steel wheels turned, grinding on sand. West Diggory began to move. People waved their hands and cheered, the noise reduction circuits on the Common Channel stopped the din down to a surge of delighted giggling. The wheels, each taller than Tash, ground round, slow as growing. West Diggory, perched on its cantilevers, inched down its eighteen tracks, tentative as an old woman stepping from a diggler. This was motion on the glacial, the geological scale. It would take ten hours for West Diggory to make its scheduled descent into the Big Dig. You had to be sure to have eaten and drunk enough because it wasn't safe to go inside. Tash had breakfasted lightly at the commons in the Raven Sorority, when the In-daughters lived together after they turned five. The semizoic fabric absorbed everything without stink or stain but it was far from cool to piss your suit. Unless you were up and out on a job. Then it was mandatory.

Music trilled on the Common Channel, a cheery little toe-tapper. Tash gritted her teeth. She knew what it heralded: the West Diggory Down. No one knew when where or who had started the tradition of the Moving Day dance: Tash suspected it was a joke that no one had recognized and so became literal. She slid behind a stanchion as her Raven sisters formed up and the boys up on the Lads' Pavilion bowed and raised their hands. Slip away slip away before it starts. Up the steps and along the clattering catwalk to the Outermost Preview. From this distant perch, a birdcage of steel at the end of a slender pier, a lantern suspended over the sand, Tash surveyed all West Diggory, her domes and gantries and pods and tubes and flapping banners and her citizens—so few of them, Tash thought—formed up into lines and squares for the dance. She tuned out the Common Channel. Strange, them stepping gaily, hand in hand, up and down the lines, do-se-doh in psuits and facemasks and total silence. The olds seemed to enjoy it. They had no dignity. Look how fat some of them were in their psuits. Tash turned away from the rituals of West Diggory to the great, subtle slope of the Big Dig, following the lines up the slope. She was on the edge of the age when you could leave West Diggory but she had heard that up there, beyond Mt Incredible, the small world curved away so quickly in all directions that the horizon was only three kilometers distant. The Big Dig held different horizons. It was a huge cone sunk into the surface of a sphere. An alternative geometry worked here. The world didn't curve away, it curved inwards, a circle over three hundred kilometers round where it met the surface of Mars. The world radiated outwards: Tash could follow the radiating spokes of the scooplines all the way of the edge of the world, and beyond, to the encircling ring-mountain of Mt Incredible that reached the edge of space. Peering along the curve of the Big Dig through the dust haze constantly thrown up by the ceaseless excavating, she could just make out the sun-glitter from the gantries of North Cutter, like West Diggory, making its slow descent deeper into the pit. A flicker of thought would up the magnification on her visor and she would be able to look clear across eighty kilometers of airspace to A.R.E.A and spy on whatever celebrations they held there, on the first and greatest of the Excavating Cities on Moving Day. Maybe she might see a girl like herself, balanced on some high and perilous perch, looking out across the bowl of the world.

The figures on the platforms and terraces broke apart, bowed to each other, lost all pattern and rhythm and became random again. Moving Day Down was over for another half-year. Tash flicked on the Common Channel. Tash liked to be apart, different, a girl of words and wit, but she also loved to be immersed in West Diggory's never-ending babble of chat and gossip and jokes and family news. Together, the Excavating Cities had a population of less than two thousand humans. Small, complex societies, isolated from the rest of the planet, gush words like springs, like torrents and floods. The river of words, the only river that Mars knew. Tash's psuit circuitry was smart enough to adjust the voices so that they spoke at the volume and distance they would have in atmosphere. Undifferentiated, the flood of West Diggory voices would have overwhelmed her. So the wall of voices did not overwhelm her. She turned her head this way, that way. Eavesdropping. There was Leyta Soshinwe-Opunyo, Queen-beeing again. Tash had seen pictures of bees like she had seen birds. On Arrival Day, when the Excavating Cities finally reached the bottom of the Big Dig, there would be birds, and bees, and even spiders. There was Great-Out-Aunt Yoto, seeming enthusiastic but always seasoned with a pinch of criticism—*oh, and another thing*: people weren't performing the dance moves right, the Engineers had mistuned the tokamaks and her titanium hip was aching, was it her or did more bits fall off West Diggory every time? They would never have allowed that in Southdelving, her family home. A sudden two-tone siren cut across the four hundred voices of West Diggory. Emergency teams slapped their psuits to warning yellow and rushed to their positions, everyone hurried to the muster points, then relaxed as the medics discovered the nature of the Emergency. The Common Channel flooded with laughter. Haramwe Odonye, during a particularly energetic caper in the West Diggory Down, had slipped and sprained his ankle.

Big Dig Figs.:

Population: one thousand eight hundred and thirty-three, divided between the four Excavating Cities of (clockwise) Southdelving, West Diggory, North Cutter and A.R.E.A (Ares Re-engineering of Environment and Atmosphere). Total Martian population: five thousand two hundred and seventeen.

Elevation: at the digging head as of Martian Year 112, Janulum 1: minus twenty-three kilometers below Martian Mean Gravity Surface (no sea level). Same date, highest point of Mt Incredible: 15 kilometers above MGS.

Diameter of the Big Dig at Martian MGS: Five hundred and sixteen kilometers

Circumference of the Big Dig at Martian MGS: One thousand six hundred and twenty-two kilometers.

Angle of Big Dig Excavation Surface: 5.754 degrees. That's pretty gentle. The Scoopline can't handle more than an eight-degree slope. To the casual human eye—one that hasn't grown up inside the gentle dish of the Big Dig, that would look almost flat. But it's not flat. That's why it's the key figure: those 5.75 degrees are going to make Mars habitable.

Date of commencement of the Big Dig: AlterMarch 23rd, Martian Year 70. Two thirty in the afternoon, on schedule, the scooplines excavated and the bucket teeth took their first bites of Isidis Planitia.

Volume of the Big Dig: as of above date: one million, eight hundred and thirteen thousand cubic kilometers. All piled up neatly into Mt Incredible, the ring-shaped mountain that surrounds the Big Dig like the wall of an old impact crater. Not entirely surrounds. Mt Incredible has been constructed with four huge valleys: Windrush, Zephyr, Cyroco and Storm of the Black Plums: howling wind-haunted, storm-scoured canyons: that same wind singing over the tombs of the Diggers who have died in the course of the great excavation, unfailingly stirring the flags and streamers of the mobile cities far below.

Total mass of Martian surface excavated in the Big Dig to date: 7.1 x 10^{15} tons.

Big Dig Figs and Facts. The numbers that shape Tash's world.

Tash was in the Orangery when the call came down through the rows of breadfruit trees. Like the Moving Day dance, the name was generally considered another joke that had run away and taken up residence in the ventilators and crawlspaces and power conduits of the Excavating City, as this baroque glass dome had never grown oranges. The rows of breadfruit and plantains and bananas and other high-carbo staples gave camouflage and opportunity for West Diggory's young people to meet and talk and scheme and flirt.

"Milaba wants to see Tash, pass it on."

"Sweto, tell Chunye that Milaba wants to see Tash."

"Qori, have you seen Tash?"

"I think she was down in the plantains, but she might have moved on to the breadfruit."

"Well tell her Milaba wants to see her."

By leaps and misunderstandings, by staggers and misapprehensions, by devious spirals of who liked whom and who was talking to whom and who wasn't and who was hooking with whom and who had finished with whom, the message spiralled in along the web of leaf-mould smelling plants to Tash, spraying the breadfruit. A simple call, a message would have reached her directly but where there are only a hundred of you, true social networking is mouth to mouth.

In-Aunt Milaba. She was a legend, a statue of woman, gracious and noble, adored far beyond West Diggory. Her dark skin was lustrous as night, her soul as star-filled. To be in her presence was to be blessed in ways you would not immediately understand but, more thrilling to Tash, was that In-Aunt Milaba was the chief service engineer for the North West sector scooplines. The summons to her office, a little glass and aluminum bubble like a bunion on one of West Diggory's steel feet, could mean only one thing. Out. Out and up.

"So Haramwe sprained his ankle."

Every part of In-Aunt Milaba's tiny office, from the hand-carved ol-ivine desk to the carafe of water that stood on it, shook to the rattle of the buckets hurtling up the scoopline. Milaba raised an eyebrow. Tash realized a response was due.

"Are his injuries debilitating?"

"Debilitating." Milaba gave a flicker of a smile. "You could say that. He'll be out for a week or so. He came down heavily, silly boy. Showing off. When is your birthday?" Tash's heart leapt.

She knew. Everyone knew everything, all the time. The game was pretending not to know.

"Octobril fifth."

"Three months." Milaba appeared to consider for a moment. "Peyko Ruebens-Opollo says for all your fancy talk you've a good head and better sense and do what you're told. That's good because I don't need attitude problems or last-minute-good-ideas when I'm out on the line."

For once the words failed Tash. They hissed from her like air from a ruptured atmosphere cell. She waved her hands in speechless delight.

"I'm taking a digger up Line 12 to Windrush Valley. The feed tokamaks have been fluctuating nastily. Probably a soft fail in a command chip set; they get a lot of radiation up there. Now I need someone with me to hold things and make tea and generally make intelligent conversation. Are you interested?"

Still the words would not come. The rule was that you did not leave the Excavating Cities until you were eight, when you were technically adult. Rules broke and bent with the frequency of scoopline breakdowns but three months was a significant proportion of the long Martian year.

Out. Out, and up. Up the line, into the windy valley. In a diggler, with In-Aunt Milaba.

"Yes, oh yes, I'd love to," Tash finally squeaked. Now Milaba unleashed the full radiance of her smile and it was like sunrise, it was solstice lights, it was the warmth of the glow-lamps in the Orangery. *I say you are an adult citizen of West Diggory, Tash Gelem-Opunyo,* the smile said, *and if I say it, all say it.*

"Be at the Outlock 12 at fourteen o'clock," Milaba said. "You do know how to make tea, don't you?"

Still not got it? It's easy, easy easy easy. Easy as a heezy, which is a Digger saying. A heezy is the lever on a scoopline bucket that, when struck by the dohbrin (which is a different type of lever found at the load-off end of the scoopline), tips the contents of the bucket down Mt Incredible. Heezy peasy easy. It's all because air has weight. Air's not nothing. It's gas—in Mars' case, carbon dioxide nitrogen argon oxygen and the leaked breathings from the hundred-and-something years that humans have scratched and scrabbled clawholds on its red earth. It has mass. It has weight. And it flows, the same way that water flows, to the lowest point. Wind is air flowing. People say, *no one knows why the wind blows.* That's stupid nonsense. Wind blows from high to low, high pressure to low pressure, high altitude to low altitude; down the slopes of mountains, through canyons and valleys. The air pressure at the bottom of the great and primeval rift of Valles Marineris is ten times that in the long-cold volcanic calderas atop Olympus Mons. Titanic gales and fog blow through that valley. The fog is because the atmospheric pressure at the bottom of the valley is enough—just enough—to allow water to exist as vapour. But that's still not enough to support big life. That's like higher than earth's highest mountain. That's fingertip-lip-exploding, eyeball-squelching, cheek-bursting pressure. Bug life yes, big life no. That's not enough to make Mars a green paradise, a home for humanity, a fertile pool of life beyond little blue Earth. What you need is deep. Thirty kilometers deep. Deeper than any place on Earth is deep. Deeper than even Olympus Mons, mightiest mountain on all the worlds, is high. And because air has weight, because atmosphere flows and the wind blows, gas will fill up the hole. That's the wind that rattles the banners and turns the rotors of West Diggory. As the gas flows the pressure grows until the day comes when the atmospheric pressure at the bottom of the hole is enough for you to walk around without a psuit, in just your skin if you have the urge and your skin is pretty enough. Earth atmospheric pressure. Pressure, that's always been the problem with making Mars habitable. Get all the gas into one place. When you've got enough of it, turning it into something you can breathe is the easy bit. That's just bugs and plants and life.

Thirty kilometers deep. The scooplines are at minus twenty-six kilometers. That's another five M-years before they hit atmospheric baseline. Then they'll level out the floor of the crater, take away some of the sides, expand the flat area, though it will all seem so flat, the atmospheric gradient so subtle, that you will seem to be walking out into breathlessness and light-headedness rather than ascending into it. Fifty years after her In-Grandfather Tayhum made the first incision, the Big Dig will be dug. Tash will be seventeen and a half when the wind rushing down the sides of the Big Dig finally fails and the rotors stop and the banners fall and the Excavating Cities finally come to a rest.

Twenty-six kilometers up-slope, In-Aunt Milaba gave the sign for Tash to throw the levers to disengage the diggler from the scoopline. Thus far the big world of outside had been a thumping disappointment to Tash. She had yet to be outside, properly outside, two-figures-in-a-Mars-scape outside, shiver-in-your-psuit outside. She had transited from plastic bubble by plastic tube to plastic bubble connected by its grip on the scoopline to home.

This was what Tash Gelem-Opunyo saw from the transparent bubble of the diggler. Sand sand sand sand sand, a rock there, sand sand sand rock rock, oh, some pebbles! Sand grit sand more grit something between pebble and grit, something between grit and sand, a bit of old abandoned machinery, wow wow wow! Dust drifted up around it. Sand. Sand. Sand. West Diggory was still visible, down the dwindling thread of the scoopline, now truly the size of a spider. The enormous, horizonless perspectives robbed Tash of anything by which she could judge movement. The sand, the buckets, the unchanging gentle gradient that went up halfway to space. Only by squinting down through the floor glass at the blurred, grainy surface did she get any sense of movement.

Twenty-six vertical kilometers equalled two hundred sixty surface kilometers equalled five and a half hours in a plastic bubble with a relative you've grown up in enforced proximity to but until now never really known or talked to. Everyone loves In-Aunt Milaba the Magnificent, that's the legend, but five hours, Aunt and Niece, Tash began to wonder if this was another wind-whisper legend blown around the corners and crannies of West Diggory. She was beautiful, a feast for the eye and soul, all those things an eight-year-old girl hopes for herself (and did Tash not share the DNA—given that the Excavating Cities gene-pool was shallow as a spit, hence all the careful arrangements of In-relatives and Out-relatives and who would be sent to one of the other Excavating Cities and who would stay), all those things a girl of almost-eight wants for herself but try as she might, and did, Tash could not engage her. Fancy funny words of the type Tash treasured. Poems. Puns. Riddles. Guessing games. Break-the-code games. Allusions and circumspect questions. Direct questions. To them all In-Aunt Milaba shook her head and smiled and bent over the controls and the monitors and checked her kit and said not a word. So tea, lots of tea, and muttering little rhymes to the rhythm of the huge balloon wheels as the scoopline hauled Diggler Six up the side of the biggest excavation in the solar system.

But now they were released from the scoopline and Milaba was standing at the steering column, driving the diggler under its own power. It was still sand sand sand and occasional rock, but Tash knew a gnaw of excitement. She was free, disconnected from the umbilicals of life for the first time. She was out in the wild world. The scoopline dwindled to a thread, to invisibility behind her, ahead she saw a notch on the edge of vision. Windrush Valley. All the wind-blown words stopped. A flaw in the horizon. A place beyond the Big Dig. Beyond that declivity was the whole curved world. In the silence In-Aunt Milaba turned from the control column.

"I think you could have a go now."

So this was what she had been waiting for, Tash to run out of words, and finally listen.

The diggler was ridiculously simple to drive. Plant your feet firmly at the drive column. Push forward to feed power to the traction motors in the wheel hubs. Pull back to brake. Yaw to steer. There was even a little holder on the side of the drive column for your tea. Tash giggled with nervous glee as she gingerly pushed forward the stick and the bubble of pressure glass slung between the giant orange tyres stuttered forward. Within thirty seconds she had it. Thirty seconds later she was pushing it, sneaking the speed bar up, looking for places where she could make the diggler skip over rocks.

"I'd go easy on that throttle," Milaba said. "The battery life is eight hours. That's why we ride the scoopline up and down again. You don't want to get stuck up here with night coming down, no traction and no heat."

Tash eased the stick back but not before the diggler hit the small boulder at which she had discreetly aimed and bounced all four wheels in the air. Milaba smiled that morning-sun smile. Then shoulder by shoulder they stood at the controls and rode up into the orange valley. The land rose up on either side, higher as they drove deeper, kilometers high. They felt like oppression to Tash, shouldering close and ominous, their heights breathless and haunted with dark things that lived in the sky. At the same time she felt hideously small and exposed in the fragile glass ornament of the diggler. The wind was rising, she could feel the diggler shake on its suspension, hear the shriek and moan through the cables. The controls fought her but she pushed the little bubble deeper and deeper into Windrush Valley. When her forearms arched and the sinews on her neck stood out from fighting the atmosphere of Mars pouring through this two-kilometer wide notch in Mt Incredible, Milaba leaned over and tapped a preprogrammed course into the computer.

"Suit up," she said. "We'll be there in ten minutes."

The tokamak station was a wind-scoured blister of construction plastic hunkering between a boulder field and a stretch of polished olivine. It was only when the diggler slowed to a stop and fired sand anchors that Tash realized that it was nearer and smaller than she had thought. It was not a distant vast city, the power plant was only slightly higher than the diggler's mammoth wheels. The wind rotor, spinning like it would suddenly leap from its pylon and spin madly away through the upper air, was no bigger than her outstretched hands.

"Mask sealed?"

Tash ran her fingers around the join with her psuit hood and give In-Aunt Milaba two thumbs up. "I'm dee-peeing the diggler." There was a high-pitched shriek of air being vented into the tanks, a whistle that ebbed into silence as the pressure dropped to match the outside environment. The scribbled-over psuit felt tight and stiff. This was true eyeball-squelch altitude. Then Milaba popped the door and Tash followed her out and down the ladder on to the wild surface of Mars.

Gods and teeth, but the wind was brutal. Tash balled her fists and squared her shoulders and lowered her head to battle through it to the yellow-and-blue-chevronned tokamak station. She could feel the sand whipping across the skin of her psuit. She didn't like to think of the semizoic skin abrading, cell by cell. She imagined it wailing in pain. A tap on the shoulder, Milaba gestured for her to hook her safety line on to the door winch. Then In-Aunt and In-Niece they punched through the big wind to the shelter of the tokamak shell. Out. Out in the world. Up high. If Tash kept walking into the wind she would pass through Windrush Valley and come to a place where the world curved away from her, not towards her. The desire to do it was unbearable. Out of the hole. All it would take would be one foot in front of another. They would take her all the way around the world and back again, to this place. The gale of possibility died. It was all, only, ever circles. Milaba tapped her again on the shoulder to remind her that there was work to be done here. Tash took the unitool and unscrewed the inspection hatch. Milaba plugged in her diagnosticators. She was glorious to watch at work, easy and absorbed. But it was long work and Tash's attention wandered to the little meandering dust-dervishes that spun up into a small tornado for a few seconds, staggered down the valley and collapsed into swirling sand.

"Willie-willies," Milaba said. "You want to be careful with those, they're tricksy. As I thought." She pointed at the readout. "A hard fail in the chip set." She pulled a new blade out of her thigh pouch and slid it into the control unit. Lights flashed green. Inside its shielded dome the tokamak grumbled and woke up with a shiver that sent the dust rising from the ground. Tash watched the wind whirl into a dozen dust-devils, dancing around each other. "Just going to check the supply line. You stay here." She headed up the valley along the line of the power cable. The dust devils swirled in towards each other. They merged. They fused. They became one, a true dust demon.

"Looks all right!" In-Aunt Milaba called.

"Milaba, I don't like the look…" The dust-demon spun towards Tash, then at the last moment veered away and tracked up the valley. "Milaba!"

Milaba hesitated. The hesitation was death. The dusty-demon bore down on her, she tried to throw herself away but it spun over her, lifted her, threw her hard and far, smashed her down on to the smooth polished olivine. Tash saw her face-plate shatter in a spray of shards and water vapour. It was random, it was mad, it was a chance in a billion, it can't happen, it was an affront to order and reason but it had and there Milaba lay on the hard olivine.

"Oh my gods oh my gods oh my gods!" For a moment Tash was paralyzed, for a moment she did not know what to do, that she could do anything, that she must do something. Then she was running up the valley. The dust-demon veered towards Tash. Tash shrieked, then it staggered away, broke itself on the boulders and spun down to dust again. The psuit would seal automatically but In-Aunt Milaba had moments before her eyeballs froze. "Oh help help help help help," Tash cried, her hands pressed to Milaba's face, trying to will heat into it. Then she saw the red button on the safety line harness. She hit it and was almost jolted off her feet as the winch on the diggler reeled Milaba in. Tash hit the Emergency Channel. "This is Diggler Six this is Diggler Six in Windrush Valley. This is an emergency." Of course it is. It's the Emergency channel. She tried to calm her voice as the winch lifted the limp Milaba into the air. "We have a suit dee-pee situation. We have a suit dee-pee."

"Hello Diggler Six. This is Diggory West Emergency Services. Please identify yourself."

"This is Tash Gelem-Opunyo. It's Milaba."

"Tash. Control here." Tash recognized Out-Uncle Yoyote's voice. "Get back. Get back here. You should have enough power, we'll send another diggler up the line to meet you, but you, darling, you have to do it. We can't get to you in time. It's up to you. Get back to us. It's all you can do."

Of course. It was. All she could do. No rescue swooping from the skies, in a world where nothing could fly. No speed-star scorching up the slope of the Big Dig in a world where the scoopline was the fastest means of transport. She was on her own.

It took all her strength to swing Milaba through the hatch into the diggler cab and seal the lock. Almost Tash popped her faceplate. Almost. She re-pressurized the diggler. Air-shriek built to a painful screech then stopped. But Milaba was so still, so cold. Her face was white with frost where her breath had frozen into her skin. It would never be the same again. Tash knelt, turned her cheek to her In-Aunt's lips. A whisper a sigh a suspicion a susurration. She was breathing. But it was cold so cold death cold Mars cold in the diggler. Tash slapped the heater up to the maximum and jigged around the tiny cab. Condensation turned the windows opaque, then cleared. Back. She had to get back. Was there an auto-return programme? Where would she find it? Where would she even begin looking? Wasting precious instants, wasting precious instants. Tash took the control column, stamped on the pedal to release the anchors and engaged the traction motors. Turning was difficult. Turning was scary. Turning forced a small moan of fear when the wind got under the diggler and she felt the right side lift. If it went over here, they were both dead.

This was not fun driving. There was no glee, no whee! At every bounce Tash tensed and clenched, fearful that the diggler would roll over and shatter like an egg, smash an axle, any number of new terrors that only appear when your life depends on everything working perfectly. *Come on come on come on.* The battery gauge was dwindling with terrifying speed. This was outside. This was the horizoned world. Where was the scoopline? Surely it hadn't been this far. *Come on come on come on.* A line on the sand. But so far. Power at twelve percent. Where had it gone what had she used it on? The heating blast? The emergency ree-pee? The burn on the winch? Call home. That would be sensible. That would be the act of a girl with a good head and better sense who did what she was told. But it would use power. Batteries at seven percent, but now she could see the scoopline, the laden buckets above, the empty buckets below, bucket after bucket after bucket. She drove the diggler on. Matching velocities with the scoopline was teeth-gritting, nerve-stretching work. Tash had to drop the diggler into the space between the buckets and hold exact speed. A push too fast would ride up on the preceding bucket. Too slow and she would be rear-ended by the bucket behind. And ever edging inwards, inwards, closer to the line as the batteries slid from green to red. Lights flashes. Tash threw the lever. The shackle engaged. Tash rolled away from the drive column to Milaba on the floor.

"Tash." A whisper a sigh a suspicion a susurration.

"It's all right, it's all right, don't talk, we're on scoopline."

"Tash, are my eyes open?"

"Yes they are."

A tiny sigh.

"Then I can't see. Tash, talk to me."

"What about?"

"I don't know. Anything. Everything. Just talk to me. We're on the line, did you say?"

"We're on the line. We're going home."

"Five hours then. Talk to me."

So she did. Tash pulled cushions and mats around her into a nest and sat holding her In-Aunt's head and she talked. She talked about her friends and her in-sisters and her out-sisters and who would go away from West Diggory and who would stay. She talked about boys and how she liked them looking at her but still wanted to be different and special, not to be taken for granted, funny-Tash, odd-Tash. She talked about whether she would marry, which she didn't think she would, not as far as she could see, and what she would do then if she didn't. She talked about the things she loved, like swimming, and cooking vegetables, and drawing and words words words. She talked about how she loved the sound and shape of words, the sound of them as something quite different from what they meant and how you could put them together to say things that could not possibly be, and how the words came to her, like they were blown on the wind, shaped from wind, the wind brought to life. She talked of these in words that weren't clever or mouth-filling, words said quietly and simply and honestly, saying what she thought and how she felt. Tash saw then a richer lode in words; beyond the beauty of their sounds and shapes and patterns was a deeper beauty of the truth they could shape. They could tell what it was to be Tash Gelem-Opunyo. Words could fly the banners and turn the rotors of a life. Milaba squeezed her hand and pushed her broken lips into a smile, and creased the corner of her white, frost-burned eyes.

The Emergency Channel chimed. Yoyote had her on visual: they were about twenty kilometers down slope from her. They were coming to get her. They would be safe soon. Well done. And there was other news, news that made his voice sound strange to Tash in Diggler Six, like he was dead and walking and talking and about to cry all at the same time. A command had come in from Isidis Excavation Command, from the High Orbital, ultimately all the way from Earth and the Isidis Development Consortium. There had been a political shift. The faction that was up was down and the faction that was down was up. The Big Dig was cancelled.

From here, every way was up. There had been no official announcement from the Council of Diggers for ceremonials or small mournings: in their ones and two, their families and kinship groups and sororities and fraternities, the people of West Diggory had decided to share the news that their world was ending, and to see the bottom of it; the base that had been their striving for three generations; the machine head. Dig Zero. Minimum elevation. So they took digglers or rode down the scoopline to the bottom of the Big Dig, and looked around them, and looked around at the digging heads of the scooplines, stilled and frozen for the first time in memory, buckets filled with their last bite of Mars turned to the sky. As they grew accustomed to the sights and wonders of the dig head, for not one in fifty of the Excavating Cities' populations worked at the minimum elevation, they saw in the distance, between the black scoopline, groups and families and societies from North Cutter and Southdelving and A.R.E.A. They waved to each other, greeting relatives they had not seen in years; the Common Channel was a flock of voices. Tash stood with her Raven Sorority sisters. They positioned themselves around her, even Queen-bee Leyta. Tash was a slam and brief heroine—perhaps the last one the Big Dig would ever have. In-Aunt Milaba had been taken to the main medical facility A.R.E.A where they were growing her new irises for her frost-blinded eyes. Her face would be scarred and patched with ugly white but her smile would always be beautiful. So the In-sisters and In-cousins stood around Tash, needing to be down at zero but not knowing why, or what to do now. The boys from the Black Obsidian Fraternity waved over and came across the sand to join the girls. *So few of us, really,* Tash thought.

"Why?" Out-cousin Sebben asked.

"Environment," said Sweto and, in the same transmission, Qori said, "Cost."

"Are they going to take us all back to Earth?" Chunye asked.

"No, they're never going to do that," Haramwe said. He walked with a stick, which made him look like an old man but at the same interesting and attractive. "That would cost too much."

"We couldn't anyway," Sweto said. "The gravity down there would kill us. We can't live anywhere but here. This is our home."

"We're Martians," Tash said. Then she put her hands up to her face mask.

"What are you doing?" Chunye, always the nervous In-cousin, cried in alarm.

"I just want to know," Tash said. "I just want to feel it, like it should be." Three taps, and the face plate fell into her waiting hands. The air was cold, shakingly cold, and still too thin to breathe and anyway, to breathe was to die on lungfuls of carbon dioxide but she could feel the wind, the real wind, the true wind in her face. Tash exhaled gently into the atmosphere gathered at the bottom of the Big Dig. The world still sloped gently away from her, all the way up the sky. Tears would freeze in an instant so she kept them to herself. Then Tash clapped the plate back over her face and fastened it to the psuit hood with her clever fingers.

"So, what do we do now?" whiny Chunye asked. Tash knelt. She pushed her fingers into the soft regolith. What else was there? What else had there ever been. A message had come down Mt Incredible, from High Orbital, from a world on the other side of the sky, from people who had never seen this, whose horizons were always curved away from them. Who were they so say? What wind blew their words and made them so strong? Here were people, whole cities, an entire civilization, in a hole. This was Mars.

"We do what we know best," Tash said, scooping up pale golden Mars in her gloved hand. "We put it all back again."

THE MAN WHO BRIDGED THE MIST

KIJ JOHNSON

Kij Johnson is the author of three novels, many short stories, and several essays. She has won the Theodore Sturgeon Memorial Award and the International Association for the Fantastic in the Arts' Crawford Award. Her short story "The Evolution of Trickster Stories Among the Dogs of North Park After the Change" was nominated for the Nebula, World Fantasy, and Hugo awards. Her story "26 Monkeys, Also the Abyss" was nominated for the Nebula, Sturgeon, and Hugo awards, and won the World Fantasy Award, while short science fiction story "Spar" won the 2009 Nebula Award.

Her novels include World Fantasy Award nominee The Fox Woman *and* Fudoki. *Coming up later this year is a new short story collection,* At the Mouth of the River of Bees.

Kit came to Nearside with two trunks and an oiled-cloth folio full of plans for the bridge across the mist. His trunks lay tumbled like stones at his feet, where the mailcoach guard had dropped them. The folio he held close, away from the drying mud of yesterday's storm.

Nearside was small, especially to a man of the capital where buildings towered seven and eight stories tall, a city so large that even a vigorous walker could not cross it in half a day. Here hard-packed dirt roads threaded through irregular spaces scattered with structures and fences. Even the inn was plain, two stories of golden limestone and blue slate tiles, with (he could smell) some sort of animals living behind it. On

521

the sign overhead, a flat, pale blue fish very like a ray curvetted against a black background.

A brightly dressed woman stood by the inn's door. Her skin and eyes were pale, almost colorless. "Excuse me," Kit said. "Where can I find the ferry to take me across the mist?" He could feel himself being weighed, but amiably: a stranger, small and very dark, in gray—a man from the east.

The woman smiled. "Well, the ferries are both on this side, at the upper dock. But I expect what you really want is someone to oar the ferry, yes? Rasali Ferry came over from Farside last night. She's the one you'll want to talk to. She spends a lot of time at The Deer's Hart. But you wouldn't like The Hart, sir," she added. "It's not nearly as nice as The Fish here. Are you looking for a room?"

"I'll be staying in Farside tonight," Kit said apologetically. He didn't want to seem arrogant. The invisible web of connections he would need for his work started here, with this first impression, with all the first impressions of the next few days.

"That's what *you* think," the woman said. "I'm guessing it'll be a day or two or more before Rasali goes back. Valo Ferry might, but he doesn't cross so often."

"I could buy out the trip's fares, if that's why she's waiting."

"It's not that," the woman said. "She won't cross the mist 'til she's ready. Until she feels it's right, if you follow me. But you can ask, I suppose."

Kit didn't follow, but he nodded anyway. "Where's The Deer's Hart?"

She pointed. "Left, then right, then down by the little boat yard."

"Thank you," Kit said. "May I leave my trunks here until I work things out with her?"

"We always stow for travelers." The woman grinned. "And cater to them, too, when they find out there's no way across the mist today."

The Deer's Hart was smaller than The Fish, and livelier. At midday the oak-shaded tables in the beer garden beside the inn were clustered with light-skinned people in brilliant clothes, drinking and tossing comments over the low fence into the boat yard next door, where, half lost in steam, a youth and two women bent planks to form the hull of a small flat-bellied boat. When Kit spoke to a man carrying two mugs of something that looked like mud and smelled of yeast, the man gestured at the yard with his chin. "Ferrys are over there. Rasali's the one in red," he said as he walked away.

"The one in red" was tall, her skin as pale as that of the rest of the locals, with a black braid so long that she had looped it around her neck to keep it out of the way. Her shoulders flexed in the sunlight as she and the youth forced a curved plank to take the skeletal hull's shape. The other woman, slightly shorter, with the ash-blond hair so common here, forced an augur through the plank and into a rib, then hammered a peg into the hole she'd made. After three pegs, the boatwrights straightened. The plank held. *Strong*, Kit thought; *I wonder if I can get them for the bridge?*

"Rasali!" a voice bellowed, almost in Kit's ear. "Man here's looking for you." Kit turned in time to see the man with the mugs gesturing, again with his chin. He sighed and walked to the waist-high fence. The boatwrights stopped to drink from blueware bowls before the one in red and the youth came over.

"I'm Rasali Ferry of Farside," the woman said. Her voice was softer and higher than he had expected of a woman as strong as she, with the fluid vowels of the local accent. She nodded to the boy beside her: "Valo Ferry of Farside, my brother's eldest." Valo was more a young man than a boy, lighter-haired than Rasali and slightly taller. They had the same heavy eyebrows and direct amber eyes.

"Kit Meinem of Atyar," Kit said.

Valo asked, "What sort of name is Meinem? It doesn't mean anything."

"In the capital, we take our names differently than you."

"Oh, like Jenner Ellar." Valo nodded. "I guessed you were from the capital—your clothes and your skin."

Rasali said, "What can we do for you, Kit Meinem of Atyar?"

"I need to get to Farside today," Kit said.

Rasali shook her head. "I can't take you. I just got here, and it's too soon. Perhaps Valo?"

The youth tipped his head to one side, his expression suddenly abstract. He shook his head. "No, not today, I don't think."

"I can buy out the fares, if that helps. It's Jenner Ellar I am here to see."

Valo looked interested but said, "No," to Rasali, and she added, "What's so important that it can't wait a few days?"

Better now than later, Kit thought. "I am replacing Teniant Planner as the lead engineer and architect for construction of the bridge over the mist. We start work again as soon as I've reviewed everything. And had a chance to talk to Jenner." He watched their faces.

Rasali said, "It's been a year since Teniant died. I was starting to think Empire had forgotten all about us, and your deliveries would be here 'til the iron rusted away."

"Jenner Ellar's not taking over?" Valo asked, frowning.

"The new Department of Roads cartel is in my name," Kit said, "but I hope Jenner will remain as my second. You can see why I would like to meet him as soon as is possible, of course. He will—"

Valo burst out, "You're going to take over from Jenner, after he's worked so hard on this? And what about us? What about *our* work?" His cheeks were flushed an angry red. *How do they conceal anything with skin like that?* Kit thought.

"Valo," Rasali said, a warning tone in her voice. Flushing darker still, the youth turned and strode away. Rasali snorted but said only: "Boys. He likes Jenner, and he has problems with the bridge, anyway."

That was worth addressing. *Later.* "So what will it take to get you to carry me across the mist, Rasali Ferry of Farside? The project will pay anything reasonable."

"I cannot," she said. "Not today, not tomorrow. You'll have to wait."

"Why?" Kit asked: reasonably enough, he thought, but she eyed him for a long moment, as if deciding whether to be annoyed.

"Have you gone across mist before?" she said at last.

"Of course."

"Not the river," she said.

"Not the river," he agreed. "It's a quarter-mile across here, yes?"

"Oh, yes." She smiled suddenly: white even teeth and warmth like sunlight in her eyes. "Let's go down and perhaps I can explain things better there." She jumped the fence with a single powerful motion, landing beside him to a chorus of cheers and shouts from the inn garden's patrons. She laughed at them, then gestured to Kit to follow her. She was well-liked, clearly. Her opinion would matter.

The boat yard was heavily shaded by low-hanging oaks and chestnuts, and bounded on the east by an open-walled shelter filled with barrels and stacks of lumber. Rasali waved at the third boat maker, who was still putting her tools away. "Tilisk Boatwright of Nearside. My brother's wife," she said to Kit. "She makes skiffs with us but she won't ferry. She's not born to it as Valo and I are."

"Where's your brother?" Kit asked.

"Dead," Rasali said, and lengthened her stride.

They walked a few streets over and then climbed a long even ridge perhaps eighty feet high, too regular to be natural. *A levee,* Kit thought, and distracted himself from the steep path by estimating the volume of earth and the labor that had been required to build it. Decades, perhaps, but how long ago? How long was it? The levee was treeless. The only feature was a slender wood tower hung with flags on the ridge, probably for signaling across the mist to Farside, since it appeared too fragile for anything else. They had storms out here, Kit knew; there'd been one the night before. How often was the tower struck by lightning?

Rasali stopped. "There."

Kit had been watching his feet. He looked up and nearly cried out as light lanced his suddenly tearing eyes. He fell back a step and shielded his face. What had blinded him was an immense band of mist reflecting the morning sun.

Kit had never seen the mist river itself, though he bridged mist before this, two simple post-and-beam structures over narrow gorges closer to the capital. From his work in Atyar, he knew what was to be known. It was not water, or anything like. It did not flow but formed somehow in the deep gorge of the great riverbed before him. It found its way many hundreds of miles north, upstream through a hundred narrowing mist creeks and streams before failing at last in shreds of drying foam that left bare patches of earth where they collected.

The mist stretched to the south as well, a deepening, thickening band that poured out at last from the river's mouth two thousand miles south to form the mist ocean, which lay on the face of the saltwater ocean. Water had to follow the river's bed to run somewhere beneath or through the mist, but there was no way to prove this.

There was mist nowhere but this river and its streams and sea, but the mist split Empire in half.

After a moment, the pain in Kit's eyes grew less, and he opened them again. The river was a quarter-mile across where they stood, a great gash of light between the levees. It seemed nearly featureless, blazing under the sun like a river of cream or of bleached silk, but as his eyes accustomed themselves, he saw the surface was not smooth but heaped and hollowed, and that it shifted slowly, almost indiscernibly, as he watched.

Rasali stepped forward, and Kit started. "I'm sorry," he said with a laugh. "How long have I been staring? It's just—I had no idea."

"No one does," Rasali said. Her eyes when he met them were amused.

The east and west levees were nearly identical, each treeless and scrub-covered, with a signal tower. The levee on their side ran down to a narrow bare bank half a dozen yards wide. There was a wooden dock and a boat ramp, a rough switchback leading down to them. Two large boats had been pulled onto the bank. Another, smaller dock was visible a hundred yards downstream, attended by a clutter of boats, sheds, and indeterminate piles covered in tarps.

"Let's go down." Rasali led the way, her words coming back to him over her shoulder. "The little ferry is Valo's. *Pearlfinder. The Tranquil Crossing*'s mine." Her voice warmed when she said the name. "Eighteen feet long, eight wide. Mostly pine, but a purpleheart keel and pearwood headpiece. You can't see it from here, but the hull's sheathed in blue-dyed fishskin. I can carry three horses or a ton and a half of cartage or fifteen passengers. Or various combinations. I once carried twenty-four hunting dogs and two handlers. Never again."

Channeled by the levees, a steady light breeze eased down from the north. The air had a smell, not unpleasant but a little sour, wild. "How can you manage a boat like this alone? Are you that strong?"

"It's as big as I can handle," she said, "but Valo helps sometimes for really unwieldy loads. You don't paddle through mist. I mostly just coax the *Crossing* to where I want it to go. Anyway, the bigger the boat, the more likely that the Big Ones will notice it—though if you *do* run into a fish, the smaller the boat, the easier it is to swamp. Here we are."

They stood on the bank. The mist streams he had bridged had not prepared him for anything like this. Those were tidy little flows, more like fog collection in hollows than this. From this angle, the river no longer seemed a smooth flow of creamy whiteness, nor even gently heaped clouds. The mist forced itself into hillocks and hollows, tight slopes perhaps twenty feet high that folded into one another. It had a surface, but it was irregular, cracked in places, or translucent in others. It didn't seem as clearly defined as that between water and air.

"How can you move on this?" Kit said, fascinated. "Or even float?" The hillock immediately before them was flattening as he watched. Beyond it something like a vale stretched out for a few dozen yards before turning and becoming lost to his eyes.

"Well, I can't, not today," Rasali said. She sat on the gunwale of her boat, one leg swinging, watching him. "I can't push the *Crossing* up those slopes or find a safe path, unless I feel it. If I went today, I know—I *know*—" she tapped her belly—"that I would find myself stranded on a pinnacle or lost in a hole. *That's* why I can't take you today, Kit Meinem of Atyar."

When Kit was a child, he had not been good with other people. He was small and easy to tease or ignore, and then he was sick for much of his seventh year and had to leave his crèche before the usual time, to convalesce in his mother's house. None of the children of the crèche came to visit him, but he didn't mind that: he had books and puzzles, and whole quires of blank paper that his mother didn't mind him defacing.

The clock in the room in which he slept didn't work, so one day he used his penknife to take it apart. He arranged the wheels and cogs and springs in neat rows on the quilt in his room, by type and then by size; by materials; by weight; by shape. He liked holding the tiny pieces, thinking of how they might have been formed and how they worked together. The patterns they made were interesting but he knew the best pattern would be the working one, when they were all put back into their right places and the clock performed its task again. He had to think that the clock would be happier that way, too.

He tried to rebuild the clock before his mother came upstairs from her counting house at the end of the day, but when he had reassembled things, there remained a pile of unused parts and it still didn't work; so he shut the clock up and hoped she wouldn't notice that it wasn't ticking. Four days more of trying things during the day and concealing his failures at night; and on the fifth day, the clock started again. One piece hadn't fit anywhere, a small brass cog. Kit still carried that cog in his pen case.

Late that afternoon, Kit returned to the river's edge. It was hotter; the mud had dried to cracked dust and the air smelled like old rags left in water too long. He saw no one at the ferry dock, but at the fisher's dock upstream, people were gathering, a score or more of men and women, with children running about.

The clutter looked even more disorganized as he approached. The fishing boats were fat coracles of leather stretched on frames, tipped bottom up to the sun and looking like giant warts. The mist had dropped so that he could see a band of exposed rock below the bank, and he could see the dock's pilings clearly, which were not vertical but set at an angle: a cantilevered deck braced into the stone underlying the bank. The wooden pilings had been sheathed in metal.

He approached a silver-haired woman doing something with a treble hook as long as her hand. "What are you catching with that?" he said.

Her forehead was wrinkled when she looked up, but she smiled when she saw him. "Oh, you're a stranger. From Atyar, dressed like that. Am I right? We catch fish—" Still holding the hook, she extended her arms as far as they would stretch. "Bigger than that, some of them. Looks like more storms, so they're going to be biting tonight. I'm Meg Threehooks.

Of Nearside, obviously."

"Kit Meinem of Atyar. I take it you can't find a bottom?" He pointed to the pilings.

Meg Threehooks followed his glance. "It's there somewhere, but it's a long way down, and we can't sink pilings because the mist dissolves the wood. Oh, and fish eat it. Same thing with our ropes, the boats, us—anything but metal and rock, really." She knotted a line around the hook's eye. The cord was dark and didn't look heavy enough for anything Kit could imagine catching on hooks that size.

"What are these made of, then?" He squatted to look at the framing under one of the coracles.

"Careful, that one's mine," Meg said. "The hides—well, and all the ropes—are fishskin. Mist fish, not water fish. Tanning takes off some of the slime, so they don't last forever either, not if they're immersed." She made a face. "We have a saying: foul as fish-slime. That's pretty nasty, you'll see."

"I need to get to Farside," Kit said. "Could I hire you to carry me across?"

"In my boat?" She snorted. "No, fishers stay close to shore. Go see Rasali Ferry. Or Valo."

"I saw them," he said ruefully.

"Thought so. You must be the new architect—city folk are always so impatient. You're so eager to be dinner for a Big One? If Rasali doesn't want to go then don't go, stands to reason."

Kit was footsore and frustrated by the time he returned to The Fish. His trunks were already upstairs, in a small cheerful room overwhelmed by a table that nearly filled it, with a stiflingly hot cupboard bed. When Kit spoke to the woman he'd talked to earlier, Brana Keep, the owner of The Fish (its real name turned out to be The Big One's Delight)—laughed. "Rasali's as hard to shift as bedrock," she said. "And truly, you would not be comfortable at The Hart."

By the next morning, when Kit came downstairs to break his fast on flatbread and pepper-rubbed fish, everyone appeared to know everything about him, especially his task. He had wondered whether there would be resistance to the project, but if there had been any, it was gone now. There were a few complaints, mostly about slow payments, a universal issue for public works; but none at all about the labor or organization. Most in the taproom seemed not to mind the bridge, and the feeling everywhere he went in town was optimistic. He'd run into more resistance elsewhere, building the small bridges.

"Well, why should we be concerned?" Brana Keep said to Kit. "You're bringing in people to work, yes? So we'll be selling room and board and clothes and beer to them. And you'll be hiring some of us, and everyone will do well while you're building this bridge of yours. I plan to be wading ankle-deep through gold by the time this is done."

"And after," Kit said, "when the bridge is complete—think of it, the first real link between the east and west sides of Empire. The only place for three thousand miles where people and trade can cross the mist easily, safely, whenever they wish. You'll be the heart of Empire in ten years. Five." He laughed a little, embarrassed by the passion that shook his voice.

"Yes, well," Brana Keep said, in the easy way of a woman who makes her living by not antagonizing customers, "we'll make that harness when the colt is born."

For the next six days, Kit explored the town and surrounding countryside.

He met the masons, a brother and sister that Teniant had selected before her death to oversee the pillar and anchorage construction on Nearside. They were quiet but competent, and Kit was comfortable not replacing them.

Kit also spoke with the Nearside rope-makers, and performed tests on their fishskin ropes and cables, which turned out even stronger than he had hoped, with excellent resistance to rot and to catastrophic and slow failure. The makers told him that the rope stretched for its first two years in use, which made it ineligible to replace the immense chains that would bear the bridge's weight; but it could replace the thousands of vertical suspender chains that would support the roadbed with a great savings in weight.

He spent much of his time watching the mist. It changed character unpredictably: a smooth rippled flow; hours later, a badland of shredding foam; still later, a field of steep dunes that joined and shifted as he watched. He thought that the river generally dropped in its bed each day under the sun, and rose after dark.

The winds were more predictable. Hedged between the levees, they streamed southward each morning and northward each evening, growing stronger toward midday and dusk, and falling away entirely in the afternoons and at night. They did not seem to affect the mist much, though they did tear shreds off that landed on the banks as dried foam.

The winds meant that there would be more dynamic load on the bridge than Teniant Planner had predicted. Kit would never criticize her work publicly and he gladly acknowledged her brilliant interpersonal skills, which had brought the town into cheerful collaboration, but he was grateful that her bridge had not been built as designed.

He examined the mist more closely, as well, by lifting a piece from the river's surface on the end of an oar. The mist was stiffer than it looked, and in bright light he thought he could see tiny shapes, perhaps creatures or plants or something altogether different. There were microscopes in the city and people who studied these things; but he had never bothered to learn more, interested only in the structure that would bridge it. In any case, living things interested him less than structures.

Nights, Kit worked on the table in his room. Teniant's plans had to be revised. He opened the folios and cases she had left behind and read everything he found there. He wrote letters, wrote lists, wrote schedules, made duplicates of everything, sent to the capital for someone to do all the subsequent copying. His new plans for the bridge began to take shape. He started to glimpse the invisible architecture that was the management of the vast project.

He did not see Rasali Ferry, except to ask each morning whether they might travel that day. The answer was always no.

One afternoon, when the clouds were heaping into anvils filled with rain, he walked up to the building site half a mile north of Nearside. For two years, off and on, carts had tracked south on the Hoic Mine Road and the West River Road, leaving limestone blocks and iron bars in untidy heaps. Huge dismantled sheerlegs lay beside a caretaker's wattle-and-daub hut. There were thousands of large rectangular blocks.

Kit examined some of the blocks. Limestone was often too chossy for large-scale construction, but this rock was sound, with no apparent flaws or fractures. There were not enough, of course, but undoubtedly more had been quarried. He had written to order resumption of deliveries, and they would start arriving soon.

Delivered years too early, the iron trusses that would eventually support the roadbed were stacked neatly, painted black to protect them from moisture, covered in oiled tarps, and raised from the ground on planks. Sheep grazed the knee-high grass that grew everywhere. When one of the sheep eyed him incuriously, Kit found himself bowing. "Forgive the intrusion," he said, and laughed: too old to be talking to sheep.

The test pit was still open, a ladder on the ground nearby. Weeds clung when he moved the ladder, as if reluctant to release it. He descended.

The pasture had not been noisy, but he was startled when he dropped below ground level and the insects and whispering grasses were suddenly silenced. The soil around him was striated shades of dun and dull yellow. Halfway down, he sliced a wedge free with his knife: lots of clay; good foundation soil, as he had been informed. The pit's bottom, some twenty feet down, looked like the walls, but crouching to dig at the dirt between his feet with his knife, he hit rock almost immediately. It seemed to be shale. He wondered how far down the water table was: Did the Nearsiders find it difficult to dig wells? Did the mist ever backwash into one? There were people at University in Atyar who were trying to understand mist, but there was still so much that could not be examined or quantified.

He collected a rock to examine in better light, and climbed from the pit in time to see a teamster leading four mules, her wagon groaning under the weight of the first new blocks. A handful of Nearsider men and women followed, rolling their shoulders and popping their joints. They called out greetings and he walked across to them.

When he got back to The Fish hours later, exhausted from helping unload the cart, and soaked from the storm that had started while he did so, there was a message from Rasali. *Dusk* was all it said.

Kit was stiff and irritable when he left for *The Tranquil Crossing*. He had hired a carrier from The Fish to haul one of his trunks down to the dock, but the others remained in his room, which he would probably keep until the bridge was done. He carried his folio of plans and paperwork himself. He was leaving duplicates of everything on Nearside, but after so much work it was hard to trust any of it to the hands of others.

The storm was over and the clouds were moving past, leaving the sky every shade between lavender and a rich purple-blue. The large moon was a crescent in the west; the smaller a half circle immediately overhead. In the fading light, the mist was a dark, smoky streak. The air smelled fresh. Kit's mood lightened, and he half-trotted down the final slope.

His fellow passengers were there before him: a prosperous-looking man with a litter of piglets in a woven wicker cage (Tengon whites, the man confided, the best bloodline in all Empire); a woman in the dark clothes fashionable in the capital, with brass-bound document cases and a folio very like Kit's; two traders with many cartons of powdered pigment; a mail courier with locked leather satchels and two guards. Nervous about their first crossing, Uni and Tom Mason greeted Kit when he arrived.

In the gathering darkness, the mist looked like bristling, tight-folded hills and coulees. Swifts darted just above it, using the wind flowing up the valley, searching for insects, he supposed. Once a sudden black shape, too quick to see clearly, appeared from below; then it, and one of the birds, was gone.

The voices of the fishers at their dock carried to him. They launched their boats, and he watched one and then another, and then a gaggle of the little coracles push themselves up a slope of the mist. There were no lamps.

"Ready, everyone?" Kit had not heard Rasali approach. She swung down into the ferry. "Hand me your gear."

Stowing and embarkation were quick though the piglets complained. Kit strained his eyes, but the coracles could no longer be seen. When he noticed Rasali waiting for him, he apologized. "I guess the fish are biting."

Rasali glanced at the river as she stowed his trunk. "Small ones. A couple of feet long only. The fishers like them bigger, five or six feet, though they don't want them too big, either. But they're not fish, not what you think fish are. Hand me that."

He hesitated a moment, then gave her the folio before stepping into the ferry. The boat sidled at his weight but sluggishly: a carthorse instead of a riding mare. His stomach lurched. "Oh!" he said.

"What?" one of the traders asked nervously. Rasali untied the rope holding them to the dock.

Kit swallowed. "I had forgotten. The motion of the boat. It's not like water at all."

He did not mention his fear, but there was no need. The others murmured assent. The courier, her dark face sharp-edged as a hawk, growled, "Every time I do this, it surprises me. I dislike it."

Rasali unshipped a scull and slid the great triangular blade into the mist, which parted reluctantly. "I've been on mist more than water but I remember the way water felt. Quick and jittery. This is better."

"Only to you, Rasali Ferry," Uni Mason said.

"Water's safer," the man with the piglets said.

Rasali leaned into the oar and the boat slid away from the dock. "Anything is safe until it kills you."

The mist absorbed the quiet sounds of shore almost immediately. One of Kit's first projects had been a stone single-arch bridge over water, far to the north in Eskje province. He had visited before construction started. He was there for five days more than he had expected, caught by a snowstorm that left nearly two feet on the ground. This reminded him of those snowy moonless nights, the air as thick and silencing as a pillow on the ears.

Rasali did not scull so much as steer. It was hard to see far in any direction except up, but perhaps it was true that the mist spoke to her, for she seemed to know where best to position the boat for the mist to carry it forward. She followed a small valley until it started to flatten and then mound up. *The Tranquil Crossing* tipped slightly as it slid a few feet to port. The mail carrier made a noise, and immediately stifled it.

Mist was a misnomer. It was denser than it seemed. Sometimes the boat seemed not to move through it so much as over its surface. Tonight it seemed like sea-wrack, the dirty foam that strong winds could whip from ocean waves. Kit reached a hand over the boat's side. The mist piled against his hand, almost dry to the touch, sliding up his forearm with a sensation he could not immediately identify. When he realized it was prickling, he snatched his arm back in and rubbed it on a fold of his coat. The skin burned. Caustic, of course.

The man with the pigs whispered, "Will they come if we talk or make noise?"

"Not to talking, or pigs' squealing," Rasali said. "They seem to like low noises. They'll rise to thunder sometimes."

One of the traders said, "What are they if they're not really fish? What do they look like?" Her voice shook. The mist was weighing on them all, all but Rasali.

"If you want to know you'll have to see one for yourself," Rasali said. "Or try to get a fisher to tell you. They gut and fillet them over the sides of their boats. No one else sees much but meat wrapped in paper, or rolls of black skin for the ropemakers and tanners."

"*You've* seen them," Kit said.

"They're broad and flat. But ugly."

"And Big Ones?" Kit asked.

Her voice was harsh. "*Them*, we don't talk about here."

No one spoke for a time. Mist—foam—heaped up at the boat's prow and parted, eased to the sides with an almost inaudible hissing. Once the mist off the port side heaved, and something dark broke the surface for a moment, followed by other dark somethings, but they were not close enough to see well. One of the merchants cried without a sound or movement, the tears on his face the only evidence.

The Farside levee showed at last, a black mass that didn't get any closer for what felt like hours. Fighting his fear, Kit leaned over the side, keeping his face away from the surface. "It can't really be bottomless," he said, half to himself. "What's under it?"

"You wouldn't hit the bottom, anyway," Rasali said.

The Tranquil Crossing eased up a long swell of mist and into a hollow. Rasali pointed the ferry along a crease and eased it forward. And then they were suddenly a stone's throw from the Farside dock and the light of its torches.

People on the dock moved as they approached. Just loudly enough to carry, a soft baritone voice called, "Rasali?"

She called back, "Ten this time, Pen."

"Anyone need carriers?" A different voice. Several passengers responded.

Rasali shipped the scull while the ferry was still some feet away from the dock, and allowed it to ease forward under its own momentum. She stepped to the prow and picked up a coiled rope there, tossing one end across the narrowing distance. Someone on the dock caught it and pulled the boat in, and in a very few moments, the ferry was snug against the dock.

Disembarking and payment was quicker than embarkation had been. Kit was the last off, and after a brief discussion he hired a carrier to haul his trunk to an inn in town. He turned to say farewell to Rasali. She and the man—Pen, Kit remembered—were untying the boat. "You're not going back already," he said.

"Oh, no." Her voice sounded loose, content, relaxed. Kit hadn't known how tense she was. "We're just going to tow the boat down to where the Twins will pull it out." She waved with one hand to the boat launch. A pair of white oxen gleamed in the night, at their heads a woman hardly darker.

"Wait," Kit said to Uni Mason and handed her his folio. "Please tell the innkeeper I'll be there soon." He turned back to Rasali. "May I help?"

In the darkness, he felt more than saw her smile. "Always."

The Red Lurcher, commonly called The Bitch, was a small but noisy inn five minutes' walk from the mist, ten (he was told) from the building site. His room was larger than at The Fish, with an uncomfortable bed and a window seat crammed with quires of ancient hand-written music. Jenner stayed here, Kit knew, but when he asked the owner (Widson Innkeep, a heavyset man with red hair turning silver), he had not seen him. "You'll be the new one, the architect," Widson said.

"Yes," Kit said. "Please ask him to see me when he gets in."

Widson wrinkled his forehead. "I don't know, he's been out late most days recently, since—" He cut himself off, looking guilty.

"—since the signals informed him that I was here," Kit said. "I understand the impulse."

The innkeeper seemed to consider something for a moment, then said slowly, "We like Jenner here."

"Then we'll try to keep him," Kit said.

When the child Kit had recovered from the illness, he did not return to the crèche—which he would have been leaving in a year in any case—but went straight to his father. Davell Meinem was a slow-talking humorous man who nevertheless had a sharp tongue on the sites of his many projects. He brought Kit with him to his work places: best for the boy to get some experience in the trade.

Kit loved everything about his father's projects: the precisely drawn plans, the orderly progression of construction, the lines and curves of brick and iron and stone rising under the endlessly random sky.

For the first year or two, Kit imitated his father and the workers, building structures of tiny beams and bricks made by the woman set to mind him, a tiler who had lost a hand some years back. Davell collected the boy at the end of the day. "I'm here to inspect the construction," he said, and Kit demonstrated his bridge or tower, or the materials he had laid out in neat lines and stacks. Davell would discuss Kit's work with great seriousness until it grew too dark to see and they went back to the inn or rented rooms that passed for home near the sites.

Davell spent nights buried in the endless paperwork of his projects, and Kit found this interesting as well. The pattern that went into building something big was not just the architectural plans or the construction itself; it was also labor schedules and documentation and materials deliveries. He started to draw his own plans, but he also made up endless correspondences with imaginary providers.

After a while, Kit noticed that a large part of the pattern that made a bridge or a tower was built entirely out of people.

The knock on Kit's door came very late that night, a preemptory rap. Kit put down the quill he was mending and rolled his shoulders to loosen them. "Yes," he said aloud as he stood.

The man who stormed through the door was as dark as Kit, though perhaps a few years younger. He wore mud-splashed riding clothes.

"I am Kit Meinem of Atyar."

"Jenner Ellar of Atyar. Show it to me." Silently Kit handed the cartel to Jenner, who glared at it before tossing it onto the table. "It took long enough for them to pick a replacement."

Might as well deal with this right now, Kit thought. "You hoped it would be you."

Jenner eyed Kit for a moment. "Yes. I did."

"You think you're the most qualified to complete the project because you've been here for the last—what is it? year?"

"I know the sites," Jenner said. "I worked with Teniant to make those plans. And then Empire sends—" He turned to face the empty hearth.

"—Empire sends someone new," Kit said to Jenner's back. "Someone with connections in the capital, influential friends but no experience with this site, this bridge. It should have been you, yes?"

Jenner was still.

"But it isn't," Kit said, and let the words hang for a moment. "I've built nine bridges in the past twenty years. Four suspension bridges, three major spans. Two bridges over mist. You've done three and the biggest span you've directed was three hundred and fifty feet, six stone arches over shallow water and shifting gravel up on Mati River."

"I know," Jenner snapped.

"It's a good bridge." Kit poured two glasses of whiskey from a stoneware pitcher by the window. "I coached down to see it before I came here. It's well made and you were on budget and nearly on schedule in spite of the drought. Better, the locals still like you. Asked how you're doing these days. Here."

Jenner took the glass Kit offered. *Good.* Kit continued, "Meinems have built bridges—and roads and aqueducts and stadia, a hundred sorts of public structures—for Empire for a thousand years." Jenner turned to speak, but Kit held up his hand. "This doesn't mean we're any better at it than Ellars. But Empire knows us—and we know Empire, how to do what we need to. If they'd given you this bridge, you'd be replaced within a year. But I can get this bridge built and I will." Kit sat and leaned forward, elbows on knees. "With you. You're talented. You know the site. You know the people. Help me make this bridge."

"It's real to you," Jenner said finally. Kit knew what he meant: *You care about this work. It's not just another tick on a list.*

"Yes," Kit said. "You'll be my second for this one. I'll show you how to deal with Atyar and I'll help you with contacts. And your next project will belong entirely to you. This is the first bridge but it isn't going to be the only one across the mist."

Together they drank. The whiskey bit at Kit's throat and made his eyes water. "Oh," he said, "that's *awful*."

Jenner laughed suddenly and met his eyes for the first time: a little wary still but willing to be convinced. "Farside whiskey is terrible. You drink much of this, you'll be running for Atyar in a month."

"Maybe we'll have something better ferried across," Kit said.

Preparations were not so far along on this side. The heaps of blocks at the construction site were not so massive, and it was harder to find local workers. In discussions between Kit, Jenner and the Near- and Farside masons who would oversee construction of the pillars, final plans materialized. This would be unique, the largest structure of its kind ever attempted: a single-span chain suspension bridge a quarter of a mile long. The basic plan remained unchanged: the bridge would be supported by eyebar-and-bolt chains, four on each side, allowed to play independently to compensate for the slight shifts that would be caused by traffic on the roadbed. The huge eyebars and their bolts were being fashioned five hundred miles away and far to the north, where iron was common and the smelting and ironworking were the best in Empire. Kit had just written to the foundries to start the work again.

The pillar and anchorage on Nearside would be built of gold limestone anchored with pilings into the bedrock; on Farside they would be pink-gray granite with a funnel-shaped foundation. The towers' heights would be nearly three hundred feet. There were taller towers back in Atyar, but none had to stand against the compression of the bridge.

The initial tests with the fishskin rope had showed it to be nearly as strong as iron, without the weight. When Kit asked the Farside tanners and ropemakers about its durability, he was taken a day's travel east to Meknai, to a waterwheel that used knotted belts of the material for its drive. The belts, he was told, were seventy-five years old and still sound. Fishskin wore like maplewood so long as it wasn't left in mist, but it required regular maintenance.

He watched Meknai's little river for a time. There had been rain recently in the foothills, and the water was quick and abrupt as light. *Water bridges are easy*, he thought a little wistfully, and then: *Anyone can bridge water*.

Kit revised the plans again, to use the lighter material where they could. Jenner crossed the mist to Nearside, to work with Daell and Stivvan Cabler on the expansion of their workshops and ropewalk.

Without Jenner (who was practically a local, as Kit was told again and again), Kit felt the difference in attitudes on the river's two banks more clearly. Most Farsiders shared the Nearsiders' attitudes: money is money and always welcome, and there was a sense of the excitement that comes of any great project; but there was more resistance here. Empire was effectively split by the river, and the lands to the east—starting with Nearside—had never seen their destinies as closely linked to Atyar in the west. They were overseen by the eastern capital, Triple; their taxes went to building necessities on their own side of the mist. Empire's grasp on the eastern lands was loose, and had never needed to be tighter.

The bridge would change things. Travel between Atyar and Triple would grow more common, and perhaps Empire would no longer hold the eastern lands so gently. Triple's lack of enthusiasm for the project showed itself in delayed deliveries of stone and iron. Kit traveled five days along the Triple road to the district seat to present his credentials to the governor, and wrote sharp letters to the Department of Roads in Triple. Things became a little easier.

It was midwinter before the design was finished. Kit avoided crossing the mist. Rasali Ferry crossed seventeen times. He managed to see her nearly every time, at least for as long as it took to drink a beer.

The second time Kit crossed, it was midmorning of an early spring day. The mist mirrored the overcast sky above: pale and flat, like a layer of fog in a dell. Rasali was loading the ferry at the upper dock when Kit arrived and to his surprise she smiled at him, her face suddenly beautiful. Kit nodded to the stranger watching Valo toss immense cloth-wrapped bales down to Rasali, then greeted the Ferrys. Valo paused for a moment but did not return Kit's greeting, only bent again to his work. Valo had been avoiding him since nearly the beginning of his time there. *Later.* With a mental shrug, Kit turned from Valo to Rasali. She was catching and stacking the enormous bales easily.

"What's in those? You throw them as if they were—"

"—paper," she finished. "The very best Ibraric mulberry paper. Light as lambswool. You probably have a bunch of this stuff in that folio of yours."

Kit thought of the vellum he used for his plans, and the paper he used for everything else: made of cotton from the south, its surface buffed until it felt hard and smooth as enamelwork. He said, "All the time."

Rasali piled on bales and more bales until the ferry was stacked three and four high. He added, "Is there going to be room for me in there?"

"Pilar Runner and Valo aren't coming with us," she said. "You'll have to sit on top of the bales, but there's room as long as you sit still and don't wobble."

As Rasali pushed away from the dock Kit asked, "Why isn't the trader coming with her paper?"

"Why would she? Pilar has a broker on the other side." Her hands busy, she tipped her head to one side, in a gesture that somehow conveyed a shrug. "Mist is dangerous."

Somewhere along the river a ferry was lost every few months: horses, people, cartage, all lost. Fishers stayed closer to shore and died less often. It was harder to calculate the impact to trade and communications of this barrier splitting Empire in half.

This journey—in daylight, alone with Rasali—was very different than Kit's earlier crossing: less frightening but somehow wilder, stranger. The cold wind down the river was cutting and brought bits of dried foam to rest on his skin, but they blew off quickly, without pain and leaving no mark. The wind fell to a breeze and then to nothing as they navigated into the mist, as if they were buried in feathers or snow.

They moved through what looked like a layered maze of thick cirrus clouds. He watched the mist along the *Crossing*'s side until they passed over a small hole like a pockmark, straight down and no more than a foot across. For an instant he glimpsed open space below them; they were floating on a layer of mist above an air pocket deep enough to swallow the boat. He rolled onto his back to stare up at the sky until he stopped shaking; when he looked again, they were out of the maze, it seemed. The boat floated along a gently curving channel. He relaxed a little and moved to watch Rasali.

"How fares your bridge?" Rasali said at last, her voice muted in the muffled air. This had to be a courtesy—everyone in town seemed to know everything about the bridge's progress—but Kit was used to answering questions to which people already knew the answers. He had found patience to be a highly effective tool.

"Farside foundations are doing well. We have maybe six more months before the anchorage is done, but pilings for the pillar's foundation are in place and we can start building. Six weeks early," Kit said, a little smugly, though this was a victory no one else would appreciate and in one case the weather was as much to be credited as any action on his part. "On Nearside, we've run into basalt that's too hard to drill easily so we sent for a specialist. The signal flags say she's arrived, and that's why I'm crossing."

She said nothing, seemingly intent on moving the great scull. He watched her for a time, content to see her shoulders flex, hear her breath forcing itself out in smooth waves. Over the faint yeast scent of the mist, he smelled her sweat, or thought he did. She frowned slightly but he could not tell whether it was due to her labor, or something in the mist, or something else. Who was she, really? "May I ask a question, Rasali Ferry of Farside?"

Rasali nodded, eyes on the mist in front of the boat.

Actually, he had several things he wished to know: about her, about the river, about the people here. He picked one almost at random. "What is bothering Valo?

"He's transparent, isn't he? He thinks you take something away from him," Rasali said. "He is too young to know what you take is unimportant."

Kit thought about it. "His work?"

"His work is unimportant?" She laughed, a sudden puff of an exhale as she pulled. "We have a lot of money, Ferrys. We own land and rent it out—The Deer's Hart belongs to my family; do you know that? He's young. He wants what we all want at his age, a chance to test himself against the world and see if he measures up. And because he's a Ferry he wants be tested against adventures. Danger. The mist. Valo thinks you take that away from him."

"But he's not immortal," Kit said. "Whatever he thinks. The river can kill him. It will, sooner or later. It—"

—*will kill you.* Kit caught himself, rolled onto his back again to look up at the sky.

In The Bitch's taproom one night, a local man had told him about Rasali's family: a history of deaths, of boats lost in a silent hissing of mist, or the rending of wood, or screams that might be human and might be a horse. "So everyone wears ash-color for a month or two, and then the next Ferry takes up the business. Rasali's still new, two years maybe. When she goes, it'll be Valo, then Rasali's youngest sister, then Valo's sister. Unless Rasali or Valo have kids by then.

"They're always beautiful," the man had added after some more porter, "the Ferrys. I suppose that's to make up for having such short lives."

Kit looked down from the paper bales at Rasali. "But you're different. You don't feel you're losing anything."

"You don't know what I feel, Kit Meinem of Atyar." Cool light moved along the muscles of her arms. Her voice came again, softer. "I am not young; I don't need to prove myself. But I will lose this. The mist, the silence."

Then tell me, he did not say. *Show me.*

She was silent for the rest of the trip. Kit thought perhaps she was angry, but when he invited her, she accompanied him to the building site.

The quiet pasture was gone. All that remained of the tall grass was struggling tufts and dirty straw. The air smelled of sweat and meat and the bitter scent of hot metal. There were more blocks here now, a lot more. The pits for the anchorage and the pillar were excavated to bedrock, overshadowed by mountains of dirt. One sheep remained, skinned and spitted, and greasy smoke rose as a boy turned it over a fire beside the temporary forge. Kit had considered the pasture a nuisance, but looking at the skewered sheep he felt a twinge of guilt.

The rest of the flock had been replaced by sturdy-looking women and men, who were using rollers to shift stones down a dugout ramp into the hole for the anchorage foundation. Dust dulled their skin and muted the bright colors of their short kilts and breastbands. In spite of the cold, sweat had cleared tracks along their muscles.

One of the workers waved to Rasali and she waved back. Kit recalled his name: Mik Rounder, very strong but he needed direction. Had they been lovers? Relationships out here were tangled in ways Kit didn't understand; in the capital such things were more formal and often involved contracts.

Jenner and a small woman knelt conferring on the exposed stone floor of the larger pit. When Kit slid down the ladder to join them, the small woman bowed slightly. Her eyes and short hair and skin all seemed to be turning the same iron-gray. "I am Liu Breaker of Hoic. Your specialist."

"Kit Meinem of Atyar. How shall we address this?"

"Your Jenner says you need some of this basalt cleared away, yes?"

Kit nodded.

Liu knelt to run her hand along the pit's floor. "See where the color and texture change along this line? Your Jenner was right: this upthrust of basalt is a problem. Here where the shale is, you can carve out most of the foundation the usual way with drills, picks. But the basalt is too hard to drill." She straightened and brushed dust from her knees. "Have you ever seen explosives used?"

Kit shook his head. "We haven't needed them for any of my projects.

I've never been to the mines, either."

"Not much good anywhere else," Liu said, "but very useful for breaking up large amounts of rock. A lot of the blocks you have here were loosed using explosives." She grinned. "You'll like the noise."

"We can't afford to break the bedrock's structural integrity."

"I brought enough powder for a number of small charges. Comparatively small."

"How—"

Liu held up a weathered hand. "I don't need to understand bridges to walk across one. Yes?"

Kit laughed outright. "Yes."

Liu Breaker was right; Kit liked the noise very much. Liu would not allow anyone close to the pit but even from what she considered a safe distance, behind huge piles of dirt, the explosion was an immense shattering thing, a crack of thunder that shook the earth. There was a second of echoing silence. After a collective gasp and some scattered screams, the workers cheered and stamped their feet. A small cloud of mingled smoke and rock-dust eased over the pit's edge, sharp with the smell of saltpeter. The birds were not happy; with the explosion, they burst from their trees and wheeled nervously.

Grinning, Liu climbed from her bunker near the pit, her face dust-caked everywhere but around her eyes, which had been protected by the wooden slit-goggles now hanging around her neck. "So far so good," she shouted over the ringing in Kit's ears. Seeing his face she laughed. "These are nothing—gnat sneezes. You should hear when we quarry granite up at Hoic."

Kit was going to speak more with her when he noticed Rasali striding away. He had forgotten she was there. He followed her, half shouting to hear himself. "Some noise, yes?"

Rasali whirled. "What are you *thinking*?" She was shaking and her lips were white. Her voice was very loud.

Taken aback, Kit answered, "We are blowing the foundations." Rage? Fear? He wished he could think a little more clearly but the sound seemed to have stunned his wits.

"And making the earth shake! The Big Ones come to thunder, Kit!"

"It wasn't thunder," he said.

"Tell me it wasn't worse!" Tears glittered in her eyes. Her voice was dulled by the echo in his ears. "They will come, I *know* it."

He reached a hand out to her. "It's a tall levee, Rasali. Even if they do, they're not going to come over that." His heart in his chest thrummed. His head was hurting. It was so hard to hear her.

"*No one* knows what they'll do! They used to destroy whole towns, drifting inland on foggy nights. Why do you think they built the levees a thousand years ago? The Big Ones—"

She stopped shouting, listening. She mouthed something but Kit could not hear her over the beating in his ears, his heart, his head. He realized suddenly that these were not the aftereffects of the explosion; the air itself was beating. He was aware at the edges of his vision of the other workers, every face turned toward the mist. There was nothing to see but the overcast sky. No one moved.

But the sky was moving.

Behind the levee the river mist was rising, dirty gray-gold against the steel-gray of the clouds in a great boiling upheaval at least a hundred feet high, to be seen over the levee. The mist was seething, breaking open in great swirls and rifts, everything moving, changing. Kit had seen a great fire once when a warehouse of linen had burned, and the smoke had poured upward and looked a little like this before it was torn apart by the wind.

Gaps opened in the mountain of mist and closed; and others opened, darker the deeper they were. And through those gaps, in the brown-black shadows at the heart of the mist, was movement.

The gaps closed. After an eternity the mist slowly smoothed and then settled back, behind the levee, and could no longer be seen. He wasn't really sure when the thrumming of the air blended back into the ringing of his ears.

"Gone," Rasali said with a sound like a sob.

A worker made one of the vivid jokes that come after fear; the others laughed, too loud. A woman ran up the levee and shouted down, "Farside levees are fine; ours are fine." More laughter: people jogged off to Nearside to check on their families.

The back of Kit's hand was burning. A flake of foam had settled and left an irregular mark. "I only saw mist," Kit said. "Was there a Big One?"

Rasali shook herself, stern now but no longer angry or afraid. Kit had learned this about the Ferrys, that their emotions coursed through them and then dissolved. "It was in there. I've seen the mist boil like that before but never so big. Nothing else could heave it up like that."

"On purpose?"

"Oh, who knows? They're a mystery, the Big Ones." She met his eyes. "I hope your bridge is very high, Kit Meinem of Atyar."

Kit looked to where the mist had been, but there was only sky. "The deck will be two hundred feet above the mist. High enough. I hope."

Liu Breaker walked up to them, rubbing her hands on her leather leggings. "So, *that's* not something that happens at Hoic. *Very* exciting. What do you call that? How do we prevent it next time?"

Rasali looked at the smaller woman for a moment. "I don't think you can. Big Ones come when they come."

Liu said, "They do not always come?"

Rasali shook her head.

"Well, cold comfort is better than no comfort, as my Da says."

Kit rubbed his temples; the headache remained. "We'll continue."

"Then you'll have to be careful," Rasali said. "Or you will kill us all."

"The bridge will save many lives," Kit said. *Yours, eventually.*

Rasali turned on her heel.

Kit did not follow her, not that day. Whether it was because subsequent explosions were smaller ("As small as they can be and still break rock," Liu said), or because they were doing other things, the Big Ones did not return, though fish were plentiful for the three months it took to plan and plant the charges, and break the bedrock.

There was also a Meinem tradition of metal-working, and Meinem reeves, and many Meinems went into fields altogether different; but Kit had known from nearly the beginning that he would be one of the building Meinems. He loved the invisible architecture of construction, looking for a compromise between the vision in his head and the sites, the materials, and the people that would make them real. The challenge was to compromise as little as possible.

Architecture was studied at University. His tutor was a materials specialist, a woman who had directed construction on an incredible twenty-three bridges. Skossa Timt was so old that her skin and hair had faded together to the white of Gani marble, and she walked with a cane she had designed herself for efficiency. She taught him much. Materials had rules, patterns of behavior: they bent or crumbled or cracked or broke under quantifiable stresses. They strengthened or destroyed one another. Even the best materials in stablest combinations did not last forever—she tapped her own forehead with one gnarled finger and laughed—but if he did his work right, they could last a thousand years or more. "But not forever," Skossa said. "Do your best, but don't forget this."

The anchorages and pillars grew. Workers came from towns up and down each bank; and locals, idle or inclined to make money from outside, were hired on the spot. Generally, the new people were welcome. They paid for rooms and food and goods of all sorts. The taverns settled into making double and then triple batches of everything, threw out new wings and stables. Nearside accepted the new people easily, the only fights late at night when people had been drinking and flirting more than they should. Farside had fist fights more frequently though they decreased steadily as skeptics gave in to the money that flowed into Farside, or to the bridge itself, its pillars too solid to be denied.

Farmers and husbanders sold their fields, and new buildings sprawled out from the towns' hearts. Some were made of wattle and daub, slapped together over stamped-earth floors that still smelled of sheep dung; others, small but permanent, went up more slowly, as the bridge builders laid fieldstones and timber in their evenings and on rest days.

The new people and locals mixed together until it was hard to tell the one from the other, though the older townfolk kept scrupulous track of who truly belonged. For those who sought lovers and friends, the new people were an opportunity to meet someone other than the men and women they had known since childhood. Many met casual lovers, and several term-partnered with new people. There was even a Nearside wedding, between Kes Tiler and a black-eyed builder from far to the south called Jolite Deveren, whatever that meant.

Kit did not have lovers. Working every night until he fell asleep over his paperwork, he didn't miss it much, except late on certain nights when thunderstorms left him restless and unnaturally alert, as though lightning ran under his skin. Some nights he thought of Rasali, wondered whether she was sleeping with someone that night or alone, and wondered if the storm had awakened her, left her restless as well.

Kit saw a fair amount of Rasali when they were both on the same side of the mist. She was clever and calm and the only person who did not want to talk about the bridge all the time.

Kit did not forget what Rasali said about Valo. Kit had been a young man himself not so many years before, and he remembered what young men and women felt, the hunger to prove themselves against the world. Kit didn't need Valo to accept the bridge—he was scarcely into adulthood and his only influence over the townspeople was based on his work, but Kit liked the youth, who had Rasali's eyes and her effortless way of moving.

Valo started asking questions, first of the other workers and then of Kit. His boat-building experience meant the questions were good ones. Kit passed on the first things he had learned as a child on his father's sites, and showed him the manipulation of the immense blocks and the tricky balance of material and plan; the strength of will that allows a man to direct a thousand people toward a single vision. Valo was too honest not to recognize Kit's mastery and too competitive not to try and meet Kit on his own ground. He came more often to visit the construction sites.

After a season, Kit took him aside. "You could be a builder if you wished."

Valo flushed. "Build things? You mean bridges?"

"Or houses or granges or retaining walls. Or bridges. You could make peoples' lives better."

"Change peoples' lives?" He frowned suddenly. "No."

"Our lives change all the time, whether we want them to or not," Kit said. "Valo Ferry of Farside, you are intelligent. You are good with people. You learn quickly. If you were interested, I could start teaching you myself or send you to Atyar to study there."

"Valo Builder…" he said, trying it out, then: "No." But after that, whenever he had time free from ferrying or building boats, he was always to be found on the site. Kit knew that the answer would be different the next time he asked. There was for everything a possibility, an invisible pattern that could be made manifest given work and the right materials. Kit wrote to an old friend or two, finding contacts that would help Valo when the time came.

The pillars and anchorages grew. Winter came, and summer, and a second winter. There were falls, a broken arm, two sets of cracked ribs. Someone on Farside had her toes crushed when one of the stones slipped from its rollers and she lost the foot. The bridge was on schedule even after the delay caused by the slow rock-breaking. There were no problems with payroll or the Department of Roads or Empire, and only minor manageable issues with the occasionally disruptive representatives from Triple or the local governors.

Kit knew he was lucky.

The first death came during one of Valo's visits.

It was early in the second winter of the bridge, and Kit had been in

Farside for three months. He had learned that winter meant gray skies and rain and sometimes snow. Soon they would have to stop the heavy work for the season. Still, it had been a good day and the workers had lifted and placed almost a hundred stones.

Valo had returned after three weeks at Nearside building a boat for Jenna Bluefish. Kit found him staring up at the slim tower through a rain so faint it felt like fog. The black opening of the roadway arch looked out of place halfway up the pillar.

Valo said, "You're a lot farther along since I was here last. How tall now?"

Kit got this question a lot. "A hundred and five feet, more or less. A third finished."

Valo smiled, shook his head. "Hard to believe it'll stay up."

"There's a tower in Atyar, black basalt and iron, five hundred feet. Five times this tall."

"It just looks so delicate," Valo said. "I know what you said, that most of the stress on the pillar is compression, but it still looks as though it'll snap in half."

"After a while you'll have more experience with suspension bridges and it will seem less….unsettling. Would you like to see the progress?"

Valo's eyes brightened. "May I? I don't want to get in the way."

"I haven't been up yet today, and they'll be finishing up soon. Scaffold or stairwell?"

Valo looked at the scaffolding against one face of the pillar, the ladders tied into place within it, and shivered. "I can't believe people go up that. Stairs, I think."

Kit followed Valo. The steep internal stair was three feet wide and endlessly turning, five steps up and then a platform, turn to the left and then five more steps and turn. Eventually the stairs would at need be lit by lanterns set into alcoves at every third turning, but today Kit and Valo felt their way up, fingers trailing along the cold damp stone, a small lantern in Valo's hand. The stairwell smelled of water and earth and the thin smell of the burning lamp oil. Some of the workers hated the stairs and preferred the ladders outside, but Kit liked it. For these few moments, he was part of his bridge, a strong bone buried deep in flesh he had created.

They came out at the top and paused a moment to look around the unfinished courses, and the black silhouette of the winch against the dulling sky. The last few workers were breaking down a sheerleg, which had been used to move blocks around the pillar. A lantern hung from a pole jammed into one of the holes the laborers would fill with rods and molten iron, later in construction. Kit nodded to them as Valo went to an edge to look down.

"It is wonderful," Valo said, smiling. "Being high like this—you can look right down into people's kitchen yards. Look, Teli Carpenter has a pig smoking."

"You don't need to see it to know that," Kit said dryly. "I've been smelling it for two days."

Valo snorted. "Can you see as far as White Peak yet?"

"On a clear day, yes," Kit said. "I was up here two—"

A heavy sliding sound and a scream. Kit whirled to see one of the workers on her back, one of the sheerleg's timbers across her chest. Loreh Tanner, a local. Kit ran the few steps to Loreh and dropped beside her. One man, the man who had been working with her, said, "It slipped—oh Loreh, please hang on," but Kit could see already that it was futile. She was pinned to the pillar, chest flattened, one shoulder visibly dislocated, unconscious, her breathing labored. Black foam bloomed from her lips in the lantern's bad light.

Kit took her cold hand. "It's all right, Loreh. It's all right." It was a lie and in any case she could not hear him, but the others would. "Get Hall," one of the workers said and Kit nodded: Hall was a surgeon. And then, "And get Obal, someone. Where's her husband?" Footsteps ran down the stairs and were lost into the hiss of rain just beginning and someone's crying and Loreh's wet breathing.

Kit glanced up. His chest heaving, Valo stood staring at the body. Kit said to him, "Help find Hall," and when the boy did not move he repeated it, his voice sharper. Valo said nothing, did not stop looking at Loreh until he spun and ran down the stairs. Kit heard shouting far below as the first messenger ran toward the town.

Loreh took a last shuddering breath and died.

Kit looked at the others around Loreh's body. The man holding Loreh's other hand pressed his face against it crying helplessly. The two other workers left here knelt at her feet, a man and a woman, huddled close, though they were not a couple. "Tell me," he said.

"I tried to stop it from hitting her," the woman said. She cradled one arm: obviously broken, though she didn't seem to have noticed. "But it just kept falling."

"She was tired. She must have gotten careless," the man said, and the broken-armed woman said, "I don't want to think about that sound." Words fell from them like blood from a cut.

Kit listened. This was what they needed right now, to speak and to be heard. So he listened, and when the others came, Loreh's husband Obal white-lipped and angry-eyed, and the surgeon Hall and six other workers, Kit listened to them as well, and gradually moved them down through the pillar and back toward the warm lights and comfort of Farside.

Kit had lost people before and it was always like this. There would be tears tonight, and anger at him and at his bridge, anger at fate for permitting this. There would be sadness and nightmares. There would be lovemaking and the holding close of children and friends and dogs—affirmations of life in the cold wet night.

His tutor at University had said, during one of her frequent digressions from the nature of materials and the principles of architecture, "Things will go wrong."

It was winter, but in spite of the falling snow they walked slowly to the coffee-house, as Skossa looked for purchase for her cane. She continued, "On long projects, you'll forget that you're not one of them. But if there's an accident? You're slapped in the face with it. Whatever you're feeling? Doesn't matter. Guilty, grieving, alone, worried about the schedule. None of it. What matters is *their* feelings. So listen to them. Respect what they're going through."

She paused then, tapped her cane against the ground thoughtfully. "No, I lie. It does matter but you will have to find your own strength, your own resources elsewhere."

"Friends?" Kit said doubtfully. He knew already that he wanted a career like his father's. He would not be in the same place for more than a few years at a time.

"Yes, friends." Snow collected on Skossa's hair but she didn't seem to notice. "Kit, I worry about you. You're good with people, I've seen it. You like them. But there's a limit for you." He opened his mouth to protest but she held up her hand to silence him. "I know. You do care. But inside the framework of a project. Right now it's your studies. Later it'll be roads and bridges. But people around you—their lives go on outside the framework. They're not just tools to your hand, even likable tools. Your life should go on, too. You should have more than roads to live for. Because if something does go wrong, you'll need what *you're* feeling to matter, to someone somewhere, anyway."

Kit walked through Farside toward the Red Lurcher. Most people were home or at one of the taverns by now, a village turned inward; but he heard footsteps running behind him. He turned quickly—it was not unknown for people reeling from a loss to strike at whatever they blamed, and sometimes that was a person.

It was Valo. Though his fists were balled, Kit could tell immediately that he was angry but that he was not looking for a fight. For a moment Kit wished he didn't need to listen, that he could just go back to his rooms and sleep for a thousand hours, but there was a stricken look in Valo's eyes: Valo, who looked so much like Rasali. He hoped that Rasali and Loreh hadn't been close.

Kit said gently, "Why aren't you inside? It's cold." As he said it, he realized suddenly that it *was* cold. The rain had settled into a steady cold flow.

"I will, I was, I mean, but I came out for a second because I thought maybe I could find you, because—" The boy was shivering too.

"Where are your friends? Let's get you inside. It'll be better there."

"No," he said. "I have to know first. It's like this always? If I do this, build things, it'll happen for me? Someone will die?"

"It might. It probably will, eventually."

Valo said an unexpected thing. "I see. It's just that she had just gotten married."

The blood on Loreh's lips, the wet sound of her crushed chest as she took her last breaths—"Yes," Kit said. "She had."

"I just…I had to know if I need to be ready for this." It seemed callous, but Ferrys were used to dying, to death. "I guess I'll find out."

"I hope you don't have to." The rain was getting heavier. "You should be inside, Valo."

Valo nodded. "Rasali—I wish she were here. She could help maybe. You should go in, too. You're shivering."

Kit watched him go. Valo had not invited him to accompany him back into the light and the warmth. He knew better than to expect that but for a moment he had permitted himself to hope otherwise.

Kit slipped through the stables and through the back door at The Bitch. Widson Innkeep, hands full of mugs for the taproom, saw him and nodded, face unsmiling but not hostile. That was good, Kit thought: as good as it would get, tonight.

He entered his room and shut the door, leaned his back to it as if holding the world out. Someone had already been in his room. A lamp had been lit against the darkness, a fire laid, and bread and cheese and a tankard of ale set by the window to stay cool.

He began to cry.

The news went across the river by signal flags. No one worked on the bridge the next day, or the day after that. Kit did all the right things, letting his grief and guilt overwhelm him only when he was alone, huddled in front of the fire in his room.

The third day, Rasali arrived from Nearside with a boat filled with crates of northland herbs on their way east. Kit was sitting in The Bitch's taproom, listening. People were coping, starting to look forward again. They should be able to get back to it soon, the next clear day. He would offer them something that would be an immediate, visible accomplishment, something different, perhaps guidelining the ramp.

He didn't see Rasali come into the taproom; only felt her hand on his shoulder and heard her voice in his ear. "Come with me," she murmured.

He looked up, puzzled, as though she were a stranger. "Rasali Ferry, why are you here?"

She said only, "Come for a walk, Kit."

It was raining but he accompanied her anyway, pulling a scarf over his head when the first cold drops hit his face.

She said nothing as they splashed through Farside. She was leading him somewhere, but he didn't care where, grateful not to have to be the decisive one, the strong one. After a time she opened a door and led him through it into a small room filled with light and warmth.

"My house," she said. "And Valo's. He's still at the boat yard. Sit."

She pointed and Kit dropped onto the settle beside the fire. Rasali swiveled a pot hanging from a bracket out of the fire and ladled something out. She handed a mug to him and sat. "So. Drink."

It was spiced porter and the warmth eased into the tightness in his chest. "Thank you."

"Talk."

"This is such a loss for you all, I know," he said. "Did you know Loreh well?"

She shook her head. "This is not for me, this is for you. Tell me."

"I'm fine," he said, and when she didn't say anything, he repeated with a flicker of anger: "I'm *fine*, Rasali. I can handle this."

"Probably you can," Rasali said. "But you're not fine. She died and it was your bridge she died for. You don't feel responsible? I don't believe it."

"Of course I feel responsible," he snapped.

The fire cast gold light across her broad cheekbones when she turned her face to him, but to his surprise she said nothing, only looked at him and waited.

"She's not the first," Kit said, surprising himself. "The first project I had sole charge of, a toll gate. Such a little project, such a silly little project to lose someone on. The wood frame for the passageway collapsed before we got the keystone in. The whole arch came down. Someone got killed." It had been a very young man, slim and tall with a limp. He was raising his little sister. She hadn't been more than ten. Running loose in the fields around the site, she had missed the collapse, the boy's death. Dafuen? Naus? He couldn't remember his name. And the girl—what had her name been? *I should remember. I owe that much to them.*

"Every time I lose someone," he said at last, "I remember the others. There've been twelve in twenty-three years. Not so many, considering. Building's dangerous. My record's better than most."

"But it doesn't matter, does it?" she said. "You still feel you killed each one of them, as surely as if you'd thrown them off a bridge yourself."

"It's my responsibility. The first one, Duar—" *that* had been his name; there it was. The name loosened something in Kit. His face warmed: tears, hot tears running down his face.

"It's all right," she said. She held him until he stopped crying.

"How did you know?" he said finally.

"I am the eldest surviving member of the Ferry family," she said. "My aunt died seven years ago. And then I watched my brother leave to cross the mist, three years ago now. It was a perfect day, calm and sunny, but he never made it. He went instead of me because on that day the river felt wrong to me. It could have been me. It should have, maybe. So I understand."

She stretched a little. "Not that most people don't. If Petro Housewright sends his daughter to select timber in the mountains, and she doesn't come back—eaten by wolves, struck by lightning, I don't know—is Petro to blame? It's probably the wolves or the lightning. Maybe it's the daughter, if she did something stupid. And it *is* Petro, a little; she wouldn't have been there at all if he hadn't sent her. And it's her mother for being fearless and teaching that to her daughter; and Thom Green for wanting a new room to his house. Everyone except maybe the wolves feels at least a little responsible. This path leads nowhere. Loreh would have died sooner or later," Rasali added softly. "We all do."

"Can you accept death so readily?" he asked. "Yours even?"

She leaned back, her face suddenly weary. "What else can I do, Kit? Someone must ferry and I am better suited than most—and by more than my blood. I love the mist, its currents and the smell of it and the power in my body as I push us all through. Petro's daughter—she did not want to die when the wolves came, I'm sure, but she loved selecting timber."

"If it comes for you?" he said softly. "Would you be so sanguine then?"

She laughed, and the pensiveness was gone. "No indeed. I will curse the stars and go down fighting. But it will still have been a wonderful thing, to cross the mist."

At University, Kit's relationships had all been casual. There were lectures that everyone attended, and he lived near streets and pubs crowded with students; but the physical students had a tradition of keeping to themselves that was rooted in the personal preferences of their predecessors, and in their own. The only people who worked harder than the engineers were the ale-makers, the University joke went. Kit and the other physical students talked and drank and roomed and slept together.

In his third year, he met Domhu Canna at the arcade where he bought vellums and paper: a small woman with a heart-shaped face and hair in black clouds that she kept somewhat confined by gray ribands. She was a philosophical student from a city two thousand miles to the east, on the coast.

He was fascinated. Her mind was abrupt and fish-quick and made connections he didn't understand. To her, everything was a metaphor, a symbol for something else. People, she said, could be better understood by comparing their lives to animals, to the seasons, to the structure of certain lyrical songs, to a gambling game.

This was another form of pattern-making, he saw. Perhaps people were like teamed oxen to be led; or like metals to be smelted and shaped to one's purpose; or as the stones for a dry-laid wall, which had to be carefully selected for shape and strength, and sorted, and placed. This last suited him best. What held them together was no external mortar but their own weight and the planning and patience of the drystone builder. But it was an inadequate metaphor. People were this, but they were all the other things as well.

He never understood what Domhu found attractive in him. They never talked about regularizing their relationship. When her studies were done halfway through his final year, she returned to her city to help found a new university, and in any case her people did not enter into term marriages. They separated amicably and with a sense of loss on his part at least, but it did not occur to him until years later that things might have been different.

The winter was rainy but there were days they could work and they did. By spring, there had been other deaths unrelated to the bridge on both banks: a woman who died in childbirth, a child who had never breathed properly in his short life; two fisherfolk lost when they capsized; several who died for the various reasons that old or sick people died.

Over the spring and summer they finished the anchorages, featureless masses of blocks and mortar anchored to the bedrock. They were buried so that only a few courses of stone showed above the ground. The anchoring bolts were each tall as a man, hidden safely behind the portals through which the chains would pass.

The Farside pillar was finished by midwinter of the third year, well before the Nearside tower. Jenner and Teniant Planner had perfected a signal system that allowed detailed technical information to pass between the banks, and documents traveled each time a ferry crossed. Rasali made sixty-eight trips back and forth. Though he spent much of his time with Kit, Valo made twenty. Kit did not cross the mist at all unless the flags told him he must.

It was early spring and Kit was in Farside when the signals went up: *Message. Imperial seal.* He went to Rasali at once.

"I can't go," she said. "I just got here yesterday. The Big Ones—"

"I have to get across and Valo's on Nearside. There's news from the capital."

"News has always waited before."

"No, it hasn't. You forced it to but news waited restlessly, pacing along the levee until we could pick it up."

"Use the flags," she said, a little impatiently.

"The seals can't be broken by anyone but me or Jenner. He's over here. I'm sorry," he said, thinking of her brother, dead four years before.

"If you die no one can read it either," she said, but they left just after dusk anyway. "If we must go, better then than earlier or later," she said.

He met her at the upper dock at dusk. The sky was streaked with bright bands of green and gold, clouds catching the last of the sun, but they radiated no light. The current down the river was steady and light. The mist between the levees was already in shadow, smooth dunes twenty feet high.

Rasali waited silently, coiling and uncoiling a rope in her hands. Beside her stood two women and a dog: dealers in spices returning from the plantations of Gloth, the dog whining and restless. Kit was burdened with document cases filled with vellum and paper, rolled tightly and wrapped in oilcloth. Rasali seated the merchants and their dog in the ferry's bow, then untied and pushed off in silence. Kit sat near her.

She stood at the stern, braced against the scull. For a moment he could pretend that this was water they moved on and he half-expected to hear sloshing, but the big paddle made no noise. It was so silent that he could hear her breath, the dog's nervous panting, and his own pulse, too fast. Then the *Crossing* slid up the long slope of a mist dune and there was no possibility that this could be anything but mist.

He heard a soft sighing, like air entering a once-sealed bottle. It was hard to see so far, but the lingering light showed him a heaving of the mist on the face of a neighboring dune, like a bubble coming to the surface of hot mud. The dome grew and then burst. There was a gasp from one of the women. A shape rolled away, too dark for Kit to see more than its length.

"What—" he said in wonder.

"Fish," Rasali breathed to Kit. "Not small ones. They are biting tonight. We should not have come."

It was night now. The first tiny moon appeared, scarcely brighter than a star, followed by other stars. Rasali oared gently through the dunes, face turned to the sky. At first he thought she was praying, but she was navigating. There were more fish now: each time the sighing sound, the dark shape half-seen. He heard someone singing, the voice carrying somehow to them, from far behind.

"The fishers," Rasali said. "They will stay close to the levees tonight. I wish...."

But she left the wish unspoken. They were over the deep mist now. He could not say how he knew this. He had a sudden vision of the bridge overhead, a black span bisecting the star-spun sky, the parabolic arch of the chains perhaps visible, perhaps not. People would stride across the river an arrow's flight overhead, unaware of this place beneath. Perhaps they would stop and look over the bridge's railings, but they would be too high to see the fish as any but small shadows, supposing they saw them at all, supposing they stopped at all. The Big Ones would be novelties, weird creatures that caused a safe little shiver, like hearing a frightening story late at night.

Perhaps Rasali saw the same thing, for she said suddenly, "Your bridge. It will change all this."

"It must. I am sorry," he said again. "We are not meant to be here on mist."

"We are not meant to cross this without passing through it. Kit—" Rasali said as if starting a sentence, and then fell silent. After a moment she began to speak again, her voice low, as though she were speaking to herself. "The soul often hangs in a balance of some sort. Tonight do I lie down in the high fields with Dirk Tanner or not? At the fair, do I buy ribbons or wine? For the new ferry's headboard, do I use camphor or pearwood? Small things, right? A kiss, a ribbon, a grain that coaxes the knife this way or that. They are not, Kit Meinem of Atyar. Our souls wait for our answer because any answer changes us. This is why I wait to decide what I feel about your bridge. I'm waiting until I know how I will be changed."

"You can never know how things will change you," Kit said.

"If you don't, you have not waited to find out." There was a popping noise barely a stone's throw to starboard. "Quiet."

On they moved. In daylight, Kit knew, the trip took less than an hour, but now it seemed much longer. Perhaps it was. He looked up at the stars and thought they had moved, but perhaps not.

His teeth were clenched as were all his muscles. When he tried to relax them, he realized it was not fear that cramped him but something else, something outside him. He heard Rasali falter. "No…."

He recognized it now, the sound that was not a sound, like the lowest pipes on an organ, a drone so low that he couldn't hear it, one that turned his bones to liquid and his muscles to flaked and rusting iron. His breath labored from his chest in grunts. His head thrummed. Moving as though through honey, he strained his hands to his head, cradling it. He could not see Rasali except as a gloom against the slightly less gloom of the mist, but he heard her pant, tiny pain-filled breaths like an injured dog.

The thrumming in his body pounded at his bones now, dissolving them. He wanted to cry out but there was no air left in his lungs. He realized suddenly that the mist beneath them was raising itself into a mound. It piled up along the boat's sides. *I never got to finish the bridge*, he thought. *And I never kissed her.* Did Rasali have any regrets?

The mound roiled and became a hill, which became a mountain obscuring part of the sky. The crest melted into curls and there was a shape inside, large and dark as night itself, that slid and followed the collapsing moist. It seemed not to move, but he knew that was only because of the size of the thing, that it took ages for its full length to pass. That was all he saw before his eyes slipped shut.

How long he lay there in the bottom of the boat, he didn't know. At some point he realized he was there. Some time later he found he could move again, his bones and muscles back to what they should be. The dog was barking. "Rasali?" he said shakily. "Are we sinking?"

"Kit." Her voice was a thread. "You're still alive. I thought we were dead."

"That was a Big One?"

"I don't know. No one has ever seen one. Maybe it was just a Fairly Large One."

The old joke. Kit choked on a weak laugh.

"Shit," Rasali said in the darkness. "I dropped the oar."

"Now what?" he said.

"I have a spare, but it's going to take longer and we'll land in the wrong place. We'll have to tie off and then walk up to get help."

I'm alive, he did not say. *I can walk a thousand miles tonight.*

It was nearly dawn before they got to Nearside. The two big moons rose just before they landed, a mile south of the dock. The spice traders and their dog went on ahead while Kit and Rasali secured the boat. They walked up together. Halfway home, Valo came down at a dead run.

"I was waiting and you didn't come—" He was pale and panting. "But they told me, the other passengers, that you made it and—"

"Valo." Rasali hugged him and held him hard. "We're safe, little one. We're here. It's done."

"I thought…." he said.

"I know," she said. "Valo, please, I am so tired. Can you get the *Crossing* up to the dock? I am going to my house and I will sleep for a day, and I don't care if the Empress herself is tapping her foot, it's going to wait." She released Valo, saluted Kit with a weary smile, and walked up the long flank of the levee. Kit watched her leave.

The "Imperial seal" was a letter from Atyar, some underling arrogating authority and asking for clarification on a set of numbers Kit had sent— scarcely worth the trip at any time, let alone across mist on a bad night. Kit cursed the capital and Empire and then sent the information, along with a tautly worded paragraph about seals and their appropriate use.

Two days later, he got news that would have brought him across the mist in any case. The caravan carrying the first eyebars and bolts was twelve miles out on the Hoic Mine Road. Kit and his ironmaster Tandreve Smith rode out to meet the wagons as they crept southward and found them easing down a gradual slope near Oud village. The carts were long and built strong, their contents covered, each pulled by a team of tough-legged oxen with patient expressions. The movement was slow, and drivers walked beside them, singing something unfamiliar to Kit's city-bred ears.

"Ox-tunes. We used to sing these at my uncle's farm," Tandreve said, and sang:

Remember last night's dream,
the sweet cold grass, the lonely cows.
You had your bollocks then.

Tandreve chuckled, and Kit with her.

One of the drivers wandered over as Kit pulled his horse to a stop. Unattended, her team moved forward anyway. "Folks," she said and nodded. A taciturn woman.

Kit swung down from the saddle. "These are the chains?"

"You're from the bridge?"

"Kit Meinem of Atyar."

The woman nodded again. "Berallit Red-Ox of Ilver. Your smiths are sitting on the tail of the last wagon."

One of the smiths, a rangy man with singed eyebrows, loped forward to meet them, and introduced himself as Jared Toss of Little Hoic. They walked beside the carts as they talked, and he threw aside a tarp to show Kit what they carried: stacks of iron eyebars, each a rod ten feet long with eyes at either end. Tandreve walked sideways as she inspected the eyebars. She and Jared soon lost themselves in a technical discussion, while Kit kept them company, leading Tandreve's forgotten horse and his own, content for the moment to let the masters talk it out. He moved a little forward until he was abreast of the oxen. *Remember last night's dream*, he thought and then: *I wonder what Rasali dreamt?*

After that night on the mist, Rasali seemed to have no bad days. She took people the day after they arrived, no matter what the weather or the mist's character. The tavern keepers grumbled at this, but the decrease in time each visitor stayed was made up for by the increase in numbers of serious-eyed men and women sent by firms in Atyar to establish offices in the towns on the river's far side. It made things easier for the bridge as well, since Kit and others could move back and forth as needed. Kit remained reluctant, more so since the near miss.

There was enough business for two boats. Valo volunteered to ferry more often but Rasali refused the help, allowing him to ferry only when she couldn't prevent it. "The Big Ones don't seem to care about me this winter," she said to him, "but I can't say they would feel the same about tender meat like you." With Kit she was more honest. "If he is to leave ferrying to go study in the capital, it's best sooner than later. Mist will be dangerous until the last ferry crosses it. And even then, even after your bridge is done."

It was Rasali only who seemed to have this protection. The fishing people had as many problems as in any year. Denis Redboat lost his coracle when it was rammed ("—by a Medium-Large One," he laughed in the tavern later: sometimes the oldest jokes really were the best), though he was fished out by a nearby boat before he had sunk too deep. The rash was only superficial but his hair grew back only in patches.

Kit sat in the crowded beer garden of The Deer's Hart watching Rasali and Valo make a little pinewood skiff in the boat yard next door. Valo had called out a greeting when Kit first sat down, and Rasali turned her head to smile at him, but after that they ignored him. Some of the locals stopped by to greet him, and the barman stayed for some time, telling him about the ominous yet unchanging ache in his back; but for most of the afternoon, Kit was alone in the sun, drinking cellar-cool porter and watching the boat take shape.

In the midsummer of the fourth year, it was rare for Kit to have all the afternoon of a beautiful day to himself. The anchorages had been finished for some months. So had the rubble-filled ramps that led to the arched passages through each pillar. The pillars themselves had taken longer, and the granite saddles that would support the chains over the towers had only just been put in place.

They were only slightly behind on Kit's deadlines for most of the materials. More than a thousand of the eyebars and bolts for the chains were laid out in rows, the iron smelling of the linseed oil used to protect them during transit. More were expected before winter. Close to the ramps were the many fishskin ropes and cables that would be needed to bring the first chain across the gap. They were irreplaceable—probably the most valuable thing on the work sites—and were treated accordingly, kept in closed tents that reeked.

Kit's high-work specialists were here, too: the men and women who would do the first perilous tasks, mostly experts who had worked on other big spans or the towers of Atyar.

Valo and Rasali were not alone in the boat yard. Rasali had sent for the ferry folk of Ubmie, a hundred miles to the south and they had arrived a few days before: a woman and her cousin, Chell and Lan Crosser. The strangers had the same massive shoulders and good looks the Ferrys had, but they shared a faraway expression of their own. The river was broader at Ubmie, deeper, so perhaps death was closer to them. Kit wondered what they thought of his task. The bridge would cut into ferry trade for many hundreds of miles on either side and Ubmie had been reviewed as a possible site for the bridge—but they must not have resented it or they would not be here.

Everything waited on the ferry folk. The next major task was to bring the lines across the river to connect the piers—fabricating the chains required temporary cables and catwalks be there first—but this could not be rushed. Rasali, Valo, and the Crossers all needed to feel at the same time that it was safe to cross. Kit tried not to be impatient. In any case he had plenty to do—items to add to lists, formal reports and polite updates to send to the many interested parties in Atyar and Triple, instructions to pass on to the ropemakers, the masons, the road-builders, the exchequer. And Jenner: Kit had written to the capital, and the Department of Roads was offering Jenner the lead on the second bridge across the river, to be built a few hundred miles to the north. Kit was to deliver the cartel the next time they were on the same side, but he was grateful the officials had agreed to leave Jenner with him until the first chain on this bridge was in place. Things to do.

He pushed all this from his mind. *Later,* he said to the things half-apologetically; *I'll deal with you later. For now just let me sit in the sun and watch other people work.*

The sun slanted peach-gold through the oak's leaves before Rasali and Valo finished for the day. The skiff was finished, an elegant tiny curve of pale wood and dying sunlight. Kit leaned against the fence as they threw a cup of water over its bow and then drew it into the shadows of the boathouse. Valo took off at a run—*so much energy, even after a long day*; ah, youth—as Rasali walked to the fence and leaned on it from her side.

"It's beautiful," he said.

She rolled her neck. "I know. We make good boats. Are you hungry?

Your busy afternoon must have raised an appetite."

He had to laugh. "We laid the capstone this morning. I *am* hungry."

"Come on, then. Thalla will feed us all."

Dinner was simple. The Deer's Hart was better known for its beer than its foods, but the stew Thalla served was savory with chervil, and thick enough to stand a spoon in. Valo had friends to be with, so they ate with Chell and Lan, who turned out to be as light-hearted as Rasali. At dusk, the Crossers left to explore the Nearside taverns, leaving Kit and Rasali to watch heat lightning in the west. The air was thick and warm, soft as wool.

"You never come up to the work sites on either side," Kit said suddenly, after a comfortable, slightly drunken silence. He inspected his earthenware mug, empty except for the smell of yeast.

Rasali had given up on the benches and sat instead on one of the garden tables. She leaned back until she lay supine, face toward the sky. "I've been busy, perhaps you noticed?"

"It's more than that. Everyone finds time here and there. And you used to."

"I did, didn't I? I just haven't seen the point, lately. The bridge changes everything, but I don't see yet how it changes me. So I wait until it's time. Perhaps it's like the mist."

"What about now?"

She rolled her head until her cheek lay against the rough wood of the tabletop: looking at him he could tell, though her eyes were hidden in shadows. What did she see, he wondered: What was she hoping to see? It pleased him but made him nervous.

"Come to the tower now, tonight," he said. "Soon everything changes. We pull the ropes across, and make the chains, and hang the supports, and lay the road—everything changes then, it stops being a project and becomes a bridge, a road. But tonight, it's still just two towers and some plans. Rasali, climb it with me. I can't describe what it's like up there—the wind, the sky all around you, the river below." He flushed at the urgency in his voice. When she remained silent, he added, "You change whether you wait for it or not."

"There's lightning," she said.

"It runs from cloud to cloud," he said. "Not to earth."

"Heat lightning." She sat up. "So show me this place."

The work site was abandoned. The sky overhead had filled with clouds lit from within by the lightning, which was worse than no light at all since it ruined their night vision. They staggered across the site, trying to plan their paths in the moments of light, doggedly moving through the darkness. "Shit," Rasali said suddenly in the darkness, then: "Tripped over something or other." Kit found himself laughing for no apparent reason.

They took the internal stairs instead of the scaffold that still leaned against the pillar's north wall. Kit knew them thoroughly, knew every irregular turn and riser; he counted them aloud to Rasali as he led her by the hand. They reached one hundred and ninety-four before they saw light from a flash of lightning overhead, two hundred and eighteen when they finally stepped onto the roof, gasping for air.

They were not alone. A woman squealed; she and the man with her grabbed clothes and blankets and bolted with their lamp down the stairs, naked and laughing. Rasali said with satisfaction, "Sera Oakfield. I'd recognize that laugh anywhere. That was Erno Bridgeman with her."

"He took his name from the bridge?" Kit asked but Rasali said only, "Oh," in a child's voice. Silent lightning painted the sky over her head in sudden strokes of purple-white, shot through what seemed a dozen layers of cloud.

"The sky is so much closer." She looked about her, walked to the edge and looked down at Nearside. Dull gold light poured from doors open to the heavy air. Kit stayed where he was, content to watch her. The light (when there was lightning) was shadowless, and her face looked young and full of wonder. After a time, she walked to his side.

They said nothing, only kissed and then made love in a nest of their discarded clothes. Kit felt the stone of his bridge against his knees, his back, still warm as skin from the day's heat. Rasali was softer than the rocks and tasted sweet.

A feeling he could not have described cracked open his chest, his throat, his belly. It had been a long time since he had been with a woman, not met his own needs; he had nearly forgotten the delight of it, the sharp rising shock of his release, the rocking ocean of hers. Even their awkwardness made him glad, because it held in it the possibility of doing this again, and better.

When they were done they talked. "You know my goal, to build this bridge," Kit looked down at her face, there and gone, in the flickering of the lightning. "But I do not know yours."

Rasali laughed softly. "Yet you have seen me succeed a thousand times, and fail a few. I wish to live well each day."

"That's not a goal," Kit said.

"Why? Because it's not yours? Which is better, Kit Meinem of Atyar? A single great victory or a thousand small ones?" And then: "Tomorrow," Rasali said. "We will take the rope across tomorrow."

"You're sure?" Kit asked.

"That's a strange statement coming from you. The bridge is all about crossing being a certainty, yes? Like the sun coming up each morning? We agreed this afternoon. It's time."

Dawn came early with the innkeeper's rap on the door. Kit woke disoriented, tangled in the sheets of his little cupboard bed. After he and Rasali had come down from the pillar, Rasali to sleep and Kit to do everything that needed to happen the night before the rope was brought across, all in the few hours left of the night. His skin smelled of Rasali but, stunned with lack of sleep, he had trouble believing their lovemaking had been real. But there was stone dust ground into his skin; he smiled and, though it was high summer, sang a spring song from Atyar as he quickly washed and dressed. He drank a bowl filled with broth in the taproom. It was tangy, lukewarm. A single small perch stared up at him from a salted eye. Kit left the fish, and left the inn.

The clouds and the lightning were gone. Early as it was the sky was already pale and hot. The news was everywhere and the entire town, or so it seemed, drifted with Kit to the work site and then flowed over the levee and down to the bank.

The river was a blinding creamy ribbon high between the banks, looking just it had the first time he had seen it; and for a minute he felt dislocated in time. High mist was seen as a good omen, and though he did not believe in omens he was nevertheless glad. There was a crowd collected on the Farside levee as well, though he couldn't see details, only movement like gnats. The signal towers' flags hung limp against the hot blue-white sky.

Kit walked down to Rasali's boat, nearly hidden in its own tight circle of watchers. As Kit approached, Valo called, "Hey, Kit!" Rasali looked up. Her smile was like welcome shade on a bright day. The circle opened to accept him.

"Greetings, Valo Ferry of Farside, Rasali Ferry of Farside," he said. When he was close enough, he clasped Rasali's hands in his own, loving their warmth despite the day's heat.

"Kit." She kissed his mouth, to a handful of muffled hoots and cheers from the bystanders and a surprised noise from Valo. She tasted like chicory.

Daell Cabler nodded absently to Kit. She was the lead ropemaker. Now she, her husband Stivvan, and the journeymen and masters they had drawn to them were inspecting the hundreds of fathoms of plaited fishskin cord, loading them without twists onto spools three feet across and loading those onto a wooden frame bolted to *The Tranquil Crossing*.

The rope was thin, not much more than a cord, narrower than Kit's smallest finger. It looked fragile, nothing like strong enough to carry its own weight for a quarter of a mile though the tests said otherwise.

Several of the stronger people from the bridge handed down small heavy crates to Valo and Chell Crosser in the bow. Silverwork from Hedeclin, and copper in bricks: the ferry was to be weighted somewhat forward, which would make the first part of the crossing more difficult but should help with the end of it as the cord paid out and took on weight from the mist.

"—We think, anyway," Valo had said, two months back when he and Rasali had discussed the plan with Kit. "But we don't know; no one's done this before." Kit had nodded, and not for the first time wished that the river had been a little less broad. Upriver, perhaps; but no, this had been the only option. He did write to an old classmate back in Atyar, a man who now taught the calculus, and presented their solution. His friend had written back to say that it looked as though it ought to work, but that he knew little of mist.

One end of the rope snaked along the ground and up the levee. No one touched the rope or even approached it, but left a narrow lane and stepped only carefully over it. Now Daell and Stivvan Cabler followed the lane back, up and over the levee, to check the rope and temporary anchor at the Nearside pillar's base.

There was a wait. People sat on the grass, or walked back to watch the Cablers. Someone brought cool broth and small beer from the fishers' tavern. Valo and Rasali and the two Crossers were remote, focused already on what came next.

And for himself? Kit was wound up, but it wouldn't do to show anything but a calm confident front. He walked among the watchers, exchanged words or a smile with each of them. He knew them all by now, even the children.

It was nearly midmorning before Daell and Stivvan returned. The ferryfolk took their positions in *The Tranquil Crossing*, two to each side, far enough apart that they could pull on different rhythms. Kit was useless freight until they got to the other side, so he sat at the bow where his weight might do some good. Uni stumbled as she was helped into the boat's stern: she would monitor the rope but as she told them all, she was nervous; she had never crossed the mist before this. "I think I'll wait 'til the catwalks go up before I return," she added. "Stivvan can sleep without me 'til then."

"Ready, Kit?" Rasali called forward.

"Yes," he said.

"Daell? Lan? Chell? Valo?" Assent all around.

"A historic moment," Valo announced. "The Day the Mist Was Bridged."

"Make yourself useful, boy," Rasali said. "Prepare to scull."

"Right," Valo said.

"Push us off," she said to the people on the dock. A cheer went up.

The dock and all the noises behind them disappeared almost immediately. The ferryfolk had been right that it was a good day for such an undertaking; the mist was a smooth series of ripples no taller than a man, and so thick that the *Crossing* rode high despite the extra weight and drag. It was the gentlest he had ever seen the river.

Kit's eyes ached from the brightness. "It will work?" Kit said, meaning the rope and their trip across the mist and the bridge itself—a question rather than a statement; unable to help himself, though he had worked the calculations himself and had Daell and Stivvan and Valo and a specialist in Atyar all double-check them, though it was a child's question. Isolated in the mist, even competence seemed tentative.

"Yes," Daell Cabler said from aft.

The rowers said little. At one point Rasali murmured into the deadened air, "To the right," and Valo and Lan Crosser changed their stroke to avoid a gentle mound a few feet high directly in their path. Mostly the *Crossing* slid steadily across the regular swells. Unlike his other trips, Kit saw no dark shapes in the mist, large or small. From here, they could not see the dock, but the levee was scattered with Farsiders waiting for the work they would do when the ferry landed. Her eyes were alight with reflections from the mist.

There was nothing he could do to help, so Kit watched Rasali scull in the blazing sun. The work got harder as the rope spooled out until she and the others panted. Shining with sweat, her skin was nearly as bright as the mist in the sunlight, and he wondered how she could bear the light without burning. Her face looked solemn, intent on the eastern shore. Then he recognized the expression: not fear, not planning, not even focus. It was joy.

How will she bear it, he thought suddenly, *when there is no more ferrying to be done?* He had known that she loved what she did but he had never realized just how much. He felt as though he had been kicked in the stomach. What would it do to her? His bridge would destroy this thing that she loved, that gave her name. How could he not have thought of that? "Rasali," he said, unable to stay silent.

"Not now," she said. The rowers panted as they dug in.

"It's like...pulling through dirt," Valo gasped.

"Quiet," Rasali snapped and then they were silent except for their laboring breath. Kit's own muscles knotted sympathetically. Foot by foot the ferry heaved forward. At some point they were close enough to the Farside upper dock that someone threw a rope to Kit and at last he could do something however inadequate. He took the rope and pulled. The rowers pushed for their final strokes. The boat slid up beside the dock. People swarmed aboard, securing the boat to the dock, the rope to a temporary anchor onshore.

Released, the Ferrys and the Crossers embraced, laughing a little dizzily. They walked up the levee toward Farside town and did not look back.

Kit left the ferry to join Jenner Ellar.

It was hard work. The rope's end had to be brought over an oiled stone saddle on the levee and down to a temporary anchor and capstan at the Farside pillar's base, a task that involved driving a team of oxen through a temporary gap Jenner had cut into the levee: a risk, but one that had to be taken.

More oxen were harnessed to the capstan. Daell Cabler was still pale and shaking from the crossing, but after a glass of something cool and dark, she and her Farside counterparts could walk the rope to look for any new weak spots, but they found none. Jenner stayed at the capstan. Daell and Kit returned to the temporary saddle in the levee, the notch polished like glass and gleaming with oil.

The rope was released from the dockside anchor. The rope over the saddle whined as it took the load and flattened, and there was a deep pinging noise as it swung out to make a single slightly curved line down from the saddle, down into the mist. The oxen at the capstan dug in.

The next hours were the tensest of Kit's life. For a time, the rope did not appear to change. The capstan moaned and clicked, and at last the rope slid by inches, by feet, through the saddle. He could do nothing but watch and yet again rework all the calculations in his mind. He did not see Rasali, but Valo came up after a time to watch the progress. Answering his questions settled Kit's nerves. The calculations were correct. He had done this before. He was suddenly starved and voraciously ate the food that Valo had brought for him. How long had it been since the broth at The Fish? Hours; most of a day.

The oxen puffed and grunted, and were replaced with new teams. Even lubricated and with leather sleeves, the rope moved reluctantly across the saddle, but it did move. And then the pressure started to ease and the rope paid through the saddle faster. The sun was westering when at last the rope lifted free of the mist. By dusk, the rope was sixty feet above it, stretched humming-tight between the Farside and Nearside levees and the temporary anchors.

Just before dark, Kit saw the flags go up on the signal tower: *secure*.

Kit worked on and then seconded projects for five years after he left University. His father knew men and women at the higher levels in the Department of Roads, and his old tutor, Skossa Timt, knew more, so many were high-profile works, but he loved all of them, even his first lead, the little toll gate where the boy, Duar, had died.

All public work—drainage schemes, roadwork, amphitheaters, public squares, sewers, alleys and mews—was alchemy. It took the invisible patterns that people made as they lived and turned them into stone and brick and wood and space. Kit built things that moved people through the invisible architecture that was his mind and his notion—and Empire's notion—of how their lives could be better.

The first major project he led was a replacement for a collapsed bridge in the Four Peaks region north of Atyar. The original had also been a chain suspension bridge but much smaller than the mist bridge, crossing only a hundred yards, its pillars only forty feet high. With maintenance, it had survived heavy use for three centuries, shuddering under the carts that brought quicksilver ore down to the smelting village of Oncalion; but after the heavy snowfalls of what was subsequently called the Wolf Winter, one of the gorge's walls collapsed, taking the north pillar with it and leaving nowhere stable to rebuild. It was easier to start over, two hundred yards upstream.

The people of Oncalion were not genial. Hard work made for hard men and women. There was a grim, desperate edge to their willingness to labor on the bridge, because their livelihood and their lives were dependent on the mine. They had to be stopped at the end of each day or, dangerous as it was, they would work through moonlit nights.

But it was lonely work, even for Kit who did not mind solitude; and when the snows of the first winter brought a halt to construction, he returned with some relief to Atyar, to stay with his father. Davell Meinem was old now. His memory was weakening though still strong enough. He spent his days constructing a vast and fabulous public maze of dry-laid stones brought from all over Empire: his final project, he said to Kit, an accurate prophecy. Skossa Timt had died during the hard cold of the Wolf Winter, but many of his classmates were still in the capital. Kit spent evenings with them, attended lectures and concerts, entering for the season into a casual relationship with an architect who specialized in waterworks.

Kit returned to the site at Oncalion as soon as the roads cleared. In his absence, through the snows and melt-off, the people of Oncalion had continued to work, laying course after course of stone in the bitter cold. The work had to be redone.

The second summer, they worked every day and moonlit nights, and Kit worked beside them.

Kit counted the bridge as a failure although it was coming in barely over budget and only a couple of months late, and no one had died. It was an ugly design; the people of Oncalion had worked hard but joylessly; and there was all his dissatisfaction and guilt about the work that had to be done anew.

Perhaps there was something in the tone of his letters to his father, for there came a day in early autumn that Davell Meinem arrived in Oncalion, riding a sturdy mountain horse and accompanied by a journeyman who vanished immediately into one of the village's three taverns. It was mid-afternoon.

"I want to see this bridge of yours," Davell said. He looked weary but straight-backed as ever. "Show it to me."

"We'll go tomorrow," Kit said. "You must be tired."

"Now," Davell said.

They walked up from the village together. It was a cool day, and bright though the road was overshadowed with pines and fir trees. Basalt outcroppings were stained dark green and black with lichens. His father moved slowly, pausing often for breath. They met a steady trickle of local people leading heavy-laden ponies. The roadbed across the bridge wasn't quite complete and could not take carts yet, but ponies could cross carrying ore in baskets. Oncalion was already smelting these first small loads.

At the bridge, Davell asked the same questions he had asked when Kit was a child playing on his work sites. Kit found himself responding as he had so many years before, eager to explain—or excuse—each decision; and always, always the ponies passing.

They walked down to the older site. The pillar had been gutted for stones so all that was left was rubble, but it gave them a good view of the new bridge: the boxy pillars, the curve of the main chains, the thick vertical suspender chains; the slight sprung arch of the bulky roadbed. It looked as clumsy as a suspension bridge ever could. Yet another pony crossed, led by a woman singing something in the local dialect.

"It's a good bridge," Davell said at last.

Kit shook his head. His father, who had been known for his sharp tongue on the work sites though never to his son, said, "A bridge is a means to an end. It only matters because of what it does. Leads from *here* to *there*. If you do your work right they won't notice it, any more than you notice where quicksilver comes from, most times. It's a good bridge because they are already using it. Stop feeling sorry for yourself, Kit."

It was a big party, that night. The Farsiders (and, Kit knew, the Nearsiders) drank and danced under the shadow of their bridge-to-be. Torchlight and firelight touched the stones of the tower base and anchorage, giving them mass and meaning, but above their light the tower was a black outline, the absence of stars. More torches outlined the tower's top, and they seemed no more than gold stars among the colder ones.

Kit walked among them. Everyone smiled or waved and offered to stand him drinks, but no one spoke much with him. It was as if the lifting of the cable had separated him from them. The immense towers had not done this; he had still been one of them, to some degree at least—the instigator of great labors but still one of them. But now, for tonight anyway, he was the man who bridged the mist. He had not felt so lonely since his first day here. Even Loreh Tanner's death had not severed him so completely from their world.

On every project, there was a day like this. It was possible that the distance came from him, he realized suddenly. He came to a place and built something, passing through the lives of people for a few months or years. He always left. A road through dangerous terrain or a bridge across mist saved lives and increased trade, but it always changed the world as well. It was his job to make a thing and then leave to make the next one—but it was also his preference not to remain and see what he had made. What would Nearside and Farside look like in ten years, in fifty? He had never returned to a previous site.

It was harder this time, or perhaps just different. Perhaps *he* was different. He was staying longer this time because of the size of the project, and he had allowed himself to belong to the country on either side of the bridge. To have more was to have more to miss when it was taken away.

Rasali—what would her life look like?

Valo danced by, his arm around a woman half a head taller than he— Rica Bridger—and Kit caught his arm. "Where is Rasali?" he shouted, then, knowing he could not be heard over the noise of drums and pipes, mouthed: *Rasali*. He didn't hear what Valo said but followed his pointing hand.

Rasali was alone, flat on her back on the river side of the levee, looking up. There were no moons, so the Sky Mist hung close overhead, a river of stars that poured east to west. Kit knelt a few feet away. "Rasali Ferry of Farside."

Her teeth flashed in the dark. "Kit Meinem of Atyar."

He lay beside her. The grass was like bad straw, coarse against his back and neck. Without looking at him she passed a jar of something. Its taste was strong as tar and Kit gasped for a moment.

"I did not mean…." he started but trailed off, unsure how to continue.

"Yes," she said and he knew she had heard the words he didn't say. Her voice contained a shrug. "Many people born into a Ferry family never cross the mist."

"But you—" He stopped, felt carefully for his words. "Maybe others don't but you do. And I think maybe you must do so."

"Just as you must build," she said softly. "That's clever of you to realize that."

"And there will be no need after this, will there? Not on boats anyway. We'll still need fishskin, so they'll still be out, but they—"

"—stay close to shore," she said.

"And you?" he asked.

"I don't know, Kit. Days come, days go. I go onto the mist or I don't. I live or I don't. There is no certainty, but there never is."

"It doesn't distress you?"

"Of course it does. I love and I hate this bridge of yours. I will pine for the mist, for the need to cross it. But I do not want to be part of a family that all die young without even a corpse for the burning. If I have a child she will not need to make the decision I did: to cross the mist and die, or to stay safe on one side of the world and never see the other. She will lose something. She will gain something else."

"Do you hate me?" he said finally, afraid of the answer, afraid of any answer she might give.

"No. Oh, no." She rolled over to him and kissed his mouth, and Kit could not say if the salt he tasted was from her tears or his own.

The autumn was spent getting the chains across the river. In the days after the crossing, the rope was linked to another, and then pulled back the way it had come, coupled now; and then there were two ropes in parallel courses. It was tricky work, requiring careful communications through the signal towers, but it was completed without event, and Kit could at last get a good night's sleep. To break the rope would have been to start anew with the long difficult crossing. Over the next days, each rope was replaced with fishskin cable strong enough to take the weight of the chains until they were secured.

The cables were hoisted to the tops of the pillars, to prefigure the path one of the eight chains would take: secured with heavy pins set in protected slots in the anchorages and then straight sharp lines to the saddles on the pillars and, two hundred feet above the mist, the long perfect catenary. A catwalk was suspended from the cables. For the first time, people could cross the mist without the boats, though few chose to do so except for the high-workers from the capital and the coast: a hundred men and women so strong and graceful that they seemed another species and kept mostly to themselves. They were directed by a woman Kit had worked with before, Feinlin. The high-workers took no surnames. Something about Feinlin reminded him of Rasali.

The weather grew colder and the days shorter, and Kit pushed hard to have the first two chains across before the winter rains began. There would be no heavy work once the ground got too wet to give sturdy purchase to the teams, and calculations to the contrary, Kit could not quite trust that cables, even fishskin cables, would survive the weight of those immense arcs through an entire winter—or that a Big One would not take one down in the unthinking throes of some winter storm.

The eyebars that would make up the chain were ten feet long and required considerable manhandling to be linked with the bolts, each larger than a man's forearm. The links became a chain, even more cumbersome. Winches pulled the chain's end up to the saddles and out onto the catwalk.

After this, the work became even more difficult and painstaking. Feinlin and her people moved individual eyebars and pins out onto the catwalks and joined them in place; a backbreaking dangerous task that had to be exactly synchronized with the work on the other side of the river so that the cable would not be stressed.

Most nights Kit worked into the darkness. When the moons were bright enough, he, the high-workers, and the bridgewrights would work in shifts, day and night.

He crossed the mist six more times that fall. The high-workers disliked having people on the catwalks, but he was the architect after all, so he crossed once that way, struggling with vertigo. After that he preferred the ferries. When he crossed once with Valo, they talked exclusively about the bridge—Valo had decided to stay until the bridge was complete and the ferries finished though his mind was already full of the capital—but the other times, when it was Rasali, they were silent, listening to the hiss of the V-shaped scull moving in the mist. His fear of the mist decreased with each day they came closer to the bridge's completion, though he couldn't say why this was.

When Kit did not work through the night and Rasali was on the same side of the mist, they spent their nights together, sometimes making love, at other times content to share drinks or play ninepins in The Hart's garden, at which Kit's proficiency surprised everyone including himself. He and Rasali did not talk again about what she would do when the bridge was complete—or what he would do, for that matter.

The hard work was worth it. It was still warm enough that the iron didn't freeze the high-workers' hands on the day they placed the final bolt. The first chain was complete.

Though work slowed through the winter, the second and third chains were in place by spring, and the others were completed by the end of the summer.

With the heavy work done, some of the workers returned to their home-places. More than half had taken the name Bridger or something similar. "We have changed things," Kit said to Jenner on one of his Nearside visits, just before Jenner left for his new work. "No," Jenner said: "*You* have changed things." Kit did not respond but held this close, and thought of it sometimes with mingled pride and fear.

The workers who remained were high-men and -women, people who did not mind crawling about on the suspension chains securing the support ropes. For the last two years, the ropemakers for two hundred miles up- and downstream from the bridge had been twisting and cutting, and looping and reweaving the ends of the fishskin cables that would support the road deck. Crates, each marked with the suspender's position in the bridge, stood in carefully sorted, labeled towers in the sheepfield.

Kit's work was now all paperwork, it seemed—so many invoices, so many reports for the capital—but he managed every day to watch the high-workers. Sometimes he climbed to the tops of the pillars and looked down into the mist and saw Rasali's or Valo's ferry, an elegant narrow shape half-hidden in tendrils of blazing white mist or pale gray fog.

Kit lost one more worker, Tommer Bullkeeper, who climbed out onto the catwalk for a drunken bet and fell, with a maniacal cry that changed into unbalanced laughter as he vanished into the mist. His wife wept in mixed anger and grief, and the townspeople wore ash-color, and the bridge continued. Rasali held Kit when he cried in his room at The Red Lurcher. "Never mind," she said. "Tommer was a good person: a drunk, but good to his sons and his wife, careful with animals. People have always died. The bridge doesn't change that."

The towns changed shape as Kit watched. Commercial envoys from every direction gathered. Many stayed in inns and homes. Some built small houses, shops, and warehouses. Many used the ferries and it became common for these businessmen and women to tip Rasali or Valo lavishly— "in hopes I never ride with you again," they would say. Valo laughed and spent this money buying beer for his friends; the letter had come from University and he would begin his studies with the winter term, so he had many farewells to make. Rasali told no one, not even Kit, what she planned to do with hers.

Beginning in the spring of the project's fifth year, they attached the road deck. Wood planks wide enough for oxen two abreast were nailed together with iron struts to give stability. The bridge was made of several hundred sections, constructed on the work sites and then hauled out by workers. Each segment had farther to go before being placed and secured. The two towns celebrated all night the first time a Nearsider shouted from her side of the bridge and was saluted by Farsider cheers. In the lengthening evenings, it became a pastime for people to walk onto the bridge and lie belly-down at its end, and look into the mist so far below them. Sometimes dark shapes moved within it but no one saw anything big enough to be a Big One. A few heedless locals dropped heavy stones from above to watch the mist twist away, opening holes into its depths, but their neighbors stopped them. "It's not respectful," one said; and, "Do you want to piss them off?" said another.

Kit asked her but Rasali never walked out with him. "I see enough from the river," she said.

Kit was Nearside, in his room in The Fish. He had lived in this room for five years, and it looked it. Plans and time tables overlapped one another, pinned to the walls. The chair by the fire was heaped with clothes, books, a length of red silk he had seen at a fair and could not resist; it had been years since he sat there. The plans in his folio and on the oversized table had been replaced with waybills and receipts for materials, payrolls, and copies of correspondence between Kit and his sponsors in the government. The window was open and Kit sat on the cupboard bed, watching a bee feel its way through the sun-filled air. He'd left half a pear on the table and he was waiting to see if the bee would find it, and thinking about the little hexagonal cells of a beehive, whether they were stronger than squares were and how he might test this.

Feet ran along the corridor. His door flew open. Rasali stood there blinking in the light, which was so golden that Kit didn't at first notice how pale she was, or the tears on her face. "What—" he said as he swung off his bed.

"Valo," she said. "The *Pearlfinder*."

He held her. The bee left, then the sun, and still he held her as she rocked silently on the bed. Only when the square of sky in the window faded to purple and the little moon's crescent eased across it, did she speak. "Ah," she said, a sigh like a gasp. "I am so tired." She fell asleep as quickly as that, with tears still wet on her face. Kit slipped from the room.

The taproom was crowded, filled with ash-gray clothes, with soft voices and occasional sobs. Kit wondered for a moment if everyone had a set of mourning clothes always at hand and what this meant about them.

Brana Keep saw Kit in the doorway and came from behind the bar to speak with him. "How is she?" she said.

"I think she's asleep right now," Kit said. "Can you give me some food for her, something to drink?"

Brana nodded, spoke to her daughter Lixa as she passed into the back, then returned. "How are *you* doing, Kit? You saw a fair amount of Valo yourself."

"Yes," Kit said. Valo chasing the children through the field of stones, Valo laughing at the top of a tower, Valo serious-eyed with a handbook of the calculus in the shade of a half-built fishing boat. "What happened?

She hasn't said anything yet."

Brana spread her hands out. "What can be said? Signal flags said he was going to cross just after midday, but he never came. When we signaled over, they said he left when they signaled."

"Could he be alive?" Kit asked, remembering the night that he and Rasali had lost the big scull, the extra hours it had taken for the crossing. "He might have broken the scull, landed somewhere downriver."

"No," Brana said. "I know, that's what we wanted to hope. But Asa, one of the strangers, the high-workers; she was working overhead and heard the boat capsize, heard him cry out. She couldn't see anything and didn't know what she had heard until we figured it out."

"Three more months," Kit said mostly to himself. He saw Brana looking at him, so he clarified: "Three more months. The bridge would have been done. This wouldn't have happened."

"This was today," Brana said, "not three months from now. People die when they die; we grieve and move on, Kit. You've been with us long enough to understand how we see these things. Here's the tray."

When Kit returned, Rasali was asleep. He watched her in the dark room, unwilling to light more than the single lamp he'd carried up with him. *People die when they die.* But he could not stop thinking about the bridge, its deck nearly finished. *Another three months. Another month.*

When she awakened, there was a moment when she smiled at him, her face weary but calm. Then she remembered and her face tightened and she started crying again. When she was done, Kit got her to eat some bread and fish and cheese and drink some watered wine. She did so obediently, like a child. When she was finished she lay back against him. Her matted hair pushed up into his mouth.

"How can he be gone?"

"I'm so sorry," Kit said. "The bridge was so close to finished. Three more months, and this wouldn't have—"

She pulled away. "What? Wouldn't have happened? Wouldn't have *had* to happen?" She stood and faced him. "His death would have been un-necessary?"

"I—" Kit began but she interrupted him, new tears streaking her face.

"He *died*, Kit. It wasn't necessary, it wasn't irrelevant, it wasn't anything except the way things are. But he's gone and I'm not and *now* what do I do, Kit? I lost my father and my aunt and my sister and my brother and my brother's son, and now I lose the mist when the bridge's done, and then what? What am I then? Who are the Ferry people then?"

Kit knew the answer. However she changed, she would still be Rasali. Her people would still be strong and clever and beautiful. The mist would still be there, and the Big Ones. But she wouldn't be able to hear these words, not yet, not for months maybe. So he held her and let his own tears slip down his face, and tried not to think.

Five years after the Oncalion bridge was completed, Davell Meinem died. Kit was two years into building an aqueduct that stretched across the Bakyar valley, a big project, and there had been problems. The first stones could not sustain both the weight of the aqueduct and the water it was meant to carry; his predecessor on the project should never have accepted them. They were a full season behind schedule, but he left anyway to return to Atyar. Some time would be required to put his father's affairs in order but mostly he did not wish to miss Twentieth-day, when Davell would be remembered.

The Grayfield was a little amphitheatre Davell had designed when he was young, matured now to a warm half-circle of white stone and grass. It was a warm day, brilliantly sunny. The air smelled of honey-cakes and incense. Kit was Davell's only child, so he stood alone at the red-tasselled archway to greet those who came. He was not surprised at how many came to honor his father, more and more until the amphitheatre overflowed, the honey-cakes all eaten and the silver bowls filled with flowers, one from each mourner. Davell Meinem had built nine bridges, three aqueducts, four major buildings, innumerable smaller projects; and beyond this many people had liked him, his good humor.

What surprised Kit was all the people who had come for *his* sake: fellow students, tutors, old lovers, even the man who ran the wine-shop he frequented when he was in the city. Many of them had never even met his father. He did not know what to think about this: he had not known that so many might care about him.

Five months later, when he was back in the Bakyar valley, a letter came to him, wrapped in dirty oiled paper and clearly from far away. It was from the miners of Oncalion. "We heard about Davell Meinem from a trader when we were asking about you," the letter said. "It was good to meet him. We are sorry for your loss."

The fairs to celebrate the opening of the bridge started days before midsummer, the official date. Representatives of Empire from Atyar polished their speeches and waited impatiently in their suite of tents, planted on hurriedly cleaned-up fields near (but not too near) Nearside. The town had bled northward until it surrounded the west pillar of the bridge. The land that had once been sheep-pasture—Sheepfield, it was now—at the foot of the pillar was crowded with fair-tents and temporary booths, cheek by jowl with more permanent shops of wood and stone selling food and space for sleeping and the sorts of products a traveler might find herself needing. Kit was proud of the streets; he had organized construction of the crosshatch of sturdy cobblestones as something to do while he waited through the bridge's final years. The new wells had been a project of Jenner's, planned from the very beginning, but Kit had seen them completed. Kit had just received a letter from Jenner with news of his new bridge up in the Keitche mountains: on schedule, a happy work site.

Kit walked alone through the fair, which had splashed up the levee and along its ridge. A few people, townspeople and workers, greeted him; but others only pointed him out to their friends (*the man who built the bridge; see there, that short dark man*); and still others ignored him completely, just another stranger in a crowd of strangers. When he had first come to build the bridge everyone in Nearside knew everyone else, local or visitor. He felt solitude settling around him again, the loneliness of coming to a strange place and building something and then leaving. The people of Nearside were moving forward into this new world he had built, the world of a bridge across the mist, but he was not going with them.

He wondered what Rasali was doing over in Farside, and wished he could see her. They had not spoken since the days after Valo's death, except once for a few minutes when he had come upon her at The Bitch. She had been withdrawn though not hostile, and he had felt unbalanced and not sought her out since.

Now, at the end of his great labor, he longed to see her. When would she cross next? He laughed. He of all people should know better: *ten minutes' walk.*

The bridge was not yet open, but Kit was the architect; the guards at the toll booth only nodded when he asked to pass and lifted the gate for him. A few people noticed and gestured as he climbed. When Uni Mason (hands filled with ribbons) shouted something he could not hear clearly, Kit smiled and waved and walked on.

He had crossed the bridge before this. The first stage of building the heavy oak frames that underlay the roadbed had been a narrow strip of planking that led from one shore to the other. Nearly every worker had found some excuse for crossing it at least once before Empire had sent people to the tollgates. Swallowing his fear of the height, Kit himself had crossed it nearly every day for the last two months.

This was different. It was no longer his bridge, but belonged to Empire and to the people of Near- and Farside. He saw it with the eyes of a stranger.

The stone ramp was a quarter-mile long, inclined gradually for carts. Kit hiked up, and the noises dropped behind and below him. The barriers that would keep animals (and people) from seeing the drop-off to either side were not yet complete: there were always things left unfinished at a bridge's opening, afterthoughts and additions. Ahead of him, the bridge was a series of perfect dark lines and arcs.

The ramp widened as it approached the pillar, and offered enough space for a cart to carefully turn onto the bridge itself. The bed of the span was barely wide enough for a cart with two oxen abreast, so Nearside and Farside would have to take turns sending wagons across. *For now,* Kit thought: *Later they can widen it, or build another. They*: it would be someone else.

The sky was overcast with high tin-colored clouds, their metallic sheen reflected in the mist below Kit. There were no railings, only fishskin ropes strung between the suspension cables that led up to the chains. Oxen and horses wouldn't like that, or the hollow sound their feet would make on the boards. Kit watched the deck roll before him in the breeze, which was constant from the southwest. The roll wasn't so bad in this wind, but perhaps they should add an iron parapet or more trusses, to lessen the twisting and make crossing more comfortable. Empire had sent a new engineer to take care of any final projects: Jeje Tesanthe. He would mention it to her.

Kit walked to one side so that he could look down. Sound dropped off behind him, deadened as it always was by the mist. He could almost imagine that he was alone. It was several hundred feet down, but there was nothing to give scale to the coiling field of hammered metal below him. Deep in the mist he saw shadows that might have been a Big One or something smaller or a thickening of the mist, and then, his eyes learning what to look for, he saw more of the shadows, as if a school of fish were down there. One separated and darkened as it rose in the mist until it exposed its back almost immediately below Kit.

It was dark and knobby, shiny with moisture, flat as a skate; and it went on forever—thirty feet long perhaps, or forty, twisting as it rose to expose its underside, or what he thought might be its underside. As Kit watched, the mist curled back from a flexing scaled wing of sorts, and then a patch that might have been a single eye or a field of eyes or something altogether different, and then a mouth like the arc of the suspension chains. The mouth gaped open to show another arc, a curve of gum or cartilage. The creature rolled and then sank and became a shadow and then nothing as the mist closed over it and settled.

Kit had stopped walking when he saw it. He forced himself to move forward again. A Big One, or perhaps just a Medium-Large One; at this height it hadn't seemed so big or so frightening. Kit was surprised at the sadness he felt.

Farside was crammed with color and fairings as well, but Kit could not find Rasali anywhere. He bought a tankard of rye beer and went to find some place alone.

Once it became dark and the Imperial representatives were safely tucked away for the night, the guards relaxed the rules and let their friends (and then any of the locals) on the bridge to look around them. People who had worked on the bridge had papers to cross without charge for the rest of their lives, but many others had watched it grow, and now they charmed or bribed or begged their way onto the bridge. Torches were forbidden because of the oil that protected the fishskin ropes but covered lamps were permitted. From his place on the levee, Kit watched the lights move along the bridge, there and then hidden by the support ropes and deck, dim and inconstant as fireflies.

"Kit Meinem of Atyar."

Kit stood and turned to the voice behind him. "Rasali Ferry of Farside." She wore blue and white, and her feet were bare. She had pulled back her dark hair with a ribbon and her pale shoulders gleamed. She glowed under the moonlight like mist. He thought of touching her, kissing her; but they had not spoken since just after Valo's death.

She stepped forward and took the mug from his hand, drank the lukewarm beer, and just like that, the world righted itself. He closed his eyes and let the feeling wash over him.

He took her hand, and they sat on the cold grass and looked out across the river. The bridge was a black net of arcs and lines. Behind it was the mist glowing blue-white in the light of the moons. After a moment, he asked, "Are you still Rasali Ferry, or will you take a new name?"

"I expect I'll take a new one." She half-turned in his arms so that he could see her face, her pale eyes. "And you? Are you still Kit Meinem, or do you become someone else? Kit Who Bridged the Mist? Kit Who Changed the World?"

"Names in the city do not mean the same thing," Kit said absently, aware that he had said this before and not caring. "*Did* I change the world?" He knew the answer already.

She looked at him for a moment as though trying to gauge his feelings. "Yes," she said slowly after a moment. She turned her face up toward the loose strand of bobbing lights: "There's your proof, as permanent as stone and sky."

"'Permanent as stone and sky,'" Kit repeated. "This afternoon—it flexes a lot, the bridge. There has to be a way to control it, but it's not engineered for that yet. Or lightning could strike it. There are a thousand things that could destroy it. It's going to come down, Rasali. This year, next year, a hundred years from now, five hundred." He ran his fingers through his hair. "All these people, they think it's forever."

"No, we don't," Rasali said. "Maybe Atyar does, but we know better here. Do you need to tell a Ferry that nothing will last? These stones will fall eventually, *these* cables—but the *dream* of crossing the mist, the dream of connection. Now that we know it can happen, it will always be here. My mother died, my grandfather. Valo." She stopped, swallowed. "Ferrys die, but there is always a Ferry to cross the mist. Bridges and ferryfolk, they are not so different, Kit." She leaned forward, across the space between them, and they kissed.

"Are you off soon?"

Rasali and Kit had made love on the levee against the cold grass. They had crossed the bridge together under the sinking moons, walked back to The Deer's Hart and bought more beer, the crowds thinner now, people gone home with their families or friends or lovers; the strangers from out of town bedding down in spare rooms, tents, anywhere they could. But Kit was too restless to sleep, and he and Rasali ended up back by the mist, down on the dock. Morning was only a few hours away, and the smaller moon had set. It was darker now and the mist had dimmed.

"In a few days," Kit said, thinking of the trunks and bags packed tight and gathered in his room at The Fish: the portfolio, fatter now, and stained with water, mist, dirt, and sweat. Maybe it was time for a new one. "Back to the capital."

There were lights on the opposite bank, fisherfolk preparing for the night's work despite the fair, the bridge. *Some things don't change.*

"Ah," she said. They both had known this. It was no surprise. "What will you do there?"

Kit rubbed his face, feeling stubble under his fingers, happy to skip that small ritual for a few days. "Sleep for a hundred years. Then there's another bridge they want, down at the mouth of the river, a place called Ulei. The mist's nearly a mile wide there. I'll start midwinter."

"A mile," Rasali said. "Can you do it?"

"I think so. I bridged this, didn't I?" His gesture took in the berms, the slim stone tower overhead, the woman beside him. She smelled sweet and salty. "There are islands by Ulei, I'm told. Low ones. That's the only reason it would be possible. So maybe a series of flat stone arches, one to the next. You? You'll keep building boats?"

"No." She leaned her head back and he felt her face against his ear. "I don't need to. I have a lot of money. The rest of the family can build boats but for me that was just what I did while I waited to cross the mist again."

"You'll miss it," Kit said. It was not a question.

Her strong hand laid over his. "Mmm," she said, a sound without implication.

"But it was the *crossing* that mattered to you, wasn't it?" Kit said, realizing it. "Just as with me, but in a different way."

"Yes," she said and after a pause. "So now I'm wondering: How big do the Big Ones get in the Mist Ocean? And lives there?"

"Nothing's on the other side," Kit said. "There's no crossing something without an end."

"Everything can be crossed. Me, I think there is an end. There's a river of water deep under the Mist River, yes? And that water runs somewhere. And all the other rivers, all the lakes—they all drain somewhere. There's a water ocean under the Mist Ocean, and I wonder whether the mist ends somewhere out there, if it spreads out and vanishes and you find you are floating on water."

"It's a different element," Kit said, turning the problem over. "So you would need a boat that works through mist, light enough with that broad belly and fishskin sheathing; but it would have to be deep-keeled enough for water."

She nodded. "I want to take a coast-skimmer and refit it, find out what's out there. Islands, Kit. Big Ones. *Huge* Ones. Another whole world maybe. I think I would like to be Rasali Ocean."

"You will come to Ulei with me?" he said but he knew already. She *would* come, for a month or a season or a year. They would sleep tumbled together in an inn very like The Fish or The Bitch, and when her boat was finished, she would sail across ocean, and he would move on to the next bridge or road. Or he might return to the capital and a position at University. Or he might rest at last.

"I will come," she said. "For a bit."

Suddenly he felt a deep and powerful emotion in his chest: overwhelmed by everything that had happened or would happen in their lives, the changes to Nearside and Farside, the ferry's ending, Valo's death, the fact that she would leave him eventually, or that he would leave her. "I'm sorry," he said.

"I'm not," she said and leaned across to kiss him, her mouth warm with sunlight and life. "It is worth it, all of it."

All those losses, but this one at least he could prevent.

"When the time comes," he said: "When you sail. I will come with you,"

A fo ben, bid bont. To be a leader, be a bridge.
  Welsh proverb

GOODNIGHT MOONS

ELLEN KLAGES

Ellen Klages is the author of the short story collection, Portable Childhoods, *and two acclaimed YA novels:* The Green Glass Sea, *which won the Scott O'Dell Award, the New Mexico Book Award, and the Lopez Award; and* White Sands, Red Menace, *which won the California and New Mexico Book awards. Her short stories have been translated into Czech, French, German, Hungarian, Japanese, and Swedish, and have been nominated for the Nebula, Hugo, World Fantasy, and Campbell awards. Her story, "Basement Magic," won a Nebula in 2005. She lives in San Francisco, in a small house full of strange and wondrous things.*

This is her Heinlein story.

'd always dreamed of living on Mars. From the first time I went to the library in Omaha and found the books with rocket ships on their spines, discovered Bradbury and Heinlein and Robinson. Later, I heard real scientists on the news saying it could happen—would happen—in my lifetime.

I didn't want to stay behind and watch.

A big dream, but I was disciplined, focused. I took physics and chemistry, ran track after school, spent my evenings stargazing from the garage roof—and my nights reading science fiction under the covers. I graduated valedictorian, with a full scholarship to MIT, and got a doctorate in mechanical engineering, then stayed on for a second degree in astrobotany. We'd need to grow food, once we arrived.

My husband was an electronics genius, but a small flaw in Pete Morrison's left eardrum grounded him early in the NASA program. We lived outside of Houston while I trained: endurance, microgravity, EVA simulations. I even survived the "vomit comet" with flying colors.

When they announced the team for the Mars mission, I made the list. Four men and two women: Archie, Paolo, Rajuk, Tom, Chandra and I were overnight celebrities. Interviews, photos, talk shows—everyone wanted to know how it felt to be the first humans to go to another planet.

Our last public appearance was at the launch of the *Sacagawea* with her payload of hydrogen and the gas extractor that would fuel our trip back. She would be waiting for us when we landed, in another thirty months. Once she was up, we disappeared for two years of training and maneuvers in Antarctica and the Gobi Desert, the most extreme conditions Earth could offer.

Pete and I said our farewells the night before the launch team was sequestered for the final countdown week. Champagne (for him), filet mignon, red roses, and a king-size bed. Then I was isolated with the others at the base, given so many last-minute shots, tests, and dry runs that I felt like a check mark on an endless to-do list.

But I made it. On a sunny Tuesday morning, the *Conestoga* roared up into a bright blue sky. Billions of people watched us set out for a new world.

Free fall was a relief after the crush of the launch. We'd be floating in zero-g for seven months. Archie and Paolo were a little green around the gills at first, but they got their sea legs soon enough. For me, it was as easy as swimming.

The tedium of a long voyage set in once we established our routine. Cramped quarters, precious little privacy, and not much to do once we were past the moon. I checked my instruments, sent data packets back to Mission Control, took my turn in the galley. Then on day 37, I tossed my cookies so suddenly there wasn't even time to grab a barf bag. Everyone laughed, no one harder than Paolo and Archie.

For three days, nothing wanted to stay down. Didn't feel like zero-g effects. More like a bug. Chandra, the medical officer, took my vitals. No fever, blood pressure normal—for these conditions. When she took an EPT stick from the supply closet, I laughed. "No way. Brand-new implant when we got back from the desert."

"Just a precaution," she said. "By the book. Anything abdominal I can rule out is a plus."

The only plus was the symbol on the stick. The second one as well.

"Jeez." Chandra whistled through her teeth. "Protocol says—"

"I know." Pregnant personnel are restricted to ground duty. Pregnant personnel assigned to flight missions are immediately reassigned. That was why we both had the implants. A one-in-a-million chance, but mine was defective.

Human error? Technical glitch? For two years, we'd gone over every phase of the mission, tens of thousands of parts, maneuvers, systems— anything could go wrong at any time. We had reams of contingency plans. Every snafu had some kind of back-up. Except this.

I zipped up my flight suit. "You have to tell Tom," I said. Another protocol. Information that might affect the crew or the mission had to be relayed to the captain.

"Yeah."

"Wait till tomorrow? I need to tell Pete first."

She put her hand on my arm. "Okay." She hesitated. "There's only one option. You know that."

I nodded. If one crew member becomes unfit to serve, the mission is aborted. It had happened once on the space station. Appendicitis. The whole crew had to evacuate back to Earth. And that wasn't possible for us, not in an orbital transit. Earth wouldn't be in the same position as when we'd left, and we didn't have enough fuel to realign. I *had* to be fit for duty.

"Tomorrow," I said.

My bunk was the only private place. I pulled the curtain across and leaned against the bulkhead, my hand on my still-flat belly. Chandra was right. And, in theory, that was a choice I'd always supported. So why did I feel like I had to pick—my dreams or my future?

This was an exploration mission. Seventeen months on the surface. We didn't have the supplies or the technology or the infrastructure to start colonizing. That was decades down the road, and only if *we* succeeded.

When the communication window opened, I sent a message to my husband. I told him what had happened and what I had to do. The fourteen-minute delay for his reply seemed endless. And when it arrived, the words on the screen surprised me. "Can't let you do that, Zoë," it said.

Before I could type my reply, the next message arrived. That one was from CNN, asking for confirmation.

Then all hell broke loose.

Tom and the rest of the crew stared at me as the queue backed up with message after message. Mission Control was furious. Two different generals sent conflicting orders from millions of miles away.

But the public response was instant and overwhelming. News sites headlined, WELCOME FIRST MARTIAN BABY! Within an hour, I was the hot topic of blogs, newscasts, and water cooler discussions all over the globe. A contest offered a million dollars for the person who named "The First Citizen of Space." It was a circus—and NASA had never been so popular.

The furor showed no signs of dying down, but at least Earth continued to rotate, and we lost the comm signal after a few hours. I went to my bunk, but didn't sleep much. When I got up, the screen held a terse communiqué from Mission Control: "Seventh crew member authorized."

I was relieved. I was scared. The rest of the crew did their best to hide their feelings. An order was an order.

The Surgeon General issued a statement. Barring any complications, the likelihood of transit-oriented problems in the next six months was low. The fetus was in a water-filled sac, exactly the sort of environment the crew had trained in for zero-g. As long as radiation levels were closely monitored, she believed a full-term pregnancy was entirely possible. Deceleration and landing, however, would require further consideration.

Would I still fit in my landing couch? What about my pressure suit— it wasn't designed to stretch. I'd never paid much attention in home economics, but the suit was just engineering, and I was able to make some alterations.

A few days shy of my eighth month, we began the descent to the surface. The baby kicked the whole way down. Fortunately, the landing was textbook: no system failures, no injuries, no unexpected terrain. And out the porthole, we could see the *Sacagawea* a hundred meters away, plumes of vapor wafting from its lower vents. Our ride home.

That first night, Rajuk broke out the bottle of whiskey he'd smuggled on board, and we toasted our places in history. I drank my share; all the medical texts said it wouldn't make much difference, not at that stage. Of course, no one knew what difference cosmic radiation and zero-g had already made.

The baby and the planet were both *terrae incognitae*.

I had studied Mars for more than twenty years. I wasn't prepared for how eerily beautiful and utterly alien it was. Everything was shades of reddish brown, no greens or blues. The horizon was too close, the sky too uniform, the lighting flat. Daylight was butterscotch, as if it were always afternoon, half an hour before dusk. At night, the two small, lumpy moons rose into the starry blackness, Phobos slowly in the west, tiny Deimos in the east.

I was restricted to the ship. For two weeks I had to watch as the others took turns out on the dusty metallic surface, kicking up puffs of iron oxide with every step. I could feel the floor vibrate as they opened the cargo bay, unloaded the rover, began to set up a base. It took a full day to anchor the *Conestoga*, turning her from a spaceship into a permanent habitat, for us, for future crews.

We had all cross-trained in each other's field, so I was busy checking schematics, logging soil samples, monitoring pressure levels and hatch seals. I gave hand signals through the porthole as Tom and Paolo unrolled my inflatable greenhouse and moved the equipment in. As soon as they connected it to the Hab and its atmosphere, I started my own work.

The first seedlings were unfurling in the hydroponics tank when my water broke.

Chandra had set up the medical facility as soon as we landed; everything was ready. Like the Russians' rats, which gestated in zero-g, my labor was long and slow. The gravity of Mars—only one third Earth's—meant less strain, but less pull when I pushed. Finally, on day 266 of the mission, Mars day 52, I heard a loud, strong cry.

"It's a girl," Chandra said a moment later. I saw a red, wrinkled face, then she was on the counter, being weighed and measured and tested. "Only five pounds, a little underweight, but otherwise she seems remarkably healthy." Chandra laid her on my chest.

A few days later, a woman in Indiana would win a million dollars for naming my baby Virginia Dare Morrison—the first child born in the New World. But as she lay there, suckling for the first time, I murmured, "Podkayne of Mars," and we just called her Poddy.

The *Conestoga* had not been stocked with infant necessities, so we had to make do. T-shirts were diapers. Archie made a mobile from some color-coded spare parts and dental floss, dangling it above the hammock that hung in my bunk. A blanket became a snugglie; while I worked, I carried her like a papoose from another, older frontier.

I breast-fed her for the first eight months, no extra draw on the closely measured rations. She got sponge baths, just like the rest of us. When she was teething, her cries filled the Hab—the bunks were only soundproofed enough to offer a bit of privacy—and the rest of the crew grumbled about lost sleep. But they watched her when it was my turn in the rotation to be outside, and she heard lullabies in four different languages.

Martian gravity is kind to toddlers. At thirteen months, Poddy massed eighteen pounds, but her chubby legs only had to support six as she pulled herself up and began to walk. It's impossible to child-proof a spacecraft, but we blocked off the lab and the stairs to the upper level of the Hab, and strung tether cords across the hatchways. She could climb like a monkey.

She bounced and hopped the length of the greenhouse, laughing at the top of her lungs and bounding about in a way no Earth baby could. I sent vids to Pete, and they were replayed everywhere; a dance called the Poddy Hop was the new craze. Plans were made for a homecoming tour the next year: FIRST MARTIAN RETURNS.

But that *was* a problem, said the doctors.

Martian gravity *might* turn out to be sufficient for healthy growth. No one knew. Poddy's stats were being studied by scientists everywhere, and would provide the data for future missions. But travel in zero-g was not a possibility, not at her age. She was still developing—bones and muscles, neurons and connections. She would never recover from seven months in free fall.

Every member of the crew already had muscle-mass and bone loss from the trip out. I'd known from day one that once the mission was over, I'd spend the next two years in hospitals and gyms trying to get as much of it back as I could.

For Poddy, they said, the loss would be irreversible. Mission Control advised: further study needed.

A month before takeoff, I got their final verdict.

Poddy could not return to Earth.

If she did, even as an adult, she would never walk again. She would be crippled by the physics of her home planet, always in excruciating pain, crushed by the mass of her own body. Her lungs might collapse, her heart might not take the strain.

"We had not planned for children," Mission Control's message ended. "We're sorry."

I read the message three times, then picked her up and kissed her hair. I'd always dreamed of living on Mars.

Future missions would bring supplies, they promised. Clothes, shoes, a helmet, a modified pressure suit with expandable sections and room to grow. From now on, they would carry extra milk and vitamins, educational materials, toys and games. Engineers had begun working on a small-scale rover. Whatever she needed.

The next ship should arrive in seven months.

Tom reassigned duties for a five-person crew. By the time the *Sacagawea* was ready for launch, Poddy was talking. Just simple words. *Mama, Hab, juice.* She waved her tiny fingers at the porthole as her aunt and uncles boarded: *Bye-bye Chanda, bye-bye Tom. Bye-bye.*

We would never see them again.

Like my great-grandmother, I was a pioneer woman, alone on the frontier. Isolated, self-sufficient by necessity. Did it matter, I wondered as I heated up our supper, whether it was a hundred miles of prairie, a thousand miles of ocean, or millions of miles of space that separated me from everything and everyone I had known?

I read to Poddy, after the meal. A picture book, uploaded a week before, drawings in primary colors of things she would never see: *tree, cat, house, father.* For her, Earth was make-believe, a fantasy world with funny green grass and the wrong color sky.

On the first of two hundred cold, black nights, Deimos and Phobos low in the sky, I sat by the porthole and cuddled my daughter, whispering as I rocked her to sleep.

Goodnight, Poddy.

Goodnight, moons.

COPYRIGHT

Night Shade Books is an Independent Publisher of Quality Science-Fiction, Fantasy and Horror

ISBN: 978-1-59780-390-8 ❧ $14.99 ❧ Look for it in e-Book!

"...A HUGE WIDESCREEN PREMISE... THE PERFECT MIX OF SPACE BATTLES AND POLITICS." — io9.com

JOHN LOVE

Faith is the name humanity has given to the unknown, seemingly invincible alien ship that has begun to harass the newly emergent Commonwealth. 300 years earlier, the same ship destroyed the Sakhran Empire, allowing the Commonwealth to expand its sphere of influence. But now Faith has returned.

The ship is as devastating as before, and its attacks leave some Commonwealth solar systems in chaos. Eventually it reaches Sakhra, now an important Commonwealth possession, and it seems like history is about to repeat itself. But this time, something is waiting: an Outsider, one of the Commonwealth's ultimate warships.

Outsiders are almost as alien as Faith—instruments of the Commonwealth, outside all normal command structures. Slender silver ships, full of functionality: drives and weapons and sentience cores, bionics and electronics, packed to almost dwarf-star density. And crewed by people of unusual abilities, often sociopaths or psychopaths. Outsiders were conceived in back alleys, built and launched in secret, and commissioned without ceremony.

Faith continues to destroy the Commonwealth's regular spacecraft and planetary defenses. With each new engagement, the Kafkaesque enemy reveals a new set of abilities.

One system away from Earth, the Outsider ship Charles Manson makes a stand. Commander Foord waits with his crew of Miscreants and sociopath, hoping to accomplish what no other human has been able to do... to destroy Faith.

Night Shade Books is an Independent Publisher of Quality Science-Fiction, Fantasy and Horror

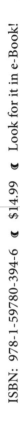

ISBN: 978-1-59780-394-6 ❦ $14.99 ❦ Look for it in e-Book!

Enormity is the strange tale of an American working in Korea, a lonely young man named Manny Lopes, who is not only physically small (in his own words, he's a "Creole shrimp"), but his work, his failed marriage, his race, all conspire to make him feel puny and insignificant—the proverbial ninety-eight-pound weakling.

Then one day an accident happens, a quantum explosion, and suddenly Manny awakens to discover that he is big—really big. In fact, Manny is enormous, a mile-high colossus! Now there's no stopping him: he's a one-man weapon of mass destruction. Yet he means well .

Enormity takes some odd turns, featuring characters like surfing gangbangers, elderly terrorists, and a North Korean assassin who thinks she's Dorothy from *The Wizard of Oz*. There's also sex, violence, and action galore, with the army throwing everything it has against the rampaging colossus that is Manny Lopes. But there's only one weapon that has any chance at all of stopping him: his wife.

Night Shade Books is an Independent Publisher of Quality Science-Fiction, Fantasy and Horror

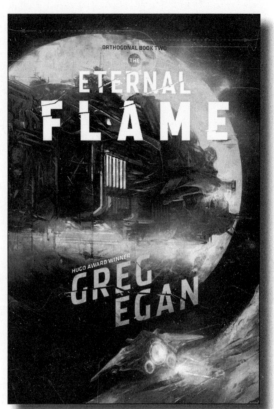

ISBN: 978-1-59780-293-2 ❦ $26.99 ❦ Look for it in e-Book!

Greg Egan's *The Clockwork Rocket* introduced readers to an exotic universe where the laws of physics are very different from our own, where the speed of light varies in ways Einstein would never allow, and where intelligent life has evolved in unique and fascinating ways. Now Egan continues his epic tale of alien beings embarked on a desperate voyage to save their world . . . .

The generation ship *Peerless* is in search of advanced technology capable of sparing their home planet from imminent destruction. In theory, the ship is traveling fast enough that it can traverse the cosmos for generations–and still return home only a few years after they departed. But a critical fuel shortage threatens to cut their urgent voyage short, even as a population explosion stretches the ship's life-support capacity to its limits.

When the astronomer Tamara discovers the Object, a meteor whose trajectory will bring it within range of the *Peerless*, she sees a risky solution to the fuel crisis. Meanwhile, the biologist Carlo searches for a better way to control fertility, despite the traditions and prejudices of their society. As the scientists clash with the ship's leaders, they find themselves caught up in two equally dangerous revolutions: one in the sexual roles of their species, the other in their very understanding of the nature of matter and energy.

The Eternal Flame lights up the mind with dazzling new frontiers of physics and biology, as only Greg Egan could imagine them.